WILLIAM DEAN HOWELLS

WILLIAM DEAN HOWELLS

NOVELS 1886–1888
The Minister's Charge
April Hopes
Annie Kilburn

THE LIBRARY OF AMERICA

The paper used in this publication meets the
minimum requirements of the American National Standard for
Information Sciences—Permanence of Paper for Printed
Library Materials, ANSI Z39.48—1984.

Distributed to the trade in the United States
and Canada by the Viking Press.

Library of Congress Catalog Number: 88-82728
For cataloging information, see end of Notes section.
ISBN 0—940450—51—8

———

First Printing
The Library of America—44

Manufactured in the United States of America

DON L. COOK
WROTE THE NOTES AND SELECTED
THE TEXTS FOR THIS VOLUME

The texts of The Minister's Charge and April Hopes
in this volume are reprinted from A Selected Edition of W. D. Howells,
published by the Indiana University Press and the Howells Edition
Editorial Board, and bear the emblem of the Center for Editions
of American Authors of the Modern Language Association.
The text of The Minister's Charge was edited by David J. Nordloh
and David Kleinman; the text of April Hopes was edited by
Don L. Cook, James P. Elliott, and David J. Nordloh.
These texts are reprinted here without change except
as noted on page 876.

Grateful acknowledgment is made to the National Endowment for the
Humanities, the Ford Foundation, and the Andrew W. Mellon
Foundation for their generous support of this series.

Contents

THE MINISTER'S CHARGE

or
The Apprenticeship of Lemuel Barker

I

ON THEIR WAY BACK to the farm-house where they were boarding, Sewell's wife reproached him for what she called his recklessness. "You had no right," she said, "to give the poor boy false hopes. You ought to have discouraged him—that would have been the most merciful way—if you knew the poetry was bad. Now, he will go on building all sorts of castles in the air on your praise, and sooner or later they will come tumbling about his ears—just to gratify your passion for saying pleasant things to people."

"I wish you had a passion for saying pleasant things to me, my dear," suggested her husband evasively.

"Oh, a nice time I should have!"

"I don't know about *your* nice time, but I feel pretty certain of my own. How do you know— Oh, *do* get up, you implacable cripple!" he broke off to the lame mare he was driving, and pulled at the reins.

"Don't saw her mouth!" cried Mrs. Sewell.

"Well, let her get up, then, and I won't. I don't like to saw her mouth; but I have to do something when you come down on me with your interminable consequences. I dare say the boy will never think of my praise again. And besides, as I was saying when this animal interrupted me with her ill-timed attempts at grazing, how do you know that I knew the poetry was bad?"

"How? By the sound of your voice. I could tell you were dishonest in the dark, David."

"Perhaps the boy knew that I was dishonest too," suggested Sewell.

"Oh, no, he didn't. I could see that he pinned his faith to every syllable."

"He used a quantity of pins, then; for I was particularly profuse of syllables. I find that it requires no end of them to make the worse appear the better reason to a poet who reads his own verses to you. But come, now, Lucy, let me off a syllable or two. I—I have a conscience, you know well enough, and if I thought— But pshaw! I've merely cheered a lonely hour for the boy, and he'll go back to hoeing potatoes to-morrow, and that will be the end of it."

"I *hope* that will be the end of it," said Mrs. Sewell, with the darkling reserve of ladies intimate with the designs of Providence.

"Well," argued her husband, who was trying to keep the matter from being serious, "perhaps he may turn out a poet yet. You never can tell where the lightning is going to strike. He has some idea of rhyme, and some perception of reason, and—yes, some of the lines *were* musical. His general attitude reminded me of Piers Plowman. Didn't he recall Piers Plowman to you?"

"I'm glad you can console yourself in that way, David," said his wife relentlessly.

The mare stopped again, and Sewell looked over his shoulder at the house, now black in the twilight, on the crest of the low hill across the hollow behind them. "I declare," he said, "the loneliness of that place almost broke my heart. There!" he added, as the faint sickle gleamed in the sky above the roof, "I've got the new moon right over my left shoulder for my pains. That's what comes of having a sympathetic nature."

The boy was looking at the new moon, across the broken gate which stopped the largest gap in the tumbled stone wall. He still gripped in his hand the manuscript which he had been reading to the minister.

"There, Lem," called his mother's voice from the house, "I guess you've seen the last of 'em for one while. I'm 'fraid you'll take cold out there'n the dew. Come in, child."

The boy obeyed. "I was looking at the new moon, mother. I saw it over my right shoulder. Did you hear—hear him," he asked in a broken and husky voice,—"hear how he praised my poetry, mother?"

"Oh, *do* make her get up, David!" cried Mrs. Sewell. "These mosquitoes are eating me alive!"

"I will saw her mouth all to the finest sort of kindling-wood, if she doesn't get up this very instant," said Sewell, jerking the reins so wildly that the mare leaped into a galvanic canter, and continued without further urging for twenty paces. "Of course, Lucy," he resumed, profiting by the opportunity for conversation which the mare's temporary activity afforded, "I should feel myself greatly to blame if I thought I had gone beyond mere kindness in my treatment of the poor fellow. But at first I couldn't realize that the stuff was so bad. Their saying that he read all the books he could get, and was writing every spare moment, gave me the idea that he *must* be some sort of literary genius in the germ, and I listened on and on, expecting every moment that he was coming to some passage with a little lift or life in it; and when he got to the end, and hadn't come to it, I couldn't quite pull myself together to say so. I had gone there so full of the wish to recognize and encourage, that I couldn't turn about for the other thing. Well! I shall know another time how to value a rural neighborhood report of the existence of a local poet. Usually there is some hardheaded cynic in the community with native perception enough to enlighten the rest as to the true value of the phenomenon; but there seems to have been none here. I ought to have come sooner to see him, and then I could have had a chance to go again and talk soberly and kindly with him, and show him gently how much he had mistaken himself. Oh, *get* up!" By this time the mare had lapsed again into her habitual absent-mindedness, and was limping along the dark road with a tendency to come to a full stop, from step to step. The remorse in the minister's soul was so keen that he could not use her with the cruelty necessary to rouse her flagging energies; as he held the reins he flapped his elbows up toward his face, as if they were wings, and contrived to beat away a few of the mosquitoes with them; Mrs. Sewell, in silent exasperation, fought them from her with the bough which she had torn from an overhanging birch-tree.

In the morning they returned to Boston, and Sewell's parish duties began again; he was rather faithfuller and busier in these than he might have been if he had not laid so much stress upon duties of all sorts, and so little upon beliefs. He declared that he envied the ministers of the good old times who had only to teach their people that they would be lost if they did not do right; it was much simpler than to make them understand that they were often to be good for reasons not immediately connected with their present or future comfort, and that they could not confidently expect to be lost for any given transgression, or even to be lost at all. He found it necessary to do his work largely in a personal way, by meeting and talking with people, and this took up a great deal of his time, especially after the summer vacation, when he had to get into relations with them anew, and to help them recover themselves from the moral lassitude into which people fall during that season of physical recuperation.

He was occupied with these matters one morning late in October when a letter came addressed in a handwriting of copybook carefulness, but showing in every painstaking stroke the writer's want of training, which, when he read it, filled Sewell with dismay. It was a letter from Lemuel Barker, whom Sewell remembered, with a pang of self-upbraiding, as the poor fellow he had visited with his wife the evening before they left Willoughby Pastures; and it inclosed passages of a long poem which Barker said he had written since he got the fall work done. The passages were not submitted for Sewell's criticism, but were offered as examples of the character of the whole poem, for which the author wished to find a publisher. They were not without ideas of a didactic and satirical sort, but they seemed so wanting in literary art beyond a mechanical facility of versification, that Sewell wondered how the writer should have mastered the notion of anything so literary as publication, till he came to that part of the letter in which Barker spoke of their having had so much sickness in the family that he thought he would try to do something to help along. The avowal of this meritorious ambition inflicted another wound upon Sewell's guilty consciousness; but what made his blood run cold was Barker's proposal to come down to Boston, if Sewell advised, and find a publisher with Sewell's assistance.

This would never do, and the minister went to his desk with the intention of dispatching a note of prompt and total discouragement. But in crossing the room from the chair into which he had sunk, with a cheerful curiosity, to read the letter, he could not help some natural rebellion against the punishment visited upon him. He could not deny that he deserved punishment, but he thought that this, to say the least, was very ill-timed. He had often warned other sinners

who came to him in like resentment that it was this very quality of inopportuneness that was perhaps the most sanative and
divine property of retribution; the eternal justice fell upon us,
he said, at the very moment when we were least able to bear
it, or thought ourselves so; but now in his own case the clear-
sighted prophet cried out and revolted in his heart. It was
Saturday morning, when every minute was precious to him
for his sermon, and it would take him fully an hour to write
that letter; it must be done with the greatest sympathy; he
had seen that this poor foolish boy was very sensitive, and yet
it must be done with such thoroughness as to cut off all hope
of anything like literary achievement for him.

At the moment Sewell reached his desk, with a spirit disciplined to the sacrifice required of it, he heard his wife's step
outside his study door, and he had just time to pull open a
drawer, throw the letter into it, and shut it again before she
entered. He did not mean finally to conceal it from her, but
he was willing to give himself breath before he faced her with
the fact that he had received such a letter. Nothing in its way
was more terrible to this good man than the righteousness of
that good woman. In their case, as in that of most other couples who cherish an ideal of dutiful living, she was the custo-
dian of their potential virtue, and he was the instrument,
often faltering and imperfect, of its application to circumstances; and without wishing to spare himself too much, he
was sometimes aware that she did not spare him enough. She
worked his moral forces as mercilessly as a woman uses the
physical strength of a man when it is placed at her direction.

"What is the matter, David?" she asked, with a keen glance
at the face he turned upon her over his shoulder.

"Nothing that I wish to talk of at present, my dear," answered Sewell, with a boldness that he knew would not avail
him if she persisted in knowing.

"Well, there would be no time if you did," said his wife.
"I'm dreadfully sorry for you, David, but it's really a case you
can't refuse. Their own minister is taken sick, and it's appointed for this afternoon at two o'clock, and the poor thing
has set her heart upon having you, and you must go. In fact, I
promised you would. I'll see that you're not disturbed this
morning, so that you'll have the whole forenoon to yourself.

But I thought I'd better tell you at once. It's only a child—a little boy. You won't have to say much."

"Oh, of course I must go," answered Sewell, with impatient resignation; and when his wife left the room, which she did after praising him and pitying him in a way that was always very sweet to him, he saw that he must begin his sermon at once, if he meant to get through with it in time, and must put off all hope of replying to Lemuel Barker till Monday at least. But he chose quite a different theme from that on which he had intended to preach. By an immediate inspiration he wrote a sermon on the text, "The tender mercies of the wicked are cruel," in which he taught how great harm could be done by the habit of saying what are called kind things. He showed that this habit arose not from goodness of heart, or from the desire to make others happy, but from the wish to spare one's self the troublesome duty of formulating the truth so that it would perform its heavenly office without wounding those whom it was intended to heal. He warned his hearers that the kind things spoken from this motive were so many sins committed against the soul of the flatterer and the soul of him they were intended to flatter; they were deceits, lies; and he besought all within the sound of his voice to try to practice with one another an affectionate sincerity, which was compatible not only with the brotherliness of Christianity, but the politeness of the world. He enforced his points with many apt illustrations, and he treated the whole subject with so much fullness and fervor, that he fell into the error of the literary temperament, and almost felt that he had atoned for his wrong-doing by the force with which he had portrayed it.

Mrs. Sewell, who did not always go to her husband's sermons, was at church that day, and joined him when some ladies who had lingered to thank him for the excellent lesson he had given them at last left him to her.

"Really, David," she said, "I wondered your congregation could keep their countenances while you were going on. Did you think of that poor boy up at Willoughby Pastures when you were writing that sermon?"

"Yes, my dear," replied Sewell gravely; "he was in my mind the whole time."

"Well, you were rather hard upon yourself; and I think I was rather too hard upon you, that time, though I *was* so vexed with you. But nothing has come of it, and I suppose there are cases where people are so lost to common sense that you can't do anything for them by telling them the truth."

"But you'd better tell it, all the same," said Sewell, still in a glow of righteous warmth from his atonement; and now a sudden temptation to play with fire seized him. "You wouldn't have excused me if any trouble had come of it."

"No, I certainly shouldn't," said his wife. "But I don't regret it altogether if it's made you see what danger you run from that tendency of yours. What in the world made you think of it?"

"Oh, it came into my mind," said Sewell.

He did not find time to write to Barker the next day, and on recurring to his letter he saw that there was no danger of his taking another step without his advice, and he began to postpone it: when he had time he was not in the mood; he waited for the time and the mood to come together, and he also waited for the most favorable moment to tell his wife that he had got that letter from Barker and to ask her advice about answering it. If it had been really a serious matter, he would have told her at once; but being the thing it was, he did not know just how to approach it, after his first concealment. He knew that, to begin with, he would have to account for his mistake in attempting to keep it from her, and would have to bear some just upbraiding for this unmanly course, and would then be miserably led to the distasteful contemplation of the folly by which he had brought this trouble upon himself. Sewell smiled to think how much easier it was to make one's peace with one's God than with one's wife; and before he had brought himself to the point of answering Barker's letter, there came a busy season in which he forgot him altogether.

II

ONE DAY in the midst of this Sewell was called from his study to see some one who was waiting for him in the reception-room, but who sent in no name by the housemaid.

"I don't know as you remember me," the visitor said, rising awkwardly, as Sewell came forward with a smile of inquiry. "My name's Barker."

"Barker?" said the minister, with a cold thrill of instant recognition, but playing with a factitious uncertainty till he could catch his breath in the presence of the calamity. "Oh, yes! How do you do?" he said; and then planting himself adventurously upon the commandment to love one's neighbor as one's self, he added: "I'm very glad to see you!"

In token of his content, he gave Barker his hand and asked him to be seated.

The young man complied, and while Sewell waited for him to present himself in some shape that he could grapple with morally, he made an involuntary study of his personal appearance. That morning, before starting from home by the milk-train that left Willoughby Pastures at 4:05, Barker had given his Sunday boots a coat of blacking, which he had eked out with stove-polish, and he had put on his best pantaloons, which he had outgrown, and which, having been made very tight a season after tight pantaloons had gone out of fashion in Boston, caught on the tops of his boots and stuck there in spite of his efforts to kick them loose as he stood up, and his secret attempts to smooth them down when he had reseated himself. He wore a single-breasted coat of cheap broadcloth, fastened across his chest with a carnelian clasp-button of his father's, such as country youth wore thirty years ago, and a belated summer scarf of gingham, tied in a breadth of knot long since abandoned by polite society.

Sewell had never thought his wife's reception-room very splendidly appointed, but Barker must have been oppressed by it, for he sat in absolute silence after resuming his chair, and made no sign of intending to open the matter upon which he came. In the kindness of his heart Sewell could not refrain from helping him on.

"When did you come to Boston?" he asked with a cheeriness which he was far from feeling.

"This morning," said Barker, briefly, but without the tremor in his voice which Sewell expected.

"You've never been here before, I suppose," suggested Sewell, with the vague intention of generalizing or particularizing the conversation, as the case might be.

Barker abruptly rejected the overture, whatever it was. "I don't know as you got a letter from me a spell back," he said.

"Yes, I did," confessed Sewell. "I did receive that letter," he repeated, "and I ought to have answered it long ago. But the fact is——" He corrected himself when it came to his saying this, and said, "I mean that I put it by, intending to answer it when I could do so in the proper way, until, I'm very sorry to say, I forgot it altogether. Yes, I forgot it, and I certainly ask your pardon for my neglect. But I can't say that as it's turned out I altogether regret it. I can talk with you a great deal better than I could write to you in regard to your"—Sewell hesitated between the words poems and verses, and finally said—"work. I have blamed myself a great deal," he continued, wincing under the hurt which he felt that he must be inflicting on the young man as well as himself, "for not being more frank with you when I saw you at home in September. I hope your mother is well?"

"She's middling," said Barker, "but my married sister that came to live with us since you was there has had a good deal of sickness in her family. Her husband's laid up with the rheumatism most of the time."

"Oh!" murmured Sewell sympathetically. "Well! I ought to have told you at that time that I could not see much hope of your doing acceptable work in a literary way; and if I had supposed that you ever expected to exercise your faculty of versifying to any serious purpose,—for anything but your own pleasure and entertainment,—I should certainly have done so. And I tell you now that the specimens of the long poem you have sent me give me even less reason to encourage you than the things you read me at home."

Sewell expected the audible crash of Barker's air-castles to break the silence which the young man suffered to follow upon these words; but nothing of the kind happened, and for all that he could see, Barker remained wholly unaffected by what he had said. It nettled Sewell a little to see him apparently so besotted in his own conceit, and he added: "But I think I had better not ask you to rely altogether upon my opinion in the matter, and I will go with you to a publisher, and you can get a professional judgment. Excuse me a moment."

He left the room and went slowly upstairs to his wife. It appeared to him a very short journey to the third story, where he knew she was decking the guest-chamber for the visit of a friend whom they expected that evening. He imagined himself saying to her when his trial was well over that he did not see why she complained of those stairs; that he thought they were nothing at all. But this sense of the absurdity of the situation which played upon the surface of his distress flickered and fled at sight of his wife bustling cheerfully about, and he was tempted to go down and get Barker out of the house, and out of Boston if possible, without letting her know anything of his presence.

"Well?" said Mrs. Sewell, meeting his face of perplexity with a penetrating glance. "What is it, David?"

"Nothing. That is—everything! Lemuel Barker is here!"

"Lemuel Barker? Who is Lemuel Barker?" She stood with the pillow-sham in her hand which she was just about to fasten on the pillow, and Sewell involuntarily took note of the fashion in which it was ironed.

"Why, surely you remember! That simpleton at Willoughby Pastures." If his wife had dropped the pillow-sham, and sunk into a chair beside the bed, fixing him with eyes of speechless reproach; if she had done anything dramatic, or said anything tragic, no matter how unjust or exaggerated, Sewell could have borne it; but she only went on tying the sham on the pillow, without a word. "The fact is, he wrote to me some weeks ago, and sent me some specimens of a long poem."

"Just before you preached that sermon on the tender mercies of the wicked?"

"Yes," faltered Sewell. "I had been waiting to show you the letter."

"You waited a good while, David."

"I know—I know," said Sewell miserably. "I was waiting—waiting—" He stopped, and then added with a burst, "I was waiting till I could put it to you in some favorable light."

"I'm glad you're honest about it at last, my dear!"

"Yes. And while I was waiting I forgot Barker's letter altogether. I put it away somewhere—I can't recollect just where, at the moment. But that makes no difference; he's here with the whole poem in his pocket, now." Sewell gained a little courage from his wife's forbearance; she knew that she could trust him in all great matters, and perhaps she thought that for this little sin she would not add to his punishment. "And what I propose to do is to make a complete thing of it, this time. Of course," he went on convicting himself, "I see that I shall inflict twice the pain that I should have done if I had spoken frankly to him at first; and of course there will be the added disappointment, and the expense of his coming to Boston. But," he added brightly, "we can save him any expense while he's here, and perhaps I can contrive to get him to go home this afternoon."

"He wouldn't let you pay for his dinner out of the house anywhere," said Mrs. Sewell. "You must ask him to dinner here."

"Well," said Sewell, with resignation; and suspecting that his wife was too much piqued or hurt by his former concealment to ask what he now meant to do about Barker, he added: "I'm going to take him round to a publisher and let him convince himself that there's no hope for him in a literary way."

"David!" cried his wife; and now she left off adjusting the shams, and erecting herself looked at him across the bed. "You don't intend to do anything so cruel."

"Cruel?"

"Yes! Why should you go and waste any publisher's time by getting him to look at such rubbish? Why should you expose the poor fellow to the mortification of a perfectly needless refusal? Do you want to shirk the responsibility—to put it on some one else?"

"No; you know I don't."

"Well, then, tell him yourself that it won't do."

"I have told him."

"What does he say?"

"He doesn't say anything. I can't make out whether he believes me or not."

"Very well, then; you've done your duty, at any rate." Mrs. Sewell could not forbear saying also: "If you'd done it at first, David, there wouldn't have been any of this trouble."

"That's true," owned her husband, so very humbly that her heart smote her.

"Well, go down and tell him he must stay to dinner, and then try to get rid of him the best way you can. Your time is really too precious, David, to be wasted in this way. You *must* get rid of him, somehow."

Sewell went back to his guest in the reception-room, who seemed to have remained as immovably in his chair as if he had been a sitting statue of himself. He did not move when Sewell entered.

"On second thoughts," said the minister, "I believe I will not ask you to go to a publisher with me, as I had intended; it would expose you to unnecessary mortification, and it would be, from my point of view, an unjustifiable intrusion upon very busy people. I must ask you to take my word for it that no publisher would bring out your poem, and it never would pay you a cent if he did." The boy remained silent as before, and Sewell had no means of knowing whether it was from silent conviction or from mulish obstinacy. "Mrs. Sewell will be down presently. She wished me to ask you to stay to dinner. We have an early dinner, and there will be time enough after that for you to look about the city."

"I shouldn't like to put you out," said Barker.

"Oh, not at all," returned Sewell, grateful for this sign of animation, and not exigent of a more formal acceptance of his invitation. "You know," he said, "that literature is a trade, like every other vocation, and that you must serve an apprenticeship if you expect to excel. But first of all you must have some natural aptitude for the business you undertake. You understand?" asked Sewell; for he had begun to doubt whether Barker understood anything. He seemed so much more stupid than he had at home; his faculties were apparently sealed up, and he had lost all the personal picturesqueness which he had when he came in out of the barn, at his mother's call, to receive Sewell.

"Yes," said the boy.

"I don't mean," continued Sewell, "that I wouldn't have you continue to make verses whenever you have the leisure for it. I think, on the contrary, that it will give a grace to your life which it might otherwise lack. We are all in daily danger of being barbarized by the sordid details of life; the constantly recurring little duties which must be done, but which we must not allow to become the whole of life." Sewell was so much pleased with this thought, when it had taken form in words, that he made a mental note of it for future use. "We must put a border of pinks around the potato-patch, as Emerson would say, or else the potato-patch is no better than a field of thistles." Perhaps because the logic of this figure rang a little false, Sewell hastened to add: "But there are many ways in which we can prevent the encroachment of those little duties without being tempted to neglect them, which would be still worse. I have thought a good deal about the condition of our young men in the country, and I have sympathized with them in what seems their want of opportunity, their lack of room for expansion. I have often wished that I could do something for them—help them in their doubts and misgivings, and perhaps find some way out of the trouble for them. I regret this tendency to the cities of the young men from the country. I am sure that if we could give them some sort of social and intellectual life at home, they would not be so restless and dissatisfied."

Sewell felt as if he had been preaching to a dead wall; but now the wall opened, and a voice came out of it, saying: "You mean something to occupy their minds?"

"Exactly so!" cried Sewell. "Something to occupy their minds. Now," he continued, with a hope of getting into some sort of human relations with his guest which he had not felt before, "why shouldn't a young man on a farm take up some scientific study, like geology, for instance, which makes every inch of earth vocal, every rock historic, and the waste places social?" Barker looked so blankly at him that he asked again, "You understand?"

"Yes," said Barker; but having answered Sewell's personal

question, he seemed to feel himself in no wise concerned with
the general inquiry which Sewell had made, and he let it lie
where Sewell had let it drop. But the minister was so well
pleased with the fact that Barker had understood anything of
what he had said, that he was content to let the notion he had
thrown out take its chance of future effect, and rising, said
briskly: "Come upstairs with me into my study, and I will
show you a picture of Agassiz. It's a very good photograph."

He led the way out of the reception-room, and tripped
lightly in his slippered feet up the steps against which Barker
knocked the toes of his clumsy boots. He was not large, nor
naturally loutish, but the heaviness of the country was in every
touch and movement. He dropped the photograph twice in
his endeavor to hold it between his stiff thumb and finger.

Sewell picked it up each time for him, and restored it to his
faltering hold. When he had securely lodged it there, he asked
sweetly: "Did you ever hear what Agassiz said when a scheme
was once proposed to him by which he could make a great
deal of money?"

"I don't know as I did," replied Barker.

" 'But, gentlemen, *I've no time to make money.*' "

Barker received the anecdote in absolute silence, standing
helplessly with the photograph in his hand; and Sewell with a
hasty sigh forbore to make the application to the ordinary
American ambition to be rich that he had intended. "That's a
photograph of the singer Nilsson," he said, cataloguing the
other objects on the chimney-piece. "She was a peasant, you
know, a country girl in Norway. That's Grévy, the President
of the French Republic; his father was a peasant. Lincoln, of
course. Sforza, throwing his hoe into the oak," he said, explaining the picture that had caught Barker's eye on the wall
above the mantel. "He was working in the field, when a band
of adventurers came by, and he tossed his hoe at the tree. If it
fell to the ground, he would keep on hoeing; if it caught in
the branches and hung there he would follow the adventurers.
It caught, and he went with the soldiers and became Duke of
Milan. I like to keep the pictures of these great Originals
about me," said Sewell, "because in our time, when we refer
so constantly to law, we are apt to forget that God is creative
as well as operative." He used these phrases involuntarily;

they slipped from his tongue because he was in the habit of saying this about these pictures, and he made no effort to adapt them to Barker's comprehension, because he could not see that the idea would be of any use to him. He went on pointing out the different objects in the quiet room, and he took down several books from the shelves that covered the whole wall, and showed them to Barker, who, however, made no effort to look at them for himself, and did not say anything about them. He did what Sewell bade him do in admiring this thing or that; but if he had been an Indian he could not have regarded them with a greater reticence. Sewell made him sit down from time to time, but in a sitting posture Barker's silence became so deathlike that Sewell hastened to get him on his legs again, and to walk him about from one point to another, as if to keep life in him. At the end of one of these otherwise aimless excursions Mrs. Sewell appeared, and infused a gleam of hope into her husband's breast. Apparently she brought none to Barker; or perhaps he did not conceive it polite to show any sort of liveliness before a lady. He did what he could with the hand she gave him to shake, and answered the brief questions she put to him about his family to precisely the same effect as he had already reported its condition to Sewell.

"Dinner's ready now," said Mrs. Sewell, for all comment. She left the expansiveness of sympathy and gratulation to her husband on most occasions, and on this she felt that she had less than the usual obligation to make polite conversation. Her two children came down-stairs after her, and as she unfolded her napkin across her lap after grace she said, "This is my son, Alfred, Mr. Barker; and this is Edith." Barker took the acquaintance offered in silence, the young Sewells smiled with the wise kindliness of children taught to be good to all manner of strange guests, and the girl cumbered the helpless country boy with offers of different dishes.

Mr. Sewell as he cut at the roast beef lengthwise, being denied by his wife a pantomimic prayer to be allowed to cut it crosswise, tried to make talk with Barker about the weather at Willoughby Pastures. It had been a very dry summer, and he asked if the fall rains had filled up the springs. He said he really forgot whether it was an apple year. He also said that he supposed they had dug all their turnips by this time. He had meant to say potatoes when he began, but he remembered that he had seen the farmers digging their potatoes before he came back to town, and so he substituted turnips; afterwards it seemed to him that dig was not just the word to use in regard to the harvesting of turnips. He wished he had said, "got your turnips in," but it appeared to make no difference to Barker, who answered, "Yes, sir," and "No, sir," and "Yes, sir," and let each subject drop with that.

III

T HE SILENCE grew so deep that the young Sewells talked together in murmurs, and the clicking of the knives on the plates became painful. Sewell kept himself from looking at Barker, whom he nevertheless knew to be changing his knife and fork from one hand to the other, as doubt after doubt took him as to their conventional use, and to be getting very little good of his dinner in the process of settling these questions. The door-bell rang, and the sound of a whispered conference between the visitor and the servant at the threshold penetrated to the dining-room. Some one softly entered, and then Mrs. Sewell called out, "Yes, yes! Come in! Come in, Miss Vane!" She jumped from her chair and ran out into the hall, where she was heard to kiss her visitor; she reappeared, still holding her by the hand, and then Miss Vane shook hands with Sewell, saying in a tone of cordial liking, "*How* d'ye do?" and to each of the young people, as she shook hands in turn with them, "How d'ye *do*, dear?" She was no longer so pretty as she must have once been; but an air of distinction and a delicate charm of manner remained to her from her fascinating youth.

Young Sewell pushed her a chair to the table, and she dropped softly into it, after acknowledging Barker's presentation by Mrs. Sewell with a kindly glance that probably divined him.

"You must dine with us," said Mrs. Sewell. "You can call it lunch."

"No, I can't, Mrs. Sewell," said Miss Vane. "I could once, and should have said with great pleasure, when I went away, that I had been lunching at the Sewells; but I can't now. I've reformed. What have you got for dinner?"

"Roast beef," said Sewell.

"Nothing I dislike more," replied Miss Vane. "What else?" She put on her glasses, and peered critically about the table.

"Stewed tomatoes, baked sweet potatoes, macaroni."

"How unimaginative! What are you going to have afterwards?"

"Cottage pudding."

"The very climax of the commonplace! Well!" Miss Vane began to pull off her gloves, and threw her veil back over her shoulder. "I will dine with you, but when I say dine, and people ask me to explain, I shall have to say 'Why, the Sewells still dine at one o'clock, you know,' and laugh over your old-fashioned habits with them. I should like to do differently, and to respect the sacredness of broken bread and that sort of thing; but I'm trying to practice with every one an affectionate sincerity, which is perfectly compatible not only with the brotherliness of Christianity, but the politeness of the world." Miss Vane looked demurely at Mrs. Sewell. "I can't make any exceptions."

The ladies both broke into a mocking laugh, in which Sewell joined with sheepish reluctance; after all, one does not like to be derided, even by one's dearest friends.

"As soon as I hear my other little sins denounced from the pulpit, I'm going to stop using profane language and carrying away people's spoons in my pocket."

The ladies seemed to think this also a very good joke, and his children laughed in sympathy, but Sewell hung his head; Barker sat bolt upright behind his plate, and stared at Miss Vane. "I never have been all but named in church before," she concluded, "and I've heard others say the same."

"Why didn't you come to complain sooner?" asked Sewell.

"Well, I have been away ever since that occasion. I went down the next day to Newport, and I've been there ever since, admiring the ribbon-planting."

"On the lawns or on the ladies?" asked Sewell.

"Both. And sowing broadcast the seeds of plain speaking. I don't know what Newport will be in another year if they all take root."

"I dare say it will be different," said Sewell. "I'm not sure it will be worse." He plucked up a little spirit, and added: "Now you see of how little importance you really are in the community; you have been gone these three weeks, and your own pastor didn't know you were out of town."

"Yes, you did, David," interposed his wife. "I told you Miss Vane was away two weeks ago."

"Did you? Well, I forgot it immediately; the fact was of no

consequence, one way or the other. How do you like that as a bit of affectionate sincerity?"

"I like it immensely," said Miss Vane. "It's delicious. I only wish I could believe you were honest." She leaned back and laughed into her handkerchief, while Sewell regarded her with a face in which his mortification at being laughed at was giving way to a natural pleasure at seeing Miss Vane enjoy herself. "What do you think," she asked, "since you're in this mood of exasperated veracity,—or pretend to be,—of the flower charity?"

"Do you mean by the barrel, or the single sack? The Graham, or the best Haxall, or the health-food cold-blast?" asked Sewell.

Miss Vane lost her power of answering in another peal of laughter, sobering off, and breaking down again before she could say, "I mean cut flowers for patients and prisoners."

"Oh, that kind! I don't think a single pansy would have an appreciable effect upon a burglar; perhaps a bunch of forget-me-nots might, or a few lilies of the valley carelessly arranged. As to the influence of a graceful little *boutonnière*, in cases of rheumatism or cholera morbus, it might be efficacious; but I can't really say."

"How perfectly cynical!" cried Miss Vane. "Don't you know how much good the flower mission has accomplished among the deserving poor? Hundreds of bouquets are distributed every day. They prevent crime."

"That shows how susceptible the deserving poor are. I don't find that a bowl of the most expensive and delicate roses in the center of a dinner-table tempers the asperity of the conversation when it turns upon the absent. But perhaps it oughtn't to do so."

"I don't know about that," said Miss Vane; "but if you had an impulsive niece to supply with food for the imagination, you would be very glad of anything that seemed to combine practical piety and picturesque effect."

"Oh, if you mean that," began Sewell more soberly, and his wife leaned forward with an interest in the question which she had not felt while the mere joking went on.

"Yes. When Sibyl came in this morning with an imperative demand to be allowed to go off and do good with flowers in the homes of virtuous poverty, as well as the hospitals and prisons, I certainly felt as if there had been an interposition, if you will allow me to say so."

Miss Vane still had her joking air, but a note of anxiety had crept into her voice.

"I don't think it will do the sick and poor any harm," said Sewell, "and it may do Sibyl some good." He smiled a little in adding: "It may afford her varied energies a little scope."

Miss Vane shook her head, and some lines of age came into her face which had not shown themselves there before. "And you would advise letting her go into it?" she asked.

"By all means," replied Sewell. "But if she's going to engage actively in the missionary work, I think you'd better go with her on her errands of mercy."

"Oh, of course, she's going to do good in person. What she wants is the sensation of doing good—of seeing and hearing the results of her beneficence. She'd care very little about it if she didn't."

"Oh, I don't know that you can say that," replied Sewell in deprecation of this extreme view. "I don't believe," he continued, "that she would object to doing good for its own sake."

"Of course she wouldn't, David! Who in the world supposed she would?" demanded his wife, bringing him up roundly at this sign of wandering, and Miss Vane laughed wildly.

"And is this what your doctrine of sincerity comes to? This fulsomeness! You're very little better than one of the wicked, it seems to me! Well, I *hoped* that you would approve of my letting Sibyl take this thing up, but such *unbounded* encouragement!"

"Oh, I don't wish to flatter," said Sewell, in the spirit of her raillery. "It will be very well for her to go round with flowers; but don't let her," he continued seriously—"don't let her imagine it's more than an innocent amusement. It would be a sort of hideous mockery of the good we ought to do one another if there were supposed to be anything more than a kindly thoughtfulness expressed in such a thing."

"Oh, if Sibyl doesn't feel that it's real, for the time being she won't care anything about it. She likes to lose herself in the illusion, she says."

"Well!" said Sewell with a slight shrug, "then we must let her get what good she can out of it as an exercise of the sensibilities."

"Oh, my dear!" exclaimed his wife. "You *don't* mean anything so abominable as that! I've heard you say that the worst thing about fiction and the theater was that they brought emotions into play that ought to be sacred to real occasions."

"Did I say that? Well, I must have been right. I——"

Barker made a scuffling sound with his boots under the table, and rose to his feet. "I guess," he said, "I shall have to be going."

They had all forgotten him, and Sewell felt as if he had neglected this helpless guest. "Why, no, you mustn't go! I was in hopes we might do something to make the day pleasant to you. I intended proposing——"

"Yes," his wife interrupted, believing that he meant to give up one of his precious afternoons to Barker, and hastening to prevent the sacrifice, "my son will show you the Public Garden and the Common, and go about the town with you." She rose too, and young Sewell, accustomed to suffer, silently acquiesced. "If your train isn't to start very soon——"

"I guess I better be going," said Barker, and Mrs. Sewell now gave her husband a look conveying her belief that Barker would be happier if they let him go. At the same time she frowned upon the monstrous thought of asking him to stay the night with them, which she detected in Sewell's face. She allowed him to say nothing but, "I'm sorry; but if you really must——"

"I guess I better," persisted Barker. He got himself somehow to the door, where he paused a moment, and contrived to pant "Well, good-day," and without effort at more cordial leave-taking, passed out.

Sewell followed him, and helped him find his hat, and made him shake hands. He went with him to the door, and, beginning to suffer afresh at the wrong he had done Barker, he detained him at the threshold. "If you still wish to see a publisher, Mr. Barker, I will gladly go with you."

"Oh, not at all, not at all. I guess I don't want to see any publisher this afternoon. Well, good-afternoon!" He turned away from Sewell's remorseful pursuit, and clumsily hurrying down the steps, he walked up the street and round the next corner. Sewell stood watching him in rueful perplexity, shading his eyes from the mild October sun with his hand; and some moments after Barker had disappeared, he remained looking after him.

When he rejoined the ladies in the dining-room they fell into a conscious silence.

"Have you been telling, Lucy?" he asked.

"Yes, I've been telling, David. It was the only way. Did you offer to go with him to a publisher again?"

"Yes, I did. It was the only way," said Sewell.

Miss Vane and his wife both broke into a cry of laughter. The former got her breath first. "So *that* was the origin of the famous sermon that turned all our heads gray with good resolutions." Sewell assented with a sickly grin. "What in the world *made* you encourage him?"

"My goodness of heart, which I didn't take the precaution of mixing with goodness of head before I used it."

Everything was food for Miss Vane's laugh, even this confession. "But what is the natural history of the boy? How came he to write poetry? What do you suppose he means by it?"

"That isn't so easy to say. As to his natural history, he lives with his mother in a tumble-down, unpainted wooden house in the deepest fastness of Willoughby Pastures. Lucy and I used to drive by it and wonder what kind of people inhabited that solitude. There were milk-cans scattered round the dooryard, and the Monday we were there a poverty-stricken wash flapped across it. The thought of the place preyed upon me till one day I asked about it at the post-office, and the postmistress told me that the boy was quite a literary character, and read everything he could lay his hands on, and 'sat up nights' writing poetry. It seemed to me a very clear case of genius, and the postmistress's facts rankled in my mind till I couldn't stand it any longer. Then I went to see him. I suppose Lucy has told you the rest?"

"Yes, Mrs. Sewell has told me the rest. But still I don't see how he came to write poetry. I believe it doesn't pay, even in extreme cases of genius."

"Ah, but that's just what this poor fellow didn't know. He

must have read somewhere, in some deleterious newspaper, about the sale of some large edition of a poem, and have had his own wild hopes about it. I don't say his work didn't show sense; it even showed some rude strength, of a didactic, satirical sort, but it certainly didn't show poetry. He might have taken up painting by a little different chance. And when it was once known about the neighborhood that he wrote poetry, his vanity was flattered——"

"Yes, I see. But wasn't there any kind soul to tell him that he was throwing his time away?"

"It appears not."

"And even the kind soul from Boston, who visited him," suggested Mrs. Sewell. "Go on, David."

"Visited him in spite of his wife's omniscience,—even the kind soul from Boston paltered with this plain duty. Even he, to spare himself the pain of hurting the boy's feelings, tried to find some of the lines better than others, and left him with the impression that he had praised them."

"Well, that was pretty bad," said Miss Vane. "You had to tell him to-day, I suppose, that there was no hope for him?"

"Yes, I had to tell him at last, after letting him waste his time and money in writing more stuff and coming to Boston with it. I've put him to needless shame, and I've inflicted suffering upon him that I can't lighten in the least by sharing."

"No, that's the most discouraging thing about pitying people. It does them no manner of good," said Miss Vane, "and just hurts you. Don't you think that in an advanced civilization we shall cease to feel compassion? Why don't you preach against common pity, as you did against common politeness?"

"Well, it isn't quite such a crying sin yet. But really, really," exclaimed Sewell, "the world seems so put together that I believe we ought to think twice before doing a good action."

"David!" said his wife warningly.

"Oh, let him go on!" cried Miss Vane, with a laugh. "I'm proof against his monstrous doctrines. Go on, Mr. Sewell."

"What I mean is this." Sewell pushed himself back in his chair, and then stopped.

"Is what?" prompted both the ladies.

"Why, suppose this boy really had some literary faculty, should I have had any right to encourage it? He was very well where he was. He fed the cows and milked them, and carried the milk to the cross-roads, where the dealer collected it and took it to the train. That was his life, with the incidental facts of cutting the hay and fodder, and bedding the cattle; and his experience never went beyond it. I doubt if his fancy ever did, except in some wild, mistaken excursion. Why shouldn't he have been left to this condition? He ate, he slept, he fulfilled his use. Which of us does more?"

"How would you like to have been in his place?" asked his wife.

"I couldn't *put* myself in his place; and therefore I oughtn't to have done anything to take him out of it," answered Sewell.

"It seems to me that's very un-American," said Miss Vane. "I thought we had prospered up to the present point by taking people out of their places."

"Yes, we have," replied the minister, "and sometimes, it seems to me, the result is hideous. I don't mind people taking themselves out of their places; but if the particles of this mighty cosmos have been adjusted by the divine wisdom, what are we to say of the temerity that disturbs the least of them?"

"I'm sure I don't know," said Miss Vane, rising. "I'm almost afraid to stir, in view of the possible consequences. But I can't sit here all day, and if Mrs. Sewell will excuse me, I'll go at once. Yes, 'I guess I better be going,' as your particle Barker says. Let us hope he'll get safely back to his infinitesimal little crevice in the cosmos. He's a very pretty particle, don't you think? That thick, coarse, wavy black hair growing in a natural bang over his forehead would make his fortune if he were a certain kind of young lady."

They followed her to the door, chatting, and Sewell looked quickly out when he opened it for her.

As she shook his hand she broke into another laugh. "Really, you looked as if you were afraid of finding him on the steps!"

"If I could only have got near the poor boy," said Sewell to his wife, as they returned within doors. "If I could only have reached him where he lives, as our slang says! But do what I would, I couldn't find any common ground where we could stand together. We were as unlike as if we were of two different species. I saw that everything I said bewildered him more and more; he couldn't understand me! Our education is unchristian, our civilization is pagan. They both ought to bring us in closer relations with our fellow-creatures, and they both only put us more widely apart! Every one of us dwells in an impenetrable solitude! We understand each other a little if our circumstances are similar, but if they are different all our words leave us dumb and unintelligible."

IV

BARKER WALKED AWAY from the minister's door without knowing where he was going, and with a heart full of hot pain. He burned with a confused sense of shame and disappointment and anger. It had turned out just as his mother had said: Mr. Sewell would be mighty different in Boston from what he was that day at Willoughby Pastures. There he made Barker think everything of his poetry, and now he pretended to tell him that it was not worth anything; and he kept hinting round that Barker had better go back home and stay there. Did he think he would have left home if there had been anything for him to do there? Had not he as much as told him that he was obliged to find something to make a living by, and help the rest? What was he afraid of? Was he afraid that Barker wanted to come and live off *him*? He could show him that there was no great danger. If he had known how, he would have refused even to stay to dinner.

What made him keep the pictures of these people who had got along, if he thought no one else ought to try? Barker guessed to himself that if that Mr. Agassiz had had to get a living off the farm at Willoughby Pastures, he would have *found* time to make money. What did Mr. Sewell mean by speaking of that Nilsson lady by her surname, without any Miss or Mrs.? Was that the way people talked in Boston?

Mr. Sewell had talked to him as if he were a baby, and did not know anything; and Barker was mad at himself for having staid half a minute after the minister had owned up that he had got the letter he wrote him. He wished he had said, "Well, that's all I want of *you*, sir," and walked right out; but he had not known how to do it. Did they think it was very polite to go on talking with that woman who laughed so much, and forget all about him? Pretty poor sort of manners to eat with her bonnet on, and tell them she hated their victuals.

Barker tried to rage against them in these thoughts, but at the bottom of all was a simple grief that he should have lost the friend whom he thought he had in the minister; the friend he had talked of and dreamed of ever since he had seen and heard him speak those cordial words; the friend he had trusted through all, and had come down to Boston counting upon so much. The tears came into his eyes as he stumbled and scuffled along the brick pavements with his uncouth country walk.

He was walking up a straight, long street, with houses just alike on both sides, and bits of grass before them, that sometimes were gay with late autumn flowers. A horse-car track ran up the middle, and the cars seemed to be tinkling by all the time, and people getting on and off. They were mostly ladies and children, and they were very well dressed. Sometimes they stared at Barker, as they crossed his way in entering or issuing from the houses, but generally no one appeared to notice him. In some of the windows there were flowers in painted pots, and in others little marble images on stands.

There were more images in the garden that Barker came to presently: an image of Washington on horseback, and some orator speaking, with his hand up, and on top of a monument a kind of Turk holding up a man that looked sick. The man was almost naked, but he was not so bad as the image of a woman in a granite basin; it seemed to Barker that it ought not to be allowed there. A great many people of all kinds were passing through the garden, and after some hesitation he went in too, and walked over the bridge that crossed the pond in the middle of the garden, where there were rowboats and boats with images of swans on them. Barker made a sarcastic reflection that Boston seemed to be a great place for images, and passed rather hurriedly through the garden on the other side of the bridge. There were beds of all kinds of flowers scattered about, and they were hardly touched by the cold yet. If he had been in better heart, he would have liked to look round a little; but he felt strange, being there all alone, and he felt very low-spirited.

He wondered if this were the Public Garden that Mrs. Sewell had spoken of, and if that kind of grove across the street were the Common. He felt much more at home in it, as he wandered up and down the walks, and finally sat down on one of the iron benches beside the path. At first he obscurely doubted whether he had any right to do so, unless he had a lady with him; most of the seats were occupied by couples who seemed to be courting, but he ventured finally to take one; nobody disturbed him, and so he remained.

It was a beautiful October afternoon; the wind, warm and dry, caught the yellow leaves from the trees overhead in little whiffs, and blew them about the grass, which the fall rains had made as green as May; and a pensive golden light streamed through the long loose boughs, and struck across the slopes of the Common. Slight buggies flashed by on the street near which he sat, and glistening carriages, with drivers dressed out in uniform like soldiers, rumbled down its slope.

While he sat looking, now at the street and now at the people sauntering and hurrying to and fro in the Common, he tried to decide a question that had mixed itself up with the formless resentment he had felt ever since Mr. Sewell played him false. It had got out in the neighborhood that he was going to Boston before he left home; his mother must have told it; and people would think he was to be gone a long time. He had warned his mother that he did not know when he should be back, before he started in the morning; and he knew that she would repeat his words to everybody who stopped to ask about him during the day, with what she had said to him in reply: "You better come home to-night, Lem; and I'll have ye a good hot supper waitin' for ye."

The question was whether he should go back on the five o'clock train, which would reach Willoughby Centre after dark, and house himself from public ignominy for one night at least, or whether self-respect did not demand that he should stay in Boston for twenty-four hours at any rate, and see if something would not happen. He had now no distinct hope of anything; but his pride and shame were holding him fast, while the homesickness tugged at his heart, and made him almost forget the poverty that had spurred him to the adventure of coming to Boston. He could see the cows coming home through the swampy meadow as plain as if they were coming across the Common; his mother was calling them; she and his sister were going to milk in his absence, and he could see her now, how she looked going out to call the cows, in her bare, gray head, gaunt of neck and cheek, in the ugly Bloomer dress in which she was not grotesque to his eyes, though it usually affected strangers with stupefaction or alarm. But it all seemed far away, as far as if it were in another planet that he had dropped out of; he was divided from it by his failure and disgrace. He thought he must stay and try for something, he did not know what; but he could not make up his mind to throw away his money for nothing; at the hotel, down by the depot, where he had left his bag, they were going to make him pay fifty cents for just a room alone.

"Any them beats 'round here been trying to come their games on *you*?"

At first Barker could not believe himself accosted, though the young man who spoke stood directly in front of him, and seemed to be speaking to him. He looked up, and the young man added, "Heigh?"

"Beats? I don't know what you mean," said Barker.

"Confidence sharps, young feller. They're 'round everywheres, and don't you forget it. Move up a little!"

Barker was sitting in the middle of the bench, and at this he pushed away from the young man, who had dropped himself sociably beside him. He wore a pair of black pantaloons, very tight in the legs, and widening at the foot so as almost to cover his boots. His coat was deeply braided, and his waistcoat was cut low, so that his plastron-scarf hung out from the shirt-bosom, which it would have done well to cover.

"I tell you, Boston's full of 'em," he said, excitedly. "One of 'em come up to me just now, and says he, 'Seems to me I've seen you before, but I can't place you.' 'Oh yes,' says I, 'I'll tell you where it was. I happened to be in the police court one morning when they was sendin' you up for three months.' I tell you he got round the corner! Might 'a' played checkers on his coat-tail. Why, what do you suppose would been the next thing if I hadn't have let him know I saw through him?" demanded the young man of Barker, who listened to this adventure with imperfect intelligence. "He'd 'a' said, 'Hain't I seen you down Kennebunk way som'eres?' And when I said, 'No, I'm from Leominster!' or wherever I was from if I was green, he'd say, 'Oh yes, so it *was* Leominster. How's the folks?' and he'd try to get me to think that *he* was from Leominster too; and then he'd want me to go off and see the sights with him; and pretty soon he'd meet a feller that 'ud dun him for that money he owed him; and he'd say he hadn't got anything with him but a check for forty dollars; and the other feller 'd say he'd got to have his money, and he'd kind of insinuate it was all a put-up job about the check for forty dollars, any way; and that 'ud make the first feller mad, and he'd take out the check, and ask him what he thought o' that; and the other feller 'd say, well, it was a good check, but it wa'n't money, and he wanted money; and then the first feller 'd say, 'Well, come along to the bank, and get your money,' and the other 'd say the bank was shut. 'Well, then,' the first feller 'd say, 'well, sir, I ain't a-goin' to ask any favor of *you*. How much *is* your bill?' and the other feller 'd say ten dollars, or fifteen, or may be twenty-five, if they thought I had that much, and the first feller 'd say, 'Well, here's a gentleman from up my way, and I guess he'll advance me that much on my check if I make it worth his while. He knows me.' And the first thing you know—he's been treatin' you, and so polite, showin' you round, and ast you to go to the theayter—you advance the money, and you keep on with the first feller, and pretty soon he asks you to hold up a minute, he wants to go back and get a cigar; and he goes round the corner, and you hold up, and *hold* up, and in about a half an hour, or may be less time, you begin to smell a rat, and you go for a policeman, and the next morning you find your name in the papers, 'One more unfortunate!' You look out fer 'em, young feller! Wish I *had* let that one go on till he done something so I could handed him over to the cops. It's a shame they're allowed to go 'round, when the cops knows 'em. Hello! There *comes* my mate, *now*." The young man spoke as if they had been talking of his mate and expecting him, and another young man, his counterpart in dress, but of a sullen and heavy demeanor very unlike his own brisk excitement, approached, flapping a bank-note in his hand. "I just been tellin' this young feller about that beat, you know."

"Oh, he's all right," said the mate. "Just seen him down on Tremont street, between two cops. Must ha' caught him in the act."

"You don't say so! Well, that's good, any way. Why! Didn't you get it changed?" demanded the young man with painful surprise as his mate handed him the bank-note.

"No, I didn't. I been to more'n twenty places, and there

ain't no small bills nowhere. The last place, I offered 'em twenty-five cents if they'd change it."

"Why didn't you offer 'em fifty? I'd 'a' give fifty, and glad to do it. Why, I've *got* to have this bill changed."

"Well, I'm sorry for you," said the mate, with ironical sympathy, "because I don't see how you're goin' to git it done. Won't you move up a little bit, young feller?" He sat down on the other side of Barker. "I'm about tired out." He took his head between his hands in sign of extreme fatigue, and drooped forward, with his eyes fixed on the ground.

Lemuel's heart beat. Fifty cents would pay for his lodging, and he could stay till the next day and prolong the chance of something turning up without too sinful a waste of money.

"How much is the bill?" he asked.

"Ten dollars," said the young man despondently.

"And will you give me fifty cents if I change it?"

"Well, I *said* I'd give fifty cents," replied the young man gloomily, "and I *will*."

"It's a bargain," said Lemuel promptly, and he took from his pocket the two five-dollar notes that formed his store, and gave them to the young man.

He looked at them critically. "How do I know they're good?" he asked. "You're a stranger to me, young feller, and how do I know you ain't tryin' to beat me?" He looked sternly at Lemuel, but here the mate interposed.

"How does *he* know that you ain't tryin' to beat *him*?" he asked contemptuously. "I never saw such a feller as you are! Here you make me run half over town to change that bill, and now when a gentleman offers to break it for you, you have to go and accuse him of tryin' to put off counterfeit money on you. If I was him I'd see you furder."

"Oh, well, I don't want any words about it. Here, take your money," said the young man. "As long as I said I'd do it, I'll do it. Here's your half a dollar." He put it, with the banknote, into Lemuel's hand, and rose briskly. "You stay here, Jimmy, till I come back. I won't be gone a minute."

He walked down the mall, and went out of the gate on Tremont street. Then the mate came to himself. "Why, I've *let* him go off with both them bills now, and he owes me one of 'em." With that he rose from Lemuel's side and hurried after his vanishing comrade; before he was out of sight he had broken into a run.

Lemuel sat looking after them, his satisfaction in the affair alloyed by dislike of the haste with which it had been transacted. His rustic mind worked slowly; it was not wholly content even with a result in its own favor, where the process had been so rapid; he was scarcely able to fix the point at which the talk ceased to be a warning against beats and became his opportunity for speculation. He did not feel quite right at having taken the fellow's half-dollar; and yet a bargain was a bargain. Nevertheless, if the fellow wanted to rue it, Lemuel would give him fifteen minutes to come back and get his money; and he sat for that space of time where the others had left him. He was not going to be mean; and he might have waited a little longer if it had not been for the behavior of two girls who came up and sat down on the same bench with him. They could not have been above fifteen or sixteen years old, and Lemuel thought they were very pretty, but they talked so, and laughed so loud, and scuffled with each other for the paper of chocolate which one of them took out of her pocket, that Lemuel, after first being abashed by the fact that they were city girls, became disgusted with them. He was a stickler for propriety of behavior among girls; his mother had taught him to despise anything like carrying-on among them, and at twenty he was as severely virginal in his morality as if he had been twelve.

People looked back at these tomboys when they had got by; and some shabby young fellows exchanged saucy speeches with them. When Lemuel got up and walked away in reproving dignity, one of the hoydens bounced into his place, and they both sent a cry of derision after him. But Lemuel would not give them the satisfaction of letting them know that he heard them, and at the same time he was not going to let them suppose that they had driven him away. He went very slowly down to the street where a great many horse-cars were passing to and fro, and waited for one marked "Fitchburg, Lowell, and Eastern Depots." He was not going to take it; but he meant to follow it on its way to those stations, in the neighborhood of which was the hotel where he had left his traveling-bag. He had told them that he might take a room there, or he might not; now since he had this half-dollar extra he thought that he would stay for the night; it probably would not be any cheaper at the other hotels.

He ran against a good many people in trying to keep the car in sight, but by leaving the sidewalk from time to time where it was most crowded, he managed not to fall very much behind; the worst was that the track went crooking and turning about so much in different streets, that he began to lose faith in its direction, and to be afraid, in spite of the sign on its side, that the car was not going to the depots after all. But it came in sight of them at last, and then Lemuel, blown with the chase but secure of his ground, stopped and rested himself against the side of a wall to get his breath. The pursuit had been very exhausting, and at times it had been mortifying; for here and there people who saw him running after the car had supposed he wished to board it, and in their good-nature had hailed and stopped it. After this had happened twice or thrice, Lemuel perceived that he was an object of contempt to the passengers in the car; but he did not know what to do about it; he was not going to pay six cents to ride when he could just as well walk, and on the other hand he dared not lose sight of the car, for he had no other means of finding his way back to his hotel.

But he was all right now, as he leaned against the housewall, panting, and mopping his forehead with his handkerchief; he saw his hotel a little way down the street, and he did not feel anxious about it.

"Gave you the slip after all," said a passer, who had apparently been interested in Lemuel's adventure.

"Oh, I didn't want to catch it," said Lemuel.

"Ah, merely fond of exercise," said the stranger. "Well, it's a very good thing, if you don't overdo it." He walked by, and then after a glance at Lemuel over his shoulder, he returned to him. "May I ask why you wanted to chase the car, if you didn't want to catch it?"

Lemuel hesitated; he did not like to confide in a total stranger; this gentleman looked kind and friendly, but he was all the more likely on that account to be a beat; the expression was probably such as a beat would put on in approaching his intended prey. "Oh, nothing," said Lemuel evasively.

"I beg your pardon," said the stranger, and he walked away with what Lemuel could only conjecture was the air of a baffled beat.

He waited till he was safely out of sight, and then followed on down the street towards his hotel. When he reached it he walked boldly up to the clerk's desk, and said that he guessed he would take a room for the night, and gave him the check for his bag that he had received in leaving it there.

The clerk wrote the number of a room against Lemuel's name in the register, and then glanced at the bag. It was a large bag of oil-cloth, a kind of bag which is by nature lank and hollow, and must be made almost insupportably heavy before it shows any signs of repletion. The shirt and pair of every-day pantaloons which Lemuel had dropped that morning into its voracious maw made no apparent effect there, as the clerk held it up and twirled it on the crook of his thumb.

"I guess I shall have to get the money for that room in advance," he said, regarding the bag very critically. However he might have been wounded by the doubt of his honesty or his solvency implied in this speech, Lemuel said nothing, but took out his ten-dollar note and handed it to the clerk. The latter said apologetically, "It's one of our rules, where there isn't baggage," and then glancing at the note he flung it quickly across the counter to Lemuel. "That won't do!"

"Won't do?" repeated Lemuel, taking up the bill.

"Counterfeit," said the clerk.

V

LEMUEL STRETCHED the note between his hands, and pored so long upon it that the clerk began to tap impatiently with his finger-tips on the register. "It won't go?" faltered the boy, looking up at the clerk's sharp face.

"It won't go here," replied the clerk. "Got anything else?"

Lemuel's head whirled; the air seemed to darken around him, as he pored again upon the note, and turned it over and over. Two tears scalded their way down his cheeks, and his lips twitched, when the clerk added, "Some beats been workin' you?" but he made no answer. His heart was hot with shame and rage, and heavy with despair. He put the note in his pocket, and took his bag and walked out of the hotel. He had not money enough to get home with now, and besides he could not bear to go back in the disgrace of such calamity. It would be all over the neighborhood, as soon as his mother could tell it; she might wish to keep it to herself for his sake, but she could not help telling it to the first person and every person she saw; she would have to go over to the neighbors to tell it. In a dreary, homesick longing he saw her crossing the familiar meadows that lay between the houses, bareheaded, in her apron, her face set and rigid with wonder at what had happened to her Lem. He could not bear the thought. He would rather die; he would rather go to sea. This idea flashed into his mind as he lifted his eyes aimlessly and caught sight of the tall masts of the coal-ships lying at the railroad wharfs, and he walked quickly in the direction of them, so as not to give himself time to think about it, so as to do it now, quick, right off. But he found his way impeded by all sorts of obstacles; a gate closed across the street to let some trains draw in and out of a station; then a lot of string teams and slow heavy-laden trucks got before him, with a turmoil of express wagons, herdics, and hacks, in which he was near being run over, and was yelled at, sworn at, and laughed at as he stood bewildered, with his lank bag in his hand. He turned and walked back past the hotel again. He felt it an escape, after all, not to have gone to sea; and now a hopeful thought struck him. He would go back to the Common and watch for those fellows who fooled him, and set the police on them, and get his money from them; they might come prowling round again to fool somebody else. He looked out for a car marked like the one he had followed down from the Common, and began to follow it on its return. He got ahead of the car whenever it stopped, so as to be spared the shame of being seen to chase it; and he managed to keep it in sight till he reached the Common. There he walked about looking for those scamps, and getting pushed and hustled by the people who now thronged the paths. At last he was tired out, and on the Beacon street mall, where he had first seen those fellows, he found the very seat where they had all sat together, and sank into it. The seats were mostly vacant now; a few persons sat there reading their evening papers. As the light began to wane, they folded up their papers and walked away, and their places were filled by young men, who at once put their arms round the young women with them, and seemed to be courting. They did not say much, if anything; they just sat there. It made Lemuel ashamed to look at them; he thought they ought to have more sense. He looked away, but he could not look away from them all, there were so many of them. He was all the time very hungry, but he thought he ought not to break into his half-dollar as long as he could help it, or till there was no chance left of catching those fellows. The night came on, the gas-lamps were lighted, and some lights higher up, like moonlight off on the other paths, projected long glares into the night and made the gas look sickly and yellow. Sitting still there while it grew later, he did not feel quite so hungry, but he felt more tired than ever. There were not so many people around now, and he did not see why he should not lie down on that seat and rest himself a little. He made feints of reclining on his arm at first, to see if he were noticed; then he stretched himself out, with his bag under his head, and his hands in his pockets clutching the money which he meant to make those fellows take back. He got a gas-lamp in range, to keep him awake, and lay squinting his eyes to meet the path of rays running down from it to him. Then he shivered, and rose up with a sudden start. The dull, rich dawn was hanging under the trees around him, while the electric lamps, like paler moons now, still burned among their tops.

The sparrows bickered on the grass and the gravel of the path around him.

He could not tell where he was at first; but presently he remembered, and looked for his bag. It was gone; and the money was gone out of both his pockets. He dropped back upon the seat, and leaning his head against the back, he began to cry for utter despair. He had hardly ever cried since he was a baby; and he would not have done it now, but there was no one there to see him.

When he had his cry out he felt a little better, and he got up and went to the pond in the hollow, and washed his hands and face, and wiped them on the handkerchief his mother had ironed for him to use at the minister's; it was still in the folds she had given it. As he shook it out, rising up, he saw that people were asleep on all the benches round the pond; he looked hopelessly at them to see if any of them were those fellows, but he could not find them. He seemed to be the only person awake on the Common, and wandered out of it and down through the empty streets, filled at times with the moony light of the waning electrics, and at times merely with the gray dawn. A man came along putting out the gas, and some milk-carts rattled over the pavement. By and by a market-wagon, with the leaves and roots of cabbages sticking out from the edges of the canvas that covered it, came by, and Lemuel followed it; he did not know what else to do, and it went so slow that he could keep up, though the famine that gnawed within him was so sharp sometimes that he felt as if he must fall down. He was going to drop into a doorway and rest, but when he came to it he found on an upper step a man folded forward like a limp bundle, snoring in a fetid, sodden sleep, and, shocked into new strength, he hurried on. At last the wagon came to a place that he saw was a market. There were no buyers yet, but men were flitting round under the long arcades of the market-houses, with lanterns under their arms, among boxes and barrels of melons, apples, potatoes, onions, beans, carrots, and other vegetables, which the country carts as they arrived continually unloaded. The smell of peaches and cantaloupes filled the air, and made Lemuel giddy as he stood and looked at the abundance. The men were not saying much; now and then one of them priced something, the owner pretended to figure on it, and then they fell into a playful scuffle, but all silently. A black cat lay luxuriously asleep on the canvas top of a barrel of melons, and the man who priced the melons asked if the owner would throw the cat in. There was a butcher's cart laden with carcasses of sheep, and one of the men asked the butcher if he called that stuff mutton. "No; imitation," said the butcher. They all seemed to be very good-natured. Lemuel thought he would ask for an apple; but he could not.

The neighboring restaurants began to send forth the smell of breakfast, and he dragged up and down till he could bear it no longer, and then went into one of them, meaning to ask for some job by which he could pay for a meal. But his shame again would not let him. He looked at the fat, white-aproned boy drawing coffee hot from a huge urn, and serving a countryman with a beefsteak. It was close and sultry in there; the open sugar-bowl was black with flies, and a scent of decaying meat came from the next cellar. "Like some nice fresh doughnuts?" said the boy to Lemuel. He did not answer; he looked around as if he had come in search of some one. Then he went out, and straying away from the market, he found himself after a while in a street that opened upon the Common.

He was glad to sit down, and he said to himself that now he would stay there, and keep a good lookout for the chaps that had robbed him. But again he fell asleep, and he did not wake now till the sun was high, and the paths of the Common were filled with hurrying people. He sat where he had slept, for he did not know what else to do or where to go. Sometimes he thought he would go to Mr. Sewell, and ask him for money enough to get home; but he could not do it; he could more easily starve.

After an hour or two he went to get a drink at a fountain he saw a little way off, and when he came back some people had got his seat. He started to look for another, and on his way he found a cent in the path, and he bought an apple with it—a small one that the dealer especially picked out for cheapness. It seemed pretty queer to Lemuel that a person should want anything for one apple. The apple when he ate it made him sick. His head began to ache, and it ached all day. Late in the afternoon he caught sight of one of those fellows at a distance; but there was no policeman near. Lemuel called out, "Stop there, you!" but the fellow began to run when he recognized Lemuel, and the boy was too weak and faint to run after him.

The day wore away and the evening came again, and he had been twenty-four hours houseless and without food. He must do something; he could not stand it any longer; there was no sense in it. He had read in the newspapers how they gave soup at the police-stations in Boston in the winter; perhaps they gave something in summer. He mustered up courage to ask a gentleman who passed where the nearest station was, and then started in search of it. If the city gave it, then there was no disgrace in it, and Lemuel had as much right to anything that was going as other people; that was the way he silenced his pride.

But he missed the place; he must have gone down the wrong street from Tremont to Washington; the gentleman had said the street that ran along the Common was Tremont, and the next was Washington. The cross-street that Lemuel got into was filled with people, going and coming, and lounging about. There were girls going along two or three together with books under their arms, and other girls talking with young fellows who hung about the doors of brightly lighted shops, and flirting with them. One of the girls, whom he had seen the day before in the Common, turned upon Lemuel as he passed, and said, "There goes my young man *now*! Good-evening, Johnny!" It made Lemuel's cheek burn; he would have liked to box her ears for her. The fellows all set up a laugh.

Towards the end of the street the crowd thickened, and there the mixture of gas and the white moony lights that glared higher up, and winked and hissed, shone upon the faces of a throng that had gathered about the doors and windows of a store a little way down the other street. Lemuel joined them, and for pure listlessness waited round to see what they were looking at. By and by he was worked inward by the shifting and changing of the crowd, and found himself looking in at the door of a room, splendidly fitted up with mirrors and marble everywhere, and colored glass and carved mahogany. There was a long counter with three men behind it, and over their heads was a large painting of a woman, worse than that image in the garden. The men were serving out liquor to the people that stood around drinking and smoking, and battening on this picture. Lemuel could not help looking, either. "What place is this?" he asked of the boy next him.

"Why, don't you know?" said the boy. "It's Jimmy Baker's. Just opened."

"Oh," said Lemuel. He was not going to let the boy see that he did not know who Jimmy Baker was. Just then something caught his eye that had a more powerful charm for him than that painting. It was a large bowl at the end of the counter which had broken crackers in it, and near it were two plates, one with cheese, and one with bits of dried fish and smoked meat. The sight made the water come into his mouth; he watched like a hungry dog, with a sympathetic working of the jaws, the men who took a bit of fish, or meat, or cheese, and a cracker, or all four of them, before or after they drank. Presently one of the crowd near him walked in and took some fish and cracker without drinking at all; he merely winked at one of the bartenders, who winked at him in return.

A tremendous tide of daring rose in Lemuel's breast. He was just going to go in and risk the same thing himself, when a voice in the crowd behind him said, "Hain't you had 'most enough, young fellow? Some the rest of us would like a chance to see now."

Lemuel knew the voice, and turning quickly, he knew the impudent face it belonged to. He did not mind the laugh raised at his expense, but launched himself across the intervening spectators, and tried to seize the scamp who had got his money from him. The scamp had recognized Lemuel too, and he fell back beyond his grasp, and then lunged through the crowd, and tore round the corner and up the street. Lemuel followed as fast as he could. In spite of the weakness he had felt before, wrath and the sense of wrong lent him speed, and he was gaining in the chase when he heard a girl's voice, "There goes one of them now!" and then a man seemed to be calling after him, "Stop, there!" He turned round, and a policeman, looking gigantic in his belted blue flannel blouse and his straw helmet, bore down upon the country boy with his club drawn, and seized him by the collar.

"You come along," he said.

"I haven't done anything," said Lemuel, submitting as he must, and in his surprise and terror losing the strength his wrath had given him. He could scarcely drag his feet over the pavement, and the policeman had almost to carry him at arm's length.

A crowd had gathered about them, and was following Lemuel and his captor, but they fell back when they reached the steps of the police station, and Lemuel was pulled up alone, and pushed in at the door. He was pushed through another door, and found himself in a kind of office. A stout man in his shirt-sleeves was sitting behind a desk within a railing, and a large book lay open on the desk. This man, whose blue waistcoat with brass buttons marked him for some sort of officer, looked impersonally at Lemuel and then at the officer, while he chewed a quill toothpick, rolling it in his lips. "What have you got there?" he asked.

"Assaulting a girl down here, and grabbing her satchel," said the officer who had arrested Lemuel, releasing his collar and going to the door, whence he called, "You come in here, lady," and a young girl, her face red with weeping and her hair disordered, came back with him. She held a crumpled straw hat with the brim torn loose, and in spite of her disordered looks she was very pretty, with blue eyes flung very wide open, and rough brown hair, wavy and cut short, almost like a boy's. This Lemuel saw in the frightened glance they exchanged.

"This the fellow that assaulted you?" asked the man at the desk, nodding his head toward Lemuel, who tried to speak; but it was like a nightmare; he could not make any sound.

"There were three of them," said the girl with hysterical volubility. "One of them pulled my hat down over my eyes and tore it, and one of them held me by the elbows behind, and they grabbed my satchel away that had a book in it that I had just got out of the library. I hadn't got it more than——"

"What name?" asked the man at the desk.

"'A Young Man's Darling,'" said the girl, after a bashful

hesitation. Lemuel had read that book just before he left home; he had not thought it was much of a book.

"The captain wants to know your name," said the officer in charge of Lemuel.

"Oh," said the girl with mortification. "Statira Dudley."

"What age?" asked the captain.

"Nineteen last June," replied the girl with eager promptness, that must have come from shame from the blunder she had made. Lemuel was twenty, the 4th of July.

"Weight?" pursued the captain.

"Well, I hain't been weighed very *lately*," answered the girl, with increasing interest. "I don't know as I been weighed since I left home."

The captain looked at her judicially.

"That so? Well, you look pretty solid. Guess I'll put you down at a hundred and twenty."

"Well, I guess it's full as *much* as that," said the girl, with a flattered laugh.

"Dunno how high you are?" suggested the captain, glancing at her again.

"Well, yes, I *do*. I am just five feet two inches and a half."

"You don't look it," said the captain critically.

"Well, I *am*," insisted the girl, with a returning gayety.

The captain apparently checked himself and put on a professional severity.

"What business—occupation?"

"Saleslady," said the girl.

"Residence?"

"No. 1334 Pleasant Avenue."

The captain leaned back in his arm-chair, and turned his toothpick between his lips, as he stared hard at the girl.

"Well, now," he said, after a moment, "you know you've got to come into court and testify to-morrow morning."

"Yes," said the girl, rather faltering, with a sidelong glance at Lemuel.

"You've got to promise to do it, or else it will be my duty to have you locked up overnight."

"Have me locked up?" gasped the girl, her wide blue eyes filling with astonishment.

"Detain you as a witness," the captain explained. "Of

course, we shouldn't put you in a cell; we should give you a good room, and if you ain't sure you'll appear in the morning——"

The girl was not of the sort whose tongues are paralyzed by terror. "Oh, I'll *sure* to appear, captain! Indeed I will, captain! You needn't lock me up, captain! Lock me *up!*" she broke off indignantly. "It would be a *pretty* idea if I was first to be robbed of my satchel and then put in prison for it overnight! A great kind of law *that* would be! Why, I never heard of such a thing! I think it's a perfect shame! I want to know if that's the way you do with poor things that you don't know about?"

"That's about the size of it," said the captain, permitting himself a smile, in which the officer joined.

"Well, it's a shame!" cried the girl, now carried far beyond her personal interest in the matter.

The captain laughed outright. "It *is* pretty rough. But what you going to do?"

"Do? Why, I'd——" But here she stopped for want of science, and added from emotion, "I'd do *any*thing before I'd do that."

"Well," said the captain, "then I understand you'll come round to the police court and give your testimony in the morning?"

"Yes," said the girl, with a vague, compassionate glance at Lemuel, who had stood there dumb throughout the colloquy.

"If you don't, I shall have to send for you," said the captain.

"Oh, I'll *come*," replied the girl, in a sort of disgust, and her eyes still dwelt upon Lemuel.

"That's all," returned the captain, and the girl, accepting her dismissal, went out.

Now that it was too late, Lemuel could break from his nightmare. "Oh, don't let her go! I ain't the one! I was running after a fellow that passed off a counterfeit ten-dollar bill on me in the Common yesterday. I never touched her satchel. I never saw her before——"

"What's that?" demanded the captain sharply.

"You've got the wrong one!" cried Lemuel. "I never did anything to the girl."

"Why, you fool!" retorted the captain angrily; "why didn't you say that when she was here, instead of standing there like a dumb animal? Heigh?"

Lemuel's sudden flow of speech was stopped at its source again. His lips were locked; he could not answer a word.

The captain went on angrily. "If you'd spoke up in time, maybe I might 'a' let you go. I don't want to do a man any harm if I can't do him some good. Next time, if you've got a tongue in your head, use it. I can't do anything for you now. I got to commit you."

He paused between his sentences, as if to let Lemuel speak, but the boy said nothing. The captain pulled his book impatiently toward him, and took up his pen.

"What's your name?"

"Lemuel Barker."

"I thought maybe there was a mistake all the while," said the captain to the officer, while he wrote down Lemuel's name. "But if a man hain't got sense enough to speak for himself, I can't put the words in his mouth. Age?" he demanded savagely of Lemuel.

"Twenty."

"Weight?"

"A hundred and thirty."

"I could see with half an eye that the girl wa'n't very sanguine about it. But what's the use? *I* couldn't tell her she was mistaken. Height?"

"Five feet six."

"Occupation?"

"I help mother carry on the farm."

"Just as I expected!" cried the captain. "Slow as a yoke of oxen. Residence?"

"Willoughby Pastures."

The captain could not contain himself. "Well, Willoughby Pastures,—or whatever your name is,—you'll get yourself into the papers *this* time, *sure*. And I must say it serves you right. If you can't speak for yourself, who's going to speak for you, do you suppose? Might send round to the girl's house—— No, she wouldn't be there, ten to one. You've got to go through now. Next time don't be such an infernal fool."

The captain blotted his book and shut it.

"We'll have to lock him up here to-night," he said to the policeman. "Last batch has gone round. Better go through him." But Lemuel had been gone through before, and the officer's search of his pockets only revealed their emptiness. The captain struck a bell on his desk. "If it ain't all right, you can make it right with the judge in the morning," he added to Lemuel.

Lemuel looked up at the policeman who had arrested him. He was an elderly man, with a kindly face, squarely fringed with a chin-beard. The boy tried to speak, but he could only repeat, "I never saw her before. I never touched her."

The policeman looked at him and then at the captain.

"Too late now," said the latter. "Got to go through the mill this time. But if it ain't right, you can make it right."

Another officer had answered the bell, and the captain indicated with a comprehensive roll of his head that he was to take Lemuel away and lock him up.

"Oh, my!" moaned the boy. As they passed the door of a small room opening on an inner corridor, a smell of coffee gushed out of it; the officer stopped, and Lemuel caught sight of two gentlemen in the room with a policeman, who was saying:

"Get a cup of coffee here when we want it. Try one?" he suggested hospitably.

"No, thank you," said one of the gentlemen, with the bland respectfulness of people being shown about an institution. "How many of you are attached to this station?"

"Eighty-one," said the officer. "Largest station in town. Gang goes on at one in the morning, and another at eight and another at six P.M." He looked inquiringly at the officer in charge of Lemuel.

"Any matches?" asked this officer.

"Everything but money," said the other, taking some matches out of his waistcoat pocket.

Lemuel's officer went ahead, lighting the gas along the corridor, and the boy followed, while the other officer brought up the rear with the visitor whom he was lecturing. They passed some neat rooms, each with two beds in it, and he answered some question: "Tramps? Not much! Give *them* a *board* when they're drunk; send 'em round to the Wayfarers' Lodge when they're sober. These officers' rooms."

Lemuel followed his officer downstairs into a basement, where on either side of a white-walled, brilliantly lighted, specklessly clean corridor, there were numbers of cells, very clean and smelling of fresh whitewash. Each had a broad low shelf in it, and a bench opposite, a little wider than a man's body. Lemuel suddenly felt himself pushed into one of them, and then a railed door of iron was locked upon him. He stood motionless in the breadth of light and lines of shade which the gas-light cast upon him through the door, and knew the gentlemen were looking at him as their guide talked.

"Well, fill up pretty well, Sunday nights. Most the arrests for drunkenness. But all the arrests before seven o'clock sent to the City Prison. Only keep them that come in afterwards."

One of the gentlemen looked into the cell opposite Lemuel's. "There seems to be only one bunk. Do you ever put more into a cell?"

"Well, hardly ever, if they're men. Lot o' women brought in 'most always ask to be locked up together for company."

"I don't see where they sleep," said the visitor. "Do they lie on the floor?"

The officer laughed. "Sleep? *They* don't want to sleep. What *they* want to do is to set up all night, and talk it over."

Both of the visitors laughed.

"Some of the cells," resumed the officer, "have two bunks, but we hardly ever put more than one in a cell."

The visitors noticed that a section of the rail was removed in each door near the floor.

"That's to put a dipper of water through, or anything," explained the officer. "There!" he continued, showing them Lemuel's door; "see how the rails are bent there? You wouldn't think a man could squeeze through there, but we found a fellow half out o' that one night—backwards. Captain came down with a rattan and made it hot for him."

The visitors laughed, and Lemuel, in his cell, shuddered.

"I never saw anything so astonishingly clean," said one of the gentlemen. "And do you keep the gas burning here all night?"

"Yes; calculate to give 'em plenty of light," said the officer, with comfortable satisfaction in the visitor's complimentary tone.

"And the sanitary arrangements seem to be perfect, doctor," said the other visitor.

"Oh, perfect."

"Yes," said the officer, "we do the best we can for 'em."

The visitors made a murmur of approbation. Their steps moved away; Lemuel heard the guide saying, "Dunno *what* that fellow's in for. Find out in the captain's room."

"He didn't look like a very abandoned ruffian," said one of the visitors, with both pity and amusement in his voice.

VI

LEMUEL STOOD and leaned his head against the wall of his cell. The tears that had come to his relief in the morning when he found that he was robbed would not come now. He was trembling with famine and weakness, but he could not lie down; it would be like accepting his fate, and every fiber of his body joined his soul in rebellion against that. The hunger gnawed him incessantly, mixed with an awful sickness.

After a long time a policeman passed his door with another prisoner, a drunken woman, whom he locked into a cell at the end of the corridor. When he came back, Lemuel could endure it no longer. "Say!" he called huskily through his door. "Won't you give me a cup of that coffee upstairs? I haven't had anything but an apple to eat for nearly two days. I don't want you to *give* me the coffee. You can take my clasp button——"

The officer went by a few steps, then he came back, and peered in through the door at Lemuel's face. "Oh! that's you?" he said; he was the officer who had arrested Lemuel.

"Yes. Please get me the coffee. I'm afraid I shall have a fit of sickness if I go much longer."

"Well," said the officer, "I guess I can get you something." He went away, and came back, after Lemuel had given up the hope of his return, with a saucerless cup of coffee, and a slice of buttered bread laid on top of it. He passed it in through the opening at the bottom of the door.

"Oh, my!" gasped the starving boy. He thought he should drop the cup, his hand shook so when he took it. He gulped the coffee and swallowed the bread in a frenzy.

"Here—here's the button," he said as he passed the empty cup out to the officer.

"I don't want your button," answered the policeman. He hesitated a moment. "I shall be round at the court in the morning, and I guess if it ain't right we can make it so."

"Thank you, sir," said Lemuel, humbly grateful.

"You lay down now," said the officer. "We sha'n't put anybody in on you to-night."

"I guess I better," said Lemuel. He crept in upon the lower

shelf and stretched himself out in his clothes, with his arm under his head for a pillow. The drunken woman at the end of the corridor was clamoring to get out. She wished to get out just half a minute, she said, and settle with that hussy; then she would come back willingly. Sometimes she sang, sometimes she swore; but with the coffee still sensibly hot in his stomach, and the comfort of it in every vein, her uproar turned into an agreeable, fantastic medley for Lemuel, and he thought it was the folks singing in church at Willoughby Pastures, and they were all asking him who the new girl in the choir was, and he was saying Statira Dudley; and then it all slipped off into a smooth, yellow nothingness, and he heard some one calling him to get up.

When he woke in the morning he started up so suddenly that he struck his head against the shelf above him, and lay staring stupidly at the iron-work of his door.

He heard the order to turn out repeated at other cells along the corridor, and he crept out of his shelf, and then sat down upon it, waiting for his door to be unlocked. He was very hungry again, and he trembled with faintness. He wondered how he should get his breakfast, and he dreaded the trial in court less than the thought of going through another day with nothing to eat. He heard the stir of the other prisoners in the cells along the corridors, the low groans and sighs with which people pull themselves together after a bad night; and he heard the voice of the drunken woman, now sober, poured out in voluble remorse, and in voluble promise of amendment for the future, to every one who passed, if they would let her off easy. She said aisy, of course, and it was in her native accent that she bewailed the fate of the little ones whom her arrest had left motherless at home. No one seemed to answer her, but presently she broke into a cry of joy and blessing, and from her cell at the other end of the corridor came the clink of crockery. Steps approached with several pauses, and at last they paused at Lemuel's door, and a man outside stooped and pushed in, through the opening at the bottom, a big bowl of baked beans, a quarter of a loaf of bread, and a tin cup full of coffee. "Coffee's extra," he said, jocosely. "Comes from the officers. You're in luck, young feller."

"I ha'n't got anything to pay for it with," faltered Lemuel.

"Guess they'll trust you," said the man. "Anyrate, I got orders to leave it." He passed on, and Lemuel gathered up his breakfast, and arranged it on the shelf where he had slept; then he knelt down before it, and ate.

An hour later an officer came and unbolted his door from the outside. "Hurry up," he said; "Maria's waiting."

"Maria?" repeated Lemuel, innocently.

"Yes," returned the officer. "Other name's Black. She don't like to wait. Come out of here."

Lemuel found himself in the corridor with four or five other prisoners, whom some officers took in charge and conducted upstairs to the door of the station. He saw no woman, but a sort of omnibus without windows was drawn up at the curbstone.

"I thought," he said to an officer, "that there was a lady waiting to see me. Maria Black," he added, seeing that the officer did not understand.

The policeman roared, and could not help putting his head in at the office door to tell the joke.

"Well, you must introduce him," called a voice from within.

"Guess you ha'n't got the name exactly straight, young man," said the policeman to Lemuel, as he guarded him down the steps. "It's Black Maria you're looking for. There she is," he continued, pointing to the omnibus, "and don't you forget it. She's particular to have folks recognize her. She's blacker'n she's painted."

The omnibus was, in fact, a sort of æsthetic drab, relieved with salmon, as Lemuel had time to notice before he was hustled into it with the other prisoners, and locked in.

There were already several there, and as Lemuel's eyes accustomed themselves to the light that came in through the little panes at the sides of the roof, he could see that they were women; and by and by he saw that two of them were the saucy girls who had driven him from his seat in the Common that day, and laughed so at him. They knew him too, and one of them set up a shrill laugh. "Hello, Johnny! That you? You don't say so? What you up for *this* time? Going down to the Island? Well, give us a call there! Do be sociable! Ward II's the address." The other one laughed, and then swore at the first for trying to push her off the seat.

Lemuel broke out involuntarily in all the severity that was native to him. "You ought to be ashamed of yourselves."

This convulsed the bold things with laughter. When they could get their breath, one of them said, "Pshaw! I know what he's up for: preaching on the Common. Say, young feller! don't you want to hold a prayer-meetin' here?"

They burst into another shriek of laughter, so wild and shrill that the driver rapped on the roof, and called down, "Dry up in there!"

"Oh, you mind your horses, and we'll look after the passengers. Go and set on his knee, Jen, and cheer him up a little."

Lemuel sat in a quiver of abhorrence. The girl appealed to remained giggling beside her companion.

"I—I pity ye!" said Lemuel.

The Irishwoman had not stopped bewailing herself and imploring right and left an easy doom. She now addressed herself wholly to Lemuel, whose personal dignity seemed to clothe him with authority in her eyes. She told him about her children, left alone with no one to look after them; the two little girls, the boy only three years old. When the van stopped at a station to take in more passengers, she tried to get out—to tell the gentlemen at the office about it, she said.

After several of these halts they stopped at the basement of a large stone building, that had a wide flight of steps in front, and columns, like the church at Willoughby Pastures, only the church steps were wood, and the columns painted pine. Here more officers took charge of them, and put them in a room where there were already twenty-five or thirty other prisoners, the harvest of the night before; and presently another vanload was brought in. There were many women among them, but here there was no laughing or joking as there had been in the van. Scarcely any one spoke, except the Irishwoman, who crept up to an officer at the door from time to time, and begged him to tell the judge to let her have it easy this time. Lemuel could not help seeing that she and most of the others were familiar with the place. Those two saucy jades who had teased him were silent, and had lost their bold looks.

After waiting what seemed a long time, the door was

opened, and they were driven up a flight of stairs into a railed inclosure at the corner of a large room, where they remained huddled together, while a man at a long desk rattled over something that ended with "God bless the commonwealth of Massachusetts." On a platform behind the speaker sat a gray-haired man in spectacles, and Lemuel knew that he was in the court-room, and that this must be the judge. He could not see much of the room over the top of the railing, but there was a buzz of voices and a stir of feet beyond, that made him think the place was full. But full or empty, it was the same to him; his shame could not be greater or less. He waited apathetically while the clerk read off the charges against the vastly greater number of his fellow-prisoners arrested for drunkenness. When these were disposed of, he read from the back of a paper, which he took from a fresh pile, "Bridget Gallagher, complained of for habitual drunkenness. Guilty or not guilty?"

"Not guilty, your hanor," answered the Irishwoman who had come from Lemuel's station. "But make it aisy for me this time, judge, and ye'll never catch me in it again. I've three helpless childer at home, your hanor, starvin' and cryin' for their mother. Holy Mary, make it aisy, judge!"

A laugh went round the room, which a stern voice checked with "Silence, there!" but which renewed itself when the old woman took the stand at the end of the clerk's long desk, while a policeman mounted a similar platform outside the rail, and gave his testimony against her. It was very conclusive, and it was not affected by the denials with which the poor woman gave herself away more and more. She had nothing to say when invited to do so except to beg for mercy; the judge made a few inquiries, apparently casual, of the policeman; then after a moment's silence, in which he sat rubbing his chin, he leaned forward and said quietly to the clerk, "Give her three months."

The woman gave a wild Irish cry, "Oh, my poor childer!" and amidst the amusement of the spectators, which the constables could not check at once, was led wailing below.

Before Lemuel could get his breath those bold girls, one after the other, were put upon the stand. The charge against them was not made the subject of public investigation; the

judge and some other elderly gentleman talked it over together; and the girls, who had each wept in pleading guilty,
were put on probation, as Lemuel understood it, and, weeping still and bridling a little, were left in charge of this elderly
gentleman, and Lemuel saw them no more.

One case followed another, and Lemuel listened with the
fascination of terror; the sentences seemed terribly severe, and
out of all proportion to the offenses. Suddenly his own name
was called. His name had been called in public places before:
at the school exhibitions, where he had taken prizes in elocu-
tion and composition; in church, once, when the minister had
mentioned him for peculiar efficiency and zeal among other
Sabbath-school teachers. It was sacred to him for his father's
sake, who fell in the war, and who was recorded in it on the
ugly, pathetic monument on the village green; and hitherto
he had made it respected and even honored, and had tried all
the harder to keep it so because his family was poor, and his
mother had such queer ways and dressed so. He dragged himself to the stand which he knew he must mount, and stole
from under his eyelashes a glance at the court-room, which
took it all in. There were some people, whom he did not
know for reporters, busy with their pencils next the railing;
and there was a semicircular table in the middle of the room
at which a large number of policemen sat, and they had their
straw helmets piled upon it, with the hats of the lawyers who
sat among them. Beyond, the seats which covered the floor
were filled with the sodden loafers whom the law offers every
morning, the best dramatic amusement in the city. Presently,
among the stupid eyes fixed upon him, Lemuel was aware of
the eyes of that fellow who had passed the counterfeit money
on him; and when this scamp got up and coolly sauntered out
of the room, Lemuel was held in such a spell that he did not
hear the charge read against him, or the clerk's repeated demand, "Guilty or not guilty?"

He was recalled to himself by the voice of the judge.
"Young man, do you understand? Are you guilty of assaulting
this lady and taking her satchel, or not?"

"Not guilty," said Lemuel, huskily; and he looked, not at
the judge, but at the pretty girl, who confronted him from a
stand at the other end of the clerk's desk, blushing to find

herself there up to her wide-flung blue eyes. Lemuel blushed
too, and dropped his eyes; and it seemed to him in a crazy
kind of way that it was impolite to have pleaded not guilty
against her accusation. He stood waiting for the testimony
which the judge had to prompt her to offer.

"State the facts in regard to the assault," he said gravely.

"I don't know as I can do it, very well," began the girl.

"We shall be satisfied if you do your best," said the judge,
with the glimmer of a smile, which spread to a laugh among
the spectators, unrebuked by the constables, since the judge
had invited it.

In this atmosphere of sympathy the girl found her tongue,
and with a confiding twist of her pretty head began again:
"Well, now, I'll tell you just how it was. I'd just got my book
out of the Public Library, and I was going down Neponset
street on my way home, hurrying along, because I see it was
beginning to be pretty late, and the first thing I know somebody pulled my hat down over my eyes, and tore the brim
half off, so I don't suppose I can ever wear it again, it's such a
lookin' thing; anyrate it ain't the one I've got on, though it's
some like it; and then the next thing, somebody grabbed
away the satchel I'd got on my arm; and as soon as I could
get my eyes clear again, I see two fellows chasin' up the street,
and I told the officer somebody'd got my book; and I knew it
was one of those fellows runnin' away, and I said, 'There they
go now,' and the officer caught the hind one, and I guess the
other one got away; and the officer told me to follow along to
the station-house, and when we got there they took my name,
and where I roomed, and my age——"

"Do you recognize this young man as one of the persons
who robbed you?" interrupted the judge, nodding his head
toward Lemuel, who now lifted his head and looked his ac-
cuser fearlessly in her pretty eyes.

"Why, no!" she promptly replied. "The first thing I knew,
he'd pulled my hat over my eyes."

"But you recognize him as one of those you saw running
away?"

"Oh, yes, he's one of *them*," said the girl.

"What made you think he had robbed you?"

"Why, because my satchel was gone!" returned the girl,

with logic that apparently amused the gentlemen of the bar.

"But why did you think *he* had taken it?"

"Because I see him running away."

"You couldn't swear that he was the one who took your satchel?"

"Why, of course not! I didn't *see* him till I saw him running. And I don't know as he was the one, now," added the girl, in a sudden burst of generosity. "And if it was to do over again, I should say as much to the officers at the station. But I got confused when they commenced askin' me who I was, and how much I weighed, and what my height was; and *he* didn't say anything; and I got to thinkin' maybe it *was*; and when they told me that if I didn't promise to appear at court in the morning they'd have to lock me up, I was only too glad to get away alive."

By this time all the blackguard audience were sharing, unchecked, the amusement of the bar. The judge put up his hand to hide a laugh. Then he said to Lemuel, "Do you wish to question the plaintiff?"

The two young things looked at each other, and both blushed. "No," said Lemuel.

The girl looked at the judge for permission, and at a nod from him left the stand and sat down.

The officer who had arrested Lemuel took the stand on the other side of the rail from him, and corroborated the girl's story; but he had not seen the assault or robbery, and could not swear to either. Then Lemuel was invited to speak, and told his story with the sort of nervous courage that came to him in extremity. He told it from the beginning, and his adventure with the two beats in the Common made the audience laugh again. Even then, Lemuel could not see the fun of it; he stopped, and the stout ushers in blue flannel sacks commanded silence. Then Lemuel related how he had twice seen one of the beats since that time, but he was ashamed to say how he had let him escape out of that very room half an hour before. He told how he had found the beat in the crowd before the saloon, and how he was chasing him up the street when he heard the young lady hollo out, "There they go now!" and then the officer arrested him.

The judge sat a moment in thought; then said quietly, "The charge is dismissed"; and before Lemuel well knew what it meant, a gate was opened at the stand, and he was invited to pass out. He was free. The officer who had arrested him shook his hand in congratulation and excuse, and the lawyers and the other policemen gave him a friendly glance. The loafers and beats of the audience did not seem to notice him. They were already intent upon a case of colored assault and battery which had been called, and which opened with the promise of uncommon richness, both of the parties being women.

Lemuel saw that girl who had accused him passing down the aisle on the other side of the room. She was with another girl, who looked older. Lemuel walked fast, to get out of their way; he did not know why, but he did not want to speak to the girl. They walked fast too, and when he got down the stairs on to the ground floor of the court-house they overtook him.

"Say!" said the older girl, "I want to speak to *you*. I think it's a down shame, the way that you've been treated; and Statira, she feels jus's I do about it; and I tell her she's got to say so. It's the least she can do, I tell her, after what she got you *in* for. My name's 'Manda Grier; I room 'th S'tira; 'n' I come 'th her this mornin' t' help keep her up; b't I *didn't* know 't was goin' to be s'ch a *perfect* flat-out!"

As the young woman rattled on she grew more and more glib; she was what they call whopper-jawed, and spoke a language almost purely consonantal, cutting and clipping her words with a rapid play of her whopper-jaw till there was nothing but the bare bones left of them. Statira was crying, and Lemuel could not bear to see her cry. He tried to say something to comfort her, but all he could think of was, "I hope you'll get your book back," and 'Manda Grier answered for her:

"Oh, I guess 't ain't the book 't she cares for. S' far forth's the book goes, I guess she can afford to buy another book, well enough. B't I tell her she's done 'n awful thing, and a thing 't she'll carry to her grave 'th her, 'n't she'll remember to her dyin' day. That's what *I* tell her."

"She ha'n't got any call to feel bad about it," said Lemuel, clumsily. "It was just a mistake." Then, not knowing what more to say, he said, being come to the outer door by this time, "Well, I wish you good-morning."

"Well, good-morning," said 'Manda Grier, and she thrust her elbow sharply into Statira Dudley's side, so that she also said faintly:

"Well, good-morning!" She was fluent enough on the witness-stand and in the police station, but now she could not find a word to say.

The three stood together on the threshold of the court-house, not knowing how to get away from one another.

'Manda Grier put out her hand to Lemuel. He took it, and, "Well, good-morning," he said again.

"Well, good-morning," repeated 'Manda Grier.

Then Statira put out her hand, and she and Lemuel shook hands, and said together, "Well, good-morning," and on these terms of high civility they parted. He went one way and they another. He did not look back, but the two girls, marching off with locked arms and flying tongues, when they came to the corner, turned to look back. They both turned inward and so bumped their heads together.

"Why, you—coot!" cried 'Manda Grier, and they broke out laughing.

Lemuel heard their laugh, and he knew they were laughing at him; but he did not care. He wandered on, he did not know whither, and presently he came to the only place he could remember.

VII

THE PLACE was the Common, where his trouble had begun. He looked back to the beginning, and could see that it was his own fault. To be sure, you might say that if a fellow came along and offered to pay you fifty cents for changing a ten-dollar bill, you had a right to take it; but there was a voice in Lemuel's heart which warned him that greed to another's hurt was sin, and that if you took too much for a thing from a necessitous person, you oppressed and robbed him. You could make it appear otherwise, but you could not really change the nature of the act. He owned this with a sigh, and he owned himself justly punished. He was still on those terms of personal understanding with the eternal spirit of right which most of us lose later in life, when we have so often seemed to see the effect fail to follow the cause, both in the case of our own misdeeds and the misdeeds of others.

He sat down on a bench, and he sat there all day, except when he went to drink from the tin cup dangling by the chain from the nearest fountain. His good breakfast kept him from being hungry for a while, but he was as aimless and as hopeless as ever, and as destitute. He would have gone home now if he had had the money; he was afraid they would be getting anxious about him there, though he had not made any particular promises about the time of returning. He had dropped a postal card into a box as soon as he reached Boston, to tell of his safe arrival, and they would not expect him to write again.

There were only two ways for him to get home: to turn tramp and walk back, or to go to that Mr. Sewell and borrow the money to pay his passage. To walk home would add intolerably to the public shame he must suffer, and the thought of going to Mr. Sewell was, even in the secret which it would remain between him and the minister, a pang so cruel to his pride that he recoiled from it instantly. He said to himself he would stand it one day more; something might happen, and if nothing happened, he should think of it again. In the mean time he thought of other things: of that girl, among the rest, and how she looked at the different times. As nearly as he could make out, she seemed to be a very fashionable girl; at any rate, she was dressed fashionably, and she was nice-looking. He did not know whether she had behaved very sensibly, but he presumed she was some excited.

Toward dark, when Lemuel was reconciling himself to another night's sleep in the open air, a policeman sauntered along the mall, and as he drew nearer the boy recognized his friendly captor. He dropped his head, but it was too late. The officer knew him, and stopped before him.

"Well," he said, "hard at it, I see."

Lemuel made no answer, but he was aware of a friendly look in the officer's face, mixed with fatherly severity.

"I was in hopes you had started back to Willoughby Pastur's before this. You don't want to get into the habit of settin' round on the Common, much. First thing you know you can't quit it. Where you goin' to put up to-night?"

"I don't know," murmured Lemuel.

"Got no friends in town you can go to?"

"No."

"Well, now, look here! Do you think you could find your way back to the station?"

"I guess so," said Lemuel, looking up at the officer questioningly.

"Well, when you get tired of this, you come round, and we'll provide a bed for you. And you get back home to-morrow, quick as you can."

"Thank you," said Lemuel. He was helpless against the advice and its unjust implication, but he could not say anything.

"Get out o' Boston, anyway, wherever you go or don't go," continued the officer. "It's a bad place."

He walked on, and left Lemuel to himself again. He thought bitterly that no one knew better than himself how luridly wicked Boston was, and that there was probably not a soul in it more helplessly anxious to get out of it. He thought it hard to be talked to as if it were his fault; as if he wished to become a vagrant and a beggar. He sat there an hour or two longer, and then he took the officer's advice, so far as concerned his going to the station for a bed, swallowing his pride as he must. He must do that, or he must go to Mr. Sewell. It was easier to accept humiliation at the hands of strangers. He found his way there with some difficulty, and slinking in at the front door, he waited at the threshold of the captain's room while he and two or three officers disposed of a respectably dressed man, whom a policeman was holding up by the collar of his coat. They were searching his pockets and taking away his money, his keys, and his pencil and pen-knife, which the captain sealed up in a large envelope, and put into his desk.

"There! take him and lock him up. He's pretty well loaded," said the captain.

Then he looked up and saw Lemuel. "Hello! Can't keep away, eh?" he demanded jocosely. "Well, we've heard about you. I told you the judge would make it all right. What's wanted? Bed? Well, here!" The captain filled up a blank which he took from a pigeon-hole; and gave it to Lemuel. "I guess that'll fix you out for the night. And to-morrow you put back to Willoughby Pastures tight as you can get there. You're on the wrong track now. First thing you know you'll be a professional tramp, and then you won't be worth the powder to blow you. I use plain talk with you because you're a beginner. I wouldn't waste my breath on that fellow behind you."

Lemuel looked round, and almost touched with his a face that shone fiery red through the rusty growth of a week's beard, and recoiled from a figure that was fouler as to shirt and coat and trousers than anything the boy had seen; though the tramps used to swarm through Willoughby Pastures before the Selectmen began to lock them up in the town poor-house and set them to breaking stone. There was no ferocity in the loathsome face; it was a vagrant swine that looked from it, no worse in its present mood than greedy and sleepy.

"Bed?" demanded the captain, writing another blank. "Never been here before, I suppose?" he continued with good-natured irony. "I don't seem to remember you."

The captain laughed, and the tramp returned a husky "Thank you, sir," and took himself off into the street.

Then the captain came to Lemuel's help. "You follow him," he said, "and you'll come to a bed by and by."

He went out, and, since he could do no better, did as he was bid. He had hardly ever seen a drunken man at Willoughby Pastures, where the prohibition law was strictly enforced; there was no such person as a thief in the whole community, and the tramps were gone long ago. Yet here was he, famed at home for the rectitude of his life and the loftiness of his aims, consorting with drunkards and thieves and tramps, and warned against what he was doing by policemen, as if he was doing it of his own will. It was very strange business. If it was *all* a punishment for taking that fellow's half-dollar, it was pretty heavy punishment. He was not going to say that it was unjust, but he would say it was hard. His spirit was now so bruised and broken that he hardly knew what to think.

He followed the tramp as far off as he could and still keep him in sight, and he sometimes thought he had lost him, in the streets that climbed and crooked beyond the Common towards the quarter whither they were going; but he reappeared, slouching and shambling rapidly on, in the glare of some electric lights that stamped the ground with shadows thick and black as if cut in velvet or burnt into the surface. Here and there some girl brushed against the boy, and gave him a joking or jeering word; her face flashed into light for a moment, and then vanished in the darkness she passed into. It was that hot October, and the night was close and still; on the steps of some of the houses groups of fat, weary women were sitting, and children were playing on the sidewalks, using the lamp-posts for goal or tag. The tramp ahead of Lemuel issued upon a brilliantly lighted little square, with a great many horse-cars coming and going in it; a church with stores on the ground floor, and fronting it on one side a row of handsome old stone houses with iron fences, and on another a great hotel, with a high-pillared portico, where men sat talking and smoking. People were waiting on the sidewalk to take the cars; a druggist's window threw its mellow lights into the street; from open cellar-ways came the sound of banjos and violins. At one of these cellar-doors his guide lingered so long that Lemuel thought he should have to find the way beyond for himself. But the tramp suddenly commanded himself from the music, the light, and the smell of strong drink, which Lemuel caught a whiff of as he followed, and turning a corner led the way to the side of a lofty building in a dark street, where they met other like shapes tending toward it from different directions.

VIII

LEMUEL ENTERED a lighted doorway from a bricked court-yard, and found himself with twenty or thirty houseless comrades in a large, square room, with benching against the wall for them to sit on. They were all silent and quelled-looking, except a young fellow whom Lemuel sat down be-side, and who, ascertaining that he was a new-comer, seemed disposed to do the honors of the place. He was not daunted by the reserve native to Lemuel, or by that distrust of strang-ers which experience had so soon taught him. He addressed him promptly as mate, and told him that the high, narrow, three-sided tabling in the middle of the room was where they would get their breakfast, if they lived.

"And I guess I shall live," he said. "I notice I 'most always live till breakfast-time, whatever else I do, or I don't do; but sometimes it don't seem as if I *could* saw my way through that quarter of a cord of wood." At a glance of inquiry which Lemuel could not forbear, he continued: "What I mean by a quarter of a cord of wood is that they let you exercise that much free in the morning, before they give you your break-fast: it's the doctor's orders. This used to be a school-house, but it's in better business now. They got a kitchen under here, that beats the Parker House; you'll smell it pretty soon. No whacking on the knuckles here any more. All serene, I tell you. You'll see. I don't know how I should got along without this institution, and I tell the manager so, every time I see him. That's him, hollering 'Next,' out of that room there. It's a name he gives all of us; he knows it's a name we'll answer to. Don't you forget it when it comes your turn."

He was younger than Lemuel, apparently, but his swarthy, large-mouthed, droll-eyed face affirmed the experience of a sage. He wore a blue flannel shirt, with loose trousers belted round his waist, and he crushed a soft felt hat between his hands; his hair was clipped close to his skull, and as he rubbed it now and then it gave out a pleasant, rasping sound.

The tramps disappeared in the order of their vicinity to the manager's door, and it came in time to this boy and Lemuel.

"You come along with me," he said, "and do as I do." When they entered the presence of the manager, who sat at a desk, Lemuel's guide nodded to him, and handed over his order for a bed.

"Ever been here before?" asked the manager, as if going through the form for a joke.

"Never." He took a numbered card which the manager gave him, and stood aside to wait for Lemuel, who made the same answer to the same question, and received his numbered card.

"Now," said the young fellow, as they passed out of another door, "we ain't either of us 'Next' any more. I'm Thirty-nine, and you're Forty, and don't you forget it. All right, boss," he called back to the manager; "I'll take care of him! This way," he said to Lemuel. "The reason why I said I'd never been here before," he explained on the way down, "was because you got to say something when he asks you. Most of 'em says last fall or last year, but I say never, because it's just as true, and he seems to like it better. We're going down to the dressing-room now, and then we're going to take a bath. Do you know why?"

"No," said Lemuel.

"Because we can't help it. It's the doctor's orders. He thinks it's the best thing you can do, just before you go to bed."

The basement was brightly lighted with gas everywhere, and a savory odor of onion-flavored broth diffused itself through the whole place.

"Smell it? You might think that was supper, but it ain't. It's breakfast. You got a bath and a night's rest as well as the quarter of a cord of wood between you and that stew. Hungry?"

"Not very," said Lemuel faintly.

"Because if you say you are they'll give you all the bread and water you can hold now. But I ruther wait."

"I guess I don't want anything to-night," said Lemuel, shrinking from the act of beggary.

"Well, I guess you won't lose anything in the long run," said the other. "You'll make it up at breakfast."

They turned into a room where eight or ten tramps were

undressing; some of them were old men, quite sodden and stupefied with a life of vagrancy and privation; others were of a dull or cunning middle-age. Two or three were as young as Lemuel and his partner, and looked as if they might be poor fellows who had found themselves in a strange city without money or work; but it was against them that they had known where to come for a night's shelter, Lemuel felt.

There were large iron hooks hanging from the walls and ceiling, and his friend found the numbers on two of them corresponding to those given Lemuel and himself, and brass checks which they hung around their necks.

"You got to hang your things on that hook, all but your shoes and stockings, and you got to hang on to *them* yourself. Forty's your number, and forty's your hook, and they give you the clothes off'n it in the morning."

He led the way through the corridor into a large room where a row of bath-tubs flanked the wall, half of them filled with bathers, who chatted in tones of subdued cheerfulness under the pleasant excitement of unlimited hot and cold water. As each new-comer appeared a black boy, perched on a window-sill, jumped down and dashed his head from a large bottle which he carried.

"Free shampoo," explained Lemuel's mate. "Doctor's orders. Only you have to do the rubbing yourself. I don't suppose *you* need it, but some the pardners here couldn't sleep without it," he continued, as Lemuel shrank a little from the bottle, and then submitted. "It's a regular night-cap."

The tramps recognized the humor of the explanation by a laugh, intended to be respectful to the establishment in its control, which spread along their line, and the black boy grinned.

"There ain't anything mean about the Wayfarer's Hotel," said the mate; and they all laughed again, a little louder.

Each man, having dried himself from his bath, was given a coarse linen night-gown; sometimes it was not quite whole, but it was always clean; and then he gathered up his shoes and stockings and went out.

"Hold on a minute," said the mate to Lemuel, when they left the bath-room. "You ought to see the kitchen." And in his night-gown, with his shoes in his hand, he led Lemuel to the open door which that delicious smell of broth came from. A vast copper-topped boiler was bubbling within, and trying to get its lid off. The odor made Lemuel sick with hunger.

"Refrigerator in the next room," the mate lectured on. "Best beef-chucks in the market; fish for Fridays—we don't make any man go against his religion in *this* house; pots of butter as big as a cheese,—none of your oleomargarine,—the real thing, every time; potatoes and onions and carrots laying around on the floor; barrels of hard-tack; and bread, like sponge,—bounce you up if you was to jump on it,—baked by the women at the Chardon Street Home. Oh, I tell you we do things in style here."

A man who sat reading a newspaper in the corner looked up sharply. "Hello, there! what's wanted?"

"Just dropped in to wish you good-night, Jimmy," said Lemuel's mate.

"You clear out!" said the man good-humoredly, as if to an old acquaintance, who must not be allowed to presume upon his familiarity.

"All right, Jimmy," said the boy. He set his left hand horizontally on its wrist at his left shoulder and cut the air with it in playful menace as the man dropped his eyes again to his paper. "They're all just so in this house," he explained to Lemuel. "No nonsense, but good-natured. *They're* all right. They know me."

He mounted two flights of stairs in front of Lemuel to a corridor, where an attendant stood examining the numbers on the brass checks hung around the tramps' necks as they came up with their shoes in their hands. He instructed them that the numbers corresponded to the cots they were to occupy, as well as the hooks where their clothes hung. Some of them seemed hardly able to master the facts. They looked wistfully, like cowed animals, into his face as he made the case clear.

Two vast rooms, exquisitely clean, like the whole house, opened on the right and left of the corridor, and presented long phalanxes of cots, each furnished with two coarse blankets, a quilt, and a thin pillow.

"Used to be school-rooms," said Lemuel's mate, in a low tone.

"Cots thirty-nine and forty," said the attendant, looking at their checks. "Right over there, in the corner."

"Come along," said the mate, leading the way, with the satisfaction of an habitué. "Best berth in the room, and about the last they reach in the morning. You see, they got to take us as we come when they call us, and the last feller in at night's the first feller out in the morning, because his bed's the nearest the door."

He did not pull down the blankets of his cot at once, but stretched himself out on the quilt that covered them. "Cool off a little first," he explained. "Well, this is what I call comfort, mate, heigh?"

Lemuel did not answer. He was watching the attendant with a group of tramps who could not find their cots.

"Can't read, I suppose," said the mate, a little disdainfully. "Well, look at that old chap, will you!" A poor fellow was fumbling with his blankets, as if he did not know quite how to manage them. The attendant had to come to his help, and tuck him in. "Well, there!" exclaimed the mate, lifting himself on his elbow to admire the scene. "I don't suppose he's ever been in a decent bed before. Hayloft's *his* style, or a board-pile." He sank down again, and went on: "Well, you do see all kinds of folks here, that's a fact. Sorry there ain't more in to-night, so's to give you a specimen. You ought to be here in the winter. Well, it ain't so lonesome now in summer as it used to be. Sometimes I used to have nearly the whole place to myself, summer nights, before they got to passin' these laws against tramps in the country, and lockin' 'em up when they ketched 'em. That drives 'em into the city summers now; because they're always sure of a night's rest and a day's board here if they ask for it. But winter's the time. You'll see all these cots full then. They let on the steam-heat, and it's comfortable; and it's always airy and healthy." The vast room was, in fact, perfectly ventilated, and the poor who housed themselves that night, and many well-to-do sojourners in hotels, had reason to envy the vagrants their free lodging.

The mate now got under his quilt, and turned his face toward Lemuel, with one hand under his cheek. "They don't let *every* body into this room, 's I was tellin' ye. This room is for the big-bugs, you know. Sometimes a drunk will get in, though, in spite of everything. Why, I've seen a drunk at the station-house, when I've been gettin' my order for a bed, stiffen up so 't the captain himself thought he was sober; and then I've followed him round here, wobblin' and corkscrewin' all over the sidewalk; and then I've seen him stiffen up in the office again, and go through his bath like a little man, and get into bed as drunk as a fish; and maybe wake up in the night with the man with the poker after him, and make things hum. Well, sir, one night there was a drunk in here that thought the man with the poker was after him, and he just up and jumped out of this window behind you—three stories from the ground."

Lemuel could not help lifting himself in bed to look at it. "Did it kill him?" he asked.

"Kill him? *No!* You can't kill a *drunk*. One night there was a drunk got loose here, and he run down-stairs into the wood-yard, and he got hold of an axe down there, and it took five men to get that axe away from that drunk. He was goin' for the snakes."

"The snakes!" repeated Lemuel. "Are there snakes in the wood-yard?"

The other gave a laugh so loud that the attendant called out, "Less noise over there!"

"I'll tell you about the snakes in the morning," said the mate; and he turned his face away from Lemuel.

The stories of the drunks had made Lemuel a little anxious; but he thought that attendant would keep a sharp lookout, so that there would not really be much danger. He was very drowsy from his bath, in spite of the hunger that tormented him, but he tried to keep awake and think what he should do after breakfast.

IX

"COME, TURN OUT!" said a voice in his ear, and he started up, to see the great dormitory where he had fallen asleep empty of all but himself and his friend.

"Make out a night's rest?" asked the latter. "Didn't I tell you we'd be the last up? Come along!" He preceded Lemuel, still drowsy, down the stairs into the room where they had undressed, and where the tramps were taking each his clothes from their hook, and hustling them on.

"What time is it, Johnny?" asked Lemuel's mate of the attendant. "I left my watch under my pillow."

"Five o'clock," said the man, helping the poor old fellow who had not known how to get into bed to put on his clothes.

"Well, that's a pretty good start," said the other. He finished his toilet by belting himself around the waist, and "Come along, mate," he said to Lemuel. "I'll show you the way to the tool-room."

He led him through the corridor into a chamber of the basement where there were bright rows of wood-saws, and ranks of saw-horses, with heaps of the latter in different stages of construction. "House self-supporting, as far as it can. We don't want to be beholden to anybody if we can help it. We make our own horses here; but we can't make our saws, or we would. Ever had much practice with the wood-saw?"

"No," said Lemuel, with a throb of homesickness, that brought back the hacked log behind the house, and the axe resting against it; "we always chopped our stove-wood."

"Yes, that's the way in the country. Well, now," said the other, "I'll show you how to choose a saw. Don't you be took in by no new saw because it's bright and looks pretty. You want to take a saw that's been filed and filed away till it ain't more'n an inch and a half deep; and then you want to tune it up, just so, like a banjo,—not too tight, and not too slack,— and then it'll slip through a stick o' wood like—lyin'." He selected a saw, and put it in order for Lemuel. "There!" He picked out another. "Here's *my* old stand-by!" He took up a saw-horse at random, to indicate that one need not be critical in that, and led through the open door into the wood-yard, where a score or two of saws were already shrilling and wheezing through the wood.

It was a wide and lofty shed, with piles of cord-wood and slabs at either end, and walled on the farther side with kindling, sawed, split, and piled up with admirable neatness. The place gave out the sweet smell of the woods from the bark of the logs and from the fresh section of their grain. A double rank of saw-horses occupied the middle space, and beside each horse lay a quarter of a cord of wood, at which the men were toiling in sullen silence for the most part, only exchanging a grunt or snarl of dissatisfaction with one another.

"Morning, mates," said Lemuel's friend cheerfully, as he entered the shed, and put his horse down beside one of the piles. "Thought we'd look in and see how you was gettin' along. Just stepped round from the Parker House while our breakfast was a-cookin'. Hope you all rested well?"

The men paused, with their saws at different slopes in the wood, and looked round. The night before, in the nakedness in which Lemuel had first seen them, the worst of them had the inalienable comeliness of nature, and their faces, softened by their relation to their bodies, were not so bad; they were not so bad, looking from their white night-gowns; but now, clad in their filthy rags, and caricatured out of all native dignity by their motley and misshapen attire, they were a hideous gang, and all the more hideous for the grin that overspread their stubbly muzzles at the boy's persiflage.

"Don't let me interrupt you, fellows," he said, flinging a log upon his horse, and dashing his saw gayly into it. "Don't mind *me*! I know you hate to lose a minute of this fun; I understand just how you feel about it, and I don't want you to stand upon ceremony with *me*. Treat me just like one of yourselves, gents. This beech-wood is the regular Nova Scotia thing, ain't it? Tough and knotty! I can't bear any of your cheap wood-lot stuff from around here. What I want is Nova Scotia wood every time. Then I feel that I'm gettin' the worth of my money." His log dropped apart on each side of his horse, and he put on another. "Well, mates," he rattled on, "this is lovely, ain't it? I wouldn't give up my little quarter of a cord of green Nova Scotia before breakfast for anything; I've got into the way of it, and I can't live without it."

The tramps chuckled at these ironies, and the attendant who looked into the yard now and then did not interfere with them.

The mate went through his stint as rapidly as he talked, and he had nearly finished before Lemuel had half done. He did not offer to help him, but he delayed the remnant of his work, and waited for him to catch up, talking all the while with gay volubility, joking this one and that, and keeping the whole company as cheerful as it was in their dull, sodden nature to be. He had a floating eye that harmonized with his queer, mobile face, and played round on the different figures, but mostly upon Lemuel's dogged, rustic industry as if it really amused him.

"What's your lay after breakfast?" he asked, as they came to the last log together.

"Lay?" repeated Lemuel.

"What you goin' to do?"

"I don't know; I can't tell yet."

"You know," said the other, "you can come back here and get your dinner, if you want to saw wood for it from ten till twelve, and you get your supper if you'll saw from five to six."

"Are you going to do that?" asked Lemuel cautiously.

"No, sir," said the other; "I can't spare the time. I'm goin' to fill up for all day at breakfast, and then I'm going up to lay round on the Common till it's time to go to the police court; and when that's over I'm goin' back to the Common ag'in, and lay round the rest of the day. I hain't got any leisure for no such nonsense as wood-sawin'. I don't mind the work, but I hate to waste the time. It's the way with most o' the pardners, unless it's the green hands. That so, pards?"

Some of them had already gone in to breakfast; the smell of the stew came out to the wood-yard through the open door. Lemuel and his friend finished their last stick at the same time, and went in together, and found places side by side at the table in the waiting-room. The attendant within its oblong was serving the men with heavy quart bowls of the steaming broth. He brought half a loaf of light, elastic bread with each, and there were platters of hard-tack set along the board, which every one helped himself from freely, and broke into his broth.

"Morning, Jimmy," said the mate, as the man brought him and Lemuel their portions. "I hate to have the dining-room chairs off a-paintin' when there's so much style about everything else, and I've got a visitor with me. But I tell him he'll have to take us as he finds us, and stand it this mornin'." He wasted no more words on his joke, but, plunging his large tin spoon into his bowl, kept his breath to cool his broth, blowing upon it with easy grace, and swallowing it at a tremendous rate, though Lemuel, after following his example, still found it so hot that it brought the tears into his eyes. It was delicious, and he was ravenous from his twenty-four hours' fast; but his companion was scraping the bottom of his bowl before Lemuel had got half-way down, and he finished his second as Lemuel finished his first.

"Just oncet more for both of us, Jimmy," he said, pushing his bowl across the board; and when the man brought them back he said, "Now I'm goin' to take it easy and enjoy myself. I can't never seem to get the good of it till about the third or fourth bowl. Too much of a hurry."

"Do they give you four bowls?" gasped Lemuel in astonishment.

"They give your four barrels, if you can hold it," replied the other proudly; "and some the mates *can*, pretty near. They got an awful tank, as a general rule, the pards has. There ain't anything mean about this house. They don't scamp the broth, and they don't shab the measure. I do wish you could see that refrigerator oncet. Never been much at sea, have you, mate?"

Lemuel said he had never been at sea at all.

The other leaned forward with his elbows on each side of his bowl, and lazily broke his hard-tack into it. "Well, I have. I was shipped when I was about eleven years old by a shark that got me drunk. I wanted to ship, but I wanted to ship on an American vessel for New Orleans. First thing I knowed I turned up on a Swedish brig bound for Venice. Ever been to It'ly?"

"No," said Lemuel.

"Well, I hain't but oncet. Oncet is enough for *me*. I run away while I was in Venice, and went ashore—if you can call it ashore; it's all water, and you got to go round in boats, gondolas they call 'em there—and went to see the American counsul, and told him I was an American boy, and tried to get him to get me off. But he couldn't do anything. If you ship under the Swedish flag you're a Swede, and the whole United States couldn't get you off. If I'd 'a' shipped under the American flag I'd 'a' been an American, I don't care if I was born in Hottentot. That's what the counsul said. I never want to see that town ag'in. I used to hear songs about Venice: 'Beautiful Venice, Bride of the Sea'; but I think it's a kind of a hole of a place. Well, what I started to say was that when I turn up in Boston now,—and I most generally do,—I don't go to no sailor boardin'-house; I break for the Wayfarer's Lodge every time. It's a temperance house, and they give you the worth o' your money."

"Come! hurry up!" said the attendant. He wiped the table impatiently with his towel, and stood waiting for Lemuel and the other to finish. All the rest had gone.

"Don't you be too fresh, pard," said the mate, with the effect of standing upon his rights. "Guess if you was on your third bowl, you wouldn't hurry."

The attendant smiled. "Don't you want to lend us a hand with the dishes?" he asked.

"Who's sick?" asked the other in his turn.

"Johnny's got a day off."

The boy shook his head. "No; I couldn't. If it was a case of sickness, of course I'd do it. But I couldn't spare the time; I couldn't really. Why, I ought to be up on the Common now."

Lemuel had listened with a face of interest.

"Don't you want to make half a dollar, young feller?" asked the attendant.

"Yes, I do," said Lemuel eagerly.

"Know how to wash dishes?"

"Yes," answered the boy, not ashamed of his knowledge, as the boy of another civilization might have been. Nothing more distinctly marks the rustic New England civilization than the taming of its men to the performance of certain domestic offices elsewhere held dishonorably womanish. The boy learns not only to milk and to keep the milk-cans clean, but to churn, to wash dishes, and to cook.

"Come around here, then," said the attendant, and Lemuel promptly obeyed.

"Well, now," said his mate, "that's right. I'd do it myself if I had the time." He pulled his soft wool hat out of his hip pocket. "Well, good-morning, pards. I don't know as I shall see you again much before night." Lemuel was lifting a large tray, heavy with empty broth-bowls. "What *time* did you say it was, Jimmy?"

"Seven o'clock."

"Well, I just got time to get there," said the other, putting on his hat, and pushing out of the door.

At the moment Lemuel was lifting his tray of empty broth-bowls, Mr. Sewell was waking for the early quarter-to-eight breakfast, which he thought it right to make—not perhaps as an example to his parishioners, most of whom had the leisure to lie later, but as a sacrifice, not too definite, to the lingering ideal of suffering. He could not work before breakfast,—his delicate digestion forbade that,—or he would have risen still earlier; and he employed the twenty minutes he had between his bath and his breakfast in skimming the morning paper.

Just at present Mr. Sewell was taking two morning papers: the "Advertiser," which he had always taken, and a cheap little one-cent paper, which had just been started, and which he had subscribed for experimentally, with the vague impression that he ought to encourage the young men who had established it. He did not like it very well. It was made up somewhat upon the Western ideal, and dealt with local matters in a manner that was at once a little more lively and a little more intimate than he had been used to. But before he had quite made up his mind to stop it, his wife had come to like it on that very account. She said it was interesting. On this point she used her conscience a little less actively than usual, and he had to make her observe that to be interesting was not the whole duty of journalism. It had become a matter of personal pride with them respectively to attack and defend the "Sunrise," as I shall call the little sheet, though that was not the name; and Mr. Sewell had lately made some gain through the character of the police reports, which the "Sunrise" had been developing into a feature. It was not that offensive matters were introduced; the worst cases were in fact rather blinked; but Sewell insisted that the tone of flippant gayety with which many facts, so serious, so tragic for their perpetrators and victims, were treated was odious. He objected to the court being called a Mill, and prisoners Grists, and the procedure Grinding; he objected to the familiar name of Uncle for the worthy gentleman to whose care certain offenders were confided on probation. He now read that department of the "Sunrise" the first thing every morning, in the hope of finding something with which to put Mrs. Sewell hopelessly in the wrong; but this morning a heading in the foreign news of the "Advertiser" caught his eye, and he laid the "Sunrise" aside to read at the breakfast-table. His wife came down in a cotton dress, as a tribute to the continued warmth of the weather, and said that she had not called the children, because it was Saturday, and they might as well have their sleep out. He liked to see her in that dress; it had a leafy rustling that was pleasant to his ear, and as she looked into the library he gayly put out his hand, which she took, and suffered herself to be drawn toward him. Then she gave him a kiss, somewhat less business-like and preoccupied than usual.

"Well, you've got Lemuel Barker off your mind at last," she divined, in recognition of her husband's cheerfulness.

"Yes, he's off," admitted Sewell.

"I hope he'll stay in Willoughby Pastures after this. Of course it puts an end to our going there next summer."

"Oh, I don't know," Sewell feebly demurred.

"*I* do," said his wife, but not despising his insincerity enough to insist that he did also. The mellow note of an apostle's bell—the gift of an æsthetic parishioner—came from below, and she said, "Well, there's breakfast, David," and went before him down the stairs.

He brought his papers with him. It would have been her idea of heightened coziness at this breakfast, which they had once a week alone together, not to have the newspapers; but she saw that he felt differently, and after a number of years of married life a woman learns to let her husband have his own way in some unimportant matters. It was so much his nature to have some sort of reading always in hand, that he was certainly more himself, and perhaps more companionable, with his papers than without them.

She merely said, "Let me take the 'Sunrise,' " when she had poured out his coffee, and he had helped her to cantaloupe and steak, and spread his "Advertiser" beside his plate. He had the "Sunrise" in his lap.

"No, you may have the 'Advertiser,' " he said, handing it over the table to her. "I was down first, and I got both the papers. I'm not really obliged to make any division, but I've seen the 'Advertiser,' and I'm willing to behave unselfishly. If you're very impatient for the police report in the 'Sunrise,' I'll read it aloud for you. I think that will be a very good test of its quality, don't you?"

He opened the little sheet, and smiled teasingly at his wife, who said, "Yes, read it aloud; I'm not at all ashamed of it."

She put the "Advertiser" in her lap, and leaned defiantly forward, while she stirred her coffee, and Sewell unfolded the little sheet, and glanced up and down its columns. "Go on! If you can't find it, I can."

"Never mind! Here it is," said Sewell, and he began to read:

" 'The mill opened yesterday morning with a smaller number of grists than usual, but they made up in quality what they lacked in quantity.'

"Our friend's metaphor seems to have weakened under him a little," commented Sewell, and then he pursued:

" 'A reasonable supply of drunks were dispatched——'

"Come, now, Lucy! you'll admit that this is horrible?" he broke off.

"No," said his wife, "I will admit nothing of the kind. It's flippant, I'll allow. Go on!"

"I can't," said Sewell; but he obeyed.

" 'A reasonable supply of drunks were dispatched, and an habitual drunk, in the person of a burly dame from Tipperary, who pleaded not guilty and then urged the "poor childer" in extenuation, was sent down the harbor for three months; Uncle Cook had been put in charge of a couple of young frailties whose hind name was woman——'

"How do you like that, my dear?" asked Sewell exultantly.

Mrs. Sewell looked grave, and then burst into a shocked laugh. "You must stop that paper, David! I can't have it about for the children to get hold of. But it *is* funny, isn't it? That will do——"

"No, I think you'd better have it all now. There can't be anything worse. It's funny, yes, with that truly infernal drollery which the newspaper wits seem to have the art of." He read on:

"——'when a case was called that brought the breath of clover-blossoms and hay-seed into the sultry court-room, and warmed the cockles of the habitués' toughened pericardiums with a touch of real poetry. This was a case of assault with intent to rob, in which a lithe young blonde, answering to the good old Puritanic name of Statira Dudley, was the complainant, and the defendant an innocent-looking, bucolic youth, yclept——' "

Sewell stopped and put his hand to his forehead.

"What is it, David?" demanded his wife. "Why don't you go on? Is it too scandalous?"

"No, no," murmured the minister.

"Well?"

"I *can't* go on. But you must read it, Lucy," he said, in quite a passion of humility. "And you must try to be merciful. That poor boy—that——"

He handed the paper to his wife, and made no attempt to escape from judgment, but sat submissive while she read the report of Lemuel's trial. The story was told throughout in the poetico-jocular spirit of the opening sentences; the reporter had felt the simple charm of the affair, only to be ashamed of it and the more offensive about it.

When she had finished Mrs. Sewell did not say anything. She merely looked at her husband, who looked really sick.

At last he said, making an effort to rise from his chair, "I must go and see him, I suppose."

"Yes, if you can find him," responded his wife with a sigh.

"Find him?" echoed Sewell.

"Yes. Goodness knows what more trouble the wretched creature's got into by this time. You saw that he was acquitted, didn't you?" she demanded in answer to her husband's stare.

"No, I didn't. I supposed he was convicted, of course."

"Well, you see it isn't so bad as it might be," she said, using a pity which she did not perhaps altogether feel. "Eat your breakfast now, David, and then go and try to look him up."

"Oh, I don't want any breakfast," pleaded the minister.

He offered to rise again, but she motioned him down in his chair. "David, you shall! I'm not going to have you going about all day with a headache. Eat! And then when you've finished your breakfast, go and find out which station that officer Baker belongs to, and he can tell you something about the boy, if any one can."

Sewell made what shift he could to grasp these practical ideas, and he obediently ate of whatever his wife bade him. She would not let him hurry his breakfast in the least, and when he had at last finished, she said: "Now you can go, David. And when you've found the boy, don't you let him out of your sight again till you've put him aboard the train for Willoughby Pastures, and seen the train start out of the depot with him. Never mind your sermon. I will be setting down the heads of a sermon, while you're gone, that will do *you* good, if you write it out, whether it helps any one else or not."

Sewell was not so sure of that. He had no doubt that his wife would set down the heads of a powerful sermon, but he questioned whether any discourse, however potent, would have force to benefit such an abandoned criminal as he felt himself, in walking down his brown-stone steps, and up the long brick sidewalk of Bolingbroke street toward the Public Garden. The beds of geraniums and the clumps of scarlet-blossomed salvia in the little grass-plots before the houses, which commonly flattered his eye with their color, had a suggestion of penal fires in them now, that needed no lingering superstition in his nerves to realize something very like perdition for his troubled soul. It was not wickedness he had been guilty of, but he had allowed a good man to be made the agency of suffering, and he was sorely to blame, for he had sinned against himself. This was what his conscience said, and though his reason protested against his state of mind as a phase of the religious insanity which we have all inherited in some measure from Puritan times, it could not help him. He went along involuntarily framing a vow that if Providence would mercifully permit him to repair the wrong he had done, he would not stop at any sacrifice to get that unhappy boy back to his home, but would gladly take any open shame or obloquy upon himself in order to accomplish this.

He met a policeman on the bridge of the Public Garden, and made bold to ask him at once if he knew an officer named Baker, and which station he could be found at. The policeman was over-rich in the acquaintance of two officers of the name of Baker, and he put his hand on Sewell's shoulder, in the paternal manner of policemen when they will be friendly, and advised him to go first to the Neponset street station, to which one of these Bakers was attached, and inquire there first. "Anyway, that's what I should do in your place."

Sewell was fulsomely grateful, as we all are in the like case; and at the station he used an urbanity with the captain which was perhaps not thrown away upon him, but which was certainly disproportioned to the trouble he was asking him to take in saying whether he knew where he could find Officer Baker.

"Yes, I do," said the captain; "you can find him in bed, upstairs. But I'd rather you wouldn't wake a man off duty if you don't have to, especially if you don't know he's the one. What's wanted?"

Sewell stopped to say that the captain was quite right, and then he explained why he wished to see Officer Baker.

The captain listened with nods of his head at the names and facts given. "Guess you won't have to get Baker up for that. I can tell you what there is to tell. I don't know where your young man is now, but I gave him an order for a bed at the Wayfarer's Lodge last night, and I guess he slept there. You a friend of his?"

"Yes," said Sewell, much questioning inwardly whether he could be truly described as such. "I wish to befriend him," he added savingly. "I knew him at home, and I am sure of his innocence."

"Oh, I guess he's *innocent* enough," said the captain. "Well, now, I tell you what you do, if you want to befriend him; you get him home quick as you can."

"Yes," said Sewell, helpless to resent the officer's authoritative and patronizing tone. "That's what I wish to do. Do you suppose he's at the Wayfarer's Lodge now?" asked Sewell.

"Can't say," said the captain, tilting himself back in his chair, and putting his quill toothpick between his lips like a cigarette. "The only way is to go and see."

"Thank you very much," said the minister, accepting his dismissal meekly, as a man vowed to ignominy should, but feeling keenly that he was dismissed, and dismissed in disgrace.

At the Lodge he was received less curtly. The manager was there with a long morning's leisure before him, and disposed to friendliness that Sewell found absurdly soothing. He turned over the orders for beds delivered by the vagrants the night before, and "Yes," he said, coming to Lemuel's name, "he slept here; but nobody knows where he is by this time. Wait a bit, sir!" he added to Sewell's fallen countenance. "There was one of the young fellows staid to help us through with the dishes this morning. I'll have him up; or maybe you'd like to go down and take a look at our kitchen? You'll find him there, if it's the one. Here's our card. We can supply you with all sorts of firewood at less cost than the dealers, and you'll be helping the poor fellows to earn an honest bed and breakfast. This way, sir!"

Sewell promised to buy his wood there, put the card respectfully into his pocket, and followed the manager downstairs, and through the basement to the kitchen. He arrived just as Lemuel was about to lift a trayful of clean soup-bowls, to carry it upstairs. After a glance at the minister, he stood still with dropped eyes.

Sewell did not know in what form to greet the boy on whom he had unwillingly brought so much evil, and he found the greater difficulty in deciding as he saw Lemuel's face hardening against him.

"Barker," he said at last, "I'm very glad to find you—I have been very anxious to find you."

Lemuel made no sign of sympathy, but stood still in his long check apron, with his sleeves rolled up to his elbow, and the minister was obliged to humble himself still further to this figure of lowly obstinacy.

"I should like to speak with you. Can I speak with you a few moments?"

The manager politely stepped into the storeroom, and affected to employ himself there, leaving Lemuel and the minister alone together.

X

SEWELL LOST no time. "I want you to go home, Barker. I feel that I am wholly to blame, and greatly to blame, for your coming to Boston with the expectation that brought you, and that I am indirectly responsible for all the trouble that has befallen you since you came. I want to be the means of your getting home, in any way you can let me."

This was a very different way of talking from the smooth superiority of address which the minister had used with him the other day at his own house. Lemuel was not insensible to the atonement offered him, and it was not from sulky stubbornness that he continued silent, and left the minister to explore the causes of his reticence unaided.

"I will go home *with* you, if you like," pursued the minister, though his mind misgave him that this was an extreme which Mrs. Sewell would not have justified him in. "I will go with you, and explain all the circumstances to your friends, in case there should be any misunderstanding—though in that event I should have to ask you to be my guest till Monday." Here the unhappy man laid hold of the sheep, which could not bring him greater condemnation than the lamb.

"I guess they won't know anything about it," said Lemuel, with whatever intention.

It seemed hardened indifference to the minister, and he felt it his disagreeable duty to say, "I am afraid they will. I read of it in the newspaper this morning, and I'm afraid that an exaggerated report of your misfortunes will reach Willoughby Pastures, and alarm your family."

A faint pallor came over the boy's face, and he stood again in his impenetrable, rustic silence. The voice that finally spoke from it said, "I guess I don't want to go home, then."

"You *must* go home!" said the minister, with more of imploring than imperiousness in his command. "What will they make of your prolonged absence?"

"I sent a postal to mother this morning. They lent me one."

"But what will you do here, without work and without means? I wish you to go home with me—I feel responsible for you—and remain with me till you can hear from your mother. I'm sorry you came to Boston; it's no place for you, as you must know by this time, and I am sure your mother will agree with me in desiring your return."

"I guess I don't want to go home," said Lemuel.

"Are you afraid that an uncharitable construction will be placed upon what has happened to you by your neighbors?" Lemuel did not answer. "I assure you that all that can be arranged. I will write to your pastor, and explain it fully. But in any event," continued Sewell, "it is your duty to yourself and your friends to go home and live it down. It would be your duty to do so even if you had been guilty of wrong, instead of the victim of misfortune."

"I don't know," said Lemuel, "as I want to go home and be the laughing-stock."

Against this point Sewell felt himself helpless. He could not pretend that the boy would not be ridiculous in the eyes of his friends, and all the more ridiculous because so wholly innocent. He could only say, "That is a thing which you must bear." And then it occurred to him to ask, "Do you feel that it is right to let your family meet the ridicule alone?"

"I guess nobody will speak to mother about it more than once," said Lemuel, with a just pride in his mother's powers of retort. A woman who, unaided and alone, had worn the Bloomer costume for twenty years in the heart of a commentative community like Willoughby Pastures, was not likely to be without a cutting tongue for her defense.

"But your sister," urged Sewell; "your brother-in-law," he feebly added.

"I guess they will have to stand it," replied Lemuel.

The minister heaved a sigh of hopeless perplexity. "What do you propose to do, then? You can't remain here without means. Do you expect to sell your poetry?" he asked, goaded to the question by a conscience peculiarly sore on that point.

It made Lemuel blush. "No, I don't expect to sell it now. They took it out of my pocket on the Common."

"I am glad of that," said the minister as simply, "and I feel bound to warn you solemnly that there is absolutely *no* hope for you in that direction."

Lemuel said nothing.

The minister stood baffled again. After a bad moment he asked, "Have you anything particular in view?"

"I don't know as I have."

"How long can you remain here?"

"I don't know exactly."

Sewell turned and followed the manager into the refrigerator room, where he had remained patiently whistling throughout this interview.

When he came back, Lemuel had carried one trayful of bowls upstairs, and returned for another load, which he was piling carefully up for safe transportation.

"The manager tells me," said Sewell, "that practically you can stay here as long as you like, if you work; but he doesn't think it desirable you should remain, nor do I. But I wish to find you here again when I come back. I have something in view for you."

This seemed to be a question, and Lemuel said, "All right," and went on piling up his bowls. He added, "I shouldn't want you to take a great deal of trouble."

"Oh, it's no trouble," groaned the minister. "Then I may depend upon seeing you here any time during the day?"

"I don't know as I'm going away," Lemuel admitted.

"Well, then, good-bye for the present," said Sewell; and after speaking again to the manager, and gratefully ordering some kindling which he did not presently need, he went out, and took his way homeward. But he stopped half a block short of his own door, and rang at Miss Vane's. To his perturbed and eager spirit it seemed nothing short of a divine mercy that she should be at home. If he had not been a man bent on repairing his wrong at any cost to others, he would hardly have taken the step he now contemplated without first advising with his wife, who, he felt sure, would have advised against it. His face did not brighten at all when Miss Vane came briskly in, with the "*How* d'ye do?" which he commonly found so cheering. She pulled up the blind and saw his knotted brow.

"What is the matter? You look as if you had got Lemuel Barker back on your hands."

"I have," said the minister briefly.

Miss Vane gave a wild laugh of delight. "You *don't* mean it!" she sputtered, sitting down before him, and peering into his face. "What *do* you mean?"

Sewell was obliged to possess Miss Vane's entire ignorance of all the facts in detail. From point to point he paused; he began really to be afraid she would do herself an injury with her laughing.

She put her hand on his arm and bowed her head forward, with her face buried in her handkerchief. "What—what—do you suppose-pose—they did with the po-po-*po*em they stole from him?"

"Well, one thing I'm sure they *didn't* do," said Sewell bitterly. "They didn't *read* it."

Miss Vane hid her face in her handkerchief, and then plucked it away, and shrieked again. She stopped, with the sudden calm that succeeds such a paroxysm, and, "Does Mrs. Sewell know all about this?" she panted.

"She knows everything, except my finding him in the dishwashing department of the Wayfarer's Lodge," said Sewell gloomily, "and my coming to you."

"Why do you come to me?" asked Miss Vane, her face twitching and her eyes brimming.

"Because," answered Sewell, "I'd rather not go to her till I have done something."

Miss Vane gave way again, and Sewell sat regarding her ruefully.

"What do you expect me to do?" She looked at him over her handkerchief, which she kept pressed against her mouth.

"I haven't the least idea what I expected you to do. I expected you to tell me. You have an inventive mind."

Miss Vane shook her head. Her eyes grew serious, and after a moment she said, "I'm afraid I'm not equal to Lemuel Barker. Besides," she added with a tinge of trouble, "I have *my* problem already."

"Yes," said the minister sympathetically. "How has the flower charity turned out?"

"She went yesterday with one of the ladies, and carried flowers to the city hospital. But she wasn't at all satisfied with the result. She said the patients were mostly disgusting old men that hadn't been shaved. I think that now she wants to try her flowers on criminals. She says she wishes to visit the prisons."

Sewell brightened forlornly. "Why not let her reform Barker?"

This sent Miss Vane off again. "Poor boy!" she sighed, when she had come to herself. "No, there's nothing that I can do for him, except to order some firewood from his bene-factors."

"I did that," said Sewell. "But I don't see how it's to help Barker exactly."

"I would gladly join in a public subscription to send him home. But you say he won't *go* home?"

"He won't go home," sighed the minister. "He's deter-mined to stay. I suspect he would accept employment, if it were offered him in the right spirit."

Miss Vane shook her head. "There's nothing I can think of except shoveling snow. And as yet it's rather warm October weather."

"There's certainly no snow to shovel," admitted Sewell. He rose disconsolately. "Well, there's nothing for it, I suppose, but to put him down at the Christian Union, and explain his checkered career to everybody who proposes to employ him."

Miss Vane could not keep the laughter out of her eyes; she nervously tapped her lips with her handkerchief, to keep it from them. Suddenly she halted Sewell in his dejected progress toward the door. "I might give him my furnace."

"Furnace?" echoed Sewell.

"Yes. Jackson has 'struck' for twelve dollars a month, and at present there is a 'lock-out,'—I believe that's what it's called. And I had determined not to yield as long as the fine weather lasted. I knew I should give in at the first frost. I will take Barker now, if you think he can manage the furnace."

"I've no doubt he can. Has Jackson really struck?" Miss Vane nodded. "He hasn't said anything to me about it."

"He probably intends to make special terms to the clergy. But he told me he was putting up the rates on all his 'fam-blies' this winter."

"If he puts them up on me, I will take Barker too," said the minister boldly. "If he will come," he added with less courage. "Well, I will go round to the Lodge, and see what he thinks of it. Of course, he can't live upon ten dollars a month, and I must look him up something besides."

"That's the only thing I can think of at present," said Miss Vane.

"Oh, you're indefinitely good to think of so much," said Sewell. "You must excuse me if my reception of your kindness has been qualified by the reticence with which Barker received mine this morning."

"Oh, do tell me about it!" cried Miss Vane.

"Some time I will. But I can assure you it was such as to make me shrink from another interview. I don't know but Barker may fling your proffered furnace in my teeth. But I'm sure we both mean well. And I thank you, all the same. Good-bye."

"Poor Mr. Sewell!" said Miss Vane, following him to the door. "May I run down and tell Mrs. Sewell?"

"Not yet," said the minister sadly. He was too insecure of Barker's reception of him to be able to enjoy the joke.

When he got back to the Wayfarer's Lodge, whither he made himself walk in penance, he found Lemuel with a book in his hand, reading, while the cook stirred about the kitchen, and the broth, which he had well under way for the midday meal, lifted the lid of its boiler from time to time and sent out a joyous whiff of steam. The place had really a coziness of its own, and Sewell began to fear that his victim had been so far corrupted by its comfort as to be unwilling to leave the refuge. He had often seen the subtly disastrous effect of bounty, and it was one of the things he trembled for in considering the question of public aid to the poor. Before he addressed Barker, he saw him entered upon the dire life of idleness and dependence, partial or entire, which he had known so many Americans even willing to lead since the first great hard times began; and he spoke to him with the asperity of anticipative censure.

"Barker!" he said, and Lemuel lifted his head from the book he was reading. "I have found something for you to do. I still prefer you should go home, and I advise you to do so. But," he added, at the look that came into Lemuel's face, "if you are determined to stay, this is the best I can do for you. It isn't a full support, but it's something, and you must look about for yourself, and not rest till you've found full work, and something better fitted for you. Do you think you can take care of a furnace?"

"Hot air?" asked Lemuel.

"Yes."

"I guess so. I took care of the church furnace last winter."

"I didn't know you had one," said the minister, brightening in the ray of hope. "Would you be willing to take care of a domestic furnace—a furnace in a private house?"

Lemuel pondered the proposal in silence. Whatever objections there were to it in its difference from the aims of his ambition in coming to Boston he kept to himself; and his ignorance of city prejudices and sophistications probably suggested nothing against the honest work to his pride. "I guess I should," he said at last.

"Well, then, come with me."

Sewell judged it best not to tell him whose furnace he was to take care of; he had an impression that Miss Vane was included in the resentment which Lemuel seemed to cherish toward him. But when he had him at her door, "It's the lady whom you saw at my house the other day," he explained. It was then too late for Lemuel to rebel, and they went in.

If there was any such unkindness in Lemuel's breast toward her, it yielded promptly to her tact. She treated him at once, not like a servant, but like a young person, and yet she used a sort of respect for his independence which was soothing to his rustic pride. She put it on the money basis at once; she told him that she should give him ten dollars a month for taking care of the furnace, keeping the sidewalk clear of snow, shoveling the paths in the back yard for the women to get at their clothes-lines, carrying up and down coal and ashes for the grates, and doing errands. She said that this was what she had always paid, and asked him if he understood and were satisfied.

Lemuel answered with one yes to both her questions, and then Miss Vane said that of course till the weather changed they should want no fire in the furnace, but that it might change any day, and they should begin at once and count October as a full month. She thought he had better go down and look at the furnace and see if it was in order; she had had the pipes cleaned, but perhaps it needed blacking; the cook would show him how it worked. She went with him to the head of the basement stairs, and calling down, "Jane, here is Lemuel, come to look after the furnace," left him and Jane to complete the acquaintance upon coming in sight of each other, and went back to the minister. He had risen to go, and she gave him her hand, while a smile rippled into laughter on her lips.

"Do you think," she asked, struggling with her mirth to keep unheard of those below, "that it is quite the work for a literary man?"

"If he is a man," said Sewell courageously, "the work won't keep him from being literary."

Miss Vane laughed at his sudden recovery of spirit, as she had laughed at his dejection; but he did not care. He hurried home, with a sermon kindling in his mind so obviously that his wife did not detain him beyond a few vital questions, and let him escape from having foisted his burden upon Miss Vane with the simple comment, "Well, we shall see how that will work."

As once before, Sewell tacitly took a hint from his own experience, and, enlarging to more serious facts from it, preached effort in the erring. He denounced mere remorse. Better not feel that at all, he taught; and he declared that what is ordinarily distinguished from remorse as repentance was equally a mere corrosion of the spirit unless some attempt at reparation went with it. He maintained that though some mischiefs—perhaps most mischiefs—were irreparable so far as restoring the original status was concerned, yet every mischief was reparable in the good will and the good deed of its perpetrator. Do what you could to retrieve yourself from error, and then, not leave the rest to Providence, but keep doing. The good, however small, must grow if tended and nurtured like a useful plant, as the evil would certainly grow like a wild and poisonous weed if left to itself. Sin, he said, was a terrible mystery; one scarcely knew how to deal with it or to attempt to determine its nature; but perhaps—he threw out the thought while warning those who heard him of its danger in some aspects—sin was not wholly an evil. We were so apt in this world of struggle and ambition to become centered solely in ourselves, that possibly the wrong done to another—the wrong that turned our thoughts from ourselves, and kept them bent in agony and despair upon the suffering we had caused another, and knew not how to mitigate—possibly this wrong, nay, certainly this wrong was good in disguise. But, returning to his original point, we were to beware how we rested in this despair. In the very extremity of our anguish, our fear, our shame, we were to gird ourselves up to reparation. Strive to do good, he preached; strive most of all to do good to those you have done harm to. His text was "Cease to do evil."

He finished his sermon during the afternoon, and in the evening his wife said they would run up to Miss Vane's. Sewell shrank from this a little, with the obscure dread that Lemuel might have turned his back upon good fortune, and abandoned the place offered him, in which case Sewell would have to give a wholly different turn to his sermon; but he consented, as indeed he must. He was as curious as his wife to know how the experiment had resulted.

Miss Vane did not wait to let them ask. "My dear," she said, kissing Mrs. Sewell and giving her hand to the minister in one, "he is a pearl! And I've kept him from mixing his native luster with Rising Sun Stove Polish by becoming his creditor in the price of a pair of overalls. I had no idea they were so cheap, and you can see that they will fade, with a few washings, to a perfect Millet blue. They were quite his own idea, when he found the furnace needed blacking, and he wanted to use the fifty cents he earned this morning toward the purchase, but I insisted upon advancing the entire dollar myself. Neatness, self-respect, awe-inspiring deference!—he is each and every one of them in person."

Sewell could not forbear a glance of triumph at his wife.

"You leave us very little to ask," said that injured woman.

"But I've left myself a great deal to tell, my dear," retorted Miss Vane, "and I propose to keep the floor; though I don't really know where to begin."

"I thought you had got past the necessity of beginning," said Sewell. "We know that the new pearl sweeps clean,"— Miss Vane applauded his mixed metaphor,—"and now you might go on from that point."

"Well, you may think I'm rash," said Miss Vane, "but I've thoroughly made up my mind to keep him."

"Dear, *dear* Miss Vane!" cried the minister. "Mrs. Sewell thinks you're rash, but I don't. What do you mean by keeping him?"

"Keeping him as a fixture—a permanency—a continuosity."

"Oh! A continuosity? I know what that is in the ordinary acceptation of the term, but I'm not sure that I follow your meaning exactly."

"Why, it's simply this," said Miss Vane. "I have long secretly wanted the protection of what Jane calls a man-body in the house, and when I saw how Lemuel had blacked the furnace, I knew I should feel as safe with him as with a whole body of troops."

"Well," sighed the minister, "you have not been rash, perhaps, but you'll allow that you've been rapid."

"No," said Miss Vane, "I won't allow that. I have simply been intuitive—nothing more. His functions are not decided yet, but it is decided that he is to stay; he's to sleep in the little room over the L, and in my tranquilized consciousness he's been there years already."

"And has Sibyl undertaken Barker's reformation?" asked Sewell.

"Don't interrupt! Don't anticipate! I admit nothing till I come to it. But after I had arranged with Lemuel I began to think of Sibyl."

"That was like some ladies I have known of," said Sewell. "You women commit yourselves to a scheme, in order to show your skill in reconciling circumstances to the irretrievable. Well?"

"*Don't* interrupt, David!" cried his wife.

"Oh, let him go on," said Miss Vane. "It's all very well, taking people into your house on the spur of the moment, and in obedience to a generous impulse; but when you reflect that the object of your good intentions slept in the Wayfarer's Lodge the night before, and in the police station the night before that, and enjoys a newspaper celebrity in connection with a case of assault and battery with intent to rob,—why, then you *do* reflect!"

"Yes," said Sewell, "that is just the point where I should begin."

"I thought," continued Miss Vane, "I had better tell Sibyl all about it, so if by any chance the neighbors' kitchens should have heard of the case—they read the police reports very carefully in the kitchens——"

"They do in some drawing-rooms," interrupted Sewell.

"It's well for you they do, David," said his wife. "Your protégé would have been in your refuge still, if they didn't."

"I see!" cried the minister. "I shall have to take the 'Sunrise' another week."

Miss Vane looked from one to the other in sympathetic ignorance, but they did not explain, and she went on.

"And if they should hear Lemuel's name, and put two and two together, and the talk should get to Sibyl—well, I thought it all over, until the whole thing became perfectly lurid, and I wished Lemuel Barker was back in the depths of Willoughby Pastures——"

"I understand," said Sewell. "Go on!"

Miss Vane did so, after stopping to laugh. "It seemed to me I couldn't wait for Sibyl to get home—she spent the night in Brookline, and didn't come till five o'clock—to tell her. I began before she had got her hat or gloves off, and she sat down with them on, and listened like a three-years' child to the Ancient Mariner, but she lost no time when she understood the facts. She went out immediately and stripped the nasturtium bed. If you could have seen it when you came in, there's hardly a blossom left. She took the decorations of Lemuel's room into her own hands at once; and if there is any saving power in nasturtiums, he will be a changed person. She says that now the great object is to keep him from feeling that he has been an outcast, and needs to be reclaimed; she says nothing could be worse for him. I don't know how she knows."

"Barker might feel that he was disgraced," said the minister, "but I don't believe that a whole system of ethics would make him suspect that he needed to be reclaimed."

"He makes me suspect that *I* need to be reclaimed," said Miss Vane, "when he looks at me with those beautiful honest eyes of his."

Mrs. Sewell asked, "Has he seen the decorations yet?"

"Not at all. They are to steal upon him when he comes in to-night. The gas is to be turned very low, and he is to notice everything gradually, so as not to get the impression that things have been done with a design upon him." She laughed in reporting these ideas, which were plainly those of the young girl. "Sh!" she whispered at the end.

A tall girl, with a slim vase in her hand, drifted in upon their group like an apparition. She had heavy black eyebrows with beautiful blue eyes under them, full of an intensity unrelieved by humor.

"Aunty!" she said severely, "have you been telling?"

"Only Mr. and Mrs. Sewell, Sibyl," said Miss Vane. "*Their* knowing won't hurt. He'll never know it."

"If he hears you laughing, he'll know it's about him. He's in the kitchen now. He's come in the back way. Do be quiet." She had given her hand without other greeting in her preoccupation to each of the Sewells in turn, and now she passed out of the room.

XI

"WHAT MAKES Lemuel such a gift," said Miss Vane, in a talk which she had with Sewell a month later, "is that he is so supplementary."

"Do you mean just in the supplementary sense of the term?"

"Well, not in the fifth-wheel sense. I mean that he supplements us, all and singular—if you will excuse the legal exactness."

"Oh, certainly," said Sewell; "I should like even more exactness."

"Yes; but before I particularize I must express my general satisfaction in him as a man-body. I had no idea that manbodies in a house were so perfectly admirable."

"I've sometimes feared that we were not fully appreciated," said Sewell. "Well?"

"The house is another thing with a man-body in it. I've often gone without little things I wanted, simply because I hated to make Jane bring them, and because I hated still worse to go after them, knowing we were both weakly and tired. Now I deny myself nothing. I make Lemuel fetch and carry without remorse, from morning till night. I never knew it before, but the man-body seems never to be tired, or ill, or sleepy."

"Yes," said Sewell, "that is often the idea of the womanbody. I'm not sure that it's correct."

"Oh, *don't* attack it!" implored Miss Vane. "You don't *know* what a blessing it is. Then, the man-body never complains, and I can't see that he expects anything more in an order than the clear understanding of it. He doesn't expect it to be accounted for in any way; the fact that you say you want a thing is enough. It is very strange. Then the moral support of the presence of a man-body is enormous. I now know that I have never slept soundly since I have kept house alone—that I have never passed a night without hearing burglars or smelling fire."

"And now?"

"And now I shouldn't mind a legion of burglars in the

house; I shouldn't mind being burned in my bed every night. I feel that Lemuel is in charge, and that nothing can happen."

"Is he really so satisfactory?" asked Sewell, exhaling a deep relief.

"He is, indeed," said Miss Vane. "I couldn't exaggerate it."

"Well, well! Don't try. We are finite, after all, you know. Do you think it can last?"

"I have thought of that," answered Miss Vane. "I don't see why it shouldn't last. I have tried to believe that I did a foolish thing in coming to your rescue, but I can't see that I did. I don't see why it shouldn't last as long as Lemuel chooses. And he seems perfectly contented with his lot. He doesn't seem to regard it as domestic service, but as domestication, and he patronizes our inefficiency while he spares it. His common sense is extraordinary—it's exemplary; it almost makes one wish to have common sense one's self." They had now got pretty far from the original proposition, and Sewell returned to it with the question, "Well, and how does he supplement you singularly?"

"Oh! oh, yes!" said Miss Vane. "I could hardly tell you without going into too deep a study of character."

"I'm rather fond of that," suggested the minister.

"Yes, and I've no doubt we should all work very nicely into a sermon as illustrations; but I can't more than indicate the different cases. In the first place, Jane's forgetfulness seems to be growing upon her, and since Lemuel came she's abandoned herself to ecstasies of oblivion."

"Yes?"

"Yes. She's quite given over remembering *any*thing, because she knows that he will remember *every*thing."

"I see. And you?"

"Well, you have sometimes thought I was a little rash."

"A little? Did I think it was a little?"

"Well, a good deal. But it was all nothing to what I've been since Lemuel came. I used to keep some slight check upon myself for Sibyl's sake; but I don't now. I know that Lemuel is there to temper, to delay, to modify the effect of every impulse, and so I am all impulse now. And I've quite ceased to rule my temper. I know that Lemuel has self-control enough for all the tempers in the house, and so I feel perfectly calm in my wildest transports of fury."

"I understand," said Sewell. "And does Sibyl permit herself a similar excess in her fancies and ambitions?"

"Quite," said Miss Vane. "I don't know that she consciously relies upon Lemuel to supplement her, any more than Jane does; but she must be unconsciously aware that no extravagance of hers can be dangerous while Lemuel is in the house."

"Unconsciously aware is good. She hasn't got tired of reforming him yet?"

"I don't know. I sometimes think she wishes he had gone a little farther in crime. Then his reformation would be more obvious."

"Yes; I can appreciate that. Does she still look after his art and literature?"

"That phase has changed a little. She thinks now that he ought to be stimulated, if anything—that he ought to read George Eliot. She's put 'Middlemarch' and 'Romola' on his shelf. She says that he looks like Tito Melema."

Sewell rose. "Well, I don't see but what your supplement is a very demoralizing element. I shall never dare to tell Mrs. Sewell what you've said."

"Oh, she knows it," cried Miss Vane. "We've agreed that you will counteract any temptation that Lemuel may feel to abuse his advantages by the ferociously self-denying sermons you preach at him every Sunday."

"Do I preach at him? Do you notice it?" asked Sewell nervelessly.

"Notice it?" laughed Miss Vane. "I should think your whole congregation would notice it. You seem to look at nobody else."

"I know it! Since he began to come, I can't keep my eyes off him. I do deliver my sermons at him. I believe I write them at him! He has an eye of terrible and exacting truth. I feel myself on trial before him. He holds me up to a standard of sincerity that is killing me. Mrs. Sewell was bad enough; I was reasonably bad myself; but this! Couldn't you keep him away? Do you think it's exactly decorous to let your manservant occupy a seat in your family pew? How do you suppose it looks to the Supreme Being?"

Miss Vane was convulsed. "I had precisely those misgivings! But Lemuel hadn't. He asked me what the number of our pew was, and I hadn't the heart—or else I hadn't the face—to tell him he mustn't sit in it. How could I? Do you think it's so very scandalous?"

"I don't know," said Sewell. "It may lead to great abuses. If we tacitly confess ourselves equal in the sight of God, how much better are we than the Roman Catholics?"

Miss Vane could not suffer these ironies to go on.

"He approves of your preaching. He has talked your sermons over with me. You oughtn't to complain."

"Oh, I don't! Do you think he's really softening a little toward me?"

"Not personally, that I know," said Miss Vane. "But he seems to regard you as a channel of the truth."

"I ought to be glad of so much," said Sewell. "I confess that I hadn't supposed he was at all of our way of thinking. They preached a very appreciable orthodoxy at Willoughby Pastures."

"I don't know about that," said Miss Vane. "I only know that he approves your theology, or your ethics."

"Ethics, I hope. I'm sure *they're* right." After a thoughtful moment the minister asked, "Have you observed that they have softened him socially at all—broken up that terrible rigidity of attitude, that dismaying retentiveness of speech?"

"I know what you mean!" cried Miss Vane, delightedly. "I believe Lemuel *is* a little more supple, a little *less* like a granite bowlder in one of his meadows. But I can't say that he's glib yet. He isn't apparently going to say more than he thinks."

"I hope he thinks more than he says," sighed the minister. "My interviews with Lemuel have left me not only exhausted but bruised, as if I had been hurling myself against a dead wall. Yes, I manage him better from the pulpit, and I certainly oughtn't to complain. I don't expect him to make any response, and I perceive that I am not *quite* so sore as after meeting him in private life."

That evening Lemuel was helping to throng the platform of an overcrowded horse-car. It was Saturday night, and he was going to the provision man up toward the South End, whom Miss Vane was dealing with for the time being, in an economical recoil from her expensive Back Bay provision man, to order a forgotten essential of the Sunday's supplies. He had already been at the grocer's, and was carrying home three or four packages to save the cart from going a third time that day to Bolingbroke street, and he stepped down into the road, when two girls came squeezing their way out of the car.

"Well, I'm glad," said one of them in a voice Lemuel knew at once, " 't there's one man's got the politeness to make a *little* grain o' room for you. Thank you, sir!" she added, with more scorn for the others than gratitude for Lemuel. "*You're* a gentleman, *any*way."

The hardened offenders on the platform laughed, but Lemuel said simply, "You're quite welcome."

"Why, land's sakes!" shouted the girl. "Well, if 'tain't you. S'tira!" she exclaimed to her companion in utter admiration. Then she added to Lemuel, "Why, I didn't s'pose but what you'd 'a' be'n back home long ago. Well, I *am* glad. Be'n in Boston ever since? Well, I want to know!"

The conductor had halted his car for the girls to get off, but, as he remarked with a vicious jerk at his bell-strap, he could not keep his car standing there while a woman was asking about the folks, and the horses started up and left Lemuel behind. "Well, there!" said 'Manda Grier. " 'F I hain't made you lose your car! I never see folks like some them conductors."

"Oh, I guess I can walk the rest of the way," said Lemuel, his face bright with a pleasure visible in the light of the lamp that brought out Statira Dudley's smiles and the forward thrust of 'Manda Grier's whopper-jaw as they turned toward the pavement together.

"Well, I guess 'f I've spoke about you once, I have a hundred times, in the last six weeks. I always told S'tira you'd be'n sure to turn up b'fore this 'f you'd be'n in Boston all the time; 'n' 't I guessed you'd got a disgust for the place, 'n' 't you wouldn't want to see it again for *one* while."

Statira did not say anything. She walked on the other side of 'Manda Grier, who thrust her in the side from time to time with a lift of her elbow, in demand of sympathy and corroboration; but though she only spoke to answer yes or no, Lemuel could see that she was always smiling or else biting her lip to keep herself from it. He thought she looked about as pretty as anybody could, and that she was again very fashionably dressed. She had on a short dolman, and a pretty hat that shaded her forehead but fitted close round, and she wore long gloves that came up on her sleeves. She had a book from the library; she walked with a little bridling movement that he found very ladylike. 'Manda Grier tilted along between them and her tongue ran and ran, so that Lemuel, when they came to Miss Vane's provision man's, could hardly get in a word to say that he guessed he must stop there.

Statira drifted on a few paces, but 'Manda Grier halted abruptly with him. "Well, 'f you're ever up our way we sh'd be much pleased to have you call, Mr. Barker," she said formally.

"I should be much pleased to do so," said Lemuel with equal state.

" 'Tain't but just a little ways round here on the Avenue," she added.

Lemuel answered, "I guess I know where it is." He did not mean it for anything of a joke, but both the girls laughed, and though she had been so silent before, Statira laughed the most.

He could not help laughing either when 'Manda Grier said, "I guess if you was likely to forget the number you could go round to the station and inquire. They got your address too."

" 'Manda Grier, you be still!" said Statira.

"S'tira said that's the way she knew you was from Willoughby Pastures. Her folks is from up that way, themselves. She says the minute she heard the name she knew it couldn't 'a' be'n you, whoever it was done it."

" 'Manda Grier!" cried Statira again.

"I tell her she don't believe 't any harm can come out the town o' Willoughby, anywheres."

" 'Manda!" cried Statira.

Lemuel was pleased, but he could not say a word. He could not look at Statira.

"Well, good-evening," said Amanda Grier.

"Well, good-evening," said Lemuel.

"Well, good-evening," said Statira.

"Well, good-evening," said Lemuel again.

The next moment they were gone round the corner, and he was left standing before the provision man's, with his packages in his hand. It did not come to him till he had transacted his business within, and was on his way home, that he had been very impolite not to ask if he might not see them home. He did not know but he ought to go back and try to find them, and apologize for his rudeness, and yet he did not see how he could do that, either; he had no excuse for it; he was afraid it would seem queer, and make them laugh. Besides, he had those things for Miss Vane, and the cook wanted some of them at once.

He could hardly get to sleep that night for thinking of his blunder, and at times he cowered under the bedclothes for shame. He decided that the only way for him to do was to keep out of their way after this, and if he ever met them anywhere, to pretend not to see them.

The next morning he went to hear Mr. Sewell preach, as usual, but he found himself wandering far from the sermon, and asking or answering this or that in a talk with those girls that kept going on in his mind. The minister himself seemed to wander, and at times, when Lemuel forced a return to him, he thought he was boggling strangely. For the first time Mr. Sewell's sermon, in his opinion, did not come to much.

While his place in Miss Vane's household was still indefinitely ascertained, he had the whole of Sunday, and he always wrote home in the afternoon, or brought up the arrears of the journal he had begun keeping; but the Sunday afternoon that followed, he was too excited to stay in and write. He thought he would go and take a walk, and get away from the things that pestered him. He did not watch where he was going, and after awhile he turned a corner, and suddenly found himself in a long street, planted with shade-trees, and looking old-fashioned and fallen from a former dignity. He perceived that it could never have been fashionable, like Bolingbroke street or Beacon; the houses were narrow and their doors opened from little, cavernous arches let into the brick fronts, and they stood flush upon the pavement. The sidewalks were full of people, mostly girls walking up and down; at the corners young fellows lounged, and there were groups before the cigar stores and the fruit stalls, which were open. It was not very cold yet, and the children who swarmed upon the low door-steps were bareheaded and often summer-clad. The street was not nearly so well kept as the streets on the Back Bay that Lemuel was more used to, but he could see that it was not a rowdy street either. He looked up at a lamp on the first corner he came to, and read Pleasant Avenue on it; then he said that the witch was in it. He dramatized a scene of meeting those girls, and was very glib in it, and they were rather shy, and Miss Dudley kept behind Amanda Grier, who nudged her with her elbow when Lemuel said he had come round to see if anybody had robbed them of their books on the way home after he left them last night.

But all the time, as he hurried along to the next corner, he looked fearfully to the right and left. Presently he began to steal guilty glances at the numbers of the houses. He said to himself that he would see what kind of a looking house they did live in, any way. It was only No. 900 odd when he began, and he could turn off if he wished long before he reached 1334. As he drew nearer he said he would just give a look at it, and then rush by. But 1334 was a house so much larger and nicer than he had expected that he stopped to collect his slow rustic thoughts, and decide whether she really lived there, or whether she had just given that number for a blind. He did not know why he should think that, though; she was dressed well enough to come out of any house.

While he lingered before the house an old man with a cane in his hand and his mouth hanging open stopped and peered through his spectacles, whose glare he fixed upon Lemuel, till he began to feel himself a suspicious character. The old man did not say anything, but stood faltering upon his stick and now and then gathering up his lower lip as if he were going to speak, but not speaking.

Lemuel cleared his throat. "Hmmn! Is this a boarding-house?"

"I don't know," crowed the old man, in a high senile note. "You want table-board or rooms?"

"I don't want board at all," began Lemuel again.

"What?" crowed the old man; and he put up his hand to his ear.

People were beginning to put their heads out of the neighboring windows, and to walk slowly as they went by, so as to hear what he and the old man were saying. He could not run away now, and he went boldly up to the door of the large house and rang.

A girl came, and he asked her, with a flushed face, if Miss Amanda Grier boarded there; somehow he could not bear to ask for Miss Dudley.

"Well," the girl said, "she *rooms* here," as if that might be a different thing to Lemuel altogether.

"Oh!" he said. "Is she in?"

"Well, you can walk in," said the girl, "and I'll see." She came back to ask, "Who shall I say called?"

"Mr. Barker," said Lemuel, and then glowed with shame because he had called himself Mister. The girl did not come back, but she hardly seemed gone before 'Manda Grier came into the room. He did not know whether she would speak to him, but she was as pleasant as could be, and said he must come right up to her and S'tira's room. It was pretty high up, but he did not notice the stairs, 'Manda Grier kept talking so; and when he got to it, and 'Manda Grier dashed the door open, and told him to walk right in, he would not have known but he was in somebody's sitting-room. A curtained alcove hid the bed, and the room was heated by a cheerful little kerosene stove; there were bright folding carpet-chairs, and the lid of the wash-stand had a cloth on it that came down to the floor, and there were plants in the window. There was a mirror on the wall, framed in black walnut with gilt molding inside, and a family-group photograph in the same kind of frame, and two chromos, and a clock on a bracket.

Statira seemed surprised to see him; the room was pretty warm, and her face was flushed. He said it was quite mild out, and she said, "Was it?" Then she ran and flung up the window, and said, "Why, so it was," and that she had been in the house all day, and had not noticed the weather.

She excused herself and the room for being in such a state; she said she was ashamed to be caught in such a looking dress, but they were not expecting company, and she did suppose 'Manda Grier would have given her time to put the room to rights a little. He could not understand why she said all this, for the whole room was clean, and Statira herself was beautifully dressed in the same dress that she had worn the night before, or one just like it; and after she had put up the window, 'Manda Grier said, "S'tira Dudley, do you want to kill yourself?" and ran and pulled aside the curtain in the corner, and took down the dolman from among other clothes that hung there, and threw it on Statira's shoulders, who looked as pretty as a pink in it. But she pretended to be too hot, and wanted to shrug it off, and 'Manda Grier called out, "Mr. Barker! *will* you make her keep it on?" and Lemuel sat dumb and motionless, but filled through with a sweet pleasure.

He tried several times to ask them if they had been robbed on the way home last night, as he had done in the scene he had dramatized; but he could not get out a word, except that it had been pretty warm all day.

Statira said, "I think it's been a very warm fall," and 'Manda Grier said, "I think the summer's goin' to spend the winter with us," and they all three laughed.

"What speeches you do make, 'Manda Grier!" said Statira.

"Well, anything better than Quaker meetin', *I* say," retorted 'Manda Grier; and then they were all three silent, and Lemuel thought of his clothes, and how fashionably both of the girls were dressed.

"I guess," said Statira, "it'll be a pretty sickly winter, if it keeps along this way. They say a green Christmas makes a fat grave-yard."

"I guess you'll see the snow fly long before Christmas," said 'Manda Grier, "or Thanksgiving either."

"I guess so, too," said Lemuel, though he did not like to seem to take sides against Statira.

She laughed as if it were a good joke, and said, " 'Tain't but about a fortnight now till Thanksgiving, anyway."

"If it comes a good fall of snow before Thanksgivin', won't you come round and give us a sleigh-ride, Mr. Barker?" asked 'Manda Grier.

They all laughed at her audacity, and Lemuel said, Yes, he

would; and she said, "We'll give you a piece of real Willoughby Center mince-pie, if you will."

They all laughed again.

" 'Manda Grier!" said Statira, in protest.

"Her folks sent her half a dozen last Thanksgivin'," persisted 'Manda Grier.

" *'Manda!*" pleaded Statira.

'Manda Grier sprang up and got Lemuel a folding-chair. "You ain't a bit comfortable in that stiff old thing, Mr. Barker."

Lemuel declared that he was perfectly comfortable, but she would not be contented till he had changed, and then she said, "Why don't you look after your company, S'tira Dudley? I should think you'd be ashamed."

Lemuel's face burned with happy shame, and Statira, who was as red as he was, stole a look at him, that seemed to say that there was no use trying to stop 'Manda Grier. But when she went on, "I don't know but it's the fashion to Willoughby Center," they both gave way again, and laughed more than ever, and Statira said, "*Well,* 'Manda Grier, what do you s'pose Mr. Barker'll think?"

She tried to be sober, but the wild girl set her and Lemuel off laughing when she retorted, "Guess he'll think what he did when he was brought up in court for highway robbery."

'Manda Grier sat upright in her chair, and acted as if she had merely spoken about the weather. He knew that she was talking that way just to break the ice, and though he would have given anything to be able to second her, he could not.

"How you do carry on, 'Manda Grier," said Statira, as helpless as he was.

"Guess I got a pretty good load to carry!" said 'Manda Grier.

They all now began to find their tongues a little, and Statira told how one season when her mother took boarders she had gone over to the Pastures with a party of summer-folks on a straw-ride and picked blueberries. She said she never saw the berries as thick as they were there.

Lemuel said he guessed he knew where the place was; but the fire had got into it last year, and there had not been a berry there this summer.

Statira said, "What a shame!" She said there were some Barkers over East Willoughby way; and she confessed that when he said his name was Barker, and he was from Willoughby Pastures, that night in the station, she thought she should have gone through the floor.

Then they talked a little about how they had both felt, but not very much, and they each took all the blame, and would not allow that the other was the least to blame. Statira said she had behaved like a perfect coot all the way through, and Lemuel said that he guessed he had been the coot, if there was any.

"I guess there was a pair of you," said 'Manda Grier; and at this association of them in 'Manda Grier's condemnation, he could see that Statira was blushing, though she hid her face in her hands, for her ears were all red.

He now rose and said he guessed he would have to be going; but when 'Manda Grier interposed and asked, "Why, what's your hurry?" he said he guessed he had not had any, and Statira laughed at the wit of this till it seemed to him she would perish.

"Well, then, you set right straight down again," said 'Manda Grier, with mock severity, as if he were an obstinate little boy; and he obeyed, though he wished that Statira had asked him to stay too.

"Why, the land sakes!" exclaimed 'Manda Grier, "have you been lettin' him keep his hat all this while, S'tira Dudley? You take it right away from him!" And Statira rose, all smiling and blushing, and said:

"Will you let me take your hat, Mr. Barker?" as if he had just come in, and made him feel as if she had pressed him to stay. She took it and went and laid it on a stand across the room, and Lemuel thought he had never seen a much more graceful person. She wore a full Breton skirt, which was gathered thickly at the hips, and swung loose and free as she stepped. When she came back and sat down, letting the back of one pretty hand fall into the palm of the other in her lap, it seemed to him impossible that such an elegant young lady should be tolerating a person dressed as he was.

"There!" began 'Manda Grier. "I guess Mr. Barker won't object a great deal to our going on, if it is Sunday. 'S kind of a Sunday game, anyways. You 'posed to games on Sunday?"

"I don't know as I am," said Lemuel.

"Now, 'Manda Grier, don't you!" pleaded Statira.

"Shall, too!" persisted 'Manda. "I guess if there's any harm in the key, there ain't any harm in the Bible, and so it comes out even. D'you ever try your fate with a key and a Bible?" she asked Lemuel.

"I don't know as I did," he answered.

"Well, it's *real* fun, 'n' it's curious how it comes out, often-times. Well, *I* don't s'pose there's anything *in* it, but it *is* curious."

"I guess we hadn't better," said Statira. "I don't believe Mr. Barker 'll care for it."

Lemuel said he would like to see how it was done, anyway.

'Manda Grier took the key out of the door, and looked at it. "That key 'll cut the leaves all to pieces."

"Can't you find some other?" suggested Statira.

"I don't know but maybe I could," said 'Manda Grier. "You just wait a half a second."

Before Lemuel knew what she was doing, she flew out of the door, and he could hear her flying down the stairs.

"Well, I *must* say!" said Statira, and then neither she nor Lemuel said anything for a little while. At last she asked, "That window trouble you any?"

Lemuel said, "Not at all," and he added, "Perhaps it's too cold for you?"

"Oh, no," said the girl, "I can't seem to get anything too cold for me. I'm the greatest person for cold weather! I'm *real* glad it's comin' winter. We had the greatest *time*, last winter," continued Statira, "with those English sparrows. Used to feed 'em crumbs, there on the window-sill, and it seemed as if they got to know we girls, and they'd hop right inside, if you'd let 'em. Used to make me feel kind of creepy to have 'em. They say it's a sign of death to have a bird come into your room, and I was always for drivin' 'em out, but 'Manda, she said she guessed the Lord didn't take the trouble to send birds round to every one, and if the rule didn't work one way it didn't work the other. You believe in signs?"

"I don't know as I do, much. Mother likes to see the new moon over her right shoulder, pretty well," said Lemuel.

"Well, I declare," said Statira, "that's just the way with *my* aunt. Now you're up here," she said, springing suddenly to her feet, "I want you should see what a nice view we got from our window."

Lemuel had it on his tongue to say that he hoped it was not going to be his last chance; he believed he would have said it if 'Manda Grier had been there; but now he only joined Statira at the window, and looked out. They had to stoop over, and get pretty close together, to see the things she wished to show him, and she kept shrugging her sack on, and once she touched him with her shoulder. He said yes to everything she asked him about the view, but he saw very little of it. He saw that her hair had a shade of gold in its brown, and that it curled in tight little rings where it was cut on her neck, and that her skin was very white under it. When she touched him, that time, it made him feel very strange; and when she glanced at him out of her blue eyes, he did not know what he was doing. He did not laugh as he did when 'Manda Grier was there.

Statira said, "Oh, excuse me!" when she touched him, and he answered, "Perfectly excusable," but he said hardly anything else. He liked to hear her talk, and he watched the play of her lips as she spoke. Once her breath came across his cheek, when she turned quickly to see if he was looking where she was pointing.

They sat down and talked, and all at once Statira exclaimed, "*Well!* I should think 'Manda Grier was *makin'* that key!"

Now, whatever happened, Lemuel was bound to say, "I don't think she's been gone very long."

"Well, you're pretty patient, I *must* say," said Statira, and he did not know whether she was making fun of him or not. He tried to think of something to say, but could not. "I hope she'll fetch a lamp, too, when she comes," Statira went on, and now he saw that it was beginning to be a little darker. Perhaps that about the lamp was a hint for him to go; but he did not see exactly how he could go till 'Manda Grier came back; he felt that it would not be polite.

"Well, there!" said Statira, as if she divined his feeling. "I shall give 'Manda Grier a *good* talking-to. I'm awfully afraid we're keeping you, Mr. Barker."

"Not at all," said Lemuel; "I'm afraid I'm keeping *you*."

"Oh, not at all," said Statira. She became rather quieter, till 'Manda Grier came back.

'Manda Grier burst into the room, with a key in one hand and a lamp in the other. "Well, I knew you two'd be holdin' Quaker's meetin'."

"We hain't at all! How'd you know we have? Have we, Mr. Barker?" returned Statira, in simultaneous admission and denial.

"Well, if you want to know, I listened outside the door," said 'Manda Grier, "and you wa'n't sayin' a word, either of you. I guess I got a key now that'll do," she added, setting down her lamp, "and I borrowed an old Bible 't I guess 'tain't go'n' to hurt a great deal."

"I don't know as I want to play it much," said Statira.

"Well, I guess you got to, now," said 'Manda Grier, "after all my trouble. Hain't she, Mr. Barker?"

It flattered Lemuel through and through to be appealed to, but he could not say anything.

"Well," said Statira, "if I got to, I got to. But you got to hold the Bible."

"You got to put the key in!" cried 'Manda Grier. She sat holding the Bible open toward Statira.

She offered to put the key in, and then she stopped. "Well! I'm great! Who are we going to find it for first?"

"Oh, company first," said 'Manda Grier.

"You company, Mr. Barker?" asked Statira, looking at Lemuel over her shoulder.

"I hope not," said Lemuel, gallantly, at last.

"Well, I declare!" said Statira.

"Quite one the family," said 'Manda Grier, and that made Statira say, " 'Manda!" and Lemuel blush to his hair. "Well, anyway," continued 'Manda Grier, "you're company enough to have your fate found first. Put in the key, S'tira."

"No, I sha'n't do it."

"Well, *I* shall, then!" She took the key from Statira, and shut the book upon it at the Song of Solomon, and bound it tightly in with a ribbon. Lemuel watched breathlessly; he was not sure that he knew what kind of fate she meant, but he thought he knew, and it made his heart beat quick. 'Manda Grier had passed the ribbon through the ring of the key, which was left outside of the leaves, and now she took hold of the key with her two forefingers. "You got to be careful not to touch the Bible with your fingers," she explained, "or the charm won't work. Now I'll say over two verses, 't where the key's put in, and Mr. Barker, you got to repeat the alphabet at the same time; and when it comes to the first letter of the right name, the Bible will drop out of my fingers, all I can do. Now, then! *Set me as a seal on thine heart*——"

"A, B, C, D," began Lemuel.

"Pshaw, now, 'Manda Grier, you stop!" pleaded Statira.

"You be still! Go on, Mr. Barker!—*As a seal upon thine arm; for love is as strong as death*—don't say the letters so fast—*jealousy as cruel as the grave*—don't look at S'tira; look at me!—*the coals thereof are coals of fire*—you're sayin' it too slow now—*which hath a most vehement flame*. I declare, S'tira Dudley, if you joggle me!—*Many waters cannot quench love; neither can the floods drown it*—you must put just so much time between every letter; if you stop on every particular one, it ain't fair—*if a man would give all the substance of his house for love*—you stop laughin', you two!—*it would be utterly consumed*. Well, there! Now we got to go it all over again, and my arm's most broke *now*."

"I don't believe Mr. Barker wants to do it again," said Statira, looking demurely at him; but Lemuel protested that he did, and the game began again. This time the Bible began to shake at the letter D, and Statira cried out, "Now, 'Manda Grier, you're making it," and 'Manda Grier laughed so that she could scarcely hold the book. Lemuel laughed too; but he kept on repeating the letters. At S the book fell to the floor, and Statira caught it up, and softly beat 'Manda Grier on the back with it. "Oh, you mean thing!" she cried out. "You did it on purpose."

'Manda Grier was almost choked with laughing.

"Do you know anybody of the name of Sarah, Mr. Barker?" she gasped, and then they all laughed together till Statira said, "Well, I shall surely die! Now, 'Manda Grier, it's your turn. And you see if I don't pay you up."

"I guess I ain't afraid any," retorted 'Manda Grier. "The book'll do what it pleases, in spite of you."

They began again, Statira holding the book this time, and Lemuel repeating as before, and he went quite through the alphabet without anything happening. "Well, I declare!" said Statira, looking grave. "Let's try it over again."

"You may try, and you may try, and you may try," said 'Manda Grier. "It won't do you any good. I hain't got any fate in that line."

"Well, that's what we're goin' to find out," said Statira; but again the verses and alphabet were repeated without effect.

"Now you satisfied?" asked 'Manda Grier.

"No, not yet. Begin again, Mr. Barker!"

He did so, and at the second letter the book dropped. Statira jumped up, and 'Manda Grier began to chase her round the room, to box her ears for her, she said. Lemuel sat looking on. He did not feel at all severe toward them, as he usually did toward girls that cut up; he did not feel that this was cutting up, in fact.

"Stop, stop!" implored Statira, "and I'll let you try it over again."

"No, it's your turn now!"

"No, I ain't going to have any," said Statira, folding her arms.

"You got to," said 'Manda Grier. "The rest of us has, and now you've got to. Hain't she got to, Mr. Barker?"

"Yes," said Lemuel, delightedly; "you've got to, Miss Dudley."

"Miss Dudley!" repeated 'Manda Grier. "How that *does* sound."

"I don't know as it sounds any worse than Mr. Barker," said Lemuel.

"Well," said 'Manda Grier, judicially, "I sh'd think it was 'bout time they was both of 'em dropped. 'T any rate, I don't want you should call me Miss Grier—Lemuel."

"Oh!" cried S'tira. "Well, you *are* getting along, 'Manda Grier!"

"Well, don't you let yourself be outdone, then, S'tira."

"I guess Mr. Barker's good enough for me awhile yet," said Statira, and she hastened to add, "The name, I mean," and at this they all laughed till Statira said, "I shall *certainly* die!" She suddenly recovered herself—those girls seemed to do everything like lightning, Lemuel observed—and said, "No, I ain't goin' to have mine told at all. I don't like it. Seems kind of wicked. I ruther talk. I never *could* make it just right to act so with the Bible."

Lemuel was pleased at that. Statira seemed prettier than ever in this mood of reverence.

"Well, don't talk too much when I'm gone," said 'Manda Grier, and before anybody could stop her, she ran out of the room. But she put her head in again to say, "I'll be back as soon's I can take this key home."

Lemuel did not know what to do. The thought of being alone with Statira again was full of rapture and terror. He was glad when she seized the door, and tried to keep 'Manda Grier.

"I—I—guess I better be going," he said.

"You sha'n't go till I get back, anyway," said 'Manda Grier hospitably. "You keep him, S'tira!"

She gave Statira a little push, and ran down the stairs.

Statira tottered against Lemuel, with that round, soft shoulder which had touched him before. He put out his arms to save her from falling, and they seemed to close round her of themselves. She threw up her face, and in a moment he had kissed her. He released her and fell back from her aghast.

She looked at him.

"I—I didn't mean to," he panted. His heart was thundering in his ears.

She put up her hands to her face, and began to cry.

"Oh, my goodness!" he gasped. He wavered a moment, then he ran out of the room.

On the stairs he met 'Manda Grier coming up. "Now, Mr. Barker, you're real mean to go!" she pouted.

"I guess I better be going," Lemuel called back, in a voice so husky that he hardly knew it for his own.

XII

LEMUEL LET HIMSELF into Miss Vane's hou
to the back gate, and sat down, still throbbing, ɪɴ ....
room over the L, and tried to get the nature of his deed, or
misdeed, before his mind. He had grown up to manhood in
an austere reverence for himself as regarded the other sex, and
in a secret fear, as exacting for them as it was worshipful, of
women. His mother had held all show of love-sickness between young people in scorn; she said they were silly things,
when she saw them soft upon one another; and Lemuel had
imbibed from her a sense of unlawfulness, of shame, in the
love-making he had seen around him all his life. These things
are very open in the country. Even in large villages they have
kissing-games at the children's parties, in the church vestries
and refectories; and as a little boy Lemuel had taken part in
such games. But as he grew older, his reverence and his fear
would not let him touch a girl. Once a big girl, much older
than he, came up behind him in the play-ground and kissed
him; he rubbed the kiss off with his hand, and scoured the
place with sand and gravel. One winter all the big boys and
girls at school began courting whenever the teacher was out
of sight a moment; at the noon-spell, some of them sat with
their arms round one another. Lemuel wandered off by himself in the snows of the deep woods; the sight of such things,
the thought of them, put him to shame for those fools, as he
tacitly called them; and now what had he done himself? He
could not tell. At times he was even proud and glad of it; and
then he did not know what would become of him. But mostly
it seemed to him that he had been guilty of an enormity that
nothing could ever excuse. He must have been crazy to do
such a thing to a young lady like that; her tear-stained face
looked her wonder at him still.

By this time she had told 'Manda Grier all about it; and he
dared not think what their thoughts of him must be. It
seemed to him that he ought to put such a monster as he was
out of the world. But all the time there was a sweetness, a joy
in his heart, that made him half frantic with fear of himself.

"Lemuel!"

He started up at the sound of Sibyl Vane's voice calling to him from the dining-room which opened into the L.

"Yes, ma'am," he answered tremulously, going to his door. Miss Vane had been obliged to instruct him to say ma'am to her niece, whom he had at first spoken of by her Christian name.

"Was that you came in a little while ago?"

"Yes, ma'am, I came in."

"Oh! And have you had your supper?"

"I—I guess I don't want any supper."

"Don't want any supper? You will be ill. Why don't you?"

"I don't know as I feel just like eating anything."

"Well, it won't do. Will you see, please, if Jane is in the kitchen?"

Lemuel came forward, full of his unfitness for the sight of men, but gathering a little courage when he found the dining-room so dark. He descended to the basement and opened the door of the kitchen, looked in, and shut it again. "Yes, ma'am, she's there."

"Oh!" Sibyl seemed to hesitate. Then she said: "Light the gas down there, hadn't you better?"

"I don't know but I had," Lemuel assented.

But before he could obey, "And Lemuel!" she called down again, "come and light it up here too, please."

"I will, as soon as I've lit it here," said Lemuel.

An imperious order came back. "You will light it here *now*, please."

"All right," assented Lemuel. When he appeared in the upper entry and flashed the gas up, he saw Sibyl standing at the reception-room door, with her finger closed into a book which she had been reading.

"You're not to say that you will do one thing when you're told to do another."

Lemuel whitened a little round the lips. "I'm not to do two things at once, either, I suppose."

Sibyl ignored this reply. "Please go and get your supper, and when you've had it come up here again. I've some things for you to do."

"I'll do them now," said Lemuel fiercely. "I don't want any supper, and I sha'n't eat any."

"Why, Lemuel, what is the matter with you?" asked the girl, in the sudden effect of motherly solicitude. "You look very strange, you seem so excited."

"I'm not hungry, that's all," said the boy doggedly. "What is it you want done?"

"Won't you please go up to the third floor," said Sibyl, in a phase of timorous dependence, "and see if everything is right there? I thought I heard a noise. See if the windows are fast, won't you?"

Lemuel turned, and she followed with her finger in her book, and her book pressed to her heart, talking. "It seemed to me that I heard steps and voices. It's very mysterious. I suppose any one could plant a ladder on the roof of the L part, and get into the windows if they were not fastened."

"Have to be a pretty long ladder," grumbled Lemuel.

"Yes," Sibyl assented, "it would. And it didn't sound exactly like burglars."

She followed him half-way up the second flight of stairs, and stood there while he explored the third story throughout.

"There ain't anything there," he reported without looking at her, and was about to pass her on the stairs in going down.

"Oh, thank you very much, Lemuel," she said, with fervent gratitude in her voice. She fetched a tremulous sigh. "I suppose it was nothing. Yes," she added hoarsely, "it must have been nothing. Oh, let *me* go down first!" she cried, putting out her hand to stop him from passing her. She resumed when they reached the ground floor again. "Aunty has gone out, and Jane was in the kitchen, and it began to grow dark while I sat reading in the drawing-room, and all at once I heard the strangest *noise*." Her voice dropped deeply on the last word. "Yes, it was very strange, indeed! Thank you, Lemuel," she concluded.

"Quite welcome," said Lemuel dryly, pushing on towards the basement stairs.

"Oh! And Lemuel! will you let Jane give you your supper in the dining-room, so that you could be here if I heard anything else?"

"I don't want any supper," said Lemuel.

The girl scrutinized him with an expression of misgiving. Then, with a little sigh, as of one who will not explore a painful mystery, she asked: "Would you mind sitting in the dining-room, then, till aunty gets back?"

"I'd just as lives sit there," said Lemuel, walking into the dark dining-room and sitting down.

"Oh, thank you very much. Aunty will be back very soon, I suppose. She's just gone to the Sewells' to tea."

She followed him to the threshold. "You must—I must—light the gas in here, for you."

"Guess I can light the gas," said Lemuel, getting up to intercept her in this service. She had run into the reception-room for a match, and she would not suffer him to prevent her.

"No, no! I insist! And Lemuel," she said, turning upon him, "I must ask you to excuse my speaking harshly to you. I was—agitated."

"Perfectly excusable," said Lemuel.

"I am afraid," said the girl, fixing him with her eyes, "that you are not well."

"Oh, yes, I'm well. I'm—pretty tired; that's all."

"Have you been walking far?"

"Yes—not very."

"The walking ought to do you good," said Sibyl with serious thoughtfulness. "I think," she continued, "you had better have some bryonia. Don't you think you had?"

"No, no! I don't want anything," protested Lemuel.

She looked at him with a feeling of baffled anxiety painted on her face; and as she turned away, she beamed with a fresh inspiration. "I will get you a book." She flew into the reception-room and back again, but she only had the book that she had herself been reading.

"Perhaps you would like to read this? I've finished it. I was just looking back through it."

"Thank you; I guess I don't want to read any, just now."

She leaned against the side of the dining-table, beyond which Lemuel sat, and searched his fallen countenance with a glance contrived to be at once piercing and reproachful. "I see," she said, "you have not forgiven me."

"Forgiven you?" repeated Lemuel blankly.

"Yes—for giving way to my agitation in speaking to you."

"I don't know," said Lemuel, with a sigh of deep inward trouble, "as I noticed anything."

"I told you to light the gas in the basement," suggested Sibyl, "and then I told you to light it up here, and then—I scolded you."

"Oh, yes," admitted Lemuel: "that." He dropped his head again.

Sibyl sank upon the edge of a chair. "Lemuel! you have something on your mind!"

The boy looked up with a startled face.

"Yes! I can see that you have," pursued Sibyl. "What have you been doing?" she demanded sternly.

Lemuel was so full of the truth that it came first to his lips in all cases. He could scarcely force it aside now with the evasion that availed him nothing. "I don't know as I've been doing anything in particular."

"I see that you don't wish to tell me!" cried the girl. "But you might have trusted me. I would have defended you, no matter what you had done—the worse the better."

Lemuel hung his head without answering.

After a while she continued: "If I had been that girl who had you arrested, and I had been the cause of so much suffering to an innocent person, I should never have forgiven myself. I should have devoted my life to expiation. I should have spent my life in going about the prisons, and finding out persons who were unjustly accused. I should have done it as a penance. Yes! even if he had been guilty!"

Lemuel remained insensible to this extreme of self-sacrifice, and she went on: "This book—it is a story—is all one picture of such a nature. There is a girl who's been brought up as the ward of a young man. He educates her, and she expects to be his wife, and he turns out to be perfectly false and unworthy in every way; but she marries him all the same, although she likes some one else, because she feels that she ought to punish herself for thinking of another, and because she hopes that she will die soon, and when her guardian finds out what she's done for him, it will reform him. It's perfectly sublime. It's—ennobling! If every one could read this book, they would be very different."

"I don't see much sense in it," said Lemuel, goaded to this comment.

"You would if you read it. When she dies—she is killed by a fall from her horse in hunting, and has just time to join the hands of her husband and the man she liked first, and tell them everything—it is wrought up so that you hold your breath. I suppose it was reading that that made me think there were burglars getting in. But perhaps you're right not to read it now, if you're excited already. I'll get you something cheerful." She whirled out of the room and back in a series of those swift, nervous movements peculiar to her. "There! that will amuse you, I know." She put the book down on the table before Lemuel, who silently submitted to have it left there. "It will distract your thoughts, if anything will. And I shall ask you to let me sit just here in the reception-room, so that I can call you if I feel alarmed."

"All right," said Lemuel, lapsing absently to his own troubled thoughts.

"Thank you very much," said Sibyl. She went away, and came back directly. "Don't you think," she asked, "that it's very strange you should never have seen or heard anything of her?"

"Heard of who?" he asked, dragging himself painfully up from the depths of his thoughts.

"That heartless girl who had you arrested."

"She *wasn't* heartless!" retorted Lemuel indignantly.

"You think so because you are generous, and can't imagine such heartlessness. Perhaps," added Sibyl, with the air of being illumined by a happy thought, "she is dead. That would account for everything. She may have died of remorse. It probably preyed upon her till she couldn't bear it any longer, and then she killed herself."

Lemuel began to grow red at the first apprehension of her meaning. As she went on, he changed color more and more.

"She is alive!" cried Sibyl. "She's alive, and you have seen her! You needn't deny it! You've seen her to-day!"

Lemuel rose in clumsy indignation. "I don't know as anybody's got any right to say what I've done, or haven't done."

"Oh, Lemuel!" cried Sibyl. "Do you think any one in this house would intrude in your affairs? But if you need a friend—a sister——"

"I don't need any sister. I want you should let me alone."

At these words, so little appreciative of her condescension, her romantic beneficence, her unselfish interest, Sibyl suddenly rebounded to her former level, which she was sensible was far above that of this unworthy object of her kindness. She rose from her chair, and pursued:

"If you need a friend—a sister—I'm sure that you can safely confide in—the cook." She looked at him a moment, and broke into a malicious laugh very unlike that of a social reformer, which rang shriller at the bovine fury which mounted to Lemuel's eyes. The rattle of a night-latch made itself heard in the outer door. Sibyl's voice began to break, as it rose: "I never expected to be treated in my own aunt's house with such perfect ingratitude and impudence—yes, impudence!—by one of her servants!"

She swept out of the room, and her aunt, who entered it, after calling to her in vain, stood with Lemuel, and heard her mount the stairs, sobbing, to her own room, and lock herself in.

"What is the matter, Lemuel?" asked Miss Vane, breathing quickly. She looked at him with the air of a judge who would not condemn him unheard, but would certainly do so after hearing him. Whether it was Lemuel's perception of this that kept him silent, or his confusion of spirit from all the late rapidly successive events, or a wish not to inculpate the girl who had insulted him, he remained silent.

"Answer me!" said Miss Vane sharply.

Lemuel cleared his throat. "I don't know as I've got anything to say," he answered finally.

"But I *insist* upon your saying something," said Miss Vane. "What is this *impudence*?"

"There hasn't been any impudence," replied Lemuel, hanging his head.

"Very well, then, you can tell me what Sibyl means," persisted Miss Vane.

Lemuel seemed to reflect upon it. "No, I can't tell you," he said at last, slowly and gently.

"You refuse to make any explanation whatever?"

"Yes."

Miss Vane rose from the chair which she had mechanically sunk into while waiting for him to speak, and ceased to be the kindly, generous soul she was, in asserting herself as a gentlewoman who had a contumacious servant to treat with. "You will wait here a moment, please."

"All right," said Lemuel. She had asked him not to receive instructions from her with that particular answer, but he could not always remember.

She went upstairs, and returned with some bank-notes that rustled in her trembling hand. "It is two months since you came, and I've paid you one month," she said, and she set her lips, and tried to govern her head, which nevertheless shook with the vehemence she was struggling to repress. She laid two ten-dollar notes upon the table, and then added a five, a little apart. "This second month was to be twenty instead of ten. I shall not want you any longer, and should be glad to have you go now—at once—to-night! But I had intended to offer you a little present at Christmas, and I will give it you now."

Lemuel took up the two ten-dollar notes without saying anything, and then after a moment laid one of them down. "It's only half a month," he said. "I don't want to be paid for any more than I've done."

"Lemuel!" cried Miss Vane. "I insist upon your taking it. I employed you by the month."

"It don't make any difference about that; I've only been here a month and a half."

He folded the notes, and turned to go out of the room. Miss Vane caught the five-dollar note from the table and intercepted him with it. "Well, then, you shall take it as a present."

"I don't want any present," said Lemuel, patiently waiting her pleasure to release him, but keeping his hands in his pockets.

"You would have taken it at Christmas," said Miss Vane. "You shall take it now."

"I shouldn't take a present any time," returned Lemuel steadily.

"You are a foolish boy!" cried Miss Vane. "You need it, and I tell you to take it."

He made no reply whatever.

"You are behaving very stubbornly—ungratefully," said Miss Vane.

Lemuel lifted his head; his lip quivered a little. "I don't think you've got any right to say I'm ungrateful."

"I don't mean ungrateful," said Miss Vane. "I mean unkind—very silly, indeed. And I wish you to take this money. You are behaving resentfully—wickedly. I am much older than you, and I tell you that you are not behaving rightly. Why don't you do what I wish?"

"I don't want any money I haven't earned."

"I don't mean the money. Why don't you tell me the meaning of what I heard? My niece said you had been impudent to her. Perhaps she didn't understand."

She looked wistfully into the boy's face.

After a long time he said, "I don't know as I've got anything to say about it."

"Very well, then, you may *go*," said Miss Vane, with all her hauteur.

"Well, good-evening," said Lemuel passively, but the eyes that he looked at her with were moist, and conveyed a pathetic reproach. To her unmeasured astonishment, he offered her his hand; her amaze was even greater—*more* infinite, as she afterwards told Sewell—when she found herself shaking it.

He went out of the room, and she heard him walking about in his room in the L, putting together his few belongings. Then she heard him go down and open the furnace-door, and she knew he was giving a final conscientious look at the fire. He closed it, and she heard him close the basement door behind him, and knew that he was gone.

She explored the L, and then she descended to the basement and mechanically looked it over. Everything that could be counted hers by the most fastidious sense of property had been left behind him in the utmost neatness. On their accustomed nail, just inside the furnace-room, hung the blue overalls. They looked like a suicidal Lemuel hanging there.

Miss Vane went upstairs slowly, with a heavy heart. Under

the hall light stood Sibyl, picturesque in the deep shadow it flung upon her face.

"Aunt Hope," she began in a tragic voice.

"Don't *speak* to me, you wicked girl!" cried her aunt, venting her self-reproach upon this victim. "It is *your* doing."

Sibyl turned with the meekness of an ostentatious scapegoat unjustly bearing the sins of her tribe, and went upstairs into the wilderness of her own thoughts again.

XIII

T HE SENSE of outrage with which Lemuel was boiling when Miss Vane came in upon Sibyl and himself had wholly passed away, and he now saw his dismissal, unjust as between that girl and him, unimpeachably righteous as between him and the moral frame of things. If he had been punished for being ready to take advantage of that fellow's necessity, and charge him fifty cents for changing ten dollars, he must now be no less obviously suffering for having abused that young lady's trust and defenselessness; only he was not suffering one-tenth as much. When he recurred to that wrong, in fact, and tried to feel sorry for it and ashamed, his heart thrilled in a curious way; he found himself smiling and exulting, and Miss Vane and her niece went out of his mind, and he could not think of anything but of being with that girl, of hearing her talk and laugh, of touching her. He sighed; he did not know what his mother would say if she knew; he did not know where he was going; it seemed a hundred years since the beginning of the afternoon.

A horse-car came by, and Lemuel stopped it. He set his bag down on the platform, and stood there near the conductor, without trying to go inside, for the bag was pretty large, and he did not believe the conductor would let him take it in.

The conductor said politely after a while, "See, 'd I get your fare?"

"No," said Lemuel. He paid, and the conductor went inside and collected the other fares.

When he came back he took advantage of Lemuel's continued presence to have a little chat. He was a short, plump, stubby-mustached man, and he looked strong and well, but he said, with an introductory sigh, "Well, sir, I get sore all over at this business. There ain't a bone in me that hain't got an ache in it. Sometimes I can't tell but what it's the ache got a bone in it, ache seems the biggest."

"Why, what makes it?" asked Lemuel, absently.

"Oh, it's this standin'; it's the hours, and changin' the hours so much. You hain't got a chance to get used to one set o' hours before they get 'em all shifted round again. Last week I was on from eight to eight; this week it's from twelve to twelve. Lord knows what it's going to be next week. And this is one o' the best lines in town, too."

"I presume they pay you pretty well," said Lemuel, with awakening interest.

"Well, they pay a dollar 'n' half a day," said the conductor.

"Why, it's more than forty dollars a month," said Lemuel.

"Well, it is," said the conductor scornfully, "if you work every day in the week. But I can't stand it more than six days out o' seven; and if you miss a day, or if you miss a trip, they dock you. No, sir. It's about the meanest business *I* ever struck. If I wa'n't a married man, 'n' if I didn't like to be regular about my meals and get 'em at home 'th my wife, I wouldn't stand it a minute. But that's where it is. It's regular."

A lady from within signaled the conductor. He stopped the car, and the lady, who had risen with her escort, remained chatting with a friend before she got out. The conductor snapped his bell for starting, with a look of patient sarcasm. "See that?" he asked Lemuel. "Some these women act as if the cars was their private carriage; and *you* got to act so *too*, or the lady complains of you, and the company bounces you in a minute. Stock's owned along the line, and they think they own *you* too. You can't get 'em to set more than ten on a side; they'll leave the car first. I'd like to catch 'em on some the South End or Cambridge cars; I'd show 'em how to pack live stock once, anyway. Yes, sir, these ladies that ride on this line think they can keep the car standin' while they talk about the opera. But you'd ought to see how they all look if a *poor* woman tried their little game. Oh, I tell you, rich people are hard."

Lemuel reflected upon the generalization. He regarded Miss Vane as a rich person; but though she had blamed him unjustly, and had used him impatiently, even cruelly, in this last affair, he remembered other things, and he said:

"Well, I don't know as I should say all of them were hard."

"Well, maybe not," admitted the conductor. "But I don't envy 'em. The way I look at it, and the way I tell my wife, I wouldn't want their money 'f I had to have the rest of it. Ain't any of 'em happy. I saw that when I lived out. No, sir; what me and my wife want to do is to find us a nice little place in the country."

At the words a vision of Willoughby Pastures rose upon Lemuel, and a lump of homesickness came into his throat. He saw the old wood-colored house, crouching black within its walls under the cold November stars. If his mother had not gone to bed yet, she was sitting beside the cooking-stove in the kitchen, and perhaps his sister was brewing something on it, potion or lotion, for her husband's rheumatism. Miss Vane had talked to him about his mother; she had said he might have her down to visit him, if everything went on right; but of course he knew that Miss Vane did not understand that his mother wore bloomers, and he made up his mind that her invitation was never to be accepted. At the same time he had determined to ask Miss Vane to let him go up and see his mother some Sunday.

" 'S fur's we go," said the conductor. " 'F you're goin' on, you want to take another car here."

"I guess I'll go back with you a little ways," said Lemuel. "I want to ask you——"

"Guess we'll have to take a back seat, then," said the conductor, leading the way through the car to the other platform; "or a standee," he added, snapping the bell. "What is it you want to ask?"

"Oh, nothing. How do you fellows learn to be conductors? How long does it take you?"

Till other passengers should come the conductor lounged against the guard of the platform in a conversational posture.

"Well, generally it takes you four or five days. You got to learn all the cross streets, and the principal places on all the lines."

"Yes?"

"It didn't take me more'n two. Boston boy."

"Yes," said Lemuel, with a fine discouragement. "I presume the conductors are mostly from Boston."

"They're from everywhere. And some of 'em are pretty streaked, I can tell you; and then the rest of us has got to suffer; throws suspicion on all of us. One fellow gets to stealin' fares, and then everybody's got to wear a bell-punch.

I never hear mine go without thinkin' it says, 'Stop thief!'
Makes me sick, I can tell you."

After a while Lemuel asked, "How do you get such a position?"

The conductor seemed to be thinking about something
else. "It's a pretty queer kind of a world, anyway, the way
everybody's mixed up with everybody else. What's the reason, if a man wants to steal, he can't steal and suffer for it
himself, without throwin' the shame and the blame on a lot
more people that never thought o' stealin'? I don't notice
much when a fellow sets out to do right that folks think
everybody else is on the square. No, sir, they don't seem to
consider that kind of complaint so catching. Now, you take
another thing: A woman goes round with the scarlet fever in
her clothes, and a whole carful of people take it home to their
children; but let a nice young girl get in, fresh as an apple,
and a perfect daisy for wholesomeness every way, and she
don't give it to a single soul on board. No, sir; it's a world I
can't see through, nor begin to."

"I never thought of it that way," said Lemuel, darkened by
this black pessimism of the conductor. He had not, practically, found the world so unjust as the conductor implied, but
he could not controvert his argument. He only said, "Maybe
the right thing makes us feel good in some way we don't
know of."

"Well, I don't want to feel good in some way I don't know
of, myself," said the conductor very scornfully.

"No, that's so," Lemuel admitted. He remained silent, with
a vague wonder flitting through his mind whether Mr. Sewell
could make anything better of the case, and then settled back
to his thoughts of Statira, pierced and confused as they were
now with his pain from that trouble with Miss Vane.

"What was that you asked me just now?" said the conductor.

"That I asked you?" Lemuel echoed. "Oh, yes! I asked you
how you got your place on the cars."

"Well, sir, you have to have recommendations—they won't
touch you without 'em; and then you have to have about
seventy-five dollars capital to start with. You got to get your
coat, and your cap, and your badge, and you got to have

about twenty dollars of your own to make change with, first off; company don't start you with a cent."

Lemuel made no reply. After a while he asked, "Do you know any good hotel, around here, where I could go for the night?"

"Well, there's the Brunswick, and there's the Van-dome," said the conductor. "They're both pretty fair houses." Lemuel looked round at the mention of the aristocratic hostelries to see if the conductor was joking. He owned to something of the kind by adding, "There's a little hotel, if you want something quieter, that ain't a great ways from here." He gave the name of the hotel, and told Lemuel how to find it.

"Thank you," said Lemuel. "I guess I'll get off here, then. Well, good-evening."

"Guess I'll have to get another nickel from you," said the conductor, snapping his bell. "New trip," he explained.

"Oh," said Lemuel, paying. It seemed to him a short ride for five cents.

He got off, and as the conductor started up the car, he called forward through it to the driver, "Wanted to try for conductor, I guess. But I guess the seventy-five dollars capital settled that little point for him."

Lemuel heard the voice but not the words. He felt his bag heavy in his hand as he walked away in the direction the conductor had given him, and he did not set it down when he stood hesitating in front of the hotel; it looked like too expensive a place for him, with its stained-glass door, and its bulk hoisted high into the air. He walked by the hotel, and then he came back to it, and mustered courage to go in. His bag, if not superb, looked a great deal more like baggage than the lank sack which he had come to Boston with; he had bought it only a few days before, in hopes of going home before long; he set it down with some confidence on the tessellated floor of cheap marble, and when a shirt-sleeved, drowsy-eyed, young man came out of a little room or booth near the door, where there was a desk, and a row of bells, and a board with keys, hanging from the wall above it, Lemuel said quite boldly that he would like a room. The man said, well, they did not much expect transients; it was more of a family-hotel, like; but he guessed they had a vacancy, and they could put him up. He brushed his shirt-sleeves down with his hands, and looked apologetically at some ashes on his trousers, and said, well, it was not much use trying to put on style, anyway, when you were taking care of a furnace and had to run the elevator yourself, and look after the whole concern. He said his aunt mostly looked after letting the rooms, but she was at church, and he guessed he should have to see about it himself. He bade Lemuel just get right into the elevator, and he put his bag into a cage that hung in one corner of the hallway, and pulled at the wire rope, and they mounted together. On the way up he had time to explain that the clerk, who usually ran the elevator when they had no elevator-boy, had kicked, and they were just between hay and grass, as you might say. He showed Lemuel into a grandiose parlor or drawing-room, enormously draped and upholstered, and furnished in a composite application of yellow jute and red plush to the ashen easy-chairs and sofa. A folding-bed in the figure of a chiffo-nier attempted to occupy the whole side of the wall and failed.

"I'm afraid it's more than I can pay," said Lemuel. "I guess I better see some other room." But the man said the room belonged to a boarder that had just gone, and he guessed they would not charge him very much for it; he guessed Lemuel had better stay. He pulled the bed down, and showed him how it worked, and he lighted two bulbous gas-burners, con-trived to burn the gas at such a low pressure that they were like two unsnuffed candles for brilliancy. He backed round over the spacious floor and looked about him with an unfa-miliar, marauding air, which had a certain boldness, but failed to impart courage to Lemuel, who trembled for fear of the unknown expense. But he was ashamed to go away, and when the man left him he went to bed, after some suspicious in-vestigation of the machine he was to sleep in. He found its comfort unmistakable. He was tired out with what had been happening, and the events of the day recurred in a turmoil that helped rather than hindered slumber; none evolved itself distinctly enough from the mass to pursue him; what he was mainly aware of was the daring question whether he could not get the place of that clerk who had kicked.

In the morning he saw the landlady, who was called Mrs.

Harmon, and who took the pay for his lodging, and said he might leave his bag awhile there in the office. She was a large, smooth, tranquil person, who seemed ready for any sort of consent; she entered into an easy conversation with Lemuel, and was so sympathetic in regard to the difficulties of getting along in the city, that he had proposed himself as clerk and been accepted almost before he believed the thing had happened. He was getting a little used to the rapidity of urban transactions, but his mind had still a rustic difficulty in keeping up with his experiences.

"I suppose," said Mrs. Harmon, "it ain't very usual to take anybody without a reference; I never do it; but so long as you haven't been a great while in the city—You ever had a place in Boston before?"

"Well, not exactly what you may call a place," said Lemuel, with a conscience against describing in that way his position at Miss Vane's. "It was only part work." He added, "I wasn't there but a little while."

"Know anybody in the city?"

"Yes," said Lemuel, reluctantly; "I know Rev. David L. Sewell, some."

"Oh, all right," said Mrs. Harmon, with eager satisfaction. "I have to be pretty particular who I have in the house. The boarders are all high-class, and I have to have all the departments accordingly. I'll see Mr. Sewell about you as soon as I get time, and I guess you can take hold right now, if you want to."

Mrs. Harmon showed him in half a minute how to manage the elevator, and then left him with general instructions to tell everybody who came upon any errand he did not understand, that she would be back in a very short time. He found pen and paper in the office, and she said he might write the letter that he asked leave to send his mother; when he mentioned his mother, she said, yes, indeed, with a burst of maternal sympathy which was imagined in her case, for she had already told Lemuel that if she had ever had any children she would not have gone into the hotel business, which she believed unfriendly to their right nurture; she said she never liked to take ladies with children.

He inclosed some money to his mother which he had intended to send, but which, before the occurrence of the good fortune that now seemed opening upon him, he thought he must withhold. He made as little as he could of his parting with Miss Vane, whom he had celebrated in earlier letters to his mother; he did not wish to afflict her on his own account, or incense her against Miss Vane, who, he felt, could not help her part in it; but his heart burned anew against Miss Sibyl while he wrote. He dwelt upon his good luck in getting this new position at once, and he let his mother see that he considered it a rise in life. He said he was going to try to get Mrs. Harmon to let him go home for Thanksgiving, though he presumed he might have to come back the same night.

His letter was short, but he was several times interrupted by the lady boarders, many of whom stopped to ask Mrs. Harmon something on their way to their rooms from breakfast. They did not really want anything, in most cases; but they were strict with Lemuel in wanting to know just when they could see Mrs. Harmon; and they delayed somewhat to satisfy a natural curiosity in regard to him. They made talk with him as he took them up in the elevator, and did what they could to find out about him. Most of them had their door-keys in their hands, and dangled them by the triangular pieces of brass which the keys were chained to; they affected some sort of *négligée* breakfast costume, and Lemuel thought them very fashionable. They nearly all snuffled and whined as they spoke; some had a soft, lazy nasal; others broke abruptly from silence to silence in voices of nervous sharpness, like the cry or the bleat of an animal; one young girl, who was quite pretty, had a high, hoarse voice, like a gander.

Lemuel did not mind all this; he talked through his nose too; and he accepted Mrs. Harmon's smooth characterization of her guests, as she called them, which she delivered in a slow, unimpassioned voice. "I never have any but the highest class people in my house—the very nicest; and I never have any jangling going on. In the first place, I never allow anybody to have anything to complain of, and then if they do complain, I'm right up and down with them; I tell them their rooms are wanted, and they understand what I mean. And I never allow any trouble among the servants; I tell them, if they are not suited, that I don't want them to stay; and if they get to quarreling among themselves, I send them all away, and get a new lot; I pay the highest wages, and I can always do it. If you want to keep up with the times at all, you have got to set a good table, and I mean to set just as good a table as any in Boston; I don't intend to let any one complain of my house on that score. Well, it's as broad as it's long: if you set a good table, you can ask a good price; and if you don't, you can't, that's all. Pay as you go, is my motto."

Mrs. Harmon sat talking in the little den beside the door which she called the office, when she returned from that absence which she had asked him to say would not be more than fifteen minutes at the outside. It had been something more than two hours, and it had ended almost clandestinely; but knowledge of her return had somehow spread through the house, and several ladies came in while she was talking, to ask when their window-shades were to be put up, or to say that they knew their gas-fixtures must be out of order; or that there were mice in their closets, for they had heard them gnawing; or that they were sure their set-bowls smelt, and that the traps were not working. Mrs. Harmon was prompt in every exigency. She showed the greatest surprise that those shades had not gone up yet; she said she was going to send round for the gas-fitter to look at the fixtures all over the house; and that she would get some potash to pour down the bowls, for she knew the drainage was perfect—it was just the pipes down *to* the traps that smelt; she advised a cat for the mice, and said she would get one. She used the greatest sympathy with the ladies, recognizing a real sufferer in each, and not attempting to deny anything. From the dining-room came at times the sound of voices, which blended in a discord loud above the clatter of crockery, but Mrs. Harmon seemed not to hear them. An excited foreigner of some sort finally rushed from this quarter, and thrust his head into the booth where Lemuel and Mrs. Harmon sat, long enough to explode some formula of renunciation upon her, which left her serenity unruffled. She received with the same patience the sarcasm of a boarder who appeared at the office-door with a bag in his hand, and said he would send an express-man for his trunk. He threw down the money for his receipted bill; and when she said she was sorry he was going, he replied that he could not stand the table any longer, and that he believed that French cook of hers had died on the way over; he was tired of the Nova Scotia temporary, who had become permanent.

A gentleman waited for the parting guest to be gone, and then said to the tranquil Mrs. Harmon: "So Mellen has kicked, has he?"

"Yes, Mr. Evans," said Mrs. Harmon; "Mr. Mellen has kicked."

"And don't you want to abuse him a little? You can to me, you know," suggested the gentleman.

He had a full beard, parted at the chin; it was almost white, and looked older than the rest of his face; his eyes were at once sad and whimsical. Lemuel tried to think where he had seen him before.

"Thank you; I don't know as it would do any good, Mr. Evans. But if he could have waited one week longer, I should have had that cook."

"Yes, that is what I firmly believe. Do you feel too much broken up to accept a ticket to the Wednesday matinée at the Museum?"

"No, I don't," said Mrs. Harmon. "But I shouldn't want to deprive Mrs. Evans of it."

"Oh, she wouldn't go," said Mr. Evans, with a slight sigh. "You had better take it. Jefferson's going to do *Bob Acres.*"

"Is that so?" asked Mrs. Harmon placidly, taking the ticket. "Well, I'm ever so much obliged to you, Mr. Evans. Mr. Evans, Mr. Barker—our new clerk," she said, introducing them.

Lemuel rose with rustic awkwardness, and shook hands with Mr. Evans, who looked at him with a friendly smile, but said nothing.

"Now Mr. Barker is here, I guess I can get the time." Mr. Evans said, well, he was glad she could, and went out of the street-door. "He's just one of the nicest gentlemen I've got," continued Mrs. Harmon, following him with her eye as far as she conveniently could without turning her head, "him and his wife both. Ever heard of the 'Saturday Afternoon'?"

"I don't know as I have," said Lemuel.

"Well, he's one of the editors. It's a kind of a Sunday paper, I guess, for all it don't come out that day. I presume he could go every night in the week to every theater in town, if he wanted to. I don't know how many tickets he's give me. Some of the ladies seem to think he's always makin' fun of them; but I can't ever feel that way. He used to board with a great friend of mine, him and his wife. They've been with me now ever since Mrs. Hewitt died; she was the one they boarded with before. They say he used to be dreadful easy-going, 'n' 't his wife was all't saved him. But I guess he's different now. Well, I must go out and see after the lunch. You watch the office and say just what I told you before."

XIV

SEWELL CHANCED to open his door to go out just as Miss
Vane put her hand on the bell-pull, the morning after she
had dismissed Lemuel. The cheer of his Monday face died out
at the unsmiling severity of hers; but he contrived to ask her
in, and said he would call Mrs. Sewell, if she would sit down
in the reception-room a moment.

"I don't know," she said, with a certain look of inquiry, not
unmixed with compassion. "It's about Lemuel."

The minister fetched a deep sigh. "Yes, I know it. But she
will have to know it sooner or later." He went to the stairway
and called her name, and then returned to Miss Vane in the
reception-room.

"Has Lemuel been here?" she asked.

"No."

"You said you knew it was about him—"

"It was my bad conscience, I suppose, and your face that
told me."

Miss Vane waited for Mrs. Sewell's presence before she un-
packed her heart. Then she left nothing in it. She ended by
saying, "I have examined and cross-examined Sibyl, but it's
like cross-questioning a chameleon; she changed color with
every new light she was put into." Here Miss Vane had got
sorrowfully back to something more of her wonted humor,
and laughed.

"Poor Sibyl!" said Mrs. Sewell.

"Poor?" retorted Miss Vane. "Not at all! I could get nothing out of either of them; but I feel perfectly sure that Lemuel
was not to blame."

"It's very possible," suggested Mrs. Sewell, "that he did say
something in his awkward way that she misconstrued into
impertinence."

Miss Vane did not seem to believe this. "If Lemuel had
given me the slightest satisfaction," she began in self-
exculpation. "But no," she broke off. "It had to be!" She rose.
"I thought I had better come and tell you at once, Mr. Sewell.
I suppose you will want to look him up, and do something
more for him. I wish if you find him you would make him

take this note." She gave the minister a ten-dollar bill. "I tried to do so, but he would not have it. I don't know what I shall do without him! He is the best and most faithful creature in the world. Even in this little time I had got to relying implicitly upon his sense, his judgment, his goodness, his—— Well! good-morning!"

She ran out of the door, and left Sewell confronted with his wife.

He did not know whether she had left him to hope or to despair, and he waited for his wife to interpret his emotion, but Mrs. Sewell tacitly refused to do this. After a dreary interval he plucked a random cheerfulness out of space, and said: "Well, if Miss Vane feels in that way about it, I don't see why the whole affair can't be arranged and Barker reinstated."

"David," returned his wife, not vehemently at all, "when you come out with those mannish ideas I don't know what to do."

"Well, my dear," said the minister, "I should be glad to come out with some womanish ideas if I had them. I dare say they would be better. But I do my poor best, under the circumstances. What is the trouble with my ideas, except that the sex is wrong?"

"You think, you men," replied Mrs. Sewell, "that a thing like that can be mended up and smoothed over, and made just the same as ever. You think that because Miss Vane is sorry she sent Barker away and wants him back, she can take him back."

"I don't see why she can't. I've sometimes supposed that the very highest purpose of Christianity was mutual forgiveness—forbearance with one another's errors."

"That's all very well," said Mrs. Sewell. "But you know that whenever I have taken a cook back, after she had shown temper, it's been an entire failure; and this is a far worse case, because there is disappointed good-will mixed up with it. I don't suppose Barker is at all to blame. Whatever has happened, you may be perfectly sure that it has been partly a bit of stage-play in Sibyl and partly a mischievous desire to use her power over him. I foresaw that she would soon be tired of reforming him. But whatever it is, it's something that you can't repair. Suppose Barker went back to them; could they ignore what's happened?"

"Of course not," Sewell admitted.

"Well, and should he ask her pardon, or she his?"

"The Socratic method is irresistible," said the minister sadly. "You have proved that nothing can be done for Barker with the Vanes. And now the question is, what *can* be done for him?"

"That's something I must leave to you, David," said his wife dispiritedly. She arose, and as she passed out of the room she added, "You will have to find him, in the *first* place, and you had better go round to the police stations and the tramps' lodging-houses and begin looking."

Sewell sighed heavily under the sarcastic advice, but acted upon it, and set forth upon the useless quest, because he did not know in the least what else to do.

All that week Barker lay, a lurking discomfort, in his soul, though as the days passed the burden grew undeniably lighter; Sewell had a great many things besides Barker to think of. But when Sunday came, and he rose in his pulpit, he could not help casting a glance of guilty fear toward Miss Vane's pew and drawing a long breath of guilty relief not to see Lemuel in it. We are so made, that in the reaction the minister was able to throw himself into the matter of his dis-course with uncommon fervor.

It was really very good matter, and he felt the literary joy in it which flatters the author even of a happily worded suppli-cation to the Deity. He let his eyes, freed from their bondage to Lemuel's attentive face, roam at large in liberal ease over his whole congregation; and when, toward the close of his sermon, one visage began to grow out upon him from the two or three hundred others, and to concentrate in itself the facial expression of all the rest, and become the only counte-nance there, it was a perceptible moment before he identified it as that of his inalienable charge. Then he began to preach at it as usual, but defiantly, and with yet a haste to be through and to get speech with it that he felt was ludicrous, and must appear unaccountable to his hearers. It seemed to him that he could not bring his sermon to a close; he ended it in a cloudy burst of rhetoric which he feared would please the nervous, elderly ladies—who sometimes blamed him for a want of emotionality—and knew must grieve the judicious. While the choir was singing the closing hymn, he contrived to beckon the sexton to the pulpit, and described and located Lemuel to him as well as he could without actually pointing him out; he said that he wished to see that young man after church, and asked the sexton to bring him to his room. The sexton did so to the best of his ability, but the young man whom he brought was not Lemuel, and had to be got rid of with apologies.

On three or four successive Sundays Lemuel's face dawned upon the minister from the congregation, and tasked his powers of impersonal appeal and mental concentration to the utmost. It never appeared twice in the same place, and when at last Sewell had tutored the sexton carefully in Lemuel's dress, he was driven to despair one morning when he saw the boy sidling along between the seats in the gallery, and sitting down with an air of satisfaction in an entirely new suit of clothes.

After this defeat the sexton said with humorous sympathy, "Well, there ain't anything for it now, Mr. Sewell, but a detective. Or else an advertisement in the Personals."

Sewell laughed with him at his joke, and took what comfort he could from the evidence of prosperity which Lemuel's new clothes offered. He argued that if Barker could afford to buy them he could not be in immediate need, and for some final encounter with him he trusted in Providence, and was not too much cast down when his wife made him recognize that he was trusting in luck. It was an ordeal to look forward to finding Lemuel sooner or later among his hearers every Sunday; but having prepared his nerves for the shock, as men adjust their sensibilities to the recurrent pain of a disease, he came to bear it with fortitude, especially as he continually reminded himself that he had his fixed purpose to get at Lemuel at last and befriend him in any and every possible way. He tried hard to keep from getting a grudge against him.

At the hotel, Lemuel remained in much of his original belief in the fashion and social grandeur of the ladies who formed the majority of Mrs. Harmon's guests. Our womankind are prone to a sort of helpless intimacy with those who

serve them; the ladies had an instinctive perception of Lemuel's trustiness, and readily gave him their confidence and
much of their history. He came to know them without being
at all able to classify them with reference to society at large, as
of that large tribe among us who have revolted from domestic
care, and have skillfully unseated the black rider who remains
mounted behind the husband of the average lady-boarder.
Some of them had never kept house, being young and newly
married, though of this sort there were those who had tried it
in flats, and had reverted to their natural condition of boarding. They advised Lemuel not to take a flat, whatever he did,
unless he wanted to perish at once. Other lady boarders had
broken up housekeeping during the first years of the war, and
had been boarding round ever since, going from hotels in the
city to hotels in the country, and back again with the change
of the seasons; these mostly had husbands who had horses,
and they talked with equal tenderness of the husbands and the
horses, so that you could not always tell which Jim or Bob
was; usually they had no children, but occasionally they had a
married daughter, or a son who lived West. There were several single ladies: one who seemed to have nothing in this
world to do but to come down to her meals, and another a
physician who had not been able, in embracing the medical
profession, to deny herself the girlish pleasure of her pet
name, and was lettered in the list of guests in the entry as Dr.
Cissie Bluff. In the attic, which had a north light favorable to
their work, were two girls, who were studying art at the Museum; one of them looked delicate at first sight, and afterwards seemed merely very gentle, with a clear-eyed pallor
which was not unhealth. A student in the Law School sat at
the table with these girls, and seemed sometimes to go with
them to concerts and lectures. From his talk, which was almost the only talk that made itself heard in the dining-room,
it appeared that he was from Wyoming Territory; he treated
the young ladies as representative of Boston and its prejudices, though apparently they were not Bostonians. There
were several serious and retiring couples, of whom one or
other was an invalid, and several who were poor, and preferred the plated gentility of Mrs. Harmon's hotel—it was
called the St. Albans; Mrs. Harmon liked the name—to the

genuine poverty of such housekeeping as they could have set up. About each of these women a home might have clung, with all its loves and cares; they were naturally like other women; but here they were ignoble particles, without attraction for one another, or apparently joy for themselves, impermanent, idle, listless; they had got rid of the trouble of housekeeping, and of its dignity and usefulness. There were a few children in the house, not at all noisy; the boys played on the sidewalk, and the little girls staid in their rooms with their mothers, and rarely took the air oftener than they.

They came down rather later to breakfast, and they seemed not to go to school; some of them had piano lessons in their rooms. Their mothers did not go out much; sometimes they went to church or the theater, and they went shopping. But they had apparently no more social than domestic life. Now and then they had a friend to lunch or dinner; if a lady was absent, it was known to Mrs. Harmon, and through her to the other ladies, that she was spending the day with a friend of hers at a hotel in Newton, or Lexington, or Woburn. In a city full of receptions, of dinner-giving, and party-going, Mrs. Harmon's guests led the lives of cloistered nuns, so far as such pleasures were concerned. Occasionally a transient had rooms for a week or two, and was continually going, and receiving visits. She became the object of a certain unenvious curiosity with the other ladies, who had not much sociability among themselves; they waited a good while before paying visits at one another's rooms, and then were very punctilious not to go again until their calls had been returned. They were all doctoring themselves; they did not talk gossip or scandal much; they talked of their diseases and physicians, and their married daughters, and of Mrs. Harmon, whom they censured for being too easy-going. Certain of them devoured novels, which they carried about clasped to their breasts with their fingers in them at the place where they were reading; they did not often speak of them, and apparently took them as people take opium.

The men were the husbands or fathers of the women, and were wholly without the domestic weight or consequence that belongs to men living in their own houses. There were certain old bachelors, among whom were two or three de-

cayed branches of good Boston families, spendthrifts, or in-
valided bankrupts. Mr. Evans was practically among the
single gentlemen, for his wife never appeared in the parlor or
dining-room, and was seen only when she went in or out,
heavily veiled, for a walk. Lemuel heard very soon that she
had suffered a shock from the death of her son on the cars;
the other ladies made much of her inability to get over it, and
said nothing would induce them to have a son of theirs go in
and out on the cars.

Among these people, such as they were, and far as they
might be from a final civilization, Lemuel began to feel an
ambition to move more lightly and quickly than he had yet
known how to do, to speak promptly, and to appear well.
Our schooling does not train us to graceful or even correct
speech; even our colleges often leave that uncouth. Many of
Mrs. Harmon's boarders spoke bad grammar through their
noses; but the ladies dressed stylishly, and the men were good
arithmeticians. Lemuel obeyed a native impulse rather than a
good example in cultivating a better address; but the incentive
to thrift and fashion was all about him. He had not been
ignorant that his clothes were queer in cut and out of date,
and during his stay at Miss Vane's he had taken much counsel
with himself as to whether he ought not to get a new suit
with his first money instead of sending it home. Now he had
solved the question, after sending the money home, by the
discovery of a place on a degenerate street, in a neighborhood
of Chinese laundries, with the polite name of Misfit Parlors,
where they professed to sell the failures of the leading tailors
of Boston, New York, and Chicago. After long study of the
window of the Parlors, Lemuel ventured within one day, and
was told, when he said he could not afford the suit he fancied,
that he might pay for it on the installment plan, which the
proprietor explained to him. In the mirror he was almost startled at the stylishness of his own image. The proprietor of the
Parlors complimented him. "You see, you've got a good figure
for a suit of clothes—what I call a ready-made figure. *You* can
go into a clothing-store anywheres and fit you."

He took the first installment of the price, with Lemuel's
name and address, and said he would send the clothes round;
but in the evening he brought them himself, and no doubt

verified Lemuel's statement by this device. It was a Saturday night, and the next morning Lemuel rose early to put them on. He meant to go to church in them, and in the afternoon he did not know just what he should do. He had hoped that some chance might bring them together again, and then he could see from the way Miss Dudley and 'Manda Grier behaved just what they thought. He had many minds about the matter himself, and had gone from an extreme of self-abhorrence to one of self-vindication, and between these he had halted at every gradation of blame and exculpation. But perhaps what chiefly kept him away was the uncertainty of his future; till he could give some shape to that, he had no courage to face the past. Sometimes he wished never to see either of those girls again; but at other times he had a longing to go and explain, to justify himself, or to give himself up to justice.

The new clothes gave him more heart than he had yet had, but the most he could bring himself to do was to walk towards Pleasant Avenue the next Sunday afternoon, which Mrs. Harmon especially gave him, and to think about walking up and down before the house. It ended in his walking up and down the block, first on one side of the street and then on the other. He knew the girls' window; Miss Dudley had shown him it was the middle window of the top story when they were looking out of it, and he glanced up at it. Then he hurried away, but he could not leave the street without stopping at the corner, to cast a last look back at the house. There was an apothecary's at that corner, and while he stood wistfully staring and going round the corner a little way, and coming back to look at the things in the apothecary's window, he saw 'Manda Grier come swiftly towards him. He wanted to run away now, but he could not; he felt nailed to the spot, and he felt the color go out of his face. She pretended not to see him at first; but with a second glance she abandoned the pretense, and at his saying faintly "Good-afternoon," she said, with freezing surprise, "Oh! good-afternoon, Mr. Barker!" and passed into the apothecary's.

He could not go now, since he had spoken, and leave all so inconclusive again; and yet 'Manda Grier had been so repellent, so cutting, in her tone and manner, that he did not know how to face her another time. When she came out he faltered, "I hope there isn't anybody sick at your house, Miss Grier."

"Oh, nobody that you'll care about, Mr. Barker," she answered airily, and began to tilt rapidly away, with her chin thrust out before her.

He made a few paces after her, and then stopped; she seemed to stop too, and he caught up with her.

"I hope," he gasped, "there ain't anything the matter with Miss Dudley?"

"Oh, nothing 't *you'll* care about," said 'Manda Grier; and she added with terrible irony, "You've b'en round to inquire so much that you hain't allowed time for any *great* change."

"Has she been sick long?" faltered Lemuel. "I didn't dare to come!" he cried out. "I've been wanting to come, but I didn't suppose you would speak to me—any of you." Now his tongue was unlocked, he ran on: "I don't know as it's any excuse—there *ain't* any excuse for such a thing! I know she must perfectly despise me, and that I'm not fit for her to look at; but I'd give anything if I could take it all back and be just where I was before. You tell her, won't you, how I feel?"

'Manda Grier, who had listened with a killingly averted face, turned sharply upon him. "You mean about stayin' away so long? I don't know as she cared a great deal, but it's a pretty queer way of showin' you cared for her."

"I didn't mean that!" retorted Lemuel; and he added by an immense effort, "I meant—the way I behaved when I was there; I meant——"

"Oh!" said 'Manda Grier, turning her face away again; she turned it so far away that the back of her head was all that Lemuel could see. "I guess you better speak to Statira about that."

By this time they had reached the door of the boarding-house, and 'Manda Grier let herself in with her latch-key. "Won't you walk in, Mr. Barker?" she said in formal tones of invitation.

"Is she well enough to see—company?" murmured Lemuel. "I shouldn't want to disturb her."

"I don't believe but what she can see you," said 'Manda Grier, for the first time relentingly.

"All right," said Lemuel, gulping the lump in his throat,

and he followed 'Manda Grier up the flights of stairs to the door of the girls' room, which she flung open without knocking.

"S'tira," she said, "here's Mr. Barker." And Lemuel, from the dark landing, where he lurked a moment, could see Statira sitting in the rocking-chair in a pretty blue dressing-gown. After a first flush she looked pale, and now and then put up her hand to hide a hoarse little cough.

XV

"WALK RIGHT IN, Mr. Barker," cried 'Manda Grier, and Lemuel entered, more awkward and sheepish in his new suit from the Misfit Parlors than he had been before in his Willoughby Pastures best clothes.

Statira merely said, "Why, Mr. Barker!" and stood at her chair where she rose. "You're quite a stranger. Won't you sit down?"

Lemuel sat down, and 'Manda Grier said, politely, "Won't you let me take your hat, Mr. Barker?" and they both treated him with so much ceremony and deference that it seemed impossible he could ever have done such a monstrous thing as kiss a young lady like Miss Dudley; and he felt that he never could approach the subject even to accept a just doom at her hands.

They all talked about the weather for a minute, and then 'Manda Grier said, "Well, I guess I shall have to go down and set this boneset to steep"; and as he rose, and stood to let her pass, she caught his arm and gave it a clutch. He did not know whether she did it on purpose, or why she did it, but somehow it said to him that she was his friend, and he did not feel so much afraid.

When she was gone, however, he returned to the weather for conversation; but when Statira said it was lucky for her that the winter held off so, he made out to inquire about her sickness, and she told him that she had caught a heavy cold; at first it seemed just to be a head-cold, but afterwards it seemed to settle on the lungs, and it seemed as if she never *could* throw it off; they had had the doctor twice; but now she was better, and the cough was nearly *all* gone.

"I guess I took the cold that day, from havin' the window open," she concluded; and she passed her hand across her lap, and looked down demurely, and then up at the ceiling, and her head twitched a little and trembled.

Lemuel knew that his hour had come, if ever it were to come, and he said hoarsely: "I guess if I made you take cold that day, it wasn't all I did. I guess I did worse than that."

She did not look at him and pretend ignorance, as 'Manda

Grier would have done; but lifting her moist eyes and then dropping them, she said, "Why, Mr. Barker, what can you mean?"

"You know what I mean," he retorted, with courage astonishing to him. "It was because I liked you so much." He could not say loved; it seemed too bold. "There's nothing else can excuse it, and I don't know as *that* can."

She put up her hands to her eyes and began to cry, and he rose and went to her and said, "Oh, don't cry, don't cry!" and somehow he took hold of her hands, and then her arms went round his neck, and she was crying on his breast.

"You'll think I'm rather of a silly person, crying so much about nothing," she said, when she lifted her head from his shoulder to wipe her eyes. "But I can't seem to help it," and she broke down again. "I presume it's because I've been sick, and I'm kind of weak yet. I know you wouldn't have done that, that day, if you hadn't have cared for me; and I wasn't mad a bit—not half as mad as I ought to have been; but when you staid away so long, and never seemed to come near any more, I didn't know what *to* think. But now I can understand just how you felt, and I don't blame you one bit; I should have done just so myself if I'd been a man, I suppose. And now it's all come right, I don't mind being sick, or anything; only when Thanksgiving came, we felt sure you'd call, and we'd got the pies nicely warmed. Oh dear!" She gave way again, and then pressed her cheek tight against his to revive herself. " 'Manda said she just knew it was because you was kind of ashamed, and I was too sick to eat any of the pies, any way; and so it all turned out for the best; and I don't want you to believe that I'm one to cry over spilt milk, especially when it's all gathered up again!"

Her happy tongue ran on, revealing, divining everything, and he sat down with her in his arms, hardly speaking a word, till her heart was quite poured out. 'Manda Grier left them a long time together, and before she came back he had told Statira all about himself since their last meeting. She was very angry at the way that girl had behaved at Miss Vane's, but she was glad he had found such a good place now, without being beholden to any one for it, and she showed that she felt a due pride in his being a hotel clerk. He described the hotel, and told what he had to do there, and about Mrs. Harmon and the fashionableness of all the guests. But he said he did not think any of the ladies went ahead of her in dress, if they came up to her; and Statira pressed her lips gratefully against his cheek, and then lifting her head held herself a little away to see him again, and said, "*You're* splendidly dressed, *too*; I noticed it the first thing when you came in. You look just as if you had always lived in Boston."

"Is that so?" asked Lemuel; and he felt his heart suffused with tender pride and joy. He told her of the Misfit Parlors and the installment plan, and she said, well, it was just splendid; and she asked him if he knew she wasn't in the store any more; and "No," she added delightedly, upon his confession of ignorance, "I'm going to work in the box-factory, after this, where 'Manda Grier works. It's better pay, and you have more control of your hours, and you can set down while you work, if you're a mind to. I think it's going to be splendid. What should you say if 'Manda Grier and me took some rooms and went to housekeepin'?"

"I don't know," said Lemuel; but in his soul he felt jealous of her keeping house with 'Manda Grier.

"Well, I don't know as we shall do it," said Statira, as if feeling his tacit reluctance.

'Manda Grier came in just then, and cast a glance of friendly satire at them. "Well, I declare!" she said, for all recognition of the situation.

Lemuel made an offer to rise, but Statira would not let him. "I guess 'Manda Grier won't mind it much."

"I guess I can stand it if you can," said 'Manda Grier; and this seemed such a witty speech that they all laughed, till, as Statira said, she thought she should die. They laughed the more when 'Manda Grier added dryly, "I presume you won't want your boneset now." She set the vessel she had brought it up in on the stove, and covered it with a saucer. "I do' know as *I* should if I was in your place. It's kind o' curious I should bring *both* remedies home with me at once." At this they all laughed a third time, till 'Manda Grier said, " 'Sh! 'sh! Do you want to raise the roof?"

She began to bustle about, and to set out a little table, and cover it with a napkin, and as she worked she talked on. "I guess if you don't want any boneset tea, a little of the other kind won't hurt any of us, and I kinder want a cup myself." She set it to steep on the stove, and it went through Lemuel's mind that she might have steeped the boneset there too, if she had thought of it; but he did not say anything, though it seemed a pretty good joke on 'Manda Grier. She ran on in that way of hers so that you never could tell whether she really meant a thing or not. "I guess if I have to manage many more cases like yours, S'tira Dudley, I shall want to lay in a whole chest of it. What do you think, Mr. Barker?"

"*Mr. Barker!*" repeated Statira.

"Well, I'm afraid to say Lemuel any more, for fear he'll fly off the handle, and never come again. What do you think, Mr. Barker, of havin' to set at that window every Sunday for the last three weeks, and keep watch of both sidewalks till you get such a crick in your neck, and your eyes so set in your head, you couldn't move either of 'em?"

"Now, 'Manda Grier!" said Statira from Lemuel's shoulder.

"Well, I don't say I had to do it, and I don't say who the young man was that I was put to look out for——"

" *'Manda!*"

"But I *do* say it's pretty hard to wait on a sick person one side the room, and keep watch for a young man the other side, both at once."

" 'Manda Grier, you're *too* bad!" pouted Statira. "Don't you believe a word she says, Mr. Barker."

"*Mr. Barker!*" repeated 'Manda Grier.

"Well, I don't care!" said Statira. "I know who I mean."

"*I* don't," said 'Manda Grier. "And I didn't know who you meant this afternoon when you was standin' watch't the window, and says you, 'There! there he is!' and I had to run so quick with the dipper of water I had in my hand to water the plants that I poured it all over the front of my dress."

"*Do* you believe her?" asked Statira.

"And I didn't know who you meant," proceeded 'Manda Grier, busy with the cups and saucers, "when you kept hurryin' me up to change it; 'Oh, quick, quick! How long you are! I know he'll get away! I *know* he will!' and I had to just *sling* on a shawl and rush out after this boneset."

"There! Now that *shows* she's makin' it all up!" cried

Statira. "She put on a sack, and I helped her on with it my-self. So there!"

"Well, if it *was* a sack! And after all, the young man was gone when I got down int' the street," concluded 'Manda Grier solemnly.

Lemuel had thought she was talking about him; but now a pang of jealousy went through him, and showed at the eyes he fixed on her.

"I don't know what I sh'd 'a' done," she resumed demurely, "if I hadn't have found Mr. Barker at the apothecary's, and got *him* to come home 'th me; but of course 'twan't the same as if it was the young man!"

Lemuel's arm fell from Statira's waist in his torment.

"Why, Lemuel!" she said in tender reproach.

"Why, you coot!" cried 'Manda Grier in utter amazement at his single-mindedness, and burst into a scream of laughter. She took the teapot from the stove, and set it on the table. "There, young man—if you *are* the young man—you better pull up to the table, and have something to start your ideas. S'tira! let him come!" and Lemuel, blushing for shame at his stupidity, did as he was bid.

"I've got the greatest mind in the world to set next to S'tira myself," said 'Manda Grier, "for fear she should miss that young man!" and now they both laughed together at Lemuel; but the girls let him sit between them, and Statira let him keep one of her hands under the table, as much as she could. "I never saw such a jealous piece! Why, I shall begin to be afraid for myself. What should you think of S'tira's going to housekeeping with me?"

"I don't believe he likes the idea one bit," Statira answered for him.

"Oh, yes, I do!" Lemuel protested.

" 'D you tell him?" 'Manda Grier demanded of her. She nodded with saucy defiance. "Well, you *have* got along! And about the box-factory?" Statira nodded again, with a look of joyous intelligence at Lemuel. "Well, what *hain't* you told, I wonder!" 'Manda Grier added seriously to Lemuel, "I think it'll be about the best thing in the world for S'tira. I see for the last six months she's been killin' herself in that store. She can't ever get a chance to set down a minute; and she's on her feet from morning till night; and I think it's more'n half that that's made her sick; I don't *say* what the other four-fifths was!"

"Now, 'Manda Grier, stop!"

"Well, that's over with now, and now we want to keep you out that store. I been lookin' out for this place for S'tira a good while. She can go onto the small boxes, if she wants to, and she can set down all the time; and she'll have a whole hour for her dinner; and she can work by the piece, and do as much or as little as she's a mind to; but if she's a mind to work she can make her five and six dollars a week, easy. Mr. Stevens's *real* nice and kind, and he looks out for the girls that ain't exactly strong—not but what S'tira's as strong as anybody, when she's well—and he don't put 'em on the green paper work, because it's got arsenic in it, and it makes your head ache, and you're liable to blood-poisonin'. One the girls fainted and had spasms, and as soon as he found it out he took her right off; and he's just like clockwork to pay. I think it'll do everything for S'tira to be along 'th me there, where I can look after her."

Lemuel said he thought so too; he did not really think at all, he was so flattered at being advised with about Statira, as if she were in his keeping and it was for him to say what was best for her; and when she seemed uncertain about his real opinion, and said she was not going to do anything he did not approve of, he could scarcely speak for rapture, but he protested that he did approve of the scheme entirely.

"But you shouldn't want we girls to set up housekeeping in rooms?" she suggested; and he said that he should, and that he thought it would be more independent and homelike.

"We're half doin' it now," said 'Manda Grier, "and I know some rooms—two of 'em—where we could get along first-rate, and not cost us much more'n half what it does here."

After she cleared up the tea-things she made another errand down-stairs, and Lemuel and Statira went back to their rocking-chair. It still amazed him that she seemed not even to make it a favor to him; she seemed to think it was a favor to her. What was stranger yet was that he could not feel that there was anything wrong or foolish about it; he thought of his mother's severity about young folks' sickishness, as she

called it, and he could not understand it. He knew that he
had never had such right and noble thoughts about girls before; perhaps Statira was better than other girls; she must
be; she was just like a child; and he must be very good himself to be anyways fit for her; if she cared so much for him,
it must be a sign that he was not so bad as he had sometimes thought. A great many things went through his mind,
the silent comment and suggestion of their talk, and all the
time while he was saying something or listening to her, he
was aware of the overwhelming wonder of her being so
frank with him, and not too proud or ashamed to have him
know how anxious she had been, ever since they first met,
for fear he did not care for her. She had always appeared so
stylish and reserved, and now she was not proud at all. He
tried to tell her how it had been with him the last three
weeks; all that he could say was that he had been afraid to
come. She laughed, and said, the idea of his being afraid of
her! She said that she was glad of everything she had gone
through. At times she lifted herself from his shoulder, and
coughed; but that was when she had been laughing or crying a little. They told each other about their families. Statira
said she had not really any folks of her own; she was just
brought up by her aunt; and Lemuel had to tell her that his
mother wore bloomers. Statira said she guessed she should
not care much for the bloomers; and in everything she tried
to make out that he was much better than she was, and just
exactly right. She already spoke of his sister by her first
name, and she entered into his whole life, as if she had always known him. He said she must come with him to hear
Mr. Sewell preach, some time; but she declared that she did
not think much of a minister who could behave the way he
had done to Lemuel. He defended Sewell, and maintained
that if it had not been for him he might not have come to
Boston, and so might never have seen her; but she held out
that she could not bear Mr. Sewell, and that she knew he
was double-faced, and everything. Lemuel said well, he did
not know that he should ever have anything more to do
with him; but he liked to hear him preach, and he guessed
he tried to do what was about right. Statira made him
promise that if ever he met Mr. Sewell again, he would not

make up to him, any way; and she would not tolerate the thought of Miss Vane.

"What you two quar'lin' about?" demanded 'Manda Grier, coming suddenly into the room; and that turned their retrospective griefs into joy again.

"I'm scoldin' him because he don't think enough of himself," cried Statira.

"Well, he seems to take it pretty meekly," said 'Manda Grier. "I guess you didn't scold very hard. Now, young man," she added to Lemuel, "I guess you better be goin'. It's five o'clock, and if you should be out after dark, and the bears should get you, I don't know what S'tira would do."

"'T ain't five yet!" pleaded Statira. "That old watch of yours is always tryin' to beat the town clock."

"Well, it's the clock that's ahead this time," said 'Manda Grier. "My watch says quarter of. Come, now, S'tira, you let him go, or he sha'n't come back any more."

They had a parting that Lemuel's mother would have called sickish, without question; but it all seemed heavenly sweet and right. Statira said now he had got to kiss 'Manda Grier too; and when he insisted, her chin knocked against his and saved her lips, and she gave him a good box on the ear.

"There, I guess that'll do for one while," she said, arranging her tumbled hair; "but there's more kisses where that came from, for both of you, if you want 'em. Coots!"

Once, when Lemuel was little, he had a fever, and he was always seeming to glide down the school-house stairs without touching the steps with his feet. He remembered this dream now, when he reached the street; he felt as if he had floated down on the air; and presently he was back in his little den at the hotel, he did not know how. He ran the elevator up and down for the ladies who called him from the different floors, and he took note of the Sunday difference in their toilet as they passed in to tea, but in the same dreamy way.

After the boarders had supped, he went in as usual with Mrs. Harmon's nephew, less cindery than on week-days, from the cellar, and Mrs. Harmon, silken smooth for her evening worship at the shrine of a popular preacher from New York. The Sunday evening before, she had heard an agnostic lecture in the Boston Theater, and she said she wished to compare notes. Her tranquillity was unruffled by the fact that the head-waitress had left, just before tea; she presumed they could get along just as well without her as with her; the boarders had spoiled her, anyway. She looked round at Lemuel's face, which beamed with his happiness, and said she guessed she should have to get him to open the dining-room doors and seat the transients the next few days, till she could get another head-waitress. It did not seem to be so much a request as a resolution; but Lemuel willingly assented. Mrs. Harmon's nephew said that so long as they did not want him to do it, he did not care who did it; and if a few of them had his furnace to look after, they would not be so anxious to kick.

XVI

LEMUEL HAD to be up early in the morning to get the bills of fare, which Mrs. Harmon called the Meanyous, written in time for the seven o'clock breakfasters; and after opening the dining-room doors with fit ceremony, he had to run backward and forward to answer the rings at the elevator, and to pull out the chairs for the ladies at the table, and slip them back under them as they sat down. The ladies at the St. Albans expected to get their money's worth; but their exactions in most things were of use to Lemuel. He grew constantly nimbler of hand and foot under them, and he grew quicker-witted; he ceased to hulk in mind and body. He did not employ this new mental agility in devising excuses and delays; he left that to Mrs. Harmon, whose conscience was easy in it; but from seven o'clock in the morning till eleven at night, when the ladies came in from the theater, he was so promptly, so comfortingly at their service, that they all said they did not see how they had ever got along without him.

His activities took the form of interruptions rather than constant occupation, and he found a good deal of broken-up time on his hands, which he passed in reading and in reveries of Statira. At the hours when the elevator was mostly in use he kept a book in it with him, and at other times he had it in the office, as Mrs. Harmon called his little booth. He remained there reading every night after the house quieted down after dinner, until it was time to lock up for the night; and several times Mr. Evans stopped and looked in at him where he sat in the bad combustion of the gas that was taking the country tan out of his cheeks. One night when he came in late, and Lemuel put his book down to take him up in the elevator, he said, "Don't disturb yourself; I'm going to walk up"; but he lingered at the door, looking in with the queer smile that always roused the ladies' fears of tacit ridicule. "I suppose you don't find it necessary," he said finally, "to chase a horse-car now, when you want to find your way to a given point?"

Lemuel reddened and dropped his head; he had already recognized in Mr. Evans the gentleman from whose kindly curiosity he had turned, that first day, in the suspicion that he might be a beat. "No," he said; "I guess I can go pretty near everywhere in Boston, now."

"Well," said Mr. Evans, "it was an ingenious system. How do you like Boston?"

"I like it first-rate, but I've not seen many other places," answered Lemuel cautiously.

"Well, if you live here long enough you won't care to see any other places; you'll know they're not worth seeing." Lemuel looked up as if he did not understand exactly, and Mr. Evans stepped in and lifted the book he had been reading. It was one he had bought at second hand while he was with Miss Vane: a tough little epitome of the philosophies in all times, the crabbed English version of a dry German original. Mr. Evans turned its leaves over. "Do you find it a very exciting story?" he asked.

"Why, it isn't a story," said Lemuel, in simple surprise.

"No?" asked Mr. Evans. "I thought it must be. Most of the young gentlemen who run the elevators I travel in read stories. Do you like this kind of reading?"

Lemuel reflected, and then he said he thought you ought to find out about such things if you got a chance.

"Yes," said the editor, musingly, "I suppose one oughtn't to throw any sort of chance away. But you're sure you don't prefer the novels? You'll excuse my asking you?"

"Oh, perfectly excusable," said Lemuel. He added that he liked a good novel too, when he could get hold of it.

"You must come to my room some day, and see if you can't get hold of one there. Or if you prefer metaphysics, I've got shelves full that you're welcome to. I suppose," he added, "you hadn't been in Boston a great while when I met you that day?"

"No," said Lemuel, dropping his head again; "I had just come."

As if he saw that something painful lurked under the remembrance of the time for Lemuel, the editor desisted.

The next morning he stopped on his way to breakfast with some books which he handed to Lemuel. "Don't feel at all obliged to read them," he said, "because I lend them to you. They won't be of the least use to you, if you do so."

"I guess that anything you like will be worth reading," said Lemuel, flattered by the trouble so chief a boarder as Mr. Evans had taken with him.

"Not if they supplied a want you didn't feel. You seem to be fond of books, and after a while you'll be wanting to lend them yourself. I'll give you a little hint that I'm too old to profit by: remember that you can lend a person more books in a day than he can read in a week."

His laugh kept Lemuel shy of him still, in spite of a willingness that the editor showed for their better acquaintance. He seemed to wish to know about Lemuel, particularly since he had recognized the pursuer of the horse-car in him, and this made Lemuel close up the more. He would have liked to talk with him about the books Evans had lent him. But when the editor stopped at the office door, where Lemuel sat reading one of them, and asked him what he thought of it, the boy felt that somehow it was not exactly his opinion that Mr. Evans was getting at; and this sense of being inspected and arranged in another's mind, though he could not formulate the operation in his own, somehow wounded and repelled him. It was not that the editor ever said anything that was not kind and friendly; he was always doing kind and friendly things, and he appeared to take a real interest in Lemuel. At the end of the first week after Lemuel had added the head-waitership to his other duties, Evans stopped in going out of the dining-room and put a dollar in his hand.

"What is it for?" asked Lemuel.

"For? Really, I don't know. It must be tribute money," said the editor in surprise, but with a rising curiosity. "I never know what it's for."

Lemuel turned red, and handed it back. "I don't know as I want any money I haven't earned."

That night, after dinner, when Evans was passing the office door on his way out of the hotel, Lemuel stopped him and said with embarrassment, "Mr. Evans, I don't want you should think I didn't appreciate your kindness this morning."

"Ah, I'm not sure it was kindness," said Evans with immediate interest. "Why didn't you take the money?"

"Well, I told you why," said Lemuel, overcoming the obscure reluctance he felt at Evans's manner as best he could.

"I've been thinking it over, and I guess I was right; but I didn't know whether I had expressed it the best way."

"The way couldn't be improved. But why did you think you hadn't earned my dollar?"

"I don't do anything but open the doors, and show people to their places; I don't call that anything."

"But if you were a waiter and served at table?"

"I wouldn't *be* one," said Lemuel, with a touch of indignation; "and I shouldn't take presents, anyway."

Evans leaned against the door-jamb.

"Have you heard of the college students who wait at the mountain hotels in vacation? They all take fees. Do you think yourself better than they are?"

"Yes, I do!" cried Lemuel.

"Well, I don't know but you are," said the editor thoughtfully. "But I think I should distinguish. Perhaps there's no shame in waiting at table, but there is in taking fees."

"Yes; that's what I meant," said Lemuel, a little sorry for his heat. "I shouldn't be ashamed to do any kind of work, and to take my pay for it; but I shouldn't want to have folks giving me money over and above, as if I was a beggar."

The editor stood looking him absently in the face. After a moment he asked, "What part of New England did you come from, Mr. Barker?"

"I came from the middle part of the State—from Willoughby Pastures."

"Do those ideas—those principles—of yours prevail there?"

"I don't know whether they do or not," said Lemuel.

"If you were sure they did, I should like to engage board there for next summer," said the editor, going out.

It was Monday night, a leisure time with him, and he was going out to see a friend, a minister, with whom Monday night was also leisure time.

After he was gone, some of the other boarders began to drop in from the lectures and concerts which they frequented in the evening. The ladies had all some favor to ask of Lemuel, some real or fancied need of his help; in return for his promise or performance, they each gave him advice. What they expressed collectively was that they should think that he would put his eyes out reading by that gas, and that he had better look out, or he would ruin his health anyway, reading so much. They asked him how much time he got for sleep; and they said that from twelve till six was not enough, and that he was just killing himself. They had all offered to lend him books; the least literary among them had a sort of house pride in his fondness for books; their sympathy with this taste of his amused their husbands, who tolerated it, but in their hearts regarded it as a womanish weakness, indicating a want of fiber in Lemuel. Mrs. Harmon, as a business woman, and therefore occupying a middle ground between the sexes, did not exactly know herself what to make of her clerk's studiousness; all that she could say was that he kept up with his work. She assumed that before Lemuel's coming she had been the sole motive power of the house; but it was really a sort of democracy, and was managed by the majority of its inmates. An element of demagoguery tampered with the Irish vote in the person of Jerry, nominally porter, but actually factotum, who had hitherto, pending the strikes of the different functionaries, filled the offices now united in Lemuel. He had never been clerk, because his literature went no further than the ability to write his name, and to read a passage of the Constitution in qualifying for the suffrage. He did not like the new order of things, but he was without a party, and helpless to do more than neglect the gong-bell when he had reason to think Lemuel had sounded it.

About eleven o'clock the law-student came in with the two girl art-students, fresh from the outside air, and gay from the opera they had been hearing. The young man told Lemuel he ought to go to see it. After the girls had opened their door, one of them came running back to the elevator, and called down to Lemuel that there was no ice-water, and would he please send some up.

Lemuel brought it up himself, and when he knocked at the door, the same girl opened it and made a pretty outcry over the trouble she had given him. "I supposed, of course, Jerry would bring it," she said contritely; and as if for some atonement she added, "Won't you come in, Mr. Barker, and see my picture?"

Lemuel stood in the gush of the gas-light hesitating, and

the law-student called out to him, jollily, "Come in, Mr. Barker, and help me play art-critic." He was standing before the picture, with his overcoat on and his hat in his hand. "First appearance on any stage," he added, and as Lemuel entered, "If I were you," he said, "I'd fire that porter out of the hotel. He's outlived his usefulness."

"It's a shame, your having to bring the water," said Miss Swan; she was the girl who had spoken before.

The other one came forward and said, "Won't you sit down?"

She spoke to Lemuel; the law-student answered, "Thank you; I don't care if I do."

Lemuel did not know whether to stay, nor what to say of Miss Swan's picture, and he thanked the young lady and remained standing.

"Oh, Jessie, *Jessie*, Jessie!" cried Miss Swan.

The other went to her, tranquilly, as if used to such vehement appeals.

"Just *see* how my poor cow looks since I painted out that grass! She hasn't got a leg to stand on!"

The law-student did nothing but make jokes about the picture. "I think she looks pretty well for a cow that you must have had to study from a milk-can—nearest you could come to a cow in Boston."

Miss Carver, the other young lady, ignored his joking, and after some criticisms on the picture left him and Miss Swan to talk it over. She talked to Lemuel, and asked him if he had read a book he glanced at on the table, and seemed willing to make him feel at ease. But she did not. He thought she was very proud, and he believed she wanted him to go, but he did not know how to go. Her eyes were so still and pure; but they dwelt very coldly upon him. Her voice was like that look put into sound; it was rather high-pitched, but very sweet and pure and cold. He hardly knew what he said; he felt hot, and he waited for some chance to get away.

At last he heard Miss Swan saying, "*Must* you go, Mr. Berry? So *soon!*" and saw her giving the student her hand, with a bow of burlesque desolation.

Lemuel prepared to go, too. All his rusticity came back upon him, and he said, "Well, I wish you good-evening."

It seemed to him that Miss Carver's still eyes looked a sort of starry scorn after him. He found that he had brought away the book they had been talking about, and he was a long time in question whether he had better take it back at once, or give it to her when she came to breakfast.

He went to bed in the same trouble of mind. Every night he had fallen asleep with Statira in his thoughts, but now it was Miss Carver that he thought of, and more and more uncomfortably. He asked himself what she would say if she saw his mother in the bloomers. She was herself not dressed so fashionably as Statira, but very nicely.

XVII

A<small>T</small> S<small>EWELL'S</small> <small>HOUSE</small> the maid told Evans to walk up into the study, without seating him first in the reception-room, as if that were needless with so intimate a friend of the family. He found Sewell at his desk, and he began at once, without the forms of greeting:

"If you don't like that other subject, I've got a new one for you, and you could write a sermon on it that would make talk."

"You look at it from the newspaper point of view," returned Sewell, in the same humor. "I'm not an 'enterprise,' and I don't want to make talk in your sense. I don't know that I want to make talk at all; I should prefer to make thought, to make feeling."

"Well," said the editor, "this would do all three."

"Would you come to hear me, if I wrote the sermon?"

"Ah, that's asking a good deal."

"Why don't you develop your idea in an article? You're always bragging that you preach to a larger congregation than I."

"I propose to let you preach to my congregation too, if you'll write this sermon. I've talked to you before about reporting your sermons in 'Saturday Afternoon.' They would be a feature; and if we could open with this one, and have a good 'incisive' editorial on it, disputing some of your positions, and treating certain others with a little satire, at the same time maintaining a very respectful attitude towards you on the whole, and calling attention to the fact that there was a strong and increasing interest in your 'utterances,' which we were the first to recognize,—it would be a card. We might agree beforehand on the points the editorial was to touch, and so make one hand wash another. See?"

"I see that journalism has eaten into your soul. What *is* your subject?"

"Well, in general terms, and in a single word, *Complicity*. Don't you think that would be rather taking? 'Mr. Sewell, in his striking sermon on Complicity,' and so forth. It would be a great hit, and it would stand a chance of sticking, like Emerson's 'Compensation.' "

"Delightful! The most amusing part is that you've really a grain of business in your bushel of chaff." Sewell wheeled about in his swivel-chair, and sat facing his guest, deeply sunken in the low easy seat he always took. "When did this famous idea occur to you?" he pursued, swinging his glasses by their cord.

"About three weeks ago, at the theater. There was one of those pieces on that make you despair of the stage, and ashamed of writing a play even to be rejected by it—a farrago of indecently amusing innuendoes and laughably vile situations, such as, if they were put into a book, would prevent its being sent through the mail. The theater apparently can still be as filthy in suggestion as it was at the Restoration, and not shock its audiences. There were all sorts of people there that night: young girls who had come with young men for an evening's polite amusement; families; middle-aged husbands and wives; respectable-looking single women; and average bachelors. I don't think the ordinary theatrical audience is of a high grade intellectually; it's third or fourth rate; but morally it seems quite as good as other public assemblages. All the people were nicely dressed, and they sat there before that nasty mess—it was an English comedy where all the jokes turn upon the belief of the characters that their wives and husbands are the parents of illegitimate offspring—and listened with as smooth self-satisfaction as if they were not responsible for it. But all at once it occurred to me that they *were* responsible, every one of them—as responsible as the players, as the author himself."

"Did you come out of the theater at that point?" asked Sewell.

"Oh, I was responsible too; but I seemed to be the only one ashamed of my share in the business."

"If you were the only one conscious of it, your merit wasn't very great," suggested the minister.

"Well, I should like the others to be conscious of it too. That's why I want you to preach my sermon. I want you to tell your people and my people that the one who buys sin or shame, or corruption of any sort, is as guilty as the one who sells it."

"It isn't a new theory," said Sewell, still refusing to give up his ironical tone. "It was discovered some time ago that this was so before God."

"Well, I've just discovered that it ought to be so before man," said Evans.

"Still, you're not the first," said Sewell.

"Yes," said the editor, "I think I am, from my peculiar stand-point. The other day a friend of mine—an upright, just, worthy man, no one more so—was telling me of a shocking instance of our national corruption. He had just got home from Europe, and he had brought a lot of dutiable things, that a customs inspector passed for a trifling sum. That was all very well, but the inspector afterwards came round with a confidential claim for a hundred dollars, and the figures to show that the legal duties would have been eight or ten times as much. My friend was glad to pay the hundred dollars; but he defied me to name any country in Europe where such a piece of official rascality was possible. He said it made him ashamed of America!" Evans leaned his head back against his chair and laughed.

"Yes," said Sewell with a sigh, and no longer feigning light-ness. "That's awful."

"Well, now," said Evans, "don't you think it your duty to help people realize that they can't regard such transactions *de haut en bas*, if they happen to have taken part in them? I have heard of the shameful condition of things down in Maine, where I'm told the French Canadians who've come in regu-larly expect to sell their votes to the highest bidder at every election. Since my new system of ethics occurred to me, I've fancied that there must have always been a shameful state of things there, if Americans could grow up in the willingness to buy votes. I want to have people recognize that there is no superiority for them in such an affair; that there's nothing but inferiority; that the man who has the money and the wit to corrupt is a far baser rascal than the man who has the igno-rance and the poverty to be corrupted. I would make this principle seek out every weak spot, every sore spot in the whole social constitution. I'm sick to death of the frauds that we practice upon ourselves in order to be able to injure others. Just consider the infernal ease of mind in which men remain concerning men's share in the social evil——"

"Ah, my dear friend, you can't expect me to consider *that* in my pulpit!" cried the minister.

"No; I couldn't consider it in my paper. I suppose we must leave that where it is, unless we can affect it by analogy, and show that there is infamy for both parties to any sin committed in common. You must select your instances in other directions, but you can find plenty of them—enough and to spare. It would give the series a tremendous send-off," said Evans, relapsing into his habitual tone, "if you would tackle this subject in your first sermon for publication. There would be money in it. The thing would make a success in the paper, and you could get somebody to reprint it in pamphlet form. Come, what do you say?"

"I should say that you had just been doing something you were ashamed of," answered Sewell. "People don't have these tremendous moral awakenings for nothing."

"And you don't think my present state of mind is a gradual outgrowth of my first consciousness of the common responsibility of actors and audience in the representation of a shameless comedy?"

"No, I shouldn't think it was," said the minister securely.

"Well, you're right." Evans twisted himself about in his chair, and hung his legs over one of the arms. "The real reason why I wish you to preach this sermon is because I have just been offering a fee to the head-waiter at our hotel."

"And you feel degraded with him by his acceptance? For it *is* a degradation."

"No, that's the strangest thing about it. I have a monopoly of the degradation, for he didn't take my dollar."

"Ah, then a sermon won't help *you*! Why wouldn't he take it?"

"He said he didn't know as he wanted any money he hadn't earned," said Evans with a touch of mimicry.

The minister started up from his lounging attitude. "Is his name—Barker?" he asked with unerring prescience.

"Yes," said Evans with a little surprise. "Do you know him?"

"Yes," returned the minister, falling back in his chair help-lessly, not luxuriously. "So well that I knew it was he almost as soon as you came into the room to-night."

"What harm have you been doing him?" demanded the editor, in parody of the minister's acuteness in guessing the guilty operation of his own mind.

"The greatest. I'm the cause of his being in Boston."

"This is very interesting," said Evans. "We are companions in crime—pals. It's a great honor. But what strikes me as being so interesting is that we appear to feel remorse for our misdeeds; and I was almost persuaded the other day by an observer of our species, that remorse had gone out, or rather had never existed, except in the fancy of innocent people; that real criminals like ourselves were afraid of being found out, but weren't in the least sorry. Perhaps, if we are sorry, it proves that we needn't be. Let's judge each other. I've told you what my sin against Barker is, and I know yours in gen-eral terms. It's a fearful thing to be the cause of a human soul's presence in Boston; but what did you do to bring it about? Who is Barker? Where did he come from? What was his previous condition of servitude? He puzzles me a good deal."

"Oh, I'll tell you," said Sewell; and he gave his personal chapter in Lemuel's history.

Evans interrupted him at one point. "And what became of the poem he brought down with him?"

"It was stolen out of his pocket, one night when he slept in the Common."

"Ah, then he can't offer it to me! And he seems very far from writing any more. I can still keep his acquaintance. Go on."

Sewell told, in amusing detail, of the Wayfarer's Lodge, where he had found Barker after supposing he had gone home. Evans seemed more interested in the place than in the minister's meeting with Lemuel there, which Sewell fancied he had painted rather well, describing Lemuel's severity and his own anxiety.

"There!" said the editor. "There you have it—a practical illustration! Our civilization has had to come to it!"

"Come to what?"

"Complicity."

Sewell made an impatient gesture.

"Don't sacrifice the consideration of a great principle," cried Evans, "to the petty effect of a good story on an appreciative listener. I realize your predicament. But don't you see that in establishing and regulating a place like that the city of Boston has instinctively sanctioned my idea? You may say that it is aiding and abetting the tramp-nuisance by giving vagrants food and shelter, but other philosophers will contend that it is—blindly perhaps—fulfilling the destiny of the future State, which will at once employ and support all its citizens; that it is prophetically recognizing my new principle of Complicity?"

"Your new principle!" cried Sewell. "You have merely given a new name to one of the oldest principles in the moral world."

"And that is a good deal to do, I can tell you," said Evans. "All the principles are pretty old now. But don't give way to an ignoble resentment of my interruption. Go on about Barker."

After some feints that there was nothing more important to tell, Sewell went on to the end; and when he had come to it, Evans shook his head. "It looks pretty black for you, but it's a beautifully perfect case of Complicity. What do you propose to do, now you've rediscovered him?"

"Oh, I don't know! I hope no more mischief. If I could only get him back on his farm!"

"Yes, I suppose that would be the best thing. But I dare say he wouldn't go back!"

"That's been my experience with him."

They talked this aspect of the case over more fully, and Evans said: "Well, I wouldn't go back to such a place myself after I'd once had a glimpse of Boston, but I suppose it's right to wish that Barker would. I hope his mother will come to visit him while he's in the hotel. I would give a good deal to see her. Fancy her coming down in her bloomers, and the poor fellow being ashamed of her! It would be a very good subject for a play. Does she wear a hat or a bonnet? What sort of head-gear goes with that 'sleek odalisque' style of dress? A turban, I suppose."

"Mrs. Barker," said the minister, unable to deny himself the fleeting comfort of the editor's humorous view of the situation, "is as far from a 'sleek odalisque' as any lady I've ever seen, in spite of her oriental costume. If I remember, her *yashmak* was not gathered at the ankles, but hung loose like occidental trousers; and the day we met, she wore simply her own hair. There was not much of it on top, and she had it cut short in the neck. She was rather a terrible figure. Her having ever been married would have been inconceivable, except for her son."

"I should like to have seen her," said Evans, laughing back in his chair.

"She was worth seeing as a survival of the superficial fermentation of the period of our social history when it was believed that women could be like men if they chose, and ought to be if they ever meant to show their natural superiority. But she was not picturesque."

"The son's very handsome. I can see that the lady boarders think him so."

"Do you find him at all remarkable otherwise? What dismayed me more than his poetry even was that when he gave that up he seemed to have no particular direction."

"Oh, he reads a good deal, and pretty serious books; and he goes to hear all the sermons and lectures in town."

"I thought he came to mine only," sighed the minister, with a retrospective suffering. "Well, what can be done for him now? I feel my complicity with Barker as poignantly as you could wish."

"Ah, you see how the principle applies everywhere!" cried the editor joyously. He added: "But I really think that for the present you can't do better than let Barker alone. He's getting on very well at Mrs. Harmon's, and although the conditions at the St. Albans are more transitory than most sublunary things, Barker appears to be a fixture. Our little system has begun to revolve round him unconsciously; he keeps us going."

"Well," said Sewell, consenting to be a little comforted. He was about to go more particularly into the facts; but Mrs. Sewell came in just then, and he obviously left the subject.

Evans did not sit down again after rising to greet her; and presently he said good-night.

She turned to her husband: "What were you talking about when I came in?"

"When you came in?"

"Yes. You both had that look—I can always tell it—of having suddenly stopped."

"Oh!" said Sewell, pretending to arrange the things on his desk. "Evans had been suggesting the subject for a sermon." He paused a moment, and then he continued hardily, "And he'd been telling me about—Barker. He's turned up again."

"Of course!" said Mrs. Sewell. "What's happened to him now?"

"Nothing, apparently, but some repeated strokes of prosperity. He has become clerk, elevator-boy, and head-waiter at the St. Albans."

"And what are you going to do about him?"

"Evans advises me to do nothing."

"Well, that's sensible, at any rate," said Mrs. Sewell. "I really think you've done quite enough, David, and now he can be left to manage for himself, especially as he seems to be doing well."

"Oh, he's doing as well as I could hope, and better. But I'm not sure that I shouldn't have personally preferred a continued course of calamity for him. I shall never be quite at peace about him till I get him back on his farm at Willoughby Pastures."

"Well, that you will never do; and you may as well rest easy about it."

"I don't know as to never doing it," said Sewell. "All prosperity, especially the prosperity connected with Mrs. Harmon's hotel, is transitory; and I may succeed yet."

"Does everything go on there in the old way, does Mr. Evans say?" Mrs. Sewell did not refer to any former knowledge of the St. Albans, but to a remote acquaintance with the character and methods of Mrs. Harmon, with whom the Sewells had once boarded. She was then freshly widowed by the loss of her first husband, and had launched her earliest boarding-house on that sea of disaster, where she had buoyantly outridden every storm and had floated triumphantly on the top of every ingulfing wave. They recalled the difficult navigation of that primitive craft, in which each of the boarders had taken a hand at the helm, and their reminiscences of her financial embarrassments were mixed with those of the unfailing serenity that seemed not to know defeat, and with fond memories of her goodness of heart, and her ideal devotion in any case of sickness or trouble.

"I should think the prosperity of Mrs. Harmon would convince the most negative of agnostics that there was an overruling Providence, if nothing else did," said Sewell. "It's so defiant of all law, so delightfully independent of causation."

"Well, let Barker alone with her, then," said his wife, rising to leave him to the hours of late reading which she had never been able to break up.

XVIII

Aᴛᴇʀ ᴀɢʀᴇᴇɪɴɢ with his wife that he had better leave Barker alone, Sewell did not feel easy in doing so. He had that ten-dollar note which Miss Vane had given him, and though he did not believe, since Evans had reported Barker's refusal of his fee, that the boy would take it, he was still constrained to do something with it. Before giving it back to her, he decided at least to see Barker and learn about his prospects and expectations. He might find some way of making himself useful to him.

In a state of independence he found Lemuel much more accessible than formerly, and their interview was more nearly amicable. Sewell said that he had been delighted to hear of Lemuel's whereabouts from his old friend Evans, and to know that they were housed together. He said that he used to know Mrs. Harmon long ago, and that she was a good-hearted, well-meaning woman, though without much forecast. He even assented to Lemuel's hasty generalization of her as a perfect lady, though they both felt a certain inaccuracy in this, and Sewell repeated that she was a woman of excellent heart, and turned to a more intimate inquest of Lemuel's life. He tried to find out how he employed his leisure time, saying that he always sympathized with young men away from home, and suggesting the reading-room and the frequent lectures at the Young Men's Christian Union for his odd moments. He learned that Lemuel had not many of these during the week, and that on Sundays he spent all the time he could get in hearing the different noted ministers. For the rest, he learned that Lemuel was very much interested in the city, and appeared to be rapidly absorbing both its present civilization and its past history. He was unsmilingly amused at the comments of mixed shrewdness and crudity which Lemuel was betrayed into at times beyond certain limits of diffidence that he had apparently set himself; at his blunders and misconceptions, at the truth divined by the very innocence of his youth and inexperience. He found out that Lemuel had not been at home since he came to Boston; he had expected to go at Thanksgiving, but it came so soon after he had got his place that he hated to ask; the folks were all well, and he would send the kind remembrances which the minister asked him to give his mother. Sewell tried to find out, in saying that Mrs. Sewell and himself would always be glad to see him, whether Lemuel had any social life outside of the St. Albans, but here he was sensible that a door was shut against him; and finally he had not the courage to do more about that money from Miss Vane than to say that from time to time he had sums intrusted him, and that if Lemuel had any pressing need of money he must borrow of him. He fancied he had managed that rather delicately, for Lemuel thanked him without severity and said he should get along now, he guessed, but he was much obliged. Neither of them mentioned Miss Vane, and upon the whole the minister was not sure that he had got much nearer the boy, after all.

Certainly he formed no adequate idea of the avidity and thoroughness with which Lemuel was learning his Boston. It was wholly a public Boston which unfolded itself during the winter to his eager curiosity, and he knew nothing of the social intricacies of which it seems solely to consist for so many of us. To him Boston society was represented by the coteries of homeless sojourners in the St. Albans; Boston life was transacted by the ministers, the lecturers, the public meetings, the concerts, the horse-cars, the policemen, the shop-windows, the newspapers, the theaters, the ships at the docks, the historical landmarks, the charity apparatus.

The effect was a ferment in his mind in which there was nothing clear. It seemed to him that he had to change his opinions every day. He was whirled round and round; he never saw the same object twice the same. He did not know whether he learned or unlearned most. With the pride that comes to youth from the mere novelty of its experiences was mixed a shame for his former ignorance, an exasperation at his inability to grasp their whole meaning.

His activities in acquainting himself with Boston interested Evans, who tried to learn just what his impression was; but this was the last thing that Lemuel could have distinctly imparted.

"Well, upon the whole," he asked, one day, "what do you

think? From what you've seen of it, which is the better place, Boston or Willoughby Pastures? If you were friendless and homeless, would you rather be cast away in the city or in the country?"

Lemuel did not hesitate about this. "In the city! They haven't got any idea in the country what's done to help folks along in the city!"

"Is that so?" asked Evans. "It's against tradition," he suggested.

"Yes, I know that," Lemuel assented. "And in the country they think the city is a place where nobody cares for you, and everybody is against you, and wants to impose upon you. Well, when I first came to Boston," he continued, with a consciousness of things that Evans did not betray his own knowledge of, "I thought so too, and I had a pretty hard time for a while. It don't seem as if people *did* care for you, except to make something out of you; but if any one happens to find out that you're in trouble, there's ten times as much done for you in the city as there is in the country."

"Perhaps that's because there are ten times as many to do it," said Evans, in the hope of provoking this impartial spirit further.

"No, it isn't that altogether. It's because they've seen ten times as much trouble, and know how to take hold of it better. I think our folks in the country have been flattered up too much. If some of them could come down here and see how things are carried on, they would be surprised. They wouldn't believe it if you told them."

"I didn't know we were so exemplary," said Evans.

"Oh, city folks have their faults too," said Lemuel, smiling in recognition of the irony.

"No! What?"

Lemuel seemed uncertain whether to say it. "Well, they're too aristocratic."

Evans enjoyed this frank simplicity. He professed not to understand, and begged Lemuel to explain.

"Well, at home, in the country, they mightn't want to do so much for you, or be so polite about it, but they wouldn't feel themselves so much above you. They're more on an equality. If I needed help, I'd rather be in town; but if I could help myself, I'd just as soon be in the country. Only," he added, "there are more chances here."

"Yes, there *are* more chances. And do you think it's better not to be quite so kind, and to be more on an equality?"

"Why, don't you?" demanded Lemuel.

"Well, I don't know," said Evans, with a whimsical affectation of seriousness. "Shouldn't you like an aristocracy if you could be one of the aristocrats? Don't you think you're opposed to aristocracy because you don't want to be under? I have spoken to be a duke when we get an order of nobility, and I find that it's a great relief. I don't feel obliged to go in for equality nearly as much as I used."

Lemuel shyly dropped the subject, not feeling himself able to cope with his elder in these railleries. He always felt his heaviness and clumsiness in talking with the editor, who fascinated him. He did not know but he had said too much about city people being aristocratic. It was not quite what he meant; he had really been thinking of Miss Carver, and how proud she was, when he said it.

Lately he had seemed to see a difference between himself and other people, and he had begun to look for it everywhere, though when he spoke to Evans he was not aware how strongly the poison was working in him. It was as if the girl had made that difference; she made it again, whatever it was, between herself and the black man who once brought her a note and a bunch of flowers from one of her young lady pupils. She was very polite to him, trying to put him at ease, just as she had been with Lemuel that night. If he came into the dining-room to seat a transient when Miss Carver was there, he knew that she was mentally making a difference between him and the boarders. The ladies all had the custom of bidding him good-morning when they came in to breakfast, and they all smiled upon him except Miss Carver; she seemed every morning as if more surprised to see him standing there at the door and showing people to their places; she looked puzzled, and sometimes she blushed, as if she were ashamed for him.

He had discovered, in fine, that there were sorts of honest work in the world which one must not do if he would keep his self-respect through the consideration of others. Once all work had been work, but now he had found that there was work which was service, and that service was dishonor. He had learned that the people who did this work were as a class apart, and were spoken of as servants, with slight that was unconscious or conscious, but never absent.

Some of the ladies at the St. Albans had tried to argue with Lemuel about his not taking the fees he refused, and he knew that they talked him over. One day, when he was showing a room to a transient, he heard one of them say to another in the next apartment, "Well, I did hate to offer it to him, just as if he was a common servant"; and the other said, "Well, I don't see what he can expect if he puts himself in the place of a servant." And then they debated together whether his quality of clerk was sufficient to redeem him from the reproach of servitude; they did not call his running the elevator anything, because a clerk might do that in a casual way without loss of dignity; they alleged other cases of the kind.

His inner life became a turmoil of suspicions, that attached themselves to every word spoken to him by those who must think themselves above him. He could see now how far behind in everything Willoughby Pastures was, and how the summer folks could not help despising the people that took them to board, and waited on them like servants in cities. He esteemed the boarders at the St. Albans in the degree that he thought them enlightened enough to contemn him for his station; and he had his own ideas of how such a person as Mr. Evans really felt toward him. He felt toward him and was interested in his reading as a person might feel toward and be interested in the attainments of some anomalous animal, a learned pig, or something of that kind.

He could look back, now, on his life at Miss Vane's, and see that he was treated as a servant, there,—a petted servant, but still a servant,—and that was what made that girl behave so to him; he always thought of Sibyl as that girl.

He would have thrown up his place at once, though he knew of nothing else he could do; he would have risked starving rather than keep it; but he felt that it was of no use; that the stain of servitude was indelible; that if he were lifted to the highest station, it would not redeem him in Miss Carver's eyes. All this time he had scarcely more than spoken with her, to return her good-mornings at the dining-room door, or to exchange greetings with her on the stairs, or to receive some charge from her in going out, or to answer some question of hers in coming in, as to whether any of the pupils who had lessons of her had been there in her absence. He made these interviews as brief as possible; he was as stiff and cold as she.

The law-student, whose full name was Alonzo W. Berry, had one joking manner for all manner of men and women, and Lemuel's suspicion could not find any offensive distinction in it toward himself; but he disabled Berry's own gentility for that reason, and easily learning much of the law-student's wild past in the West from so eager an autobiographer, he could not comfort himself with his friendship. While the student poured out his autobiography without stint upon Lemuel, his shyness only deepened upon the boy. There were things in his life for which he was in equal fear of discovery: his arrest and trial in the police court, his mother's queerness, and his servile condition at Miss Vane's. The thought that Mr. Sewell knew about them all made him sometimes hate the minister, till he reflected that he had evidently told no one of them. But he was always trembling lest they should somehow become known at the St. Albans; and when Berry was going on about himself, his exploits, his escapes, his loves,—chiefly his loves,—Lemuel's soul was sealed within him; a vision of his disgraces filled him with horror.

But in the delight of talking about himself, Berry was apparently unaware that Lemuel had not reciprocated his confidences. He celebrated his familiarity with Miss Swan and her friend, though no doubt he had the greater share of the acquaintance,—that was apt to be the case with him,—and from time to time he urged Lemuel to come up and call on them with him.

"I guess they don't want *me* to call," said Lemuel with feeble bitterness at last, one evening after an elaborate argument from Berry to prove that Lemuel had the time, and that he just knew they would be glad to see him.

"Why?" demanded Berry, and he tried to get Lemuel's reason; but when Lemuel had stated that belief, he could not have given the reason for it on his death-bed. Berry gave the conundrum up for the time, but he did not give Lemuel up; he had an increasing need of him as he advanced in a passion for Miss Swan, which, as he frankly prophesied, was bound to bring him to the popping-point sooner or later; he debated with himself in Lemuel's presence all the best forms of popping, and he said that it was simply worth a ranch to be able to sing to him,

> "She's a darling,
> She's a daisy,
> She's a dumpling,
> She's a lamb,"

and to feel that he knew who *she* was. He usually sang this refrain to Lemuel when he came in late at night after a little supper with some of the fellows, that had left traces of its cheer on his bated breath. Once he came down-stairs alone in the elevator, in his shirt-sleeves and stocking-feet, for the purpose of singing it after Lemuel had thought him in bed.

Every Sunday afternoon during the winter Lemuel went to see Statira, and sometimes in the evening he took her to church. But she could not understand why he always wanted to go to a different church; she did not see why he should not pick out one church and stick to it: the ministers seemed to be all alike, and she guessed one was pretty near as good as another. 'Manda Grier said she guessed they were all Lemuel to her; and Statira said well, she guessed that was pretty much so. She no longer pretended that he was not the whole world to her, either with him or with 'Manda Grier; she was so happy from morning till night, day in and day out, that 'Manda Grier said if she were in her place she should be afraid something would happen.

Statira worked in the box-factory now; she liked it a great deal better than the store, and declared that she was ever so much stronger. The cough lingered still, but none of them noticed it much; she called it a cold, and said she kept catching more. 'Manda Grier told her that she could throw it off soon enough if she would buy a few clothes for warmth and not so many for looks; but they did not talk this over before Lemuel. Before he came Statira took a soothing mixture that she got of the apothecary, and then they were all as bright and gay as could be, and she looked so pretty that he said he could not get used to it. The housekeeping experiment was a great success; she and 'Manda Grier had two rooms now, and they lived better than ever they had, for less money. Of course, Statira said, it was not up to the St. Albans, which Lemuel had told them of at first a little braggingly. In fact she liked to have him brag of it, and of the splendors of his position and surroundings. She was very curious, but not envious of anything, and it became a joke with her and 'Manda Grier, who pretended to despise the whole affair.

At first it flattered Lemuel to have her admire his rise in life so simply and ardently; but after a while it became embarrassing, in proportion as it no longer seemed so superb to him. She was always wanting him to talk of it; after a few Sundays, with the long hours they had passed in telling each other all they could think of about themselves, they had not much else to talk of. Now that she had him to employ her fancy, Statira no longer fed it on the novels she used to devour. He brought her books, but she did not read them; she said that she had been so busy with her sewing she had no time to read; and every week she showed him some pretty new thing she had been making, and tried it on for him to see how she looked in it. Often she seemed to care more to rest with her head on his shoulder, and not talk at all; and for a while this was enough for him too, though sometimes he was disappointed that she did not even let him read to her out of the books she neglected. She would not talk over the sermons they heard together; but once when Mr. Evans offered him tickets for the theater, and Lemuel had got the night off and taken Statira, it seemed as if she would be willing to sit up till morning and talk the play over.

Nothing else ever interested her so much, except what one of the girls in the box-factory had told her about going down to the beach, summers, and waiting on table. This girl had been at Old Orchard, where they had splendid times, with one veranda all to themselves and the gentlemen-help; and in the afternoon the girls got together on the beach—or the grass right in front of the hotel—and sewed. They got nearly as much as they did in the box-factory; and then the boarders all gave you something extra; some of them gave as much as a dollar a week apiece. The head-waiter was a college student, and a perfect gentleman; he was always dressed up in a dress-suit and a white silk neck-tie. Statira said that next summer she wanted they should go off somewhere, she and 'Manda Grier, and wait on table together; and she knew Lemuel could easily get the head-waiter's place, after the St. Albans. She should not want he should be clerk, because then they could not have such good times, for they would be more separated.

Lemuel heard her restively through, and then broke out fiercely and told her that he had seen enough of waiting on table at the St. Albans for him never to want her to do it; and that the boarders who gave money to the waiters despised them for taking it. He said that he did not consider just help-ing Mrs. Harmon out the same as being head-waiter, and that he would not be a regular waiter for any money: he would rather starve.

Statira did not understand; she asked him meekly if he were mad at her, he seemed so; and he had to do what he could to cheer her up.

'Manda Grier took Statira's part pretty sharply. She said it was one thing to live out in a private family—that *was* a dis-grace, if you could keep the breath of life in you any other way—and it was quite another to wait in a hotel; and she did not want to have any one hint round that she would let Statira demean herself. Lemuel was offended by her manner, and her assumption of owning Statira. She defended him, but he could not tell her how he had changed; the influences were perhaps too obscure for him to have traced them all himself; after the first time he had hardly mentioned the art-student girls to her. There were a great many things that Statira could not understand. She had been much longer in the city than Lemuel, but she did not seem to appreciate the difference be-tween that and the country. She dressed very stylishly; no one went beyond her in that; but in many things he could see that she remained countrified. Once on a very mild April evening, when they were passing through the Public Garden, she wished him to sit on a vacant seat they came to. All the others were occupied by young couples who sat with their arms around each other.

"No, no!" shuddered Lemuel, "I don't want people should take you for one of these servant-girls."

"Why, Lem, how proud you're getting!" she cried with easy acquiescence. "You're awfully stuck up! Well, then, you've got to take a horse-car; I can't walk any further."

XIX

LEMUEL had found out about the art-students from Berry. He said they were no relation to each other, and had not even been acquainted before they met at the art-school; he had first met them at the St. Albans. Miss Swan was from the western part of the State, and Miss Carver from down Plymouth way. The latter took pupils, and sometimes gave lessons at their houses; she was, to Berry's thinking, not half the genius and not half the duck that Miss Swan was, though she was a duck in her way too. Miss Swan, as nearly as he could explain, was studying art for the fun of it, or the excitement, for she was well enough off; her father was a lawyer out there, and Berry believed that a rising son-in-law in his own profession would be just the thing for the old man's declining years. He said he should not be very particular about settling down to practice at once; if his wife wanted to go to Europe awhile, and kind of tenderfoot it round for a year or two in the art-centers over there, he would let the old man run the business a little longer; sometimes it did an old man good. There was no hurry; Berry's own father was not excited about his going to work right away; he had the money to run Berry and a wife too, if it came to that; Miss Swan understood that. He had not told her so in just so many words, but he had let her know that Alonzo W. Berry, Senior, was not borrowing money at two per cent. a month any more. He said he did not care to make much of a blow about that part of it till he was ready to act, and he was not going to act till he had a dead-sure thing of it; he was having a very good time as it went along, and he guessed Miss Swan was too; no use to hurry a girl, when she was on the right track.

Berry invented these axioms apparently to put himself in heart; in the abstract he was already courageous enough. He said that these Eastern girls were not used to having any sort of attention; that there was only about a tenth or fifteenth of a fellow to every girl, and that it tickled one of them to death to have a whole man around. He was not meanly exultant at their destitution. He said he just wished one of these pretty

179

Boston girls—nice, well dressed, cultured, and brought up to
be snubbed and neglected by the tenths and fifteenths of men
they had at home—could be let loose in the West, and have a
regular round-up of fellows. Or no, he would like to have
about five thousand fellows from out there, that never expected a woman to look at them, unloaded in Boston, and see
them open their eyes. "Wouldn't one of 'em get home alive, if
kindness could kill 'em. I never saw such a place! I can't get
used to it! It makes me tired. *Any* sort of fellow could get
married in Boston!"

Berry made no attempt to reconcile his uncertainty as to his
own chances with this general theory, but he urged it to
prove that Miss Swan and Miss Carver would like to have
Lemuel call; he said they had both said they wished they
could paint him. He had himself sustained various characters
in costume for them, and one night he pretended that they
had sent him down for Lemuel to help out with a certain
group. But they received him with a sort of blankness which
convinced him that Berry had exceeded his authority; there
was a helplessness at first, and then an indignant determination to save him from a false position even at their own cost,
which Lemuel felt rather than saw. Miss Carver was foremost
in his rescue; she devoted herself to this, and left Miss Swan
to punish Berry, who conveyed from time to time his sense
that he was "getting it," by a wink to Lemuel.

An observer with more social light might have been more
puzzled to account for Berry's toleration by these girls, who
apparently associated with him on equal terms. Since he was
not a servant, he *was* their equal in Lemuel's eyes; perhaps his
acceptance might otherwise be explained by the fact that he
was very amusing, chivalrously harmless, and extremely kind-
hearted and useful to them. One must not leave out of the
reckoning his open devotion for Miss Swan, which in itself
would do much to approve him to her, and commend him to
Miss Carver, if she were a generous girl, and very fond of her
friend. It is certain that they did tolerate Berry, who made
them laugh even that night in spite of themselves, till Miss
Swan said, "Well, what's the use?" and stopped trying to discipline him. After that they had a very sociable evening,
though Lemuel kept his distance, and would not let them

include him, knowing what the two girls really thought of him. He would not take part in Berry's buffooneries, but talked soberly and rather austerely with Miss Carver; and to show that he did not feel himself an inferior, whatever she might think, he was very sarcastic about some of the city ways and customs they spoke of. There were a good many books about—novels mostly, but not the kind Statira used to read, and poems; Miss Carver said she liked to take them up when she was nervous from her work; and if the weather was bad, and she could not get out for a walk, a book seemed to do her almost as much good. Nearly all the pictures about in the room seemed to be Miss Swan's; in fact, when Lemuel asked about them, and tried to praise them in such a way as not to show his ignorance, Miss Carver said she did very little in color; her lessons were all in black and white. He would not let her see that he did not know what this was, but he was ashamed, and he determined to find out; he determined to get a drawing-book, and learn something about it himself. To his thinking, the room was pretty harum-scarum. There were shawls hung upon the walls, and rugs, and pieces of cloth, which sometimes had half-finished paintings fastened to them; there were paintings standing round the room on the floor, sometimes right side out, and sometimes faced to the walls; there were two or three fleeces and fox-pelts scattered about instead of a carpet; and there were two easels, and stands with paints all twisted up in lead tubes on them. He compared the room with Statira's, and did not think much of it at first.

Afterwards it did not seem so bad; he began to feel its picturesqueness, for he went there again, and let the girls sketch him. When Miss Swan asked him that night if he would let them he wished to refuse; but she seemed so modest about it, and made it such a great favor on his part, that he consented; she said she merely wished to make a little sketch in color, and Miss Carver a little study of his head in black and white; and he imagined it a trifling affair that could be dispatched in a single night. They decided to treat his head as a Young Roman head; and at the end of a long sitting, beguiled with talk and with thoughtful voluntaries from Berry on his banjo, he found that Miss Carver had rubbed her study nearly all out with a piece of bread, and Miss Swan said she should want to try a perfectly new sketch with the shoulders draped; the coat had confused her; she would not let any one see what she had done, though Berry tried to make her let him.

Lemuel looked a little blank when she asked him for another sitting; but Berry said, "Oh, you'll have to come, Barker. Penalty of greatness, you know. Have you in Williams & Everett's window; notices in all the papers. 'The exquisite studies, by Miss Swan and Miss Carver, of the head of the gentlemanly and accommodating clerk of the St. Albans, as a Roman Youth.' Chromoed as a Christmas card by Prang, and photograph copies everywhere. You're all right, Barker."

One night Miss Swan said, in rapture with some momentary success, "Oh, I'm perfectly in love with this head!"

Berry looked up from his banjo, which he ceased to strum. "Hello, hello, hel-*lo!*"

Then the two broke into a laugh, in which Lemuel helplessly joined.

"What—what is it?" asked Miss Carver, looking up absently from her work.

"Nothing; just a little outburst of passion from our young friend here," said Berry, nodding his head toward Miss Swan.

"What does it mean, Mad?" asked Miss Carver in the same dreamy way, continuing her work.

"Yes, Madeline," said Berry, "explain yourself."

"Mr. Berry!" cried Miss Swan, warningly.

"That's me; Alonzo W., Jr. Go on!"

"You forget yourself," said the girl with imperfect severity.

"Well, you forgot me first," said Berry with affected injury. "Ain't it hard enough to sit here night after night, strumming on the old banjo, while another fellow is going down to posterity as a Roman Youth with a red shawl round his neck, without having to hear people say they're in love with that head of his?"

Miss Carver now stopped her work, and looked from her friend, with her head bowed in laughter on the back of her hand, to that of Berry bent in burlesque reproach upon her, and then at Lemuel, who was trying to control himself.

"But I can tell you what, Miss Swan; you spoke too late, as

the man said when he swallowed the chicken in the fresh egg. Mr. Barker has a previous engagement. That so, Barker?"

Lemuel turned fire-red, and looked round at Miss Carver, who met his glance with her clear gaze. She turned presently to make some comment on Miss Swan's sketch, and then, after working a little while longer, she said she was tired, and was going to make some tea.

The girls both pressed Lemuel to stay for a cup, but he would not; and Berry followed him downstairs to explain and apologize.

"It's all right," said Lemuel. "What difference would it make to them whether I was engaged or not?"

"Well, I suppose as a general rule a girl would rather a fellow wasn't," philosophized Berry. He whistled ruefully, and Lemuel drawing a book toward him in continued silence, he rose from the seat he had taken on the desk in the little office, and said, "Well, I guess it'll all come out right. Come to think of it, *I* don't know anything about your affairs, and I can tell 'em so."

"Oh, it don't matter."

He had pulled the book toward him as if he were going to read, but he could not read; his head was in a whirl. After a first frenzy of resentment against Berry, he was now angry at himself for having been so embarrassed. He thought of a retort that would have passed it all off lightly; then he reflected again that it was of no consequence to these young ladies whether he was engaged or not, and at any rate it was nobody's business but his own. Of course he was engaged to Statira, but he had hardly thought of it in that way. 'Manda Grier had joked about the time when she supposed she should have to keep old maid's hall alone; when she first did this Lemuel thought it delightful, but afterwards he did not like it so much; it began to annoy him that 'Manda Grier should mix herself up so much with Statira and himself. He believed that Statira would be different, would be more like other ladies (he generalized it in this way, but he meant Miss Swan and Miss Carver), if she had not 'Manda Grier there all the time to keep her back. He convinced himself that if it were not for 'Manda Grier, he should have had no trouble in telling Statira that the art-students were sketching him; and that he had not done so yet because he hated to have 'Manda ask her so much about them, and call them that Swan girl and that Carver girl, as she would be sure to do, and clip away the whole evening with her questions and her guesses. It was now nearly a fortnight since the sketching began, and he had let one Sunday night pass without mentioning it. He could not let another pass, and he knew 'Manda Grier would say they were a good while about it, and would show her ignorance, and put Statira up to asking all sorts of things. He could not bear to think of it, and he let the next Sunday night pass without saying anything to Statira. The sittings continued; but before the third Sunday came Miss Swan said she did not see how she could do anything more to her sketch, and Miss Carver had already completed her study. They criticised each other's work with freedom and good humor, and agreed that the next thing was to paint it out and rub it out.

"No," said Berry; "what you want is a fresh eye on it. I've worried over it as much as you have,—suffered more, I believe,—and Barker can't tell whether he looks like a Roman Youth or not. Why don't you have up old Evans?"

Miss Swan took no apparent notice of this suggestion; and Miss Carver, who left Berry's snubbing entirely to her, said nothing. After a minute's study of the pictures, Miss Swan suggested, "If Mr. Barker had any friends he would like to show them to?"

"Oh, no, thank you," returned Lemuel hastily, "there isn't anybody," and again he found himself turning very red.

"Well, I don't know how we can thank you enough for your patience, Mr. Barker," said the girl.

"Oh, don't mention it. I've—I've enjoyed it," said Lemuel.

"Game—every time," said Berry; and their evening broke up with a laugh.

The next morning Lemuel stopped Miss Swan at the door of the breakfast-room, and said, "I've been thinking over what you said last night, and I *should* like to bring some one—a lady friend of mine—to see the pictures."

"Why, certainly, Mr. Barker. Any time. Some evening?" she suggested.

"Should you mind it if I came to-morrow night?" he asked; and he thought it right to remind her, "It's Sunday night."

"Oh, not at all! To-morrow night, by all means! We shall both be at home, and very glad to see you." She hurried after Miss Carver, loitering on her way to their table, and Lemuel saw them put their heads together, as if they were whispering. He knew they were whispering about him, but they did not laugh; probably they kept themselves from laughing. In coming out from breakfast, Miss Swan said, "I hope your friend isn't *very* critical, Mr. Barker?" and he answered confusedly, "Oh, not at all, thank you." But he said to himself that he did not care whether she was trying to make fun of him or not, he knew what he had made up his mind to do.

Statira did not seem to care much about going to see the pictures, when he proposed it to her the next evening. She asked why he had been keeping it such a great secret, and he could not pretend, as he had once thought he could, that he was keeping it as a surprise for her. "Should *you* like to see 'em, 'Manda?" she asked with languid indifference.

"I d' know as I care much about Lem's picture, s' long 's we've got *him* around," 'Manda Grier whipped out, "but I *should* like t' see those celebrated girls 't we 've heard s' much about."

"Well," said Statira carelessly, and they went into the next room to put on their wraps. Lemuel, vexed to have 'Manda Grier made one of the party, and helpless to prevent her going, walked up and down, wondering what he should say when he arrived with this unexpected guest.

But Miss Swan received both of the girls very politely, and chatted with 'Manda Grier, whose conversation, in defiance of any sense of superiority that the Swan girl or the Carver girl might feel, was a succession of laconic snaps, sometimes witty, but mostly rude and contradictory.

Miss Carver made tea, and served it in some pretty cups which Lemuel hoped Statira might admire, but she took it without noticing, and in talking with Miss Carver she drawled, and said "N-y-e-e-e-s," and "I don't know as I d-o-o-o," and "Well, I should think as m-u-u-ch," with a prolongation of all the final syllables in her sentences which he had not observed in her before, and which she must have borrowed for the occasion for the gentility of the effect. She tried to refer everything to him, and she and 'Manda Grier talked together as much as they could, and when the others spoke of him as Mr. Barker, they called him Lem. They did not look at anything, or do anything to betray that they found the studio, on which Lemuel had once expatiated to them, different from other rooms.

At last Miss Swan abruptly brought out the studies of Lemuel's head, and put them in a good light; 'Manda Grier and Statira got into the wrong place to see them.

'Manda blurted out, "Well, he looks 's if he'd had a fit of sickness in *that* one"; and perhaps, in fact, Miss Carver had refined too much upon a delicate ideal of Lemuel's looks.

"So he d-o-o-es!" drawled Statira. "And how funny he looks with that red thing o-o-o-n!"

Miss Swan explained that she had thrown that in for the color, and that they had been fancying him in the character of a young Roman.

"You think he's got a Roman n-o-o-se?" asked Statira through her own.

"I think Lem's got a kind of a pug, m'self," said 'Manda Grier.

"Well, 'Manda Grier!" said Statira.

Lemuel could not look at Miss Carver, whom he knew to be gazing at the two girls from the little distance to which she had withdrawn; Miss Swan was biting her lip.

"So that's the celebrated St. Albans, is it?" said 'Manda Grier, when they got in the street. "Don't know's I really ever expected to see the inside 'f it. You notice the kind of oil-cloth they had on that upper entry, S'tira?"

They did not mention Lemuel's pictures, or the artists; and he scarcely spoke on the way home.

When they parted, Statira broke out crying and would not let him kiss her.

XX

I'M AFRAID your little friend at the St. Albans isn't altogether happy of late," said Evans toward the end of what
he called one of his powwows with Sewell. Their talk had
taken a vaster range than usual, and they both felt the need,
that people know in dealing with abstractions, of finally getting the ground beneath their feet again.

"Ah?" asked Sewell, with a twinge that allayed his satisfaction in this. "What's the matter with him?"

"Oh, the knowledge of good and evil, I suspect."

"I hope there's nothing wrong," said Sewell, anxiously.

"Oh, no. I used the phrase because it came easily. Just what
I mean is that I'm afraid his view of our social inequalities
is widening and deepening, and that he experiences the dissatisfaction of people who don't command that prospect
from the summit. I told you of his censure of our aristocratic
constitution?"

"Yes," said Sewell, with a smile.

"Well, I'm afraid he feels it more and more. If I can judge
from the occasional distance and *hauteur* with which he treats
me, he is humiliated by it. Nothing makes a man so proud as
humiliation, you know."

"That's true!"

"There are a couple of pretty girls at the St. Albans, art-
students, who have been painting Barker. So I learn from a
reformed cow-boy of the plains who is with us as a law-
student, and is about with one of the young ladies a good
deal. They're rather nice girls; quite nice, in fact; and there's
no harm in the cow-boy, and a good deal of fun. But if
Barker had conceived of being painted as a social inferior and
had been made to feel that he was merely a model, and if he
had become at all aware that one of the girls was rather
pretty—they both are——"

"I see!"

"I don't say it's so. But he seems low-spirited. Why don't
you come round and cheer him up—get into his confidence——"

"Get into the center of the earth!" cried Sewell. "I never saw such an inapproachable creature!"

Evans laughed. "He *is* rather remote. The genuine American youth is apt to be so, especially if he thinks you mean him a kindness. But there ought to be some way of convincing him that he need not feel any ignominy in his employment. After so many centuries of Christianity and generations of Democracy, it ought to be very simple to convince him that there is nothing disgraceful in showing people to their places at table."

"It isn't," said the minister, soberly.

"No, it isn't," said Evans. "I wonder," he added thoughtfully, "why we despise certain occupations? We don't despise a man who hammers stone or saws boards; why should we despise a barber? Is the care of the human head intrinsically less honorable than the shaping of such rude material? Why do we still contemn the tailor who clothes us, and honor the painter who portrays us in the same clothes? Why do we despise waiters? I tried to make Barker believe that I respected all kinds of honest work. But I lied; I despised him for having waited on table. Why have all manner of domestics fallen under our scorn, and come to be stigmatized in a lump as servants?"

"Ah, I don't know," said the minister. "There *is* something in personal attendance upon us that dishonors; but the reasons of it are very obscure; *I* couldn't give them. Perhaps it's because it's work that in a simpler state of things each of us would do for himself, and in this state is too proud to do."

"That doesn't cover the whole ground," said Evans.

"And you think that poor boy is troubled — is really suffering from a sense of inferiority to the other young people?"

"Oh, I don't say certainly. Perhaps not. But if he were, what should you say was the best thing for him to do? Remain a servant; cast his lot with these outcasts; or try to separate and distinguish himself from them, as we all do? Come; we live in the world, which isn't so bad, though it's pretty stupid. He couldn't change it. Now, what ought he to do?"

Sewell mused awhile without answering anything. Then he said with a smile, "It's very much simpler to fit people for the other world than for this, don't you think?"

"Yes, it is. It was a cold day for the clergy when it was imagined that they ought to do both."

"Well," said Sewell, rising to follow his friend to the door, "I will come to see Barker, and try to talk with him. He's a very complicated problem. I supposed that I had merely his material prosperity to provide for, after getting him down here; but if I have to reconcile him to the constitution of society!"

"Yes," said Evans. "I wish you'd let me know the result of your labors. I think I could make a very incisive article on the subject. The topic is always an attractive one. There is nobody who doesn't feel that somebody else is taking on airs with him, and ought to have his comb cut. Or, if you should happen to prove to Barker that his ignominy is in accordance with the Development Theory, and is a necessary Survival, or something of that sort, don't you see what a card it would be for us with the better classes?"

They went down-stairs together, and at the street door Evans stopped again. "Or, I'll tell you what. Make it a simple study of Barker's mind—a sort of psychological interview; and then with what I've been able to get from him we can present the impression that Boston makes upon a young, fresh, shrewd mind. That would be something rather new, wouldn't it? Come! the 'Afternoon' would make it worth your while. And then you could work it into a sermon afterwards."

"You shameless reprobate!" said Sewell, laying his hand affectionately on his friend's arm.

There was nothing in Lemuel's case that seemed to him urgent, and he did not go to see him at once. In the mean time, Fast Day came, and Lemuel got away at last to pay his first visit home.

"Seems to me ye ain't lookin' over and above well, Lem," was the first thing his mother said to him, even before she noticed how well he was dressed.

His new spring overcoat, another prize from the Misfit Parlors, and his new pointed-toe shoes and Derby hat, with the suit of clothes he had kept so carefully all through the winter, were not the complete disguise he had fancied they might be at Willoughby Pastures. The depot-master had known him as soon as he got out of the cars, and ignored his splendor in recognizing him. He said, "Hello, Lem!" and had not time to reconcile himself to the boy's changed appearance before Lemuel hurried away with the bag he had bought so long before for the visit. He met several people on his way home from the depot: two of them were women, and one of these said she knew as soon as she looked at him who it was, and the other said she should have known it was Lem Barker as far as she could see him. She asked him if he was home for good now.

His mother pushed back his thick hair with her hard old hand as she spoke to him, and then she pressed his head down upon her neck, which was mostly collar-bone. But Lemuel could hear her heart beat, and the tears came into his eyes.

"Oh, I'm all right, mother," he said huskily, though he tried to say it cheerfully. He let her hold his head there the longer because mixed with his tenderness for her was a horror of her bloomers, which he was not at once able to overcome. When he gained courage to look, he saw that she had them on, but now he had the strength to bear it.

"Ye had any breakfast?" she asked; and when he said that he had got a cup of coffee at Fitchburg, she said, well, she must get him something; and she drew him a cup of Japan tea, and made him some milk-toast and picked-fish, talking all the time, and telling him how his sister and her husband had gone to the village to have one of her teeth drawn. They had got along through the winter pretty well; but she guessed that they would have had more to complain of if it had not been for him. This was her way of acknowledging the help Lemuel had given them every week, and it was casually sandwiched between an account of an Indian Spirit treatment, which Reuben had tried for his rheumatism, and a question whether Lemuel had seen anything of that Mind Cure down to Boston.

But when he looked about the room, and saw here and there the simple comforts and necessaries which his money had bought the sick man and the two helpless women, his heart swelled with joy and pride; and he realized the pleasure we all feel in being a good genius. At times it had come pretty hard to send the greater part of his week's wages home, but now he was glad he had done it. The poor, coarse food which his mother had served him as a treat; the low, cracked ceilings; the waving floor, covered with rag carpet; the sagging doors, and the old-fashioned trim of the small-paned windows, were all very different from the luxurious abundance, the tessellated pavement, and the tapestry brussels, the lofty studding, and the black walnut moldings of the St. Albans; and Lemuel felt the difference with a curious mixture of pride and remorse in his own escape from the meanness of his home. He felt the self-reproach to which the man who rises without raising with him all those dear to him is destined in some measure all his life. His interests and associations are separated from theirs, but if he is not an ignoble spirit, the ties of affection remain unweakened; he cares for them with a kind of indignant tenderness, and calls himself to account before them in the midst of pleasures which they cannot share, or even imagine.

Lemuel's mother did not ask him much about his life in Boston; she had not the materials for curiosity about it; but he told her everything that he thought she could understand. She recurred to his hopes when he left home and their disappointment in Sewell, and she asked if Lemuel ever saw him nowadays. She could not reconcile herself to his reconciliation with Sewell, whom she still held to have behaved treacherously. Then she went back to Lemuel's looks, and asked him if he kept pretty well; and when he answered that he did, she smoothed with her hand the knot between her eyes, and did not question him further.

He had the whole forenoon with his mother, and he helped her to get the dinner, as he used to do, pulling the stove-wood out of the snow-drift that still imbedded part of the wood-pile, though the snow was all gone around Boston. It was thawing under the dull, soft April sky, and he saw the first bluebird perched on the clothes-line when he went out for the wood; his mother said there had been lots of them. He walked about the place, and into the barn, taking in the forlornness and shabbiness; and then he went up into the room over the shed, where he used to study and write. His heart ached with self-pity.

He realized as he had not done at a distance how dependent this wretched home was upon him; and after meaning the whole morning to tell his mother about Statira, he decided that he was keeping it from her, not merely because he was ashamed to tell her that he was engaged, but because it seemed such a crazy thing, for a person in his circumstances, if it was really an engagement. He had not seen Statira since that night when he brought her to look at the pictures the art-students had made of him. He felt that he had not parted with her kindly, and he went to see her the night before he started home, though it was not Sunday; but he had found her door locked, and this made him angry with her, he could not have said just why. If he told his mother about Statira now, what should he tell her? He compromised by telling her about the two girls that had painted his likeness.

His mother seemed not to care a great deal about the picture. She said, "I don't want you should let any girl make a fool of you, Lem."

"Oh, no," he answered; and went and looked out of the window.

"I don't say but what they're nice girls enough, but in your place you no need to throw yourself away."

Lemuel thought of the awe of Miss Carver in which he lived, and the difference between them; and he could have laughed at his mother's ignorant pride. What would she say if she knew that he was engaged to a girl that worked in a box-factory? But probably she would not think that studying art and teaching it was any better. She evidently believed that his position in the St. Albans was superior to that of Miss Carver.

His sister and her husband came home before they had finished dinner. His sister had her face all tied up to keep from taking cold after having her tooth drawn, and Lemuel had to go out and help his rheumatic brother-in-law put up the horse. When they came in, his brother-in-law did not wash his hands before going to the table, and Lemuel could not keep his eyes off his black and broken finger-nails; his mother's and sister's nails were black too. It must have been so when he lived at home.

His sister could not eat; she took some tea, and went to bed. His brother-in-law pulled off his boots after dinner, and put up his stocking-feet on the stove-hearth to warm them.

There was no longer any chance to talk with his mother indoors, and he asked her if she would not like to come out; it was very mild. She put on her bonnet, and they strolled down the road. All the time Lemuel had to keep from looking at her bloomers. When they met any one driving, he had to keep himself from trying to look as if he were not with her, but was just out walking alone.

The day wore heavily away. His brother-in-law's rheumatism came on toward evening, and his sister's face had swollen, so that it would not do for her to go out. Lemuel put on some old clothes he found in his room, and milked the cows himself.

"Like old times, Lem," said his mother, when he came in.

"Yes," he assented quietly.

He and his mother had tea together, but pretty soon afterwards she seemed to get sleepy; and Lemuel said he had been up early and he guessed he would go to bed. His mother said she guessed she would go too.

After he had blown out his light, she came in to see if he were comfortable. "I presume it seems a pretty poor place to you, Lem," she said, holding her lamp up and looking round.

"I guess if it's good enough for you it is for me," he answered evasively.

"No, it ain't," she said. "I always b'en used to it, and I can see from your talk that you've got used to something different already. Well, it's right, Lem. You're a good boy, and I want you should get the good of Boston, all you can. We don't any of us begrutch it to ye; and what I came up to say now was, don't you scrimp yourself down there to send home to us. We got a roof over our heads, and we can keep soul and body together somehow; we always have, and we don't need a great deal. But I want you should keep yourself nicely dressed down to Boston, so't you can go with the best; I don't want you should feel anyways meechin' on account of your clothes. You got a good figure, Lem; you take after your father. Sometimes I wish you was a little bigger; but *he* wa'n't; and he had a big spirit. He wa'n't afraid of anything; and they said if he'd come out o' that battle where he was killed, he'd 'a' b'en a captain. He was a good man."

She had hardly ever spoken so much of his father before; he

knew now by the sound of her voice in the dim room that the tears must be in her eyes; but she governed herself and went on.

"What I wanted to say was, don't you keep sendin' so much o' your money home, child. It's yours, and I want you should have it. Most of it goes for patent medicines, anyway, when it gets here; we can't keep Reuben from buying 'em, and he's always changin' doctors. And I want you should hold yourself high, Lem. You're as good as anybody. And don't you go with any girls, especially, that ain't of the best. You're gettin' to that time o' life when you'll begin to think about 'em; but don't you go and fall in love with the first little pop-pet you see, because she's got pretty eyes and curly hair."

It seemed to Lemuel as if she must know about Statira, but of course she did not. He lay still, and she went on.

"Don't you go and get engaged, or any such foolishness, in a hurry, Lem. Them art-student girls you was tellin' about, I presume they're all right enough; but you wait awhile. Young men think it's a kind of miracle if a girl likes 'em, and they're ready to go crazy over it; but it's the most natural thing she can do. You just wait awhile. When you get along a little further, you can pick and choose for yourself. I don't know as I should want you should marry for money; but don't you go and take up with the first thing comes along, because you're afraid to look higher. What's become o' that nasty thing that talked so to you at that Miss Vane's?"

Lemuel said that he had never seen Sibyl or Miss Vane since; but he did not make any direct response to the anxieties his mother had hinted at. Her pride in him, so ignorant of all the reality of his life in the city, crushed him more than the sight and renewed sense of the mean conditions from which he had sprung. What if he should tell her that Miss Carver, whom she did not want him to marry in a hurry, regarded him as a servant, and treated him as she would treat a black man? What if she knew that he was as good as engaged to marry a girl that could no more meet Miss Carver on the same level than she could fly? He could only tell his mother not to feel troubled about him; that he was not going to get married in any great hurry; and pretend to be sleepy and turn his head away.

She pulled the covering up round his neck and tucked it in with her strong, rough old hand, whose very tenderness hurt.

He had expected to stay the greater part of the next day, but he took an earlier train. His sister was still laid up; she thought she must have taken cold in her jaw; her husband, rumpled, unshaven, with a shawl over his shoulders, cowered about the cook-stove for the heat. He began to hate this poverty and suffering, to long for escape from it to the life which at that distance seemed so rich and easy and pleasant; he trembled lest something might have happened in his absence to throw him out of his place.

All the way to Boston he was under the misery of the home that he was leaving; his mother's pride added to the burden of it. But when the train drew in sight of the city, and he saw the steeples and chimneys, and the thin masts of the ships printed together against the horizon, his heart rose. He felt equal to it, to anything in it.

He arrived in the middle of the afternoon, and he saw no one at the hotel except the Harmons till toward dinner-time. Then the ladies coming in from shopping had a word of welcome for him; some of them stopped and shook hands at the office, and when they began to come down to dinner they spoke to him, and there again some of them offered their hands; they said it seemed an age since he had gone.

The art-students came down with Berry, who shook hands so cordially with him that perhaps they could not help it. Miss Carver seemed to hesitate, but she gave him her hand too, and she asked, as the others had done, whether he had found his family well.

He did not know what to think. Sometimes he felt as if people were trying to make a fool of him, almost. He remained blushing and smiling to himself after the last of them had gone in to dinner. He did not know what Miss Carver meant, but her eyes seemed to have lost that cold distance, and to have come nearer to him.

Late at night Berry came to him where he sat at his desk. "Well, Barker, I'm glad you're back again, old man. Feels as if you'd been gone a month of Sundays. Didn't know whether we should have you with us this *first* evening."

Lemuel grew hot with consciousness, and did not make it better for himself by saying, "I don't know what you mean."

"Well, I don't suppose *I* should in your *place*," returned Berry. "It's human nature. It's all right. What did the ladies think of the 'Roman Youth' the other night? The distinguished artists weren't sure exactly, and I thought I could make capital with one of 'em if I could find out. Yes, that's my little game, Barker; that's what I dropped in for; Bismarck style of diplomacy. I'll tell you why they want to know, if you won't give me away: Miss Swan wanted to give her 'bit of color'—that's what she calls it—to one of the young ladies; but she's afraid she didn't like it."

"I guess they liked it well enough," said Lemuel, thinking with shame that Statira had not had the grace to say a word of either of the pictures; he attributed this to 'Manda Grier's influence.

"Well, that's good, so far as it goes," said Berry. "But now, to come down to particulars, what did they *say*? That's what Miss Swan will ask *me*."

"I don't remember just what they said," faltered Lemuel.

"Well, they must have said something," insisted Berry, jocosely. "Give a fellow some little clew, and I can piece it out for myself. What did *she* say? I don't ask which she *was*, but I have my suspicions. All I want to know is what she *said*. Anything like beautiful middle distance, or splendid chiaroscuro, or fine perspective, or exquisite modeling? Come, now! Try to think, Barker." He gave Lemuel time, but to no purpose. "Well," he resumed with affected dejection, "I'll have to try to imagine it; I guess I can; I haven't worked my imagination much since I took up the law. But look here, Barker," he continued more briskly, "now you open up a little. Here I've been giving you my confidence ever since I saw you—forcing it on you; and you know just how far I'm gone on Miss Swan, to the hundredth part of an inch; but I don't know enough of your affections to swear that you've got any. Now, which one is it? Don't be mean about it. I won't give you away. Honest Injun!"

Lemuel was goaded to desperation. His face burned, and the perspiration began to break out on his forehead. He did not know how to escape from this pursuit.

"Which is it, Barker?" repeated his tormentor. "I know it's human nature to deny it, though I never could understand why; if I was engaged, the Sunday papers should have it about as quick!"

"I'm *not* engaged!" cried Lemuel.

"You ain't?" yelled Berry.

"No!"

"Give me your hand! Neither am I!"

He shook Lemuel's helpless hand with mock-heroic fervor. "We are brothers from this time forth, Barker! You can't imagine how closely this tie binds you to me, Barker. Barker, we are one; with no particular prospect, as far as I am concerned, of ever being more."

He offered to dramatize a burst of tears on Lemuel's shoulder; but Lemuel escaped from him.

"Stop! Quit your fooling! What if somebody should come in?"

"They won't," said Berry, desisting, and stretching himself at ease in the only chair besides Lemuel's with which the office was equipped. "It's too late for 'em. Now o'er the one half world nature seems dead-ah, and wicked dreams abuse the curtained sleep-ah. We are safe here from all intrusion, and I can lay bare my inmost thoughts to you, Barker, if I happen to have any. Barker, I'm awfully glad you're not engaged to either of those girls—or both. And it's not altogether because I enjoy the boon companionship of another unengaged man, but it's partly because I don't think—shall I say it?"

"Say what?" asked Lemuel, not without some prescience.

"Well, you can forgive the brotherly frankness, if you don't like it. I don't think they're quite up to you."

Lemuel gave a sort of start, which Berry interpreted in his own way.

"Now, hold on! I know just how you feel. Been there myself. I have seen the time, too, when I thought any sort of a girl was too good for Alonzo W., Jr. But I don't now. I think A. W., Jr., is good enough for the best. I may be mistaken; I was, the other time. But we all begin that way; and the great object is not to keep on that way. See? Now, I suppose you're in love—puppy love—with that little thing. Probably the first girl you got acquainted with after you came to Boston, or maybe a sweet survival of the Willoughby Pastures period. All right. Perfectly natural, in either case. But don't you let it go any further, my dear boy; old man, don't you let it go any further. Pause! Reflect! Consider! Love wisely, but not too well! Take the unsolicited advice of a sufferer."

Pride, joy, shame, remorse, mixed in Lemuel's heart, which eased itself in an involuntary laugh at Berry's nonsense.

"Now, what I want you to do—dear boy, or old man, as the case may be—is to regard yourself in a new light. Regard yourself, for the sake of the experiment, as too good for any girl in Boston. No? Can't fetch it? Try again!"

Lemuel could only laugh foolishly.

"Well, now, that's singular," pursued Berry. "I supposed you could have done it without the least trouble. Well, let's try something a little less difficult. Look me in the eye, and regard yourself as too good, for example, for Miss Carver. Ha!"

An angry flush spread over Lemuel's embarrassed face. "I wish you'd behave yourself," he stammered.

"In any other cause I would," said Berry, solemnly. "But I must be cruel to be kind. Seriously, old man, if you can't think yourself too good for Miss Carver, I wish you'd think yourself good enough. Now, I'm not saying anything against the Willoughby episode, mind. That has its place in the wise economy of nature, just like anything else. But there ain't any outcome in it for you. You've got a future before you, Barker, and you don't want to go and load up with a love affair that you'll keep trying to unload as long as you live. No, sir! Look at me! I know I'm not an example in some things, but in this little business of correctly placed affections I could give points to Solomon. Why am I in love with M. Swan? Because I can't help it for one thing, and because for another thing she can do more to develop the hidden worth and unsuspected powers of A. W., Jr., than any other woman in the world. She may never feel that it's her mission, but she can't shake my conviction that way; and I shall stay undeveloped to prove that I was right. Well, now, what you want, my friend, is development, and you can't get it where you've been going. She hain't got it on hand. And what you want to do is not to take something else in its place—tender heart, steadfast affections, loyalty; they've got 'em at every shop in town; they're a drug in the market. You've got to say, 'No development, heigh? Well, I'll just look round awhile, and if I can't find it at some of the other stores I'll come back and take some of that steadfast affection. You say it won't come off? Or run in washing?' See?"

"You ought to be ashamed of yourself," said Lemuel, trying to summon an indignant feeling, and laughing with a strange pleasure at heart. "You've got no right to talk to me that way. I want you should leave me alone!"

"Well, since you're so pressing, I will go," said Berry, easily. "But if I find you at our next interview sitting under the shade of the mustard-tree whose little seed I have just dropped, I shall feel that I have not labored in vain. 'She's a darling, she's a daisy, she's a dumpling, she's a lamb!' I refer to Miss Swan, of course; but on other lips the terms are equally applicable to Miss Carver, and don't you forget it!"

He swung out of the office with a mazurka step. His silk hat, gayly tilted on the side of his head, struck against the door-jamb, and fell rolling across the entry floor. Lemuel laughed wildly. At twenty these things are droll.

XXI

A WEEK PASSED, and Lemuel had not tried to see Statira again. He said to himself that even when he had tried to do what was right, and to show those young ladies how much he thought of her by bringing her to see their pictures, she had acted very ungratefully, and had as good as tried to quarrel with him. Then, when he went to see her before his visit home, she was out; she had never been out before when he called.

Now, he had told Berry that they were not engaged. At first this shocked him as if it were a lie. Then he said to himself that he had a right to make that answer because Berry had no right to ask the questions that led to it. Then he asked himself if he really were engaged to Statira. He had told her that he liked her better than any one else in the world, and she had said as much to him. But he pretended that he did not know whether it could be called an engagement.

There was no one who could solve the question for him, and it kept asking itself that whole week, and especially when he was with Miss Carver, as happened two or three times through Berry's connivance. Once he had spent the greater part of an evening in the studio, where he talked nearly all the time with Miss Carver, and he found out that she was the daughter of an old ship's captain at Corbitant; her mother was dead, and her aunt had kept house for her father. It was an old, square house that her grandfather built, in the days when Corbitant had direct trade with France. She described it minutely, and told how a French gentleman had died there in exile at the time of the French Revolution, and who was said to haunt the house; but Miss Carver had never seen any ghosts in it. They all began to talk of ghosts and weird experiences; even Berry had had some strange things happen to him in the West. Then the talk broke in two again, and Lemuel sat apart with Miss Carver, who told at length the plot of a story she had been reading; it was a story called "Romola," and she said she would lend it to Lemuel; she said she did not see how any one could bear to be the least selfish or untrue after reading it. That made Lemuel feel cold; but he could not break away from her charm. She sat where the shaded lamp threw its soft light on one side of her face; it looked almost like the face of a spirit, and her eyes were full of a heavenly gentleness.

Lemuel asked himself how he could ever have thought them proud eyes. He asked himself at the same time, and perpetually, whether he was really engaged to Statira or not. He thought how different this evening was from those he spent with her. She could not talk about anything but him and her dress; and 'Manda Grier could not do anything but say saucy things which she thought were smart. Miss Swan was really witty; it was as good as the theater to hear her and Berry going on together. Berry was pretty bright; there was no denying it. He sang to his banjo that night; one of the songs was Spanish; he had learnt it in New Mexico.

Lemuel began to understand better how such nice young ladies could go with Berry. At first, after Berry talked so to him that night in the office against Statira, he determined that he would keep away from him; but Berry was so sociable and good-natured that he could not. The first thing he knew, Lemuel was laughing at something Berry said, and then he could not help himself.

Berry was coming now, every chance he had, to talk about the art-students. He seemed to take it for granted that Lemuel was as much interested in Miss Carver as he was himself in Miss Swan; and Lemuel did begin to speak of her in a shy way. Berry asked him if he had noticed that she looked like that Spanish picture of the Virgin that Miss Swan had pinned up next to the door; and Lemuel admitted that there was some resemblance.

"Notice those eyes of hers, so deep, and sorry for everybody in general? If it was anybody in particular, *that* fellow would be in luck. Oh, she's a dumpling, there's no mistake about it! 'Nymph, in thy orisons be all my sins remembered!' That's Miss Carver's style. She looks as if she just *wanted* to forgive somebody something. I'm afraid you ain't wicked enough, Barker. Look here! What's the reason we can't make up a little party for the Easter service at the Catholic cathedral Sunday night? The girls would like to go, I know."

"No, no, I can't! I mustn't!" said Lemuel; and he remained

steadfast in his refusal. It would be the second Sunday night that he had not seen Statira, and he felt that he must not let it pass so. Berry went off to the cathedral with the art-students; and he kept out of the way till they were gone.

He said to himself that he would go a little later than usual to see Statira, to let her know that he was not so very anxious; but when he found her alone, and she cried on his neck, and owned that she had not behaved as she should that night when she went to see the pictures, and that she had been afraid he hated her, and was not coming any more, he had staid away so long, his heart was melted, and he did everything to soothe and comfort her, and they were more loving together than they had been since the first time.

'Manda Grier came in, and said through her nose, like an old countrywoman, " 'The falling out of faithful friends renewing is of love!' " and Statira exclaimed in the old way, " *'Manda!*" that he had once thought so cunning, and rested there in his arms with her cheek tight pressed against his.

She did not talk; except when she was greatly excited about something, she rarely had anything to say. She had certain little tricks, poutings, bridlings, starts, outcries, which had seemed the most bewitching things in the world to Lemuel. She tried all these now, unaffectedly enough, in listening to his account of his visit home, and so far as she could she vividly sympathized with him.

He came away heavy and unhappy. Somehow, these things no longer sufficed for him. He compared this evening with the last he had spent with the art-students, which had left his brain in a glow, and kept him awake for hours with luminous thoughts. But he had got over that unkindness to Statira, and he was glad of that. He pitied her now, and he said to himself that if he could get her away from 'Manda Grier, and under the influence of such girls as Miss Swan and Miss Carver, it would be much better for her. He did not relent toward 'Manda Grier; he disliked her more than ever, and in the friendship which he dramatized between Statira and Miss Carver, he saw her cast adrift without remorse.

Sewell had told him that he was always at leisure Monday night, and the next evening Lemuel went to pay his first visit to the minister since his first day in Boston. It was early, and

Evans, who usually came that evening, had not arrived yet; but Sewell had him in his thought when he hurried forward to meet his visitor.

"Oh, is it you, Mr. Barker?" he asked, in a note of surprise. "I am glad to see you. I had been intending to come and look you up again. Will you sit down? Mr. Evans was here the other night, and we were talking of you. I hope you are well?"

"Very well, thank you," said Lemuel, taking the hand the minister offered, and then taking the chair he indicated. Sewell did not know exactly whether to like the greater ease which Lemuel showed in his presence; but there was nothing presumptuous in it, and he could not help seeing the increased refinement of the young man's beauty. The knot between his eyes gave him interest, while it inflicted a vague pang upon the minister. "I have been at home since I saw you." Lemuel looked down at his neat shoes to see if they were in fit state for the minister's study-carpet, and Sewell's eye, sympathetically following, wandered to the various details of Lemuel's simple and becoming dress,—the light spring suit which he had indulged himself in at the Misfit Parlors since his mother had bidden him keep his money for himself and not send so much of it home.

"Ah, have you?" cried the minister. "I hope you found your people all well? How is the place looking? I suppose the season isn't quite so advanced as it is with us."

"There's some snow in the woods yet," said Lemuel, laying the stick he carried across the hat-brim on his knees. "Mother was well; but my sister and her husband have had a good deal of sickness."

"Oh, I'm sorry for that," said Sewell, with the general sympathy which Evans accused him of keeping on tap professionally. "Well, how did you like the looks of Willoughby Pastures compared with Boston? Rather quieter, I suppose."

"Yes, it was quieter," answered Lemuel.

"But the first touch of spring must be very lovely there! I find myself very impatient with these sweet, early days in town. I envy you your escape to such a place."

Lemuel opposed a cold silence to the lurking didacticism of these sentences, and Sewell hastened to add, "And I wish I could have had your experience in contrasting the country and the town, after your long sojourn here, on your first return home. Such a chance can come but once in a lifetime, and to very few."

"There are some pleasant things about the country," Lemuel began.

"Oh, I am sure of it!" cried Sewell, with cheerful aimlessness.

"The stillness was a kind of rest, after the noise here. I think any one might be glad to get back to such a place——"

"I was sure you would," interrupted Sewell.

"If he was discouraged or broken down any way," Lemuel calmly added.

"Oh!" said Sewell. "You mean that you found more sympathy among your old friends and neighbors than you do here?"

"No," said Lemuel bluntly. "That's what city people think. But it's all a mistake. There isn't half the sympathy in the country that there is in the city. Folks pry into each other's business more, but they don't really care so much. What I mean is that you could live cheaper, and the fight isn't so hard. You might have to use your hands more, but you wouldn't have to use your head hardly at all. There isn't so much opposition—competition."

"Oh," said Sewell, a second time. "But this competition—this struggle—in which one or the other must go to the wall, isn't that painful?"

"I don't know as it is," answered Lemuel, "as long as you're young and strong. And it don't always follow that one must go to the wall. I've seen some things where both got on better."

Sewell succumbed to this worldly wisdom. He was frequently at the disadvantage men of cloistered lives must be, in having his theories in advance of his facts. He now left this point, and covertly touched another that had come up in his last talk with Evans about Barker. "But you find in the country, don't you, a greater equality of social condition? People are more on a level, and have fewer artificial distinctions."

"Yes, there's that," admitted Lemuel. "I've worried a good deal about that, for I've had to take a servant's place in a good many things, and I've thought folks looked down on me for it, even when they didn't seem to intend to do it. But I guess it isn't so bad as I thought when I first began to notice it. Do you suppose it is?" His voice was suddenly tense with personal interest in the question which had ceased to be abstract.

"Oh, certainly not," said the minister, with an ease which he did not feel.

"I presume I had what you may call a servant's place at Miss Vane's," pursued Lemuel unflinchingly, "and I've been what you may call head waiter at the St. Albans since I've been there. If a person heard afterwards, when I had made out something, if I ever did, that I had been a servant, would they—they—despise me for it?"

"Not unless they were very silly people," said Sewell, cordially, "I can assure you."

"But if they had ever seen me doing a servant's work, wouldn't they always remember it, no matter what I was afterwards?" Sewell hesitated, and Lemuel hurried to add, "I ask because I've made up my mind not to be anything but clerk after this."

Sewell pitied the simple shame, the simple pride. "That isn't the question for you to ask, my dear boy," he answered gently, and with an affection which he had never felt for his charge before. "There's another question, more important, and one which you must ask yourself: '*Should I care if they did?*' After all, the matter's in your own hands. Your soul's always your own till you do something wrong."

"Yes, I understand that." Lemuel sat silently thoughtful, fingering his hat-band. It seemed to Sewell that he wished to ask something else, and was mustering his courage; but if this was so, it exhaled in a sigh, and he remained silent.

"I should be sorry," pursued the minister, "to have you dwell upon such things. There are certain ignoble facts in life which we can best combat by ignoring them. A slight of almost any sort ceases to be when you cease to consider it." This did not strike Sewell as wholly true when he had said it, and he was formulating some modification of it in his mind, when Lemuel said:

"I presume a person can help himself some by being

ashamed of caring for such things, and that's what I've tried to do."

"Yes, that's what I meant——"

"I guess I've exaggerated the whole thing, some. But if a thing is so, thinking it ain't won't unmake it."

"No," admitted Sewell, reluctantly. "But I should be sorry, all the same, if you let it annoy—grieve you. What has pleased me in what I've been able to observe in you has been your willingness to take hold of any kind of honest work. I liked finding you with your coat off washing dishes, that morning, at the Wayfarer's Lodge, and I liked your going at once to Miss Vane's in a—as you did——"

"Of course," Lemuel interrupted, "I could do it before I knew how it was looked at here."

"And couldn't you do it now?"

"Not if there was anything else."

"Ah, that's the great curse of it; that's what I deplore," Sewell broke out, "in our young people coming from the country to the city. They must all have some genteel occupation! I don't blame them; but I would gladly have saved you this experience—this knowledge—if I could. I felt that I had done you a kind of wrong in being the means, however indirectly and innocently, of your coming to Boston, and I would willingly have done anything to have you go back to the country. But you seemed to distrust me—to find something hostile in me—and I did not know how to influence you."

"Yes, I understand that," said Lemuel. "I couldn't help it, at first. But I've got to see it all in a different light since then. I know that you meant the best by me. I know now that what I wrote wasn't worth anything, and just how you must have looked at it. I didn't know some things then that I do now; and since I have got to know a little more I have understood better what you meant by all you said."

"I am very glad," said Sewell, with sincere humility, "that you have kept no hard feeling against me."

"Oh, not at all. It's all right now. I couldn't explain very well that I hadn't come to the city just to be in the city, but because I had to do something to help along at home. You didn't seem to understand that there wa'n't anything there for me to take hold of."

"No, I'm afraid I didn't, or wouldn't, quite understand that; I was talking and acting, I'm afraid, from a preconceived notion." Lemuel made no reply, not having learned yet to utter the pleasant generalities with which city people left a subject; and after a while Sewell added, "I am glad to have seen your face so often at church. You have been a great deal in my mind, and I have wished to do something to make your life happy and useful to you in the best way here, but I haven't quite known how." At this point Sewell realized that it was nearly eight months since Lemuel had come to Boston, and he said contritely, "I have not made the proper effort, I'm afraid; but I did not know exactly how to approach you. You were rather a difficult subject," he continued, with a smile in which Lemuel consented to join, "but now that we've come to a clearer understanding"— He broke off and asked, "Have you many acquaintances in Boston?"

Lemuel hesitated, and cleared his throat. "Not many."

Something in his manner prompted the minister to say, "That is such a very important thing for young men in a strange place. I wish you would come oftener to see us hereafter. Young men, in the want of companionship, often form disadvantageous acquaintances, which they can't shake off afterwards, when they might wish to do so. I don't mean evil acquaintance; I certainly couldn't mean that in your case; but frivolous ones, from which nothing high or noble can come—nothing of improvement or development."

Lemuel started at the word and blushed. It was Berry's word. Sewell put his own construction on the start and the blush.

"Especially," he went on, "I should wish any young man whom I was interested in to know refined and noble women." He felt that this was perhaps, in Lemuel's case, too much like prescribing port wine and carriage exercise to an indigent patient, and he added, "If you cannot know such women, it is better to know none at all. It is not what women say or do, so much as the art they have of inspiring a man to make the best of himself. The accidental acquaintances that young people are so apt to form are in most cases very detrimental. There is no harm in them of themselves, perhaps, but all irregularity in the life of the young is to be deplored."

"Do you mean," asked Lemuel, with that concreteness which had alarmed Sewell before, "that they ought to be regularly introduced?"

"I mean that a young girl who allowed a young man to make her acquaintance outside of the—the—social sanctions would be apt to be a silly or romantic person, at the best. Of course, there are exceptions. But I should be very sorry if any young man I knew—no; why shouldn't I say *you* at once?—should involve himself in any such way. One thing leads to another, especially with the young; and the very fact of irregularity, of romance, of strangeness in an acquaintance, throws a false glamour over the relation, and appeals to the sentiments in an unwarranted degree."

"Yes, that is so," said Lemuel.

The admission stimulated Sewell in the belief that he had a clew in his hand which it was his duty to follow up. "The whole affair loses proportion and balance. The fancy becomes excited, and some of the most important interests—the very most important interests of life—are committed to impulse." Lemuel remained silent, and it seemed the silence of conviction. "A young man is better for knowing women older than himself, more cultivated, devoted to higher things. Of course, young people must see each other, must fall in love, and get married; but there need be no haste about such things. If there is haste—if there is rashness, thoughtlessness—there is sure to be unhappiness. Men are apt to outgrow their wives intellectually, if their wives' minds are set on home and children, as they should be; and allowance for this ought to be made, if possible. I would rather that in the beginning the wife should be the mental superior. I hope it will be several years yet before you think seriously of such things, but when the time comes, I hope you will have seen some young girl—there are such for every one of us—whom it is civilization and enlightenment, refinement, and elevation, simply to know. On the other hand, a silly girl's influence is degrading and ruinous. She either drags those attached to her down to her own level, or she remains a weight and a clog upon the life of a man who loves her."

"Yes," said Lemuel, with a sigh which Sewell interpreted as that of relief from danger recognized in time.

He pursued eagerly: "I could not warn any one too earnestly against such an entanglement."

Lemuel rose and looked about with a troubled glance.

Sewell continued: "Any such marriage—a marriage upon any such conditions—is sure to be calamitous; and if the conditions are recognized beforehand, it is sure to be iniquitous. So far from urging the fulfillment of even a promise, in such a case, I would have every such engagement broken, in the interest of humanity—of morality——"

Mrs. Sewell came into the room, and gave a little start of surprise, apparently not mixed with pleasure, at seeing Lemuel. She had never been able to share her husband's interest in him, while insisting upon his responsibility; she disliked him not logically, but naturally, for the wrong and folly which he had been the means of her husband's involving himself in; Miss Vane's kindliness toward Lemuel, which still survived, and which expressed itself in questions about him whenever she met the minister, was something that Mrs. Sewell could not understand. She now said, "Oh! Mr. Barker!" and coldly gave him her hand. "Have you been well? Must you go?"

"Yes, thank you. I have got to be getting back. Well, good-evening." He bowed to the Sewells.

"You must come again to see me," said the minister, and looked at his wife.

"Yes, it has been a very long time since you were here," Mrs. Sewell added.

"I haven't had a great deal of time to myself," said Lemuel, and he contrived to get himself out of the room.

Sewell followed him down to the door, in the endeavor to say something more on the subject his wife had interrupted, but he only contrived to utter some feeble repetitions. He came back in vexation, which he visited upon Lemuel. "Silly fellow!" he exclaimed.

"What has he been doing now?" asked Mrs. Sewell, with reproachful discouragement.

"Oh, I don't know! I suspect that he's been involving himself in some ridiculous love affair!" Mrs. Sewell looked a silent inculpation. "It's largely conjecture on my part, of course,—he's about as confiding as an oyster!—but I fancy I have said some things in a conditional way that will give him pause. I suspect from his manner that he has entangled himself with some other young simpleton, and that he's ashamed of it, or tired of it, already. If that's the case, I have hit the nail on the head. I told him that a foolish, rash engagement was better broken than kept. The foolish marriages that people rush into are the greatest bane of life!"

"And would you really have advised him, David," asked his wife, "to break off an engagement if he had made one?"

"Of course I should! I——"

"Then I am glad I came in in time to prevent your doing anything so wicked."

"Wicked?" Sewell turned from his desk, where he was about to sit down, in astonishment.

"Yes! Do you think that nobody else is to be considered in such a thing? What about the poor, silly girl if he breaks off with her? Oh, you men are all alike! Even the best! You think it is a dreadful thing for a young man to be burdened with a foolish love affair at the beginning of his career; but you never think of the girl whose whole career is spoiled, perhaps, if the affair is broken off! Hasn't she any right to be considered?"

"I should think," said Sewell, distinctly daunted, "that they were equally fortunate if it were broken off."

"Oh, my dear, you know you don't think anything of the kind! If he has more mind than she has, and is capable of doing something in the world, he goes on and forgets her; but she remembers him. Perhaps it's her one chance in life to get married—to have a home. You know very well that in a case of that kind—a rash engagement, as you call it—both are to blame; and shall one do all the suffering? Very probably his fancy was taken first, and he followed her up, and flattered her into liking him; and now shall he leave her because he's tired of her?"

"Yes," said Sewell, recovering from the first confusion which his wife's unexpected difference of opinion had thrown him into, "I should think that was the very best reason in the world why he should leave her. Would his marrying make matters worse or better if he were tired of her? As for wickedness, I should feel myself guilty if I did not do my utmost to

prevent marriages between people when one or other wished
to break their engagement, and had not the moral courage to
do so. There is no more pernicious delusion than that one's
word ought to be kept in such an affair, after the heart has
gone out of it, simply because it's been given."

"David!"

But Sewell was not to be restrained. "I am right about this,
Lucy, and you know it. Half the miserable marriages in the
world could be prevented, if there were only some frank and
fearless adviser at hand to say to the foolish things that if they
no longer fully and freely love each other they can commit no
treason so deadly as being true to their word. I wish," he now
added, "that I could be the means of breaking off every marriage that the slightest element of doubt enters into beforehand. I should leave much less work for the divorce courts.
The trouble comes from that crazy and mischievous principle
of false self-sacrifice that I'm always crying out against. If a
man has ceased to love the woman he has promised to
marry—or *vice versa*—the best possible thing they can do,
the only righteous thing, is not to marry."

Mrs. Sewell could not deny this. She directed an oblique
attack from another quarter, as women do, while affecting not
to have changed her ground at all. "Very well, then, David, I
wish you would have nothing to do with that crazy and mischievous principle yourself. I wish you would let this ridiculous Barker of yours alone from this time forth. He has found
a good place, where he is of use, and where he is doing very
well. Now I think your responsibility is fairly ended. I hope
you won't meddle with his love affairs, if he has any; for if
you do, you will probably have your hands full. He is very
good-looking, and all sorts of silly little geese will be falling in
love with him."

"Well, so far his love troubles are purely conjectural," said
Sewell, with a laugh. "I'm bound to say that Barker himself
didn't say a word to justify the conjecture that he was either
in love or wished to be out of it. However, I've given him
some wholesome advice, which he'll be all the better for
taking, merely as a prophylactic, if nothing else."

"I am tired of him," sighed Mrs. Sewell. "Is he going to
keep perpetually turning up, in this way? I hope you were not

very pressing with him in your invitations to him to call again?"

Sewell smiled. "You were not, my dear."

"You let him take too much of your time. I was so provoked, when I heard you going on with him, that I came down to put an end to it."

"Well, you succeeded," said Sewell easily. "Don't you think he's greatly improved in the short time he's been in the city?"

"He's very well dressed. I hope he isn't extravagant."

"He's not only well dressed, but he's beginning to be well spoken. I believe he's beginning to observe that there is such a thing as not talking through the nose. He still says, 'I don't know *as*,' but most of the men they turn out of Harvard say that; I've heard some of the professors say it."

Mrs. Sewell was not apparently interested in this.

XXII

THAT NIGHT Lemuel told Mrs. Harmon that she must not expect him to do anything thenceforward but look after the accounts and the general management; she must get a head-waiter, and a boy to run the elevator. She consented to this, as she would have consented to almost anything else that he proposed.

He had become necessary to the management of the St. Albans in every department; and if the lady boarders felt that they could not now get on without him, Mrs. Harmon was even more dependent. With her still nominally at the head of affairs, and controlling the expenses as a whole, no radical reform could be effected. But there were details of the outlay in which Lemuel was of use, and he had brought greater comfort into the house for less money. He rejected her old and simple device of postponing the payment of debt as an economical measure, and substituted cash dealings with new purveyors. He gradually but inevitably took charge of the store-room, and stopped the waste there; early in his administration he had observed the gross and foolish prodigality with which the portions were sent from the carving-room, and after replacing Mrs. Harmon's nephew there, he established a standard portion that gave all the needed variety, and still kept the quantity within bounds. It came to his taking charge of this department entirely, and as steward he carved the meats, and saw that nothing was in a way to become cold before he opened the dining-room doors as head-waiter.

His activities promoted the leisure which Mrs. Harmon had always enjoyed, and which her increasing bulk fitted her to adorn. Her nephew willingly relinquished the dignity of steward. He said that his furnaces were as much as he wanted to take care of; especially as in former years, when it had begun to come spring, he had experienced a stress of mind in keeping the heat just right, when the ladies were all calling down the tubes for more of it or less of it, which he should now be very glad not to have complicated with other cares. He said that now he could look forward to the month of May with some pleasure.

The guests, sensibly or insensibly, according to their several temperaments, shared the increased ease that came from Lemuel's management. The service was better in every way; their beds were promptly made, their rooms were periodically swept; every night when they came up from dinner they found their pitchers of ice-water at their doors. This change was not accomplished without much of that rebellion and renunciation which was known at the St. Albans as kicking. Chambermaids and table-girls kicked, but they were replaced by Lemuel, who went himself to the intelligence office, and pledged the new ones to his rule beforehand. There was even some kicking among the guests, who objected to the new portions, and to having a second bill sent them if the first remained unpaid for a week; but the general sense of the hotel was in Lemuel's favor.

He had no great pleasure in the reform he had effected. His heart was not in it, except as waste and disorder and carelessness were painful to him. He suffered to promote a better state of things, as many a woman whose love is for books or pictures or society suffers for the perfection of her housekeeping, and sacrifices her tastes to achieve it. He would have liked better to read, to go to lectures, to hear sermons; with the knowledge of Mr. Evans's life as an editor and the incentive of a writer near him, he would have liked to try again if he could not write something, though the shame of his failure in Mr. Sewell's eyes had burned so deep. Above all, since he had begun to see how city people regarded the kind of work he had been doing, he would have liked to get out of the hotel business altogether, if he could have been sure of any other.

As the spring advanced his cares grew lighter. Most of the regular boarders went away to country hotels and became regular boarders there. Their places were only partially filled by transients from the South and West, who came and went, and left Lemuel large spaces of leisure, in which he read, or deputed Mrs. Harmon's nephew to the care of the office and pursued his studies of Boston, sometimes with Mr. Evans,— whose newspaper kept him in town, and who liked to prowl about with him, and to frequent the odd summer entertainments,—but mostly alone. They became friends after a fashion, and were in each other's confidence as regarded their opinions and ideas, rather than their history; now and then Evans dropped a word about the boy he had lost, or his wife's health, but Lemuel kept his past locked fast in his breast.

The art-students had gone early in the summer, and Berry had left Boston for Wyoming at the end of the spring term of the law school. He had not been able to make up his mind to pop before Miss Swan departed, but he thought he should fetch it by another winter; and he had got leave to write to her, on condition, he said, that he should conduct the whole correspondence himself.

Miss Carver had left Lemuel dreaming of her as an ideal, yet true, with a slow, rustic constancy, to Statira. For all that had been said and done, he had not swerved explicitly from her. There was no talk of marriage between them, and could not be; but they were lovers still, and when Miss Carver was gone, and the finer charm of her society was unfelt, he went back to much of the old pleasure he had felt in Statira's love. The resentment of her narrow-mindedness, the shame for her ignorance passed; the sense of her devotion remained.

'Manda Grier wanted her to go home with her for part of the summer, but she would not have consented if Lemuel had not insisted. She wrote him back ill-spelt, scrawly little letters, in one of which she told him that her cough was all gone, and she was as well as ever. She took a little more cold when she returned to town in the first harsh September weather, and her cough returned, but she said she did not call it anything now.

The hotel began to fill up again for the winter. Berry preceded the art-students by some nervous weeks, in which he speculated upon what he should do if they did not come at all. Then they came, and the winter passed, with repetitions of the last winter's events, and a store of common memories that enriched the present, and insensibly deepened the intimacy in which Lemuel found himself. He could not tell whither the present was carrying him; he only knew that he had drifted so far from the squalor of his past, that it seemed like the shadow of a shameful dream.

He did not go to see Statira so often as he used; and she was patient with his absences, and defended him against

'Manda Grier, who did not scruple to tell her that she believed the fellow was fooling with her, and who could not
always keep down a mounting dislike of Lemuel in his presence. One night toward spring, when he returned early from
Statira's, he found Berry in the office at the St. Albans. "That
you, old man?" he asked. "Well, I'm glad you've come. Just
going to leave a little Billy Ducks for you here, but now I
needn't. The young ladies sent me down to ask if you had a
copy of Whittier's poems; they want to find something in it. I
told 'em Longfellow would do just as well, but I couldn't
seem to convince 'em. They say he didn't write the particular
poem they want."

"Yes, I've got Whittier's poems here," said Lemuel, unlock-
ing his desk. "It belongs to Mr. Evans; I guess he won't care
if I lend it."

"Well, now, I tell you what," said Berry; "don't you let a
borrowed book like that go out of your hands. Heigh? You
just bring it up yourself. See?" He winked the eye next
Lemuel with exaggerated insinuation. "They'll respect you all
the more for being so scrupulous, and I guess they won't be
very much disappointed on general principles if you come
along. There's lots of human nature in girls—the best of 'em.
I'll tell 'em I left you lookin' for it. I don't mind a lie or two in
a good cause. But you hurry along up, now."

He was gone before Lemuel could stop him; he could not
do anything but follow.

It appeared that it was Miss Swan who wished to see the
poem; she could not remember the name of it, but she was
sure she should know it if she saw it in the index. She mingled these statements with her greetings to Lemuel, and Miss
Carver seemed as glad to see him. She had a little more color
than usual, and they were all smiling, so that he knew Berry
had been getting off some of his jokes. But he did not care.

Miss Swan found the poem as she had predicted, and,
"Now all keep still," she said, "and I'll read it." But she suddenly added, "Or no; you read it, Mr. Barker, won't you?"

"If Barker ain't just in voice to-night, *I'll* read it," suggested
Berry.

But she would not let him make this diversion. She ignored
his offer, and insisted upon Lemuel's reading. "Jessie says you

read beautifully. That passage in 'Romola,' " she reminded him; but Lemuel said it was only a few lines, and tried to excuse himself. At heart he was proud of his reading, and he ended by taking the book.

When he had finished the two girls sighed.

"Isn't it beautiful, Jessie?" said Miss Swan.

"Beautiful!" answered her friend.

Berry yawned.

"Well, I don't see much difference between that and a poem of Longfellow's. Why wouldn't Longfellow have done just as well? Honestly, now! Why isn't one poem just as good as another, for all practical purposes?"

"It is, for some people," said Miss Swan.

Berry figured an extreme anguish by writhing in his chair. Miss Swan laughed in spite of herself, and they began to talk in their usual banter, which Miss Carver never took part in, and which Lemuel was quite incapable of sharing. If it had come to savage sarcasm or a logical encounter, he could have held his own, but he had a natural weight and slowness that disabled him from keeping up with Berry's light talk; he envied it, because it seemed to make everybody like him, and Lemuel would willingly have been liked.

Miss Carver began to talk to him about the book, and then about Mr. Evans. She asked him if he went much to his rooms, and Lemuel said no, not at all, since the first time Mr. Evans had asked him up. He said, after a pause, that he did not know whether he wanted him to come.

"I should think he would," said Miss Carver. "It must be very gloomy for him, with his wife such an invalid. He seems naturally such a gay person."

"Yes, that's what I think," said Lemuel.

"I wonder," said the girl, "if it seems to you harder for a naturally cheerful person to bear things, than for one who has always been rather melancholy?"

"Yes, it does!" he answered with the pleasure and surprise young people have in discovering any community of feeling; they have thought themselves so utterly unlike each other. "I wonder why it should?"

"I don't know; perhaps it isn't so. But I always pity the cheerful person the most."

They recognized an amusing unreason in this, and laughed. Miss Swan across the room had caught the name.

"Are you talking of Mrs. Evans?"

Berry got his banjo down from the wall, where Miss Swan allowed him to keep it as bric-à-brac, and began to tune it.

"I don't believe it agrees with this banjoseph being an object of virtue," he said. "What shall it be, ladies? Something light and gay, adapted to disperse gloomy reflections?" He played a fandango. "How do you like that? It has a tinge of melancholy in it, and yet it's lively too, as a friend of mine used to say about the Dead March."

"Was his name Berry?" asked Miss Swan.

"Not Alonzo W., Jr.," returned Berry tranquilly, and he and Miss Swan began to joke together.

"I know a friend of Mr. Evans's," said Lemuel to Miss Carver. "Mr. Sewell. Have you ever heard him preach?"

"Oh, yes, indeed. We go nearly every Sunday morning."

"I nearly always go in the evening now," said Lemuel. "Don't you like him?"

"Yes," said the girl. "There's something about him — I don't know what — that doesn't leave you feeling how bad you are, but makes you want to be better. He helps you so; and he's so clear. And he shows that he's had all the mean and silly thoughts that you have. I don't know — it's as if he were talking for each person alone."

"Yes, that is exactly the way I feel!" Lemuel was proud of the coincidence. He said, to commend himself further to Miss Carver, "I have just been round to see him."

"I should think you would value his acquaintance beyond anything," said the girl. "Is he just as earnest and simple as he is in the pulpit?"

"He's just the same, every way." Lemuel went a little further: "I knew him before I came to Boston. He boarded one summer where we live." As he spoke he thought of the gray, old, unpainted house, and of his brother-in-law with his stocking-feet on the stove-hearth, and his mother's bloomers; he thought of his arrest, and his night in the police-station, his trial, and the Wayfarer's Lodge; and he wondered that he could think of such things and still look such a girl in the face. But he was not without the strange

joy in their being unknown to her which reserved and latent
natures feel in mere reticence, and which we all experience in
some degree when we talk with people and think of our undiscovered lives.

They went on a long time, matching their opinions and
feelings about many things, as young people do, and fancying
that much of what they said was new with them. When he
came away after ten o'clock, he thought of one of the things
that Sewell had said about the society of refined and noble
women: it was not so much what they said or did that
helped; it was something in them that made men say and do
their best, and help themselves to be refined and noble men,
to make the most of themselves in their presence. He believed
that this was what Miss Carver had done, and he thought
how different it was with him when he came away from an
evening with Statira. Again he experienced that compassion
for her, in the midst of his pride and exultation; he asked
himself what he could do to help her; he did not see how she
could be changed.

Berry followed him downstairs, and wanted to talk the
evening over.

"I don't see how I'm going to stand it much longer,
Barker," he said. "I shall have to pop pretty soon or die, one
of the two; and I'm afraid either one'll kill me. Wasn't she
lovely to-night? Honey in the comb, sugar in the gourd, *I*
say! I wonder what it is about popping, anyway, that makes it
so hard, Barker? It's simply a matter of business, if you come
to boil it down. You offer a fellow so many cattle, and let him
take 'em or leave 'em. But if the fellow happens to have on a
long, slim, olive-green dress of some color, and holds her
head like a whole floral tribute on a stem, and *you* happen to
be the cattle you're offering, you can't feel so independent
about it, somehow. Well, what's the use? She's a daisy, if ever
there was one. Ever notice what a peculiar blue her eyes
are?"

"Blue?" said Lemuel. "They're brown."

"Look here, old man," said Berry compassionately, "do you
think I've come down here to fool away my time talking
about Miss Carver? We'll take some Saturday afternoon for
that, when we haven't got anything else to do; but it's Miss

Swan that has the floor at present. What were you two talking about over there, so long? I can't get along with Miss Carver worth a cent."

"I hardly know what we did talk about," said Lemuel dreamily.

"Well, I've got the same complaint. I couldn't tell you ten words that Madeline said—in thine absence let me call thee Madeline, sweet!—but I knew it was making an immortal spirit of me, right straight along, every time. The worst thing about an evening like this is, it don't seem to last any time at all. Why, when those girls began to put up their hands to hide their yawns, I felt like I was just starting in for a short call. I wish I could have had a good phonograph around. I'd put it on my sleepless pillow, and unwind its precious record all through the watches of the night." He imitated the thin phantasmal squeak of the instrument in repeating a number of Miss Swan's characteristic phrases. "Yes, sir, a pocket phonograph is the thing I'm after."

"I don't see how you can talk the way you do," said Lemuel, shuddering inwardly at Berry's audacious freedom, and yet finding a certain comfort in it.

"That's just the way I felt myself at first. But you'll get over it as you go along. The nicest thing about their style of angel is that they're perfectly human, after all. You don't believe it now, of course, but you will."

It only heightened Lemuel's conception of Miss Carver's character to have Berry talk so lightly and daringly of her, in her relation to him. He lay long awake after he went to bed, and in the turmoil of his thoughts one thing was clear: so pure and high a being must never know anything of his shameful past, which seemed to dishonor her through his mere vicinity. He must go far from her, and she must not know why; but long afterwards Mr. Sewell would tell her, and then she would understand. He owed her this all the more because he could see now that she was not one of the silly persons, as Mr. Sewell called them, who would think meanly of him for having, in his ignorance and inexperience, done a servant's work. His mind had changed about that, and he wondered that he could ever have suspected her of such a thing.

About noon the next day the street-door was opened hesitatingly, as if by some one not used to the place; and when Lemuel looked up from the *menus* he was writing, he saw the figure of one of those tramps who from time to time presented themselves and pretended to want work. He scanned the vagabond sharply, as he stood molding a soft hat on his hands, and trying to superinduce an air of piteous appeal upon the natural gayety of his swarthy face. "Well! what's wanted?"

A dawning conjecture that had flickered up in the tramp's eyes flashed into full recognition.

"Why, mate!"

Lemuel's heart stood still. "What—what do you want here?"

"Why, don't you know me, mate?"

All his calamity confronted Lemuel.

"No," he said, but nothing in him supported the lie he had uttered.

"Wayfarer's Lodge?" suggested the other cheerfully. "Don't you remember?"

"No——"

"I guess you do," said the mate easily. "Anyway, I remember you."

Lemuel's feeble defense gave way. "Come in here," he said, and he shut the door upon the intruder and himself, and submitted to his fate. "What is it?" he asked huskily.

"Why, mate! what's the matter? Nobody's goin' to hurt you," said the other encouragingly. "What's your lay here?"

"Lay?"

"Yes. Got a job here?"

"I'm the clerk," said Lemuel, with the ghost of his former pride of office.

"Clerk?" said the tramp with good-humored incredulity. "Where's your diamond pin? Where's your rings?" He seemed willing to prolong the playful inquiry. "Where's your patent-leather boots?"

"It's not a common hotel. It's a sort of a family hotel, and I'm the clerk. What do you want?"

The young fellow lounged back easily in his chair. "Why, I *did* drop in to beat the house out of a quarter if I could, or may be ten cents. Thank you, sir. God bless you, sir." He interrupted himself to burlesque a professional gratitude. "That style of thing, you know. But I don't know about it now. Look here, mate! what's the reason you couldn't get me a job here too? I been off on a six months' cruise since I saw you, and I'd like a job on shore first-rate. Couldn't you kind of ring me in for something? I ain't afraid of work, although I never did pretend to love it. But I should like to reform now, and get into something steady. Heigh?"

"There isn't anything to do—there's no place for you," Lemuel began.

"Oh, pshaw, now, mate, you think!" pleaded the other. "I'll take any sort of a job; I don't care what it is. I ain't got any o' that false modesty about me. Been round too much. And I don't want to go back to the Wayfarer's Lodge. It's a good place, and I know my welcome's warm and waitin' for me, between two hot plates; but the thing of it is, it's demoralizin'. That's what the chaplain said just afore I left the—ship, 'n' I promised him I'd give work a try, anyway. Now you just think up something! I ain't in any hurry." In proof he threw his soft hat on the desk, and took up one of the *menus*. "This your bill of fare? Well, it ain't bad! Vurmiselly soup, boiled holibut, roast beef, roast turkey with cranberry sauce, roast pork with apple sauce, chicken croquettes, ditto patties, three kinds of pie; bread puddin', both kinds of sauce; ice cream, nuts, and coffee. Why, mate!"

Lemuel sat dumb and motionless. He could see no way out of the net that had entangled him. He began feebly to repeat, "There isn't anything," when some one tried the door.

"Mr. Barker!" called Mrs. Harmon. "You in there?"

He made it worse by waiting a moment before he rose and opened the door. "I didn't know I'd locked it." The lie came unbidden; he groaned inwardly to think how he was telling nothing but lies. Mrs. Harmon did not come in. She glanced with a little question at the young fellow who had gathered his hat from the table, and risen with gay politeness.

It was a crisis of the old sort; the elevator-boy had kicked, and Mrs. Harmon said, "I just stopped to say that I was going out and I could stop at the intelligence office myself to get an elevator-boy——"

The mate took the word with a joyous laugh at the coincidence. "It's just what me and Mr. Barker was talkin' about! I'm from up his way, and I've just come down to Boston to see if I couldn't look up a job; and he was tellin' me, in here, about your wantin' a telegraph—I mean a elevator-boy, but he didn't think it would suit me. But I should like to give it a try, anyway. It's pretty dull up our way, and I got to do something. Mr. Barker'll tell you who I am."

He winked at Lemuel with the eye not exposed to Mrs. Harmon, and gave her a broad, frank, prepossessing smile.

"Well, of course," said Mrs. Harmon smoothly, "any friend of Mr. Barker's——"

"We just been talkin' over old times in here," interrupted the mate. "I guess it was me shoved that bolt in. I didn't want to have anybody see me talkin' with him till I'd got some clothes that would be a little more of a credit to him."

"Well, that's right," said Mrs. Harmon appreciatively. "I always like to have everybody around my house looking neat and respectable. I keep a first-class house, and I don't have any but first-class help, and I expect them to dress accordingly, from the highest to the lowest."

"Yes, ma'am," said the mate, "that's the way I felt about it myself, me and Mr. Barker both; and he was just tellin' me that if I was a mind to give the elevator a try, he'd lend me a suit of *his* clothes."

"Very well, then," said Mrs. Harmon; "if Mr. Barker and you are a mind to fix it up between you——"

"Oh, we are!" said the mate. "There won't be any trouble about that."

"I don't suppose I need to stop at the intelligence office. I presume Mr. Barker will show you how to work the elevator. He helped us out with it himself at first."

"Yes, that's what he said," the other chimed in. "But I guess I better go and change my clothes first. Well, mate," he added to Lemuel, "I'm ready when you're ready."

Lemuel rose trembling from the chair where he had been chained, as it seemed to him, while the mate and Mrs. Harmon arranged their affair with his tacit connivance. He had not spoken a word; he feared so much to open his lips lest another lie should come out of them, that his sense of that danger was hardly less than his terror at the captivity in which he found himself.

"Yes," said Mrs. Harmon, "I'll look after the office till you get back. Mr. Barker'll show you where you can sleep."

"Thank you, ma'am," said the mate, with gratitude that won upon her.

"And I'm glad," she added, "that it's a friend of Mr. Barker's that's going to have the place. We think everything of Mr. Barker here."

"Well, you can't think more of him than what we do up home," rejoined the other with generous enthusiasm.

In Lemuel's room he was not less appreciative. "Why, mate, it does me good to see how you've got along. I got to write a letter home at once, and tell the folks what friends you've got in Boston. I don't believe they half understand it." He smiled joyously upon Lemuel, who stood stock still, with such despair in his face that probably the wretch pitied him.

"Look here, mate, don't you be afraid now! I'm on the reform lay with all my might, and I mean business. I ain't a-goin' to do you any harm, you bet your life. These your things?" he asked, taking Lemuel's winter suit from the hooks where they hung, and beginning to pull off his coat. He talked on while he changed his dress. "I was led away, and I got my come-uppings, or the other fellow's come-uppings, for *I* wa'n't to blame any, and I always said so, and I guess the judge would say so too, if it was to do over again."

A frightful thought stung Lemuel to life. "The judge? Was it a passenger-ship?"

The other stopped buttoning Lemuel's trousers round him to slap himself on the thigh. "Why, mate! don't you know enough to know what a *sea voyage* is? Why, I've been down to the *Island* for the last six months! Hain't you never heard it called a sea voyage? Why, we *always* come off from a cruise when we git back! You don't mean to say you never *been* one?"

"Oh, my goodness!" groaned Lemuel. "Have—have you been in prison?"

"Why, of course."

"Oh, what am I going to do?" whispered the miserable creature to himself.

The other heard him. "Why, you hain't got to do anything! I'm on the reform, and you might leave everything layin' around loose, and I shouldn't touch it. Fact! You ask the ship's chaplain."

He laughed in the midst of his assertions of good resolutions, but sobered to the full extent, probably, of his face and nature, and tying Lemuel's cravat on at the glass, he said, solemnly, "Mate, it's all right. I'm on the reform."

XXIII

L EMUEL'S FRIEND entered upon his duties with what may almost be called artistic zeal. He showed a masterly touch in managing the elevator from the first trip. He was ready, cheerful, and obliging; he lacked nothing but a little more reluctance and a Seaside Library novel to be a perfect elevator-boy.

The ladies liked him at once; he was so pleasant and talkative, and so full of pride in Lemuel that they could not help liking him; and several of them promptly reached that stage of confidence where they told him, as an old friend of Lemuel's, they thought Lemuel read too much, and was going to kill himself if he kept on a great deal longer. The mate said he thought so too, and had noticed how bad Lemuel looked the minute he set eyes on him. But, he asked, what was the use? He had said everything he could to him about it. He was always just so, up at home. As he found opportunity he did what he could to console Lemuel with furtive winks and nods.

Lemuel dragged absently and haggardly through the day. In the evening he told Mrs. Harmon that he had to go round and see Mr. Sewell a moment. It was then nine o'clock, and she readily assented; she guessed Mr. Williams—he had told her his name was Williams—could look after the office while he was gone. Mr. Williams was generously glad to do so. Behind Mrs. Harmon's smooth, large form, he playfully threatened her with his hand leveled at his shoulder; but even this failed to gladden Lemuel.

It was half-past nine when he reached the minister's house, and the maid had a visible reluctance at the door in owning that Mr. Sewell was at home. Mrs. Sewell had instructed her not to be too eagerly candid with people who came so late; but he was admitted, and Sewell came down from his study to see him in the reception-room.

"What is the matter?" he asked at once, when he caught sight of Lemuel's face; "has anything gone wrong with you, Mr. Barker?" He could not help being moved by the boy's looks; he had a fleeting wish that Mrs. Sewell were there to see him, and be moved too; and he prepared himself as he might to treat the trouble which he now expected to be poured out.

"Yes," said Lemuel, "I want to tell you; I want you to tell me what to do."

When he had put the case fully before the minister, his listener was aware of wishing that it had been a love-trouble, such as he foreboded at first.

He drew a long and deep breath, and before he began to speak he searched himself for some comfort or encouragement, while Lemuel anxiously scanned his face.

"Yes—yes! I see your—difficulty," he began, making the futile attempt to disown any share in it. "But perhaps—perhaps it isn't so bad as it seems. Perhaps no harm will come. Perhaps he really means to do well; and if you are vigilant in—in keeping him out of temptation——" Sewell stopped, sensible that he was not coming to anything, and rubbed his forehead.

"Do you think," asked Lemuel, dry-mouthed with misery, "that I ought to have told Mrs. Harmon at once?"

"Why, it is always best to be truthful and above-board—as a principle," said the minister, feeling himself somehow dragged from his moorings.

"Then I had better do it yet!"

"Yes," said Sewell, and he paused. "Yes. That is to say— As the mischief is done— Perhaps—perhaps there is no haste. If you exercise vigilance— But if he has been in prison— Do you know what he was in for?"

"No. I didn't know he had been in at all till we got to my room. And then I couldn't ask him—I was afraid to."

"Yes," said Sewell, kindly if helplessly.

"I was afraid, if I sent him off—or tried to—that he would tell about my being in the Wayfarer's Lodge that night, and they would think I had been a tramp. I could have done it, but I thought he might tell some lie about me; and they might get to know about the trial——"

"I see," said Sewell.

"I hated to lie," said Lemuel piteously, "but I seemed to have to."

There was another yes on the minister's tongue; he kept it

back; but he was aware of an instant's relief in the speculation—the question presented itself abstractly—as to whether
it was ever justifiable or excusable to lie. Were the Jesuitical
casuists possibly right in some slight, shadowy sort? He came
back to Lemuel groaning in spirit. "No—no—no!" he
sighed; "we mustn't admit that you *had* to lie. We must never
admit that." A truth flashed so vividly upon him that it
seemed almost escape. "What worse thing could have come
from telling the truth than has come from withholding it?
And that would have been some sort of end, and this—this is
only the miserable beginning."

"Yes," said Lemuel, with all desirable humility. "But I
couldn't see it at once."

"Oh, I don't blame you; I don't blame *you*," said Sewell. "It
was a sore temptation. I blame *myself*!" he exclaimed, with
more comprehensiveness than Lemuel knew; but he limited
his self-accusal by adding, "I ought to have told Mrs. Harmon
myself what I knew of your history; but I refrained because I
knew you had never done any harm, and I thought it cruel
that you should be dishonored by your misfortunes in a relation where you were usefully and prosperously placed; and
so—and so I didn't. But perhaps I was wrong. Yes, I was
wrong. I have only allowed the burden to fall more heavily
upon you at last."

It was respite for Lemuel to have some one else accusing
himself, and he did not refuse to enjoy it. He left the minister
to wring all the bitterness he could for himself out of his final
responsibility. The drowning man strangles his rescuer.

Sewell looked up, and loosened his collar as if really stifling. "Well, well. We must find some way out of it. I will
see—see what can be done for you to-morrow."

Lemuel recognized his dismissal. "If you say so, Mr. Sewell,
I will go straight back and tell Mrs. Harmon all about it."

Sewell rose too. "No—no. There is no such haste. You had
better leave it to me now. I will see to it—in the morning."

"Thank you," said Lemuel. "I hate to give you so much
trouble."

"Oh," said Sewell, letting him out at the street-door, and
putting probably less thought and meaning into the polite
words than they had ever contained before, "it's no trouble."

He went upstairs to his study, and found Mrs. Sewell waiting there. "Well, *now*—what, David?"

"Now what?" he feebly echoed.

"Yes. What has that wretched creature come for now?"

"You may well call him a wretched creature," sighed Sewell.

"Is he really engaged? Has he come to get you to marry him?"

"I think he'd rather have me bury him at present." Sewell sat down, and, bracing his elbow on his desk, rested his head heavily on his hand.

"Well," said his wife, with a touch of compassion tempering her curiosity.

He began to tell her what had happened, and he did not spare himself in the statement of the case. "There you have the whole affair now. And a very pretty affair it is. But, I declare," he concluded, "I can't see that any one is to blame for it."

"No one, David?"

"Well, Adam, finally, of course. Or Eve. Or the Serpent," replied the desperate man.

Seeing him at this reckless pass, his wife forbore reproach, and asked, "What are you going to do?"

"I am going around there in the morning to tell Mrs. Harmon all about Barker."

"She will send him away instantly."

"I dare say."

"And what will the poor thing do?"

"Goodness knows."

"I'm afraid Badness knows. It will drive him to despair."

"Well, perhaps not—perhaps not," sighed the minister. "At any rate, we must not *let* him be driven to despair. You must help me, Lucy."

"Of course."

Mrs. Sewell was a good woman, and she liked to make her husband feel it keenly.

"I knew that it must come to that," she said. "Of course, we must not let him be ruined. If Mrs. Harmon insists upon his going at once—as I've no doubt she will—you must bring him here, and we must keep him till he can find some other home." She waited, and added, for a final stroke of merciless beneficence, "He can have Alfred's room, and Alf can take the front attic."

Sewell only sighed again. He knew she did not mean this.

Barker went back to the St. Albans, and shrunk into as small space in the office as he could. He pulled a book before him and pretended to read, hiding the side of his face toward the door with the hand that supported his head. His hand was cold as ice, and it seemed to him as if his head were in a flame. Williams came and looked in at him once, and then went back to the stool which he occupied just outside the elevator-shaft, when not running it. He whistled softly between his teeth, with intervals of respectful silence, and then went on whistling in absence of any whom it might offend.

Suddenly a muffled clamor made itself heard from the depths of the dining-room, like that noise of voices which is heard behind the scenes at the theater when an armed mob is about to burst upon the stage. Irish tones, high, windy, and angry, yells, and oaths defined themselves, and Mrs. Harmon came obesely hurrying from the dining-room toward the office, closely followed by Jerry, the porter. When upon duty, or, as some of the boarders contended, when in the right humor, he blacked the boots, and made the hard-coal fires, and carried the trunks up and down stairs. When in the wrong humor, he had sometimes been heard to swear at Mrs. Harmon, but she had excused him in this eccentricity because, she said, he had been with her so long. Those who excused it with her on these grounds conjectured arrears of wages as another reason for her patience. His outbreaks of bad temper had the Celtic uncertainty; the most innocent touch excited them, as sometimes the broadest snub failed to do so; and no one could foretell what direction his zigzag fury would take. He had disliked Lemuel from the first, and had chafed at the subordination into which he had necessarily fallen. He was now yelling after Mrs. Harmon, to know if she was not satisfied with *wan* gutther-snoipe, that she must nades go and pick up another, and whether the new wan was going to be too good too to take prisints of money for his worruk from the boarthers, and put all the rest of the help under the caumpliment of refusin' ut, or else demanin' themselves by takin' ut? If this was the case, he'd have her to know that she couldn't

kape anny other help; and the quicker she found it out the
betther. Mrs. Harmon was trying to appease him by promising to see Lemuel at once, and ask him about it.

The porter raised his voice an octave. "D'ye think I'm a
loyar, domn ye? Don't ye think I'm tellin' the thruth?"

He followed her to the little office, whither she had retreated on a purely mechanical fulfillment of her promise to
speak to Lemuel, and crowded in upon them there.

"Here he is now!" he roared in his frenzy. "He's too good
to take the money that's offered to 'um! He's too good to be
waither! He wannts to play the gintleman! He thinks 'umself
too good to do what the other servants do, that's been tin
times as lahng in the house!"

At the noise some of the ladies came hurrying out of the
public parlor to see what the trouble was. The street-door
opened, and Berry entered with the two art-students. They
involuntarily joined the group of terrified ladies.

"What's the row?" demanded Berry. "Is Jerry on the kick?"

No one answered. Lemuel stood pale and silent, fronting
the porter, who was shaking his fist in his face. He had not
heard anything definite in the outrage that assailed him. He
only conjectured that it was exposure of Williams's character,
and the story of his own career in Boston.

"Why don't you fire him out of there, Barker?" called the
law-student. "Don't be afraid of him!"

Lemuel remained motionless; but his glance sought the
pitying eyes of the assembled women, and then dropped before the amaze that looked at him from those of Miss Carver.
The porter kept roaring out his infamies.

Berry spoke again.

"Mrs. Harmon, do you want that fellow in there?"

"No, goodness knows I don't, Mr. Berry."

"All right." Berry swung the street-door open with his left
hand, and seemed with the same gesture to lay his clutch
upon the porter's collar. "Fire him out myself!" he exclaimed, and with a few swiftly successive jerks and bumps,
the burly shape of the porter was shot into the night. "I want
you to get me an officer, Jerry," he said, putting his head out
after him. "There's been a blackguard makin' a row here.
Never mind your hat! Go!"

"Oh, my good gracious, Mr. Berry!" gasped Mrs. Harmon, "what have you done?"

"If it's back pay, Mrs. Harmon, we'll pass round the hat. Don't you be troubled. That fellow wasn't fit to be in a decent house."

Berry stopped a moment and looked at Lemuel. The art-students did not look at him at all; they passed on upstairs with Berry.

The other ladies remained to question and to comment. Mrs. Harmon's nephew, to whom the uproar seemed to have penetrated in his basement, came up and heard the story from them. He was quite decided. He said that Mr. Berry had done right. He said that he was tired of having folks damn his aunt up hill and down dale; and that if Jerry had kept on a great deal longer, he would have said something to him himself about it.

The ladies justified him in the stand he took; they returned to the parlor to talk it all over, and he went back to his basement. Mrs. Harmon, in tears, retired to her room, and Lemuel was left standing alone in his office. The mate stole softly to him from the background of the elevator, where he had kept himself in safety during the outbreak.

"Look here, mate. This thing been about your ringin' me in here?"

"Oh, go away, go away!" Lemuel huskily entreated.

"Well, that's what I intend to do. I don't want to stay here and git you into no more trouble, and I know that's what's been done. You never done me no harm, and I don't want to do you none. I'm goin' right up to your room to git my clo'es, and then I'll skip."

"It won't do any good now. It'll only make it worse. You'd better stay now. You must."

"Well, if you say so, mate."

He went back to his elevator, and Lemuel sat down at his desk, and dropped his face upon his arms there. Toward eleven o'clock Evans came in and looked at him, but without speaking; he must have concluded that he was asleep; he went upstairs, but after a while he came down again and stopped again at the office door, and looked in on the haggard boy, hesitating as if for the best words. "Barker, Mr. Berry has been telling me about your difficulty here. I know all about you—from Mr. Sewell." Lemuel stared at him. "And I will stand your friend, whatever people think. And I don't blame you for not wanting to be beaten by that ruffian; you could have stood no chance against him; and if you had thrashed him it wouldn't have been a great triumph."

"I wish he had killed me," said Lemuel from his dust-dry throat.

"Oh, no; that's foolish," said the elder, with patient, sad kindness. "Who knows whether death is the end of trouble? We must live things down, not lie them down." He put his arm caressingly across the boy's shoulder.

"I can never live this down," said Lemuel. He added passionately, "I wish I could die!"

"No," said Evans. "You must cheer up. Think of next Saturday. It will soon be here, and then you'll be astonished that you felt so bad on Tuesday."

He gave Lemuel a parting pressure with his arm, and turned to go upstairs.

At the same moment the figure of Mrs. Harmon's nephew, distracted, violent, burst up through the door leading to the basement.

"Good heavens!" exclaimed the editor, "is Mr. Harmon going to kick?"

"The house is on fire!" yelled the apparition.

A thick cloud of smoke gushed out of the elevator-shaft, and poured into the hall, which it seemed to fill instantly. It grew denser, and in another instant a wild hubbub began. The people appeared from every quarter, and ran into the street, where some of the ladies began calling up at the windows to those who were still in their rooms. A stout little old lady came to an open window, and paid out hand over hand a small cable, on which she meant to descend to the pavement; she had carried this rope about with her many years against the exigency to which she was now applying it. Within, the halls and the stairway became the scene of frantic encounter between wives and husbands rushing down to save themselves, and then rushing back to save their forgotten friends. Many appeared in the simple white in which they had left their beds, with the addition of such shawls or rugs as chance suggested. A house was opened to the fugitives on the other side of the street, and the crowd that had collected could not repress its applause when one of them escaped from the hotel-door and shot across. It applauded impartially men, women, and children, and, absorbed in the spectacle, no one sounded the fire-alarm; the department began to be severely condemned among the bystanders before the engines appeared.

Most of the ladies, in their escape or their purpose of rescue, tried each to possess herself of Lemuel, and keep him solely in her interest. "Mr. Barker! Mr. Barker! Mr. Barker!" was called for in various sopranos and contraltos, till an outsider took up the cry and shouted "Barker! Barker! Speech! Speech!" This made him very popular with the crowd, who in their enjoyment of the fugitives were unable to regard the fire seriously. A momentary diversion was caused by an elderly gentleman who came to the hotel-door, completely dressed except that he was in his stockings, and demanded Jerry. The humorist who had called for a speech from Lemuel volunteered the statement that Jerry had just gone round the corner to see a man. "I want him," said the old gentleman savagely. "I want my boots; I can't go about in my stockings."

Cries for Jerry followed; but in fact the porter had forgotten all his grudges and enmities; he had reappeared, in perfect temper, and had joined Lemuel and Berry in helping to get the women and children out of the burning house.

The police had set a guard at the door, in whom Lemuel recognized the friendly old officer who had arrested him. "All out?" asked the policeman.

The smoke, which had reddened and reddened, was now a thin veil drawn over the volume of flame that burned strongly and steadily up the well of the elevator, and darted its tongues out to lick the framework without. The heat was intense. Mrs. Harmon came panting and weeping from the dining-room with some unimportant pieces of silver, driven forward by Jerry and her nephew.

They met the firemen, come at last, and pulling in their hose, who began to play upon the flames; the steam filled the place with a dense mist.

Lemuel heard Berry ask him through the fog, "Barker, where's old Evans?"

"Oh, I don't know!" he lamented back. "He must have gone up to get Mrs. Evans."

He made a dash toward the stairs. A fireman caught him and pulled him back. "You can't go up; smoke's thick as hell up there." But Lemuel pulled away, and shot up the stairs. He heard the firemen stop Berry.

"You can't go, I tell you! Who's runnin' this fire anyway, I'd like to know?"

He ran along the corridor which Evans's apartment opened upon. There was not much smoke there; it had drawn up the elevator-well, as if in a chimney.

He burst into the apartment and ran to the inner room, where he had once caught a glimpse of Mrs. Evans sitting by the window.

Evans stood leaning against the wall, with his hand at his breast. He panted, "Help her—help——"

"Where *is* she? Where *is* she?" demanded Lemuel.

She came from an alcove in the room, holding a handkerchief drenched with cologne in her hand, which she passed to her husband's face. "Are you better now? Can you come, dear? Rest on me!"

"I'm—I'm all right! Go—go! I can get along——"

"I'll go when *you* go," said Mrs. Evans. She turned to Lemuel. "Mr. Evans fainted; but he is better now." She took his hand with a tender tranquillity that ignored all danger or even excitement, and gently chafed it.

"But come—come!" cried Lemuel. "Don't you know the house is on fire?"

"Yes, I know it," she replied. "We must get Mr. Evans down. You must help me." Lemuel had seldom seen her before; but he had so long heard and talked of her hopeless invalidism that she was like one risen from the dead, in her sudden strength and courage, and he stared at the miracle of her restoration. It was she who claimed and bore the greater share of the burden in getting her husband away. He was helpless; but in the open air he caught his breath more fully, and at last could tremulously find his way out of the sympathetic crowd. "Get a carriage," she said to Lemuel; and then she added, as it drove up and she gave an address, "I can manage him now."

Evans weakly pressed Lemuel's hand from the seat to which he had helped him, and the hack drove away. Lemuel looked crazily after it a moment, and then returned to the burning house.

Berry called to him from the top of the outside steps, "Barker, have you seen that partner of yours?"

Lemuel ran up to him. "No!"

"Well, come in here. The elevator's dropped, and they're afraid he went down with it."

"I know he didn't! He wouldn't be such a fool!"

"Well, we'll know when they get the fire under."

"I thought I saw something in the elevator, and as long as you don't know where he is——" said a fireman.

"Well," said Berry, "if you've got the upper hands of this thing, I'm going to my room a minute."

Lemuel followed him upstairs, to see if he could find Williams. The steam had ascended and filled the upper halls; little cascades of water poured down the stairs, falling from step to step; the long strips of carpeting in the corridors swam in the deluge which the hose had poured into the building, and a rain of heavy drops burst through the ceilings.

Most of the room-doors stood open, as the people had flung them wide in their rush for life. At the door of Berry's room a figure appeared, which he promptly seized by the throat.

"Don't be in a hurry!" he said, as he pushed it into the room. "I want to see you."

It was Williams.

"I want to see what you've got in your pockets. Hold on to him, Barker."

Lemuel had no choice. He held Williams by the arms while Berry went through him, as he called the search. He found upon him whatever small articles of value there had been in his room.

The thief submitted without a struggle, without a murmur.

Berry turned scornfully to Lemuel. "This a friend of yours, Mr. Barker?"

Still the thief did not speak, but he looked at Lemuel.

"Yes," he dryly gasped.

"Well!" said Berry, staring fiercely at him for a moment. "If it wasn't for something old Evans said to me about you, a little while ago, I'd hand you both over to the police."

Williams seemed to bear the threat with philosophic resignation, but Lemuel shrank back in terror. Berry laughed.

"Why, you *are* his pal. Go along! I'll get Jerry to attend to you."

Lemuel slunk downstairs with Williams. "Look here, mate," said the rogue; "I guess I ha'n't used you just right."

Lemuel expected himself to cast the thief off with bitter rejection. But he heard himself saying hopelessly, "Go away, and try to behave yourself," and then he saw the thief make the most of the favor of heaven and vanish through the crowd.

He would have liked to steal away too; but he remained, and began mechanically helping again wherever he saw help needed. By and by Berry came out; Lemuel thought that he would tell some policeman to arrest him; but he went away without speaking to any one.

In an hour the firemen had finished their share of the havoc, and had saved the building. They had kept the fire to the elevator-shaft and the adjoining wood-work, and but for the water they had poured into the place the ladies might have returned to their rooms, which were quite untouched by the flames. As it was, Lemuel joined with Jerry in fetching such things to them as their needs or fancies suggested; the refugees across the way were finally clothed by their efforts, and were able to quit their covert indistinguishable in dress from any of the other boarders.

The crowd began to go about its business. The engines had disappeared from the little street with exultant shrieks; in the morning the insurance companies would send their workmen to sweep out the extinct volcano, and mop up the shrunken deluge, preparatory to ascertaining the extent of the damage done; in the mean time the police kept the boys and loafers out of the building, and the order that begins to establish itself as soon as chaos is confessed took possession of the ruin.

But it was all the same a ruin and a calamitous conclusion for the time being. The place that had been in its grotesque and insufficient fashion a home for so many homeless people was uninhabitable; even the Harmons could not go back to it.

The boarders had all scattered, but Mrs. Harmon lingered, dwelling volubly upon the scene of disaster. She did not do much else; she was not without a just pride in it, but she was not puffed up by all the sympathy and consolation that had been offered her. She thought of others in the midst of her own troubles, and she said to Lemuel, who had remained working with Jerry under her direction in putting together such things as she felt she must take away with her:

"Well, I don't know as I feel much worse about myself than I do about poor Mr. Evans. Why, I've got the ticket in my pocket now that he give me for the Wednesday matinée! I do wonder how he's gettin' along! I guess they've got you to thank, if they're alive to tell the tale. What *did* you do to get that woman out alive?" Lemuel looked blankly at her, and did not answer. "And Mr. Evans too! You must have had your hands full, and that's what I told the reporters; but I told 'em I guessed you'd be equal to it if any one would. Why, I don't suppose Mrs. Evans has been out of her room for a month, or hardly stepped her foot to the floor. Well, I don't want to see many people look as he did when you first got him out the house."

"Well, I don't know as I want to see many more fires where I live," said her nephew, as if with the wish to be a little more accurate.

Jerry asked Lemuel to watch Mrs. Harmon's goods while he went for a carriage, and said sir to him. It seemed to Lemuel that this respect, and Mrs. Harmon's unmerited praises, together with the doom that was secretly upon him, would drive him wild.

XXIV

THE EVENING after the fire Mrs. Sewell sat talking it over with her husband, in the light of the newspaper reports, which made very much more of Lemuel's part in it than she liked. The reporters had flattered the popular love of the heroic in using Mrs. Harmon's version of his exploits, and represented him as having been most efficient and daring throughout, and especially so in regard to the Evanses.

"Well, that doesn't differ materially from what they told us themselves," said Sewell.

"You know very well, David," retorted his wife, "that there couldn't have been the least danger at any time; and when he helped her to get Mr. Evans downstairs, the fire was nearly all out."

"Very well, then; he would have saved their lives if it had been necessary. It was a case of potential heroism, that contained all the elements of self-sacrifice."

Mrs. Sewell could not deny this, but she was not satisfied. She was silent a moment before she asked, "What do you suppose that wretched creature will do now?"

"I think very likely he will come to me," answered Sewell.

"I dare say." The bell rang. "And I suppose that's he now!"

They listened and heard Miss Vane's voice at the door, asking for them.

Mrs. Sewell ran down the stairs and kissed her. "Oh, I'm *so* glad you came. Isn't it wonderful? I've just come from them, and she's taking the whole care of him, as if he had always been the sick one, and she strong and well."

"What do you mean, Lucy? He isn't ill!"

"Who isn't?"

"What are you talking about?"

"About Mr. Evans——"

"Oh!" said Miss Vane, with cold toleration. She arrived at the study door and gave Sewell her hand. "I scarcely knew him, you know; I only met him casually here. I've come to see," she added nervously, "if you know where Lemuel is, Mr. Sewell. Have you seen anything of him since the fire? How nobly he behaved! But I never saw anything he wasn't equal to!"

"Mrs. Sewell objects to his saving human life," said Sewell, not able to deny himself.

"I don't see how you can take the slightest interest in him," began Mrs. Sewell, saying a little more than she meant.

"You would, my dear," returned Miss Vane, "if you had wronged him as I have."

"Or as I," said Sewell.

"I'm thankful I haven't, then," said his wife. "It seems to me that there's nothing else of him. As to his noble behavior, it isn't possible you believe these newspaper accounts? He didn't save any one's life; there was no danger!"

Miss Vane, preoccupied with her own ideal of the facts, stared at her without replying, and then turned to Sewell.

"I want to find him and ask him to stay with me till he can get something else to do." Sewell's eyebrows arched themselves involuntarily. "Sibyl has gone to New York for a fortnight; I shall be quite alone in the house, and I shall be very glad of his company," she explained to the eyebrows, while ignoring them. Her chin quivered a little, as she added, "I shall be *proud* of his company. I wish him to understand that he is my *guest*."

"I suppose I shall see him soon," said Sewell, "and I will give him your message."

"Will you tell him," persisted Miss Vane, a little hysterically, "that if he is in any way embarrassed I insist upon his coming to me immediately—at *once?*"

Sewell smiled, "Yes."

"I know that I'm rather ridiculous," said Miss Vane, smiling in sympathy, "and I don't blame Mrs. Sewell for not entering into my feelings. Nobody could, who hadn't felt the peculiar Lemuel-glamour."

"I don't imagine he's embarrassed in any way," said Sewell. "He seems to have the gift of lighting on his feet. But I'll tell him how peremptory you are, Miss Vane."

"Well, upon my word," cried Mrs. Sewell, when Miss Vane had taken leave of them in an exaltation precluding every re-current attempt to enlighten her as to the true proportions of Lemuel's part in the fire, "I really believe people like to be made fools of. Why didn't *you* tell her, David, that he had done nothing?"

"What would have been the use? She has her own theory of the affair. Besides, he did do something; he did his duty, and my experience is that it's no small thing to do. It wasn't his fault that he didn't do more."

He waited some days for Lemuel to come to him, and he inquired each time he went to see the Evanses if they knew where he was. But they had not heard of him since the night of the fire.

"It's his shyness," said Evans; "I can understand how if he thought he had put me under an obligation he wouldn't come near me—and couldn't."

Evans was to go out of town for a little while; the proprietors of the "Saturday Afternoon" insisted upon his taking a rest, and they behaved handsomely about his salary. He did not want to go, but his wife got him away finally, after he had failed in two or three attempts at writing.

Lemuel did not appear to Sewell till the evening of the day when the Evanses left town. It seemed as if he had waited till they were gone, so that he could not be urged to visit them. At first the minister scolded him a little for his neglect; but Lemuel said he had heard about them, and knew they were getting along all right. He looked as if he had not been getting along very well himself; his face was thin, and had an air at once dogged and apprehensive. He abruptly left talking of Evans, and said, "I don't know as you heard what happened that night before the fire just after I got back from your house?"

"No, I hadn't."

Lemuel stopped. Then he related briefly and clearly the whole affair, Sewell interrupting him from time to time with murmurs of sympathy, and "Tchk, tchk, tchk!" and "Shocking, shocking!" At the end he said, "I had hoped somehow that the general calamity had swallowed up your particular trouble in it. Though I don't know that general calamities ever do that with particular troubles," he added, more to himself than to Lemuel; and he put the idea away for some future sermon.

"Mr. Evans stopped and said something to me that night.

He said we had to live things down, and not die them down; he wanted I should wait till Saturday before I was sure that I couldn't get through Tuesday. He said, How did we know that death was the end of trouble?"

"Yes," said the minister with a smile of fondness for his friend; "that was like Evans all over."

"I sha'n't forget those things," said Lemuel. "They've been in my head ever since. If it hadn't been for them, I don't know what I should have done."

He stopped, and after a moment's inattention Sewell perceived that he wished to be asked something more. "I hope," he said, "that nothing more has been going wrong with you?" and as he asked this he laid his hand affectionately on the young man's shoulder, just as Evans had done. Lemuel's eyes dimmed and his breath thickened. "What has become of the person—the discharged convict?"

"I guess I had better tell you," he said; and he told him of the adventure with Berry and Williams.

Sewell listened in silence, and then seemed quite at a loss what to say; but Lemuel saw that he was deeply afflicted. At last he asked, lifting his eyes anxiously to Sewell's, "Do you think I did wrong to say the thief was a friend of mine, and get him off that way?"

"That's a very difficult question," sighed Sewell. "You had a duty to society."

"Yes, I've thought of that since!"

"If I had been in your place, I'm afraid I should be glad not to have thought of it in time; and I'm afraid I'm glad that, as it is, it's too late. But doesn't it involve you with him in the eyes of the other young man?"

"Yes, I presume it does," said Lemuel. "I shall have to go away."

"Back to Willoughby Pastures?" asked Sewell, with not so much faith in that panacea for Lemuel's troubles as he had once had.

"No, to some other town. Do you know of anything I could get to do in New York?"

"Oh, no, no!" said the minister. "You needn't let this banish you. We must seek this young Mr.—"

"Berry."

"—Mr. Berry out and explain the matter to him."

"Then you'll have to tell him all about me?"

"Yes. Why not?"

Lemuel was silent, and looked down.

"In the mean time," pursued the minister, "I have a message for you from Miss Vane. She has heard, as we all have, of your behavior during the fire——"

"It wasn't anything," Lemuel interrupted. "There wasn't the least danger; and Mrs. Evans did it all herself, anyway. It made me sick to see how the papers had it. It's a shame!"

Sewell smiled. "I'm afraid you couldn't make Miss Vane think so; but I can understand what you mean. She has never felt quite easy about the way—the terms—on which she parted with you. She has spoken to me several times of it, and—ah—expressed her regret; and now, knowing that you have been—interrupted in your life, she is anxious to have you come to her——"

An angry flash lighted up Lemuel's face. "I couldn't go back there! I wouldn't do any such work again."

"I don't mean that," Sewell hastened to say. "Miss Vane wished me to ask you to come as her guest until you could find something—Miss Sibyl Vane has gone to New York——"

"I'm very much obliged to her," said Lemuel, "but I shouldn't want to give her so much trouble, or any one. I—I liked her very much, and I shouldn't want she should think I didn't appreciate her invitation."

"I will tell her," said the minister. "I had no great hope you would see your way to accepting it. But she will be glad to know that you received it." He added, rather interrogatively than affirmatively, "In the right spirit."

"Oh, yes," said Lemuel. "Please to tell her I did."

"Thank you," said Sewell with bland vagueness. "I don't know that I've asked yet where you are staying at present?"

"I'm at Mrs. Nash's, 13 Canary Place. Mrs. Harmon went there first."

"Oh! And are you looking forward to rejoining her in a new place?"

"I don't know as I am. I don't know as I should want to go into a hotel again."

Sewell manifested a little embarrassment. "Well, you won't

forget your promise to let me be of use to you—pecuniarily, if you should be in need of a small advance at any time."

"Oh, no! But I've got enough money for a while yet—till I can get something to do." He rose, and after a moment's hesitation he said, "I don't know as I want you should say anything to that fellow about me. To Mr. Berry, I mean."

"Oh! certainly not," said Sewell, "if you don't wish it."

Whatever it was in that reticent and elusive soul which prompted this request, the minister now felt that he could not know; but perhaps the pang that Lemuel inflicted on himself had as much transport as anguish in it. He believed that he had forever cut himself off from the companionship that seemed highest and holiest on earth to him; he should never see that girl again; Berry must have told Miss Swan, and long before this Miss Carver had shuddered at the thought of him as the accomplice of a thief. But he proudly said to himself that he must let it all go; for if he had not been a thief, he had been a beggar and a menial, he had come out of a hovel at home, and his mother went about like a scarecrow, and it mattered little what kind of shame she remembered him in.

He thought of her perpetually now, and, in those dialogues which we hold in revery with the people we think much about, he talked with her all day long. At first, when he began to do this, it seemed a wrong to Statira; but now, since the other was lost to him beyond other approach, he gave himself freely up to the mystical colloquies he held with her, as the devotee abandons himself to imagined converse with a saint. Besides, if he was in love with Statira, he was not in love with Jessie; that he had made clear to himself; for his feeling toward her was wholly different.

Most of the time, in these communings, he was with her in her own home, down at Corbitant, where he fancied she had gone, after the catastrophe at the St. Albans, and he sat there with her on a porch at the front door, which she had once described to him, and looked out under the silver poplars at the vessels in the bay. He formed himself some image of it all from pictures of the seaside which he had seen; and there were times when he tried to go back with her into the life she had led there as a child. Perhaps his ardent guesses at this were as near reality as anything that could be made to appear, for, after her mother and brothers and sisters had died out of the wide old house, her existence there was as lonely as if she had been a little ghost haunting it. She had inherited her mother's temperament with her father's constitution; she was the child born to his last long absence at sea and her mother's last solitude at home. When he returned, he found his wife dead and his maiden sister caring for the child in the desolate house.

This sister of Captain Carver's had been disappointed, as the phrase is, when a young girl; another girl had won her lover from her. Her disappointment had hardened her to the perception of the neighbors; and, by a strange perversion of the sympathies and faculties, she had turned from gossip and censure, from religion, and from all the sources of comfort that the bruised heart of Corbitant naturally turned to, and found such consolation as came to her in books, that is to say romances, and especially the romances that celebrated and deified such sorrow as her own. She had been a pretty little thing when young, and Jessie remembered her as pretty in her early old age. At heart she must still have been young when her hair was gray, for she made a friend and companion of the child, and they fed upon her romances together. When the aunt died, the child, who had known no mother but her, was stricken with a grief so deep and wild that at first her life and then her mind was feared for. To get her away from the associations and influences of the place, her father sent her to school in the western part of the State, where she met Madeline Swan, and formed one of those friendships which are like passions between young girls. During her long absence, her father married again; and she was called home to his deathbed. He was dead when she arrived; he had left a will that made her dependent on her stepmother. When Madeline Swan wrote to announce that she was coming to Boston to study art, Jessie Carver had no trouble in arranging with her stepmother, by the sacrifice of her final claim on her father's estate, to join her friend there, with a little sum of money on which she was to live till she should begin to earn something.

Her life had been a series of romantic episodes; Madeline said that if it could be written out it would be fascinating; but she went to work very practically, and worked hard. She had not much feeling for color; but she drew better than her friend, and what she hoped to do was to learn to illustrate books.

One evening, after a day of bitter-sweet reveries of Jessie, Lemuel went to see Statira. She and 'Manda Grier were both very gay, and made him very welcome. They had tea for him; Statira tried all her little arts, and 'Manda Grier told some things that had happened in the box-factory. He could not help laughing at them; they were really very funny; but he felt somehow that it was all a preparation for something else. At last the two girls made a set at him, as 'Manda Grier called it, and tried to talk him into their old scheme of going to wait on table at some of the country hotels, or the seaside. They urged that now, while he was out of a place, it was just the time to look up a chance.

He refused, at first kindly, and at last angrily; and he would have gone away in this mood if Statira had not said that she would never say another word to him about it, and hung upon his neck, while 'Manda Grier looked on in sullen resentment. He came away sick and heavy at heart. He said to himself that they would be willing to drag him into the mire; they had no pride; they had no sense; they did not know anything and they could not learn. He tried to get away from them to Miss Carver in his thoughts; but the place where he had left her was vacant and he could not conjure her back. Out of the void, he was haunted by a look of grieving reproach and wonder from her eyes.

XXV

T HAT EVENING Sewell went to see an old parishioner of his who lived on the Hill, and who among his eccentricities had the habit of occupying his city house all summer long, while his family flitted with other people of fashion to the seashore. That year they talked of taking a cottage for the first time since they had sold their own cottage at Nahant, in a day of narrow things now past. The ladies urged that he ought to come with them, and not think of staying in Boston now that he had a trouble of the eyes which had befallen him, and Boston would be so dull if he could not get about freely and read as usual.

He answered that he would rather be blind in Boston than telescopic at Beverly, or any other summer resort; and that as for the want of proper care, which they urged, he did not think he should lack in his own house, if they left him where he could reach a bell. His youngest daughter, a lively little blonde, laughed with a cousin of his wife's who was present, and his wife decorously despaired. The discussion of the topic was rather premature, for they were not thinking of going to Beverly before the middle of May, if they took the cottage; but an accident had precipitated it, and they were having it out, as people do, each party in the hope that the other would yield if kept at long enough before the time of final decision came.

"Do you think," said the husband and father, who looked a whimsical tyrant at the worst, but was probably no easier to manage for his whimsicality, "that I am going to fly in the face of prosperity, and begin to do as other people wish because I'm pecuniarily able to do as I please?"

The little blonde rose decisively from the low chair where she had been sitting. "If papa has begun to *reason* about it, we may as well yield the point for the present, mamma. Come, Lily! Let us leave him to Cousin Charles."

"Oh, but I say!" cried Cousin Charles, "if I'm to stay and fight it out with him, I've got to know which side I'm on."

"You're on the right side," said the young lady over her shoulder; "you always are, Cousin Charles."

Cousin Charles, in the attempt to kiss his hand toward his flatterer, pulled his glasses off his nose by their cord. "Bromfield," he said, "I don't see but this commits me against you." And then, the ladies having withdrawn, the two men put on that business air with which our sex tries to atone to itself for having unbent to the lighter minds of the other; heaven knows what women do when the men with whom they have been talking go away.

"If you should happen to stay in town," continued the cousin treacherously, "I shall be very glad, for I don't know but I shall be here the greater part of the summer myself."

"I shall stay," said the other, "but there won't be anything casual about it."

"What do you hear from Tom?" asked the cousin, feeling about on the mantel for a match. He was a full-bodied, handsome, amiable-looking old fellow, whose breath came in quick sighs with this light exertion. He had a blond complexion, and what was left of his hair, a sort of ethereal down on the top of his head, and some cherished fringes at the temples, was turning the yellowish gray that blond hair becomes.

The other gentleman, stretched at ease in a deep chair, with one leg propped on a cricket, had the distinction of long forms, which the years had left in their youthful gracility; his snow-white mustache had been allowed to droop over the handsome mouth, whose teeth were beginning to go. "They're on the other side of the clock," he said, referring to the matches. He added, with another glance at his relative, "Charles, you ought to bant. It's beginning to affect your wind."

"*Beginning!* Your memory's going, Bromfield. But they say there's a new system that allows you to eat everything. I'm waiting for that. In the mean time, I've gone back to my baccy."

"They've cut mine off," sighed the other. "Doesn't it affect your heart?"

"Not a bit. But what do you do, now you can't smoke and your eyes have given out?"

"I bore myself. I had a letter from Tom yesterday," said the sufferer, returning to the question that his cousin's obesity had diverted him from. "He's coming on in the summer."

"Tom's a lucky fellow," said the cousin. "I wish you had insisted on my taking some of that stock of his when you bought in."

"Yes, you made a great mistake," said the other with whimsical superiority. "You should have taken my advice. You would now be rolling in riches, as I am, with a much better figure for it."

The cousin smoked a while. "Do you know, I think Tom's about the best fellow I ever knew."

"He's a good boy," said the other, with the accent of a father's pride and tenderness.

"Going to bring his pretty chickens and their dam?" asked the cousin, parting his coat-skirts to the genial influence of the fire.

"No; it's a short visit. They're going into the Virginia mountains for the summer." A man-servant came in and said something in a low voice. "Heigh? What? Why, of course! Certainly! By all means! Show him in! Come in, parson; come in!" called the host to his yet unseen visitor, and he held out his hand for Sewell to take when he appeared at the door. "Glad to see you! I can't get up,—a little gouty to-day,—but Bellingham's on foot. *His* difficulty is sitting down."

Bellingham gave the minister a near-sighted man's glare through his glasses, and then came eagerly forward and shook hands. "Oh, Mr. Sewell! I hope you've come to put up some job on Corey. Don't spare him! With Kanawha Paint Co. at the present figures he merits any demand that Christian charity can make upon him. The man's prosperity is disgraceful."

"I'm glad to find you here, Mr. Bellingham," said Sewell, sitting down.

"Oh, is it double-barreled?" pleaded Bellingham.

"I don't know that it's a deadly weapon of any kind," returned the minister. "But if one of you can't help me, perhaps the other can."

"Well, let us know what the job is," said Corey. "We refuse to commit ourselves beforehand."

"I shall have to begin at the beginning," said Sewell warningly, "and the beginning is a long way off."

"No matter," said Bellingham, adventurously. "The farther off, the better. I've been dining with Corey—he gives you a very good dinner now, Corey does—and I'm just in the mood for a deserving case."

"The trouble with Sewell is," said Corey, "that he doesn't always take the trouble to have them deserving. I hope this is interesting, at least."

"I suspect you'll find it more interesting than I shall," said the minister, inwardly preparing himself for the amusement which Lemuel's history always created in his hearers. It seemed to him, as he began, that he was always telling this story, and that his part in the affair was always becoming less and less respectable. No point was lost upon his hearers; they laughed till the ladies in the drawing-room above wondered what the joke could be.

"At any rate," said Bellingham, "the fellow behaved magnificently at the fire. I read the accounts of it."

"I think his exploits owe something to the imagination of the reporters," said Sewell. "He tells a different story, himself."

"Oh, of course!" said Bellingham.

"Well; and what else?" asked Corey.

"There isn't any more. Simply he's out of work, and wants something to do—anything to do—anything that isn't menial."

"Ah, that's a queer start of his," said Bellingham, thoughtfully. "I don't know but I like that."

"And do you come to such effete posterity as we are for help in a case like that?" demanded Corey. "Why, the boy's an Ancestor!"

"So he is! Why, so he is—so he is!" said Bellingham, with delight in the discovery. "Of course he is!"

"All you have to do," pursued Corey, "is to give him time, and he'll found a fortune and a family, and his children's children will be cutting ours in society. Half of our great people have come up in that way. Look at the Blue-book, where our nobility is enrolled; it's the apotheosis of farm-boys, mechanics, inside-men, and I don't know what!"

"But in the mean time this ancestor is now so remote that he has nothing to do," suggested Sewell. "If you give him time you kill him."

"Well, what do you want me to do? Mrs. Corey is thinking

of setting up a Buttons. But you say this boy has a soul above buttons. And besides, he's too old."

"Yes."

"Look here, Bromfield," said Bellingham, "why don't you get *him* to read to you?"

Corey glanced from his cousin to the minister, whose face betrayed that this was precisely what he had had in his own mind.

"Is that the job?" asked Corey.

Sewell nodded boldly.

"He would read through his nose, wouldn't he? I couldn't stand that. I've stopped talking through mine, you know."

"Why, look here, Bromfield!" said Bellingham for the second time. "Why don't you let me manage this affair for you? I'm not of much use in the world, but from time to time I like to do my poor best; and this is just one of the kind of things I think I'm fitted for. I should like to see this young man. When I read in the newspapers of some fellow who has done a fine thing, I always want to see what manner of man he is; and I'm glad of any chance that throws him in my way."

"Your foible's notorious, Charles. But I don't see why you keep my cigars all to yourself," said Corey.

"My dear fellow," said Bellingham, making a hospitable offer of the cigar-box from the mantel, "you said they'd cut you off."

"Ah, so they have. I forgot. Well, what's your plan?"

"My plan," said Bellingham, "is to have him to breakfast with me, and interview him generally, and get him to read me a few passages, without rousing his suspicions. Heigh?"

"I don't know that I believe much in your plan," said Corey. "I should like to hear what my spiritual adviser has to say."

"I shouldn't know what to advise, exactly," said Sewell. "But I won't reject any plan that gives my client a chance."

"Isn't client rather euphuistic?" asked Corey.

"It is, rather. But I've got into the habit of handling Barker very delicately, even in thought. I'm not sure he'll come," added Sewell, turning to Bellingham.

"Oh, yes, he will," said Bellingham. "Tell him it's business. There won't be anybody there. Will nine be too late for him?"

"I imagine he's more accustomed to half-past five at home, and seven here."

"Well, we'll say nine, anyway. I can't imagine the cause that would get me up earlier. Here!" He turned to the mantel and wrote an invitation upon his card, and handed it to Sewell. "Please give him that from me, and beg him to come. I really want to see him, and if he can't read well enough for this fastidious old gentleman, we'll see what else he can do. Corey tells me he expects Tom on this summer," he concluded, in dismissal of Lemuel as a topic.

"Ah," said Sewell, putting the card in his pocket, "I'm very glad to hear that."

He had something, but not so much, of the difficulty in overcoming Lemuel's reluctance that he had feared, and on the morning named Lemuel presented himself at the address on Bellingham's card exactly at nine. He had the card in his hand, and he gave it to the man who opened the street door of the bachelors' apartment house where Bellingham lived. The man read it carefully over, and then said, "Oh, yes; second floor," and, handing it back, left Lemuel to wander upstairs alone. He was going to offer the card again at Bellingham's door, but he had a dawning misgiving. Bellingham had opened the door himself, and, feigning to regard the card as offered by way of introduction, he gave his hand cordially, and led him into the cozy room where the table was already laid for breakfast.

"Glad to see you—glad to see you, Mr. Barker. Give me your coat. Ah, I see you scorn the effeminacy of half-season things. Put your hat anywhere. The advantage of bachelors' quarters is that you *can* put anything anywhere. We haven't a woman on the premises, and you can fancy how unmolested we are."

Lemuel had caught sight of one over the mantel, who had nothing but her water-colors on, and was called an "Étude"; but he no longer trembled, for evil or for good, in such presences. "That's one of those Romano-Spanish things," said Bellingham, catching the direction of his eye. "I forget the fellow's name; but it isn't bad. We're pretty snug here," he added, throwing open two doors in succession, to show the extent of his apartment. "Here you have the dining-room and drawing-room and library in one; and here's my bedroom, and here's my bath."

He pulled an easy-chair up toward the low fire for Lemuel. "But perhaps you're hot from walking? Sit wherever you like."

Lemuel chose to sit by the window. "It's very mild out," he said, and Bellingham did not exact anything more of him. He talked at him, and left Lemuel to make his mental inventory of the dense Turkey rugs on the slippery hard-wood floor, the pictures on the walls, the deep, leather-lined seats, the bric-à-brac on the mantel, the tall, colored chests of drawers in two corners, the delicate china and quaint silver on the table.

Presently steps were heard outside, and Bellingham threw open the door as he had to Lemuel, and gave a hand to each of the two guests whom he met on his threshold.

"Ah, Meredith! Good-morning, venerable father!" He drew them in. "Let me introduce you to Mr. Barker, Mr. Meredith. Mr. Barker, the Rev. Mr. Seyton. You fellows are pretty prompt."

"We're pretty hungry," said Mr. Meredith. "I don't know that we should have got here if we hadn't leaned up against each other as we came along. Several policemen regarded us suspiciously, but Seyton's cloth protected us."

"It was terrible, coming up Beacon street with an old offender like Meredith, at what he considered the dead hour of the night," said Mr. Seyton. "I don't know what I should have done if any one had been awake to see us."

"You shall have breakfast instantly," said Bellingham, touching an annunciator, and awakening a distant electric titter somewhere.

Mr. Seyton came toward Lemuel, who took the young ritualist for a Catholic priest, but was not proof against the sweet friendliness which charmed every one with him, and was soon talking at more ease than he had felt from all Bellingham's cordial intention. He was put at his host's right hand when they sat down, and Mr. Seyton was given the foot, so that they continued their talk.

"Mr. Bellingham tells me you know my friend Sewell," said the clergyman.

Lemuel's face kindled. "Oh, yes! Do you know him too?"

"Yes, I've known him a long time. He's a capital fellow, Sewell is."

"I think he's a great preacher," ventured Lemuel.

"Ah—well—yes? Is he? I've never heard him lecture," said Mr. Seyton, looking down at his bread.

"I swear, Seyton," said Meredith, across the table, "when you put on that ecclesiastical superciliousness of yours, I want to cuff you."

"I've no doubt he'd receive it in a proper spirit," said Bellingham, who was eating himself hot and red from the planked shad before him. "But you mustn't do it here."

"Of course," said Mr. Seyton, "Sewell is a very able man, and no end of a good fellow, but you can't expect me to admit he's a priest."

He smiled in sweet enjoyment of his friend's wrath. Lemuel observed that he spoke with an accent different from the others, which he thought very pleasant, but he did not know it for that neat utterance which the Anglican church bestows upon its servants.

"He's no Jesuit," growled Meredith.

"I'm bound to say he's not a pagan, either," laughed the clergyman.

"These gentlemen exchange these little knocks," Bellingham explained to Lemuel's somewhat puzzled look, "because they were boys together at school and college, and can't realize that they've grown up to be lights of the bar and the pulpit." He looked round at the different plates. "Have some more shad?" No one wanted more, it seemed, and Bellingham sent it away by the man, who replaced it with broiled chicken before Bellingham, and lamb chops in front of Mr. Seyton. "This is all there is," the host said.

"It's enough for me," said Meredith, "if no one else takes anything."

But in fact there was also an omelet, and bread and butter delicious beyond anything that Lemuel had tasted; and there was a bouquet of pink radishes with fragments of ice dropped among olives, and other facts of a polite breakfast. At the close came a dish of what Bellingham called premature strawberries.

"Why! they're actually *sweet!*" said Meredith, "and they're as natural as emery-bags."

"Yes, they're all you say," said Bellingham. "You can have strawberries any time nowadays after New Year's, if you send far enough for them; but to get them ripe and sound, or distinguishable from small turnips in taste, is another thing."

Lemuel had never imagined a breakfast like that; he wondered at himself for having respected the cuisine of the St. Albans. It seemed to him that he and the person he had been—the farm boy, the captive of the police, the guest of the Wayfarer's Lodge, the servant of Miss Vane, and the head-waiter at the hotel—could not be the same person. He fell into a strange revery, while the talk, in which he had shared so little, took a range far beyond him. Then he looked up, and found all the others' eyes upon him, and heard Bellingham saying, "I fancy Mr. Barker can tell us something about that," and at Lemuel's mystified stare he added, "About the amount of smoke at a fire that a man could fight through. Mr. Seyton was speaking of the train that was caught in the forest fires, down in Maine, the other day. How was it with you at the St. Albans?"

Lemuel blushed. It was clear that Mr. Bellingham had been reading that ridiculous newspaper version of his exploit. "There was hardly any smoke at all, where I was. It didn't seem to have got into the upper entries much."

"That's just what I was saying!" triumphed Bellingham. "If a man has anything to do, he can get on. That's the way with the firemen. It's the rat-in-a-trap *idea* that paralyzes. Do you remember your sensations at all, when you were coming through the fire? Those things are very curious, sometimes," Bellingham suggested.

"There was no fire where I was," said Lemuel, stoutly, but helpless to make a more comprehensive disclaimer.

"I imagine you wouldn't notice that, any more than the smoke," said Bellingham, with a look of satisfaction in his hero for his other guests. "It's a sort of ecstasy. Do you remember that fellow of Bret Harte's, in 'How Christmas came to Simpson's Bar,' who gets a shot in his leg, or something, when he's riding to get the sick boy a Christmas present, and doesn't know it till he drops off his horse in a faint when he gets back?" He jumped actively up from the table, and found the book on his shelf. "There!" He fumbled for his glasses without finding them. "Will you be kind enough to read the passage, Mr. Barker? I think I've found the page. It's marked." He sat down again, and the others waited.

Lemuel read, as he needs must, and he did his best.

"Ah, that's very nice. Glad you didn't dramatize it; the drama ought to be in the words, not the reader. I like your quiet way."

"Harte seems to have been about the last of the story-tellers to give us the great, simple heroes," said Seyton.

When the others were gone, and Lemuel, who had been afraid to go first, rose to take himself away, Bellingham shook his hand cordially and said, "I hope you weren't bored? The fact is, I rather promised myself a *tête-à-tête* with you, and I told Mr. Sewell so; but I fell in with Seyton and Meredith yesterday—you can't help falling in with one when you fall in with the other; they're inseparable when Seyton's in town— and I couldn't resist the temptation to ask them."

"Oh, no, I wasn't bored at all," said Lemuel.

"I'm very glad. But—sit down a moment. I want to speak to you about a little matter of business. Mr. Sewell was telling us something of you the other night, at my cousin Bromfield Corey's, and it occurred to me that you might be willing to come and read to him. His eyes seem to be on the wane, some way, and he's rather sleepless. He'd give you a bed, and sometimes you'd have to read to him in the night; you'd take your meals where you like. How does it strike you, supposing the 'harnsome pittance' can be arranged?"

"Why, if you think I can do it," began Lemuel.

"Of course I do. You don't happen to read French?"

Lemuel shook his head hopelessly. "I studied Latin some at school——"

"Ah! Well! I don't think he'd care for Latin. I think we'd better stick to English for the present."

Bellingham arranged for Lemuel to go with him that after-noon to his cousin's and make, as he phrased it, a stagger at the job.

XXVI

THE STAGGER seemed to be sufficiently satisfactory. Corey could not repress some twinges at certain characteristics of Lemuel's accent, but he seemed, in a critical way, to take a fancy to him, and he was conditionally installed for a week.

Corey was pleased from the beginning with Lemuel's good looks, and justified himself to his wife with an Italian proverb: *"Novanta su cento, chi è bello di fuori è buono di dentro."* She had heard that proverb before, and she had always considered it shocking; but he insisted that most people married upon no better grounds, and that what sufficed in the choice of a husband or wife was enough for the choice of an intellectual nurse. He corrected Lemuel's pronunciation where he found it faulty, and amused himself with Lemuel's struggles to conceal his hurt vanity, and his final good sense in profiting by the correction. But Lemuel's reading was really very good; it was what, even more than his writing, had given him a literary reputation in Willoughby Pastures; and the old man made him exercise it in widely different directions. Chiefly, however, it was novels that he read, which, indeed, are the chief reading of most people in our time; and as they were necessarily the novels of our language, his elder was not obliged to use that care in choosing them which he must have exacted of himself in the fiction of other tongues. He liked to hear Lemuel talk, and he used the art of getting at the boy's life by being frank with his own experience. But this was not always successful, and he was interested to find Lemuel keeping doors that Sewell's narrative had opened carefully closed against him. He betrayed no consciousness that they existed, and Lemuel maintained intact the dignity and pride which come from the sense of ignominy well hidden.

The week of probation had passed without interrupting their relation, and Lemuel was regularly installed, and began to lead a life which was so cut off from his past in most things that it seemed to belie it. He found himself dropped in the midst of luxury stranger to him than the things they read of in those innumerable novels. The dull, rich colors in the walls and the heavily rugged floors and dark-wooded leathern seats of the library where he read to the old man; the beautiful forms of the famous bronzes, and the Italian saints and martyrs in their baroque or gothic frames of dim gold; the low shelves with their ranks of luxurious bindings, and all the seriously elegant keeping of the place, flattered him out of his strangeness; and the footing on which he was received in this house, the low-voiced respect with which the man-servant treated him, the master's light, cordial frankness, the distant graciousness of the mistress, and the unembarrassed, unembarrassing kindliness of the young ladies, both so much older than himself, contributed to an effect that afterwards deepened more and more, and became a vital part of the struggle which he was finally to hold with himself.

The first two or three days he saw no one but Mr. Corey, and but for the women's voices in the other parts of the house, he might have supposed himself in another bachelor's apartments, finer and grander than Bellingham's. He was presented to Mrs. Corey when she came into the library, but he did not see the daughters of the house till he was installed in it. After that, his acquaintance with them seemed to go no further. They were all polite and kind when they met him, in the library or on the stairs, but they showed no curiosity about him; and his never meeting them at table helped to keep him a stranger to them under the same roof. He ate at a boarding-house in a neighboring street, but he slept at the Coreys' after he had read their father asleep, and then, going out to his late breakfast, he did not return till Mr. Corey had eaten his own, much later.

He wondered at first that neither of those young ladies read to their father, not knowing the disability for mutual help that riches bring. Later, he saw how much Miss Lily Corey was engrossed with charity and art, and how constantly Miss Nannie Corey was occupied with social cares, and was perpetually going and coming in their performance. Then he saw that they could not have rendered nor their father have received from his family the duty which he was paid to do, as they must have done if they had been poorer. But they were all fond of one another, and the father had a way of joking with his daughters, especially the youngest; and they talked with a freedom of themselves which puzzled Lemuel. It appeared from what they said, at different times, that they had not always been so rich, or that they had once had money, and then less, and now much more. It appeared, also, that their prosperity was due to a piece of luck, and that the young Mr. Corey, whom they expected in the summer, had brought it about. His father was very proud of him, and, getting more and more used to Lemuel's companionship, he talked a great deal about his Tom, as he called him, and about Tom's wife, and his wife's family, who were somehow, Lemuel inferred, not all that his own family could wish them, but very good people. Once when Mr. Corey was talking of them, Mrs. Corey came in upon them, and seemed to be uneasy, as if she thought he was saying too much. But the daughters did not seem to care, especially the youngest.

He found out that Mr. Corey used to be a painter, and had lived a long time in Italy when he was young, and he recalled with a voluptuous thrill of secrecy that Williams had once been in Italy. Mr. Corey seemed to think better of it than Williams; he liked to talk of Rome and Florence, and of Venice, which Williams had said was a kind of hole. The old man said this or that picture was of this or that school, and vague lights of knowledge and senses of difference that flattered Lemuel's intellectual vanity stole in upon him. He began to feel that the things Mr. Corey had lived for were the great and high objects of life.

He now perceived how far from really fine or fashionable anything at the St. Albans had been, and that the simplicity of Miss Vane's little house, which the splendor of the hotel had eclipsed in his crude fancy, was much more in harmony with the richness of Mr. Corey's. He oriented himself anew, and got another view of the world which he had dropped into. Occasionally he had glimpses of people who came to see the Coreys, and it puzzled him that this family, which he knew so kind and good, took with others the tone hard and even cynical which seemed the prevailing tone of society; when their acquaintances went away they dropped back, as if with relief, into their sincere and amiable fashions of speech. Lemuel asked himself if every one in the world was playing a part; it did not seem to him that Miss Carver had been; she was always the same, and always herself. To be one's self appeared to him the best thing in the world, and he longed for it the more as he felt that he too was insensibly beginning to play a part. Being so much in this beautiful and luxurious house, where every one was so well dressed and well mannered, and well kept in body and mind, and passing from his amazement at all its appointments into the habit of its comfortable beauty, he forgot more and more the humility and the humiliations of his past. He did not forget its claims upon him; he sent home every week the greater part of his earnings, and he wrote often to his mother; but now, when he could have got the time to go home and see her, he did not go. In the exquisite taste of his present environment, he could scarcely believe in that figure, grizzled, leathern and gaunt, and costumed in a grotesque unlikeness to either sex. Sometimes he played with the fantastic supposition of some other origin for himself, romantic and involved like that of some of the heroes he was always reading of, which excluded her.

Another effect of this multifarious literature through which his duties led him was the awakening of the ambition to write, stunned by his first disastrous adventures in Boston, and dormant almost ever since, except as it had stirred under the promptings of Evans's kindly interest. But now it did not take the form of verse; he began to write moralistic essays, never finished, but full of severe comment on the folly of the world as he saw it. Sometimes they were examinations of himself, and his ideas and principles, his doctrines and practice, penetrating quests such as the theologians of an earlier day used to address to their consciences.

Meantime, the deeply underlying mass of his rustic crudity and raw youth took on a far higher polish than it had yet worn. Words dropped at random in the talk he now heard supplied him with motives and shaped his actions. Once Mr. Bellingham came in laughing about a sign which he saw in a back street, of Misfit Parlors, and Lemuel spent the next week's salary for a suit at a large clothing store, to replace the dress Sewell had thought him so well in. He began insensibly to ape the manners of those about him.

It drew near the time when the ladies of the Corey family were to leave town, where they had lingered much longer than they meant, in the hope that Mr. Corey might be so much better, or so much worse, that he would consent to go to the shore with them. But his disabilities remained much the same, and his inveterate habits indomitable. By this time that trust in Lemuel which never failed to grow up in those near him, reconciled the ladies to the obstinate resolution of the master of the house to stay in it as usual. They gave up the notion of a cottage, and they were not going far away, nor for long at any one time; in fact, one or other of them was always in the house. Mrs. Corey had grown into the habit of confidence with Lemuel concerning her husband's whims and foibles; and this motherly frankness from a lady so stately and distant at first was a flattery more poisonous to his soul than any other circumstance of his changed life.

It came July, and even Sewell went away then. He went with a mind at rest concerning Lemuel's material prospects, and his unquestionable usefulness and acceptability; but something, at the bottom of his satisfaction, teased him still; a dumb fear that the boy was extravagant, a sense that he was somehow different, and not wholly for the better, from what he had been. He had seen, perhaps, nothing worse in him than that growth of manner which amused Corey.

"He is putting us on," he said to Bellingham, one day, "and making us fit as well as he can. I don't think we're altogether becoming, but that's our fault, probably. I can't help thinking that if we were of better cut and material we should show to better effect upon that granite soul. I wish Tom were here. I've an idea that Tom would fit him like a glove. Charles, why don't *you* pose as a model for Barker?"

"I don't see why I'm not a very good model without posing," said Bellingham. "What do you want me to do for him? Take him to the club? Barker's *not* very conversational."

"You don't take him on the right topics," said Corey, not minding that he had left the point. "I assure you that Barker, on any serious question that comes up in our reading, has a clear head and an apt tongue of his own. It isn't our manners alone that he emulates. I can't find that any of us ever dropped an idea or suggestion of value that Barker didn't pick it up, and turn it to much more account than the owner. He's as true as a Tuscan peasant, as proud as an Indian, and as quick as a Yankee."

"Ah! I *hoped* you wouldn't go abroad for that last," said Bellingham.

"No; and it's delightful, seeing the great variety of human nature there is in every human being here. Our life isn't stratified; perhaps it never will be. At any rate, for the present, we're all in vertical sections. But I always go back to my first notion of Barker: he's ancestral, and he makes me feel like degenerate posterity. I've had the same sensation with Tom; but Barker seems to go a little farther back. I suppose there's such a thing as getting too far back in these Origin of Species days; but he isn't excessive in that or in anything. He's confoundedly temperate, in fact; and he's reticent; he doesn't allow any unseemly intimacy. He's always turning me out-of-doors."

"Of course! But what can we old fellows hope to know of what's going on in any young one? Talk of strangeness! I'd undertake to find more in common with a florid old fellow of fifty from the red planet Mars than with any young Bostonian of twenty."

"Yes; but it's the youth of my sires that I find so strange in Barker. Only, theoretically, there's no Puritanism. He's a thorough believer in Sewell. I suspect he could formulate Sewell's theology a great deal better than Sewell could."

XXVII

STATIRA and 'Manda Grier had given up their plan of getting places in a summer hotel when Lemuel absolutely refused to take part in it, and were working through the summer in the box-factory. Lemuel came less regularly to see them now, for his Sunday nights had to be at Mr. Corey's disposition; but Statira was always happy in his coming, and made him more excuses than he had thought of, if he had let a longer interval than usual pass. He could not help feeling the loveliness of her patience, the sweetness of her constancy; but he disliked 'Manda Grier more and more, and she grew stiffer and sharper with him. Sometimes the aimlessness of his relation to Statira hung round him like a cloud, which he could not see beyond. When he was with her he contented himself with the pleasure he felt in her devotion, and the tenderness this awakened in his own heart; but when he was away from her there was a strange disgust and bitterness in these.

Sometimes, when Statira and 'Manda Grier took a Saturday afternoon off, he went with them into the country on one of the horse-car lines, or else to some matinée at a garden-theater in the suburbs. Statira liked the theater better than anything else; and she used to meet other girls whom she knew there, and had a gay time. She introduced Lemuel to them, and after a few moments of high civility and distance they treated him familiarly, as Statira's beau. Their talk, after that he was now used to, was flat and foolish, and their pert ease incensed him. He came away bruised and burning, and feeling himself unfit to breathe the refined and gentle air to which he returned in Mr. Corey's presence. Then he would vow in his heart never to expose himself to such things again; but he could not tell Statira that he despised the friends she was happy with; he could only go with a reluctance it was not easy to hide, and atone by greater tenderness for a manner that wounded her. One day toward the end of August, when they were together at a suburban theater, Statira wandered off to a pond there was in the grounds with some other girls who had asked him to go and row them, and had called him a bear for refusing, and told him to look out for Barnum. They left him sitting alone with 'Manda Grier, at a table where they had all been having ice-cream at his expense; and though it was no longer any pleasure to be with her, it was better than to be with them, for she was not a fool, at any rate. Statira turned round at a little distance to mock them with a gesture and a laugh, and the laugh ended in a cough, long and shattering, so that one of her companions had to stop with her, and put her arm round her till she could recover herself and go on.

It sent a cold thrill through Lemuel, and then he turned angry. "What is it Statira does to keep taking more cold?"

"Oh, I guess 'tain't 'ny *more* cold," said 'Manda Grier.

"What do you mean?"

"I guess 'f you cared a great deal you'd noticed that cough 'f hers before now. 'Tain't done it any too much good workin' in that arsenic paper all summer long."

'Manda Grier talked with her face turned away from him.

It provoked him more and more. "I *do* care," he retorted, eager to quarrel, "and you know it. Who got her into the box-factory, I should like to know?"

"*I* did!" said 'Manda Grier, turning sharply on him, "and you *kept* her there; and between us we've killed her."

"How have I kept her there, I should like to know?"

" 'F you'd done's she wanted you should, she might 'a' been at some pleasant place in the country—the mount'ns, or somewhere 't she'd been ov'r her cough by this time. But no! You was too nasty proud for that, Lemuel Barker!"

A heavy load of guilt dropped upon Lemuel's heart, but he flung it off, and he retorted furiously, "You ought to have been ashamed of yourself to ever want her to take a servant's place."

"Oh, a servant's place! If she'd been ashamed of a servant when you came meechin' round her, where'd you been, I sh'd like to know? And now I wish she had; 'n' if she wa'n't such a little fool, 'n' all wrapped in you, the way 't she is, I could wish't she'd never set eyes on you again, servant or no servant. But I presume it's too late now, and I presume she's got to go on suff'rin' for you and wonderin' what she's done to offend you when you don't come, and what she's done when you do, with your stuck-up, masterful airs, and your double-faced ways. But don't you try to pretend to me, Lemuel Barker, 't you care the least mite for her any more, 'f you ever did, because it won't go down! 'N' if S'tira wa'n't such a perfect little blind fool, she could see 't you didn't care for her any more than the ground 't you walk on, 'n' 't you'd be glad enough if she was under it, if you couldn't be rid of her any other way!" 'Manda Grier pulled her handkerchief out and began to cry into it.

Lemuel was powerfully shaken by this attack; he did feel responsible for Statira's staying in town all summer; but the spectacle of 'Manda Grier publicly crying at his side in a place like that helped to counteract the effect of her words. " 'Sh! Don't cry!" he began, looking fearfully round him. "Every-body'll see you!"

"I don't care! Let them!" sobbed the girl. "If they knowed what I know, and could see you *not* cryin', I guess they'd think you looked worse than I do!"

"You don't understand—I can explain—"

"No, you can't explain, Mr. Barker!" said 'Manda Grier, whipping down her handkerchief and fiercely confronting him across the table. "You can't explain anything so's to blind *me* any longer! I was a big fool to ever suppose you had any heart *in* you; but when you came round at first, and was so meek you couldn't say your soul was your own, and was so glad if S'tira spoke to you, or looked at you, that you was ready to go crazy, I *did* suppose there was some *little* some-thing to you! And yes, I helped you on, all I could, and helped you to fool that poor thing that you ain't worthy to kiss the ground she walks on, Lord forgive me *for* it! But it's all changed now! You seem to think it's the greatest favor if you come round once a fortnight, and set and let her talk to you, and show you how she dotes upon you, the poor little silly coot! And if you ever speak a word, it's like the Lord unto Moses, it's so grand! But I understand! You've got other friends now! *You after that art-student?* Oh, you can blush and try to turn it off! I've seen you blush before, and I know you! And I know you're in love with that girl, and you're just waitin' to break off with S'tira; but you hain't got the spirit to up and do it like a man! You want to let it lag along, and *lag* along, and see 'f something won't happen to get you out of it! *You waitin' for her to die?* Well, you won't have to wait long! But if I was a man, I'd spoil your beauty for you first!"

The torrent of her words rolled him on, bruising and tearing his soul, which their truth pierced like jagged points. From time to time he opened his lips to protest or deny, but no words came, and in his silence a fury of scorn for the poor, faithful, scolding thing, so just, so wildly unjust, gathered head in him.

"Be still!" he ground between his teeth. "Be still, you——" He stopped for the word, and that saved him from the outrage he had meant to pay her back with. He rose from the table. "You can tell Statira what you've said to me. I'm going home."

He rushed away; the anger was like strong drink in his brain; he was like one drunk all the way back to the city in the car.

He could not go to Mr. Corey's at once; he felt as if physically besmeared with shame; he could not go to his boarding-house; it would have been as if he had shown himself there in a coat of tar and feathers. Those insolent, true, degrading words hissed in his ears, and stung him incessantly. They accused, they condemned with pitiless iteration; and yet there were instants when he knew himself guiltless of all the wrong of which in another sense he knew himself guilty. In his room, he renewed the battle within himself that he had fought so long in his wanderings up and down the street, and he conquered himself at last into the theory that Statira had authorized or permitted 'Manda Grier to talk to him in that way. This simplified the whole affair: it offered him the release which he now knew he had longed for. As he stretched himself in the sheets at daybreak, he told himself that he need never see either of them again. He was free.

XXVIII

L EMUEL WENT through the next day in that license of revolt which every human soul has experienced in some
measure at some time. We look back at it afterwards, and see
it a hideous bondage. But for the moment Lemuel rejoiced in
it; and he abandoned himself boldly to thoughts that had
hitherto been a furtive and trembling rapture.

In the afternoon, when he was most at leisure, he walked
down to the Public Garden, and found a seat on a bench near
the fountain where the Venus had shocked his inexperience
the first time he saw her; he remembered that simple boy with
a smile of pity, and then went back into his cloud of revery.
There, safely hid from trouble and wrong, he told his ideal
how dear she was to him, and how she had shaped and governed his life, and made it better and nobler from the first
moment they had met. The fumes of the romances which he
had read mixed with the love-born delirium in his brain: he
was no longer low, but a hero of lofty line, kept from his
rightful place by machinations that had failed at last, and now
he was leading her, his bride, into the ancient halls which
were to be their home, and the source of beneficence and
hope to all the poor and humbly-born around them. His eyes
were so full of this fantastic vision, the soul of his youth dwelt
so deeply within this dream-built tabernacle, that it was with
a shock of anguish he saw coming up the walk towards him
the young girl herself. His airy structure fell in ruins around
him; he was again common and immeasurably beneath her;
she was again in her own world, where, if she thought of him
at all, it must be as a squalid vagabond and the accomplice of
a thief. If he could have escaped, he would, but he could not
move; he sat still and waited, with fallen eyes, for her to pass
him.

At sight of him she hesitated and wavered; then she came
towards him, and at a second impulse held out her hand,
smiling with a radiant pleasure.

"I didn't know it was you, at first," she said. "It seems so
strange to see any one that I know!"

"I didn't expect to see you, either," he stammered out,

getting somehow upon his feet and taking her hand, while his face burned, and he could not keep his eyes on hers; "I—didn't know you were here."

"I've only been here a few days. I'm drawing at the Museum. I've just got back. Have you been here all summer?"

"Yes—all summer. I hope you've been well—I suppose you've been away——"

"Yes, I've just got back," she repeated.

"Oh, yes! I meant that!"

She smiled at his confusion, as kindly as the ideal of his day-dream. "I've been spending the summer with Madeline, and I've spent most of it out-of-doors, sketching. Have you been well?"

"Yes—not very; oh, yes, I'm well——" She had begun to move forward with the last question, and he found himself walking with her. "Did she—has Miss Swan come back with you?" he asked, looking her in the eyes with more question than he had put into his words.

"No, I don't think she'll come back this winter," said the girl. "You know," she went on, coloring a little, "that she's married now?"

"No," said Lemuel.

"Yes. To Mr. Berry. And I have a letter from him for you."

"Was he there with you, this summer?" asked Lemuel, ignoring alike Berry's marriage and the letter from him.

"Oh, yes; of course! And I liked him better than I used to. He is very good, and if Madeline didn't have to go so far West to live! He will know how to appreciate her, and there are not many who can do that! Her father thinks he has a great deal of ability. Yes, if Madeline *had* to get married!"

She talked as if convincing and consoling herself, and there was an accent of loneliness in it all that pierced Lemuel's pre-occupation; he had hardly noted how almost pathetically glad she was to see him. "You'll miss her here," he ventured.

"Oh, I don't dare to think of it!" cried the girl. "I don't know what I shall do! When I first saw you, just now, it brought up Madeline and last winter so that it seemed too much to bear!"

They had walked out of the Garden across Charles street, and were climbing the slope of Beacon street Mall, in the

Common. "I suppose," she continued, "the only way will be to work harder, and try to forget it. They wanted me to go out and stay with them; but of course I couldn't. I shall work, and I shall read. I shall not find another Madeline Swan! You must have been reading a great deal this summer, Mr. Barker," she said, in turning upon him from her bereavement. "Have you seen any of the old boarders? Or Mrs. Harmon? I shall never have another winter like that at the poor old St. Albans!"

Lemuel made what answer he could. There was happiness enough in merely being with her to have counterbalanced all the pain he was suffering; and when she made him partner of her interests and associations, and appealed to their common memories in confidence of his sympathy, his heavy heart stirred with strange joy. He had supposed that Berry must have warned her against him; but she was treating him as if he had not. Perhaps he had not, and perhaps he had done so, and this was her way of showing that she did not believe it. He tried to think so; he knew it was a subterfuge, but he lingered in it with a fleeting, fearful pleasure. They had crossed from the Common, and were walking up under the lindens of Chestnut street, and from time to time they stopped in the earnestness of their parley, and stood talking, and then loitered on again, in the summer security from over-sight which they were too rapt to recognize. They reached the top of the hill, and came to a door where she stopped. He fell back a pace. "Good-bye——" It was eternal loss, but it was escape.

She smiled in timorous hesitation. "Won't you come in? And I will get Mr. Berry's letter."

She opened the door with a latch-key, and he followed her within; a servant girl came half-way up the basement stairs to see who it was, and then went down. She left him in the dim parlor a moment, while she went to get the letter. When she returned, "I have a little room for my work at the top of the house," she said, "but it will never be like the St. Albans. There's no one else here yet, and it's pretty lonesome—without Madeline."

She sank into a chair, but he remained standing, and seemed not to heed her when she asked him to sit down. He put Berry's letter into his pocket without looking at it, and she rose again.

She must have thought he was going, and she said, with a smile of gentle trust, "It's been like having last winter back again to see you. We thought you must have gone home right after the fire; we didn't see anything of you again. We went ourselves in about a week."

Then she did not know, and he must tell her himself.

"Did Mr. Berry say anything about me—at the fire—that last day?" he began bluntly.

"No!" she said, looking at him with surprise; there was a new sound in his voice. "He had no need to say anything! I wanted to tell you—to write and tell you—how much I honored you for it—how ashamed I was for misunderstanding you just before, when——"

He knew that she meant when they all pitied him for a coward.

Her voice trembled; he could tell that the tears were in her eyes. He tried to put the sweetness of her praise from him. "Oh, it wasn't that that I meant," he groaned; and he wrenched the words out. "That fellow who said he was a friend of mine, and got into the house that way, was a thief; and Mr. Berry caught him robbing his room the day of the fire, and treated me as if I knew it, and was helping him on——"

"Oh!" cried the girl. "How cruel! How could he do that?"

Lemuel could not suffer himself to take refuge in her generous faith now.

"When I first came to Boston I had my money stolen, and there were two days when I had nothing to eat; and then I was arrested by mistake for stealing a girl's satchel; and when I was acquitted, I slept the next night in the tramps' lodging-house, and that fellow was there, and when he came to the St. Albans I was ashamed to tell where I had known him, and so I let him pass himself off for my friend."

He kept his eyes fixed on hers, but he could not see them change from their pity of him, or light up with a sense of any squalor in his history.

"And I used to think that *my* life had been hard!" she cried. "Oh, how much you have been through!"

"And after that," he pursued, "Mr. Sewell got me a place, a sort of servant's place, and when I lost that I came to be the man-of-all-work at the St. Albans."

In her eyes the pity was changing to admiration; his confession which he had meant to be so abject had kindled her fancy like a boastful tale.

"How little we know about people and what they have suffered! But I thank you for telling me this—oh, yes!—and I shall always think of myself with contempt. How easy and pleasant my life has been! And you——"

She stopped, and he stood helpless against her misconception. He told her about the poverty he had left at home, and the wretched circumstance of his life, but she could not see it as anything but honorable to his present endeavor. She listened with breathless interest to it all, and, "Well," she sighed at last, "it will always be something for you to look back to, and be proud of. And that girl—did she never say or do anything to show that she was sorry for that cruel mistake? Did you ever see her afterwards?"

"Yes," said Lemuel, sick at heart, and feeling how much more triumphantly he could have borne ignominy and rejection than this sweet sympathy. She seemed to think he would say something more, but he turned away from her, and after a little silence of expectance she let him go, with promises to come again which she seemed to win from him for his own sake.

In the street he took out Berry's letter and read it.

"DEAR OLD MAN: I've been trying to get off a letter to you almost any time the last three months, but I've been round so much, and upside down so much since I saw you—out to W. T. and on my head in Western Mass.—that I've not been able to fetch it. I don't know as I could fetch it now, if it wasn't for the prospective Mrs. A. W. B., Jr., standing over me with a revolver, and waiting to see me do it. I've just been telling her about that little interview of ours with Williams, that day, and she thinks I ought to be man enough to write and say that I guess I was all wrong about you; I had a sneaking idea of the kind from the start almost, but if a fellow's proud at all, he's proud of his mistakes, and he hates to give them up. I'm pretty badly balled up, now, and I can't seem to get the right words about remorse, and so forth; but you know how it is yourself. I *am* sorry, there's no two ways about that; but I've kept my suspicions as well as my regrets to myself, and now I do the best thing I can by way of reparation. I send this letter by Miss Carver. She hasn't read it, and she don't know what it's all about; but I guess you'd better tell her. Don't spare yours truly,

"A. W. BERRY, JR."

The letter did not soften Lemuel at all towards Berry, and he was bitterly proud that he had spoken without this bidding, though he had seemed to speak to no end that he had expected. After a while he lost himself in his day-dreams again, and in the fantastic future which he built up this became a great source of comfort to him and to his ideal. Now he parted with her in sublime renunciation, and now he triumphed over all the obstacles between them; but, whatever turn he willed his fortunes to take, she still praised him, and he prided himself that he had shown himself at his worst to her of his own free impulse. Sewell praised him for it in his revery; Mr. Corey and Mr. Bellingham both made him delicate compliments upon his noble behavior, which he feigned had somehow become known to them.

XXIX

AT THE USUAL HOUR he was at Mr. Corey's house, where he arrived footsore and empty from supperless wanderings, but not hungry and not weary. The serving-man at the door met him with the message that Mr. Corey had gone to dine at his club and would not be at home till late. He gave Lemuel a letter, which had all the greater effect from being presented to him on the little silver tray employed to bring up the cards and notes of the visitors and correspondents of the family. The envelope was stamped in that ephemeral taste which configured the stationery of a few years ago with the lines of alligator leather, and it exhaled a perfume so characteristic that it seemed to breathe Statira visibly before him. He knew this far better than the poor, scrawly, uncultivated handwriting which he had seen so little. He took the letter, and, turning from the door, read it by the light of the next street lamp.

> "Dear Lemuel—Manda Grier has told me what she said to you and Ime about crazy about it dear Lem I want you should come and see mee O Lem you dont Suppose i could of let Manda Grier talk to you that way if I had of none it but of course you dident only do Say so I give her a real good goen over and she says shes sory she done it i dont want any body should care for mee without itse there free will but I shall alwayes care for you if you dont care for me dont come but if you do Care I want you should come as soon as ever you can I can explane everything Manda Grier dident mean anything but for the best but sometimes she dont know what she is sayin O Lem you mussent be mad But if you are and you dont want to come ennymore dont come But O i hope you wouldent let such a thing set you againste mee recollect that I never done or Said anything to set you against me.
>
> "STATIRA."

A cruel disgust mingled with the remorse that this letter brought him. Its illiteracy made him ashamed, and the helpless fondness it expressed was like a millstone hanged about his neck. He felt the deadly burden of it drag him down.

A passer-by on the other side of the street coughed slightly in the night air, and a thought flashed through Lemuel, from which he cowered as if he had found himself lifting his hand against another's life.

His impulse was to turn and run, but there was no escape on any side. It seemed to him that he was like that prisoner he had read of, who saw the walls of his cell slowly closing together upon him, and drawing nearer and nearer till they should crush him between them. The inexperience of youth denies it perspective; in that season of fleeting and unsubstantial joys, of feverish hopes, despair wholly darkens a world which after years find full of chances and expedients.

If Mr. Sewell had been in town there might have been some hope through him; or if Mr. Evans were there; or even if Berry were at hand, it would be some one to advise with, to open his heart to in his extremity. He walked down into Bolingbroke street, knowing well that Mr. Sewell was not at home, but pretending to himself, after the fashion of the young, that if he should see a light in his house it would be a sign that all should come out right with him, and if not, it would come out wrong. He would not let himself lift his eyes to the house front till he arrived before it. When he looked his heart stood still; a light streamed bright and strong from the drawing-room window.

He hurried across the street and rang; and after some delay, in which the person coming to the door took time to light the gas in the hall, Mr. Sewell himself opened to him. They stood confronted in mutual amazement, and then Sewell said, with a cordiality which he did not keep free from reluctance, "Oh—Mr. Barker! Come in! Come in!" But after they had shaken hands, and Lemuel had come in, he stood there in the hall with him, and did not offer to take him up to his study. "I'm so glad to have this glimpse of you! How in the world did you happen to come?"

"I was passing and saw the light," said Lemuel.

Sewell laughed. "To be sure! We never have any idea how far our little candle throws its beams! I'm just here for the night, on my way from the mountains to the sea; I'm to be the 'supply' in a friend's pulpit at New Bedford; and I'm here quite alone in the house, scrambling a sermon together. But I'm *so* glad to see you! You're well, I hope? You're looking a

little thin, but that's no harm. Do you enjoy your life with
Mr. Corey? I was sure you would. When you come to know
him, you will find him one of the best of men—kindly,
thoughtful, and sympathetic. I've felt very comfortable about
your being with him, whenever I've thought of you, and you
may be sure that I've thought of you often. What about our
friends of the St. Albans? Do you see Mrs. Harmon? You
knew the Evanses had gone to Europe."

"Yes; I got a letter from him yesterday."

"He didn't pick up so fast as they hoped, and he concluded
to try the voyage. I hear very good accounts of him. He said
he was going to write you. Well! And Mr. Corey is well?" He
smiled more beamingly upon Lemuel, who felt that he wished
him to go, and stood haplessly trying to get away.

In the midst of his own uneasiness Sewell noted Lemuel's.
"Is there anything--something—you wished to speak with
me about?"

"No. No, not anything in particular. I just saw the light,
and——"

Sewell took his hand and wrung it with affection. "It was
so good of you to run in and see me. Don't fancy it's been
any disturbance. I'd got into rather a dim place in my work,
but since I've been standing here with you—ha, ha, ha! those
things do happen so curiously!—the whole thing has become
perfectly luminous. I'm delighted you're getting on so nicely.
Give my love to Mr. Corey. I shall see you soon again. We
shall all be back in a little over a fortnight. Glad of this
moment with you, if it's *only* a moment! Good-bye!"

He wrung Lemuel's hand again, this time in perfect sincerity, and eagerly shut him out into the night.

The dim place had not become so luminous to him as it
had to the minister. A darkness, which the obscurity of the
night faintly typified, closed round him, pierced by one ray
only, and from this he tried to turn his face. It was the
gleam that lights up every labyrinth where our feet wander
and stumble, but it is not always easy to know it from those
false lights of feeble-hearted pity, of mock-sacrifice, of sick
conscience, which dance before us to betray to worse misery
yet.

Some sense of this, broken and faltering, reached Lemuel

where he stood, and tried to deal faithfully with his problem. In that one steadfast ray he saw that whatever he did he must not do it for himself; but what his duty was he could not make out. He knew now, if he had not known before, that whatever his feeling for Statira was, he had not released himself from her, and it seemed to him that he could not release himself by any concern for his own advantage. That notion with which he had so long played, her insufficiency for his life now and for the needs of his mind hereafter, revealed itself in its real cruelty. The things that Mr. Sewell had said, that his mother had said, that Berry had said, in what seemed a fatal succession, and all to the same effect, against throwing himself away upon some one inadequate to him at his best, fell to the ground like withered leaves, and the fire of that steadfast ray consumed them.

But whom to turn to for counsel now? The one friend in whom he had trusted, to whom he had just gone ready to fling down his whole heart before him, had failed him, failed him unwittingly, unwillingly, as he had failed him once before, but this time in infinitely greater stress. He did not blame him now, fiercely, proudly, as he had once blamed him, but again he wandered up and down the city streets, famished and outcast through his defection.

It was late when he went home, but Mr. Corey had not yet returned, and he had time to sit down and write the letter which he had decided to send to Statira, instead of going to see her. It was not easy to write, but after many attempts he wrote it.

> "DEAR STATIRA: You must not be troubled at what Amanda said to me. I assure you that, although I was angry at first, I am entirely willing to overlook it at your request. She probably spoke hastily, and I am now convinced that she spoke without your authority. You must not think that I am provoked at you.
>
> "I received your letter this evening; and I will come to see you very soon.
>
> "LEMUEL BARKER."

The letter was colder than he meant to make it, but he felt that he must above all be honest, and he did not see how he could honestly make it less cold. When it came to Statira's hands she read it silently to herself, over and over again, while her tears dripped upon it.

'Manda Grier was by, and she watched her till she could bear the sight no longer. She snatched the letter from the girl's hands, and ran it through, and then she flung it on the ground. "Nasty, cold-hearted, stuck-up, shameless thing!"

"Oh, don't, 'Manda; don't, 'Manda!" sobbed Statira, and she plunged her face into the pillows of the bed where she sat.

"Shameless, cold-hearted, stuck-up, nasty thing!" said 'Manda Grier, varying her denunciation in the repetition, and apparently getting fresh satisfaction out of it in that way. "Don't? St'ira Dudley, if you was a woman—if you was *half* a woman—you'd never speak to that little corpse-on-ice again."

"Oh, 'Manda, don't call him names! I can't bear to have you!"

"Names? If you was anybody at all, you wouldn't *look* at him! You wouldn't *think* of him!"

"Oh, 'Manda, 'Manda! You know I can't let you talk so," moaned Statira.

"Talk? I could talk my *head* off! 'You must not think I was provoked with you,'" she mimicked Lemuel's dignity of diction in mincing falsetto. "'I will come to see you very soon.' Miserable, worthless, conceited whipper-snapper!"

"Oh, 'Manda, you'll break my heart if you go on so!"

"Well, then, give him up! He's goin' to give you up."

"Oh, he ain't; you know he ain't! He's just busy, and I know he'll come. I'll bet you he'll be here to-morrow. It'll kill me to give him up."

She had lifted herself from the pillow, and she began to cough.

"He'll kill you anyway," cried 'Manda Grier, in a passion of pity and remorse. She ran across the room to get the medicine which Statira had to take in these paroxysms. "There, there! Take it! I sha'n't say anything more about him."

"And do you take it all back?" gasped Statira, holding the proffered spoon away.

"Yes, yes! But *do* take your med'cine, St'ira, 'f you don't want to die where you set."

"And do you think he'll come?"

"Yes, he'll come."

"Do you say it just to get me to take the medicine?"

"No, I really do believe he'll come."

"Oh, 'Manda, 'Manda!" Statira took her medicine, and then wildly flung her arms round 'Manda Grier's neck, and began to sob and to cry there. "Oh, how hard I *am* with you, 'Manda! I should think if *I* was as hard with everybody else, they'd perfectly hate me."

"*You* hard!"

"Yes, and that's why he hates me. He does hate me. You said he did."

"No, St'ira, I didn't. You never was hard to anybody, and the meanest old iceberg in creation couldn't hate you."

"Then you think he does care for me?"

"Yes."

"And you know he'll come soon?"

"Yes."

"To-morrow?"

"Yes, to-morrow."

"Oh, 'Manda, oh, 'Manda!"

XXX

LEMUEL HAD PROMISED himself that if he could gain a little time he should be able better to decide what it was right for him to do. His heart lifted as he dropped the letter into the box, and he went through the chapters which Mr. Corey asked him to read, after he came in, with an ease incredible to himself. In the morning he woke with a mind that was almost cheerful. He had been honest in writing that letter, and so far he had done right; he should keep his word about going soon to see Statira, and that would be honest too. He did not look beyond this decision, and he felt as we all do more or less vaguely when we have resolved to do right, that he had the merit of a good action.

Statira showed herself so glad to see him that he could not do less than seem to share her joy in their making-up, as she called it, though he insisted that there had been no quarrel between them; and now there began for him a strange double life, the fact of which each reader must reject or accept according to the witness of his own knowledge.

He renewed as far as he could the old warmth of his feeling for Statira, and in his compunction experienced a tenderness for her that he had not known before, the strange tenderness that some spirits feel for those they injure. He went oftener than ever to see her, he was very good to her, and cheered her with his interest in all her little interests; he petted her and comforted her; but he escaped from her as soon as he could, and when he shut her door behind him he shut her within it. He made haste to forget her, and to lose himself in thoughts that were never wholly absent even in her presence. Sometimes he went directly from her to Jessie, whose innocent Bohemianism kept later hours, and who was always glad to see him whenever he came. She welcomed him with talk that they thought related wholly to the books they had been reading, and to the things of deep psychological import which they suggested. He seldom came to her without the excuse of a book to be lent or borrowed; and he never quitted her without feeling inspired with the wish to know more and to be more: he seemed to be lifted to purer and clearer regions of thought. She received him in the parlor, but their evenings commonly ended in her little studio, whither some errand took them, or some intrusion of the other boarders banished them. There he read to her poems or long chapters out of the essayists or romancers; or else they sat and talked about the strange things they had noticed in themselves that were like the things they found in their books. Once when they had talked a long while in this strain, he told how when he first saw her he thought she was very proud and cold.

She laughed gayly. "And I used to be afraid of you," she said. "You used to be always reading there in your little office. Do you think I'm very proud now?"

"Are you very much afraid of me now?" he retorted.

They laughed together.

"Isn't it strange," she said, "how little we really know about people in the world?"

"Yes," he answered. "I wonder if it will ever be different. I've been wrong about nearly every one I've met since I came to Boston."

"And I have too!" she cried, with that delight in the coincidence of experience which the young feel so keenly.

He had got the habit with his growing ease in her presence, of walking up and down the room, while she sat, forgetful of everything but the things they were saying, and followed him with her eyes. As he turned about in his walk, he saw how pretty she was, with her slender form cased in the black silk she wore. Her eyes were very bright, and her soft lips, small and fine, were red.

He faltered, and lost the thread of his speech. "I forgot what I was going to say!"

She clasped her hands over her laughing face a moment. "And I don't remember what you were saying!" They both laughed a long time at this; it seemed incomparably droll, and they became better comrades.

They spent the rest of the evening in laughing and joking.

"I didn't know you were so fond of laughing," he said, when he went away.

"And I always supposed you were very solemn," she replied.

This again seemed the drollest thing in the world.

"Well, I always was," he said.

"And I don't know when I've laughed so much before!" She stood at the head of the stairs, and held her lamp up for him to find his way down.

Again looking back, he saw her in the grace that had bewildered him before.

When he came next they met very seriously, but before the evening was past they were laughing together; and so it happened now whenever he came. They both said how strange it was that laughing with any one seemed to make you feel so much better acquainted. She told of a girl at school that she had always disliked till one day something made them laugh, and after that they became the greatest friends.

He tried to think of some experience to match this, but he could not; he asked her if she did not think that you always felt a little gloomy after you had been laughing a great deal. She said, yes; after that first night when they laughed so, she felt so depressed that she was sure she was going to have bad news from Madeline. Then she said she had received a letter from Madeline that morning, and she and Mr. Berry had both wished her to give him their regards if she ever saw him. This, when she had said it, seemed a very good joke too; and they laughed at it a little consciously, till he boldly bade her tell them he came so very seldom that she did not know when she could deliver their message.

She answered that she was afraid Madeline would not believe that; and then it came out that he had never replied to Berry's letter.

She said, "Oh! Is that the way you treat your correspondents?" and he was ashamed to confess that he had not forgiven Berry.

"I will write to him to-night, if you say so," he answered hardily.

"Oh, you must do what you think best," she said, lightly refusing the responsibility.

"Whatever you say will be best," he said with a sudden, passionate fervor that surprised himself.

She tried to escape from it. "Am I so infallible as that?"

"You are for me!" he retorted.

A silence followed, which she endeavored to break, but she

sat still across the little table from him where the shaded lamp spread its glow, leaving the rest of the room, with its red curtains and its sketches pinned about, in a warm, luxurious shadow. Her eyes fell, and she did not speak.

"It must sound very strange to you, I know," he went on; "and it's strange to me too; but it seems to me that there isn't anything I've done without my thinking whether you would like me to do it."

She rose involuntarily. "You make me ashamed to think that you're so much mistaken about me! I know how we all influence each other—I know I always try to be what I think people expect me to be—I can't be myself—I know what you mean; but you—you must be yourself, and not let——" She stopped in her wandering speech, in strange agitation, and he rose too.

"I hope you're not offended with me!"

"Offended? Why? Why do you—go so soon?"

"I thought you were going," he answered stupidly.

"Why, I'm at *home!*"

They looked at each other, and then they broke into a happy laugh.

"Sit down again! I don't know what I got up for. It must have been to make some tea. Did you know Madeline had bequeathed me her tea-kettle—the one we had at the St. Albans?" She bustled about, and lit the spirit-lamp under the kettle.

"Blow out that match!" he cried. "You'll set your dress on fire!" He caught her hand, which she was holding with the lighted match in it at her side, after the manner of women with lighted matches, and blew it out himself.

"Oh, thank you!" she said indifferently. "Can you take it without milk!"

"Yes, I like it so."

She got out two of the cups he remembered, and he said, "How much like last winter that seems!"

And "Yes, doesn't it?" she sighed.

The lamp purred and fretted under the kettle, and in the silence in which they waited, the elm tree that rose from the pavement outside seemed to look in consciously upon them.

When the kettle began to sing, she poured out the two

cups of tea, and in handing him his their fingers touched, and she gave a little outcry. "Oh! Madeline's precious cup! I thought it was going to drop!"

The soft night-wind blew in through the elm leaves, and their rustling seemed the expression of a profound repose, an endless content.

XXXI

THE NEXT NIGHT Lemuel went to see Statira, without promising himself what he should say or do, but if he were to tell her everything, he felt that she would forgive him more easily than 'Manda Grier. He was aware that 'Manda always lay in wait for him, to pierce him at every undefended point of conscience. Since the first break with her, there had never been peace between them, and perhaps not kindness for long before that. Whether or not she felt responsible for having promoted Statira's affair with him, and therefore bound to guard her to the utmost from suffering by it, she seemed always to be on the alert to seize any advantage against him. Sometimes Statira accused her of trying to act so hatefully to him that he would never come any more; she wildly blamed her; but the faithful creature was none the less constant and vigilant on that account. She took patiently the unjust reproaches which Statira heaped upon her like a wayward child, and remitted nothing of her suspicion or enmity towards Lemuel. Once, when she had been very bitter with him, so bitter that it had ended in an open quarrel between them, Statira sided with him against her, and when 'Manda Grier flounced out of the room she offered him, if he wished, to break with her, and never to speak to her again, or have anything more to do with such a person. But at this his anger somehow fell; and he said no, she must not think of such a thing; that 'Manda Grier had been her friend long before he was, and that, whatever she said to him, she was always good and true to her. Then Statira fell upon his neck and cried, and praised him, and said he was a million times more to her than 'Manda Grier, but she would do whatever he said; and he went away sick at heart.

When he came now, with his thoughts clinging to Jessie, 'Manda Grier hardly gave him time for the decencies of greeting. She was in a high nervous exaltation, and Statira looked as if she had been crying.

"What's become o' them art-students you used to have 't the St. Albans?" she began, her whopper-jaw twitching with excitement, and her eyes glaring vindictively upon Lemuel.

He had sat down near Statira on the lounge, but she drew a little away from him in a provisional fashion, as if she would first see what came of 'Manda Grier's inquisition.

"Art-students?" he repeated aimlessly, while he felt his color go.

"Yes!" she snapped. "Them girls 't used to be 't the St. Albans, 't you thought so wonderful!"

"I didn't know I thought they were very wonderful."

"Can't you answer a civil question?" she demanded, raising her voice.

"I haven't heard any," said Lemuel with sullen scorn.

"Oh! Well!" she sneered. "I forgot that you've b'en used to goin' with such fine folks that you can't bear to be spoken to in plain English."

" 'Manda!" began Statira, with an incipient whimper.

"You be still, S'tira Dudley! Mr. Barker," said the poor foolish thing in the mincing falsetto which she thought so cutting, "have you any idea what's become of your young lady artist friends,—them that took your portrait as a Roman youth, you know?"

Lemuel made no answer whatever, for a time. Then, whether he judged it best to do so, or was goaded to the defiance by 'Manda Grier's manner, he replied, "Miss Swan and Miss Carver? Miss Swan is married, and lives in Wyoming Territory now." Before he had reached the close of the sentence he had controlled himself sufficiently to be speaking quite calmly.

"Oh, indeed, Mr. Barker! And may I ask where Miss Carver is? She married and livin' in Wyoming Territory too?"

"No," said Lemuel quietly. "She's not married. She's in Boston."

"Indeed! Then it *was* her I see in the Garden to-day, S'tira! She b'en back long, Mr. Barker?"

"About a month, I think," said Lemuel.

"Quite a spell! *You* seen her, Mr. Barker?"

"Yes, quite often."

"I want to know! She still paintin' Roman Boys, Mr. Barker? Didn't seem to make any great out at it last winter! But practice makes perfect, they say. I s'pose *you* seen her in the Garden too?"

"I usually see her at home," said Lemuel. "*You* probably receive your friends on the benches in the Garden, but young ladies prefer to have them call at their residences." He astonished himself by this brutality, he who was all gentleness with Miss Carver.

"Very well, Mr. Barker! That's all right. That's all I wanted to know. Never mind about where I meet my friends. Wherever it is, they're *gentlemen*; and they ain't generally goin' with three or four other girls 't the same time."

"No, one like you would be enough," retorted Lemuel.

Statira sat cowering away from the quarrel, and making little ineffectual starts as if to stay it. Heretofore their enmity had been covert if not tacit, in her presence.

Lemuel saw her wavering, and the wish to show 'Manda his superior power triumphed over every other interest and impulse in him. He got upon his feet. "There is no use in this sort of thing going on any longer. I came here because I thought I was wanted. If it's a mistake, it's easy enough to mend it, and it's easy not to make it again. I wish you good-evening."

Statira sprang from the lounge, and flung her arms around his neck. "No, no! You sha'n't go! You mustn't go, Lem! I know you're all right, and I won't have you talked to so! I ain't a bit jealous, Lem; indeed I ain't. I know you wouldn't fool with me, any more than I would with you; and that's what I tell 'Manda Grier, I'll leave it to her if I don't. I don't care who you go with, and I hain't, never since that first time. I know you ain't goin' to do anything underhanded. Don't go, Lem; oh, *don't* go!"

He was pulling towards the door; her trust, her fond generosity drove him more than 'Manda Grier's cutting tongue: that hurt his pride, his vanity, but this pierced his soul; he had only a blind, stupid will to escape from it.

Statira was crying; she began to cough; she released his neck from her clasp, and reeled backward to the lounge, where she would have fallen, if 'Manda Grier had not caught her. The paroxysm grew more violent; a bright stream of blood sprang from her lips.

"Run! Run for the doctor! Quick, Lemuel! Oh, quick!" implored 'Manda Grier, forgetting all enmity in her terror.

Statira's arms wavered towards him, as if to keep him, but he turned and ran from the house, cowed and conscience-stricken by the sight of that blood, as if he had shed it.

He did not expect to see Statira alive when he came back with the doctor whom he found at the next apothecary's. She was lying on the lounge, white as death, but breathing quietly, and her eyes sought him with an eagerness that turned to a look of tender gratitude at the look they found in his.

The doctor bent over her for her pulse and her respiration; then when he turned to examine the crimson handkerchief which 'Manda Grier showed him, Lemuel dropped on his knees beside her, and put his face down to hers.

With her lips against his cheek, she made, "Don't go!"

And he whispered, "No, I'll not leave you now!"

The doctor looked round with the handkerchief still in his hand, as if doubting whether to order him away from her. Then he mutely questioned 'Manda Grier with a glance which her glance answered. He shrugged his shoulders, with a puzzled sigh. An expression of pity crossed his face, which he hardened into one of purely professional interest, and he went on questioning 'Manda Grier in a low tone.

Statira had slipped her hand into Lemuel's, and she held it fast, as if in that clasp she were holding on to her chance of life.

XXXII

S EWELL RETURNED to town for the last time in the third week of September, bringing his family with him.

This was before the greater part of his oddly assorted congregation had thought of leaving the country, either the rich cottagers whose family tradition or liberal opinions kept them in his church, or the boarding and camping elements who were uniting a love of cheapness with a love of nature in their prolonged sojourn among the woods and fields. Certain families, perhaps half of his parish in all, were returning because the schools were opening, and they must put their children into them; and it was both to minister to the spiritual needs of these and to get his own children back to their studies that the minister was at home so early.

It was, as I have hinted already, a difficult and laborious season with him; he himself was always a little rusty in his vocation after his summer's outing and felt weakened rather than strengthened by his rest. The domestic machine started reluctantly; there was a new cook to be got in, and Mrs. Sewell had to fight a battle with herself, in which she invited him to share, before she could settle down for the winter to the cares of housekeeping. The wide skies, the dim mountain slopes, the long, delicious drives, the fresh mornings, the sweet, silvery afternoons of their idle country life, haunted their nerves and enfeebled their wills.

One evening in the first days of this moral disability, while Sewell sat at his desk trying to get himself together for a sermon, Barker's name was brought up to him.

"Really," said his wife, who had transmitted it from the maid, "I think it's time you protected yourself, David. You can't let this go on forever. He has been in Boston nearly two years now; he has regular employment, where, if there's anything in him at all, he ought to prosper and improve without coming to you every other night. What *can* he want now?"

"I'm sure I don't know," said the minister, leaning back in his chair, and passing his hand wearily over his forehead.

"Then send down and excuse yourself. Tell him you're busy, and ask him to come another time!"

"Ah, you know I can't do that, my dear."

"Very well, then; I will go down and see him. You sha'n't be interrupted."

"Would you, my dear? That would be very kind of you! Do get me off some way; tell him I'm coming to see him very soon." He went stupidly back to his writing without looking to see whether his wife had meant all she said; and after a moment's hesitation she descended in fulfillment of her promise; or, perhaps rather it was a threat.

She met Lemuel not unkindly, for she was a kind-hearted woman; but she placed duty before charity even, and she could not help making him feel that she was there in the discharge of a duty. She explained that Mr. Sewell was very unusually busy that evening, and had sent her in his place, and hoped soon to see him. She bade Lemuel sit down, and he obeyed, answering all the questions as to the summer and his occupations and health, and his mother's health, which she put to him in proof of her interest in him; in further evidence of it, she gave him an account of the Sewell family's doings since they last met. He did not stay long, and she returned slowly and pensively to her husband.

"Well?" he asked, without looking round.

"Well, it's all right," she answered, with rather a deep breath. "He didn't seem to have come for anything in particular; I told him that if he wished specially to speak with you, you would come down."

Sewell went on with his writing, and after a moment his wife said, "But you must go and see him very soon, David; you must go to-morrow."

"Why?"

"He looks wretchedly, though he says he's very well. It made my heart ache. He looks perfectly wan and haggard. I wish," she burst out, "I wish I had let you go down and see him!"

"Why—why, what was the matter?" asked Sewell, turning about now. "Did you think he had something on his mind?"

"No, but he looked fairly sick. Oh, I wish he had never come into our lives!"

"I'm afraid he hasn't got much good from us," sighed the minister. "But I'll go round and look him up in the morning. His trouble will keep overnight, if it's a real trouble. There's that comfort, at least. And now, do go away, my dear, and leave me to my writing."

Mrs. Sewell looked at him, but turned and left him, apparently reserving whatever sermon she might have in her mind till he should have finished his.

The next morning he went to inquire for Lemuel at Mr. Corey's. The man was sending him away from the door with the fact merely that Lemuel was not then in the house, when the voice of Mr. Corey descending the stairs called from within: "Is that you, Sewell? Don't go away! Come in!"

The old gentleman took him into the library, and confessed in a bit of new slang, which he said was delightful, that he was all balled up by Lemuel's leaving him, and asked Sewell what he supposed it meant.

"Left you? Meant?" echoed Sewell.

When they got at each other it was understood that Lemuel, the day before, had given up his employment with Mr. Corey, expressing a fit sense of all his kindness and a fit regret at leaving him, but alleging no reasons for his course; and that this was the first that Sewell knew of the affair.

"It must have been that which he came to see me about last night," he said with a sort of anticipative remorse. "Mrs. Sewell saw him—I was busy."

"Well! Get him to come back, Sewell," said Mr. Corey, with his whimsical imperiousness; "I can't get on without him. All my moral and intellectual being has stopped like a watch."

Sewell went to the boarding-house where Lemuel took his meals, but found that he no longer came there and had left no other address. He knew nowhere else to ask, and he went home to a day of latent trouble of mind, which whenever it came to the light defined itself as helpless question and self-reproach in regard to Barker.

That evening as he sat at tea, the maid came with the announcement that there was a person in the reception-room who would not send in any name, but wished to see Mr. Sewell, and would wait.

Sewell threw down his napkin, and said, "I'll bring him in to tea."

Mrs. Sewell did not resist; she bade the girl lay another plate.

Sewell was so sure of finding Lemuel in the reception-room, that he recoiled in dismay from the girlish figure that turned timidly from the window to meet him with a face thickly veiled. He was vexed too; here, he knew from the mystery put on, was one of those cases of feminine trouble, real or unreal, which he most disliked to meddle with.

"Will you sit down?" he said as kindly as he could, and the girl obeyed.

"I thought they would let me wait. I didn't mean to interrupt you," she began, in a voice singularly gentle and unaffected.

"Oh, no matter!" cried Sewell. "I'm very glad to see you."

"I thought you could help me. I'm in great trouble— doubt——"

The voice was almost childlike in its appealing innocence.

Sewell sat down opposite the girl and bent sympathetically forward. "Well?"

She waited a moment. Then, "I don't know how to begin," she said hoarsely, and stopped again.

Sewell was touched. He forgot Lemuel; he forgot everything but the heartache which he divined before him, and his Christ-derived office, his holy privilege, of helping any in want of comfort or guidance. "Perhaps," he said, in his loveliest way,—the way that had won his wife's heart, and that still provoked her severest criticism for its insincerity, it was so purely impersonal,—"perhaps that isn't necessary, if you mean beginning at the beginning. If you've any trouble that you think I can advise you in, perhaps it's better for both of us that I shouldn't know very much of it."

"Yes?" murmured the girl, questioningly.

"I mean that if you tell me much, you will go away feeling that you have somehow parted with yourself, that you're no longer in your own keeping, but in mine; and you know that in everything our help must really come from within our own free consciences."

"Yes," said the girl again, from behind the veil which completely hid her face. She now hesitated a long time. She put her handkerchief under her veil; and at last she said, "I know what you mean." Her voice quivered pathetically; she tried to control it. "Perhaps," she whispered huskily, after another interval, "I can put it in the form of a question."

"That would be best," said Sewell.

She hesitated; the tears fell down upon her hands behind her veil; she no longer wiped them. "It's because I've often — heard you; because I know you will tell me what's true and right——"

"Your own heart must do that," said the minister, "but I will gladly help you all I can."

She did not heed him now, but continued as if rapt quite away from him.

"If there was some one — something — if there was something that it would be right for you to do — to have, if there was no one else; but if there were some one else that had a right first——" She broke off and asked abruptly, "Don't you think it is always right to prefer another — the interest of another to your own?"

Sewell could not help smiling. "There is only one thing for us to do when we are in any doubt or perplexity," he said cheerily, "and that is the unselfish thing."

"Yes," she gasped; she seemed to be speaking to herself. "I saw it, I knew it! Even if it kills us, we must do it! Nothing ought to weigh against it! Oh, I thank you!"

Sewell was puzzled. He felt dimly that she was thanking him for anguish and despair. "I'm afraid that I don't quite understand you."

"I thought I told you," she answered, with a certain reproach and a fall of courage in view of the fresh effort she must make. It was some moments before she could say "If you knew that some one — some one who was — everything to you — and that you knew — believed——"

At fifty it is hard to be serious about these things, and it was well for the girl that she was no longer conscious of Sewell's mood.

"—Cared for you; and if you knew that before he had cared for you, there had been some else — some else that he was as much to as he was to you, and that couldn't give him up, what—should you——"

Sewell fetched a long sigh of relief; he had been afraid of a much darker problem than this. He almost smiled.

"My dear child,"—she seemed but a child there before the mature man with her poor little love-trouble, so intricate and hopeless to her, so simple and easy to him,—"that depends upon a great many circumstances."

He could feel through her veil the surprise with which she turned to him: "You said, whenever we are in doubt, we must act unselfishly."

"Yes, I said that. But you must first be sure what is really selfish——"

"I *know* what is selfish in this case," said the girl with a sublimity which, if foolish, was still sublimity. "She is sick— it will kill her to lose him— You have said what I expected, and I thank you, thank you, *thank* you! And I will do it! Oh, don't fear now but I shall; I *have* done it! No matter," she went on in her exaltation, "no matter how much we care for each other, now!"

"No," said Sewell, decidedly. "That doesn't follow. I have thought of such things; there was such a case within my experience once,"—he could not help alleging this case, in which he had long triumphed,—"and I have always felt that I did right in advising against a romantic notion of self-sacrifice in such matters. You may commit a greater wrong in that than in an act of apparent self-interest. You have not put the case fully before me, and it isn't necessary that you should, but if you contemplate any rash sacrifice, I warn you against it."

"You said that we ought to act unselfishly."

"Yes, but you must beware of the refined selfishness which shrinks from righteous self-assertion because it is painful. You must make sure of your real motive; you must consider whether your sacrifice is not going to do more harm than good. But why do you come to me with your trouble? Why don't you go to your father—your mother?"

"I have none."

"Ah——"

She had risen and pushed by him to the outer door, though he tried to keep her. "Don't be rash," he urged. "I advise you to take time to think of this——"

She did not answer; she seemed now only to wish to escape, as if in terror of him.

She pulled open the door, and was gone.

Sewell went back to his tea, bewildered, confounded.

"What's the matter? Why didn't he come in to tea with you?" asked his wife.

"Who?"

"Barker."

"What Barker?"

"David, what *is* the matter?"

Sewell started from his daze, and glanced at his children: "I'll tell you by and by, Lucy."

XXXIII

A MONTH PASSED, and Sewell heard nothing of Lemuel. His charge, always elusive and evanescent, had now completely vanished, and he could find no trace of him. Mr. Corey suggested advertising. Bellingham said, why not put it in the hands of a detective? He said he had never helped work anything up with a detective; he rather thought he should like to do it. Sewell thought of writing to Barker's mother at Willoughby Pastures, but he postponed it; perhaps it would alarm her if Barker were not there. Sewell had many other cares and duties; Lemuel became more and more a good intention of the indefinite future. After all, he had always shown the ability to take care of himself, and except that he had mysteriously disappeared there was no reason for anxiety about him.

One night his name came up at a moment when Sewell was least prepared by interest or expectation to see him. He smiled to himself, in running downstairs, at the reflection that he never seemed quite ready for Barker. But it was a relief to have him turn up again; there was no question of that, and Sewell showed him a face of welcome that dropped at sight of him. He scarcely knew the gaunt, careworn face or the shabby figure before him, in place of the handsome, well-dressed young fellow whom he had come to greet. There seemed a sort of reversion in Barker's whole presence to the time when Sewell first found him in that room; and in whatever trouble he now was, the effect was that of his original rustic constraint.

Trouble there was of some kind, Sewell could see at a glance, and his kind heart prompted him to take Lemuel's hand between both of his. "Why, my dear boy!" he began; but he stopped and made Lemuel sit down, and waited for him to speak, without further question or comment.

"Mr. Sewell," the young man said abruptly, "you told me once you—that you sometimes had money put into your hands that you could lend."

"Yes," replied Sewell, with eager cordiality.

"Could I borrow about seventy-five dollars of you?"

"Why, certainly, Barker!" Sewell had not so much of what he called his flying-charity fund by him, but he instantly resolved to advance the difference out of his own pocket.

"It's to get me an outfit for horse-car conductor," said Lemuel. "I can have the place if I can get the outfit."

"Horse-car conductor!" reverberated Sewell. "What in the world for?"

"It's work I can do," answered Lemuel, briefly, but not resentfully.

"But there are so many other things—better—fitter—more profitable! Why did you leave Mr. Corey? I assure you that you have been a great loss to him—in every way. You don't know how much he valued you, personally. He will be only too glad to have you come back."

"I can't go back," said Lemuel. "I'm going to get married."

"Married!" cried Sewell in consternation.

"My—the lady that I'm going to marry—has been sick ever since the first of October, and I haven't had a chance to look up any kind of work. But she's better now, and I've heard of this place I can get. I don't like to trouble you; but—everything's gone—I've got my mother down here helping take care of her; and I must do something. I don't know just when I can pay you back, but I'll do it sometime."

"Oh, I'm sure of that," said Sewell, from the abyss of hopeless conjecture into which these facts had plunged him; his wandering fancy was dominated by the presence of Lemuel's mother with her bloomers in Boston. "I—I hope there's nothing serious the trouble with your—the lady?" he said, rubbing away with his hand the smile that came to his lips in spite of him.

"It's lung trouble," said Lemuel, quietly.

"Oh!" responded Sewell. "Well! Well!" He shook himself together, and wondered what had become of the impulse he had felt to scold Barker for the idea of getting married. But such a course now seemed not only far beyond his province,—he heard himself saying that to Mrs. Sewell in self-defense when she should censure him for not doing it,—but utterly useless in view of the further complications. "Well! This is great news you tell me—a great surprise. You're—you're going to take an important step—— You—you——

Of course, of course! You must have a great many demands upon you, under the circumstances. Yes, yes! And I'm very glad you came to me. If your mind is quite made up about——"

"Yes, I've thought it over," said Lemuel. "The lady has had to work all her life, and she—she isn't used to what I thought—what I intended—any other kind of people; and it's better for us both that I should get some kind of work that won't take me away from her too much——" He dropped his head, and Sewell with a flash of intelligence felt a thrill of compassionate admiration for the poor, foolish, generous creature, for so Lemuel complexly appeared to him.

Again he forbore question or comment.

"Well—well! we must look you up, Mrs. Sewell and I. We must come to see your—the lady." He found himself falling helplessly into Lemuel's way of describing her. "Just write me your address here,"—he put a scrap of paper before Lemuel on the davenport,—"and I'll go and get you the money."

He brought it back in an envelope which held a very little more than Lemuel had asked for—Sewell had not dared to add much—and Lemuel put it in his pocket.

He tried to say something; he could only make a husky noise in his throat.

"Good-night!" said Sewell, pressing his hand with both of his again, at the door. "We shall come very soon."

"MARRIED!" said Mrs. Sewell, when he returned to her; and then she suffered a silence to ensue, in which it seemed to Sewell that his inculpation was visibly accumulating mountains vast and high. *"What did you say?"*

"Nothing," he answered, almost gayly; the case was so far beyond despair. "What should *you* have said?"

XXXIV

LEMUEL got a conductor's overcoat and cap at half-price from a man who had been discharged, and put by the money saved to return to Sewell when he should come. He entered upon his duties the next morning, under the instruction of an old conductor, who said "Hain't I seen you som'eres before?" and he worked all day, taking money and tickets, registering fares, helping ladies on and off the car, and monotonously journeying back and forth over his route. He went on duty at six o'clock in the morning, after an early breakfast that 'Manda Grier and his mother got him, for Statira was not strong enough yet to do much, and he was to be relieved at eight. At nightfall, after two half-hour respites for dinner and tea, he was so tired that he could scarcely stand.

"Well, how do you like it, as fur's you've gone?" asked the instructing conductor, in whom Lemuel had recognized an old acquaintance. "Sweet life, ain't it? There! That switch hain't worked again! Jump off, young man, and put your shoulder to the wheel!"

The car had failed to take the right-hand turn where the line divided; it had to be pushed back, and while the driver tugged and swore under his breath at his horses, Lemuel set himself to push the car.

" 'S no use!" said the driver finally. "I got to hitch 'em on at the other end, and pull her back."

He uncoupled the team from the front of the car, and swung round with it. Lemuel felt something strike him on the leg, and he fell down. He scrambled to his feet again, but his left leg doubled under him; it went through his mind that one of the horses must have lashed out and broken it; then everything seemed to stop.

The world began again for him in the apothecary's shop where he had been carried, and from which he was put into an ambulance, by a policeman. It stopped again, as he whirled away; it renewed itself in anguish, and ceased in bliss as he fainted from the pain or came to.

They lifted him up some steps, at last, and carried him into a high, bright room, where there were two or three cots, and a long glass case full of surgical instruments. They laid him on a cot, and some one swiftly and skillfully undressed him. A surgeon had come in, and now he examined Lemuel's leg. He looked once or twice at his face.

"This is a pretty bad job. I can't tell how bad till you've had the ether. Will you leave it to me?"

"Yes. But do the best you can for me."

"You may be sure I will."

Lemuel believed that they meant to cut off his leg. He knew that he had a right to refuse and to take the consequences, but he would not; he had no right to choose death, when he had others to live for.

He woke deathly sick at first, and found himself lying in bed, one of the two rows in a long room, where there were some quiet women in neat caps and seersucker dresses going about, with bowls of food and bottles of medicine.

Lemuel still felt his leg, and the pain in it, but he had heard how mutilated men felt their lost limbs all their lives, and he was afraid to make sure by the touch of his hand.

A nurse who saw his eyes open came to him. He turned them upon her, but he could not speak. She must have understood. "The doctor thinks he can save your leg for you; but it's a bad fracture. You must be careful to keep very still."

He fell asleep; and life began again for him, in the midst of suffering and death. He saw every day broken and mangled men, drunk with ether, brought up as he had been, and laid in beds; he saw the priest of the religion to which most of the poor and lowly still belong, go and come among the cots, and stand by the pillows where the sick feebly followed him in the mystical gestures which he made on his brow and breast; he learned to know the use of the white linen screen which was drawn about a bed to hide the passing of a soul; he became familiar with the helpless sympathy, the despair of the friends who came to visit the sick and dying.

He had not lacked for more attention and interest from his own than the rules of the hospital allowed. His mother and 'Manda Grier came first, and then Statira when they would let her. She thought it hard that she was not suffered to do the least thing for him; she wished to take him away to their own rooms, where she could nurse him twice as well. At first she cried whenever she saw him, and lamented over him, so that the head nurse was obliged to explain to her that she disturbed the patients, and could not come any more unless she controlled herself. She promised, and kept her word; she sat quietly by his pillow and held his hand, when she came, except when she put up her own to hide the cough which she could not always restrain. The nurse told her that of course she was not accountable for the cough, but she had better try to check it. Statira brought troches with her, and held them in her mouth for this purpose.

Lemuel's family was taken care of in this time of disaster. The newspapers had made his accident promptly known, and not only Sewell, but Miss Vane and Mrs. Corey had come to see if they could be of any use.

One day a young girl brought a bouquet of flowers and set it by Lemuel's bed, when he seemed asleep. He suddenly opened his eyes, and saw Sibyl Vane for the first time since their quarrel.

She put her finger to her lip, and smiled with the air of a lady benefactress; then, with a few words of official sympathy, she encouraged him to get well, and flitted to the next bed, where she bestowed a jacqueminot rosebud on a Chinaman dying of cancer.

Sewell came often to see him, at first in the teeth of his mother's obvious hostility, but with her greater and greater relenting. Nothing seemed gloomier than the outlook for Lemuel, but Sewell had lived too long not to know that the gloom of an outlook has nothing to do with a man's real future. It was impossible, of course, for Lemuel to go back to Mr. Corey's now with a sick wife, who would need so much of his care. Besides, he did not think it desirable on other accounts. He recurred to what Lemuel had said about getting work that should not take him too far away from the kind of people his betrothed was used to, and he felt a pity and respect for the boy whom life had already taught this wisdom, this resignation. He could see that before his last calamity had come upon him, Barker was trying to adjust his ambition to his next duty, or rather to subordinate it; and the conviction that he was right gave Sewell courage to think that he would yet somehow succeed. It also gave him courage to resist, on Barker's behalf, the generous importunities of some who would have befriended him. Mr. Corey and Charles Bellingham drove up to the hospital one day to see Lemuel; and when Sewell met them the same evening, they were full of enthusiasm. Corey said that the effect of the hospital, with its wards branching from the classistic building in the center, was delightfully Italian; it was like St. Peter's on a small scale, and he had no idea how interesting the South End was; it was quite a bit of foreign travel to go up there. Bellingham had explored the hospital throughout; he said he had found it the thing to do—it was a thing for everybody to do; he was astonished that he had never done it before. They united in praising Barker, and they asked what could be done for him. Corey was strenuous for his coming back to him; at any rate, they must find something for him. Bellingham favored the notion of doing something for his education; a fellow like that could come to almost anything.

Sewell shook his head. "All that's impossible now. With that girl——"

"Oh, confound her!" cried Bellingham.

"I was rather disappointed at not seeing his mother," said Corey. "I had counted a good deal, I find, upon Mrs. Barker's bloomers."

"With a girl like that for his wife," pursued Sewell, "the conditions are all changed. He must cleave to her in mind as well as body, and he must seek the kind of life that will unite them more and more, not less and less. In fact, he was instinctively doing so when this accident happened. That's what marriage means."

"Oh, not always," suggested Corey.

"He must go back to Willoughby Pastures," Sewell concluded, "to his farm."

"Oh, come now!" said Bellingham, with disgust.

"If that sort of thing is to go on," said Corey, "what is to become of the ancestry of the future *élite* of Boston? I counted upon Barker to found one of our first families. Besides, any Irishman could take his farm and do better with it. The farm would be meat to the Irishman, and poison to Barker, now that he's once tasted town."

"Yes, I know all that," said Sewell, sadly. "I once thought the greatest possible good I could do Barker, after getting him to Boston, was to get him back to Willoughby Pastures; but if that was ever true, the time is past. Now, it merely seems the only thing possible. When he gets well, he will still have an invalid wife on his hands; he must provide her a home; she could have helped him once, and would have done so, I've no doubt; but now she must be taken care of."

"Look here!" said Bellingham. "What's the reason these things can't be managed as they are in the novels? In any well-regulated romance that cough of hers would run into quick consumption and carry Barker's fiancée off in six weeks; and then he could resume his career of usefulness and prosperity here, don't you know. He could marry some one else and found that family that Corey wants."

They all laughed, Sewell ruefully.

"As it is," said Corey, "I suppose she'll go on having hemorrhages to a good old age, and outlive him, after being a clog and burden to him all his life. Poor devil! What in the world possesses him to want to marry her? But I suppose the usual thing."

This gave Sewell greater discomfort than the question of Lemuel's material future. He said listlessly, "Oh, I suppose so," but he was far from thinking precisely that. He had seen Lemuel and the young girl together a great deal, and a painful misgiving had grown up in his mind. It seemed to him that while he had seen no want of patience and kindness towards her in Lemuel, he had not seen the return of her fondness, which, silly as it was in some of its manifestations, he thought he should be glad of in him. Yet he was not sure. Barker was always so self-contained that he might very well feel more love for her than he showed; and, after all, Sewell rather weakly asked himself, was the love so absolutely necessary?

When he repeated this question in his wife's presence, she told him she was astonished at him.

"You know that it is *vitally* necessary! It's all the more necessary, if he's so superior to her, as you say. I can't think what's become of your principles, my dear!"

"I do: you've got them," said Sewell.

"I really believe I have," said his wife, with that full conviction of righteousness which her sex alone can feel. "I have always heard you say that marriage without love was not only sinful in itself, but the beginning of sorrow. Why do you think now that it makes no difference?"

"I suppose I was trying to adapt myself to circumstances," answered Sewell, frankly at least. "Let's hope that my facts are as wrong as my conclusions. I'm not sure of either. I suppose if I saw him idolizing so slight and light a person as she seems to be, I should be more disheartened about his future than I am now. If he overvalued her, it would only drag him lower down."

"Oh, his future! Drag him down! Why don't you think of *her*, going up there to that dismal wilderness, to spend her days in toil and poverty, with a half-crazy mother-in-law, and a rheumatic brother-in-law, in such a looking hovel?" Mrs. Sewell did not group these disadvantages conventionally, but they were effective. "You have allowed your feelings about that baffling creature to blind you to everything else, David. Why should you care so much for his future, and nothing for hers? Is that so very bright?"

"I don't think that either is dazzling," sighed the minister. Yet Barker's grew a little lighter as he familiarized himself with it, or rather with Barker. He found that he had a plan for getting a teacher's place in the academy, if they reopened it, at Willoughby Pastures, as they talked of doing, under the impulse of such a course in one of the neighboring towns, and that he was going home, in fancy at least, with purposes of enlightenment and elevation which would go far to console him under such measure of disappointment as they must bring. Sewell hinted to Barker that he must not be too confident of remodeling Willoughby Pastures upon the pattern of Boston.

"Oh, no; I don't expect that," said Lemuel. "What I mean is that I shall always try to remember myself what I've learnt here—from the kind of men I've seen, and the things that I know people are all the time doing for others. I told you once that they haven't got any idea of that in the country. I don't expect to preach it into them; they wouldn't like it if I did; and they'd make fun of it; but if I could try to *live* it?"

"Yes," said Sewell, touched by this young enthusiasm.

"I don't know as I can all the time," said Lemuel. "But it seems to me that that's what I've learnt here, if I've learnt anything. I think the world's a good deal better than I used to."

"Do you, indeed, my dear boy?" asked Sewell, greatly interested. "It's a pretty well meaning world—I hope it is."

"Yes, that's what I mean," said Lemuel. "I presume it ain't perfect—isn't, I should say," and Sewell smiled. "Mr. Corey was always correcting me on that. But if I were to do nothing but pass along the good that's been done me since I came here, I should be kept busy the rest of my life."

Sewell knew that this emotion was largely the physical optimism of convalescence; but he could not refuse the comfort it gave him to find Barker in such a mood, and he did not conceive it his duty to discourage it. Lofty ideals, if not indulged at the expense of lowly realities, he had never found hurtful to any; and it was certainly better for Barker to think too well than too ill of Boston, if it furnished him incentives to unselfish living. He could think of enough things in the city to warrant a different judgment, but if Barker's lesson from his experience there was this, Sewell was not the person to weaken its force with him. He said, with a smile of reserved comment, "Well, perhaps you'll be coming back to us, some day."

"I don't look forward to that," said Lemuel soberly; and then his face took a sterner cast, as if from the force of his resolution. "The first thing I've got to do after I've made a home for her is to get Statira away from the town where she can have some better air, and see if she can't get her health back. It'll be time enough to talk of Boston again when she's fit to live here."

The minister's sympathetic spirit sank again. But his final parting with Barker was not unhopeful. Lemuel consented to accept from him a small loan, to the compass of which he reduced the eager bounty of Miss Vane and Mr. Corey, representing that more would be a burden and an offense to Barker. Statira and his mother came with him to take leave of the Sewells.

They dismounted from the horse-car at the minister's door; and he saw, with sensibility, the two women helping Lemuel off; he walked with a cane, and they went carefully on either side of him. Sewell hastened to meet them at the door himself, and he was so much interested in the spectacle of this mutual affection that he failed at first to observe that Mrs. Barker wore the skirts of occidental civilization instead of the bloomers which he had identified her with.

"She *says* she's goin' to put 'em on again as soon as she gets back to Willoughby," the younger woman explained to Mrs. Sewell in an aside, while the minister was engaged with Lemuel and his mother. "But I tell her as long as it ain't the fashion in Boston, I guess she hadn't better *he*-e-e-re." Statira had got on her genteel prolongation of her last syllables again. "I guess I shall get along with her. She's kind of queer when you first get acquainted, but she's *real* good-*heart*-e-e-d." She was herself very prettily dressed, and though she looked thin, and at times gave a deep, dismal cough, she was so bright and gay that it was impossible not to feel hopeful about her. She became very confidential with Mrs. Sewell, whom she apparently brevetted Lemuel's best friend, and obliged to a greater show of interest in him than she had ever felt. She told her the whole history of her love affair, and of how much 'Manda Grier had done to help it on at first, and then how she had wanted her to break off with Lemuel. "But," she concluded, "*I* think we're goin' to get along real nice together. I don't know as we shall live all in the same *hou*-ou-se; I guess it'll be the best thing for Lem and I if we can board till we get some little of our health back; I'm more scared for him than what I am for my-*se*-e-lf. I don't presume but what we shall both miss the city some; but he might be out of a job all winter in town; I shouldn't want he should go back on them *ca*-a-rs. Most I hate is leavin' 'Manda Grier; she is the one that I've roomed with ever since I first came to Boston; but Lem and her don't get on very well; they hain't really either of 'em *got* anything against each other, now, but they don't *like* very *we*-e-ll; and, of course, I got to have the friends that he wants me to have, and that's what 'Manda Grier says *to*-o-o; and so it's just as well we're goin' to be where they won't *cla*-a-sh."

She talked to Mrs. Sewell in a low voice; but she kept her eyes upon Lemuel all the time; and when Sewell took him and his mother the length of the front drawing-room away, she was quite distraught, and answered at random till he came back.

Sewell did not know what to think. Would this dependence warm her betrothed to greater tenderness than he now showed, or would its excess disgust him? He was not afraid that Lemuel would ever be unkind to her; but he knew that in marriage kindness was not enough. He looked at Lemuel, serious, thoughtful, refined in his beauty by suffering; and then his eye wandered to Statira's delicate prettiness, so sweet, so full of amiable cheerfulness, so undeniably light and silly. What chiefly comforted him was the fact of an ally whom the young thing had apparently found in Lemuel's mother. Whether that grim personage's ignorant pride in her son had been satisfied with a girl of Statira's style and fashion, and proved capableness in housekeeping, or whether some fancy for butterfly prettiness lurking in the fastnesses of the old woman's rugged nature had been snared by the gay face and dancing eyes, it was apparent that she at least was in love with Statira. She allowed herself to be poked about, and re-arranged as to her shawl and the narrow-brimmed youthful hat which she wore on the peak of her skull, and she soft-ened to something like a smile at the touch of Statira's quick hands.

They had all come rather early to make their parting visit at the Sewells', for the Barkers were going to take the two o'clock train for Willoughby Pastures, while Statira was to re-main in Boston till he could make a home for her. Lemuel promised to write as soon as he should be settled, and tell Sewell about his life and his work; and Sewell, beyond ear-shot of his wife, told him he might certainly count upon see-ing them at Willoughby in the course of the next summer. They all shook hands several times. Lemuel's mother gave her hand from under the fringe of her shawl, standing bolt up-right at arm's length off, and Sewell said it felt like a collec-tion of corn-cobs.

XXXV

WELL?" said Sewell's wife, when they were gone.
"Well," he responded; and after a moment he said,
"There's this comfort about it, which we don't always have in
such cases: there doesn't seem to be anybody else. It would be
indefinitely worse if there were."

"Why, of course. What in the world are you thinking
about?"

"About that foolish girl who came to me with her miserable love-trouble. I declare, I can't get rid of it. I feel morally
certain that she went away from me and dismissed the poor
fellow who was looking to her love to save him."

"At the cost of some other poor creature who'd trusted and
believed in him till his silly fancy changed? I hope for the
credit of women that she did. But you may be morally certain
she did nothing of the kind. Girls don't give up all their hopes
in life so easily as that. She might think she would do it,
because she had read of such things, and thought it was fine,
but when it came to the pinch, she wouldn't."

"I hope not. If she did she would commit a great error, a
criminal error."

"Well, you needn't be afraid. Look at Mrs. Tom Corey.
And that was her own sister!"

"That was different. Corey had never thought of her sister,
much less made love to her, or promised to marry her. Besides, Mrs. Corey had her father and mother to advise her,
and support her in behaving sensibly. And this poor creature
had nothing but her own novel-fed fancies, and her crazy conscience. She thought that because she inflicted suffering upon
herself she was acting unselfishly. Really, the fakirs of India
and the Penitentes of New Mexico are more harmless, for they
don't hurt any one else. If she has forced some poor fellow
into a marriage like this of Barker's, she's committed a deadly
sin. She'd better driven him to suicide, than condemned him
to live a lie to the end of his days. No doubt she regarded it as
a momentary act of expiation. That's the way her romances
taught her to look at loveless marriage—as something spec-

tacular, transitory, instead of the enduring, degrading squalor that it is!"

"What in the world are you talking about, David? I should think *you* were a novelist yourself, by the wild way you go on! You have no proof whatever that Barker isn't happily engaged. I'm sure he's got a much better girl than he deserves, and one that's fully his equal. She's only too fond of that dry stick. Such a girl as the one you described,— like that mysterious visitor of yours,— what possible relation could she have with him? She was a lady!"

"Yes, yes! Of course it's absurd. But everybody seems to be tangled up with everybody else. My dear, will you give me a cup of tea? I think I'll go to writing at once."

Before she left her husband to order his tea Mrs. Sewell asked, "And do you think you have got through with him now?"

"I have just begun with him," replied Sewell.

His mind, naturally enough in connection with Lemuel, was running upon his friend Evans, and the subject they had once talked of in that room. It was primarily in thinking of him that he began to write his sermon on Complicity, which made a great impression at the time, and had a more lasting effect as enlarged from the newspaper reports, and reprinted in pamphlet form. His evolution from the text, "Remember them that are in bonds as bound with them," of a complete philosophy of life, was humorously treated by some of his critics as a phase of Darwinism, but upon the whole the sermon met with great favor. It not only strengthened Sewell's hold upon the affections of his own congregation, but carried his name beyond Boston, and made him the topic of editorials in the Sunday editions of leading newspapers as far off as Chicago. It struck one of those popular moods of intelligent sympathy when the failure of a large class of underpaid and worthy workers to assert their right to a living wage against a powerful monopoly had sent a thrill of respectful pity through every generous heart in the country; and it was largely supposed that Sewell's sermon referred indirectly to the telegraphers' strike. Those who were aware of his habit of seeking to produce a personal rather than a general effect, of his belief that you can have a righteous public only by the slow process of having righteous men and women, knew that he meant something much nearer home to each of his hearers, when he preached the old Christ-humanity to them, and enforced again the lesson that no one for good or for evil, for sorrow or joy, for sickness or health, stood apart from his fellows, but each was bound to the highest and the lowest by ties that centered in the hand of God. No man, he said, sinned or suffered to himself alone; his error and his pain darkened and afflicted men who never heard of his name. If a community was corrupt, if an age was immoral, it was not because of the vicious, but the virtuous who fancied themselves indifferent spectators. It was not the tyrant who oppressed, it was the wickedness that had made him possible. The gospel—Christ—God, so far as men had imagined him, —was but a lesson, a type, a witness from everlasting to everlasting of the spiritual unity of man. As we grew in grace, in humanity, in civilization, our recognition of this truth would be transfigured from a duty to a privilege, a joy, a heavenly rapture. Many men might go through life harmlessly without realizing this, perhaps, but sterilely; only those who had had the care of others laid upon them, lived usefully, fruitfully. Let no one shrink from such a burden, or seek to rid himself of it. Rather let him bind it fast upon his neck, and rejoice in it. The wretched, the foolish, the ignorant whom we found at every turn, were something more; they were the messengers of God, sent to tell his secret to any that would hear it. Happy he in whose ears their cry for help was a perpetual voice, for that man, whatever his creed, knew God, and could never forget him. In his responsibility for his weaker brethren he was Godlike, for God was but the impersonation of loving responsibility, of infinite and never-ceasing care for us all.

When Sewell came down from his pulpit, many people came up to speak to him of his sermon. Some of the women's faces showed the traces of tears, and each person had made its application to himself. There were two or three who had heard between the words. Old Bromfield Corey, who was coming a good deal more to church since his eyes began to fail him, because it was a change and a sort of relief from being read to, said:

"I didn't know that they had translated it Barker in the revised version. Well, you must let me know how he's getting on, Sewell, and give me a chance at the revelation too, if he ever gets troublesome to you again."

Miss Vane was standing at the door with his wife when Sewell came out. She took his hand and pressed it.

"Do you think I threw away my chance?" she demanded. She had her veil down, and at first Sewell thought it was laughter that shook her voice, but it was not that.

He did not know quite what to say, but he did say, "He was sent to *me*."

As they walked off alone, his wife said:

"Well, David, I hope you haven't preached away all your truth and righteousness."

"I know what you mean, my dear," answered Sewell humbly. He added, "You shall remind me, if I seem likely to forget." But he concluded seriously, "If I thought I could never do anything more for Barker, I should be very unhappy; I should take it as a sign that I had been recreant to my charge."

XXXVI

THE MINISTER heard directly from Barker two or three times during the winter, and as often through Statira, who came to see Mrs. Sewell. Barker had not got the place he had hoped for at once, but he had got a school in the country a little way off, and he was doing something; and he expected to do better.

The winter proved a very severe one. "I guess it's just as well I staid in town," said Statira, the last time she came, with a resignation which Mrs. Sewell, fond of the ideal in others, as most ladies are, did not like. " 'Manda Grier says 'twould killed me up there; and I d' know but what it would. I done so well here, since the cold weather set in, that 'Manda Grier she thinks I hadn't better get married right away; well, not till it comes summer, anyway. I tell her I guess she don't want I should get married at all, after all she done to help it along first off. Her and Mr. Barker don't seem to get along very well."

Now that Statira felt a little better acquainted with Mrs. Sewell, she dropped the genteel elongation of her final syllables, and used such vernacular forms of speech as came first to her. The name of 'Manda Grier seemed to come in at every fourth word with her, and she tired Mrs. Sewell with visits which she appeared unable to bring to a close of herself.

A long relief from them ended in an alarm for her health with Mrs. Sewell, who went to find her. She found her still better than before, and Statira frankly accounted for her absence by saying that 'Manda thought she had better not come any more till Mrs. Sewell returned some of her calls. She laughed, and then she said:

"I don't know as you'd found me here if you'd come much later. 'Manda Grier don't want I should be here in the east winds, now it's comin' spring so soon; and she's heard of a chance at a box factory in Philadelphia. She wants I should go there with her, and I don't know but what it *would* be about the best thing."

Mrs. Sewell could not deny the good sense of the plan, though she was sensible of liking Statira less and less for it.

The girl continued: "Lem—Mr. Barker, I *should* say—wants I should come up *there*, out the east winds. But 'Manda Grier she's opposed to it; she thinks I'd ought to have more of a mild climate, and he better come down *there* and get a school, if he wants me *to-*o." Statira broke into an impartial little titter. "I'm sure I don't know which of 'em 'll win the day!"

Mrs. Sewell's report of this speech brought a radiant smile of relief to Sewell's face. "Ah, well, then! That settles it! I feel perfectly sure that 'Manda Grier will win the day. That poor, sick, flimsy little Statira is completely under 'Manda Grier's thumb, and will do just what she says, now that there's no direct appeal from her will to Barker's; they will never be married. Don't you see that it was 'Manda Grier's romance in the beginning, and that when she came to distrust, to dislike Barker, she came to dislike her romance too—to hate it?"

"Well, don't *you* romance him, David," said Mrs. Sewell, only conditionally accepting his theory.

Yet it may be offered to the reader as founded in probability and human nature. In fact, he may be assured here that the marriage which eventually took place was not that of Lemuel and Statira; though how the union, which was not only happiness for those it joined, but whatever is worthier and better in life than happiness, came about, it is aside from the purpose of this story to tell, and must be left for some future inquiry.

THE END

APRIL HOPES

I

FROM HIS PLACE on the floor of the Hemenway Gymnasium Mr. Elbridge Mavering looked on at the Class Day gayety with the advantage which his stature gave him over most people there. Hundreds of these were pretty girls, in a great variety of charming costumes, such as the eclecticism of modern fashion permits, and all sorts of ingenious compromises between walking dress and ball dress. It struck him that the young men on whose arms they hung, in promenading around the long oval within the crowd of stationary spectators, were very much younger than students used to be, whether they wore the dress-coats of the Seniors or the cutaways of the Juniors and Sophomores; and the young girls themselves did not look so old as he remembered them in his day. There was a band playing somewhere, and the galleries were well filled with spectators seated at their ease, and intent on the party-colored turmoil of the floor, where from time to time the younger promenaders broke away from the ranks into a waltz, and after some turns drifted back, smiling and controlling their quick breath, and resumed their promenade. The place was intensely light, in the candor of a summer day which had no reserves; and the brilliancy was not broken by the simple decorations. Ropes of wild laurel twisted up the pine posts of the aisles, and swung in festoons overhead; masses of tropical plants in pots were set along between the posts on one side of the room; and on the other were the lunch tables, where a great many people were standing about, eating chicken and salmon salads, or strawberries and ice-cream, and drinking claret-cup. From the whole rose that blended odor of viands, of flowers, of stuffs, of toilet perfumes, which is the characteristic expression of all social festivities, and which exhilarates or depresses according as one is new or old to it.

Elbridge Mavering kept looking at the faces of the young men as if he expected to see a certain one; then he turned his eyes patiently upon the faces around him. He had been introduced to a good many persons, but he had come to that time of life when an introduction, unless charged with some special

interest, only adds the pain of doubt to the wearisome encounter of unfamiliar people; and he had unconsciously put
on the severity of a man who finds himself without acquaintance where others are meeting friends, when a small man with
a neatly trimmed reddish-gray beard and prominent eyes
stopped in front of him, and saluted him with the "Hello,
Mavering!" of a contemporary.

His face, after a moment of question, relaxed into joyful
recognition. "Why, John Munt! is that you?" he said, and he
took into his large moist palm the dry little hand of his friend,
while they both broke out into the incoherencies of people
meeting after a long time. Mr. Mavering spoke in a voice soft
yet firm, and with a certain thickness of tongue, which gave a
boyish charm to his slow utterance, and Mr. Munt used the
sort of bronchial snuffle sometimes cultivated among us as a
chest tone. But they were cut short in their intersecting questions and exclamations by the presence of the lady who detached herself from Mr. Munt's arm as if to leave him the
freer for his hand-shaking.

"Oh!" he said, suddenly recurring to her, "let me introduce
you to Mrs. Pasmer, Mr. Mavering," and the latter made a
bow that creased his waistcoat at about the height of Mrs.
Pasmer's pretty little nose.

His waistcoat had the curve which waistcoats often describe
at his age; and his heavy shoulders were thrown well back to
balance this curve. His coat hung carelessly open; the Panama
hat in his hand suggested a certain habitual informality of
dress, but his smoothly shaven large handsome face, with its
jaws slowly ruminant upon nothing, intimated the consequence of a man accustomed to supremacy in a subordinate
place.

Mrs. Pasmer looked up to acknowledge the introduction
with a sort of pseudo-respectfulness which it would be hard
otherwise to describe. Whether she divined or not that she
was in the presence of a magnate of some sort, she was rather
superfluously demure in the first two or three things she said,
and was all sympathy and interest in the meeting of these old
friends. They declared that they had not seen each other for
twenty years, or, at any rate, not since '59. She listened while
they disputed about the exact date, and looked from time to

time at Mr. Munt, as if for some explanation of Mr. Mavering; but Munt himself, when she saw him last, had only just begun to commend himself to society, which had since so fully accepted him, and she had so suddenly, the moment before, found herself hand in glove with him that she might well have appealed to a third person for some explanation of Munt. But she was not a woman to be troubled much by this momentary mystification, and she was not embarrassed at all when Munt said, as if it had all been prearranged, "Well, now, Mrs. Pasmer, if you'll let me leave you with Mr. Mavering a moment, I'll go off and bring that unnatural child *to* you; no use dragging you round through *this* crowd any longer."

He made a gesture intended in the American manner to be at once polite and jocose, and was gone, leaving Mrs. Pasmer a little surprised, and Mr. Mavering in some misgiving, which he tried to overcome by pressing his jaws together two or three times without speaking. She had no trouble in getting in the first remark. "Isn't all this charming, Mr. Mavering?" She spoke in a deep low voice, with a caressing manner, and stood looking up at Mr. Mavering with one shoulder shrugged and the other drooped, and a tasteful composition of her fan and hands and handkerchief at her waist.

"Yes, ma'am, it is," said Mr. Mavering. He seemed to say ma'am to her with a public or official accent, which sent Mrs. Pasmer's mind fluttering forth to poise briefly at such conjectures as, "Congressman from a country district? judge of the Common Pleas? bank president? railroad superintendent? leading physician in a large town?—no, Mr. Munt said Mister," and then to return to her pretty blue eyes, and to centre there in that pseudo-respectful attention under the arch of her neat brows and her soberly crinkled gray-threaded brown hair and her very appropriate bonnet. A bonnet, she said, was much more than half the battle after forty, and it was now quite after forty with Mrs. Pasmer; but she was very well dressed otherwise. Mr. Mavering went on to say, with a deliberation that seemed an element of his unknown dignity, whatever it might be, "A number of the young fellows together can give a much finer spread, and make more of the day, in a place like this, than we used to do in our rooms."

"Ah, then you're a Harvard man too!" said Mrs. Pasmer to

herself, with surprise, which she kept to herself, and she said to Mavering: "Oh, yes, indeed! It's altogether better. *Aren't* they nice-looking fellows?" she said, putting up her glasses to look at the promenaders.

"Yes," Mr. Mavering assented. "I suppose," he added, out of the consciousness of his own relation to the affair—"I suppose you've a son somewhere here?"

"Oh dear no!" cried Mrs. Pasmer, with a mingling, super-human, but, for her, of ironical deprecation and derision. "Only a daughter, Mr. Mavering."

At this feat of Mrs. Pasmer's, Mr. Mavering looked at her with question as to her precise intention, and ended by re-peating, hopelessly, "Only a daughter?"

"Yes," said Mrs. Pasmer, with a sigh of the same irony, "only a poor, despised young girl, Mr. Mavering."

"You speak," said Mr. Mavering, beginning to catch on a little, "as if it were a misfortune," and his dignity broke up into a smile that had its queer fascination.

"Why, isn't it?" asked Mrs. Pasmer.

"Well, I shouldn't have thought so."

"Then you *don't* believe that all that old-fashioned chivalry and devotion have gone out? You *don't* think the young men are all spoiled nowadays, and expect the young ladies to offer *them* attentions?"

"No," said Mr. Mavering, slowly, as if recovering from the shock of the novel ideas. "Do you?"

"Oh, I'm such a stranger in Boston—I've lived abroad so long—that I don't know. One hears all kinds of things. But I'm *so* glad you're not one of those—pessimists!"

"Well," said Mr. Mavering, still thoughtfully, "I don't know that I can speak by the card exactly. I can't say how it is now. I haven't been at a Class Day spread since my own Class Day; I haven't even been at Commencement more than once or twice. But in my time here we didn't expect the young ladies to show us attentions; at any rate, we didn't wait for them to do it. We were very glad to be asked to meet them, and we thought it an honor if the young ladies would let us talk or dance with them, or take them to picnics. I don't think that any of them could complain of want of attention."

"Yes," said Mrs. Pasmer, "that's what I preached, that's

what I prophesied, when I brought my daughter home from Europe. I told her that a girl's life in America was one long triumph; but they say now that girls have more attention in London even than in Cambridge. One hears such dreadful things!"

"Like what?" asked Mr. Mavering, with the unserious interest which Mrs. Pasmer made most people feel in her talk.

"Oh, it's too vast a subject. But they tell you about charming girls moping the whole evening through at Boston parties, with no young men to talk with, and sitting from the beginning to the end of an assembly and not going on the floor once. They say that unless a girl fairly throws herself at the young men's heads she isn't noticed. It's this terrible disproportion of the sexes that's at the root of it, I suppose; it reverses everything. There aren't enough young men to go half round, and they know it, and take advantage of it. I suppose it began in the war."

He laughed, and, "I should think," he said, laying hold of a single idea out of several which she had presented, "that there would always be enough young men in Cambridge to go round."

Mrs. Pasmer gave a little cry. "In Cambridge!"

"Yes; when I was in college our superiority was entirely numerical."

"But that's all passed *long* ago, from what I hear," retorted Mrs. Pasmer. "I know very well that it used to be thought a great advantage for a girl to be brought up in Cambridge, because it gave her independence and ease of manner to have so many young men attentive to her. But they say the students all go into Boston now, and if the Cambridge girls want to meet them, they have to go there too. Oh, I assure you that, from what I hear, they've changed all that since *our* time, Mr. Mavering."

Mrs. Pasmer was certainly letting herself go a little more than she would have approved of in another. The result was apparent in the jocosity of this heavy Mr. Mavering's reply.

"Well, then, I'm glad that I was of our time, and not of this wicked generation. But I presume that unnatural supremacy of the young men is brought low, so to speak, after marriage?"

Mrs. Pasmer let herself go a little further. "Oh, give us an equal chance," she laughed, "and we can always take care of ourselves, and something more. They say," she added, "that the young married women now have all the attention that girls could wish."

"H'm!" said Mr. Mavering, frowning. "I think I should be tempted to box my boy's ears if I saw him paying another man's wife attention."

"What a Roman father!" cried Mrs. Pasmer, greatly amused, and letting herself go a little further yet. She said to herself that she really must find out who this remarkable Mr. Mavering was, and she cast her eye over the hall for some glimpse of the absent Munt, whose arm she meant to take, and whose ear she meant to fill with questions. But she did not see him, and something else suggested itself. "He probably wouldn't let you see him, or if he did, you wouldn't know it."

"How not know it?"

Mrs. Pasmer did not answer. "One hears such dreadful things. What do you say—or you'll think I'm a terrible gossip—"

"Oh no," said Mr. Mavering, impatient for the dreadful thing, whatever it was.

Mrs. Pasmer resumed: "—to the young married women meeting last winter just after a lot of pretty girls had come out, and magnanimously resolving to give the Buds a chance in society?"

"The Buds?"

"Yes, the Rose-buds—the *débutantes*; it's an odious little word, but everybody uses it. Don't you think that's a strange state of things for America? But I can't believe all those things," said Mrs. Pasmer, flinging off the shadow of this lurid social condition. "*Isn't* this a pretty scene?"

"Yes, it *is*," Mr. Mavering admitted, withdrawing his mind gradually from a consideration of Mrs. Pasmer's awful instances. "Yes!" he added, in final self-possession. "The young fellows certainly do things in a great deal better style nowadays than we used to."

"Oh, yes, indeed! And all those pretty girls *do* seem to be having such a good time!"

"Yes; they don't have the despised and rejected appearance that you'd like to have one believe."

"Not in the least!" Mrs. Pasmer readily consented. "They look radiantly happy. It shows that you can't trust anything that people say to you." She abandoned the ground she had just been taking without apparent shame for her inconsistency. "I fancy it's pretty much as it's always been: if a girl is attractive, the young men find it out."

"Perhaps," said Mr. Mavering, unbending with dignity, "the young married women have held another meeting, and resolved to give the Buds one more chance."

"Oh, there are some pretty mature Roses here," said Mrs. Pasmer, laughing evasively. "But I suppose Class Day can never be taken from the young girls."

"I hope not," said Mr. Mavering. His wandering eye fell upon some young men bringing refreshments across the nave toward them, and he was reminded to ask Mrs. Pasmer, "Will you have something to eat?" He had himself had a good deal to eat, before he took up his position at the advantageous point where John Munt had found him.

"Why, yes, thank you," said Mrs. Pasmer. "I ought to say, 'An ice, please,' but I'm really hungry, and—"

"I'll get you some of the salad," said Mr. Mavering, with the increased liking a man feels for a woman when she owns to an appetite. "Sit down here," he added, and he caught a vacant chair toward her. When he turned about from doing so, he confronted a young gentleman coming up to Mrs. Pasmer with a young lady on his arm, and making a very low bow of relinquishment.

II

THE MEN looked smilingly at each other without saying anything, and the younger took in due form the introduction which the young lady gave him.

"My mother, Mr. Mavering."

"Mr. Mavering!" cried Mrs. Pasmer, in a pure astonishment, before she had time to color it with a polite variety of more conventional emotions. She glanced at the two men, and gave a little "Oh?" of inquiry and resignation, and then said, demurely, "Let me introduce *you* to Mr. Mavering, Alice," while the young fellow laughed nervously, and pulled out his handkerchief, partly to hide the play of his laughter, and partly to wipe away the perspiration which a great deal more laughing had already gathered on his forehead. He had a vein that showed prominently down its centre, and large, mobile, girlish blue eyes under good brows, an arched nose, and rather a long face and narrow chin. He had beautiful white teeth; as he laughed, these were seen set in a jaw that contracted very much toward the front. He was tall and slim, and he wore with elegance the evening dress which Class Day custom prescribes for the Seniors; in his button-hole he had a club button.

"I shall not have to ask an introduction to Mr. Mavering; and you've robbed me of the pleasure of giving him one to you, Mrs. Pasmer," he said.

She heard the young man in the course of a swift review of what she had said to his father, and with a formless resentment of the father's not having told her he had a son there; but she answered with the flattering sympathy she had the use of, "Oh, but you won't miss one pleasure out of so many to-day, Mr. Mavering; and think of the little dramatic surprise!"

"Oh, perfect," he said, with another laugh. "I told Miss Pasmer as we came up."

"Oh, then you were *in* the surprise, Alice!" said Mrs. Pasmer, searching her daughter's eyes for confession or denial of this little community of interest. The girl smiled slightly upon the young man, but not disapprovingly, and made no other answer to her mother, who went on: "Where in the world have you been? Did Mr. Munt find you? Who told you where I was? Did you see me? How did you know I was here? Was there ever anything so droll?" She did not mean her questions to be answered, or at least not then, for while her daughter continued to smile rather more absently, and young Mavering broke out continuously in his nervous laugh, and his father stood regarding him with visible satisfaction, she hummed on, turning to the young man: "But I'm quite appalled at Alice's having monopolized even for a few minutes a whole Senior—and probably an official Senior at that," she said, with a glance at the pink and white club button in his coat lapel, "and I can't let you stay another instant, Mr. Mavering. I know very well how many demands you have upon you, and you must go back directly to your sisters and your cousins and your aunts, and all the rest of them; you must indeed."

"Oh no! Don't drive me away, Mrs. Pasmer," pleaded the young man, laughing violently, and then wiping his face. "I assure you that I've no encumbrances of any kind here except my father, and he seems to have been taking very good care of himself." They all laughed at this, and the young fellow hurried on: "Don't be alarmed at my button; it only means a love of personal decoration, if that's where you got the notion of my being an official Senior. This isn't my spread; I shall hope to welcome you at Beck Hall after the Tree; and I *wish* you'd let me be of use to you. Wouldn't you like to go round to some of the smaller spreads? I think it would amuse you. And have you got tickets to the Tree, to see us make fools of ourselves? It's worth seeing, Mrs. Pasmer, I assure you."

He rattled on very rapidly, but with such a frankness in his urgency, such amiable kindliness, that Mrs. Pasmer could not feel that it was pushing. She looked at her daughter, but she stood as passive in the transaction as the elder Mavering. She was taller than her mother, and as she waited, her supple figure described that fine lateral curve which one sees in some Louis Quinze portraits; this effect was enhanced by the fashion of her dress of pale sage green, with a wide stripe or sash of white dropping down the front, from her delicate waist. The same simple combination of colors was carried up into her hat, which surmounted darker hair than Mrs. Pasmer's, and a complexion of wholesome pallor; her eyes were gray and grave, with black brows, and her face, which was rather narrow, had a pleasing irregularity in the sharp jut of the nose; in profile the parting of the red lips showed well back into the cheek.

"I don't know," said Mrs. Pasmer, in her own behalf; and she added in his, "about letting you take so much trouble," so smoothly that it would have been quite impossible to detect the point of union in the two utterances.

"Well, don't call it names, anyway, Mrs. Pasmer," pleaded the young man. "I thought it was nothing but a pleasure and a privilege—"

"The fact is," she explained, neither consenting nor refusing, "that we were expecting to meet some friends who had tickets for us"—young Mavering's face fell—"and I can't imagine what's happened."

"Oh, let's hope something dreadful," he cried.

"Perhaps you know them," she delayed further. "Professor Saintsbury?"

"Well, rather! Why, they were here about an hour ago—both of them. They must have been looking for you."

"Yes; we were to meet them here. We waited to come out with other friends, and I was afraid we were late." Mrs. Pasmer's face expressed a tempered disappointment, and she looked at her daughter for indications of her wishes in the circumstances; seeing in her eye a willingness to accept young Mavering's invitation, she hesitated more decidedly than she had yet done, for she was, other things being equal, quite willing to accept it herself. But other things were not equal, and the whole situation was very odd. All that she knew of Mr. Mavering the elder was that he was the old friend of John Munt, and she knew far too little of John Munt, except that he seemed to go everywhere, and to be welcome, not to feel that his introduction was hardly a warrant for what looked like an impending intimacy. She did not dislike Mr. Mavering; he was evidently a country person of great self-respect, and no doubt of entire respectability. He seemed very intelligent too. He was a Harvard man; he had rather a cultivated manner, or else naturally a clever way of saying things. But all that was really nothing, if she knew no more about him, and she certainly did not. If she could only have asked her daughter who it was that presented young Mavering to her, that might have formed some clew, but there was no earthly chance of asking this, and, besides, it was probably one of those hap-hazard introductions that people give on such occasions. Young Mavering's behavior gave her still greater question: his self-possession, his entire absence of anxiety, or any expectation of rebuff or snub, might be the ease of unimpeachable social acceptance, or it might be merely adventurous effrontery; only something ingenuous and good in the young fellow's handsome face forbade this conclusion. That his face was so handsome was another of the complications. She recalled, in the dream-like swiftness with which all these things passed through her mind, what her friends had said to Alice about her being sure to meet her fate on Class Day, and she looked at her again to see if she had met it.

"Well, mamma?" said the girl, smiling at her mother's look.

Mrs. Pasmer thought she must have been keeping young Mavering waiting a long time for his answer. "Why, of course, Alice. But I really don't know what to do about the Saintsburys." This was not in the least true, but it instantly seemed so to Mrs. Pasmer, as a plausible excuse will when we make it.

"Why, I'll tell you what, Mrs. Pasmer," said young Mavering, with a cordial unsuspicion that both won and reassured her, "we'll be sure to find them at some of the spreads. Let me be of that much use, anyway; you must."

"We really oughtn't to let you," said Mrs. Pasmer, making a last effort to cling to her reluctance, but feeling it fail, with a sensation that was not disagreeable. She could not help being pleased with the pleasure that she saw in her daughter's face.

Young Mavering's was radiant. "I'll be back in just half a minute," he said, and he took a gay leave of them in running to speak to another student at the opposite end of the hall.

III

"YOU MUST allow me to get you something to eat first, Mrs. Pasmer," said the elder Mavering.

"Oh no, thank you," Mrs. Pasmer began. But she changed her mind and said, "Or, yes, I will, Mr. Mavering: a very little salad, please." She had really forgotten her hunger, as a woman will in the presence of any social interest, but she suddenly thought his going would give her a chance for two words with her daughter, and so she sent him. As he creaked heavily across the smooth floor of the nave, "Alice," she whispered, "I don't know exactly what I've done. Who introduced this young Mr. Mavering to you?"

"Mr. Munt."

"*Mr. Munt!*"

"Yes; he came for me; he said you sent him. He introduced Mr. Mavering, and he was very polite. Mr. Mavering said we ought to go up into the gallery and see how it looked; and Mr. Munt said he'd been up, and Mr. Mavering promised to bring me back to him, but he was not there when we got back. Mr. Mavering got me some ice-cream first, and then he found you for me."

"Really," said Mrs. Pasmer to herself, "the combat thickens!" To her daughter she said, "He's very handsome."

"He laughs too much," said the daughter. Her mother recognized her uncandor with a glance. "But he waltzes well," added the girl.

"Waltzes?" echoed the mother. "Did you *waltz* with him, Alice?"

"Everybody else was dancing. He asked me for a turn or two, and of course I did it. What difference?"

"Oh, none—none. Only—I didn't see you."

"Perhaps you weren't looking."

"Yes, I was looking all the time."

"What *do* you mean, mamma?"

"Well," said Mrs. Pasmer, in a final despair, "we don't know anything about them."

"We're the only people here who don't, then," said her daughter. "The ladies were bowing right and left to him all

326

the time, and he kept asking me if I knew this one and that one, and all I could say was that some of them were distant cousins, but I wasn't acquainted with them. I should think he'd wonder who *we* were."

"Yes," said the mother, thoughtfully.

"There! he's laughing with that other student. But don't look!"

Mrs. Pasmer saw well enough out of the corner of her eye the joking that went on between young Mavering and his friend, and it did not displease her to think that it probably referred to Alice. While the young man came hurrying back to them she glanced at the girl standing near her with a keenly critical inspection, from which she was able to exclude all maternal partiality, and justly decided that she was one of the most effective girls in the place. That costume of hers was perfect. Mrs. Pasmer wished now that she could have compared it more carefully with other costumes; she had noticed some very pretty ones; and a feeling of vexation that Alice should have prevented this by being away so long just when the crowd was densest qualified her satisfaction. The people were going very fast now. The line of the oval in the nave was broken into groups of lingering talkers, who were conspicuous to each other, and Mrs. Pasmer felt that she and her daughter were conspicuous to all the rest where they stood apart, with the two Maverings converging upon them from different points, the son nodding and laughing to friends of both sexes as he came, the father wholly absorbed in not spilling the glass of claret punch which he carried in one hand, and not falling down on the slippery floor with the plate of salad which he bore in the other. She had thoughts of feigning unconsciousness; she would have had no scruple in practising this or any other social stratagem, for though she kept a conscience in regard to certain matters—what she considered essentials—she lived a thousand little lies every day, and taught her daughter by precept and example to do the same. You must seem to be looking one way when you were really looking another; you must say this when you meant that; you must act as if you were thinking one thing when you were thinking something quite different; and all to no end, for, as she constantly said, people always know perfectly well what you were about, whichever way you looked or whatever you said, or no matter how well you acted the part of thinking what you did not think. Now, although she seemed not to look, she saw all that has been described at a glance, and at another she saw young Mavering slide easily up to his father and relieve him of the plate and glass, with a laugh as pleasant and a show of teeth as dazzling as he had bestowed upon any of the ladies he had passed. She owned to her recondite heart that she liked this in young Mavering, though at the same time she asked herself what motive he really had in being so polite to his father before people. But she had no time to decide; she had only time to pack the question hurriedly away for future consideration, when young Mavering arrived at her elbow, and she turned with a little "Oh!" of surprise so perfectly acted that it gave her the greatest pleasure.

IV

I DON'T THINK my father would have got here alive with these things," said young Mavering. "Did you see how I came to his rescue?"

Mrs. Pasmer instantly threw away all pretext of not having seen. "Oh yes! my heart was in my mouth when you bore down upon him, Mr. Mavering. It was a beautiful instance of filial devotion."

"Well, do sit down now, Mrs. Pasmer, and take it comfortably," said the young fellow; and he got her one of the many empty chairs, and would not give her the things, which he put in another, till she sat down and let him spread a napkin over her lap.

"Really," she said, "I feel as if I were stopping all the wheels of Class Day. Am I keeping them from closing the Gymnasium, Mr. Mavering?"

"Not quite," said the young man, with one of his laughs. "I don't believe they will turn us out, and I'll see that they don't lock us in. Don't hurry, Mrs. Pasmer. I'm only sorry you hadn't something sooner."

"Oh, your father proposed getting me something a good while ago."

"Did he? Then I wonder you haven't had it. He's usually on time."

"You're both very energetic, I think," said Mrs. Pasmer.

"He's the father of his son," said the young fellow, assuming the merit with a bow of burlesque modesty.

It went to Mrs. Pasmer's heart. "Let's hope he'll never forget that," she said, in an enjoyment of the excitement and the salad that was beginning to leave her question of these Maverings a light, diaphanous cloud on the verge of the horizon.

The elder Mavering had been trying, without success, to think of something to say to Miss Pasmer, and had twice cleared his throat for that purpose. But this comedy between his son and the young lady's mother seemed so much lighter and brighter than anything he could have said that he said nothing, and looked on with his mouth set in its queer smile, while the girl listened with the gravity of a daughter who sees that her mother is losing her head. Mrs. Pasmer buzzed on in her badinage with the young man, and allowed him to go for a cup of coffee before she rose from her chair, and shook out her skirts with an air of pleasant expectation of whatever should come next.

He came back without it. "The coffee urn has dried up here, Mrs. Pasmer. But you can get some at the other spreads; they'd be inconsolable if you didn't take something everywhere."

They all started toward the door, but the elder Mavering said, holding back a little, "Dan, I think I'll go and see—"

"Oh no, you mustn't, father," cried the young man, laying his hand with caressing entreaty on his father's coat sleeve. "I don't want you to go anywhere till you've seen Professor Saintsbury. We shall be sure to meet him at some of the spreads. I want you to have that talk with him—" He corrected himself for the instant's deflection from the interests of his guest, and added, "I want you to help me hunt him up for Mrs. Pasmer. Now, Mrs. Pasmer, you're not to think it's the least trouble, or anything but a boon, much less *say* it," he cried, turning to the deprecation in Mrs. Pasmer's face. He turned away from it to acknowledge the smiles and bows of people going out of the place, and he returned their salutations with charming heartiness.

In the vestibule they met the friends they were going in search of.

V

WITH MR. MAVERING, of course!" exclaimed Mrs. Saintsbury. "I might have known it." Mrs. Pasmer would have given anything she could think of to be able to ask why her friend might have known it; but for the present they could only fall upon each other with flashes of self-accusal and explanation, and rejoicing for their deferred and now accomplished meeting. The professor stood by with the satirical smile with which men witness the effusion of women. Young Mavering, after sharing the ladies' excitement fully with them, rewarded himself by an exclusive moment with Miss Pasmer.

"You *must* get Mrs. Pasmer to let me show you all of Class Day that a Senior can. I didn't know what a perfect serpent's tooth it was to be one before. Mrs. Saintsbury," he broke off, "have you got tickets for the Tree? Ah, she doesn't hear me!"

Mrs. Saintsbury was just then saying to the elder Mavering: "I'm so glad you decided to come to-day. It would have been a shame if none of you were here." She made a feint of dropping her voice, with a glance at Dan Mavering. "He's *such* a nice boy," which made him laugh, and cry out:

"Oh, now! Don't poison my father's mind, Mrs. Saintsbury."

"Oh, some one would be sure to tell him," retorted the professor's wife, "and he'd better hear it from a friend."

The young fellow laughed again, and then he shook hands with some ladies going out, and asked were they going so soon, from an abstract hospitality, apparently, for he was not one of the hosts; and so turned once more to Miss Pasmer. "We must get away from here, or the afternoon will get away from us, and leave us nothing to show for it. Suppose we make a start, Miss Pasmer?"

He led the way with her out of the vestibule, banked round with pots of palm and fern, and down the steps into the glare of the Cambridge sunshine, blown full, as is the case on Class Day, of fine Cambridge dust, which had drawn a delicate gray veil over the grass of the Gymnasium lawn, and mounted in light clouds from the wheels powdering it finer and finer in

331

the street. Along the sidewalks dusty hacks and carriages were
ranged, and others were driving up to let people dismount at
the entrances to the college yard. Within the temporary
picket-fences, secluding a part of the grounds for the students
and their friends, were seen stretching from dormitory to dormitory long lines of Chinese lanterns, to be lit after nightfall,
swung between the elms. Groups of ladies came and went,
nearly always under the escort of some student; the caterers'
carts, disburdened of their ice-creams and salads, were withdrawn under the shade in the street, and their drivers lounged
or drowsed upon the seats; now and then a black waiter,
brilliant as a bobolink in his white jacket and apron, appeared
on some errand; the large, mild Cambridge policemen kept
the entrances to the yard with a benevolent vigilance which
was not harsh with the little Irish children coming up from
the Marsh in their best to enjoy the sight of other people's
pleasure.

"Isn't it a perfect Class Day?" cried young Mavering, as he
crossed Kirkland Street with Miss Pasmer, and glanced down
its vaulted perspective of elms, through which the sunlight
broke, and lay in the road in pools and washes as far as the
eye reached. "Did you ever see anything bluer than the sky
to-day? I feel as if we'd ordered the weather, with the rest of
the things, and I had some credit for it as host. Do make it a
little compliment, Miss Pasmer; I assure you I'll be very modest about it."

"Ah, I think it's fully up to the occasion," said the girl,
catching the spirit of his amiable satisfaction. "Is it the usual
Class Day weather?"

"You spoil everything by asking that," cried the young
man; "it obliges me to make a confession—it's *always* good
weather on Class Day. There haven't been more than a dozen
bad Class Days in the century. But you'll admit that there
can't have been a *better* Class Day than this?"

"Oh yes; it's certainly the pleasantest Class Day *I've* seen,"
said the girl; and now when Mavering laughed she laughed
too.

"Thank you so much for saying that! I hope it will pass off
in unclouded brilliancy; it will, if I can make it. Why, hallo!
They're on the other side of the street yet, and looking about

as if they were lost." He pulled his handkerchief from his pocket, and waved it at the others of their party.

They caught sight of it, and came hurrying over through the dust.

Mrs. Saintsbury said, apparently as the sum of her consultations with Mrs. Pasmer: "The Tree is to be at half past five, and after we've seen a few spreads I'm going to take the ladies home for a little rest."

"Oh no; *don't* do that," pleaded the young man. After making this protest he seemed not to have anything to say immediately in support of it. He merely added: "This is Miss Pasmer's first Class Day, and I want her to see it all."

"But you'll have to leave us very soon to get yourself ready for the Tree," suggested the professor's lady, with a motherly prevision.

"I shall want just fifteen minutes for that."

"I know better, Mr. Mavering," said Mrs. Saintsbury, with finality. "You will want a good three-quarters of an hour to make yourself as disreputable as you'll look at the Tree, and you'll have to take time for counsel and meditation. You may stay with us just half an hour, and then we shall part inexorably. I've seen a great many more Class Days than you have, and I know what they are in their demands upon the Seniors."

"Oh, well! Then we won't think about the time," said the young man, starting on with Miss Pasmer.

"Well, don't undertake too much," said the lady. She came last in the little procession, with the elder Mavering, and her husband and Mrs. Pasmer preceded her.

"What?" young Mavering called back, with his smiling face over his shoulder.

"She says not to bite off more than you can chew," the professor answered for her.

Mavering broke into a conscious laugh, but full of delight, and with his handkerchief to his face had almost missed the greeting of some ladies who bowed to him. He had to turn round to acknowledge it, and he was saluting and returning salutations pretty well all along the line of their progress.

"I'm afraid you'll think I'm everybody's friend but my own, Miss Pasmer, but I assure you all this is purely accidental. I don't know so many people, after all; only all that I *do* know seem to be here this morning."

"I don't think it's a thing to be sorry for," said the girl. "I wish *we* knew more people. It's rather forlorn—"

"Oh, *will* you let me introduce some of the fellows to you? They'll be *so* glad."

"If you'll tell them how forlorn I said I was," said the girl, with a smile.

"Oh, no, no, no! I understand that. And I assure you that I didn't suppose— But of course!" he arrested himself in the superfluous reassurance he was offering, "All that goes without saying. Only there are some of the fellows coming back to the law school, and if you'll allow me—"

"We shall be very happy indeed, Mr. Mavering," said Mrs. Pasmer, behind him.

"Oh, thank you ever so much, Mrs. Pasmer." This was occasion for another burst of laughter with him. He seemed filled with the intoxication of youth, whose spirit was in the bright air of the day and radiant in the young faces everywhere. The paths intersecting one another between the different dormitories under the drooping elms were thronged with people coming and going in pairs and groups; and the academic fête, the prettiest flower of our tough old Puritan stem, had that charm, at once sylvan and elegant, which enraptures in the pictured fables of the Renaissance. It falls at that moment of the year when the old university town, often so commonplace and sometimes so ugly, becomes briefly and almost pathetically beautiful under the leafage of her hovering elms and in the perfume of her syringas, and bathed in this joyful tide of youth that overflows her heart. She seems fit then to be the home of the poets who have loved her and sung her, and the regret of any friend of the humanities who has left her.

"Alice," said Mrs. Pasmer, leaning forward a little to speak to her daughter, and ignoring a remark of the professor's, "did you *ever* see so many pretty costumes?"

"Never," said the girl, with equal intensity.

"Well, it makes you feel that you *have* got a country, after all," sighed Mrs. Pasmer, in a sort of apostrophe to her European self. "You see splendid dressing abroad, but it's mostly upon old people who ought to be sick and ashamed of their pomps and vanities. But here it's the young girls who dress; and how lovely they are! I thought they were charming in the Gymnasium, but I see you must get them out-of-doors to have the full effect. Mr. Mavering, are they always so prettily dressed on Class Day?"

"Well, I'm beginning to feel as if it wouldn't be exactly modest for me to say so, whatever I think. You'd better ask Mrs. Saintsbury; she pretends to know all about it."

"No, I'm bound to say they're not," said the professor's wife, candidly. "Your daughter," she added, in a low tone for all to hear, "decides that question."

"I'm so glad you said that, Mrs. Saintsbury," said the young man. He looked at the girl, who blushed with a pleasure that seemed to thrill to the last fibre of her pretty costume.

She could not say anything, but her mother asked, with an effort at self-denial: "Do you think so really? It's one of those London things. They have so much taste there now," she added, yielding to her own pride in the dress.

"Yes; I supposed it must be," said Mrs. Saintsbury. "*We* used to come in muslins and tremendous hoops—don't you remember?"

"Did you look like your photographs?" asked young Mavering, over his shoulder.

"Yes; but we didn't know it then," said the professor's wife.

"Neither did we," said the professor. "We supposed that there had never been anything equal to those hoops and white muslins."

"Thank you, my dear," said his wife, tapping him between the shoulders with her fan. "Now don't go any further."

"Do you mean about our first meeting here on Class Day?" asked her husband.

"They'll think so now," said Mrs. Saintsbury, patiently, with a playful threat of consequences in her tone.

"When I first saw the present Mrs. Saintsbury," pursued the professor—it was his joking way of describing her, as if there had been several other Mrs. Saintsburys—"she was dancing on the green here."

"Ah, they don't dance on the green any more, I hear," sighed Mrs. Pasmer.

"No, they don't," said the other lady; "and I think it's just as well. It was always a ridiculous affectation of simplicity."

"It must have been rather public," said young Mavering, in a low voice, to Miss Pasmer.

"It doesn't seem as if it could ever have been in character quite," she answered.

"We're a thoroughly in-doors people," said the professor. "And it seems as if we hadn't really begun to get well as a race till we had come in out of the weather."

"How can you say that on a day like this?" cried Mrs. Pasmer. "I didn't suppose any one could be so unromantic."

"Don't flatter him," cried his wife.

"Does he consider that a compliment?"

"Not personally," he answered. "But it's the first duty of a Professor of Comparative Literature to be unromantic."

"I don't understand," faltered Mrs. Pasmer.

"He will be happy to explain, at the greatest possible length," said Mrs. Saintsbury. "But you sha'n't spoil our pleasure *now*, John."

They all laughed, and the professor looked proud of the wit at his expense; the American husband is so, and the public attitude of the American husband and wife toward each other is apt to be amiably satirical; their relation seems never to have lost its novelty, or to lack droll and surprising contrasts for them.

Besides these passages with her husband, Mrs. Saintsbury kept up a full flow of talk with the elder Mavering, which Mrs. Pasmer did her best to overhear, for it related largely to his son, whom it seemed, from the father's expressions, the Saintsburys had been especially kind to.

"No, I assure you," Mrs. Pasmer heard her protest, "Mr. Saintsbury has been very much interested in him. I hope he has not put any troublesome ideas into his head. Of course he's very much interested in literature, from his point of view, and he's glad to find any of the young men interested in it, and that's apt to make him overdo matters a little."

"Dan wished me to talk with him, and I shall certainly be

glad to do so," said the father, but in a tone which conveyed to Mrs. Pasmer the impression that though he was always open to conviction, his mind was made up on this point, whatever it was.

VI

THE PARTY went to half a dozen spreads, some of which were on a scale of public grandeur approaching that of the Gymnasium, and others of a subdued elegance befitting the more private hospitalities in the students' rooms. Mrs. Pasmer was very much interested in these rooms, whose luxurious appointments testified to the advance of riches and of the taste to apply them since she used to visit students' rooms in far-off Class Days. The deep window nooks and easy-chairs upholstered in the leather that seems sacred alike to the seats and the shelves of libraries; the æsthetic bookcases, low and topped with bric-à-brac; the etchings and prints on the walls, which the elder Mavering went up to look at with a mystifying air of understanding such things; the foils crossed over the chimney, and the mantel with its pipes, and its photographs of theatrical celebrities tilted about over it—spoke of conditions mostly foreign to Mrs. Pasmer's memories of Harvard. The photographed celebrities seemed to be chosen chiefly for their beauty, and for as much of their beauty as possible, Mrs. Pasmer perceived, with an obscure misgiving of the sort which an older generation always likes to feel concerning the younger, but with a tolerance, too, which was personal to herself; it was to be considered that the massive thought and honest amiability of Salvini's face, and the deep and spiritualized power of Booth's, varied the effect of these companies of posturing nymphs.

At many places she either met old friends with whom she clamored over the wonder of their encounter there, or was made acquainted with new people by the Saintsburys. She kept a mother's eye on her daughter, to whom young Mavering presented everybody within hail or reach, and whom she could see, whenever she looked at her, a radiant centre of admiration. She could hear her talk sometimes, and she said to herself that really Alice was coming out; she had never heard her say so many good things before; she did not know it was in her. She was very glad then that she had let her wear that dress; it was certainly distinguished, and the girl carried it off, to her mother's amusement, with the air of a superb

lady of the period from which it dated. She thought what a
simple child Alice really was, all the time those other children,
the Seniors, were stealing their glances of bold or timid worship at her, and doubtless thinking her a brilliant woman
of the world. But there could be no mistake that she was a
success.

Part of her triumph was of course due to Mrs. Saintsbury,
whose chaperonage, Mrs. Pasmer could see, was everywhere
of effect. But it was also largely due to the vigilant politeness
of young Mavering, who seemed bent on making her have a
good time, and who let no chance slip him. Mrs. Pasmer felt
his kindness truly; and she did not feel it the less because she
knew that there was but one thing that could, at his frankly
selfish age, make a young fellow wish to make a girl have a
good time; except for that reason he must be bending the
whole soul of egotistic youth to making some other girl have
a good time. But all the same, it gave her pause when some
one to whom she was introduced spoke to her of her friends
the Maverings, as if they were friends of the oldest standing
instead of acquaintances of very recent accident. She did not
think of disclaiming the intimacy, but "Really I shall die of
these Maverings," she said to herself, "unless I find out something about them pretty soon."

"I'm not going to take you to the Omicron spread, Mrs.
Pasmer," said young Mavering, coming up to her with such
an effect of sympathetic devotion that she had to ask herself,
"*Are* they my friends, the Maverings?" "The Saintsburys have
been there already, and it *is* a little *too* common." The tone of
superiority gave Mrs. Pasmer courage. "They're good fellows,
and all that, but I want you to see the best. I suppose it will
get back to giving the spreads all in the fellows' rooms again.
It's a good deal pleasanter, don't you think?"

"Oh yes, indeed," assented Mrs. Pasmer, though she had
really been thinking the private spreads were not nearly so
amusing as the large spread she had seen at the Gymnasium.
She had also wondered where all Mr. Mavering's relations
and friends were, and the people who had social claims on
him, that he could be giving up his Class Day in this reckless
fashion to strangers. Alice would account for a good deal, but
she would not account for everything. Mrs. Pasmer would

have been willing to take him from others, but if he were so anomalous as to have no one to be taken from, of course it lessened his value as a trophy. These things went in and out of her mind, with a final resolution to get a full explanation from Mrs. Saintsbury, while she stood and smiled her winning assent up into the young man's handsome face.

Mrs. Saintsbury caught sight of them, and as if suddenly reminded of a forgotten duty, rushed vividly upon them.

"Mr. Mavering, I shall not let you stay with us another minute. You must go to your room now and get ready. You ought to have a little rest."

He broke out in his laugh. "Do you think I want to go and lie down awhile, like a lady before a party?"

"I'm sure you'd be the stronger for it," said Mrs. Saintsbury. "But go, upon any theory. Don't you see there isn't a Senior left?"

He would not look round. "They've gone to other spreads," he said. "But now I'll tell you: it *is* pretty near time, and if you'll take me to my room, I'll go."

"You're a spoiled boy," said Mrs. Saintsbury. "But I want Mrs. Pasmer to see the room of a *real* student—a reading man, and all that—and we'll come, to humor you."

"Well, come upon any theory," said young Mavering.

His father, and Professor Saintsbury, who had been instructed by his wife not to lose sight of her, were at hand, and they crossed to that old hall which keeps its favor with the students in spite of the rivalry of the newer dormitories—it would be hard to say why. Mrs. Pasmer willingly assented to its being much better, out of pure complaisance, though the ceilings were low and the windows small, and it did not seem to her that the Franklin stove and the æsthetic papering and painting of young Mavering's room brought it up to the level of those others that she had seen. But with her habit of saying some friendly lying thing, no matter what her impressions were, she exclaimed, "Oh, how cozy!" and glad of the word, she went about from one to another, asking, "*Isn't* this cozy?"

Mrs. Saintsbury said: "It's supposed to be the cell of a recluse; but it *is* cozy—yes."

"It looks as if some hermit had been using it as a store-room," said her husband; for there were odds and ends of furniture and clothes and boxes and hand-bags scattered about the floor.

"I forgot all about them when I asked you," cried Mavering, laughing out his delight. "They belong to some fellows that are giving spreads in their rooms, and I let them put them in here."

"Do you commonly let people put things in your room that they want to get rid of?" asked Mrs. Pasmer.

"Well, not when I'm expecting company."

"He couldn't refuse even then, if they pressed the matter," said Mrs. Saintsbury, lecturing upon him to her friend.

"I'm afraid you're too amiable altogether, Mr. Mavering. I'm sure you let people impose upon you," said the other lady. "You have been letting *us* impose upon you."

"Ah! now that proves you're *all* wrong, Mrs. Pasmer."

"It proves that you know how to say things very prettily."

"Oh, thank you. I know when I'm having a good time, and I do my best to enjoy it." He ended with the nervous laugh which seemed habitual with him.

"He *does* laugh a good deal," thought Mrs. Pasmer, surveying him with smiling steadiness. "I suppose it tires Alice. Some of his teeth are filled at the sides. That vein in his forehead—they say that means genius." She said to him: "I hope you know when others are having a good time too, Mr. Mavering? You ought to have that reward."

They both looked at Alice. "Oh, I should be so happy to think you hadn't been bored with it all, Mrs. Pasmer," he returned, with deep feeling.

Alice was looking at one of the sketches which were pretty plentifully pinned about the wall, and apparently seeing it, and apparently listening to what Professor Saintsbury was saying; but her mother believed from a tremor of the ribbons on her hat that she was conscious of nothing but young Mavering's gaze and the sound of his voice.

"We've been delighted, simply enchanted," said Mrs. Pasmer. And she thought: "Now if Alice were to turn round just as she stands, he could see all the best points of her face. I wonder what she really thinks of him? What is it you have there, Alice?" she asked, aloud.

The girl turned her face over her shoulder so exactly in the way her mother wished that Mrs. Pasmer could scarcely re-press a cry of joy. "A sketch of Mr. Mavering's."

"Oh, how very interesting!" said Mrs. Pasmer. "Do you sketch, Mr. Mavering? But of course." She pressed forward, and studied the sketch inattentively. "How very, very good!" she buzzed deep in her throat, while, with a glance at her daughter, she thought, "How impassive Alice is! But she behaves with great dignity. Yes. Perhaps that's best. And are you going to be an artist?" she asked of Mavering.

"Not if it can be prevented," he answered, laughing again.

"But his laugh is very pleasant," reflected Mrs. Pasmer. "*Does* Alice dislike it so much?" She repeated aloud, "If it can be prevented?"

"They think I might spoil a great lawyer in the attempt."

"Oh, I see. And are you going to be a lawyer? But to be a great *painter*! And America has so few of them." She knew quite well that she was talking nonsense, but she was aware through her own indifference to the topic that he was not minding what she said, but was trying to bring himself into talk with Alice again. The girl persistently listened to Professor Saintsbury.

"Is she punishing him for something?" her mother asked herself. "What can it be for? Does she think he's a little too pushing? Perhaps he is a little pushing." She reflected, with an inward sigh, that she would know whether he was if she only knew more about him.

He did the honors of his room very simply and nicely, and he said it was pretty rough to think this was the last of it. After which he faltered, and something occurred to Mrs. Saintsbury.

"Why, we're keeping you! It's time for you to dress for the Tree. John"—she reproached her husband—"how could you let us do it?"

"Far be it from me to hurry ladies out of other people's houses—especially ladies who have put themselves in charge of other people."

"No, *don't* hurry," pleaded Mavering; "there's plenty of time."

"How much time?" asked Mrs. Saintsbury.

He looked at his watch. "Well, a good quarter of an hour."

"And I was to have taken Mrs. Pasmer and Alice home for a little rest before the Tree!" cried Mrs. Saintsbury. "And now we must go at once, or we shall get no sort of places."

In the civil and satirical parley which followed, no one answered another, but Mavering bore as full a part as the elder ladies, and only his father and Alice were silent; his guests got themselves out of his room. They met at the threshold a young fellow, short and dark and stout, in an old tennis suit. He fell back at sight of them, and took off his hat to Mrs. Saintsbury.

"Why, Mr. Boardman!"

"Don't be bashful, Boardman!" young Mavering called out. "Come in and show them how I shall look in five minutes."

Mr. Boardman took his introductions with a sort of main-force self-possession, and then said, "You'll have to look it in less than five minutes now, Mavering. You're come for."

"What? Are they ready?"

"We must fly," panted Mrs. Saintsbury, without waiting for the answer, which was lost in the incoherencies of all sorts of *au revoirs* called after and called back.

VII

"T HAT IS ONE THING," said Mrs. Saintsbury, looking swiftly round to see that the elder Mavering was not within hearing, as she hurried ahead with Mrs. Pasmer, "that I can't stand in Dan Mavering. Why couldn't he have warned us that it was getting near the time? Why should he have gone on pretending that there was no hurry? It isn't insincerity exactly, but it isn't candor; no, it's uncandid. Oh, I suppose it's the artistic temperament—never coming straight to the point."

"What do you mean?" asked Mrs. Pasmer, eagerly.

"I'll tell you some time." She looked round and halted a little for Alice, who was walking detached and neglected by the preoccupation of the two elderly men. "I'm afraid you're tired," she said to the girl.

"Oh no."

"Of course not, on Class Day. But I hope we shall get seats. What weather!"

The sun had not been oppressive at any time during the day, though the crowded buildings had been close and warm, and now it lay like a painted light on the grass and paths over which they passed to the entrance of the grounds around the Tree. Holden Chapel, which enclosed the space on the right as they went in, shed back the sun from its brick-red flank, rising unrelieved in its venerable ugliness by any touch of the festive preparations; but to their left and diagonally across from them high stagings supported tiers of seats along the equally unlovely red bulks of Hollis and of Harvard. These seats, and the windows in the stories above them, were densely packed with people, mostly young girls dressed in a thousand enchanting shades and colors, and bonneted and hatted to the last effect of fashion. They were like vast terraces of flowers to the swift glance, and here and there some brilliant parasol, spread to catch the sun on the higher ranks, was like a flaunting poppy, rising to the light and lolling out above the blooms of lower stature. But the parasols were few, for the two halls flung wide curtains of shade over the greater part of the spectators, and across to the foot of the chapel, while a piece of the carpentry whose simplicity seems part of the Class Day tradition shut out the glare and the uninvited public, striving to penetrate the enclosure next the street. In front of this yellow pine wall, with its ranks of benches, stood the Class Day Tree, girded at ten or fifteen feet from the ground with a wide band of flowers.

Mrs. Pasmer and her friends found themselves so late that if some gentlemen who knew Professor Saintsbury had not given up their places they could have got no seats. But this happened, and the three ladies had harmoniously blended their hues with those of the others in that bank of bloom, and the gentlemen had somehow made away with their obstructiveness in different crouching and stooping postures at their feet, when the Junior Class filed into the green enclosure amidst the 'rahs of their friends, and sank in long ranks on the grass beside the chapel. Then the Sophomores appeared, and were received with cheers by the Juniors, with whom they joined, as soon as they were placed, in heaping ignominy upon the Freshmen. The Seniors came last, grotesque in the variety of their old clothes, and a fierce uproar of 'rahs and yells met them from the students squatted upon the grass, as they loosely grouped themselves in front of the Tree; the men of the younger classes formed in three rings, and began circling in different directions around them.

Mrs. Pasmer bent across Mrs. Saintsbury to her daughter: "Can you make out Mr. Mavering among them, Alice?"

"No. Hush, mamma!" pleaded the girl.

With the subsidence of the tumult in the other classes, the Seniors had broken from the stoical silence they kept through it, and were now with an equally serious clamor applauding the first of a long list of personages, beginning with the President, and ranging through their favorites in the faculty, down to Billy the Postman. The leader who invited them to this expression of good feeling exacted the full tale of nine cheers for each person he named, and before he reached the last the 'rahs came in gasps from their dry throats.

In the midst of the tumult the Marshal flung his hat at the elm; then the rush upon the tree took place, and the scramble for the flowers. The first who swarmed up the trunk were promptly plucked down by the legs and flung upon the ground, as if to form a base there for the operations of the rest, who surged and built themselves up around the elm in an irregular mass. From time to time some one appeared clambering over heads and shoulders to make a desperate lunge and snatch at the flowers, and then fall back into the fluctuant heap again. Yells, cries, and clappings of hands came from the students on the ground and the spectators in the seats, involuntarily dying away almost to silence as some stronger or wilfuler aspirant held his own on the heads and shoulders of the others, or was stayed there by his friends among them till he could make sure of a handful of the flowers. A rush was made upon him when he reached the ground; if he could keep his flowers from the hands that snatched at them, he staggered away with the fragments. The wreath began to show wide patches of the bark under it; the surging and struggling crowd below grew less dense; here and there one struggled out of it and walked slowly about, panting pitiably.

"Oh, I wonder they don't kill each other!" cried Mrs. Pasmer. "Isn't it terrible?" She would not have missed it on any account; but she liked to get all she could out of her emotions.

"They never get hurt," said Mrs. Saintsbury. "Oh, look! There's Dan Mavering!"

The crowd at the foot of the tree had closed densely, and a wilder roar went up from all the students. A tall, slim young fellow, lifted on the shoulders of the mass below, and staying himself with one hand against the tree, rapidly stripped away the remnants of the wreath, and flung them into the crowd under him. A single tuft remained; the crowd was melting away under him in a scramble for the fallen flowers; he made a crooked leap, caught the tuft, and tumbled with it headlong.

"Oh!" breathed the ladies on the benches, with a general suspiration lost in the 'rahs and clappings, as Mavering reappeared with the bunch of flowers in his hand. He looked dizzily about, as if not sure of his course; then his face, flushed and heated, with the hair pulled over the eyes, brightened with recognition, and he advanced upon Mrs. Saintsbury's party with rapid paces, each of which Mrs. Pasmer commentated with inward conjecture.

"Is he bringing the flowers to Alice? Isn't it altogether too conspicuous? Has he really the right to do it? What will people think? Will he give them to me for her, or will he hand them directly to her? Which should I prefer him to do? I wonder if I know?"

When she looked up with the air of surprise mixed with deprecation and ironical disclaimer which she had prepared while these things were passing through her mind, young Mavering had reached them, and had paused in a moment's hesitation before his father. With a bow of affectionate burlesque, from which he lifted his face to break into laughter at the look in all their eyes, he handed the tattered nosegay to his father.

"Oh, how delightful! how delicate! how perfect!" Mrs. Pasmer confided to herself.

"I think this must be for you, Mrs. Pasmer," said the elder Mavering, offering her the bouquet with a grave smile at his son's whim.

"Oh, no, indeed!" said Mrs. Pasmer. "For Mrs. Saintsbury, of course." She gave it to her, and Mrs. Saintsbury at once transferred it to Miss Pasmer.

"They wish me to pass this to you, Alice;" and at this consummation Dan Mavering broke into a happy laugh.

"Mrs. Saintsbury, you always do the right thing at once," he cried.

"That's more than I can say of *you*, Mr. Mavering," she retorted.

"Oh, thank you, Mr. Mavering!" said the girl, receiving the flowers. It was as if she had been too intent upon them and him to have noticed the little comedy that had conveyed them to her.

VIII

As soon after Class Day as Mrs. Pasmer's complaisant sense of the decencies would let her, she went out from Boston to call on Mrs. Saintsbury in Cambridge, and thank her for her kindness to Alice and herself. "She will know well enough what I *come* for," she said to herself, and she felt it the more important to ignore Mrs. Saintsbury's penetration by every polite futility; this was due to them both; and she did not go till the second day after.

Mrs. Saintsbury came down into the darkened, syringa-scented library to find her, and gave her a fan.

"You still live, Jenny," she said, kissing her gayly.

They called each other by their girl names, as is rather the custom in Boston with ladies who are in the same set, whether they are great friends or not. In the more changeful society of Cambridge, where so many new people are constantly coming and going in connection with the college, it is not so much the custom; but Mrs. Saintsbury was Boston-born, as well as Mrs. Pasmer, and was Cantabrigian by marriage—though this is not saying that she was not also thoroughly so by convincement and usage: she now rarely went into Boston society.

"Yes, Etta—just. But I wasn't sure of it," said Mrs. Pasmer, "when I woke yesterday. I was a mere aching jelly!"

"And Alice?"

"Oh, I don't think she had any physical consciousness. She was a mere rapturous memory!"

"She *did* have a good time, didn't she?" said Mrs. Saintsbury, in a generous retrospect. "I think she was on her feet every moment in the evening. It kept me from getting tired, to watch her."

"I was afraid you'd be quite worn out. I'd no idea it was so late. It must have been nearly half past seven before we got away from the Beck Hall spread, and then by the time we had walked round the college grounds—how extremely pretty the lanterns were, and how charming the whole effect was!—it must have been nine before the dancing began. Well, we owe it all to *you*, Etta."

348

"I don't know what you mean by owing. I'm always glad of an excuse for Class Day. And it was Dan Mavering who really managed the affair."

"He was *very* kind," said Mrs. Pasmer, with a feeling which was chiefly gratitude to her friend for bringing in his name so soon. Now that it had been spoken, she felt it perfectly decorous to throw aside the outer integument of pretence, which if it could have been entirely exfoliated would have caused Mrs. Pasmer morally to disappear, like an onion stripped of its successive laminæ.

"What did you mean," she asked, leaning forward, with her face averted, "about his having the artistic temperament? Is he going to be an artist? I should hope not." She remembered without shame that she had strongly urged him to consider how much better it would be to be a painter than a lawyer, in the dearth of great American painters.

"He could be a painter if he liked—up to a certain point," said Mrs. Saintsbury. "Or he could be any one of half a dozen other things—his last craze was journalism; but you know what I mean by the artistic temperament: it's that inability to be explicit; that habit of leaving things vague and undefined, and hoping they'll somehow come out as you want them of themselves; that way of taking the line of beauty to get at what you wish to do or say, and of being very finicking about little things and lax about essentials. That's what I mean by the artistic temperament."

"Yes; that's terrible," sighed Mrs. Pasmer, with the abstractly severe yet personally pitying perception of one whose every word and act was sincere and direct. "I know just what you mean. But how does it apply to Mr. Mavering?"

"It doesn't, exactly," returned her friend. "And I'm always ashamed when I say, or even think, anything against Dan Mavering. He's sweetness itself. We've known him ever since he came to Harvard, and I must say that a more constant and lovely fellow I never saw. It wasn't merely when he was a Freshman, and he had that home feeling hanging about him still that makes all the Freshmen so appreciative of anything you do for them; but all through the Sophomore and Junior years, when they're so taken up with their athletics and their societies and their college life generally that they haven't a moment for people that have been kind to them, he was just as faithful as ever."

"How nice!" cried Mrs. Pasmer.

"Yes, indeed! And all the allurements of Boston society haven't taken him from us altogether. You can't imagine how much this means till you've been at home awhile and seen how the students are petted and spoiled nowadays in the young society."

"Oh, I've heard of it," said Mrs. Pasmer. "And is it his versatility and brilliancy, or his amiability, that makes him such a universal favorite?"

"Universal favorite? I don't know that he's that."

"Well, popular, then."

"Oh, he's certainly very much liked. But, Jenny, there *are* no universal favorites in Harvard now, if there *ever* were: the classes are altogether too big. And it wouldn't be ability, and it wouldn't be amiability alone, that would give a man any sort of leadership."

"What in the world would it be?"

"That question, more than anything else, shows how long you've been away, Jenny. It would be family—family, with a judicious mixture of the others, and with money."

"Is it possible? But of course—I remember! Only at their age one thinks of students as being all hail-fellow-well-met with each other—"

"Yes; it's hard to realize how conventional they are—how very much worldlier than the world—till one sees it as one does in Cambridge. They pique themselves on it. And Mr. Saintsbury"—she was one of those women whom everything reminds of their husbands—"says that it isn't a bad thing altogether. He says that Harvard is just like the world; and even if it's a little more so, these boys have got to live in the world, and they had better know what it is. You may not approve of the Harvard spirit, and Mr. Saintsbury doesn't sympathize with it; he only says it's the world's spirit. Harvard men—the swells—are far more exclusive than Oxford men. A student, *comme il faut*, wouldn't at all like to be supposed to know another student whom *we* valued for his brilliancy, unless he was popular and well known in college."

"Dear me!" cried Mrs. Pasmer. "But of course! It's perfectly natural, with young people. And it's well enough that they should begin to understand how things really are in the world early; it will save them from a great many disappointments."

"I assure you we have very little to teach Harvard men in those matters. They could give any of us points. Those who are of good family and station know how to protect themselves by reserves that the others wouldn't dare to transgress. But a merely rich man couldn't rise in their set any more than a merely gifted man. He could get on to a certain point by toadying, and some do; but he would never get to be popular, like Dan Mavering."

"And what makes him popular?—to go back to the point we started from," said Mrs. Pasmer.

"Ah, that's hard to say. It's—quality, I suppose. I don't mean social quality, exactly; but personal charm. He never had a mean thought; of course we're all *full* of mean thoughts, and Dan is too; but his first impulse is always generous and sweet, and at his age people act a great deal from impulse. I don't suppose he ever met a human being without wanting to make him like him, and trying to do it."

"Yes, he certainly makes you like him," sighed Mrs. Pasmer. "But I understand that he can't make people like him without family or money; and I don't understand that he's one of those *nouveaux riches* who are giving Harvard such a reputation for extravagance nowadays."

There was an inquiring note in Mrs. Pasmer's voice; and in the syringa-scented obscurity, which protected the ladies from the expression of each other's faces, Mrs. Saintsbury gave a little laugh of intelligence, to which Mrs. Pasmer responded by a murmur of humorous enjoyment at being understood.

"Oh no! He isn't one of *those*. But the Maverings have plenty of *money*," said Mrs. Saintsbury, "and Dan's been very free with it, though not lavish. And he came here with a reputation for popularity from a very good school, and that always goes a great way in college."

"Yes?" said Mrs. Pasmer, feeling herself getting hopelessly adrift in these unknown waters, but reposing a pious confidence in her pilot.

"Yes; if a sufficient number of his class said he was the best fellow in the world, he would be pretty sure to be chosen one of the First Ten in the 'Dickey.' "

"What mysteries!" gasped Mrs. Pasmer, disposed to make fun of them, but a little overawed all the same. "What in the world is the 'Dickey'?"

"It's the society that the Freshmen are the most eager to get into. They're chosen, ten at a time, by the old members, and to be one of the first ten—the only Freshmen chosen—is something quite ineffable."

"I see." Mrs. Pasmer fanned herself, after taking a long breath. "And when he had got into the—"

"Then it would depend upon himself, how he spent his money, and all that, and what sort of society success he was in Boston. That has a great deal to do with it from the first. Then another thing is caution—discreetness; not saying anything censorious or critical of other men, no matter what they do. And Dan Mavering is the perfection of prudence, because he's the perfection of good-nature."

Mrs. Pasmer had apparently got all of these facts that she could digest. "And who *are* the Maverings?"

"Why, it's an old Boston name—"

"It's *too* old, isn't it? Like Pasmer. There are no Maverings in Boston that *I* ever heard of."

"No; the name's quite died out just here, I believe; but it's old, and it bids fair to be replated at Ponkwasset Falls."

"At Ponk—"

"That's where they have their mills, or factories, or shops, or whatever institution they make wall-paper in."

"Wall-paper!" cried Mrs. Pasmer, austerely. After a moment she asked: "And is wall-paper the 'thing' now? I mean—" She tried to think of some way of modifying the commonness of her phrase, but did not. After all, it expressed her meaning.

"It isn't the extreme of fashion, of course. But it's manufacturing, and it isn't disgraceful. And the Mavering papers are very pretty, and you can live with them without becoming anæmic, or having your face twitch."

"Face twitch?" echoed Mrs. Pasmer.

"Yes: arsenical poisoning."

"Oh! Conscientious as well as æsthetic. I see. And does Mr. Mavering put his artistic temperament into them?"

"His father does. He's a very interesting man. He has the best taste in certain things—he knows more about etchings, I suppose, than any one else in Boston."

"Is it possible! And does he live at Ponkwasset Falls? It's in Rhode Island, isn't it?"

"New Hampshire. Yes; the whole family live there."

"The whole family? Are there many of them? I'd fancied, somehow, that Mr. Mavering was the only— Do tell me about them, Etta," said Mrs. Pasmer, leaning back in her chair, and fanning herself with an effect of impartial interest, to which the dim light of the room lent itself.

"He's the only son. But there are daughters, of course—very cultivated girls."

"And is he—is the elder Mr. Mavering a—I don't know what made me think so—a widower?"

"Well, no—not exactly."

"Not exactly? He's not a *grass*-widower, I hope?"

"No, indeed. But his wife's a helpless invalid, and always has been. He's perfectly devoted to her; and he hurried home yesterday, though he wanted very much to stay for Commencement. He's never away from her longer than he can help. She's bedridden; and you can see from the moment you enter it that it's a man's house. Daughters can't change that, you know."

"Have you been there?" asked Mrs. Pasmer, surprised that she was getting so much information, but eager for more. "Why, how long have you known them, Etta?"

"Only since Dan came to Harvard. Mr. Saintsbury took a fancy to him from the start, and the boy was so fond of him that they were always insisting upon a visit; and last summer we stopped there on our way to the mountains."

"And the sisters—do they stay there the whole year round? Are they countrified?"

"One doesn't live in the country without being countrified," said Mrs. Saintsbury. "They're rather quiet girls, though they've been about a good deal—to Europe with friends, and to New York in the winter. They're older than Dan; they're more like their father. Are you afraid of that draught at the window?"

"Oh no; it's delicious. And he's like the mother?"

"Yes."

"Then it's the father who has the artistic taste—he gets that from him; and the mother who has the—"

"Temperament—yes."

"How extremely interesting! And so he's going to be a lawyer. Why lawyer, if he's got the talent and the temperament of an artist? Does his father wish him to be a lawyer?"

"His father wishes him to be a wall-paper maker."

"And the young man compromises on the law. I see," said Mrs. Pasmer. "And you say he's been going into Boston a great deal? Where does he go?"

The ladies entered into this social inquiry with a zest which it would be hard to make the reader share, or perhaps to feel the importance of. It is enough that it ended in the social vindication of Dan Mavering. It would not have been enough for Mrs. Pasmer that he was accepted in the best Cambridge houses; she knew of old how people were accepted in Cambridge for their intellectual brilliancy or solidity, their personal worth, and all sorts of things, without consideration of the mystical something which alone gives vogue in Boston.

"How superb Alice was!" Mrs. Saintsbury broke off, abruptly. "She has such a beautiful manner—such repose."

"Repose? Yes," said her mother, thoughtfully. "But she's very intense. And I don't see where she gets it. Her father has repose enough, but he has *no* intensity; and I'm *all* intensity, and no repose. I don't believe much in all this heredity business; do you, Etta? I'm no more like my mother than Alice is like me."

"I think she has the Hibbins face," said Mrs. Saintsbury.

"Oh! she's got the Hibbins *face*," said Mrs. Pasmer, with a disdain of tone which she did not at all feel; the tone was mere absent-mindedness.

She was about to revert to the question of Mavering's family, when the door-bell rang, and another visitor interrupted her talk with Mrs. Saintsbury.

IX

MRS. PASMER'S husband looked a great deal older than herself, and by operation of a well-known law of compensation, he was lean and silent, while she was plump and voluble. He had thick eyebrows, which remained black after his hair and beard had become white, and which gave him an aspect of fierceness, expressive of nothing in his character. It was from him that their daughter got her height, and, as Mrs. Pasmer freely owned, her distinction.

Soon after their marriage the Pasmers had gone to live in Paris, where they remained faithful to the fortunes of the Second Empire till its fall, with intervals of return to their own country of a year or two years at a time. After the fall of the empire they made their sojourn in England, where they lived upon the edges and surfaces of things, as Americans must in Europe everywhere, but had more permanency of feeling than they had known in France, and something like a real social status. At one time it seemed as if they might end their days there; but that which makes Americans different from all other peoples, and which finally claims their allegiance for their own land, made them wish to come back to America, and to come back to Boston. After all, their place in England was strictly inferior, and must be. They knew titles and consorted with them, but they had none themselves, and the English constancy which kept their friends faithful to them after they had become an old story, was correlated with the English honesty which never permitted them to mistake themselves for even the lowest of the nobility. They went out last, and they did not come in first, ever.

The invitations, upon these conditions, might have gone on indefinitely, but they did not imply a future for the young girl in whom the interests of her parents centred. After being so long a little girl, she had become a great girl, and then all at once she had become a young lady. They had to ask themselves, the mother definitely and the father formlessly, whether they wished their daughter to marry an Englishman, and their hearts answered them, like true Republican hearts, Not an untitled Englishman, while they saw no prospect of her getting any other. Mrs. Pasmer philosophized the case with a clearness and a courage which gave her husband a series of twinges analogous to the toothache, for a man naturally shrinks from such bold realizations. She said Alice had the beauty of a beauty, and she had the distinction of a beauty, but she had not the principles of a beauty; there was no use pretending that she had. For this reason the Prince of Wales's set, so accessible to American loveliness with the courage of its convictions, was beyond her; and the question was whether there was money enough for a younger son, or whether, if there was, a younger son was worth it.

However this might be, there was no question but there was now less money than there had been, and a great deal less. The investments had not turned out as they promised; not only had dividends been passed, but there had been permanent shrinkages. What was once an amiable competency from the pooling of their joint resources had dwindled to a sum that needed a careful eye both to the income and the outgo. Alice's becoming a young lady had increased their expenses by the suddenly mounting cost of her dresses, and of the dresses which her mother must now buy for the different rôle she had to sustain in society. They began to ask themselves what it was for, and to question whether, if she could not marry a noble Englishman, Alice had not better marry a good American.

Even with Mrs. Pasmer this question was tacit, and it need not be explained to any one who knows our life that in her most worldly dreams she intended at the bottom of her heart that her daughter should marry for love. It is the rule that Americans marry for love, and the very rare exception that they marry for anything else; and if our divorce courts are so busy in spite of this fact, it is perhaps because the Americans also unmarry for love, or perhaps because love is not so sufficient in matters of the heart as has been represented in the literatures of people who have not been able to give it so fair a trial. But whether it is all in all in marriage, or only a very marked essential, it is certain that Mrs. Pasmer expected her daughter's marriage to involve it. She would have shrunk from intimating anything else to her as from a gross indecency; and she could not possibly, by any finest insinuation, have made her a partner in her designs for her happiness. That, so far as Alice was concerned, was a thing which was to fall to her as from heaven; for this also is part of the American plan. We are the children of the poets, the devotees of the romancers, so far as that goes, and however material and practical we are in other things, in this we are a republic of shepherds and shepherdesses, and we live in a golden age, which if it sometimes seems an age of inconvertible paper, is certainly so through no want of faith in us.

Though the Pasmers said that they ought to go home for Alice's sake, they both understood that they were going home experimentally, and not with the intention of laying their bones in their native soil, unless they liked it, or found they could afford it. Mrs. Pasmer had no illusions in regard to it. She had learned from her former visits home that it was frightfully expensive; and during the fifteen years which they had spent chiefly abroad, she had observed the gradual decay of that distinction which formerly attended returning sojourners from Europe. She had seen them cease gradually from the romantic reverence which once clothed them, and decline through a gathering indifference into something like slight and compassion, as people who had not been able to make their place or hold their own at home; and she had taught herself so well how to pocket the superiority natural to the Europeanized American before arriving at consciousness of this disesteem, that she paid a ready tribute to people who had always staid at home.

In fact Mrs. Pasmer was a flatterer, and it cannot be claimed for her that she flattered adroitly always. But adroitness in flattery is not necessary for its successful use. There is no morsel of it too gross for the condor gullet and the ostrich stomach of human vanity; there is no society in which it does not give the utterer instant honor and acceptance in greater or less degree. Mrs. Pasmer, who was very good-natured, had not all the occasion for it that she made, but she employed it because she liked it herself, and knowing how absolutely worthless it was from her own tongue, prized it from others. Yet she could have rested perfectly safe without it in her social position, which she found unchanged by years of absence. She had not been a Hibbins for nothing, and she was not a

Pasmer for nothing, though why she should have been either
for something it would not be easy to say.

But while confessing the foibles of Mrs. Pasmer, it would
not be fair to omit from the tale of her many virtues the final
conscientiousness of her openly involuted character. Not to
mention other things, she instituted and practised economies
as alien to her nature as to her husband's, and in their narrow-
ing affairs she kept him out of debt. She was prudent; she was
alert; and while presenting to the world all the outward effect of a butterfly, she possessed many of the best qualities of
the bee.

With his senatorial presence, his distinction of person and
manner, Mr. Pasmer was inveterately selfish in that province
of small personal things where his wife left him unmolested.
In what related to his own comfort and convenience he was
undisputed lord of himself. It was she who ordered their
comings and goings, and decided in which hemisphere they
should sojourn from time to time, and in what city, street,
and house, but always with the understanding that the
kitchen and all the domestic appointments were to her husband's mind. He was sensitive to degrees of heat and cold,
and luxurious in the matter of lighting, with a fine nose for
plumbing. If he had not occupied himself so much with these
details, he was the sort of man to have thought Mrs. Pasmer,
with her buzz of activities and pretences, rather a tedious little
woman. He had some delicate tastes, if not refined interests,
and was expensively fond of certain sorts of bric-à-brac; he
spent a great deal of time in packing and unpacking it, and he
had cases stored in Rome and London and Paris; it had been
one of his motives in consenting to come home that he might
get them out, and set up the various objects of bronze and
porcelain in cabinets. He had no vices, unless absolute idleness ensuing uninterruptedly upon a remotely demonstrated
unfitness for business can be called a vice. Like other people
who have always been idle, he did not consider his idleness a
vice. He rather plumed himself upon it, for the man who has
done nothing all his life naturally looks down upon people
who have done or are doing something. In Europe he had
not all the advantage of this superiority which such a man has
here; he was often thrown with other idle people, who had

been useless for so many generations that they had almost ceased to have any consciousness of it. In their presence Pasmer felt that his uselessness had not that passive elegance which only ancestral uselessness can give; that it was positive, and to that degree vulgar.

A life like his was not one which would probably involve great passions or affections, and it would be hard to describe exactly the feeling with which he regarded his daughter. He liked her, of course, and he had naturally expected certain things of her, as a lady-like intelligence, behavior, and appearance; but he had never shown any great tenderness for her, or even pride in her. She had never given him any displeasure, however, and he had not shared his wife's question of mind at a temporary phase of Alice's development when she showed a decided inclination for a religious life. He had apparently not observed that the girl had a pensive temperament in spite of the effect of worldly splendor which her mother contrived for her, and that this pensiveness occasionally deepened to gloom. He had certainly never seen that in a way of her own she was very romantic. Mrs. Pasmer had seen it, with amusement sometimes, and sometimes with anxiety, but always with the courage to believe that she could cope with it when it was necessary.

Whenever it was necessary she had all the moral courage she wanted; it seemed as if she could have it or not as she liked; and in coming home she had taken a flat instead of a house, though she had not talked with her friends three minutes without perceiving that the moment when flats had promised to assert their social equality with houses in Boston was past forever. There were, of course, cases in which there could be no question of them; but for the most part they were plainly regarded as makeshifts, the resorts of people of small means, or the defiances or errors of people who had lived too much abroad. They stamped their occupants as of transitory and fluctuant character; good people might live in them, and did, as good people sometimes boarded; but they could not be regarded as forming a social base, except in rare instances. They presented peculiar difficulties in calling, and for any sort of entertainment they were too—not public, perhaps, but—evident.

In spite of these objections Mrs. Pasmer took a flat in the Cavendish, and she took it furnished from people who were going abroad for a year.

X

MRS. PASMER stood at the drawing-room window of this apartment, the morning after her call upon Mrs. Saintsbury, looking out on the passage of an express-wagon load of trunks through Cavendish Square, and commenting the fact with the tacit reflection that it was quite time she should be getting away from Boston too, when her daughter, who was looking out of the other window, started significantly back.

"What is it, Alice?"

"Nothing! Mr. Mavering, I think, and that friend of his—"

"Which friend? But where? Don't look! They will think we were watching them. I can't see them at all. Which way were they going?" Mrs. Pasmer dramatized a careless unconsciousness to the Square, while vividly betraying this anxiety to her daughter.

Alice walked away to the farthest part of the room. "They are coming this way," she said, indifferently.

Before Mrs. Pasmer had time to prepare a conditional mood, adapted either to their coming that way or going some other, she heard the janitor below in colloquy with her maid in the kitchen, and then the maid came in to ask if she should say the ladies were at home. "Oh, certainly," said Mrs. Pasmer, with a caressing politeness that anticipated the tone she meant to use with Mavering and his friend. "Were you going, Alice? Better stay. It would be awkward sending out for you. You look well enough."

"Well!"

The young men came in, Mavering with his nervous laugh first, and then Boardman with his twinkling black eyes, and his main-force self-possession.

"We couldn't go away as far as New London without coming to see whether you had really survived Class Day," said the former, addressing his solicitude to Mrs. Pasmer. "I tried to find out from Mrs. Saintsbury, but she was very non-committal." He laughed again, and shook hands with Alice, whom he now included in his inquiry.

"I'm glad she was," said Mrs. Pasmer—inwardly wondering

what he meant by going to New London—"if it sent you to ask in person." She made them sit down, and she made as little as possible of the young ceremony they threw into the transaction. To be cozy, to be at ease instantly, was Mrs. Pasmer's way. "We've not only survived, we've taken a new lease of life from Class Day. I'd forgotten how charming it always was. Or perhaps it didn't use to be so charming? I don't believe they have anything like it in Europe. Is it always so brilliant?"

"I don't know," said Mavering. "I really believe it *was* rather a nice one."

"Oh, we were both enraptured," cried Mrs. Pasmer.

Alice added a quiet "Yes, indeed," and her mother went on: "And we thought the Beck Hall spread was the crowning glory of the whole affair. We owe ever so much to your kindness."

"Oh, not at all," said Mavering.

"But we were talking afterward, Alice and I, about the sudden transformation of all that dishevelled crew around the Tree into the imposing swells—may I say howling swells?—"

"Yes, *do* say howling, Mrs. Pasmer!" implored the young man.

"—Whom we met afterward at the spread," she concluded. "How did you manage it all? Mr. Irving in the *Lyons Mail* was nothing to it. We thought we had walked directly over from the Tree; and there you were, all ready to receive us, in immaculate evening dress."

"It *was* pretty quick work," modestly admitted the young man. "Could you recognize any one in that hurly-burly round the Tree?"

"We didn't till you rose, like a statue of Victory, and began grabbing for the spoils from the heads and shoulders of your friends. Who was your pedestal?"

Mavering put his hand on his friend's broad shoulder and gave him a playful push.

Boardman turned up his little black eyes at him, with a funny gleam in them.

"Poor Mr. Boardman!" said Mrs. Pasmer.

"It didn't hurt him a bit," said Mavering, pushing him. "He liked it."

"Of *course* he did," said Mrs. Pasmer, implying, in flattery of Mavering, that Boardman might be glad of the distinction; and now Boardman looked as if he were not. She began to get away in adding, "But I wonder you don't kill each other."

"Oh, we're not so easily killed," said Mavering.

"And what a fairy scene it was at the spread!" said Mrs. Pasmer, turning to Boardman. She had already talked its splendors over with Mavering the same evening. "I thought we should never get out of the Hall; but when we did get out of the window upon that tapestried platform, and down on the tennis ground, with Turkey rugs to hide the bare spots in it—" She stopped as people do when it is better to leave the effect to the listener's imagination.

"Yes, I think it was rather nice," said Boardman.

"Nice?" repeated Mrs. Pasmer; and she looked at Mavering. "Is that the famous Harvard Indifferentism?"

"No, no, Mrs. Pasmer! It's just his personal envy. He wasn't in the spread, and of course he doesn't like to hear any one praise it. Go on!" They all laughed.

"Well, even Mr. Boardman will admit," said Mrs. Pasmer, "that nothing could have been prettier than that pavilion at the bottom of the lawn, and the little tables scattered about over it, and all those charming young creatures under that lovely evening sky."

"Ah! Even Boardman can't deny that. We *did* have the nicest crowd; didn't we?"

"Well," said Mrs. Pasmer, playfully checking herself in a ready adhesion, "that depends a good deal upon where Mr. Boardman's spread was."

"Thank you," said Boardman.

"He wasn't spreading anywhere," cried his friend. "Except himself—he was spreading himself everywhere."

"Then I think I should prefer to remain neutral," said Mrs. Pasmer, with a mock prudence which pleased the young men. In the midst of the pleasure she was giving and feeling she was all the time aware that her daughter had contributed but one remark to the conversation, and that she must be seeming very stiff and cold. She wondered what she meant, and whether she disliked this little Mr. Boardman, or whether she was again trying to punish Mr. Mavering for something, and if so, what it was. Had he offended her in some way the other day? At any rate, she had no right to show it. She longed for some chance to scold the girl, and tell her that it would not do, and make her talk. Mr. Mavering was merely a friendly acquaintance, and there could be no question of anything personal. She forgot that between young people the social affair is always trembling to the personal affair.

In the little pause which these reflections gave her mother, the girl struck in, with the coolness that always astonished Mrs. Pasmer, and as if she had been merely waiting till some phase of the talk interested her.

"Are many of the students going to the race?" she asked Boardman.

"Yes; nearly everybody. That is—"

"The race?" queried Mrs. Pasmer.

"Yes, at New London," Mavering broke in. "Don't you know? The University race—Harvard and Yale."

"Oh—oh yes," cried Mrs. Pasmer, wondering how her daughter should know about the race, and she not. "Had they talked it over together on Class Day?" she asked herself. She felt herself, in spite of her efforts to keep even with them, left behind and left out, as later age must be distanced and excluded by youth. "Are you gentlemen going to row?" she asked Mavering.

"No; they've ruled the tubs out this time; and we should send anything else to the bottom."

Mrs. Pasmer perceived that he was joking, but also that they were not of the crew; and she said that if that was the case she should not go.

"Oh, don't let that keep you away! Aren't you going? I hoped you were going," continued the young man, speaking with his eyes on Mrs. Pasmer, but with his mind, as she could see by his eyes, on her daughter.

"No, no."

"Oh, *do* go, Mrs. Pasmer!" he urged. "I wish you'd go along to chaperon us."

Mrs. Pasmer accepted the notion with amusement. "I should think you might look after each other. At any rate, I think I must trust you to Mr. Boardman this time."

"Yes; but he's going on business," persisted Mavering, as if for the pleasure he found in fencing with the air, "and he can't look after me."

"On business?" said Mrs. Pasmer, dropping her outspread fan on her lap, incredulously.

"Yes; he's going into journalism—he's gone into it," laughed Mavering; "and he's going down to report the race for the *Events*."

"Really?" asked Mrs. Pasmer, with a glance at Boardman, whose droll embarrassment did not contradict his friend's words. "How splendid!" she cried. "I had heard that a great many Harvard men were taking up journalism. I'm so glad of it! It will do everything to elevate its tone."

Boardman seemed to suffer under these expectations a little, and he stole a glance of comical menace at his friend.

"Yes," said Mavering; "you'll see a very different tone about the fires, and the fights, and the distressing accidents, in the *Events* after this."

"What does he mean?" she asked Boardman, giving him unavoidably the advantage of the caressing manner which was in her mind for Mavering.

"Well, you see," said Boardman, "we have to begin pretty low down."

"Oh, but *all* departments of our press need reforming, don't they?" she answered, consolingly. "One hears such shocking things about our papers abroad. I'm sure that the more Harvard men go into them the better. And how splendid it is to have them going into politics the way they are! They're going into politics too, aren't they?" She looked from one young man to the other with an idea that she was perhaps shooting rather wild, and an amiable willingness to be laughed at if she were. "Why don't *you* go into politics, Mr. Mavering?"

"Well, the fact is—"

"So many of the young University men do in England," said Mrs. Pasmer, fortifying her position.

"Well, you see, they haven't got such a complete machine in England—"

"Oh yes, that dreadful machine!" sighed Mrs. Pasmer, who had heard of it, but did not know in the least what it was.

"Do you think the Harvard crew will beat this time?" Alice asked of Boardman.

"Well, to tell you the truth—"

"Oh, but you must never believe him when he begins that way!" cried Mavering. "To be sure they will beat. And you ought to be there to see it. Now why won't you come, Mrs. Pasmer?" he pleaded, turning to her mother.

"Oh, I'm afraid we must be getting away from Boston by that time. It's very tiresome, but there seems to be nobody left; and one can't stay quite alone, even if you're sick of moving about. Have you ever been—we think of going there—to Campobello?"

"No; but I hear that it's charming, there. I had a friend who was there last year, and he said it was charming. The only trouble is it's so far. You're pretty well on the way to Europe when you get there. You know it's all hotel life?"

"Yes. It's quite a new place, isn't it?"

"Well, it's been opened up several years. And they say it isn't like the hotel life anywhere else; it's charming. And there's the very nicest class of people."

"Very nice Philadelphia people, I hear," said Mrs. Pasmer; "and Baltimore. Don't you think it's well," she asked, deferentially, and under correction, if she were hazarding too much, "to see somebody besides Boston people sometimes—if they're nice? That seems to be one of the great advantages of living abroad."

"Oh, I think there are nice people everywhere," said the young man, with the bold expansion of youth.

"Yes," sighed Mrs. Pasmer. "We saw two such charming young people coming in and out of the hotel in Rome. We were sure they were English. And they were from Chicago! But there are not *many* Western people at Campobello, are there?"

"I really don't know," said Mavering. "How is it, Boardman? Do many of your people go there?"

"You know you do make it so frightfully expensive with your money," said Mrs. Pasmer, explaining with a prompt effect of having known all along that Boardman was from the West. "You drive us poor people all away."

"I don't think *my* money would do it," said Boardman, quietly.

"Oh, you wait till you're a Syndicate Correspondent," said Mavering, putting his hand on his friend's shoulder, and rising by aid of it. He left Mrs. Pasmer to fill the chasm that had so suddenly yawned between her and Boardman; and while she tumbled into it every sort of flowery friendliness and compliment, telling him she should look out for his account of the race with the greatest interest, and expressing the hope that he would get as far as Campobello during the summer, Mavering found some minutes for talk with Alice. He was graver with her, far graver than with her mother, not only because she was a more serious nature, but because they were both young, and youth is not free with youth except by slow and cautious degrees. In that little space of time they talked of pictures, apropos of some on the wall, and of books, because of those on the table.

"Oh yes," said Mrs. Pasmer when they paused, and she felt that her piece of difficult engineering had been quite successful, "Mrs. Saintsbury was telling me what a wonderful connoisseur of etchings your father is."

"I believe he does know something about them," said the young man, modestly.

"And he's gone back already?"

"Oh yes. He never stays long away from my mother. I shall be going home myself as soon as I get back from the race."

"And shall you spend the summer there?"

"Part of it. I always like to do that."

"Perhaps when you get away you'll come as far as Campobello—with Mr. Boardman," she added.

"Has Boardman promised to go?" laughed Mavering. "He will promise anything. Well, I'll come to Campobello if you'll come to New London. *Do* come, Mrs. Pasmer!"

The mother stood watching the two young men from the window as they made their way across the Square together. She had now, for some reason, no apparent scruple in being seen to do so.

"How ridiculous that stout little Mr. Boardman is with

him!" said Mrs. Pasmer. "He hardly comes up to his shoulder. Why in the world should he have brought him?"

"I thought he was very pleasant," said the girl.

"Yes, yes, of course. And I suppose he'd have felt that it was rather pointed coming alone."

"Pointed?"

"Young men are so queer! Did you like that kind of collar he had on?"

"I didn't notice it."

"So very, *very* high."

"I suppose he has rather a long neck."

"Well, what *did* you think of his urging us to go to the race? Do you think he meant it? Do you think he intended it for an invitation?"

"I don't think he meant anything; or if he did, I think he didn't know what."

"Yes," said Mrs. Pasmer, vaguely; "that must be what Mrs. Saintsbury meant by the artistic temperament."

"I like people to be sincere, and not to say things they don't mean, or don't know whether they mean or not," said Alice.

"Yes, of course, that's the best way," admitted Mrs. Pasmer. "It's the *only* way," she added, as if it were her own invariable practice. Then she added, further, "I wonder what he did mean?"

She began to yawn, for after her simulation of vivid interest in them the visit of the young men had fatigued her. In the midst of her yawn her daughter went out of the room, with an impatient gesture, and she suspended the yawn long enough to smile, and then finished it.

XI

AFTER FIRST GOING to the Owen, at Campobello, the Pasmers took rooms at the Ty'n-y-Coed, which is so much gayer, even if it is not so characteristic of the old Welsh Admiral's baronial possession of the island. It is characteristic enough, and perched on its bluff overlooking the bay, or whatever the body of water is, it sees a score of pretty isles and long reaches of mainland coast, with a white marble effect of white-painted wooden Eastport, nestled in the wide lap of the shore, in apparent luxury and apparent innocence of smuggling and the manufacture of herring sardines. The waters that wrap the island in morning and evening fogs temper the air of the latitude to a Newport softness in summer, with a sort of inner coolness that is peculiarly delicious, lulling the day with long calms and light breezes, and after nightfall commonly sending a stiff gale to try the stops of the hotel gables and casements, and to make the cheerful blaze on its public hearths acceptable. Once or twice a day the Eastport ferry-boat arrives, with passengers from the southward, at a floating wharf that sinks or swims half a hundred feet on the mighty tides of the Northeast; but all night long the island is shut up to its own memories and devices. The pretty romance of the old sailor who left England to become a sort of feudal seigneur here, with a holding of the entire island, and its fisher-folk for his villeins, forms a picturesque background for the æsthetic leisure and society in the three hotels remembering him and his language in their names, and housing with a few cottages all the sojourners on the island. By day the broad hotel piazzas shelter such of the guests as prefer to let others make their excursions into the heart of the island, and around its rocky, sea-beaten borders; and at night, when the falling mists have brought the early dark, and from light-house to light-house the fog-horns moan and low to one another, the piazzas cede to the corridors and the parlors and smoking-rooms. The life does not greatly differ from other sea-side hotel life on the surface, and if one were to make distinctions one would perhaps begin by saying that hotel society there has much of the tone of cottage society elsewhere, with a little more accessibility. As the reader doubtless knows, the great mass of Boston society, thoughtful of its own weight and bulk, transports itself down the North Shore scarcely farther than Manchester at the farthest; but there are more courageous or more detachable spirits who venture into more distant regions. These contribute somewhat toward peopling Bar Harbor in the summer, but they scarcely characterize it in any degree; while at Campobello they settle in little daring colonies, whose self-reliance will enlist the admiration of the sympathetic observer. They do not refuse the knowledge of other colonies of other stirps and origins, and they even combine in temporary alliance with them. But, after all, Boston speaks one language, and New York another, and Washington a third, and though the several dialects have only slight differences of inflection, their moral accents render each a little difficult for the others. In fact, every society is repellent of strangers in the degree that it is sufficient to itself, and is incurious concerning the rest of the world. If it has not the elements of self-satisfaction in it, if it is uninformed and new and restless, it is more hospitable than an older society which has a sense of merit founded upon historical documents, and need no longer go out of itself for comparisons of any sort, knowing that if it seeks anything better it will probably be disappointed. The natural man, the savage, is as indifferent to others as the exclusive, and those who accuse the coldness of the Bostonians, and their reluctant or repellent behavior toward unknown people, accuse not only civilization, but nature itself.

That love of independence which is notable in us even in our most acquiescent phases at home is perhaps what brings these cultivated and agreeable people so far away, where they can achieve a sort of sylvan urbanity without responsibility, and without that measuring of purses which attends the summer display elsewhere. At Campobello one might be poor with almost as little shame as in Cambridge, if one were cultivated. Mrs. Pasmer, who seldom failed of doing just the right thing for herself, had promptly divined the advantages of Campobello for her family. She knew, by dint of a little inquiry, and from the volunteer information of enthusiasts who had been there the summer before, just who was likely to be there during the summer with which she now found herself confronted. Campobello being yet a new thing, it was not open to the objection that you were sure to meet such and such people, more or less common or disagreeable, there; whatever happened, it could be lightly handled in retrospect as the adventure of a partial and fragmentary summer when really she hardly cared where they went.

They did not get away from Boston before the middle of July, and after the solitude they left behind them there, the Owen at first seemed very gay. But when they had once or twice compared it with the Ty'n-y-Coed, riding to and fro in the barge which formed the connecting link with the Saturday evening hops of the latter hotel, Mrs. Pasmer decided that, from Alice's point of view, they had made a mistake, and she repaired it without delay. The young people were, in fact, all at the Ty'n-y-Coed, and though she found the Owen perfectly satisfying for herself and Mr. Pasmer, she was willing to make the sacrifice of going to a new place: it was not a great sacrifice for one who had dwelt so long in tents.

There were scarcely any young girls at the Owen, and no young men, of course. Even at the Ty'n-y-Coed, where young girls abounded, it would not be right to pretend that there were young men enough. Nowhere, perhaps, except at Bar Harbor, is the long-lost balance of the sexes trimmed in New England; and even there the observer, abstractly delighting in the young girls and their dresses at that grand love-exchange of Rodick's, must question whether the adjustment is perfectly accurate.

At Campobello there were not more than half enough young men, and there was not enough flirtation to affect the prevailing social mood of the place: an unfevered, expectationless tranquillity, in which to-day is like yesterday, and to-morrow cannot be different. It is a quiet of light reading and slowly, brokenly murmured, contented gossip for the ladies, of old newspapers and old stories and luxuriously meditated cigars for the men, with occasional combinations for a steam-launch cruise among the eddies and islands of the nearer waters, or a voyage further off in the Bay of Fundy to the Grand Menan, and a return for the late dinner which marks the high civilization of Campobello, and then an evening of more reading and gossip and cigars, while the night wind whistles outside, and the brawl and crash of the balls among the tenpins comes softened from the distant alleys. There are pleasant walks, which people seldom take, in many directions, and there are drives and bridle-paths all through the dense, sad, Northern woods which still savagely clothe the greater part of the island to its further shores, where there are shelves and plateaus of rock incomparable for picnicking. One need ask nothing better, in fact, than to stroll down the sylvan road that leads to the Owen, past the little fishing village with its sheds for curing herring, and the pale blue smoke and appetizing savor escaping from them; and past the little chapel with which the old Admiral attested his love of the Established rite. On this road you may sometimes meet a little English bishop from the Provinces, in his apron and knee-breeches; and there is a certain bridge over a narrow estuary, where in the shallow land-locked pools of the deeply ebbing tide you may throw stones at sculpin, and witness the admirable indifference of those fish to human cruelty and folly. In the middle distance you will see a group of herring weirs, which with their coronals of tufted saplings form the very most picturesque aspect of any fishing industry. You may now and then find an artist at this point, who, crouched over his easel, or hers, seems to agree with you about the village and the weirs.

But Alice Pasmer cared little more for such things than her mother did, and Mrs. Pasmer regarded Nature in all her aspects simply as an adjunct of society, or an occasional feature of the *entourage*. The girl had no such worldly feeling about it, but she found slight sympathy in the moods of earth and sky with her peculiar temperament. This temperament, whose recondite origin had almost wholly broken up Mrs. Pasmer's faith in heredity, was like other temperaments, not always in evidence, and Alice was variously regarded as cold, or shy, or proud, or insipid, by the various other temperaments brought in contact with her own. She was apt to be liked, because she was as careful of others as she was of herself, and she never was childishly greedy about such admiration as she won, as girls often are, perhaps because she did not care for it. Up to this time it is doubtful if her heart had been touched even by the fancies that shake the surface of the soul of youth, and perhaps it was for this reason that her seriousness at first fretted Mrs. Pasmer with a vague anxiety for her future.

Mrs. Pasmer herself remained inalienably Unitarian, but she was aware of the prodigious growth which the Church had been making in society, and when Alice showed her inclination for it, she felt that it was not at all as if she had developed a taste for orthodoxy; when finally it did not seem likely to go too far, it amused Mrs. Pasmer that her daughter should have taken so intensely to the Anglican rite.

In the hotel it attached to her by a common interest several of the ladies who had seen her earnestly responsive at the little Owen chapel—ladies left to that affectional solitude which awaits long widowhood through the death or marriage of children; and other ladies, younger, but yet beginning to grow old with touching courage. Alice was especially a favorite with the three or four who represented their class and condition at the Ty'n-y-Coed, and who read the best books read there, and had the gentlest manners. There was a tacit agreement among these ladies, who could not help seeing the difference in the temperaments of the mother and daughter, that Mrs. Pasmer did not understand Alice; but probably there were very few people except herself whom Mrs. Pasmer did not understand quite well. She understood these ladies and their compassion for Alice, and she did not in the least resent it. She was willing that people should like Alice for any reason they chose, if they did not go too far. If they went too far, Mrs. Pasmer was quite able to stop them; and with her little flutter of futile deceits, her irreverence for every form of human worth, and her trust in a providence which had seldom betrayed her, she smiled at the cult of Alice's friends, as she did at the girl's seriousness, which also she felt herself able to keep from going too far.

While she did not object to the sympathy of these ladies, whatever inspired it, she encouraged another intimacy which grew up contemporaneously with theirs, and which was frankly secular and practical, though the girl who attached herself to Alice with one of those instant passions of girlhood was also in every exterior observance a strict and diligent Church woman. The difference was through the difference of

Boston and New York in everything: the difference between
the idealizing and the realizing tendency. The elderly and
middle-aged Boston women who liked Alice had been
touched by something high yet sad in the beauty of her face
at church; the New York girl promptly owned that she had
liked her effect the first Sunday she saw her there, and she
knew in a minute she never got those things on this side; her
obeisances and genuflections throughout the service, much
more profound and punctilious than those of any one else
there, had apparently not prevented her from making a thorough study of Alice's costume and a correct conjecture as to
its authorship.

Miss Anderson, who claimed a collateral Dutch ancestry by
the Van Hook, tucked in between her non-committal family
name and the Julia given her in christening, was of the ordinary slender make of American girlhood, with dull blond
hair, and a dull blond complexion, which would have left her
face uninteresting if it had not been for the caprice of her
nose in suddenly changing from the ordinary American regularity, after getting over its bridge, and turning out distinctly
retroussé. This gave her profile animation and character; you
could not expect a girl with that nose to be either irresolute
or commonplace, and for good or for ill Miss Anderson was
decided and original. She carried her figure, which was no
great things of a figure as to height, with vigorous erectness;
she walked with long strides, knocking her skirts into fine
eddies and tangles as she went; and she spoke in a bold, deep
voice, with tones like a man's in it, all the more amusing and
fascinating because of the perfectly feminine eyes with which
she looked at you, and the nervous, feminine gestures which
she used while she spoke.

She took Mrs. Pasmer into her confidence with regard to
Alice at an early stage of their acquaintance, which from the
first had a patronizing or rather protecting quality in it, which
we often see from lower to higher; the lower owns itself less
fine, but knows itself shrewder, and more capable of coping
with actualities.

"I think she's moybid, Alice is," she said. "She isn't moybid
in the usual sense of the woyd, but she expects more of herself
and of the woyld generally than anybody's going to get out

of it. She thinks she's going to get as much as she gives, and that's a great mistake, Mrs. Pasmey," she said, with that peculiar liquefaction of the canine letter which the New-Yorkers alone have the trick of, and which it would be tiresome and futile to try to represent throughout her talk.

"Oh yes, I quite agree with you," said Mrs. Pasmer, deep in her throat, and reserving deeper still her enjoyment of this early wisdom of Miss Anderson's.

"Now, even at chuych—she carries the same spirit into the chuych. She doesn't make allowance for human nature, and the chuych *does*."

"Oh, certainly!" Mrs. Pasmer agreed.

"She isn't like a peyson that's been brought up in the chuych. It's more like the old Puyitan spirit.—Excuse me, Mrs. Pasmey!"

"Yes, indeed! Say anything you like about the Puritans!" said Mrs. Pasmer, delighted that as a Bostonian she should be thought to care for them.

"I always forget that *you're* a Bostonian," Miss Anderson apologized.

"Oh, thank you!" cried Mrs. Pasmer.

"I'm going to try to make her like other giyls," continued Miss Anderson.

"Do," said Alice's mother, with the effect of wishing her joy of the undertaking.

"If there were a few young men about, a little over seventeen and a little under fifty, it would be easier," said Miss Anderson, thoughtfully. "But how are you going to make a giyl like other giyls when there are no young men?"

"That's very true," said Mrs. Pasmer, with an interest which she of course did her best to try to make impersonal. "Do you think there will be more, later on?"

"They will have to hu'y up if they are comin'," said Miss Anderson. "It's the middle of August now, and the hotel closes the second week in September."

"Yes," said Mrs. Pasmer, vaguely, looking at Alice. She had just appeared over the brow of the precipice, along whose face the arrivals and departures by the ferry-boat at Campobello obliquely ascend and descend.

She came walking swiftly toward the hotel, and, for her, so

excitedly that Mrs. Pasmer involuntarily rose and went to meet her at the top of the broad hotel steps.

"What is it, Alice?"

"Oh, nothing! I thought I saw Mr. Munt coming off the boat."

"Mr. Munt?"

"Yes." She would not stay for farther question.

Her mother looked after her with the edge of her fan over her mouth till she disappeared in the depths of the hotel corridor; then she sat down near the steps, and chatted with some half-grown boys lounging on the balustrade, and waited for Munt to come up over the brink of the precipice. Dan Mavering came with him, running forward with a polite eagerness at sight of Mrs. Pasmer. She distributed a skilful astonishment equally between the two men she had equally expected to see, and was extremely cordial with them, not only because she was pleased with them, but because she was still more pleased with her daughter's being, after all, like other girls, when it came to essentials.

XII

ALICE CAME DOWN to lunch in a dress which reconciled the sea-side and the drawing-room in an effect entirely satisfactory to her mother, and gave her hand to both of the gentlemen without the affectation of surprise at seeing either.

"I saw Mr. Munt coming up from the boat," she said in answer to Mavering's demand for some sort of astonishment from her. "I wasn't certain that it was you."

Mrs. Pasmer, whose pretences had been all given away by this simple confession, did not resent it, she was so much pleased with her daughter's evident excitement at the young man's having come. Without being conscious of it, perhaps, Alice prettily assumed the part of hostess from the moment of their meeting, and did the honors of the hotel with a tacit implication of knowing that he had come to see her there. They had only met twice, but now, the third time, meeting after a little separation, their manner toward each other was as if their acquaintance had been making progress in the interval. She took him about quite as if he had joined their family party, and introduced him to Miss Anderson and to all her particular friends, for each of whom, within five minutes after his presentation, he contrived to do some winning service. She introduced him to her father, whom he treated with deep respect and said Sir to. She showed him the bowling-alley, and began to play tennis with him.

Her mother, sitting with John Munt on the piazza, followed these polite attentions to Mavering with humorous satisfaction, which was qualified as they went on.

"Alice," she said to her, at a chance which offered itself during the evening, and then she hesitated for the right word.

"Well, mamma?" said the girl, impatiently stopping on her way to walk up and down the piazza with Mavering; she had run in to get a wrap and a Tam-o'-Shanter cap.

"Don't—*over*do the honors."

"What do you mean, mamma?" asked the girl, dropping her arms before her, and letting the shawl trail on the floor. "Don't you think he was very kind to us on Class Day?"

377

Her mother laughed. "But every one mayn't know it's gratitude."

Alice went out, but she came back in a little while, and went up to her room without speaking to any one.

The fits of elation and depression with which this first day passed for her succeeded one another during Mavering's stay. He did not need Alice's chaperonage long. By the next morning he seemed to know and to like everybody in the hotel, where he enjoyed a general favor which at that moment had no exceptions. In the afternoon he began to organize excursions and amusements with the help of Miss Anderson.

The plans all referred to Alice, who accepted and approved with an authority which every one tacitly admitted, just as every one recognized that Mavering had come to Campobello because she was there. Such a phase is perhaps the prettiest in the history of a love affair. All is yet in solution; nothing has been precipitated in word or fact. The parties to it even reserve a final construction of what they themselves say or do; they will not own to their hearts that they mean exactly this or that. It is this phase which in its perfect freedom is the most American of all; under other conditions it is an instant, perceptible or imperceptible; under ours it is a distinct stage, unhurried by any outside influences.

The nearest approach to a definition of the situation was in a talk between Mavering and Mrs. Pasmer, and this talk, too, light and brief, might have had no such intention as her fancy assigned his part of it.

She recurred to something that had been said on Class Day about his taking up the law immediately, or going abroad first for a year.

"Oh, I've abandoned Europe altogether for the present," he said, laughing. "And I don't know but I may go back on the law too."

"Indeed! Then you *are* going to be an artist?"

"Oh no; not so bad as that. It isn't settled yet, and I'm off here to think it over awhile before the law school opens in September. My father wants me to go into his business, and turn my powers to account in designing wall-papers."

"Oh, how very interesting!" At the same time Mrs. Pasmer ran over the whole field of her acquaintance without finding another wall-paper maker in it. But she remembered what Mrs. Saintsbury had said: it was manufacturing. This reminded her to ask if he had seen the Saintsburys lately, and he said, no; he believed they were still in Cambridge, though. "And we shall actually see a young man," she said, finally, "in the act of deciding his own destiny!"

He laughed for pleasure in her persiflage. "Yes; only don't say anything. Nobody else knows it."

"Oh, no, indeed. Too much flattered, Mr. Mavering. Shall you let me know when you've decided? I shall be dying to know, and I shall be too high-minded to ask."

It was not then too late to adapt *Pinafore* to any exigency of life, and Mavering said, "You will learn from the expression of my eyes."

XIII

THE WITNESSES of Mavering's successful efforts to make everybody like him were interested in his differentiation of the attentions he offered every age and sex from those he paid Alice. But while they all agreed that there never was a sweeter fellow, they would have been puzzled to say in just what this difference consisted, and much as they liked him, the ladies of her cult were not quite satisfied with him till they decided that it was marked by an anxiety, a timidity, which was perfectly fascinating in a man so far from bashfulness as he. That is, he did nice things for others without asking; but with her there was always an explicit pause, and an implicit prayer and permission, first. Upon this condition they consented to the glamour which he had for her, and which was evident to every one probably but to herself and to him.

Once agreeing that no one was good enough for Alice Pasmer, whose qualities they felt that only women could really appreciate, they were interested to see how near Mavering could come to being good enough; and as the drama played itself before their eyes, they pleased themselves in analyzing its hero.

"He is not bashful, certainly," said one of a little group who sat midway of the piazza while Alice and Mavering walked up and down together. "But don't you think he's modest? There's that difference, you know."

The lady addressed waited so long before answering that the young couple came abreast of the group, and then she had to wait till they were out of hearing. "Yes," she said then, with a tender, sighing thoughtfulness, "I've felt that in him. And I really think he is a very lovable nature. The only question would be whether he wasn't *too* lovable."

"Yes," said the first lady, with the same kind of suspiration, "I know what you mean. And I suppose they ought to be something more alike in disposition."

"Or sympathies?" suggested the other.

"Yes, or sympathies."

A third lady laughed a little. "Mr. Mavering has so many sympathies that he ought to be like her in some of them."

"Do you mean that he's *too* sympathetic—that he isn't sincere?" asked the first—a single lady of forty-nine, a Miss Cotton, who had a little knot of conscience between her pretty eyebrows, tied there by the unremitting effort of half a century to do and say exactly the truth, and to find it out.

Mrs. Brinkley, whom she addressed, was of that obesity which seems often to incline people to sarcasm. "No, I don't think he's insincere. I think he always means what he says and does— Well, do you think a little more concentration of good-will would hurt him for Miss Pasmer's purpose—if she has it?"

"Yes, I see," said Miss Cotton. She waited, with her kind eyes fixed wistfully upon Alice, for the young people to approach and get by. "I wonder what the men think of him?"

"You might ask Miss Anderson," said Mrs. Brinkley.

"Oh, do you think they tell her?"

"Not that exactly," said Mrs. Brinkley, shaking with good-humored pleasure in her joke.

"Her voice—oh, yes. She and Alice are great friends, of course."

"I should think," said Mrs. Stamwell, the second speaker, "that Mr. Mavering would be jealous sometimes—till he looked twice."

"Yes," said Miss Cotton, obliged to admit the force of the remark, but feeling that Mr. Mavering had been carried out of the field of her vision by the turn of the talk. "I suppose," she continued, "that he wouldn't be so well liked by other young men as she is by other girls, do you think?"

"I don't think, as a rule," said Mrs. Brinkley, "that men are half so appreciative of one another as women are. It's most amusing to see the open scorn with which two young fellows treat each other if a pretty girl introduces them."

All the ladies joined in the laugh with which Mrs. Brinkley herself led off. But Miss Cotton stopped laughing first.

"Do you mean," she asked, "that if a gentleman were generally popular with gentlemen it would be—"

"Because he wasn't generally so with women? Something like that—if you'll leave Mr. Mavering out of the question. Oh, how very good of them!" she broke off, and all the ladies glanced at Mavering and Alice where they had stopped at the farther end of the piazza, and were looking off. "Now I can probably finish before they get back here again. What I do mean, Miss Cotton, is that neither sex willingly accepts the favorites of the other."

"Yes," said Miss Cotton, admissively.

"And all that saves Miss Pasmer is that she has not only the qualities that women like in women, but some of the qualities that men like in them. She's thoroughly human."

A little sensation, almost a murmur, not wholly of assent, went round that circle which had so nearly voted Alice a saint.

"In the first place, she likes to please men."

"Oh!" came from the group.

"And that makes them like her—if it doesn't go too far, as her mother says."

The ladies all laughed, recognizing a common turn of phrase in Mrs. Pasmer.

"I should think," said Mrs. Stamwell, "that she would believe a little in heredity if she noticed that in her daughter;" and the ladies laughed again.

"Then," Mrs. Brinkley resumed concerning Alice, "she has a very pretty face, an extremely pretty face; she has a tender voice, and she's very, very graceful—in rather an odd way; perhaps it's only a fascinating awkwardness. Then she dresses—or her mother dresses her—exquisitely."

The ladies, with another sensation, admitted the perfect accuracy with which these points had been touched.

"That's what men like, what they fall in love with, what Mr. Mavering's in love with this instant. It's no use women's flattering themselves that they don't, for they *do*. The rest of the virtues and graces and charms are for women. If that serious girl could only know the silly things that that amiable simpleton is taken with in her, she'd—"

"Never speak to him again?" suggested Miss Cotton.

"No, I don't say that. But she would think twice before marrying him."

"And then do it," said Mrs. Stamwell, pensively, with eyes that seemed looking far into the past.

"Yes, and quite right to do it," said Mrs. Brinkley. "I don't know that we should be very proud ourselves if we confessed just what caught our fancy in our husbands. For my part I shouldn't like to say how much a light hat that Mr. Brinkley happened to be wearing had to do with the matter."

The ladies broke into another laugh, and then checked themselves, so that Mrs. Pasmer, coming out of the corridor upon them, naturally thought they were laughing at her. She reflected that if she had been in their place she would have shown greater tact by not stopping just at that instant. But she did not mind. She knew that they talked her over, but having a very good conscience, she simply talked them over in return.

"Have you seen my daughter within a few minutes?" she asked.

"She was with Mr. Mavering at the end of the piazza a moment ago," said Mrs. Brinkley. "They must have just gone round the corner of the building."

"Oh," said Mrs. Pasmer. She had a novel, with her finger between its leaves, pressed against her heart, after the manner of ladies coming out on hotel piazzas. She sat down and rested it on her knee, with her hand over the top.

Miss Cotton bent forward, and Mrs. Pasmer lifted her fingers to let her see the name of the book.

"Oh yes," said Miss Cotton. "But he's so terribly pessimistic, don't you think?"

"What is it?" asked Mrs. Brinkley.

"*Fumée*," said Mrs. Pasmer, laying the book title upward on her lap for every one to see.

"Oh yes," said Mrs. Brinkley, fanning herself. "Tourguénief. That man gave me the worst quarter of an hour with his *Lisa* that I ever had."

"That's the same as the *Nichée des Gentilshommes*, isn't it?" asked Mrs. Pasmer, with the involuntary superiority of a woman who reads her Tourguénief in French.

"I don't know. I had it in English. I don't build my ships to cross the sea in, as Emerson says; I take those I find built."

"Ah! I was already on the other side," said Mrs. Pasmer, softly. She added: "I must get *Lisa*. I like a good heart-break; don't you? If that's what gave you the bad moment."

"Heart-*break*? Heart-*crush*! Where Lavretsky comes back old to the scene of his love for Lisa, and strikes that chord on

the piano—well, I simply wonder that I'm alive to recom-
mend the book to you."

"Do you know," said Miss Cotton, very deferentially, "that
your daughter always made me think of Lisa?"

"Indeed!" cried Mrs. Pasmer, not wholly pleased, but gratified that she was able to hide her displeasure. "You make me
very curious."

"Oh, I doubt if you'll see more than a mere likeness of
temperament," Mrs. Brinkley interfered, bluntly. "All the conditions are so different. There couldn't be an American Lisa.
That's the charm of these Russian tragedies. You feel that
they're so perfectly true there, and so perfectly impossible
here. Lavretsky would simply have got himself divorced from
Varvara Pavlovna, and no clergyman could have objected to
marrying him to Lisa."

"That's what I mean by his pessimism," said Miss Cotton.
"He leaves you no hope. And I think that despair should
never be used in a novel except for some good purpose; don't
you, Mrs. Brinkley?"

"Well," said Mrs. Brinkley, "I was trying to think what
good purpose despair could be put to, in a book or out of it."

"I don't think," said Mrs. Pasmer, referring to the book in
her lap, "that he leaves you altogether in despair here, unless
you'd rather he'd run off with Irene than married Tatiana."

"Oh, I certainly didn't wish that," said Miss Cotton, in self-
defence, as if the shot had been aimed at her.

"The book ends with a marriage; there's no denying that,"
said Mrs. Brinkley, with a reserve in her tone which caused
Mrs. Pasmer to continue for her:

"And marriage means happiness—in a book."

"I'm not sure that it does in this case. The time would
come, after Litvinof had told Tatiana everything, when she
would have to ask herself, and not once only, what sort of
man it really was who was willing to break his engagement,
and run off with another man's wife, and whether he could
ever repent enough for it. She could make excuses for him,
and would, but at the bottom of her heart— No, it seems to
me that there, almost for the only time, Tourguénief permitted himself an amiable weakness. All that part of the book has
the air of begging the question."

"But don't you see," said Miss Cotton, leaning forward in the way she had when very earnest, "that he means to show that her love is strong enough for all that?"

"But he doesn't, because it isn't. Love isn't strong enough to save people from unhappiness through each other's faults. Do you suppose that so many married people are unhappy in each other because they don't *love* each other? No; it's because they *do* love each other that their faults are such a mutual torment. If they were indifferent, they wouldn't mind each other's faults. Perhaps that's the reason why there are so many American divorces; if they didn't care, like Europeans, who don't marry for love, they could stand it."

"Then the moral is," said Mrs. Pasmer, at her lightest, through the surrounding gravity, "that as all Americans marry for love, only Americans who have been very good ought to get married."

"I'm not sure that the have-been goodness is enough either," said Mrs. Brinkley, willing to push it to the absurd. "You marry a man's future as well as his past."

"Dear me! You are terribly *exigeante*, Mrs. Brinkley," said Mrs. Pasmer.

"One can afford to be so—in the abstract," answered Mrs. Brinkley.

They all stopped talking and looked at John Munt, who was coming toward them, and each felt a longing to lay the matter before him. There was probably not a woman among them but had felt more, read more, and thought more than John Munt, but he was a man, and the mind of a man is the court of final appeal for the wisest women. Till some man has pronounced upon their wisdom, they do not know whether it is wisdom or not.

Munt drew up his chair, and addressed himself to the whole group through Mrs. Pasmer: "We are thinking of getting up a little picnic to-morrow."

XIV

THE DAY of the picnic struggled till ten o'clock to peer through the fog that wrapt it with that remote damp and coolness and that nearer drouth and warmth which some fogs have. The low pine groves hung full of it, and it gave a silvery definition to the gossamer threads running from one grass spear to another in spacious net-works over the open levels of the old fields that stretch back from the bluff to the woods. At last it grew thinner, somewhere over the bay; then you could see the smooth water through it; then it drifted off in ragged fringes before a light breeze; when you looked landward again it was all gone there, and seaward it had gathered itself in a low, dun bank along the horizon. It was the kind of fog that people interested in Campobello admitted as apt to be common there, but claimed as a kind of local virtue when it began to break away. They said that it was a very dry fog, not like Newport, and asked you to notice that it did not wet you at all.

Four or five carriages, driven by the gentlemen of the party, held the picnic, which was destined for that beautiful cove on the Bay of Fundy where the red granite ledges, smooth-washed by ages of storm and sun, lend themselves to such festivities as if they had been artificially fashioned into shelves and tables. The whole place is yet so new to men that this haunt has not acquired that air of repulsive custom which the egg-shells and broken bottles and sardine boxes of many seasons give. Or perhaps the winter tempests heap the tides of the bay over the ledge, and wash it clean of these vulgar traces of human resort, and enable it to offer as fresh a welcome to the picnics of each successive summer as if there had never been a picnic in that place before.

This was the sense that Mavering professed to have received from it, when he jumped out of the beach wagon in which he had preceded the other carriages through the weird forest lying between the fringe of farm fields and fishing villages on the western shore of the island and these lonely coasts of the bay. As far as the signs of settled human habitation last, the road is the good hard country road of New

England, climbing steep little hills, and presently leading through long tracts of woodland. But at a certain point beyond the farthest cottage you leave it, and plunge deep into the heart of the forest, vaguely traversed by the wheel path carried through since the island was opened to summer sojourn. Road you can hardly call it, remembering its curious pauses and hesitations when confronted with stretches of marshy ground, and its staggering progress over the thick stubble of saplings through which it is cut. The progress of teams over it is slow, but there is such joy of wildness in the solitudes it penetrates that if the horses had any gait slower than a walk, one might still wish to stay them. It is a Northern forest, with the air of having sprung quickly up in the fierce heat and haste of the Northern summers. The small firs are set almost as dense as rye in a field, and in their struggle to the light they have choked one another so that there is a strange blight of death and defeat on all that vigor of life. Few of the trees have won any lofty growth; they seem to have died and fallen when they were about to outstrip the others in size, and from their decay a new sylvan generation riots rankly upward. The surface of the ground is thinly clothed with a deciduous under-growth, above which are the bare, spare stems of the evergreens, and then their limbs thrusting into one another in a sombre tangle, with locks of long yellowish-white moss, like the gray pendants of the Southern pines, dripping from them and draining their brief life.

In such a place you must surrender yourself to its influences, profoundly yet vaguely melancholy, or you must resist them with whatever gayety is in you, or may be conjured out of others. It was conceded that Mavering was the life of the party, as the phrase goes. His light-heartedness, as kindly and sympathetic as it was inexhaustible, served to carry them over the worst places in the road of itself. He jumped down and ran back, when he had passed a bad bit, to see if the others were getting through safely; the least interesting of the party had some proof of his impartial friendliness; he promised an early and triumphant emergence from all difficulties; he started singing, and sacrificed himself in several tunes, for he could not sing well; his laugh seemed to be always coming back to Alice, where she rode late in the little procession; several times, with the deference which he delicately qualified for her, he came himself to see if he could not do something for her.

"Miss Pasmer," croaked her friend Miss Anderson, who always began in that ceremonious way with her, and got to calling her Alice farther along in the conversation, "if you don't drop something for that poor fellow to run back two or three miles and get, pretty soon, I'll do it myself. It's peyfectly disheaytening to see his disappointment when you tell him theye's nothing to be done."

"He seems to get over it," said Alice, evasively. She smiled with pleasure in Miss Anderson's impeachment, however.

"Oh, he keeps coming, if that's what you mean. But do drop an umbrella, or a rubber, or something, next time, just to show a proper appreciation."

But Mavering did not come any more. Just before they got to the cove, Miss Anderson leaned over again to whisper in Alice's ear, "I told you he was huyt. Now you must be very good to him the rest of the time."

Upon theory a girl of Alice Pasmer's reserve ought to have resented this intervention, but it is not probable she did. She flushed a little, but not with offence, apparently; and she was kinder to Mavering, and let him do everything for her that he could invent in transferring the things from the wagons to the rocks.

The party gave a gayety to the wild place which accented its proper charm, as they scattered themselves over the ledges on the bright shawls spread upon the level spaces. On either hand craggy bluffs hemmed the cove in, but below the ledge it had a pebbly beach strewn with drift-wood, and the Bay of Fundy gloomed before it with small fishing-craft tipping and tilting on the swell in the foreground, and dim sail melting into the dun fog-bank at the horizon's edge.

The elder ladies of the party stood up, or stretched themselves on the shawls, as they found this or that posture more restful after their long drive; one, who was skilled in making coffee, had taken possession of the pot, and was demanding fire and water for it. The men scattered themselves over the beach, and brought her drift enough to roast an ox; two of them fetched water from the spring at the back of the ledge, whither they then carried the bottles of ale to cool in its thrilling pool. Each after his or her fashion symbolized a return to nature by some act or word of self-abandon.

"You ought to have brought heavier shoes," said Mrs. Pasmer, with a serious glance at her daughter's feet. "Well, never mind," she added. "It doesn't matter if you *do* spoil them."

"Really," cried Mrs. Brinkley, casting her sandals from her, "I will not be enslaved to rubbers in such a sylvan scene as this, at any rate."

"Look at Mrs. Stamwell!" said Miss Cotton. "She's actually taken her hat off."

Mrs. Stamwell had not only gone to this extreme, but had tied a lightly fluttering handkerchief round her hair. She said she should certainly not put on that heavy thing again till she got in sight of civilization.

At these words Miss Cotton boldly drew off her gloves and put them in her pocket.

The young girls, slim in their blue flannel skirts and their broad white canvas belts, went and came over the rocks. There were some children in the party, who were allowed to scream uninterruptedly in the games of chase and hide-and-seek which they began to play as soon as they found their feet after getting out of the wagons.

Some of the gentlemen drove a stake into the beach, and threw stones at it, to see which could knock off the pebble balanced on its top. Several of the ladies joined them in the sport, and shrieked and laughed when they made wild shots with the missiles the men politely gathered for them.

Alice had remained with Mavering to help the hostess of the picnic lay the tables, but her mother had followed those who went down to the beach. At first Mrs. Pasmer looked on at the practice of the stone-throwers with disapproval; but suddenly she let herself go in this, as she did in other matters that her judgment condemned, and began to throw stones herself; she became excited, and made the wildest shots of any, accepting missiles right and left, and making herself dangerous to everybody within a wide circle. A gentleman who had fallen a victim to her skill said, "Just wait, Mrs. Pasmer, till I get in front of the stake."

The men became seriously interested, and worked themselves red and hot; the ladies soon gave it up, and sat down on the sand and began to talk. They all owned themselves hungry, and from time to time they looked up anxiously at the preparations for lunch on the ledge, where white napkins were spread, with bottles at the four corners to keep them from blowing away. This use of the bottles was considered very amusing; the ladies tried to make jokes about it, and the desire to be funny spread to certain of the men who had quietly left off throwing at the stake because they had wrenched their shoulders; they succeeded in being merry. They said they thought that coffee took a long time to boil.

A lull of expectation fell upon all; even Mavering sat down on the rocks near the fire, and was at rest a few minutes, by order of Miss Anderson, who said that the sight of his activity tired her to death.

"I wonder why always boiled ham at a picnic?" said the lady who took a final plate of it from a basket. "Under the ordinary conditions, few of us can be persuaded to touch it."

"It seems to be dear to nature, and to nature's children," said Mrs. Brinkley. "Perhaps because their digestions are strong."

"Don't you wish that something could be substituted for it?" asked Miss Cotton.

"There have been efforts to replace it with chicken and tongue in sandwiches," said Mrs. Brinkley; "but I think they've only measurably succeeded—about as temperance drinks have in place of the real strong waters."

"On the boat coming up," said Mavering, "we had a troupe of genuine darky minstrels. One of them sang a song about ham that rather took me.

> " 'Ham, good old ham!
> Ham is de best ob meat;
> It's always good and sweet;
> You can bake it, you can boil it,
> You can fry it, you can broil it—
> Ham, good old ham!' "

"*Oh*, how good!" sighed Mrs. Brinkley. "How sincere! How native! Go on, Mr. Mavering, forever."

"I haven't the materials," said Mavering, with his laugh. "The rest was *da capo*. But there was another song, about a colored lady:

" 'Six foot high and eight foot round,
    Holler ob her foot made a hole in de ground.' "

"Ah, that's an old friend," said Mrs. Brinkley. "I remember hearing of that colored lady when I was a girl. But it's a fine flight of the imagination. What else did they sing?"

"I can't remember. But there was something they danced— to show how a rheumatic old colored uncle dances."

He jumped nimbly up, and sketched the stiff and limping figure he had seen. It was over in a flash. He dropped down again, laughing.

"Oh, how wonderfully good!" cried Mrs. Brinkley, with frank joy. "Do it again."

"Encore! Oh, encore!" came from the people on the beach.

Mavering jumped to his feet, and burlesqued the profuse bows of an actor who refuses to repeat; he was about to drop down again amidst their wails of protest.

"No, don't sit down, Mr. Mavering," said the lady who had introduced the subject of ham. "Get some of the young ladies and go and gather some blueberries for the dessert. There are all the necessaries of life here, but none of the luxuries."

"I'm at the service of the young ladies as an escort," said Mavering, gallantly, with an infusion of joke. "Will you come and pick blueberries under my watchful eyes, Miss Pasmer?"

"They've gone to pick blueberries," called the lady through her tubed hand to the people on the beach, and the younger among them scrambled up the rocks for cups and bowls to follow them.

Mrs. Pasmer had an impulse to call her daughter back, and to make some excuse to keep her from going. She was in an access of decorum, naturally following upon her late outbreak, and it seemed a very pronounced thing for Alice to be going off into the woods with the young man; but it would have been a pronounced thing to prevent her, and so Mrs. Pasmer submitted.

"Isn't it delightful," asked Mrs. Brinkley, following them with her eyes, "to see the charm that gay young fellow has for that serious girl? She looked at him while he was dancing as if she couldn't take her eyes off him, and she followed him as if he drew her by an invisible spell. Not that spells are ever *visible*," she added, saving herself. "Though this one *seems* to be," she added further, again saving herself.

"Do you really think so?" pleaded Miss Cotton.

"Well, I *say* so, whatever I think. And I'm not going to be caught up on the tenter-hooks of conscience as to *all* my meanings, Miss Cotton. I don't *know* them all. But I'm not one of the Aliceolators, you know."

"No; of course not. But shouldn't you— Don't you think it would be a great pity— She's *so* superior, so *very* uncommon in every way, that it hardly seems— Ah, I should so like to see some one really *fine*—not a coarse fibre in him, don't you know. Not that Mr. Mavering's coarse. But beside her he does seem so light!"

"Perhaps that's the reason she likes him."

"No, no! I can't believe that. She *must* see more in him than we can."

"I dare say she thinks she does. At any rate, it's a perfectly evident case on both sides; and the frank way he's followed her up here, and devoted himself to her, as if—well, not as if she were the only girl in the world, but incomparably the best—is certainly not common."

"No," sighed Miss Cotton, glad to admit it; "that's beautiful."

XV

IN THE EDGE of the woods and the open spaces among the trees the blueberries grew larger and sweeter in the late Northern summer than a more southern sun seems to make them. They hung dense upon the low bushes, and gave them their tint through the soft gray bloom that veiled their blue. Sweet-fern in patches broke their mass here and there, and exhaled its wild perfume to the foot or skirt brushing through it.

"I don't think there's anything much prettier than these clusters; do you, Miss Pasmer?" asked Mavering, as he lifted a bunch pendent from the little tree before he stripped it into the bowl he carried. "And see! it spoils the bloom to gather them." He held out a handful, and then tossed them away. "It ought to be managed more æsthetically for an occasion like this. I'll tell you what, Miss Pasmer: are you used to blueberrying?"

"No," she said; "I don't know that I ever went blueberrying before. Why?" she asked.

"Because, if you haven't, you wouldn't be very efficient perhaps, and so you might resign yourself to sitting on that log and holding the berries in your lap, while I pick them."

"But what about the bowls, then?"

"Oh, never mind them. I've got an idea. See here!" He clipped off a bunch with his knife, and held it up before her, tilting it this way and that. "Could anything be more graceful? My idea is to serve the blueberry on its native stem at this picnic. What do you think? Sugar would profane it, and of course they've only got milk enough for the coffee."

"Delightful!" Alice arranged herself on the log, and made a lap for the bunch. He would not allow that the arrangement was perfect till he had cushioned the seat and carpeted the ground for her feet with sweet-fern.

"Now you're something *like* a wood-nymph," he laughed. "Only, wouldn't a *real* wood-nymph have an apron?" he asked, looking down at her dress.

"Oh, it won't hurt the dress. You must begin now, or they'll be calling us."

He was standing and gazing at her with a distracted enjoyment of her pose. "Oh, yes, yes," he answered, coming to himself, and he set about his work.

He might have got on faster if he had not come to her with nearly every bunch he cut at first, and when he began to deny himself this pleasure he stopped to admire an idea of hers.

"Well, that's charming—making them into bouquets."

"Yes, isn't it?" she cried, delightedly, holding a bunch of the berries up at arm's-length to get the effect.

"Ah, but you must have some of this fern and this tall grass to go with it. Why, it's sweet-grass—the sweet-grass of the Indian baskets!"

"Is it?" She looked up at him. "And do you think that the mixture would be better than the modest simplicity of the berries, with a few leaves of the same?"

"No; you're right; it wouldn't," he said, throwing away his ferns. "But you'll want something to tie the stems with; you must use the grass." He left that with her, and went back to his bushes. He added, from beyond a little thicket, as if what he said were part of the subject, "I was afraid you wouldn't like my skipping about there on the rocks, doing the colored uncle."

"Like it?"

"I mean—I—you thought it undignified—trivial—"

She said, after a moment: "It was *very* funny; and people do all sorts of things at picnics. That's the pleasure of it, isn't it?"

"Yes, it is; but I know you don't always like that kind of thing."

"Do I seem so very severe?" she asked.

"Oh no, not severe. I should be afraid of you if you were. I shouldn't have dared to come to Campobello."

He looked at her across the blueberry bushes. His gay speech meant everything or nothing. She could parry it with a jest, and then it would mean nothing. She let her head droop over her work, and made no answer.

"I wish you *could* have seen those fellows on the boat," said Mavering.

"Hello, Mavering!" called the voice of John Munt, from another part of the woods.

"Alice!—Miss Pasmer!" came that of Miss Anderson.

He was going to answer, when he looked at Alice. "We'll let them see if they can find us," he said, and smiled.

Alice said nothing at first; she smiled too. "You know more about the woods than I do. I suppose if they keep looking—"

"Oh yes." He came toward her with a mass of clusters which he had clipped. "How fast you do them!" he said, standing and looking down at her. "I wish you'd let me come and make up the withes for you when you need them."

"No, I couldn't allow that on any account," she answered, twisting some stems of the grass together.

"Well, will you let me hold the bunches while you tie them, or tie them while you hold them?"

"No."

"This once, then?"

"This once, perhaps."

"How little you let me do for you!" he sighed.

"That gives you a chance to do more for other people," she answered; and then she dropped her eyes, as if she had been surprised into that answer. She made haste to add: "That's what makes you so popular with—everybody."

"Ah, but I'd rather be popular with somebody!"

He laughed, and then they both laughed together consciously; and still nothing or everything had been said. A little silly silence followed, and he said, for escape from it, "I never saw such berries before, even in September, on the top of Ponkwasset."

"Why, is it a mountain?" she asked. "I thought it was a—falls."

"It's both," he said.

"I suppose it's very beautiful, isn't it? All America seems so lovely, so large."

"It's pretty in the summer. I don't know that I shall like it there in the winter, if I conclude to— Did your—did Mrs. Pasmer tell you what my father wants me to do?"

"About going there to—manufacture?"

Mavering nodded. "He's given me three weeks to decide whether I would like to do that or go in for law. That's what I came up here for."

There was a little pause. She bent her head down over the clusters she was grouping. "Is the light of Campobello particularly good on such questions?" she asked.

"I don't mean that exactly, but I wish you could help me to some conclusion."

"I?"

"Yes; why not?"

"It's the first time I've ever had a business question referred to me."

"Well, then, you can bring a perfectly fresh mind to it."

"Let me see," she said, affecting to consider. "It's really a very important matter?"

"It is to me."

After a moment she looked up at him. "I should think that you wouldn't mind living there if your business was there. I suppose it's being idle in places that makes them dull. I thought it was dull in London. One ought to be glad— oughtn't he?—to live in any place where there's something to do."

"Well, that isn't the way people usually feel," said Mavering. "That's the kind of a place most of them fight shy of."

Alice laughed with an undercurrent of protest, perhaps because she had seen her parents' whole life, so far as she knew it, passed in this sort of struggle. "I mean that I hate my own life because there seems nothing for me to do with it. I like to have people do something."

"Do you really?" asked Mavering, soberly, as if struck by the novelty of the idea.

"Yes!" she said, with exaltation. "If I were a man—"

He burst into a ringing laugh. "Oh no; *don't!*"

"Why?" she demanded, with provisional indignation.

"Because then there wouldn't be any Miss Pasmer."

It seemed to Alice that this joking was rather an unwarranted liberty. Again she could not help joining in his light-heartedness; but she checked herself so abruptly, and put on a look so austere, that he was quelled by it.

"I mean," he began—"that is to say—I mean that I don't understand why ladies are always saying that. I am sure they can do what they like, as it is."

"Do you mean that everything is open to them now?" she asked, disentangling a cluster of the berries from those in her lap, and beginning a fresh bunch.

"Yes," said Mavering. "Something like that—yes. They can do anything they like. Lots of them do."

"Oh yes, I know," said the girl. "But people don't like them to."

"Why, what would you like to be?" he asked.

She did not answer, but sorted over the clusters in her lap. "We've got enough now, haven't we?" she said.

"Oh, not half," he said. "But if you're tired you must let me make up some of the bunches."

"No, no! I want to do them all myself," she said, gesturing his offered hands away, with a little nether appeal in her laughing refusal.

"So as to feel that you've been of some use in the world?" he said, dropping contentedly on the ground near her, and watching her industry.

"Do you think that would be very wrong?" she asked. "What made that friend of yours—Mr. Boardman—go into journalism?"

"Oh, virtuous poverty. You're not thinking of becoming a newspaper woman, Miss Pasmer!"

"Why not?" She put the final cluster into the bunch in hand, and began to wind a withe of sweet-grass around the stems. He dropped forward on his knees to help her, and together they managed the knot. They were both flushed a little when it was tied, and were serious. "Why shouldn't one be a newspaper woman, if Harvard graduates are to be journalists?"

"Well, you know, only a certain kind are."

"What kind?"

"Well, not exactly what you'd call the gentlemanly sort."

"I thought Mr. Boardman was a great friend of yours?"

"He is. He is one of the best fellows in the world. But you must have seen that he wasn't a swell."

"I should think he'd be glad he was doing something at once. If I were a—" She stopped, and they laughed together. "I mean that I should hate to be so long getting ready to do something as men are."

"Then you'd rather begin making wall-paper at once than studying law?"

"Oh, I don't say that. I'm not competent to advise. But I should like to feel that I was doing something. I suppose it's hereditary." Mavering stared a little. "One of my father's sisters has gone into a sisterhood. She's in England."

"Is she a—Catholic?" asked Mavering.

"She isn't a *Roman* Catholic."

"Oh yes!" He dropped forward on his knees again to help her tie the bunch she had finished. It was not so easy as the first.

"Oh, thank you!" she said, with unnecessary fervor.

"But you shouldn't like to go into a sisterhood, I suppose?" said Mavering, ready to laugh.

"Oh, I don't know. Why not?" She looked at him with a flying glance, and dropped her eyes.

"Oh, no reason, if you have a fancy for that kind of thing."

"That kind of thing?" repeated Alice, severely.

"Oh, I don't mean anything disrespectful to it," said Mavering, throwing his anxiety off in the laugh he had been holding back. "And I *beg* your pardon. But I *don't* suppose you're in earnest."

"Oh no, I'm not in earnest," said the girl, letting her wrists fall upon her knees, and the clusters drop from her hands. "I'm not in earnest about anything; that's the truth—that's the shame. Wouldn't you like," she broke off, "to be a priest, and go round among these people up here on their frozen islands in the winter?"

"No," shouted Mavering, "I certainly shouldn't. I don't see how anybody stands it. Ponkwasset Falls is bad enough in the winter, and compared to this region Ponkwasset Falls is a metropolis. I believe in getting all the good you can out of the world you were born in—of course without hurting anybody else." He stretched his legs out on the bed of sweet-fern, where he had thrown himself, and rested his head on his hand lifted on his elbow. "I think this is what this place is fit for—a picnic; and I wish every one well out of it for nine months of the year."

"I don't," said the girl, with a passionate regret in her

voice. "It would be heavenly here with— But you—no, you're different. You always want to share your happiness."

"I shouldn't call that happiness. But don't you?" asked Mavering.

"No. I'm selfish."

"You don't expect me to believe that, I suppose."

"Yes," she went on, "it must be selfishness. You don't believe I'm so, because you can't imagine it. But it's true. If I were to be happy, I should be very greedy about it; I couldn't endure to let any one else have a part in it. So it's best for me to be wretched, don't you see—to give myself up entirely to doing for others, and not expect any one to do anything for me; then I can be of some use in the world. That's why I should like to go into a sisterhood."

Mavering treated it as the best kind of joke, and he was confirmed in this view of it by her laughing with him, after a first glance of what he thought mock piteousness.

XVI

THE CLOUDS sailed across the irregular space of pale blue Northern sky which the break in the woods opened for them overhead. It was so still that they heard, and smiled to hear, the broken voices of the others who had gone to get berries in another direction—Miss Anderson's hoarse murmur and Munt's artificial bass. Some words came from the party on the rocks.

"Isn't it perfect?" cried the young fellow, in utter content.

"Yes, *too* perfect," answered the girl, rousing herself from the reverie in which they had both lost themselves, she did not know how long. "Shall you gather any more?"

"No; I guess there's enough. Let's count them." He stooped over on his hands and knees, and made as much of counting the bunches as he could. "There's about one bunch and a half apiece. How shall we carry them? We ought to come into camp as impressively as possible."

"Yes," said Alice, looking into his face with dreamy absence. It was going through her mind, from some romance she had read, What if he were some sylvan creature, with that gayety, that natural gladness and sweetness of his, so far from any happiness that was possible to her? Ought not she to be afraid of him? She was thinking she was not afraid.

"I'll tell you," he said. "Tie the stems of all the bunches together, and swing them over a pole, like grapes of Eshcol. Don't you know the picture?"

"Oh yes."

"Hold on! I'll get the pole." He cut a white birch sapling, and swept off its twigs and leaves, then he tied the bunches together, and slung them over the middle of the pole.

"Well?" she asked.

"Now we must rest the ends on our shoulders."

"Do you think so?" she asked, with the reluctance that complies.

"Yes, but not right away. I'll carry them out of the woods, and we'll form the procession just before we come in sight."

Every one on the ledge recognized the tableau when it appeared, and saluted it with cheers and hand-clapping. Mrs. Pasmer bent a look on her daughter which she faced impenetrably.

"Where have you been?" "We thought you were lost!" "We were just organizing a search expedition!" different ones shouted at them.

The lady with the coffee-pot was kneeling over it with her hand on it. "Have some coffee, you poor things! You must be almost starved."

"We looked about for you everywhere," said Munt, "and shouted ourselves dumb."

Miss Anderson passed near Alice. "I knew where you were all the time!"

Then the whole party fell to praising the novel conception of the bouquets of blueberries, and the talk began to flow away from Alice and Mavering in various channels.

All that had happened a few minutes ago in the blueberry patch seemed a far-off dream; the reality had died out of the looks and words.

He ran about from one to another, serving every one; in a little while the whole affair was in his hospitable hands, and his laugh interspersed and brightened the talk.

She got a little back of the others, and sat looking wistfully out over the bay, with her hands in her lap.

"Hold on just half a minute, Miss Pasmer! don't move!" exclaimed the amateur photographer, who is now of all excursions; he jumped to his feet and ran for his apparatus. She sat still, to please him, but when he had developed his picture, in a dark corner of the rocks roofed with a water-proof, he accused her of having changed her position. "But it's going to be splendid," he said, with another look at it.

He took several pictures of the whole party, for which they fell into various attitudes of consciousness. Then he shouted to a boat-load of sailors who had beached their craft while they gathered some drift for their galley fire. They had flung their arm-loads into the boat, and had bent themselves to shove it into the water.

"Keep still! don't move!" he yelled at them, with the im-

periousness of the amateur photographer, and they obeyed
with the helplessness of his victims. But they looked round.

"Oh, idiots!" groaned the artist.

"I always wonder what that kind of people think of us kind
of people," said Mrs. Brinkley, with her eye on the photographer's subjects.

"Yes, I wonder what they do?" said Miss Cotton, pleased
with the speculative turn which the talk might take from this.
"I suppose they envy us?" she suggested.

"Well, not all of them; and those that do, not respectfully.
They view us as the possessors of ill-gotten gains, who would
be in a very different place if we had our deserts."

"Do you really think so?"

"Yes, I *think* so; but I don't know that I *really* think so.
That's another matter," said Mrs. Brinkley, with the whimsical resentment which Miss Cotton's conscientious pursuit
seemed always to rouse in her.

"I supposed," continued Miss Cotton, "that it was only
among the poor in the cities, who have been misled by agitators, that the well-to-do classes were regarded with suspicion."

"It seems to have begun a great while ago," said Mrs. Brinkley, "and not exactly with agitators. It was considered very
difficult for us to get into the kingdom of heaven, you know."

"Yes, I know," assented Miss Cotton.

"And there certainly are some things against us. Even when
the chance was given us to sell all we had and give it to the
poor, we couldn't bring our minds to it, and went away ex-
ceeding sorrowful."

"I wonder," said Miss Cotton, "whether those things were
ever intended to be taken literally?"

"Let's hope not," said John Munt, seeing his chance to
make a laugh.

Mrs. Stamwell said, "Well, I shall take another cup of coffee, at any rate," and her hardihood raised another laugh.

"That always seems to me the most pitiful thing in the
whole Bible," said Alice, from her place. "To see the right so
clearly, and not to be strong enough to do it."

"My dear, it happens every day," said Mrs. Brinkley.

"I always felt sorry for that poor fellow, too," said Mavering. "He seemed to be a good fellow, and it was pretty hard lines for him."

Alice looked round at him with deepening gravity.

"Confound those fellows!" said the photographer, glancing at his hastily developed plate. "They moved."

XVII

THE PICNIC party gathered itself up after the lunch, and while some of the men, emulous of Mavering's public spirit, helped some of the ladies to pack the dishes and baskets away under the wagon seats, others threw a corked bottle into the water, and threw stones at it. A few of the ladies joined them, but nobody hit the bottle, which was finally left bobbing about on the tide.

Mrs. Brinkley addressed the defeated group, of whom her husband was one, as they came up the beach toward the wagons. "Do you think that display was calculated to inspire the lower middle classes with respectful envy?"

Her husband made himself spokesman for the rest: "No; but you can't tell how they'd have felt if we'd hit it."

They now all climbed to a higher level, grassy and smooth, on the bluff, from which there was a particular view; and Mavering came, carrying the wraps of Mrs. Pasmer and Alice, with which he associated his overcoat. A book fell out of one of the pockets when he threw it down.

Miss Anderson picked the volume up. "Browning! He reads Browning! Superior young man!"

"Oh, don't say *that!*" pleaded Mavering.

"Oh, read something aloud!" cried another of the young ladies.

"Isn't Browning rather serious for a picnic?" he asked, with a glance at Alice; he still had a doubt of the effect of the rheumatic uncle's dance upon her, and would have been glad to give her some other æsthetic impression of him.

"Oh no!" said Mrs. Brinkley, "nothing is more appropriate to a picnic than conundrums; they always have them. Choose a good tough one."

"I don't know anything tougher than the 'Legend of Pornic'—or lovelier," he said, and he began to read, simply, and with a passionate pleasure in the subtle study, feeling its control over his hearers.

The gentlemen lay smoking about at their ease; at the end a deep sigh went up from the ladies, cut short by the question which they immediately fell into.

They could not agree, but they said, one after another: "But you read beautifully, Mr. Mavering!" "Beautifully!" "Yes, indeed!"

"Well, I'm glad there is one point clear," he said, putting the book away, and "I'm afraid you'll think I'm rather sentimental," he added, in a low voice to Alice, "carrying poetry around with me."

"Oh, no!" she replied, intensely; "I *thank* you."

"I thank *you*," he retorted, and their eyes met in a deep look.

One of the outer circle of smokers came up with his watch in his hand, and addressed the company, "Do you know what time it's got to be? It's four o'clock."

They all sprang up with a clamor of surprise.

Mrs. Pasmer, under cover of the noise, said, in a low tone, to her daughter, "Alice, I think you'd better keep a little more with me now."

"Yes," said the girl, in a sympathy with her mother in which she did not always find herself.

But when Mavering, whom their tacit treaty concerned, turned toward them, and put himself in charge of Alice, Mrs. Pasmer found herself dispossessed by the charm of his confidence, and relinquished her to him. They were going to walk to the Castle Rocks by the path that now loses and now finds itself among the fastnesses of the forest, stretching to the loftiest outlook on the bay. The savage woodland is penetrated only by this forgetful path, that passes now and then over the bridge of a ravine, and offers to the eye on either hand the mystery deepening into wilder and weirder tracts of solitude. The party resolved itself into twos and threes, and these straggled far apart, out of conversational reach of one another. Mrs. Pasmer found herself walking and talking with John Munt.

"Mr. Pasmer hasn't much interest in these excursions," he suggested.

"No; he never goes," she answered, and by one of the agile intellectual processes natural to women she arrived at the question, "You and the Maverings are old friends, Mr. Munt?"

"I can't say about the son, but I'm his father's friend, and I suppose that I'm *his* friend too. Everybody seems to be so," suggested Munt.

"Oh yes," Mrs. Pasmer assented; "he appears to be a universal favorite."

"We used to expect great things of Elbridge Mavering in college. We were rather more romantic than the Harvard men are nowadays, and we believed in one another more than they do. Perhaps we idealized one another. But, anyway, our class thought Mavering could do anything. You know about his taste for etchings?"

"Yes," said Mrs. Pasmer, with a sigh of deep appreciation. "What gifted people!"

"I understand that the son inherits all his father's talent."

"He sketches delightfully."

"And Mavering wrote. Why, he was our class poet!" cried Munt, remembering the fact with surprise and gratification to himself. "He was a tremendous satirist."

"Really? And he seems so amiable now."

"Oh, it was only on paper."

"Perhaps he still keeps it up—on *wall*-paper?" suggested Mrs. Pasmer.

Munt laughed at the little joke with a good-will that flattered the veteran flatterer. "I should like to ask him that some time. Will you lend it to me?"

"Yes, if such a sayer of good things will deign to borrow—"

"Oh, Mrs. Pasmer!" cried Munt, otherwise speechless.

"And the mother? Do you know Mrs. Mavering?"

"Mrs. Mavering I've never seen."

"Oh!" said Mrs. Pasmer, with a disappointment for which Munt tried to console her.

"I've never even been at their place. He asked me once, a great while ago; but you know how those things are. I've heard that she used to be very pretty and very gay. They went about a great deal, to Saratoga and Cape May and such places—rather out of our beat."

"And now?"

"And now she's been an invalid for a great many years. Bedridden, I believe. Paralysis, I think."

"Yes; Mrs. Saintsbury said something of the kind."

"Well," said Munt, anxious to add to the store of knowledge which this remark let him understand he had not materially increased, "I think Mrs. Mavering was the origin of the wall-paper—or her money. Mavering was poor; her father had started it, and Mavering turned in his talent."

"How very interesting! And is that the reason—its being ancestral—that Mr. Mavering wishes his son to go into it?"

"Is he going into it?" asked Munt.

"He's come up here to think about it."

"I should suppose it would be a very good thing," said Munt.

"What a very remarkable forest!" said Mrs. Pasmer, examining it on either side, and turning quite round. This gave her, from her place in the van of the straggling procession, a glimpse of Alice and Dan Mavering far in the rear.

"Don't you know," he was saying to the girl at the same moment, "it's like some of those Doré illustrations to the 'Inferno,' or the *Wandering Jew*."

"Oh yes. I was trying to think what it was made me think I had seen it before," she answered. "It must be that. But how strange it is!" she exclaimed, "that sensation of having been there before—in some place before where you can't possibly have been."

"And do you feel it here?" he asked, as vividly interested as if they two had been the first to notice the phenomenon which has been a psychical consolation to so many young observers.

"Yes," she cried.

"I hope I was with you," he said, with a sudden turn of levity, which did not displease her, for there seemed to be a tender earnestness lurking in it. "I couldn't bear to think of your being alone in such a howling wilderness."

"Oh, I was with a large picnic," she retorted, gayly. "You might have been among the rest. I didn't notice."

"Well, the next time, I wish you'd look closer. I don't like being left out." They were so far behind the rest that he devoted himself entirely to her, and they had grown more and more confidential. They came to a narrow foot-bridge over a deep gorge. The hand-rail had fallen away. He sprang forward and gave her his hand for the passage.

"Who helped you over here?" he demanded. "Don't say *I* didn't."

"Perhaps it was you," she murmured, letting him keep the fingers to which he clung a moment after they had crossed the bridge. Then she took them away, and said: "But I can't be sure. There were so many others."

"Other fellows?" he demanded, placing himself before her on the narrow path, so that she could not get by. "Try to remember, Miss Pasmer. This is very important. It would break my heart if it was really some one else." She stole a glance at his face, but it was smiling, though his voice was so earnest. "I want to help you over all the bad places, and I don't want any one else to have a hand in it."

The voice and the face still belied each other, and between them the girl chose to feel herself trifled with by the artistic temperament. "If you'll please step out of the way, Mr. Mavering," she said, severely, "I shall not need anybody's help just here."

He instantly moved aside, and they were both silent, till she said, as she quickened her pace to overtake the others in front, "I don't see how you can help liking nature in such a place as this."

"I can't—human nature," he said. It was mere folly, and an abstract folly at that; but the face that she held down and away from him flushed with sweet consciousness as she laughed.

On the cliff beetling above the bay, where she sat to look out over the sad Northern sea, lit with the fishing sail they had seen before, and the surge washed into the rocky coves far beneath them, he threw himself at her feet, and made her alone in the company that came and went and tried this view and that from the different points where the picnic hostess insisted they should enjoy it. She left the young couple to themselves, and Mrs. Pasmer seemed to have forgotten that she had bidden Alice to be a little more with her.

Alice had forgotten it too. She sat listening to Mavering's talk with a certain fascination, but not so much apparently because the meaning of the words pleased her as the sound of his voice, the motion of his lips in speaking, charmed her. At first he was serious and even melancholy, as if he were afraid he had offended her; but apparently he soon believed that he had been forgiven, and began to burlesque his own mood, but still with a deference and a watchful observance of her changes of feeling which was delicately flattering in its way. Now and then when she answered something it was not always to the purpose; he accused her of not hearing what he said, but she would have it that she did, and then he tried to test her by proofs and questions. It did not matter for anything that was spoken or done; speech and action of whatever sort were mere masks of their young joy in each other, so that when he said, after he had quoted some lines befitting the scene they looked out on, "Now was that from Tennyson or from Tupper?" and she answered, "Neither; it was from Shakespeare," they joined in the same happy laugh, and they laughed now and then without saying anything. Neither this nor that made them more glad or less; they were in a trance, vulnerable to nothing but the summons which must come to leave their dream behind, and issue into the waking world.

In hope or in experience such a moment has come to all, and it is so pretty to those who recognize it from the outside that no one has the heart to hurry it away while it can be helped. The affair between Alice and Mavering had evidently her mother's sanction, and all the rest were eager to help it on. When the party had started to return, they called to them, and let them come behind together. At the carriages they had what Miss Anderson called a new deal, and Alice and Mavering found themselves together in the rear seat of the last.

The fog began to come in from the sea, and followed them through the woods. When they emerged upon the highway it wrapped them densely round, and formed a little world, cozy, intimate, where they two dwelt alone with these friends of theirs, each of whom they praised for delightful qualities. The horses beat along through the mist, in which there seemed no progress, and they lived in a blissful arrest of time. Miss Anderson called back from the front seat, "My ear buyns; you're talkin' about me."

"Which ear?" cried Mavering.

"Oh, the left, of couyse."

"Then it's merely habit, Julie. You ought to have heard the nice things we were saying about you," Alice called.

"I'd like to hear *all* the nice things you've been saying."

This seemed the last effect of subtle wit. Mavering broke out in his laugh, and Alice's laugh rang above it.

Mrs. Pasmer looked involuntarily round from the carriage ahead.

"They seem to be having a good time," said Mrs. Brinkley, at her side.

"Yes; I hope Alice isn't overdoing."

"I'm afraid you're dreadfully tired," said Mavering to the girl, in a low voice, as he lifted her from her place when they reached the hotel through the provisional darkness, and found that after all it was only dinner-time.

"Oh no. I feel as if the picnic were just beginning."

"Then you will come to-night?"

"I will see what mamma says."

"Shall I ask her?"

"Oh, perhaps not," said the girl, repressing his ardor, but not severely.

XVIII

THEY WERE GOING to have some theatricals at one of the cottages, and the lady at whose house they were to be given made haste to invite all the picnic party before it dispersed. Mrs. Pasmer accepted with a mental reservation, meaning to send an excuse later if she chose; and before she decided the point she kept her husband from going after dinner into the reading-room, where he spent nearly all his time over a paper and a cigar, or in sitting absolutely silent and unoccupied, and made him go to their own room with her.

"There is something that I must speak to you about," she said, closing the door, "and you must decide for yourself whether you wish to let it go any further."

"What go any further?" asked Mr. Pasmer, sitting down and putting his hand to the pocket that held his cigar case with the same series of motions.

"No, don't smoke," she said, staying his hand impatiently. "I want you to think."

"How can I think if I don't smoke?"

"Very well; smoke, then. Do you want this affair with young Mavering to go any farther?"

"Oh!" said Pasmer, "I thought you had been looking after that." He had in fact relegated that to the company of the great questions exterior to his personal comfort which she always decided.

"I have been looking after it, but now the time has come when you must, as a father, take some interest in it."

Pasmer's noble mask of a face, from the point of his full white beard to his fine forehead, crossed by his impressive black eyebrows, expressed all the dignified concern which a father ought to feel in such an affair; but what he was really feeling was a grave reluctance to have to intervene in any way. "What do you want me to say to him?" he asked.

"Why, I don't know that he's going to ask you anything. I don't know whether he's said anything to Alice yet," said Mrs. Pasmer, with some exasperation.

Her husband was silent, but his silence insinuated a degree

of wonder that she should approach him prematurely on such
a point.

"They have been thrown together all day, and there is no
use to conceal from ourselves that they are very much taken
with each other."

"I thought," Pasmer said, "that you said that from the beginning. Didn't you want them to be taken with each other?"

"That is what you are to decide."

Pasmer silently refused to assume the responsibility.

"Well?" demanded his wife, after waiting for him to speak.

"Well what?"

"What do you decide?"

"What is the use of deciding a thing when it is all over?"

"It isn't over at all. It can be broken off at any moment."

"Well, break it off, then, if you like."

Mrs. Pasmer resumed the responsibility with a sigh. She felt
the burden, the penalty, of power, after having so long enjoyed its sweets, and she would willingly have abdicated the
sovereignty which she had spent her whole married life in
establishing. But there was no one to take it up. "No, I shall
not break it off," she said, resentfully; "I shall let it go on."
Then, seeing that her husband was not shaken by her threat
from his long-confirmed subjection, she added: "It isn't an
ideal affair, but I think it will be a very good thing for Alice.
He is not what I expected, but he is thoroughly nice, and I
should think his family was nice. I've been talking with Mr.
Munt about them to-day, and he confirms all that Etta Saintsbury said. I don't think there can be any doubt of his intentions in coming here. He isn't a particularly artless young
man, but he's been sufficiently frank about Alice since he's
been here." Her husband smoked on. "His father seems to
have taken up the business from the artistic side, and Mr.
Mavering won't be expected to enter into the commercial part
at once. If it wasn't for Alice, I don't believe he would think
of the business for a moment; he would study law. Of course
it's a little embarrassing to have her engaged at once before
she's seen anything of society here, but perhaps it's all for the
best, after all: the main thing is that she should be satisfied,
and I can see that she's only too much so. Yes, she's very
much taken with him; and I don't wonder. He is charming."

It was not the first time that Mrs. Pasmer had reasoned in this round; but the utterance of her thoughts seemed to throw a new light on them, and she took a courage from them that they did not always impart. She arrived at the final opinion expressed, with a throb of tenderness for the young fellow whom she believed eager to take her daughter from her, and now for the first time she experienced a desolation in the prospect, as if it were an accomplished fact. She was morally a bundle of finesses, but at the bottom of her heart her daughter was all the world to her. She had made the girl her idol, and if, like some other heathen, she had not always used her idol with the greatest deference, if she had often expected the impossible from it, and made it pay for her disappointment, still she had never swerved from her worship of it. She suddenly asked herself, What if this young fellow, so charming and so good, should so wholly monopolize her child that she should no longer have any share in her? What if Alice, who had so long formed her first care and chief object in life, should contentedly lose herself in the love and care of another, and both should ignore her right to her? She answered herself with a pang that this might happen with any one Alice married, and that it would be no worse, at the worst, with Dan Mavering than with another, while her husband remained impartially silent. Always keeping within the lines to which his wife's supremacy had driven him, he felt safe there, and was not to be easily coaxed out of them.

Mrs. Pasmer rose and left him, with his perfect acquiescence, and went into her daughter's room. She found Alice there, with a pretty evening dress laid out on her bed. Mrs. Pasmer was very fond of that dress, and at the thought of Alice in it her spirits rose again.

"Oh, are you going, Alice?"

"Why yes," answered the girl. "Didn't you accept?"

"Why yes," Mrs. Pasmer admitted. "But aren't you tired?"

"Oh, not in the least. I feel as fresh as I did this morning. Don't you want me to go?"

"Oh yes, certainly, I want you to go—if you think you'll enjoy it."

"Enjoy it? Why, why shouldn't I enjoy it, mamma? What

are you thinking about? It's going to be the greatest kind of fun."

"But do you think you ought to look at everything simply as fun?" asked the mother, with unwonted didacticism.

"How everything? What are you thinking about, mamma?"

"Oh, nothing! I'm so glad you're going to wear that dress."

"Why, of course! It's my best. But what are you driving at, mamma?"

Mrs. Pasmer was really seeking in her daughter that comfort of a distinct volition which she had failed to find in her husband, and she wished to assure herself of it more and more, that she might share with some one the responsibility which he had refused any part in.

"Nothing. But I'm glad you wish so much to go." The girl dropped her hands and stared. "You must have enjoyed yourself to-day," she added, as if that were an explanation.

"Of course I enjoyed myself! But what has that to do with my wanting to go to-night?"

"Oh, nothing. But I hope, Alice, that there is one thing you have looked fully in the face."

"What thing?" faltered the girl, and now showed herself unable to confront it by dropping her eyes.

"Well, whatever you may have heard or seen, nobody else is in doubt about it. What do you suppose has brought Mr. Mavering here?"

"I don't know." The denial not only confessed that she did know, but it informed her mother that all was as yet tacit between the young people.

"Very well, then, *I* know," said Mrs. Pasmer; "and there is one thing that you must know before long, Alice."

"What?" she asked, faintly.

"Your own mind," said her mother. "I don't ask you what it is, and I shall wait till you tell me. Of course I shouldn't have let him stay here if I had objected—"

"Oh, mamma!" murmured the girl, dyed with shame to have the facts so boldly touched, but not, probably, too deeply displeased.

"Yes. And I know that he would never have thought of going into that business if he had not expected—hoped—"

"Mamma!"

"And you ought to consider—"

"Oh, don't! don't! don't!" implored the girl.

"That's all," said her mother, turning from Alice, who had hidden her face in her hands, to inspect the costume on the bed. She lifted one piece of it after another, turned it over, looked at it, and laid it down. "You can never get such a dress in this country."

She went out of the room, as the girl dropped her face in the pillow. An hour later they met equipped for the evening's pleasure. To the keen glance that her mother gave her, the daughter's eyes had the brightness of eyes that have been weeping, but they were also bright with that knowledge of her own mind which Mrs. Pasmer had desired for her. She met her mother's glance fearlessly, even proudly, and she carried her stylish costume with a splendor to which only occasions could stimulate her. They dramatized a perfect unconsciousness to each other, but Mrs. Pasmer was by no means satisfied with the decision which she had read in her daughter's looks. Somehow it did not relieve her of the responsibility, and it did not change the nature of the case. It was gratifying, of course, to see Alice the object of a passion so sincere and so ardent; so far the triumph was complete, and there was really nothing objectionable in the young man and his circumstances, though there was nothing very distinguished. But the affair was altogether different from anything that Mrs. Pasmer had imagined. She had supposed and intended that Alice should meet some one in Boston, and go through a course of society before reaching any decisive step. There was to be a whole season in which to look the ground carefully over, and the ground was to be all within certain well-ascertained and guarded precincts. But this that had happened was outside of these precincts, or at least on their mere outskirts. Class Day, of course, was all right; and she could not say that the summer colony at Campobello was not thoroughly and essentially Boston; and yet she felt that certain influences, certain sanctions, were absent. To tell the truth, she would not have cared for the feelings of Mavering's family in regard to the matter, except as they might afterward concern Alice, and the time had not come when she could recognize their existence in regard to the affair; and yet she could have wished that even as it was his family could have seen and approved it from the start. It would have been more regular.

With Alice it was a simpler matter, and of course deeper. For her it was only a question of himself and herself; no one else existed to the sublime egotism of her love. She did not call it by that name; she did not permit it to assert itself by any name; it was a mere formless joy in her soul, a trustful and blissful expectance, which she now no more believed he could disappoint than that she could die within that hour. All the rebellion that she had sometimes felt at the anomalous attitude exacted of her sex in regard to such matters was gone. She no longer thought it strange that a girl should be expected to ignore the admiration of a young man till he explicitly declared it, and should then be fully possessed of all the materials of a decision on the most momentous question in life; for she knew that this state of ignorance could never really exist; she had known from the first moment that he had thought her beautiful. To-night she was radiant for him. Her eyes shone with the look in which they should meet and give themselves to each other before they spoke—the look in which they had met already, in which they had lived that whole day.

XIX

THE EVENING'S entertainment was something that must fail before an audience which was not very kind. They were to present a burlesque of classic fable, and the parts, with their general intention, had been distributed to the different actors; but nothing had been written down, and beyond the situations and a few points of dialogue, all had to be improvised. The costumes and properties had been invented from such things as came to hand. Sheets sculpturesquely draped the deities who took part; a fox-pelt from the hearth did duty as the leopard-skin of Bacchus; a feather duster served Neptune for a trident; the lyre of Apollo was a dust pan; a gull's breast furnished Jove with his gray beard.

The fable was adapted to modern life, and the scene had been laid in Campobello, the peculiarities of which were to be satirized throughout. The principal situation was to be a passage between Jupiter, represented by Mavering, and Juno, whom Miss Anderson personated; it was to be a scene of conjugal reproaches and reprisals, and to end in reconciliation, in which the father of the gods sacrificed himself on the altar of domestic peace by promising to bring his family to Campobello every year.

This was to be followed by a sketch of the Judgment of Paris, in which Juno and Pallas were to be personated by two young men, and Miss Anderson took the part of Venus.

The pretty drawing-room of the Trevors—young people from Albany and cousins of Miss Anderson—was curtained off at one end for a stage, and beyond the sliding doors which divided it in half were set chairs for the spectators. People had come in whatever dress they liked; the men were mostly in morning coats; the ladies had generally made some attempt at evening toilet, but they joined in admiring Alice Pasmer's costume, and one of them said that they would let it represent them all, and express what each might have done if she would. There was not much time for their tributes; all the lamps were presently taken away and set along the floor in front of the curtain as foot-lights, leaving the company in a darkness which Mrs. Brinkley pronounced sepulchral. She made her reproaches to the master of the house, who had effected this transposition of the lamps. "I was just thinking some very pretty and valuable things about your charming cottage, Mr. Trevor: a rug on a bare floor, a trim of varnished pine, a wall with half a dozen simple etchings on it, an open fire, and a mantel-piece without bric-à-brac, how entirely satisfying it all is! And how it upbraids us for heaping up upholstery as we do in town!"

"Go on," said the host. "Those are beautiful thoughts."

"But I *can't* go on in the dark," retorted Mrs. Brinkley. "You can't think in the dark, much less talk! Can *you*, Mrs. Pasmer?" Mrs. Pasmer, with Alice next her, sat just in front of Mrs. Brinkley.

"No," she assented; "but if I could—*you* can think anywhere, Mrs. Brinkley—Mrs. Trevor's lovely house would inspire me to it."

"Two birds with one stone—thank you, Mrs. Pasmer, for my part of the compliment. Pick yourself up, Mr. Trevor."

"Oh, thank you, *I'm* all right," said Trevor, panting after the ladies' meanings, as a man must. "I suppose thinking and talking in the dark is a good deal like smoking in the dark."

"No; thinking and talking are not at all like smoking under any conditions. Why in the world *should* they be?"

"Oh, I can't get any fun out of a cigar unless I can see the smoke," the host explained.

"Do you follow him, Mrs. Pasmer?"

"Yes, perfectly."

"Thank you, Mrs. Pasmer," said Trevor.

"I'll get you to tell me how you did it some time," said Mrs. Brinkley. "But your house is a gem, Mr. Trevor."

"*Isn't* it?" cried Trevor. "I want my wife to live here the year round." It was the Trevors' first summer in their cottage, and the experienced reader will easily recognize his mood. "But she's such a worldly spirit she won't."

"Oh, I don't know about the year *round*. Do you, Mrs. Pasmer?"

"*I* should," said Alice, with the suddenness of youth, breaking into the talk which she had not been supposed to take any interest in.

"*Is* it proper to kiss a young lady's hand?" said Trevor, gratefully, appealing to Mrs. Brinkley.

"It isn't very customary in the nineteenth century," said Mrs. Brinkley. "But you might kiss her fan. He might kiss her fan, mightn't he, Mrs. Pasmer?"

"Certainly. Alice, hold out your fan instantly."

The girl humored the joke, laughing.

Trevor pressed his lips to the perfumed sticks. "I will tell Mrs. Trevor," he said, "and that will decide her."

"It will decide her not to come here at all next year if you tell her all."

"He never tells me all," said Mrs. Trevor, catching so much of the talk as she came in from some hospitable cares in the dining-room. "They're incapable of it. What has he been doing now?"

"Nothing. Or I will tell you when we are *alone*, Mrs. Trevor," said Mrs. Brinkley, with burlesque sympathy. "We oughtn't to have a scene on *both* sides of the foot-lights."

A boyish face, all excitement, was thrust out between the curtains forming the proscenium of the little theatre. "All ready, Mrs. Trevor?"

"Yes, all ready, Jim."

He dashed the curtains apart, and marred the effect of his own disappearance from the scene by tripping over the long legs of Jove, stretched out to the front, where he sat on Mrs. Trevor's richest rug, propped with sofa cushions on either hand.

"So perish all the impious race of Titans, enemies of the gods!" said Mavering, solemnly, as the boy fell sprawling. "Pick the earth-born giant up, Vulcan, my son."

The boy was very small for his age; every one saw that the accident had not been premeditated, and when Vulcan appeared, with an exaggerated limp, and carried the boy off, a burst of laughter went up from the company.

It did not matter what the play was to have been after that; it all turned upon the accident. Juno came on, and began to reproach Jupiter for his carelessness. "I've sent Mercury upstairs for the aynica; but he says it's no use: that boy won't be able to pass ball for a week. How often have I told you not to sit with your feet out that way! I knew you'd huyt somebody."

"I didn't *have* my feet out," retorted Jupiter. "Besides," he added, with dignity, and a burlesque of marital special pleading which every wife and husband recognized, "I *always* sit with my feet out so, and I always will, so long as I've the spirit of a god."

"Isn't he delicious?" buzzed Mrs. Pasmer, leaning backward to whisper to Mrs. Brinkley; it was not that she thought what Dan had just said was so very funny, but people are immoderately applausive of amateur dramatics, and she was feeling very fond of the young fellow.

The improvisation went wildly and adventurously on, and the curtains dropped together amidst the facile acclaim of the audience.

"It's very well for Jupiter that he happened to think of the curtain," said Mrs. Brinkley. "They couldn't have kept it up at that level much longer."

"Oh, do you think so?" softly murmured Mrs. Pasmer. "It seemed as if they could have kept it up all night if they liked."

"I doubt it. Mr. Trevor," said Mrs. Brinkley to the host, who had come up for her congratulations, "do you always have such brilliant performances?"

"Well, we have so far," he answered, modestly; and Mrs. Brinkley laughed with him. This was the first entertainment at Trevor cottage.

" 'Sh!" went up all round them, and Mrs. Trevor called across the room, in a reproachful whisper loud enough for every one to hear, "My dear!—enjoying . yourself!" while Mavering stood between the parted curtains waiting for the attention of the company.

"On account of an accident to the call-boy and the mental exhaustion of some of the deities, the next piece will be omitted, and the performance will begin with the one after. While the audience is waiting, Mercury will go round and take up a collection for the victim of the recent accident, who will probably be indisposed for life. The collector will be accompanied by a policeman, and may be safely trusted."

He disappeared behind the curtain with a *pas* and a swirl of his draperies like the Lord Chancellor in *Iolanthe*, and the audience again abandoned itself to applause.

"How very witty he is!" said Miss Cotton, who sat near John Munt. "Don't you think he's really witty?"

"Yes," Munt assented, critically. "But you should have known his father."

"Oh, do *you* know his father?"

"I was in college with him."

"Oh, do tell me about him, and all Mr. Mavering's family. We're so interested, you know, on account of— Isn't it pretty to have that little love idyl going on here? I wonder— I've been wondering all the time—what she thinks of all this. Do you suppose she quite likes it? His costume is so *very* remarkable!" Miss Cotton, in the absence of any lady of her intimate circle, was appealing confidentially to John Munt.

"Why, do you think there's anything serious between them?" he asked, dropping his head forward as people do in church when they wish to whisper to some one in the same pew.

"Why, yes, it seems so," murmured Miss Cotton. "His admiration is quite undisguised, isn't it?"

"A man never can tell," said Munt. "We have to leave those things to you ladies."

"Oh, every one's talking of it, I assure you. And you know his family?"

"I knew his father once rather better than anybody else."

"Indeed!"

"Yes." Munt sketched rather a flattered portrait of the elder Mavering, his ability, his goodness, his shyness, which he had always had to make such a hard fight with. Munt was sensible of an access of popularity in knowing Dan Mavering's people, and he did not spare his colors.

"Then it isn't from his father that he gets everything. He isn't in the least shy," said Miss Cotton.

"That must be the mother."

"And the mother?"

"The mother I don't know."

Miss Cotton sighed. "Sometimes I wish that he did show a little more trepidation. It would seem as if he were more alive to the *great* difference that there is between Alice Pasmer and other girls."

Munt laughed a man's laugh. "I guess he's pretty well alive to that, if he's in love with her."

"Oh, in a certain way, of course, but not in the highest way. Now, for instance, if he felt all her fineness as—as *we* do, I *don't* believe he'd be willing to appear before her just like that." The father of the gods wore a damask tablecloth of a pale golden hue and a classic pattern; his arms were bare, and rather absurdly white; on his feet a pair of lawn-tennis shoes had a very striking effect of sandals. "It seems to me," Miss Cotton pursued, "that if he *really* appreciated her in the *highest* way, he would wish never to do an undignified or trivial thing in her presence."

"Oh, perhaps it's that that pleases her in him. They say we're always taken with opposites."

"Yes—do you think so?" asked Miss Cotton.

The curtains were flung apart, and the Judgment of Paris followed rather tamely upon what had gone before, though the two young fellows who did Juno and Minerva were very amusing, and the dialogue was full of hits. Some of the audience, an appreciative minority, were of opinion that Mavering and Miss Anderson surpassed themselves in it; she promised him the most beautiful and cultured wife in Greece. "That settles it," he answered. They came out arm in arm, and Paris, having put on a striped tennis coat over his short-sleeved Greek tunic, moved round among the company for their congratulations, Venus ostentatiously showing the apple she had won.

"I can haydly keep from eating it," she explained to Alice, before whom she dropped Mavering's arm. "I'm awfully hungry. It's hayd woyk."

Alice stood with her head drawn back, looking at the excited girl with a smile, in which seemed to hover somewhere a latent bitterness.

Mavering, with a flushed face and a flying tongue, was exchanging sallies with her mother, who smothered him in flatteries.

Mrs. Trevor came toward the group and announced supper. "Mr. Paris, will you take Miss Aphrodite out?"

Miss Anderson swept a low bow of renunciation, and tacitly relinquished Mavering to Alice.

"Oh, no, no!" said Alice, shrinking back from him, with an intensification of her uncertain smile. "A mere mortal?"

"Oh, how very good!" said Mrs. Trevor.

There began to be, without any one's intending it, that sort of tacit misunderstanding which is all the worse because it can only follow upon a tacit understanding like that which had established itself between Alice and Mavering. They laughed and joked together gayly about all that went on; they were perfectly good friends; he saw that she and her mother were promptly served; he brought them salad and ice-cream and coffee himself, only waiting officially upon Miss Anderson first, and Alice thanked him, with the politest deprecation of his devotion; but if their eyes met, it was defensively, and the security between them was gone. Mavering vaguely felt the loss, without knowing how to retrieve it, and it made him go on more desperately with Miss Anderson. He laughed and joked recklessly, and Alice began to mark a more explicit displeasure with her. She made her mother go rather early.

On her part, Miss Anderson seemed to find reason for resentment in Alice's bearing toward her. As if she had said to herself that her frank loyalty had been thrown away upon a cold and unresponsive nature, and that her harmless follies in the play had been met with unjust suspicions, she began to make reprisals, she began in dead earnest to flirt with Mavering. Before the evening passed she had made him seem taken with her; but how justly she had done this, and with how much fault of his, no one could have said. There were some who did not notice it at all, but these were not people who knew Mavering, or knew Alice very well.

XX

THE NEXT MORNING Alice was walking slowly along the road toward the fishing village, when she heard rapid, plunging strides down the wooded hill-side on her right. She knew them for Mavering's, and she did not affect surprise when he made a final leap into the road, and shortened his pace beside her.

"May I join you, Miss Pasmer?"

"I am only going down to the herring-houses," she began.

"And you'll let me go with you?" said the young fellow. "The fact is—you're always so frank that you make everything else seem silly—I've been waiting up there in the woods for you to come by. Mrs. Pasmer told me you had started this way, and I cut across lots to overtake you, and then, when you came in sight, I had to let you pass before I could screw my courage up to the point of running after you. How is that for open-mindedness?"

"It's a very good beginning, I should think."

"Well, don't you think you ought to say now that you're sorry you were so formidable?"

"Am I so formidable?" she asked, and then recognized that she had been trapped into a leading question.

"You are to me. Because I would like always to be sure that I had pleased you, and for the last twelve hours I've only been able to make sure that I hadn't. That's the consolation I'm going away with. I thought I'd get you to confirm my impression explicitly. That's why I wished to join you."

"Are you—were you going away?"

"I'm going by the next boat. What's the use of staying? I should only make bad worse. Yesterday I hoped— But last night spoiled everything. Miss Pasmer," he broke out, with a rush of feeling, "you must know why I came up here to Campobello."

His steps took him a little ahead of her, and he could look back into her face as he spoke. But apparently he saw nothing in it to give him courage to go on, for he stopped, and then continued, lightly: "And I'm going away because I feel that

424

I've made a failure of the expedition. I knew that you were supremely disgusted with me last night; but it will be a sort of comfort if you'll tell me so."

"Oh," said Alice, "everybody thought it was very brilliant, I'm sure."

"And you thought it was a piece of buffoonery. Well, it was. I wish you'd say so, Miss Pasmer; though I didn't mean the playing entirely. It would be something to start from, and I want to make a beginning—turn over a new leaf. Can't you help me to inscribe a good resolution of the most iron-clad description on the stainless page? I've lain awake all night composing one. Wouldn't you like to hear it?"

"I can't see what good that would do," she said, with some relenting toward a smile, in which he instantly prepared himself to bask.

"But you will when I've done it. Now listen!"

"Please don't go on." She cut him short with a return to her severity, which he would not recognize.

"Well, perhaps I'd better not," he consented. "It's rather a *long* resolution, and I don't know that I've committed it perfectly yet. But I do assure you that if you were disgusted last night, you were not the only one. I was immensely disgusted myself; and why I wanted you to tell me so was because when I have a strong pressure brought to bear I can brace up, and do almost anything," he said, dropping into earnest. Then he rose lightly again, and added, "You have no idea how unpleasant it is to lie awake all night throwing dust in the eyes of an accusing conscience."

"It must have been, if you didn't succeed," said Alice, dryly.

"Yes, that's it—that's just the point. If I'd succeeded, I should be all right, don't you see. But it was a difficult case." She turned her face away, but he saw the smile on her cheek, and he laughed as if this were what he had been trying to make her do. "I got beaten. I had to give up, and own it. I had to say that I had thrown my chance away, and I had better take myself off." He looked at her with a real anxiety in his gay eyes.

"The boat goes just after lunch, I believe," she said, indifferently.

"Oh yes, I shall have time to get *lunch* before I go," he said, with bitterness. "But lunch isn't the only thing; it isn't even the main thing, Miss Pasmer."

"No?" She hardened her heart.

He waited for her to say something more, and then he went on. "The question is whether there's time to undo last night, abolish it, erase it from the calendar of recorded time— sponge it out, in short—and get back to yesterday afternoon." She made no reply to this. "Don't you think it was a very pleasant picnic, Miss Pasmer?" he asked, with pensive respectfulness.

"Very," she answered, dryly.

He cast a glance at the woods that bordered the road on either side. "That weird forest—I shall never forget it."

"No; it was something to remember," she said.

"And the blueberry patch? We mustn't forget the blueberry patch."

"There were a great many blueberries."

She walked on, and he said, "And that bridge—you don't have that feeling of having been *here* before?"

"No."

"Am I walking too fast for you, Miss Pasmer?"

"No; I like to walk fast."

"But wouldn't you like to sit down? On this way-side log, for example?" He pointed it out with his stick. "It seems to invite repose, and I know you must be tired."

"I'm not tired."

"Ah, that shows that *you* didn't lie awake grieving over your follies all night. I hope you rested well, Miss Pasmer." She said nothing. "If I thought—if I could hope that you hadn't, it would be a bond of sympathy, and I would give almost anything for a bond of sympathy just now, Miss Pasmer. Alice!" he said, with sudden seriousness. "I know that I'm not worthy even to think of you, and that you're whole worlds above me in every way. It's that that takes all heart out of me, and leaves me without a word to say when I'd like to say so much. I would like to speak—tell you—"

She interrupted him. "I wish to speak to you, Mr. Mavering, and tell you that—I'm very tired, and I'm going back to the hotel. I must ask you to let me go back alone."

"Alice, I love you."

"I'm sorry you said it—sorry, sorry."

"Why?" he asked, with hopeless futility.

"Because there can be no love between us—not friendship even—not acquaintance."

"I shouldn't have asked for your acquaintance, your friendship, if—" His words conveyed a delicate reproach, and they stung her, because they put her in the wrong.

"No matter," she began, wildly. "I didn't mean to wound you. But we must part, and we must never see each other again."

He stood confused, as if he could not make it out or believe it. "But yesterday—"

"It's to-day now."

"Ah, no! It's last night. And I can explain."

"No!" she cried. "You shall not make me out so mean and vindictive. I don't care for last night, nor for anything that happened." This was not true, but it seemed so to her at the moment; she thought that she really no longer resented his association with Miss Anderson and his separation from herself in all that had taken place.

"Then what is it?"

"I can't tell you. But everything is over between us—that's all."

"But yesterday—and all these days past—you seemed—"

"It's unfair of you to insist—it's ungenerous, ungentlemanly."

That word, which from a woman's tongue always strikes a man like a blow in the face, silenced Mavering. He set his lips and bowed, and they parted. She turned upon her way, and he kept the path which she had been going.

It was not the hour when the piazzas were very full, and she slipped into the dim hotel corridor undetected, or at least undetained. She flung into her room, and confronted her mother.

Mrs. Pasmer was there looking into a trunk that had overflowed from her own chamber. "What is the matter?" she said to her daughter's excited face.

"Mr. Mavering—"

"Well?"

"And I refused him."

Mrs. Pasmer was one of those ladies who in any finality have a keen retrovision of all the advantages of a different conclusion. She had been thinking, since she told Dan Mavering which way Alice had gone to walk, that if he were to speak to her now, and she were to accept him, it would involve a great many embarrassing consequences; but she had consoled herself with the probability that he would not speak so soon after the effects of last night, but would only try at the furthest to make his peace with Alice. Since he had spoken, though, and she had refused him, Mrs. Pasmer instantly saw all the pleasant things that would have followed in another event. "Refused him?" she repeated, provisionally, while she gathered herself for a full exploration of all the facts.

"Yes, mamma; and I can't talk about it. I wish never to hear his name again, or to see him, or to speak to him."

"Why, of course not," said Mrs. Pasmer, with a fine smile, from the vantage-ground of her superior years, "if you've refused him." She left the trunk which she had been standing over, and sat down, while Alice swept to and fro before her excitedly. "But why did you refuse him, my dear?"

"Why? Because he's detestable—perfectly ignoble."

Her mother probably knew how to translate these exalted expressions into the more accurate language of maturer life. "Do you mean last night?"

"Last night?" cried Alice, tragically. "No. Why should I care for last night?"

"Then I don't understand what you mean," retorted Mrs. Pasmer. "What did he say?" she demanded, with authority.

"Mamma, I can't talk about it—I won't."

"But you must, Alice. It's your duty. Of course I must know about it. What did he say?"

Alice walked up and down the room with her lips firmly closed; like Mavering's lips, it occurred to her, and then she opened them, but without speaking.

"What did he say?" persisted her mother, and her persistence had its effect.

"Say?" exclaimed the girl, indignantly. "He tried to make *me* say."

"I see," said Mrs. Pasmer. "Well?"

"But I *forced* him to speak, and then—I rejected him. That's all."

"Poor fellow!" said Mrs. Pasmer. "He was afraid of you."

"And that's what made it the more odious. Do you think I *wished* him to be afraid of me? Would that be any pleasure? I should hate myself if I had to *quell* anybody into being unlike themselves." She sat down for a moment, and then jumped up again, and went to the window, for no reason, and came back.

"Yes," said her mother, impartially, "he's light, and he's roundabout. He couldn't come straight at anything."

"And would you have me accept such a—being?"

Mrs. Pasmer smiled a little at the literary word, and continued: "But he's very sweet, and he's as good as the day's long, and he's very fond of you, and—I thought you liked him."

The girl threw up her arms across her eyes. "Oh, how can you say such a thing, mamma?"

She dropped into a chair at the bedside, and let her face fall into her hands, and cried.

Her mother waited for the gust of tears to pass before she said, "But if you feel so about it—"

"Mamma!" Alice sprang to her feet.

"It needn't come from you. I could make some excuse to see him—write him a little note—"

"Never!" exclaimed Alice, grandly. "What I've done I've done from my reason, and my feelings have nothing to do with it."

"Oh, very well," said her mother, going out of the room, not wholly disappointed with what she viewed as a respite, and amused by her daughter's tragics. "But if you think that the feelings have nothing to do with such a matter, you're very much mistaken." If she believed that her daughter did not know her real motives in rejecting Dan Mavering, or had not been able to give them, she did not say so.

The little group of Aliceolaters on the piazza who began to canvass the causes of Mavering's going before the top of his hat disappeared below the bank on the path leading to the ferry-boat were of two minds. One faction held that he was going because Alice had refused him, and that his gayety up to the last moment was only a mask to hide his despair. The other side contended that if he and Alice were not actually engaged, they understood each other, and he was going away because he wanted to tell his family, or something of that kind. Between the two opinions Miss Cotton wavered with a sentimental attraction to either. "What do you really think?" she asked Mrs. Brinkley, arriving from lunch at the corner of the piazza where the group was seated.

"Oh, what does it matter, at their age?" she demanded.

"But they're just of the age when it does happen to matter," suggested Mrs. Stamwell.

"Yes," said Mrs. Brinkley, "and that's what makes the whole thing so perfectly ridiculous. Just think of two children, one of twenty and the other of twenty-three, proposing to decide their life-long destiny in such a vital matter! Should we trust their judgment in regard to the smallest business affair? Of course not. They're babes in arms, morally and mentally speaking. People haven't the data for being wisely in love till they've reached the age when they haven't the least wish to be so. Oh, I suppose I thought that I was a grown woman too when I was twenty; I can look back and see that I did; and what's more preposterous still, I thought Mr. Brinkley was a man at twenty-four. But we were no more fit to accept or reject each other at that infantile period—"

"Do you really think so?" asked Miss Cotton, only partially credulous of Mrs. Brinkley's irony.

"Yes, it does seem out of all reason," admitted Mrs. Stamwell.

"Of course it is," said Mrs. Brinkley. "If she has rejected him, she's done a very safe thing. Nobody should be allowed to marry before fifty. Then if people married it would be because they *knew* that they loved each other."

Miss Cotton reflected a moment. "It *is* strange that such an important question should have to be decided at an age when the judgment is so far from mature. I never happened to look at it in that light before."

"Yes," said Mrs. Brinkley—and she made herself comfortable in an arm-chair commanding a stretch of the bay over which the ferry-boat must pass—"but it's only part and parcel of the whole affair. I'm sure that no *grown* person can see the ridiculous young things—inexperienced, ignorant, feather-brained—that nature intrusts with children, their im-mortal little souls and their extremely perishable little bodies, without rebelling at the whole system. When you see what most young mothers are, how perfectly unfit and incapable, you wonder that the whole race doesn't teeth and die. Yes, there's one thing I feel pretty sure of—that, as matters are arranged *now*, there oughtn't to be mothers at all, there ought to be only grandmothers."

The group all laughed, even Miss Cotton, but she was the first to become grave. At the bottom of her heart there was a doubt whether so light a way of treating serious things was not a little wicked.

"Perhaps," she said, "we shall have to go back to the idea that engagements and marriages are not intended to be regu-lated by the judgment, but by the affections."

"I don't know what's intended," said Mrs. Brinkley, "but I know what is. In ninety-nine cases out of a hundred the affec-tions have it their own way, and I must say I don't think the judgment could make a greater mess of it. In fact," she con-tinued, perhaps provoked to the excess by the deprecation she saw in Miss Cotton's eye, "I consider every broken engage-ment nowadays a blessing in disguise."

Miss Cotton said nothing. The other ladies said, "Why, Mrs. *Brinkley!*"

"Yes. The thing has gone altogether too far. The pendulum has swung in that direction out of all measure. We are married too much. And as a natural consequence we are divorced too much. The whole case is in a nutshell: if there were no mar-riages, there would be no divorces, and *that* great abuse would be corrected, at any rate."

All the ladies laughed, Miss Cotton more and more sorrow-fully. She liked to have people talk as they do in genteel novels. Mrs. Brinkley's bold expressions were a series of violent shocks to her nature, and imparted a terrible vibration to the fabric of her whole little rose-colored ideal world; if they had not been the expressions of a person whom a great many un-questionable persons accepted, who had such an undoubted standing, she would have thought them very coarse. As it was, they had a great fascination for her. "But in a case like that of"—she looked round and lowered her voice—"our young friends, I'm sure you couldn't rejoice if the engagement were broken off."

"Well, I'm not going to be 'a mush of concession,' as Emerson says, Miss Cotton. And, in the first place, how do you know they're engaged?"

"Ah, I don't; I didn't mean that they were. But wouldn't it be a little pathetic if, after all that we've seen going on, his coming here expressly on her account, and his perfect devotion to her for the past two weeks, it should end in nothing?"

"Two weeks isn't a very long time to settle the business of a lifetime."

"No."

"Perhaps she's proposed delay; a little further acquaintance."

"Oh, of course that would be perfectly right. Do you think she did?"

"Not if she's as wise as the rest of us would have been at her age. But I think she ought."

"Yes?" said Miss Cotton, semi-interrogatively.

"Do *you* think his behavior last night would naturally impress her with his wisdom and constancy?"

"No, I can't say that it would; but—"

"And this Alice of yours is rather a severe young person. She has her ideas, and I'm afraid they're rather heroic. She'd be just with him, of course. But there's nothing a man dreads so much as justice—some men."

"Yes," pursued Miss Cotton, "but that very disparity—I know they're *very* unlike—don't you think—"

"Oh yes, I know the theory about that. But if they were exactly alike in temperament, they'd be sufficiently unlike for the purposes of counterparts. That was arranged once for all when male and female created He them. I've no doubt their fancy was caught by all the kinds of difference they find in each other; that's just as natural as it's silly. But the misunderstanding, the trouble, the quarrelling, the wear and tear of spirit, that they'd have to go through before they assimilated—it makes me tired, as the boys say. No: I hope, for the young man's own sake, he's got his *congé*."

"But he's so kind, so good—"

"My dear, the world is surfeited with kind, good men.

There are half a dozen of them at the other end of the piazza smoking; and there comes another to join them," she added, as a large figure, semi-circular in profile, advanced itself from a doorway toward a vacant chair among the smokers. "The very soul of kindness and goodness." She beckoned toward her husband, who caught sight of her gesture. "Now I can tell you all his mental processes. First, surprise at seeing some one beckoning; then astonishment that it's I, though who else should beckon him? then wonder what I can want; then conjecture that I may want him to come here; then pride in his conjecture; rebellion; compliance."

The ladies were in a scream of laughter as Mr. Brinkley lumbered heavily to their group.

"What is it?" he asked.

"Do you believe in broken engagements? Now quick—off-hand!"

"Who's engaged?"

"No matter."

"Well, you know *Punch's* advice to those about to marry?"

"I know—chestnuts," said his wife, scornfully. They dismissed each other with tender bluntness, and he went in to get a match.

"Ah, Mrs. Brinkley," said one of the ladies, "it would be of no use for you to preach broken engagements to any one who saw you and Mr. Brinkley together."

They fell upon her, one after another, and mocked her with the difference between her doctrine and practice; and they were all the more against her because they had been perhaps a little put down by her whimsical sayings.

"Yes," she admitted. "But we've been thirty years coming to the understanding that you all admire so much; and do you think it was worth the time?"

XXI

MAVERING KEPT UP until he took leave of the party of young people who had come over on the ferry-boat to Eastport for the frolic of seeing him off. It was a tremendous *tour de force* to accept their company as if he were glad of it, and to respond to all their gay nothings gayly; to maintain a sunny surface on his turbid misery. They had tried to make Alice come with them, but her mother pleaded a bad headache for her; and he had to parry a hundred sallies about her, and from his sick heart humor the popular insinuation that there was an understanding between them, and that they had agreed together she should not come. He had to stand about on the steam-boat wharf and listen to amiable innuendoes for nearly an hour before the steamer came in from St. John. The fond adieux of his friends, their offers to take any message back, lasted during the interminable fifteen minutes that she lay at her moorings, and then he showed himself at the stern of the boat, and waved his handkerchief in acknowledgment of the last parting salutations on shore.

When it was all over, he went down into his state-room, and shut himself in, and let his misery roll over him. He felt as if there were a flood of it, and it washed him to and fro, one gall of shame, of self-accusal, of bitterness, from head to foot. But in it all he felt no resentment toward Alice, no wish to wreak any smallest part of his suffering upon her. Even while he had hoped for her love, it seemed to him that he had not seen her in all that perfection which she now had in irreparable loss. His soul bowed itself fondly over the thought of her; and stung as he was by that last cruel word of hers, he could not upbraid her. That humility which is love casting out selfishness, the most egotistic of the passions triumphing over itself—Mavering experienced it to the full. He took all the blame. He could not see that she had ever encouraged him to hope for her love, which now appeared a treasure heaven-far beyond his scope; he could only call himself fool, and fool, and fool, and wonder that he could have met her in the remoteness of that morning with the belief that but for the follies of last night she might have answered him differently. He believed now that, whatever had gone before, she must still have rejected him. She had treated his presumption very leniently; she had really spared him.

It went on, over and over. Sometimes it varied a little, as when he thought of how, when she should tell her mother, Mrs. Pasmer must laugh. He pictured them both laughing at him; and then Mr. Pasmer—he had scarcely passed a dozen words with him—coming in and asking what they were laughing at, and their saying, and his laughing too.

At other times he figured them as incensed at his temerity, which must seem to them greater and greater, as now it seemed to him. He had never thought meanly of himself, and the world so far had seemed to think well of him; but because Alice Pasmer was impossible to him, he felt that it was an unpardonable boldness in him to have dreamed of her. What must they be saying of his having passed from the ground of society compliments and light flirtation to actually telling Alice that he loved her?

He wondered what Mrs. Pasmer had thought of his telling her that he had come to Campobello to consider the question whether he should study law or go into business, and what motive she had supposed he had in telling her that. He asked himself what motive he had, and tried to pretend that he had none. He dramatized conversations with Mrs. Pasmer in which he laughed it off.

He tried to remember all that had passed the day before at the picnic, and whether Alice had done or said anything to encourage him, and he could not find that she had. All her trust and freedom was because she felt perfectly safe with him from any such disgusting absurdity as he had been guilty of. The ride home through the mist, with its sweet intimacy, that parting which had seemed so full of tender intelligence, were parts of the same illusion. There had been nothing of it on her side from the beginning but a kindliness which he had now flung away forever.

He went back to the beginning, and tried to remember the point where he had started in this fatal labyrinth of error. She had never misled him, but he had misled himself from the first glimpse of her.

Whatever was best in his light nature, whatever was generous and self-denying, came out in this humiliation. From the vision of her derision he passed to a picture of her suffering from pity for him, and wrung with a sense of the pain she had given him. He promised himself to write to her, and beg her not to care for him, because he was not worthy of that. He framed a letter in his mind, in which he posed in some noble attitudes, and brought tears into his eyes by his magnanimous appeal to her not to suffer for the sake of one so unworthy of her serious thought. He pictured her greatly moved by some of the phrases, and he composed for her a reply, which led to another letter from him, and so to a correspondence and a long and tender friendship. In the end he died suddenly, and then she discovered that she had always loved him. He discovered that he was playing the fool again, and he rose from the berth where he had tumbled himself. The state-room had that smell of parboiled paint which state-rooms have, and reminded him of the steamer in which he had gone to Europe when a boy, with the family, just after his mother's health began to fail.

He went down on the deck near the ladies' saloon, where the second-class passengers were gathered listening to the same band of plantation negroes who had amused him so much on the eastward trip. The passengers were mostly pock-marked Provincials, and many of them were women; they lounged on the barrels of apples neatly piled up, and listened to the music without smiling. One of the negroes was singing to the banjo, and another began to do the rheumatic uncle's break-down. Mavering said to himself: "I can't stand that. Oh, what a fool I am! Alice, I love you. Oh, merciful heavens! Oh, infernal jackass! Ow! Gaw!"

At the bow of the boat he found a gang of Italian laborers returning to the States after some job in the Provinces. They smoked their pipes and whined their Neapolitan dialect together. It made Mavering think of Dante, of the "Inferno," to which he passed naturally from his self-denunciation for having been an infernal jackass. The inscription on the gate of hell ran through his mind. He thought he would make his life, his desolate, broken life, a perpetual exile, like Dante's. At the same time he ground his teeth, and muttered: "Oh, what a fool I am! Oh, idiot! beast! Oh! oh!" The pipes reminded him to smoke, and he took out his cigarette case. The Italians looked at him; he gave all the cigarettes among them, without keeping any for himself. He determined to spend the miserable remnant of his life in going about doing good and bestowing alms.

He groaned aloud, so that the Italians noticed it, and doubtless spoke of it among themselves. He could not understand their dialect, but he feigned them saying respectfully compassionate things. Then he gnashed his teeth again, and cursed his folly. When the bell rang for supper he found himself very hungry, and ate heavily. After that he went out in front of the cabin, and walked up and down, thinking, and trying not to think. The turmoil in his mind tired him like a prodigious physical exertion.

Toward ten o'clock the night grew rougher. The sea was so phosphorescent that it broke in sheets and flakes of pale bluish flame from the bows and wheel-houses, and out in the dark the waves revealed themselves in flashes and long gleams of fire. One of the officers of the boat came and hung with Mavering over the guard. The weird light from the water was reflected on their faces, and showed them to each other.

"Well, I never saw anything like this before. Looks like hell; don't it?" said the officer.

"Yes," said Mavering. "Is it uncommon?"

"Well, I should *say* so. I guess we're going to have a picnic."

Mavering thought of blueberries, but he did not say anything.

"I guess it's going to be a regular circus."

Mavering did not care. He asked, incuriously, "How do you find your course in such weather?"

"Well, we guess where we are, and then give her so many turns of the wheel." The officer laughed, and Mavering laughed too. He was struck by the hollow note in his laugh; it seemed to him pathetic; he wondered if he should now always laugh so, and if people would remark it. He tried another laugh; it sounded mechanical.

He went to bed, and was so worn out that he fell asleep and began to dream. A face came up out of the sea, and brooded over the waters, as in that picture of Vedder's which he calls "Memory," but the hair was not blond; it was the color of those phosphorescent flames, and the eyes were like it. "Horrible! horrible!" he tried to shriek, but he cried, "Alice, I love you." There was a burglar in the room, and he was running after Miss Pasmer. Mavering caught him, and tried to beat him; his fists fell like bolls of cotton; the burglar drew his breath in with a long, washing sound like water.

Mavering woke deathly sick, and heard the sweep of the waves. The boat was pitching frightfully. He struggled out into the saloon, and saw that it was five o'clock. In five hours more it would be a day since he told Alice that he loved her; it now seemed very improbable. There were a good many half-dressed people in the saloon, and a woman came running out of her state-room straight to Mavering. She was in her stocking feet, and her hair hung down her back.

"Oh! *are* we going down?" she implored him. "Have we struck? Oughtn't we to pray—somebody? Shall I wake the children?"

Mavering reassured her, and told her there was no danger.

"Well, then," she said, "I'll go back for my shoes."

"Yes, better get your shoes."

The saloon rose round him and sank. He controlled his sickness by planting a chair in the centre and sitting in it with his eyes shut. As he grew more comfortable he reflected how he had calmed that woman, and he resolved again to spend his life in doing good. "Yes, that's the only ticket," he said to himself, with involuntary frivolity. He thought of what the officer had said, and he helplessly added, "Circus ticket—reserved seat." Then he began again, and loaded himself with execration.

The boat got into Portland at nine o'clock, and Mavering left her, taking his hand-bag with him, and letting his trunk go on to Boston.

The officer who received his ticket at the gang-plank noticed the destination on it, and said, "Got enough?"

"Yes, for one while." Mavering recognized his acquaintance of the night before.

"Don't like picnics very much?"

"No," said Mavering, with abysmal gloom. "They don't

agree with me. Never did." He was aware of trying to make his laugh bitter. The officer did not notice.

Mavering was surprised, after the chill of the storm at sea, to find it rather a warm, close morning in Portland. The restaurant to which the hackman took him as the best in town was full of flies; they bit him awake out of the dreary reveries he fell into while waiting for his breakfast. In a mirror opposite he saw his face. It did not look haggard; it looked very much as it always did. He fancied playing a part through life—hiding a broken heart under a smile. "Oh, you incorrigible ass!" he said to himself, and was afraid he had said it to the young lady who brought him his breakfast, and looked haughtily at him from under her bang. She was very thin, and wore a black jersey.

He tried to find out whether he had spoken aloud by addressing her pleasantly. "It's pretty cool this morning."

"What say?"

"Pretty cool."

"Oh yes. But it's pretty *clo*-ose," she replied, in her Yankee cantilation. She went away and left him to the bacon and eggs he had ordered at random. There was a fly under one of the slices of bacon, and Mavering confined himself to the coffee.

A man came up in a white cap and jacket from a basement in the front of the restaurant, where confectionery was sold, and threw down a mass of malleable candy on a marble slab, and began to work it. Mavering watched him, thinking fuzzily all the time of Alice, and holding long, fatiguing dialogues with the people at the Ty'n-y-Coed, whose several voices he heard.

He said to himself that it was worse than yesterday. He wondered if it would go on getting worse every day.

He saw a man pass the door of the restaurant who looked exactly like Boardman as he glanced in. The resemblance was explained by the man's coming back, and proving to be really Boardman.

XXII

M AVERING SPRANG at him with a demand for the reason of his being there.

"I thought it was you as I passed," said Boardman, "but I couldn't make sure—so dark back here."

"And I thought it was you, but I couldn't believe it," said Mavering, with equal force, cutting short an interior conversation with Mr. Pasmer, which had begun to hold itself since his first glimpse of Boardman.

"I came down here to do a sort of one-horse yacht race to-day," Boardman explained.

"Going to be a yacht race? Better have some breakfast. Or better not—*here*. Flies under your bacon."

"Rough on the flies," said Boardman, snapping the bell which summoned the spectre in the black jersey, and he sat down. "What are you doing in Portland?"

Mavering told him, and then Boardman asked him how he had left the Pasmers. Mavering needed no other hint to speak, and he spoke fully, while Boardman listened with an agreeable silence, letting the hero of the tale break into self-scornful groans and doleful laughs, and ease his heart with grotesque, inarticulate noises, and made little or no comments.

By the time his breakfast came Boardman was ready to say, "I didn't suppose it was so much of a mash."

"I didn't either," said Mavering, "when I left Boston. Of course I knew I was going down there to see her, but when I got there it kept going on, just like anything else, up to the last moment. I didn't realize till it came to the worst that I had become a mere pulp."

"Well, you won't stay so," said Boardman, making the first vain attempt at consolation. He lifted the steak he had ordered, and peered beneath it. "All right this time, anyway."

"I don't know what you mean by staying so," replied Mavering, with gloomy rejection of the comfort offered.

"You'll see that it's all for the best; that you're well out of it. If she could throw you over, after leading you on—"

"But she *didn't* lead me on!" exclaimed Mavering. "Don't you understand that it was all my mistake from the first? If I hadn't been perfectly besotted I should have seen that she was only tolerating me. Don't you see? Why, hang it, Boardman, I must have had a kind of consciousness of it under my thick-skinned conceit, after all, for when I came to the point—when I *did* come to the point—I hadn't the sand to stick to it like a man, and I tried to get her to help me. Yes, I can see that I did now. I kept fooling about, and fooling about, and it was because I had that sort of prescience—or whatever you call it—that I was mistaken about it from the very beginning."

He wished to tell Boardman about the events of the night before; but he could not. He said to himself that he did not care about their being hardly to his credit; but he did not choose to let Alice seem to have resented anything in them; it belittled her, and claimed too much for him. So Boardman had to proceed upon a partial knowledge of the facts.

"I don't suppose that boomerang way of yours, if that's what you mean, was of much use," he said.

"Use? It ruined me! But what are you going to do? How are you going to presuppose that a girl like Miss Pasmer is interested in an idiot like you? I mean me, of course." Mavering broke off with a dolorous laugh. "And if you can't presuppose it, what are you going to do when it comes to the point? You've *got* to shilly-shally, and *then* you've got to go it blind. I tell you it's a leap in the dark."

"Well, then, if you've got yourself to blame—"

"*How* am I to blame, I should like to know?" retorted Mavering, rejecting the first offer from another of the censure which he had been heaping upon himself: the irritation of his nerves spoke. "I *did* speak out at last—when it was too late. Well, let it all go," he groaned, aimlessly. "*I* don't care. But *she* isn't to blame. I don't think I could admire anybody very much who admired *me*. No, sir. She did just right. I was a fool, and she couldn't have treated me differently."

"Oh, I guess it'll come out all right," said Boardman, abandoning himself to mere optimism.

"How come all right?" demanded Mavering, flattered by the hope he refused. "It's come right now. I've got my deserts; that's all."

"Oh no, you haven't. What harm have you done? It's all

right for you to think small beer of yourself, and I don't see
how you could think anything else just at present. But you
wait awhile. When did it happen?"

Mavering took out his watch. "One day, one hour, twenty
minutes, and fifteen seconds ago."

"Sure about the seconds? I suppose you didn't hang round
a great while afterward?"

"Well, people don't generally," said Mavering, with scorn.

"Never tried it," said Boardman, looking critically at his
fried potatoes before venturing upon them. "If you had staid,
perhaps she might have changed her mind," he added, as if
encouraged to this hopeful view by the result of his scrutiny.

"Where did you get your fraudulent reputation for common-sense, Boardman?" retorted Mavering, who had followed his examination of the potatoes with involuntary interest. "She won't change her mind; she isn't one of that kind.
But she's the one woman in this world who could have made
a man of *me*, Boardman."

"Is that so?" asked Boardman, lightly. "Well, she *is* a good-
looking girl."

"She's divine!"

"What a dress that was she had on Class Day!"

"I never think what she has on. She makes everything perfect, and then makes you forget it."

"She's got style; there's no mistake about that."

"Style!" sighed Mavering; but he attempted no exempli-
fication.

"She's awfully graceful. What a walk she's got!"

"Oh, don't, don't, Boardman! All that's true, and all that's
nothing—nothing to her goodness. She's so *good*, Boardman!
Well, *I* give it up! She's religious. You wouldn't think that,
maybe; you can't imagine a pretty girl religious. And she's all
the more intoxicating when she's serious; and when she's forgotten your whole worthless existence she's ten thousand
times more fascinating than any other girl when she's going
right for you. There's a kind of look comes into her eyes—
kind of absence, rapture, don't you know—when she's serious, that brings your heart right into your mouth. She makes
you think of some of those pictures— I want to tell you what
she said the other day at a picnic when we were off getting

blueberries, and you'll understand that she isn't like other girls—that she has a soul full of—of—you know what, Boardman. She has high thoughts about everything. I don't believe she's ever had a mean or ignoble impulse—she couldn't have." In the business of imparting his ideas confidentially Mavering had drawn himself across the table toward Boardman, without heed to what was on it.

"Look out! You'll be into my steak first thing you know."

"Oh, confound your steak!" cried Mavering, pushing the dish away. "What difference does it make? I've lost her, anyway."

"I don't believe you've lost her," said Boardman.

"What's the reason you don't?" retorted Mavering, with contempt.

"Because, if she's the serious kind of a girl you say she is, she wouldn't let you come up there and dangle round a whole fortnight without letting you know she didn't like it, unless she *did* like it. Now you just go a little into detail."

Mavering was quite willing. He went so much into detail that he left nothing to Boardman's imagination. He lost the sense of its calamitous close in recounting the facts of his story at Campobello; he smiled and blushed and laughed in telling certain things; he described Miss Anderson and imitated her voice; he drew heads of some of the ladies on the margin of a newspaper, and the tears came into his eyes when he repeated the cruel words which Alice had used at their last meeting.

"Oh, well, you must brace up," said Boardman. "I've got to go now. She didn't mean it, of course."

"Mean what?"

"That you were ungentlemanly. Women don't know half the time how hard they're hitting."

"I guess she meant that she didn't want me, anyway," said Mavering, gloomily.

"Ah, I don't know about that. You'd better ask her the next time you see her. Good-by." He had risen, and he offered his hand to Mavering, who was still seated.

"Why, I've half a mind to go with you."

"All right, come along. But I thought you might be going right on to Boston."

"No; I'll wait and go on with you. How do you go to the race?"

"In the press boat."

"Any women?"

"No; we don't send them on this sort of duty."

"That settles it. I have got all I want of that particular sex for the time being." Mavering wore a very bitter air as he said this; it seemed to him that he would always be cynical; he rose, and arranged to leave his bag with the restaurateur, who put it under the counter, and then he went out with his friend.

The sun had come out, and the fog was burning away; there was life and lift in the air, which the rejected lover could not refuse to feel, and he said, looking round, and up and down the animated street, "I guess you're going to have a good day for it."

The pavement was pretty well filled with women who had begun shopping. Carriages were standing beside the pavement; a lady crossed the pavement from a shop door toward a coupé just in front of them with her hands full of light packages; she dropped one of them, and Mavering sprang forward instinctively and picked it up for her.

"Oh, *thank* you!" she said, with the deep gratitude which society cultivates for the smallest services. Then she lifted her drooped eyelashes, and, with a flash of surprise, exclaimed, "Mr. Mavering!" and dropped all her packages that she might shake hands with him.

Boardman sauntered slowly on, but saw with a backward glance Mavering carrying the lady's packages to the coupé for her; saw him lift his hat there, and shake hands with somebody in the coupé, and then stand talking beside it. He waited at the corner of the block for Mavering to come up, affecting an interest in the neck-wear of a furnisher's window.

In about five minutes Mavering joined him.

"Look here, Boardman! Those ladies have snagged onto me."

"Are there two of them?"

"Yes, one inside. And they want me to go with *them* to see the race. Their father's got a little steam-yacht. They want you to go too."

Boardman shook his head.

"Well, that's what I told them—told them that you had to go on the press boat. They said they wished they were going on the press boat too. But I don't see how I can refuse. They're ladies that I met Class Day, and I ought to have shown them a little more attention then; but I got so taken up with—"

"I see," said Boardman, showing his teeth, fine and even as grains of pop-corn, in a slight sarcastic smile. "Sort of poetical justice," he suggested.

"Well, it is—sort of," said Mavering, with a shamefaced consciousness. "What train are you going back on?"

"Seven o'clock."

"I'll be there."

He hurried back to rejoin the ladies, and Boardman saw him, after some parley and laughter, get into the coupé, from which he inferred that they had turned down the little seat in front, and made him take it; and he inferred that they must be very jolly, sociable girls.

He did not see Mavering again till the train was on its way, when he came in, looking distraughtly about for his friend. He was again very melancholy, and said dejectedly that they had made him stay to dinner, and had then driven him down to the station, bag and all. "The old gentleman came too. I was in hopes I'd find you hanging round somewhere, so that I could introduce you. They're awfully nice. None of that infernal Boston stiffness. The one you saw me talking with is married, though."

Boardman was writing out his report from a little book with short-hand notes in it. There were half a dozen other reporters in the car busy with their work. A man who seemed to be in authority said to one of them, "Try to throw in a little humor."

Mavering pulled his hat over his eyes, and leaned his head on the back of his seat, and tried to sleep.

XXIII

A⊤ HIS FATHER'S agency in Boston he found, the next morning, a letter from him saying that he expected to be down that day, and asking Dan to meet him at the Parker House for dinner. The letter intimated the elder Mavering's expectation that his son had reached some conclusion in the matter they had talked of before he left for Campobello.

It gave Dan a shiver of self-disgust and a sick feeling of hopelessness. He was quite willing now to do whatever his father wished, but he did not see how he could face him and own his defeat.

When they met, his father did not seem to notice his despondency, and he asked him nothing about the Pasmers, of course. That would not have been the American way. Nothing had been said between the father and son as to the special advantages of Campobello for the decision of the question pending when they saw each other last; but the son knew that the father guessed why he chose that island for the purpose; and now the elder knew that if the younger had anything to tell him he would tell it, and if he had not he would keep it. It was tacitly understood that there was no objection on the father's part to Miss Pasmer; in fact, there had been a glimmer of humorous intelligence in his eye when the son said he thought he should run down to Bar Harbor, and perhaps to Campobello, but he had said nothing to betray his consciousness.

They met in the reading-room at Parker's, and Dan said, "Hello, father," and his father answered, "Well, Dan;" and they shyly touched the hands dropped at their sides as they pressed together in the crowd. The father gave his boy a keen glance, and then took the lead into the dining-room, where he chose a corner table, and they disposed of their hats on the window-seat.

"All well at home?" asked the young fellow, as he took up the bill of fare to order the dinner. His father hated that, and always made him do it.

"Yes, yes; as usual, I believe. Minnie is off for a week at the mountains; Eunice is at home."

"Oh! How would you like some green goose, with apple-sauce, sweet-potatoes, and succotash?"

"It seems to me that was pretty good, the last time. All right, if you like it."

"I don't know that I care for anything much. I'm a little off my feed. No soup," he said, looking up at the waiter bending over him; and then he gave the order. "I think you may bring me half a dozen Blue Points, if they're good," he called after him.

"Didn't Bar Harbor agree with you—or Campobello?" asked Mr. Mavering, taking the opening offered him.

"No, not very well," said Dan; and he said no more about it, leaving his father to make his own inferences as to the kind or degree of the disagreement.

"Well, have you made up your mind?" asked the father, resting his elbows on either side of his plate, and putting his hands together softly, while he looked across them with a cheery kindness at his boy.

"Yes, I have," said Dan, slowly.

"Well?"

"I don't believe I care to go into the law."

"Sure?"

"Yes."

"Well, that's all right, then. I wished you to choose freely, and I suppose you've done so."

"Oh yes."

"I think you've chosen wisely, and I'm very glad. It's a weight off my mind. I think you'll be happier in the business than you would in the law; I think you'll enjoy it. You needn't look forward to a great deal of Ponkwasset Falls, unless you like."

"I shouldn't mind going there," said Dan, listlessly.

"It won't be necessary—at first. In fact, it won't be desirable. I want you to look up the business at this end a little."

Dan gave a start. "In Boston?"

"Yes. It isn't in the shape I want to have it. I propose to open a place of our own, and to put you in charge." Something in the young man's face expressed reluctance, and his father asked, kindly, "Would that be distasteful to you?"

"Oh no. It isn't the *thing* I object to, but I don't know that

I care to be in Boston." He lifted his face and looked his father full in the eyes, but with a gaze that refused to convey anything definite. Then the father knew that the boy's love affair had gone seriously wrong.

The waiter came with the dinner, and made an interruption in which they could be naturally silent. When he had put the dinner before them, and cumbered them with superfluous service, after the fashion of his kind, he withdrew a little way, and left them to resume their talk.

"Well," said the elder, lightly, as if Dan's not caring to be in Boston had no particular significance for him, "I don't know that I care to have you settle down to it immediately. I rather think I'd like to have you look about first a little. Go to New York, go to Philadelphia, and see their processes there. We can't afford to get old-fashioned in our ways. I've always been more interested by the æsthetic side of the business, but you ought to have a taste for the mechanism, from your grandfather; your mother has it."

"Oh, yes, sir. I think all that's very interesting," said Dan.

"Well, go to France, and see how those fellows do it. Go to London, and look up William Morris."

"Yes, that would be very nice," admitted the young fellow, beginning to catch on. "But I didn't suppose—I didn't expect to begin life with a picnic." He entered upon his sentence with a jocular buoyancy, but at the last word, which he fatally drifted upon, his voice fell. He said to himself that he was greatly changed; that he should never be gay and bright again; there would always be this undercurrent of sadness; he had noticed the undercurrent yesterday when he was laughing and joking with those girls at Portland.

"Oh, I don't want you to buckle down at once," said his father, smiling. "If you'd decided upon the law, I should have felt that you'd better not lose time. But as you're going into the business, I don't mind your taking a year off. It won't be lost time if you keep your eyes open. I think you'd better go down into Italy and Spain. Look up the old tapestries and stamped leathers. You may get some ideas. How would you like it?"

"First-rate. *I* should like it," said Dan, rising on the waft of his father's suggestion, but gloomily lapsing again. Still, it was pleasing to picture himself going about through Europe with a broken heart, and he did not deny himself the consolation of the vision.

"Well, there's nobody to *dis*like it," said his father, cheerily. He was sure now that Dan had been jilted; otherwise he would have put forth some objection to a scheme which must interrupt his love-making. "There's no reason why, with our resources, we shouldn't take the lead in this business."

He went on to speak more fully of his plans, and Dan listened with a nether reference of it all to Alice, but still with a surface intelligence on which nothing was lost.

"Are you going home with me to-morrow?" asked his father as they rose from the table.

"Well, perhaps not to-morrow. I've got some of my things to put together in Cambridge yet, and perhaps I'd better look after them. But I've a notion I'd better spend the winter at home, and get an idea of the manufacture before I go abroad. I might sail in January; they say it's a good month."

"Yes, there's sense in that," said his father.

"And perhaps I won't break up in Cambridge till I've been to New York and Philadelphia. What do you think? It's easier striking them from here."

"I don't know but you're right," said his father, easily.

They had come out of the dining-room, and Dan stopped to get some cigarettes in the office. He looked mechanically at the theatre bills over the cigar case. "I see Irving's at the 'Boston.'"

"Oh, you don't say!" said his father. "Let's go and see him."

"If you wish it, sir," said Dan, with pensive acquiescence. All the Maverings were fond of the theatre, and made any mood the occasion or the pretext of going to the play. If they were sad, they went; if they were gay, they went. As long as Dan's mother could get out-of-doors she used to have herself carried to a box in the theatre whenever she was in town; now that she no longer left her room, she had a dominant passion for hearing about actors and acting; it was almost a work of piety in her husband and children to see them and report to her.

His father left him the next afternoon, and Dan, who had

spent the day with him looking into business for the first time, with a running accompaniment of Alice in all the details, remained to uninterrupted misery. He spent the evening in his room, too wretched even for the theatre. It is true that he tried to find Boardman, but Boardman was again off on some newspaper duty; and after trying at several houses in the hope, which he knew was vain, of finding any one in town yet, he shut himself up with his thoughts. They did not differ from the thoughts of the night before, and the night before that, but they were calmer, and they portended more distinctly a life of self-abnegation and solitude from that time forth. He tested his feelings, and found that it was not hurt vanity that he was suffering from; it was really wounded affection. He did not resent Alice's cruelty; he wished that she might be happy; he could endure to see her happy.

He wrote a letter to the married one of the two ladies he had spent the day with in Portland, and thanked them for making pass pleasantly a day which he would not otherwise have known how to get through. He let a soft, mysterious melancholy pervade his letter; he hinted darkly at trouble and sorrow of which he could not definitely speak. He had the good sense to tear his letter up when he had finished it, and to send a short, sprightly note instead, saying that if Mrs. Frobisher and her sister came to Boston at the end of the month, as they had spoken of doing, they must be sure to let him know. Upon the impulse given him by this letter he went more cheerfully to bed, and fell instantly asleep.

During the next three weeks he bent himself faithfully to the schemes of work his father had outlined for him. He visited New York and Philadelphia, and looked into the business and the processes there; and he returned to Ponkwasset Falls to report and compare his facts intelligently with those which he now examined in his father's manufactory for the first time. He began to understand how his father, who was a man of intellectual and artistic interests, should be fond of the work.

He spent a good deal of time with his mother, and read to her, and got upon better terms with her than they usually were. They were very much alike, and she objected to him that he was too light and frivolous. He sat with his sisters, and took an interest in their pursuits. He drove them about with his father's sorrels, and resumed something of the old relations with them which the selfish years of his college life had broken off. As yet he could not speak of Campobello or of what had happened there; and his mother and sisters, whatever they thought, made no more allusion to it than his father had done.

They mercifully took it for granted that matters must have gone wrong there, or else he would speak about them, for there had been some gay banter among them concerning the objects of his expedition before he left home. They had heard of the heroine of his Class Day, and they had their doubts of her, such as girls have of their brothers' heroines. They were not inconsolably sorry to have her prove unkind; and their mother found in the probable event another proof of their father's total want of discernment where women were concerned, for the elder Mavering had come home from Class Day about as much smitten with this mysterious Miss Pasmer as Dan was. She talked it over indignantly with her daughters; they were glad of Dan's escape, but they were incensed with the girl who could let him escape, and they inculpated her in a high degree of heartless flirtation. They knew how sweet Dan was, and they believed him most sincere and good. He had been brilliantly popular in college, and he was as bright as he could be. What was it she chose not to like in him? They vexed themselves with asking how or in what way she thought herself better. They would not have had her love Dan, but they were hot against her for not loving him.

They did not question him, but they tried in every way to find out how much he was hurt, and they watched him in every word and look for signs of change to better or worse, with a growing belief that he was not very much hurt.

It could not be said that in three weeks he forgot Alice, or had begun to forget her; but he had begun to reconcile himself to his fate, as people do in their bereavements by death. His consciousness habituated itself to the facts as something irretrievable. He no longer framed in his mind situations in which the past was restored. He knew that he should never love again, but he had moments, and more and more of them, in which he experienced that life had objects besides love.

There were times when he tingled with all the anguish of the first moment of his rejection, when he stopped in whatever he was doing, or stood stock-still, as a man does when arrested by a physical pang, breathless, waiting. There were other times when he went about steeped in gloom so black that all the world darkened with it, and some mornings when he woke he wished that the night had lasted forever, and felt as if the daylight had uncovered his misery and his shame to every one. He never knew when he should have these moods, and he thought he should have them as long as he lived. He thought this would be something rather fine. He had still other moods, in which he saw an old man with a gray mustache, like Colonel Newcome, meeting a beautiful white-haired lady; the man had never married, and he had not seen this lady for fifty years. He bent over and kissed her hand.

"You idiot!" said Mavering to himself. Throughout he kept a good appetite. In fact, after that first morning in Portland, he had been hungry three times a day with perfect regularity. He lost the idea of being sick; he had not even a furred tongue. He fell asleep pretty early, and he slept through the night without a break. He had to laugh a good deal with his mother and sisters, since he could not very well mope without expecting them to ask why, and he did not wish to say why. But there were some laughs which he really enjoyed with the Yankee foreman of the works, who was a droll, after a common American pattern, and said things that were killingly funny, especially about women, of whom his opinions were sarcastic.

Dan Mavering suffered, but not solidly. His suffering was short, and crossed with many gleams of respite and even joy. His disappointment made him really unhappy, but not wholly so; it was a genuine sorrow, but a sorrow to which he began to resign himself even in the monotony of Ponkwasset Falls, and which admitted the thought of Mrs. Frobisher's sister by the time business called him to Boston.

XXIV

BEFORE THE END of the first week after Dan came back to town, that which was likely to happen whenever chance brought him and Alice together had taken place.

It was one of the soft days that fall in late October, when the impending winter seems stayed, and the warm breath of the land draws seaward and over a thousand miles of Indian summer. The bloom came and went in quick pulses over the girl's temples as she sat with her head thrown back in the corner of the car, and from moment to moment she stirred slightly as if some stress of rapture made it hard for her to get her breath; a little gleam of light fell from under her fallen eyelids into the eyes of the young man beside her, who leaned forward slightly and slanted his face upward to meet her glances. They said some words, now and then, indistinguishable to the others; in speaking they smiled slightly. Sometimes her hand wavered across her lap; in both their faces there was something beyond happiness—a transport, a passion, the brief splendor of a supreme moment.

They left the car at the Arlington Street corner of the Public Garden, and followed the winding paths diagonally to the further corner on Charles Street.

"How stupid we were to get into that ridiculous horse-car!" she said. "What in the world possessed us to do it?"

"I can't imagine," he answered. "What a waste of time it was! If we had walked, we might have been twice as long coming. And now you're going to send me off so soon!"

"I don't send you," she murmured.

"But you want me to go."

"Oh no! But you'd better."

"I can't do anything against your wish."

"I wish it—for your own good."

"Ah, do let me go home with you, Alice!"

"Don't ask it, or I must say yes."

"Part of the way, then?"

"No; not a step! You must take the first car for Cambridge. What time is it now?"

"You can see by the clock in the Providence Depot."

"But I wish you to go by *your* watch, now. Look!"

"Alice!" he cried, in pure rapture.

"Look!"

"It's a quarter of one."

"And we've been three hours together already! Now you must simply fly. If you came home with me I should be sure to let you come in, and if I don't see mamma alone first, I shall die. Can't you understand?"

"No; but I can do the next best thing: I can misunderstand. You want to be rid of me."

"Shall you be rid of *me* when we've parted?" she asked, with an inner thrill of earnestness in her gay tone.

"Alice!"

"You know I didn't *mean* it, Dan."

"Say it again."

"What?"

"Dan."

"Dan, love! Dan, dearest!"

"Ah!"

"Will that car of yours never come? I've promised myself not to leave you till it does, and if I stay here any longer I shall go wild. I can't believe it's happened. Say it again!"

"Say what?"

"That—"

"That I love you? That we're engaged?"

"I don't believe it. I can't." She looked impatiently up the street. "Oh, there comes your car! Run! Stop it!"

"I don't run to stop cars." He made a sign, which the conductor obeyed, and the car halted at the further crossing.

She seemed to have forgotten it, and made no movement to dismiss him. "Oh, doesn't it seem too good to be standing here talking in this way, and people think it's about the weather, or society?" She set her head a little on one side, and twirled the open parasol on her shoulder.

"Yes, it does. Tell me it's true, love!"

"It's true. How splendid you are!" She said it with an effect for the world outside of saying it was a lovely day.

He retorted, with the same apparent *nonchalance*, "How beautiful you are! How good! How divine!"

The conductor, seeing himself apparently forgotten, gave his bell a vicious snap, and his car jolted away.

She started nervously. "There! you've lost your car, Dan."

"Have I?" asked Mavering, without troubling himself to look after it.

She laughed now, with a faint suggestion of unwillingness in her laugh. "What are you going to do?"

"Walk home with you."

"No, indeed; you know I can't let you."

"And are you going to leave me here alone on the street corner, to be run over by the first bicycle that comes along?"

"You can sit down in the Garden, and wait for the next car."

"No; I would rather go back to the Art Museum, and make a fresh start."

"To the Art Museum?" she murmured, tenderly.

"Yes. Wouldn't you like to see it again?"

"Again? I should like to pass my whole life in it!"

"Well, walk back with me a little way. There's no hurry about the car."

"Dan!" she said, in a helpless compliance, and they paced very, very slowly along the Beacon Street path in the Garden. "This is ridiculous."

"Yes, but it's delightful."

"Yes, that's what I meant. Do you suppose any one ever—ever—"

"Made love there before?"

"How can you say such things? Yes. I always supposed it would be—somewhere else."

"It *was* somewhere else—once."

"Oh, I meant—the second time."

"Then you *did* think there was going to be a second time?"

"How do I know? I wished it. Do you like me to say that?"

"I wish you would never say anything else."

"Yes; there can't be any harm in it now. I thought that if you had ever—liked me, you would still—"

"So did I; but I couldn't believe that you—"

"Oh, *I* could."

"Alice!"

"Don't you like my confessing it? You asked me to."

"Like it!"

"How silly we are!"

"Not half so silly as we've been for the last two months. I think we've just come to our senses. At least I have."

"Two months," she sighed. "Has it really been so long as that?"

"Two years! Two centuries! It was back in the Dark Ages when you refused me."

"Dark Ages! I should think so! But don't say refused. It wasn't *refusing*, exactly."

"What was it, then?"

"Oh, I don't know. Don't speak of it now."

"But, Alice, why did you refuse me?"

"Oh, I don't know. You mustn't ask me now. I'll tell you some time."

"Well, come to think of it," said Mavering, laughing it all lightly away, "there's no hurry. Tell me why you accepted me to-day."

"I—I couldn't help it. When I saw you I wanted to fall at your feet."

"What an idea! I didn't want to fall at yours. I was awfully mad. I shouldn't have spoken to you if you hadn't stopped me and held out your hand."

"Really? Did you really hate me, Dan?"

"Well, I haven't exactly doted on you since we last met."

She did not seem offended at this. "Yes, I suppose so. And I've gone on being fonder and fonder of you every minute since that day. I wanted to call you back when you had got half-way to Eastport."

"I wouldn't have come. It's bad luck to turn back."

She laughed at his drolling. "How funny you are! Now I'm of rather a gloomy temperament. Did you know it?"

"You don't look it."

"Oh, but I am. Just now I'm rather excited and—happy."

"So glad!"

"Go on! go on! I like you to make fun of me."

The benches on either side were filled with nurse-maids in charge of baby-carriages, and of young children who were digging in the sand with their little beach shovels, and playing their games back and forth across the walk unrebuked by the indulgent policemen. A number of them had enclosed a square in the middle of the path with four of the benches, which they made believe was a fort. The lovers had to walk round it; and the children, chasing one another, dashed into them headlong, or backing off from pursuit, bumped up against them. They did not seem to know it, but walked slowly on without noticing: they were not aware of an occasional benchful of rather shabby young fellows who stared hard at the stylish girl and well-dressed young man talking together in such intense low tones, with rapid interchange of radiant glances.

"Oh, as to making fun of you, I was going to say—" Mavering began, and after a pause he broke off with a laugh. "I forget what I was going to say."

"Try to remember."

"I can't."

"How strange that we should have both happened to go to the Museum this morning!" she sighed. Then, "Dan," she broke in, "do you suppose that heaven is any different from this?"

"I hope not—if I'm to go there."

"Hush, dear; you mustn't talk so."

"Why, you provoked me to it."

"Did I? Did I really? Do you think I tempted you to do it? Then I must be wicked, whether I knew I was doing it or not. Yes."

The break in her voice made him look more keenly at her, and he saw the tears glimmer in her eyes. "Alice!"

"No; I'm not good enough for you. I always said that."

"Then don't say it any more. That's the only thing I won't let you say."

"Do you forbid it, really? Won't you let me even think it?"

"No, not even think it."

"How lovely you are! Oh! I *like* to be commanded by you."

"Do you? You'll have lots of fun, then. I'm an awfully commanding spirit."

"I didn't suppose you were so humorous—always. I'm afraid you won't like me. I've no sense of fun."

"And I'm a little too funny sometimes, I'm afraid."

"No, you never are. When?"

"That night at the Trevors'. You didn't like it."

"I thought Miss Anderson was rather ridiculous," said Alice. "I don't like buffoonery in women."

"Nor I in men," said Mavering, smiling. "I've dropped it."

"Well, now we must part. I must go home at once," said Alice. "It's perfectly insane."

"Oh no, not yet; not till we've said something else; not till we've changed the subject."

"What subject?"

"Miss Anderson."

Alice laughed and blushed, but she was not vexed. She liked to have him understand her. "Well, now," she said, as if that were the next thing, "I'm going to cross here at once and walk up the other pavement, and you must go back through the Garden; or else I shall never get away from you."

"May I look over at you?"

"You may glance, but you needn't expect me to return your glance."

"Oh no."

"And I want you to take the very first Cambridge car that comes along. I *command* you to."

"I thought you wanted *me* to do the commanding."

"So I do—in essentials. If you command me not to cry when I get home, I won't."

She looked at him with an ecstasy of self-sacrifice in her eyes.

"Ah, I sha'n't do that. I can't tell what would happen. But—Alice!"

"Well, what?" She drifted closely to him, and looked fondly up into his face. In walking they had insensibly drawn nearer together, and she had been obliged constantly to put space between them. Now, standing at the corner of Arlington Street, and looking tentatively across Beacon, she abandoned all precautions.

"What? I forget. Oh yes! I love you!"

"But you said that before, dearest!"

"Yes; but just now it struck me as a very novel idea. What if your mother shouldn't like the idea?"

"Nonsense! you know she perfectly idolizes you. She did

from the first. And doesn't she know how I've been behaving about you ever since I—lost you?"

"How *have* you behaved? Do tell me, Alice."

"Some time; not now," she said; and with something that was like a gasp, and threatened to be a sob, she suddenly whipped across the road. He walked back to Charles Street by the Garden path, keeping abreast of her, and not losing sight of her for a moment, except when the bulk of a string team watering at the trough beside the pavement intervened. He hurried by, and when he had passed it he found himself exactly abreast of her again. Her face was turned toward him; they exchanged a smile, lost in space. At the corner of Charles Street he deliberately crossed over to her.

"Oh, dearest *love*! why did you come?" she implored.

"Because you signed to me."

"I *hoped* you wouldn't see it. If we're *both* to be so weak as this, what are we going to do? But I'm glad you came. Yes: I was frightened. They must have overheard us there when we were talking."

"Well, *I* didn't say anything I'm ashamed of. Besides, I shouldn't care much for the opinion of those nurses and babies."

"Of course not. But people must have seen us. Don't stand here talking, Dan! *Do* come on!" She hurried him across the street, and walked him swiftly up the incline of Beacon Street. There, in her new fall suit, with him, glossy-hatted, faultlessly gloved, at a fit distance from her side, she felt more in keeping with the social frame of things than in the Garden path, which was really only a shade better than the Beacon Street Mall of the Common. "Do you suppose anybody saw us that knew us?"

"I hope so! Don't you want people to know it?"

"Yes, of course. They will *have* to know it—in the right way. Can you *believe* that it's only half a year since we met? It won't be a year till Class Day."

"I don't believe it, Alice. I can't recollect anything before I knew you."

"Well, now, as time is so confused, we must try to live for eternity. We must try to help each other to be *good*. Oh, when I think what a happy girl I am, I feel that I should be the most ungrateful person under the sun not to be good. Let's try to make our lives perfect—*perfect!* They *can* be. And we mustn't live for each other alone. We must try to *do* good as well as *be* good. We must be kind and forbearing with every one."

He answered, with tender seriousness, "My life's in your hands, Alice. It shall be whatever you wish."

They were both silent in their deep belief of this. When they spoke again, she began, gayly: "I shall never get over the wonder of it. How strange that we should meet at the Museum!" They had both said this already, but that did not matter; they had said nearly everything two or three times. "How *did* you happen to be there?" she asked, and the question was so novel that she added, "I haven't asked you before."

He stopped, with a look of dismay that broke up in a hopeless laugh. "Why, I went there to meet some people—some ladies. And when I saw you I forgot all about them."

Alice laughed too; this was a part of their joy, their triumph.

"Who were they?" she asked, indifferently, and only to heighten the absurdity by realizing the persons.

"You don't know them," he said. "Mrs. Frobisher and her sister, of Portland. I promised to meet them there and go out to Cambridge with them."

"What will they think?" asked Alice. "It's too amusing."

"They'll think I didn't come," said Mavering, with the easy conscience of youth and love; and again they laughed at the ridiculous position together. "I remember now I was to be at the door, and they were to take me up in their carriage. I wonder how long they waited? You put everything else out of my head."

"Do you think I'll keep it out?" she asked, archly.

"Oh yes; there *is* nothing else but you now."

The eyes that she dropped, after a glance at him, glistened with tears.

A lump came into his throat. "Do you suppose," he asked, huskily, "that we can ever misunderstand each other again?"

"Never. I see everything clearly now. We shall trust each other implicitly, and at the least thing that isn't clear we can speak. Promise me that you'll speak."

"I will, Alice. But after this all will be clear. We shall deal with each other as we do with ourselves."

"Yes; that will be the way."

"And we mustn't wait for question from each other. We shall know—we shall feel—when there's any misgiving, and then the one that's caused it will speak."

"Yes," she sighed, emphatically. "How perfectly you say it! But that's because you feel it—because you are good."

They walked on, treading the air in a transport of fondness for each other. Suddenly he stopped.

"Miss Pasmer, I feel it my duty to warn you that you're letting me go home with you."

"Am I? How noble of you to tell me, Dan; for I know you don't want to tell. Well, I might as well. But I sha'n't let you come in. You won't try, will you? Promise me you won't try."

"I shall only want to come in the first door."

"What for?"

"What for? Oh, for half a second."

She turned away her face.

He went on. "This engagement has been such a very public affair, so far, that I think I'd like to see my *fiancée* alone for a moment."

"I don't know what in the world you can have to say more."

He went into the first door with her, and then he went with her upstairs to the door of Mrs. Pasmer's apartment. The passages of the Cavendish were not well lighted; the little lane or alley that led down to this door from the stairs landing was very dim.

"So dark here!" murmured Alice, in a low voice, somewhat tremulous.

"But not *too* dark."

XXV

SHE BURST into the room where her mother sat looking over some house-keeping accounts. His kiss and his name were upon her lips; her soul was full of him.

"Mamma!" she panted.

Her mother did not look round. She could have had no premonition of the vital news that her daughter was bringing, and she went on comparing the first autumn month's provision bill with that of the last spring month, and trying to account for the difference.

The silence, broken by the rattling of the two bills in her mother's hands as she glanced from one to the other through her glasses, seemed suddenly impenetrable, and the prismatic world of the girl's rapture burst like a bubble against it. There is no explanation of the effect outside of temperament and overwrought sensibilities. She stared across the room at her mother, who had not heard her, and then she broke into a storm of tears.

"Alice!" cried her mother, with that sanative anger which comes to rescue women from the terror of any sudden shock. "What is the matter with you?—what do you mean?" She dropped both of the provision bills to the floor and started toward her daughter.

"Nothing—nothing! Let me go. I want to go to my room." She tried to reach the door beyond her mother.

"Indeed you shall *not!*" cried Mrs. Pasmer. "I will not have you behaving so! What has happened to you? Tell me. You have frightened me half out of my senses."

The girl gave up her efforts to escape, and flung herself on the sofa, with her face in the pillow, where she continued to sob. Her mother began to relent at the sight of her passion. As a woman and as a mother she knew her daughter, and she knew that this passion, whatever it was, must have vent before there could be anything intelligible between them. She did not press her with further question, but set about making her a little more comfortable on the sofa; she pulled the pillow straight, and dropped a light shawl over the girl's shoulders, so that she should not take cold.

462

Then Mrs. Pasmer had made up her mind that Alice had met Mavering somewhere, and that this outburst was the retarded effect of seeing him. During the last six weeks she had assisted at many phases of feeling in regard to him, and knew more clearly than Alice herself the meaning of them all. She had been patient and kind, with the resources that every woman finds in herself when it is the question of a daughter's ordeal in an affair of the heart which she has favored.

The storm passed as quickly as it came, and Alice sat upright, casting off the wraps. But once checked with the fact on her tongue, she found it hard to utter it.

"What is it, Alice?—what is it?" urged her mother.

"Nothing. I—Mr. Mavering—we met—I met him at the Museum, and—we're engaged! It's really so. It seems like raving, but it's true. He came with me to the door; I wouldn't let him come in. Don't you believe it? Oh, we are! indeed we are! Are you glad, mamma? You *know* I couldn't have lived without him."

She trembled on the verge of another outbreak.

Mrs. Pasmer sacrificed her astonishment in the interest of sanity, and returned, quietly: "Glad, Alice? You know that I think he's the sweetest and best fellow in the world."

"Oh, mamma!"

"But are you sure—"

"Yes, yes. I'm not crazy; it isn't a dream. He was there—and I met him—I couldn't run away—I put out my hand; I couldn't help it—I thought I should give way; and he took it; and then—then we were engaged. I don't know what we said. I went in to look at the 'Joan of Arc' again, and there was no one else there. He seemed to feel just as I did. I don't know whether either of us spoke. But we knew we were engaged, and we began to talk."

Mrs. Pasmer began to laugh. To her irreverent soul only the droll side of the statement appeared.

"Don't, mamma!" pleaded Alice, piteously.

"No, no; I won't. But I hope Dan Mavering will be a little more definite about it when I'm allowed to see him. Why couldn't he have come in with you?"

"It would have killed me. I couldn't let him see me cry, and I knew I should break down."

"He'll have to see you cry a great many times, Alice," said her mother, with almost unexampled seriousness.

"Yes, but not yet—not so soon. He must think I'm very gloomy, and I want to be always bright and cheerful with him. He knows why I wouldn't let him come in; he knew I was going to have a cry."

Mrs. Pasmer continued to laugh.

"Don't, mamma!" pleaded Alice.

"No, I won't," replied her mother, as before. "I suppose he was mystified. But now, if it's really settled between you, he'll be coming here soon to see your papa and me."

"Yes—to-night."

"Well, it's very sudden," said Mrs. Pasmer. "Though I suppose these things always seem so."

"Is it too sudden?" asked Alice, with misgiving. "It seemed so to me when it was going on, but I couldn't stop it."

Her mother laughed at her simplicity. "No, when it begins once, nothing can stop it. But you've really known each other a good while, and for the last six weeks at least you've known your own mind about him pretty clearly. It's a pity you couldn't have known it before."

"Yes, that's what *he* says. He says it was such a waste of time. Oh, *everything* he says is perfectly fascinating!"

Her mother laughed and laughed again.

"What is it, mamma? Are you laughing at me?"

"Oh no. What an idea!"

"He couldn't seem to understand why I didn't say yes the first time if I meant it." She looked down dreamily at her hands in her lap, and then she said, with a blush and a start, "They're very queer, don't you think?"

"Who?"

"Young men."

"Oh, *very*."

"Yes," Alice went on, musingly. "Their *minds* are so different. Everything they say and do is so unexpected, and yet it seems to be just right."

Mrs. Pasmer asked herself if this single-mindedness was to go on forever, but she had not the heart to treat it with her natural levity. Probably it was what charmed Mavering with the child. Mrs. Pasmer had the firm belief that Mavering was not single-minded, and she respected him for it. She would not spoil her daughter's perfect trust and hope by any of the cynical suggestions of her own dark wisdom, but entered into her mood, as such women are able to do, and flattered out of her every detail of the morning's history. This was a feat which Mrs. Pasmer enjoyed for its own sake, and it fully satisfied the curiosity which she naturally felt to know all. She did not comment upon many of the particulars; she opened her eyes a little at the notion of her daughter sitting for two or three hours and talking with a young man in the galleries of the Museum, and she asked if anybody they knew had come in. When she heard that there were only strangers, and very few of them, she said nothing; and she had the same consolation in regard to the walking back and forth in the Garden. She was so full of potential escapades herself, so apt to let herself go at times, that the fact of Alice's innocent self-forgetfulness rather satisfied a need of her mother's nature; she exulted in it when she learned that there were only nurses and children in the Garden.

"And so you think you won't take up art this winter?" she said, when, in the process of her cross-examination, Alice had left the sofa and got as far as the door, with her hat in her hand and her sacque on her arm.

"No."

"And the Sisters of St. James—you won't join them, either?"

The girl escaped from the room.

"Alice! Alice!" her mother called after her; and she came back. "You haven't told me how he happened to be there."

"Oh, that was the most amusing part of it. He had gone there to keep an appointment with two ladies from Portland. They were to take him up in their carriage and drive out to Cambridge, and when he saw *me* he forgot all about them."

"And what became of them?"

"We don't know. Isn't it ridiculous?"

If it appeared other or more than this to Mrs. Pasmer, she did not say. She merely said, after a moment, "Well, it was certainly devoted, Alice," and let her go.

XXVI

MAVERING CAME in the evening, rather excessively well dressed, and with a hot face and cold hands. While he waited, nominally alone, in the little drawing-room for Mr. Pasmer, Alice flew in upon him for a swift embrace, which prolonged itself till the father's step was heard outside the door, and then she still had time to vanish by another: the affair was so nicely adjusted that if Mavering had been in his usual mind he might have fancied the connivance of Mrs. Pasmer.

He did not say what he had meant to say to Alice's father, but it seemed to serve the purpose, for he emerged presently from the sound of his own voice, unnaturally clamorous, and found Mr. Pasmer saying some very civil things to him about his character and disposition, so far as they had been able to observe it, and their belief and trust in him. There seemed to be something provisional or probational intended, but Dan could not make out what it was, and finally it proved of no practical effect. He merely inferred that the approval of his family was respectfully expected, and he hastened to say, "Oh, that's all right, sir." Mr. Pasmer went on with more civilities, and lost himself in dumb conjecture as to whether Mavering's father had been in the class before him or the class after him in Harvard. He used his black eyebrows a good deal during the interview, and Mavering conceived an awe of him greater than he had felt at Campobello, yet not unmixed with the affection in which the newly accepted lover embraces even the relations of his betrothed. From time to time Mr. Pasmer looked about with the vague glance of a man unused to being so long left to his own guidance; and one of these appeals seemed at last to bring Mrs. Pasmer through the door, to the relief of both the men, for they had improvidently despatched their business, and were getting out of talk. Mr. Pasmer had, in fact, already asked Dan about the weather outside when his wife appeared.

Dan did not know whether he ought to kiss her or not, but Mrs. Pasmer did not in the abstract seem like a very kissing kind of person, and he let himself be guided by this impression, in the absence of any fixed principle applying to the case. She made some neat remark concerning the probable settlement of the affair with her husband, and began to laugh and joke about it in a manner that was very welcome to Dan; it did not seem to him that it ought to be treated so solemnly.

But though Mrs. Pasmer laughed and joked, he was aware of her meaning business, business in the nicest sort of a way, but business after all, and he liked her for it. He was glad to be explicit about his hopes and plans, and told what his circumstances were so fully that Mrs. Pasmer, whom his frankness gratified and amused, felt obliged to say that she had not meant to ask so much about his affairs, and he must excuse her if she had seemed to do so. She had her own belief that Mavering would understand, but she did not mind that. She said that of course, till his own family had been consulted, it must not be considered seriously, that Mr. Pasmer insisted upon that point; and when Dan vehemently asserted the acquiescence of his family beforehand, and urged his father's admiration for Alice in proof, she reminded him that his mother was to be considered, and put Mr. Pasmer's scruples forward as her own reason for obduracy. In her husband's presence she attributed to him, with his silent assent, all sorts of reluctances and delicate compunctions; she gave him the importance which would have been naturally a husband's due in such an affair, and ingratiated herself more and more with the young man. She ignored Mr. Pasmer's withdrawal when it took place, after a certain lapse of time, and as the moment had come for that, she began to let herself go. She especially approved of the idea of going abroad, and confessed her disappointment with her present experiment of America, where it appeared there was no leisure class of men sufficiently large to satisfy the social needs of Mr. Pasmer's nature, and she told Dan that he might expect them in Europe before long. Perhaps they might all three meet him there. At this he betrayed so clearly that he now intended his going to Europe merely as a sequel to his marrying Alice, while he affected to fall in with all Mrs. Pasmer said, that she grew fonder than ever of him for his ardor and his futile duplicity. If it had been in Dan's mind to take part in the rite, Mrs. Pasmer was quite ready at this point to embrace him with motherly tenderness. Her tough little heart was really in her throat with sympathy when she made an errand for the photograph of an English vicarage, which they had hired the summer of the year before, and she sent Alice back with it alone.

It seemed so long since they had met that the change in Alice did not strike him as strange or as too rapidly operated. They met with the fervor natural after such a separation, and she did not so much assume as resume possession of him. It was charming to have her do it, to have her act as if they had always been engaged, to have her try to press down the cowlick that started capriciously across his crown, and to straighten his neck-tie, and then to drop beside him on the sofa; it thrilled and awed him; and he silently worshipped the superior composure which her sex has in such matters. Whatever was the provisional interpretation which her father and mother pretended to put upon the affair, she apparently had no reservations, and they talked of their future as a thing assured. The Dark Ages, as they agreed to call the period of despair forever closed that morning, had matured their love till now it was a rapture of pure trust. They talked as if nothing could prevent its fulfilment, and they did not even affect to consider the question of his family's liking it or not liking it. She said that she thought his father was delightful, and he told her that his father had taken the greatest fancy to her at the beginning, and knew that Dan was in love with her. She asked him about his mother, and she said just what he could have wished her to say about his mother's sufferings, and the way she bore them. They talked about Alice's going to see her.

"Of course your father will bring your sisters to see me first."

"Is that the way?" he asked. "You may depend upon his doing the right thing, whatever it is."

"Well, *that's* the right thing," she said. "I've thought it out; and that reminds me of a duty of ours, Dan?"

"A duty?" he repeated, with a note of reluctance for its untimeliness.

"Yes. Can't you think what?"

"No; I didn't know there was a duty left in the world."

"It's full of them."

"Oh, don't say that, Alice!" He did not like this mood so well as that of the morning, but his dislike was only a vague discomfort—nothing formulated or distinct.

"Yes," she persisted; "and we must do them. You must go to those ladies you disappointed so this morning, and apologize—explain."

Dan laughed. "Why, it wasn't such a very iron-clad engagement as all that, Alice. They said they were going to drive out to Cambridge over the Milldam, and I said I was going out there to get some of my traps together, and they could pick me up at the Art Museum if they liked. Besides, how *could* I explain?"

She laughed consciously with him. "Of course. But," she added, ruefully, "I *wish* you hadn't disappointed them."

"Oh, they'll get over it. If I hadn't disappointed them, I shouldn't be here, and I shouldn't like that. Should you?"

"No; but I wish it hadn't happened. It's a blot, and I didn't want a blot on this day."

"Oh, well, it isn't very much of a blot, and I can easily wipe it off. I'll tell you what, Alice! I can write to Mrs. Frobisher, when our engagement comes out, and tell her how it was. She'll enjoy the joke, and so will Miss Wrayne. They're jolly and easy-going; they won't mind."

"How long have you known them?"

"I met them on Class Day, and then I saw them—the day after I left Campobello." Dan laughed a little.

"How, saw them?"

"Well, I went to a yacht race with them. I happened to meet them in the street, and they wanted me to go; and I was all broken up, and—I went."

"Oh!" said Alice. "The day after I—you left Campobello?"

"Well—yes."

"And I was thinking of you all that day as— And I couldn't bear to look at anybody that day, or speak!"

"Well, the fact is, I—I was distracted, and I didn't know what I was doing. I was desperate; I didn't care."

"How did you find out about the yacht race?"

"Boardman told me. Boardman was there."

"Did he know the ladies? Did he go too?"

"No. He was there to report the race for the *Events*. He went on the press boat."

"Oh!" said Alice. "Was there a large party?"

"No, no. Not very. Just ourselves, in fact. They were awfully kind. And they made me go home to dinner with them."

"They must have been rather peculiar people," said Alice. "And I don't see how—so soon—" She could not realize that Mavering was then a rejected man, on whom she had voluntarily renounced all claim. A retroactive resentment which she could not control possessed her with the wish to punish those bold women for being agreeable to one who had since become everything to her, though then he was ostensibly nothing.

In a vague way Dan felt her displeasure with that passage of his history, but no man could have fully imagined it.

"I couldn't tell half the time what I was saying or eating. I talked at random and ate at random. I guess they thought something was wrong; they asked me who was at Campobello."

"Indeed!"

"But you may be sure I didn't give myself away. I was awfully broken up," he concluded, inconsequently.

She liked his being broken up, but she did not like the rest. She would not press the question further now. She only said, rather gravely, "If it's such a short acquaintance, can you write to them in that familiar way?"

"Oh yes! Mrs. Frobisher is one of that kind."

Alice was silent a moment before she said, "I think you'd better not write. Let it go," she sighed.

"Yes, that's what I think," said Dan. "Better let it go. I guess it will explain itself in the course of time. But I don't want any blots around." He leaned over and looked her smilingly in the face.

"Oh no," she murmured; and then suddenly she caught him round the neck, crying and sobbing. "It's only—because I wanted it to be—perfect. Oh, I wonder if I've done right? Perhaps I oughtn't to have taken you, after all; but I do love you—dearly, dearly! And I was *so* unhappy when I'd lost you. And now I'm afraid I shall be a trial to you—nothing but a trial."

The first tears that a young man sees a woman shed for love of him are inexpressibly sweeter than her smiles. Dan choked with tender pride and pity. When he found his voice he raved out with incoherent endearments that she only made him more and more happy by her wish to have the affair perfect, and that he wished her always to be exacting with him, for that would give him a chance to do something for her, and all that he desired, as long as he lived, was to do more and more for her, and to do just what she wished.

At the end of his vows and entreaties she lifted her face radiantly and bent a smile upon him as sunny as that with which the sky after a summer storm denies that there has ever been rain in the world.

"Ah! you—" He could say no more. He could not be more enraptured than he was. He could only pass from surprise to surprise, from delight to delight. It was her love of him which wrought these miracles. It was all a miracle, and no part more wonderful than another. That she, who had seemed as distant as a star, and divinely sacred from human touch, should be there in his arms, with her head on his shoulder, where his kiss could reach her lips, not only unforbidden, but eagerly welcome, was impossible, and yet it was true. But it was no more impossible and no truer than that a being so poised, so perfectly self-centred as she, should already be so helplessly dependent upon him for her happiness. In the depths of his soul he invoked awful penalties upon himself if ever he should betray her trust, if ever he should grieve that tender heart in the slightest thing, if from that moment he did not make his whole life a sacrifice and an expiation.

He uttered some of these exalted thoughts, and they did not seem to appear crazy to her. She said yes, they must make their separate lives offerings to each other, and their joint lives an offering to God. The tears came into his eyes at these words of hers: they were so beautiful and holy and wise. He agreed that one ought always to go to church, and that now he should never miss a service. He owned that he had been culpable in the past. He drew her closer to him—if that were possible—and sealed his words with a kiss.

But he could not realize his happiness then, or afterward,

when he walked the streets under the thinly misted moon of that Indian summer night.

He went down to the *Events* office when he left Alice, and found Boardman, and told him that he was engaged, and tried to work Boardman up to some sense of the greatness of the fact. Boardman showed his fine white teeth under his spare mustache, and made acceptable jokes, but he did not ask indiscreet questions, and Dan's statement of the fact did not seem to give it any more verity than it had before. He tried to get Boardman to come and walk with him and talk it over; but Boardman said he had just been detailed to go and work up the case of a Chinaman who had suicided a little earlier in the evening.

"Very well, then; I'll go with *you*," said Mavering. "How can you live in such a den as this?" he asked, looking about the little room before Boardman turned down his incandescent electric. "There isn't anything big enough to hold *me* but all out-doors."

In the street he linked his arm through his friend's, and said he felt that he had a right to know all about the happy ending of the affair, since he had been told of that miserable phase of it at Portland. But when he came to the facts he found himself unable to give them with the fulness he had promised. He only imparted a succinct statement as to the where and when of the whole matter, leaving the how of it untold.

The sketch was apparently enough for Boardman. For all comment, he reminded Mavering that he had told him at Portland it would come out all right.

"Yes, you did, Boardman; that's a fact," said Dan; and he conceived a higher respect for the penetration of Boardman than he had before.

They stopped at a door in a poor court which they had somehow reached without Mavering's privity. "Will you come in?" asked Boardman.

"What for?"

"Chinaman."

"Chinaman?" Then Mavering remembered. "Good heavens! no. What have I got to do with him?"

"Both mortal," suggested the reporter.

The absurdity of this idea, though a little grisly, struck Dan as a good joke. He hit the companionable Boardman on the shoulder, and then gave him a little hug, and remounted his path of air, and walked off on it.

XXVII

MAVERING FIRST WOKE in the morning with the mechanical recurrence of that shame and grief which each day had brought him since Alice refused him. Then with a leap of the heart came the recollection of all that had happened yesterday. Yet lurking within this rapture was a mystery of regret: a reasonless sense of loss, as if the old feeling had been something he would have kept. Then this faded, and he had only the longing to see her, to realize in her presence and with her help the fact that she was his. An unspeakable pride filled him, and a joy in her love. He tried to see some outward vision of his bliss in the glass; but, like the mirror which had refused to interpret his tragedy in the Portland restaurant, it gave back no image of his transport; his face looked as it always did, and he and the reflection laughed at each other.

He asked himself how soon he could go and see her. It was now seven o'clock: eight would be too early, of course; it would be ridiculous; and nine—he wondered if he might go to see her at nine. Would they have done breakfast? Had he any right to call before ten? He was miserable at the thought of waiting till ten: it would be three hours. He thought of pretexts—of inviting her to go somewhere, but that was absurd, for he could see her at home all day if he liked; of carrying her a book, but there could be no such haste about a book; of going to ask if he had left his cane, but why should he be in such a hurry for his cane? All at once he thought he could take her some flowers—a bouquet to lay beside her plate at breakfast. He dramatized himself charging the servant who should take it from him at the door not to say who left it; but Alice would know, of course, and they would all know; it would be very pretty. He made Mrs. Pasmer say some flattering things of him, and he made Alice blush deliciously to hear them. He could not manage Mr. Pasmer very well, and he left him out of the scene: he imagined him shaving in another room; then he remembered his wearing a full beard.

He dressed himself as quickly as he could, and went down into the hotel vestibule, where he had noticed people selling flowers the evening before, but there was no one there with them now, and none of the florists' shops on the street were open yet. He could not find anything till he went to the Providence Depot, and the man there had to take some of his yesterday's flowers out of the refrigerator where he kept them; he was not sure they would be very fresh; but the heavy rose-buds had fallen open, and they were superb. Dan took all there were, and when they had been sprinkled with water, and wrapped in cotton batting, and tied round with paper, it was still only quarter of eight, and he left them with the man till he could get his breakfast at the depot restaurant. There it had a consoling effect of not being so early; many people were already breakfasting, and when Dan said, with his order, "Hurry it up, please," he knew that he was taken for a passenger just arrived or departing. By a fantastic impulse he ordered eggs and bacon again; he felt it a fine derision of the past and a seal of triumph upon the present to have the same breakfast after his acceptance as he had ordered after his rejection; he would tell Alice about it, and it would amuse her. He imagined how he would say it, and she would laugh; but she would be full of a ravishing compassion for his past suffering. They were long bringing the breakfast; when it came he despatched it so quickly that it was only a quarter after eight when he paid his check at the counter. He tried to be five minutes more getting his flowers, but the man had them all ready for him, and it did not take him ten seconds. He had said he would carry them at nine; but thinking it over on a bench in the Garden, he decided that he had better go sooner: they might breakfast earlier, and there would be no fun if Alice did not find the roses beside her plate; that was the whole idea. It was not till he stood at the door of the Pasmer apartment that he reflected that he was not accomplishing his wish to see Alice by leaving her those flowers; he was a fool, for now he would have to postpone coming a little, because he had already come.

The girl who answered the bell did not understand the charge he gave her about the roses, and he repeated his words. Some one passing through the room beyond seemed to hesitate and pause at the sound of his voice. Could it be

Alice? Then he should see her, after all! The girl looked over her shoulder and said, "Mrs. Pasmer."

Mrs. Pasmer came forward, and he fell into a complicated explanation and apology. At the end she said, "You had better give them yourself." They were in the room now, and Mrs. Pasmer let herself go. "Stay and breakfast with us, Mr. Mavering. We shall be so glad to have you. We were just sitting down."

Alice came in, and they decorously shook hands. Mrs. Pasmer turned away a smile at their decorum. "I will see that there's a place for you," she said, leaving them.

They were instantly in each other's arms. It seemed to him that all this had happened because he had so strongly wished it.

"What is it, Dan? What did you come for?" she asked.

"To see if it was really true, Alice. I couldn't believe it."

"Well—let me go—you mustn't—it's too silly. Of course it's true." She pulled herself free. "Is my hair tumbled? You oughtn't to have come; it's ridiculous; but I'm glad you came. I've been thinking it all over, and I've got a great many things to say to you. But come to breakfast now."

She had a business-like way of treating the situation that was more intoxicating than sentiment would have been, and gave it more actuality.

Mrs. Pasmer was alone at the table, and explained that Alice's father never breakfasted with them, or very seldom. "Where are your flowers?" she asked Alice.

"Flowers? What flowers?"

"That Mr. Mavering brought."

They all looked at one another. Dan ran out and brought in his roses.

"They were trying to get away in the excitement, I guess, Mrs. Pasmer; I found them behind the door." He had flung them there, without knowing it, when Mrs. Pasmer left him with Alice.

He expected her to join him and her mother in being amused at this, but he was as well pleased to have her touched at his having brought them, and to turn their gayety off in praise of the roses. She got a vase for them, and set it on the table. He noticed for the first time the pretty house dress she had on, with its barred corsage and under-skirt, and the heavy silken rope knotted round it at the waist, and dropping in heavy tufts or balls in front.

The breakfast was Continental in its simplicity, and Mrs. Pasmer said that they had always kept up their Paris habit of a light breakfast, even in London, where it was not so easy to follow foreign customs as it was in America. She was afraid he might find it too light. Then he told all about his morning's adventure, ending with his breakfast at the Providence Depot. Mrs. Pasmer entered into the fun of it, but she said it was for only once in a way, and he must not expect to be let in if he came at that hour another morning. He said no; he understood what an extraordinary piece of luck it was for him to be there; and he was there to be bidden to do whatever they wished. He said so much in recognition of their goodness that he became abashed by it. Mrs. Pasmer sat at the head of the table, and Alice across it from him, so far off that she seemed parted from him by an insuperable moral distance. A warm flush seemed to rise from his heart into his throat and stifle him. He wished to shed tears. His eyes were wet with grateful happiness in answering Mrs. Pasmer that he would not have any more coffee. "Then," she said, "we will go into the drawing-room;" but she allowed him and Alice to go alone.

He was still in that illusion of awe and of distance, and he submitted to the interposition of another table between their chairs.

"I wish to talk with you," she said, so seriously that he was frightened, and said to himself: "Now she is going to break it off. She has thought it over, and she finds she can't endure me."

"Well?" he said, huskily.

"You oughtn't to have come here, you know, this morning."

"I know it," he vaguely conceded. "But I didn't expect to get in."

"Well, now you're here, we may as well talk. You must tell your family at once."

"Yes; I'm going to write to them as soon as I get back to my room. I couldn't, last night."

"But you *mustn't* write; you must go—and prepare their minds."

"Go?" he echoed. "Oh, *that* isn't necessary! My father knows about it from the beginning, and I guess they've all talked it over. Their *minds* are prepared." The sense of his immeasurable superiority to any one's opposition began to dissipate Dan's unnatural awe; at the pleading face which Alice put on, resting one cheek against the back of one of her clasped hands, and leaning on the table with her elbows, he began to be teased by that silken rope round her waist.

"But you don't understand, dear," she said; and she said "dear" as if they were old married people. "You must go to see them, and tell them; and then some of them must come to see me—your father and sisters."

"Why, of course." His eye now became fastened to one of the fluffy silken balls.

"And then mamma and I must go to see your mother, mustn't we?"

"It'll be very nice of you—yes. You know she can't come to you."

"Yes, that's what I thought, and— What are you looking at?" she drew herself back from the table and followed the direction of his eye with a woman's instinctive apprehension of disarray.

He was ashamed to tell. "Oh, nothing. I was just thinking."

"What?"

"Well, I don't know. That it seems so strange any one else should have anything to do with it—my family and yours. But I suppose they must. Yes, it's all right."

"Why, of course. If your family didn't like it—"

"It wouldn't make any difference to me," said Dan, resolutely.

"It would to me," she retorted, with tender reproach. "Do you suppose it would be pleasant to go into a family that didn't like you? Suppose papa and mamma didn't like you?"

"But I thought they did," said Mavering, with his mind still partly on the rope and the fluffy ball, but keeping his eyes away.

"Yes, they do," said Alice. "But your family don't know me at all; and your father's only seen me once. Can't you understand? I'm afraid we don't look at it seriously enough—earnestly—and oh, I do wish to have everything done as it should be! Sometimes, when I think of it, it makes me tremble. I've been thinking about it all the morning, and—and—praying."

Dan wanted to fall on his knees to her. The idea of Alice in prayer was fascinating.

"I wish our life to begin with others, and not with ourselves. If we're intrusted with so much happiness, doesn't it mean that we're to do good with it—to give it to others as if it were money?"

The nobleness of this thought stirred Dan greatly; his eyes wandered back to the silken rope; but now it seemed to him an emblem of voluntary suffering and self-sacrifice, like a devotee's hempen girdle. He perceived that the love of this angelic girl would elevate him and hallow his whole life if he would let it. He answered her, fervently, that he would be guided by her in this as in everything; that he knew he was selfish, and he was afraid he was not very good; but it was not because he had not wished to be so; it was because he had not had any incentive. He thought how much nobler and better this was than the talk he had usually had with girls. He said that of course he would go home and tell his people; he saw now that it would make them happier if they could hear it directly from him. He had only thought of writing because he could not bear to think of letting a day pass without seeing her; but if he took the early morning train he could get back the same night, and still have three hours at Ponkwasset Falls, and he would go the next day, if she said so.

"Go to-day, Dan," she said, and she stretched out her hand impressively across the table toward him. He seized it with a gush of tenderness, and they drew together in their resolution to live for others. He said he would go at once. But the next train did not leave till two o'clock, and there was plenty of time. In the mean while it was in the accomplishment of their high aims that they sat down on the sofa together and talked of their future; Alice conditioned it wholly upon his people's approval of her, which seemed wildly unnecessary to Mavering, and amused him immensely.

"Yes," she said, "I know you will think me strange in a

great many things; but I shall never keep anything from you, and I'm going to tell you that I went to matins this morning."

"To matins?" echoed Dan. He would not quite have liked her a Catholic; he remembered with relief that she had said she was not a Roman Catholic; though, when he came to think, he would not have cared a great deal. Nothing could have changed her from being Alice.

"Yes, I wished to consecrate the first morning of our engagement; and I'm always going. Don't you like it?" she asked, timidly.

"Like it!" he said. "I'm going with you."

"Oh no!" she turned upon him. "*That* wouldn't do." She became grave again. "I'm glad you approve of it, for I should feel that there was something wanting to our happiness. If marriage is a sacrament, why shouldn't an engagement be?"

"It is," said Dan, and he felt that it was holy; till then he had never realized that marriage was a sacrament, though he had often heard the phrase.

At the end of an hour they took a tender leave of each other, hastened by the sound of Mrs. Pasmer's voice without. Alice escaped from one door before her mother entered by the other. Dan remained, trying to look unconcerned, but he was sensible of succeeding so poorly that he thought he had better offer his hand to Mrs. Pasmer at once. He told her that he was going up to Ponkwasset Falls at two o'clock, and asked her to please remember him to Mr. Pasmer.

She said she would, and asked him if he were to be gone long.

"Oh no; just overnight—till I can tell them what's happened." He felt it a comfort to be trivial with Mrs. Pasmer, after bracing up to Alice's ideals. "I suppose they'll have to know."

"What an exemplary son!" said Mrs. Pasmer. "Yes, I suppose they will."

"I supposed it would be enough if I wrote, but Alice thinks I'd better report in person."

"I think you had, indeed! And it will be a good thing for you both to have the time for clarifying your ideas. Did she tell you she had been at matins this morning?" A light of laughter trembled in Mrs. Pasmer's eyes, and Mavering could not keep a responsive gleam out of his own. In an instant the dedication of his engagement by morning prayer ceased to be a high and solemn thought, and became deliciously amusing; and this laughing Alice over with her mother did more to realize the fact that she was his than anything else had yet done.

In that dark passage outside he felt two arms go tenderly round his neck, and a soft shape strain itself to his heart. "I know you have been laughing about me. But you may. I'm yours now, even to laugh at, if you want."

"You are mine to fall down and worship," he vowed, with an instant revulsion of feeling.

Alice didn't say anything; he felt her hand fumbling about his coat lapel. "Where *is* your breast pocket?" she asked; and he took hold of her hand, which left a carte-de-visite-shaped something in his.

"It isn't very good," she murmured, as well as she could, with her lips against his cheek, "but I thought you'd like to show them some proof of my existence. I shall have none of yours while you're gone."

"Oh, Alice! you think of everything!"

His heart was pierced by the soft reproach implied in her words; he had not thought to ask her for her photograph, but she had thought to give it; she must have felt it strange that he had not asked for it, and she had meant to slip it in his pocket and let him find it there. But even his pang of self-upbraiding was a part of his transport. He seemed to float down the stairs; his mind was in a delirious whirl. "I shall go mad," he said to himself in the excess of his joy; "I shall die!"

XXVIII

THE PARTING SCENE with Alice persisted in Mavering's thought far on the way to Ponkwasset Falls. He now succeeded in saying everything to her: how deeply he felt her giving him her photograph to cheer him in his separation from her; how much he appreciated her forethought in providing him with some answer when his mother and sisters should ask him about her looks. He took out the picture, and pretended to the other passengers to be looking very closely at it, and so managed to kiss it. He told her that now he understood what love really was; how powerful; how it did conquer everything; that it had changed him, and made him already a better man. He made her refuse all merit in the work.

When he began to formulate the facts for communication to his family, love did not seem so potent; he found himself ashamed of his passion, or at least unwilling to let it be its own excuse even; he had a wish to give it almost any other appearance. Until he came in sight of the station and the Works, it had not seemed possible for any one to object to Alice. He had been going home as a matter of form to receive the adhesion of his family. But now he was forced to see that she might be considered critically, even reluctantly. This would only be because his family did not understand how perfect Alice was; but they might not understand.

With his father there would be no difficulty. His father had seen Alice and admired her; he would be all right. Dan found himself hoping this rather anxiously, as if from the instinctive need of his father's support with his mother and sisters. He stopped at the Works when he left the train, and found his father in his private office beyond the bookkeeper's picket-fence, which he penetrated, with a nod to the accountant.

"Hello, Dan!" said his father, looking up; and "Hello, father!" said Dan. Being alone, the father and son not only shook hands, but kissed each other, as they used to do in meeting after an absence when Dan was younger.

He had closed his father's door with his left hand in giving his right, and now he said at once, "Father, I've come home to tell you that I'm engaged to be married."

Dan had prearranged his father's behavior at this announcement, but he now perceived that he would have to modify the scene if it were to represent the facts. His father did not brighten all over and demand, "Miss Pasmer, of course?" He contrived to hide whatever start the news had given him, and was some time in asking, with his soft lisp, "Isn't that rather sudden, Dan?"

"Well, not for me," said Dan, laughing uneasily. "It's—you know her, father—Miss Pasmer."

"Oh yes," said his father, certainly not with displeasure, and yet not with enthusiasm.

"I've had ever since Class Day to think it over, and it—came to a climax yesterday."

"And then you stopped thinking," said his father—to gain time, it appeared to Dan.

"Yes, sir," said Dan. "I haven't thought since."

"Well," said his father, with an amusement which was not unfriendly. He added, after a moment, "But I thought that had been broken off," and Dan's instinct penetrated to the lurking fact that his father must have talked the rupture over with his mother, and not wholly regretted it.

"There was a kind of—hitch at one time," he admitted; "but it's all right now."

"Well, *well*," said his father, "this is great news—great news," and he seemed to be shaping himself to the new posture of affairs, while giving it a conditional recognition. "She's a beautiful creature."

"Isn't she?" cried Dan, with a little break in his voice, for he had found his father's manner rather trying. "And she's good too. I assure you that she is—she is simply perfect every way."

"Well," said the elder Mavering, rising and pulling down the rolling top of his desk, "I'm glad to hear it, for your sake, Dan. Have you been up at the house yet?"

"No; I'm just off the train."

"How is her mother—how is Mrs. Pasmer? All well?"

"Yes, sir," said Dan; "they're all very well. You don't know Mr. Pasmer, I believe, sir, do you?"

"Not since college. What sort of person is he?"

"He's very refined and quiet. Very handsome. Very courteous. Very nice indeed."

"Ah! that's good," said Elbridge Mavering, with the effect of not having been very attentive to his son's answer.

They walked up the long slope of the hill-side on which the house stood, overlooking the valley where the Works were, and fronting the plateau across the river where the village of operatives' houses was scattered. The paling light of what had been a very red sunset flushed them, and brought out the picturesqueness which the architect, who designed them for a particular effect in the view from the owner's mansion, had intended.

A good carriage road followed the easiest line of ascent toward this edifice, and reached a gateway. Within it began to describe a curve bordered with asphalted footways to the broad veranda of the house, and then descended again to the gate. The grounds enclosed were planted with deciduous shrubs, which had now mostly dropped their leaves, and clumps of firs darkening in the evening light, with the gleam of some garden statues shivering about the lawn next the house. The breeze grew colder and stiffer as the father and son mounted toward the mansion, which Dan used to believe was like a château, with its Mansard-roof and dormer-windows and chimneys. It now blocked its space sharply out of the thin pink of the western sky, and its lights sparkled with a wintry keenness which had often thrilled Dan when he climbed the hill from the station in former home-comings. Their brilliancy gave him a strange sinking of the heart for no reason. He and his father had kept up a sort of desultory talk about Alice, and he could not have said that his father had seemed indifferent; he had touched the affair only too acquiescently; it was painfully like everything else. When they came in full sight of the house, Dan left the subject, as he realized presently, from a reasonless fear of being overheard.

"It seems much later here, sir, than it does in Boston," he said, glancing round at the maples, which stood ragged, with half their leaves blown from them.

"Yes; we're in the hills, and we're further north," answered his father. "There's Minnie."

Dan had seen his sister on the veranda, pausing at sight of him, and puzzled to make out who was with her father. He had an impulse to hail her with a shout, but he could not. In his last walk with her he had told her that he should never marry, and they had planned to live together. It was a joke; but now he felt as if he had come to rob her of something, and he walked soberly on with his father.

"Why, Dan, you good-for-nothing fellow!" she called out when he came near enough to be unmistakable, and ran down the steps to kiss him. "What in the world are you doing here? When did you come? Why didn't you hollo, instead of letting me stand here guessing? You're not sick, are you?"

The father got himself in-doors unnoticed in the excitement of the brother's arrival. This would have been the best moment for Dan to tell his sister of his engagement; he knew it, but he parried her curiosity about his coming; and then his sister Eunice came out, and he could not speak. They all went together into the house, flaming with naphtha gas, and with the steam heat already on, and Dan said he would take his bag to his room, and then come down again. He knew he had left them to think that there was something very mysterious in his coming, and while he washed away the grime of his journey he was planning how to appear perfectly natural when he should get back to his sisters. He recollected that he had not asked either them or his father how his mother was, but it was certainly not because his mind was not full of her. Alice now seemed very remote from him, further even than his gun, or his boyish collection of moths and butterflies, on which his eye fell in roving about his room. For a bitter instant it seemed to him as if they were all alike toys, and in a sudden despair he asked himself what had become of his happiness. It was scarcely half a day since he had parted in transport from Alice.

He made pretexts to keep from returning at once to his sisters, and it was nearly half an hour before he went down to them. By that time his father was with them in the library, and they were waiting tea for him.

XXIX

A FAMILY of rich people in the country, apart from intellectual interests, is apt to gormandize; and the Maverings always sat down to a luxurious table, which was most abundant and tempting at the meal they called tea, when the invention of the Portuguese man-cook was taxed to supply the demands of appetites at once eager and fastidious. They prolonged the meal as much as possible in winter, and Dan used to like to get home just in time for tea when he came up from Harvard; it was always very jolly, and he brought a boy's hunger to its abundance. The dining-room, full of shining light, and heated from the low-down grate, was a pleasant place. But now his spirits failed to rise with the physical cheer; he was almost bashfully silent; he sat cowed in the presence of his sisters, and careworn in the place where he used to be so gay and bold. They were waiting to have him begin about himself, as he always did when he had been away, and were ready to sympathize with his egotism, whatever new turn it took. He mystified them by asking about them and their affairs, and by dealing in futile generalities, instead of launching out with any business that he happened at the time to be full of. But he did not attend to their answers to his questions; he was absent-minded, and only knew that his face was flushed, and that he was obviously ill at ease.

His younger sister turned from him impatiently at last. "Father, what *is* the matter with Dan?"

Her bold recognition of their common constraint broke it down. Dan looked at his father with helpless consent, and his father said, quietly, "He tells me he's engaged."

"What nonsense!" said his sister Eunice.

"Why, Dan!" cried Minnie; and he felt a reproach in her words which the words did not express. A silence followed, in which the father alone went on with his supper. The girls sat staring at Dan with incredulous eyes. He became suddenly angry.

"I don't know what's so very extraordinary about it, or why there should be such a pother," he began; and he knew that he was insolently ignoring abundant reasons for pother, if there had been any pother. "*Yes*, I'm engaged."

He expected now that they would believe him, and ask whom he was engaged to; but apparently they were still unable to realize it. He was obliged to go on. "I'm engaged to Miss Pasmer."

"To Miss *Pasmer!*" repeated Eunice.

"But I thought—" Minnie began, and then stopped.

Dan commanded his temper by a strong effort, and condescended to explain. "There *was* a misunderstanding, but it's all right now; I only met her yesterday, and—it's all right." He had to keep on ignoring what had passed between him and his sisters during the month he spent at home after his return from Campobello. He did not wish to do so; he would have been glad to laugh over that epoch of ill-concealed heartbreak with them; but the way they had taken the fact of his engagement made it impossible. He was forced to keep them at a distance; they forced him. "I'm glad," he added, bitterly, "that the news seems to be so agreeable to my family. Thank you for your cordial congratulations." He swallowed a large cup of tea, and kept looking down.

"How silly!" said Eunice, who was much the oldest of the three. "Did you expect us to fall upon your neck before we could believe it wasn't a hoax of father's?"

"A hoax!" Dan burst out.

"I suppose," said Minnie, with mock meekness, "that if we're to be devoured, it's no use saying we didn't roil the brook. I'm sure *I* congratulate you, Dan, with all my heart," she added, with a trembling voice.

"*I* congratulate Miss Pasmer," said Eunice, "on securing such a very reasonable husband."

When Eunice first became a young lady she was so much older than Dan that in his mother's absence she sometimes authorized herself to box his ears, till she was finally overthrown in battle by the growing boy. She still felt herself so much his tutelary genius that she could not let the idea of his engagement awe her, or keep her from giving him a needed lesson. Dan jumped to his feet, and passionately threw his napkin on his chair.

"There, that will do, Eunice!" interposed the father. "Sit

down, Dan, and don't be an ass, if you *are* engaged. Do you expect to come up here with a bomb-shell in your pocket and explode it among us without causing any commotion? We all desire your happiness, and we are glad if you think you've found it, but we want to have time to realize it. We had only adjusted our minds to the apparent fact that you *hadn't* found it when you were here before." His father began very severely, but when he ended with this recognition of what they had all blinked till then, they laughed together.

"My pillow isn't dry yet, with the tears I shed for you, Dan," said Minnie, demurely.

"*I* shall have to countermand my mourning," said Eunice, "and wear louder colors than ever. Unless," she added, "Miss Pasmer changes her mind again."

This divination of the past gave them all a chance for another laugh, and Dan's sisters began to reconcile themselves to the fact of his engagement, if not to Miss Pasmer. In what was abstractly so disagreeable there was the comfort that they could joke about his happiness; they had not felt free to make light of his misery when he was at home before. They began to ask all the questions they could think of as to how and when, and they assimilated the fact more and more in acquiring these particulars and making a mock of them and him.

"Of course you haven't got her photograph," suggested Eunice. "You know we've never had the pleasure of meeting the young lady yet."

"Yes," Dan owned, blushing, "I have. She thought I might like to show it to mother. But it isn't—"

"A very good one—they never are," said Minnie.

"And it was taken several years ago—they always are," said Eunice.

"And she doesn't photograph well, anyway."

"And this one was just after a long fit of sickness."

Dan drew it out of his pocket, after some fumbling for it, while he tolerated their gibes.

Eunice put her nose to it. "I hope it's *your* cigarettes it smells of," she said.

"Yes; she doesn't use the weed," answered Dan.

"Oh, I didn't mean *that*, exactly," returned his sister,

holding the picture off at arm's-length, and viewing it critically with contracted eyes.

Dan could not help laughing. "I don't think it's been near any other cigar case," he answered, tranquilly.

Minnie looked at it very near to, covering all but the face with her hand. "Dan, she's *lovely!*" she cried, and Dan's heart leaped into his throat as he gratefully met his sister's eyes.

"You'll *like* her, Min."

Eunice took the photograph from her for a second scrutiny. "She's certainly very stylish. Rather a beak of a nose, and a little too bird-like on the whole. But she isn't so bad. Is it like her?" she asked, with a glance at her father.

"I might say—after looking," he replied.

"True! I didn't know but Dan had shown it to you as soon as you met. He seemed to be in such a hurry to let us all know."

The father said, "I don't think it flatters her," and he looked at it more carefully. "Not much of her mother there?" he suggested to Dan.

"No, sir; she's more like her father."

"Well, after all this excitement, I believe I'll have another cup of tea, and take something to eat, if Miss Pasmer's photograph doesn't object," said Eunice, and she replenished her cup and plate.

"What colored hair and eyes has she, Dan?" asked Minnie.

He had to think so as to be exact. "Well, you might say they were black, her eyebrows are so dark. But I believe they're a sort of grayish-blue."

"Not an uncommon color for eyes," said Eunice, "but rather peculiar for hair."

They got to making fun of the picture, and Dan told them about Alice and her family; the father left them at the table, and then came back with word from Dan's mother that she was ready to see him.

XXX

By eight o'clock in the evening the pain with which every day began for Mrs. Mavering was lulled, and her jarred nerves were stayed by the opiates till she fell asleep about midnight. In this interval the family gathered into her room, and brought her their news and the cheer of their health. The girls chattered on one side of her bed, and their father sat with his newspaper on the other, and read aloud the passages which he thought would interest her, while she lay propped among her pillows, brilliantly eager for the world opening this glimpse of itself to her shining eyes. That was on her good nights when the drugs did their work, but there were times when they failed, and the day's agony prolonged itself through the evening, and the sleep won at last was a heavy stupor. Then the sufferer's temper gave way under the stress; she became the torment she suffered, and tore the hearts she loved. Most of all she afflicted the man who had been so faithful to her misery, and maddened him to reprisals, of which he afterward abjectly repented. Her tongue was sharpened by pain, and pitilessly skilled to inculpate and to punish; it pierced and burned like fire; but when a good day came again she made it up to the victims by the angelic sweetness and sanity which they felt was her real self; the cruelty was only the mask of her suffering.

When she was better they brought to her room anybody who was staying with them, and she liked them to be jolly in the spacious chamber. The pleasantest things of the house were assembled, and all its comforts concentrated, in the place which she and they knew she should quit but once. It was made gay with flowers and pictures; it was the *salon* for those fortunate hours when she became the lightest and blithest of the company in it, and made the youngest guest forget that there was sickness or pain in the world by the spirit with which she ignored her own. Her laugh became young again; she joked; she entered into what they were doing and reading and thinking, and sent them away full of the sympathy which in this mood of hers she had for every mood in others. Girls sighed out their wonder and envy to her daughters when they left her; the young men whom she captivated with her divination of their passions or ambitions went away celebrating her supernatural knowledge of human nature. The next evening after some night of rare and happy excitement, the family saw her nurse carrying the pictures and flowers and vases out of her room, in sign of her renunciation of them all, and assembled silently, shrinkingly, in her chamber, to take each their portion of her anguish, of the blame and the penalty. The household adjusted itself to her humors, for she was supreme in it.

When Dan used to come home from Harvard she put on a pretty cap for him, and distinguished him as company by certain laces hiding her wasted frame, and giving their pathetic coquetry to her transparent wrists. He was her favorite, and the girls acknowledged him so, and made their fun of her for spoiling him. He found out as he grew up that her broken health dated from his birth, and at first this deeply affected him; but his young life soon lost the keenness of the impression, and he loved his mother because she loved him, and not because she had been dying for him so many years.

As he now came into her room, and the waiting-woman went out of it with her usual "Well, Mr. Dan!" the tenderness which filled him at sight of his mother was mixed with that sense of guilt which had tormented him at times ever since he met his sisters. He was going to take himself from her; he realized that.

"Well, Dan!" she called, so gayly that he said to himself, "No, father hasn't told her anything about it," and was instantly able to answer her as cheerfully, "Well, mother!"

He bent over her to kiss her, and the odor of the clean linen mingling with that of the opium, and the cologne with which she had tried to banish its scent, opened to him one of those vast reaches of associations which perfumes can unlock, and he saw her lying there through those years of pain, as many as half his life, and suddenly the tears gushed into his eyes, and he fell on his knees, and hid his face in the bedclothes and sobbed.

She kept smoothing his head, which shook under her thin hand, and saying, "Poor Dan! poor Dan!" but did not question him. He knew that she knew what he had come to tell her, and that his tears, which had not been meant for that, had made interest with her for him and his cause, and that she was already on his side.

He tried boyishly to dignify the situation when he lifted his face, and he said, "I didn't mean to come boohooing to you in this way, and I'm ashamed of myself."

"I know, Dan; but you've been wrought up, and I don't wonder. You mustn't mind your father and your sisters. Of course they're rather surprised, and they don't like your taking yourself from them—we none of us do."

At these honest words Dan tried to become honest too. At least he dropped his pretence of dignity, and became as a little child in his simple greed for sympathy. "But it isn't necessarily that; is it, mother?"

"Yes, it's all that, Dan; and it's all right, because it's that. We don't like it, but our not liking it has nothing to do with its being right or wrong."

"I supposed that father would have been pleased, anyway, for he has seen her, and—and— Of course the girls haven't, but I think they might have trusted my judgment a little. I'm not quite a fool."

His mother smiled. "Oh, it isn't a question of the wisdom of your choice; it's the unexpectedness. We all saw that you were very unhappy when you were here before, and we supposed it had gone wrong."

"It had, mother," said Dan. "She refused me at Campobello. But it was a misunderstanding, and as soon as we met—"

"I knew you had met again, and what you had come home for, and I told your father so, when he came to say you were here."

"Did you, mother?" he asked, charmed at her having guessed that.

"Yes. She must be a good girl to send you straight home to tell us."

"You knew I wouldn't have thought of that myself," said Dan, joyously. "I wanted to *write*; I thought that would do just as well. I hated to leave her, but she made me come. She is the best, and the wisest, and the most unselfish— Oh, mother, I can't tell you about her! You must see her. You can't realize her till you see her, mother. You'll like each other, I'm sure of that. You're just alike." It seemed to Dan that they were exactly alike.

"Then perhaps we sha'n't," suggested his mother. "Let me see her picture."

"How did you know I had it? If it hadn't been for her, I shouldn't have brought any. She put it into my pocket just as I was leaving. She said you would all want to see what she looked like."

He had taken it out of his pocket, and he held it, smiling fondly upon it. Alice seemed to smile back at him. He had lost her in the reluctance of his father and sisters; and now his mother—it was his mother who had given her to him again. He thought how tenderly he loved his mother.

When he could yield her the photograph she looked long and silently at it. "She has a great deal of character, Dan."

"There you've hit it, mother! I'd rather you would have said that than anything else. But don't you think she's beautiful? She's the gentlest creature, when you come to know her! I was awfully afraid of her at first. I thought she was very haughty. But she isn't at all. She's really very self-depreciatory; she thinks she isn't good enough for me. You ought to hear her talk, mother, as I have. She's full of the noblest ideals—of being of some use in the world, of being self-devoted, and—all that kind of thing. And you can see that she's capable of it. Her aunt's in a Protestant sisterhood," he said, with a solemnity which did not seem to communicate itself to his mother, for Mrs. Mavering smiled. Dan smiled too, and said: "But I can't tell you about Alice, mother. She's perfect." His heart overflowed with proud delight in her, and he was fool enough to add, "She's so *affectionate!*"

His mother kept herself from laughing. "I dare say she is, Dan—with *you.*" Then she hid all but her eyes with the photograph and gave way.

"What a donkey!" said Dan, meaning himself. "If I go on, I shall disgust you with her. What I mean is that she isn't at all proud, as I used to think she was."

"No girl *is*, under the circumstances. She has all she can do to be proud of you."

"Do you *think* so, mother?" he said, enraptured with the

notion. "I've done my best—or my worst—not to give her any reason to be so."

"She doesn't want any—the less the better. You silly boy! Don't you suppose she wants to make you out of the whole cloth, just as you do with her? She doesn't want any facts to start with; they'd be in the way. Well, now, I can make out, with your help, what the young lady is; but what are the father and mother? They're rather important in these cases."

"Oh, they're the nicest kind of people," said Dan, in optimistic generalization. "You'd like *Mrs.* Pasmer. She's awfully nice."

"Do you say that because you think I wouldn't?" asked his mother. "Isn't she rather sly and humbugging?"

"Well, yes, she is, to a certain extent," Dan admitted, with a laugh. "But she doesn't mean any harm by it. She's extremely kind-hearted."

"To *you*? I dare say. And Mr. Pasmer is rather under her thumb?"

"Well, yes, you might say thumb," Dan consented, feeling it useless to defend the Pasmers against this analysis.

"We *won't* say *heel*," returned his mother; "we're too polite. And your father says he had the reputation in college of being one of the most selfish fellows in the world. He's never done anything since but lose most of his money. He's been absolutely idle and useless all his days." She turned her vivid blue eyes suddenly upon her son's.

Dan winced. "You know how hard father is upon people who haven't done anything. It's a mania of his. Of course Mr. Pasmer doesn't show to advantage where there's no—no leisure class."

"Poor man!"

Dan was going to say, "He's very amiable, though," but he was afraid of his mother's retorting, "To *you*?" and he held his peace, looking chapfallen.

Whether his mother took pity on him or not, her next sally was consoling. "But your Alice may not take after either of them. Her father is the worst of his breed, it seems; the rest are useful people, from what your father knows, and there's a great deal to be hoped for collaterally. She had an uncle in college at the same time who was everything that her father was not."

"One of her aunts is in one of those Protestant religious houses in England," repeated Dan.

"Oh!" said his mother, shortly. "I don't know that I like *that* particularly. But probably she isn't useless there. Is Alice very religious?"

"Well, I suppose," said Dan, with a smile for the devotions that came into his thought, "she's what would be called 'Piscopal pious."

Mrs. Mavering referred to the photograph, which she still held in her hand. "Well, she's pure and good, at any rate. I suppose you look forward to a long engagement?"

Dan was somewhat taken aback at a supposition so very contrary to what was in his mind. "Well, I don't know. Why?"

"It might be said that you are very young. How old is Agnes—Alice, I mean?"

"Twenty-one. But now, look here, mother! It's no use considering such a thing in the abstract, is it?"

"No," said his mother, with a smile for what might be coming.

"This is the way I've been viewing it; I may say it's the way Alice has been viewing it—or Mrs. Pasmer, rather."

"Decidedly Mrs. Pasmer, rather. Better be honest, Dan."

"I'll do my best. I was thinking, hoping, that is, that as I'm going right into the business—have gone into it already, in fact—and could begin life at once, that perhaps there wouldn't be much sense in waiting a great while."

"Yes?"

"That's all. That is, if you and father are agreed." He reflected upon this provision, and added, with a laugh of confusion and pleasure: "It seems to be so very much more of a family affair than I used to think it was."

"You thought it concerned just you and her?" said his mother, with arch sympathy.

"Well, yes."

"Poor fellow! *She* knew better than that, you may be sure. At any rate, her mother did."

"What Mrs. Pasmer doesn't know isn't probably worth

knowing," said Dan, with an amused sense of her omniscience.

"I thought so," sighed his mother, smiling too. "And now
you begin to find out that it concerns the families in all their
branches on both sides."

"Oh, if it stopped at the families and their ramifications!
But it seems to take in society and the general public."

"So it does—more than you can realize. You can't get married to yourself alone, as young people think; and if you don't
marry happily, you sin against the peace and comfort of the
whole community."

"Yes, that's what I'm chiefly looking out for now. I don't
want any of those people in Central Africa to suffer. That's
the reason I want to marry Alice at the earliest opportunity.
But I suppose there'll have to be a Mavering embassy to the
high contracting powers of the other part now?"

"Your father and one of the girls had better go down."

"Yes?"

"And invite Mr. and Mrs. Pasmer and their daughter to
come up here."

"All on probation?"

"Oh no. If *you're* pleased, Dan—"

"I am, mother—measurably." They both laughed at his
mild way of putting it.

"—Why, then it's to be supposed that we're all pleased.
You needn't bring the whole Pasmer family home to live with
you, if you *do* marry them all."

"No," said Dan, and suddenly he became very distraught. It
flashed through him that his mother was expecting him to
come home with Alice to live, and that she would not be at all
pleased with his scheme of a European sojourn, which Mrs.
Pasmer had so cordially adopted. He was amazed that he had
not thought of that, but he refused to see any difficulty which
his happiness could not cope with.

"No, there's that view of it," he said, jollily; and he buried
his momentary anxiety out of sight, and, as it were, danced
upon its grave. Nevertheless, he had a desire to get quickly
away from the spot. "I hope the Mavering embassy won't be
a great while getting ready to go," he said. "Of course it's
all right; but I shouldn't want an appearance of reluctance

exactly, you know, mother; and if there should be much of an interval between my getting back and their coming on, don't you know, why, the cat might let herself out of the bag."

"What cat?" asked his mother, demurely.

"Well, you know, you *haven't* received my engagement with unmingled enthusiasm, and—and I suppose they would find it out from me—from my manner; and—and I *wish* they'd come along pretty soon, mother."

"Poor boy! I'm afraid the cat got out of the bag when Mrs. Pasmer came to the years of discretion. But you sha'n't be left a prey to her. They shall go back with you. Ring the bell, and let's talk it over with them now."

Dan joyfully obeyed. He could see that his mother was all on fire with interest in his affair, and that the idea of somehow circumventing Mrs. Pasmer by prompt action was fascinating her.

His sisters came up at once, and his father followed a moment later. They all took their cue from the mother's gayety, and began talking and laughing, except their father, who sat looking on with a smile at their lively spirits and the jokes of which Dan became the victim. Each family has its own fantastic medium, in which it gets affairs to relieve them of their concrete seriousness, and the Maverings now did this with Dan's engagement, and played with it as an airy abstraction. They debated the character of the embassy which was to be sent down to Boston on their behalf, and it was decided that Eunice had better go with her father, as representing more fully the age and respectability of the family: at first glance the Pasmers would take her for Dan's mother, and this would be a tremendous advantage.

"And if I like the ridiculous little chit," said Eunice, "I think I shall let Dan marry her at once. I see no reason why he shouldn't, and I couldn't stand a long engagement; I should break it off."

"I guess there are others who will have something to say about that," retorted the younger sister. "I've always wanted a long engagement in this family, and as there seems to be no chance for it with the ladies, I wish to make the most of Dan's. I always like it where the hero gets sick and the heroine nurses him. I want Dan to get sick, and have Alice come here and take care of him."

"No; this marriage must take place at once. What do you say, father?" asked Eunice.

Her father sat, enjoying the talk, at the foot of the bed, with a tendency to doze. "You might ask Dan," he said, with a lazy cast of his eye toward his son.

"Dan has nothing to do with it."

"Dan shall not be consulted."

The two girls stormed upon their father with their different reasons.

"Now I will tell you— Girls, be still!" their mother broke in. "Listen to me: I have an idea."

"Listen to her: she has an idea!" echoed Eunice, in recitative.

"Will you be quiet?" demanded the mother.

"We will be du-u-mb!"

When they became so, at the verge of their mother's patience, of which they knew the limits, she went on: "I think Dan had better get married at once."

"There, Minnie!"

"But what does Dan say?"

"I will—make the sacrifice," said Dan, meekly.

"Noble boy! That's exactly what Washington said to *his* mother when *she* asked him not to go to sea," said Minnie.

"And then he went into the militia, and made it all right with himself that way," said Eunice. "Dan can't play his filial piety on *this* family. Go on, mother."

"I want him to bring his wife home, and live with us," continued his mother.

"In the L part!" cried Minnie, clasping her hands in rapture. "I've always said what a perfect little apartment it was by itself."

"Well, don't say it again, then," returned her sister. "Always is often enough. Well, in the L part— Go on, mother! Don't ask where you were, when it's so exciting."

"I don't care whether it's in the L part or not. There's plenty of room in the great barn of a place everywhere."

"But what about his taking care of the business in Boston?" suggested Eunice, looking at her father.

"There's no hurry about that."

"And about the excursion to æsthetic centres abroad?" Minnie added.

"That could be managed," said her father, with the same ironical smile.

The mother and the girls went on wildly planning Dan's future for him. It was all in a strain of extravagant burlesque. But he could not take his part in it with his usual zest. He laughed and joked too, but at the bottom of his heart was an uneasy remembrance of the different future he had talked over with Mrs. Pasmer so confidently. But he said to himself buoyantly at last that it would come out all right. His mother would give in, or else Alice could reconcile her mother to whatever seemed really best.

He parted from his mother with fond gayety. His sisters came out of the room with him.

"I'm perfectly sore with laughing," said Minnie. "It seems like old times—doesn't it, Dan?—such a gale with mother."

XXXI

AN ENGAGEMENT must always be a little incredible at first to the families of the betrothed, and especially to the family of the young man; in the girl's, the mother, at least, will have a more realizing sense of the situation. If there are elder sisters who have been accustomed to regard their brother as very young, he will seem all the younger because in such a matter he has treated himself as if he were a man; and Eunice Mavering said, after seeing the Pasmers, "Well, Dan, it's all well enough, I suppose, but it seems too ridiculous."

"What's ridiculous about it, I should like to know?" he demanded.

"Oh, I don't know. Who'll look after you when you're married? Oh, I forgot Ma'am Pasmer!"

"I guess we shall be able to look after ourselves," said Dan, a little sulkily.

"Yes, if you'll be allowed to," insinuated his sister.

They spoke at the end of a talk, in which he had fretted at the reticence of both his sister and his father concerning the Pasmers, whom they had just been to see. He was vexed with his father, because he felt that he had been influenced by Eunice, and had somehow gone back on him. He was vexed and he was grieved because his father had left them at the door of the hotel without saying anything in praise of Alice, beyond the generalities that would not carry favor with Eunice; and he was depressed with a certain sense of Alice's father and mother, which seemed to have imparted itself to him from the others, and to be the Mavering opinion of them. He could no longer see Mrs. Pasmer harmless if trivial, and good-hearted if inveterately scheming; he could not see the dignity and refinement which he had believed in Mr. Pasmer; they had both suffered a sort of shrinkage or collapse, from which he could not rehabilitate them. But this would have been nothing if his sister's and his father's eyes, through which he seemed to have been looking, had not shown him Alice in a light in which she appeared strange and queer almost to eccentricity. He was hurt at this effect from their want of sympathy, his pride was touched, and he said to himself that he should not fish for Eunice's praise; but he found himself saying, without surprise, "I suppose you will do what you can to prejudice mother and Min."

"Isn't that a little previous?" asked Eunice. "Have I said anything against Miss Pasmer?"

"You *haven't* because you *couldn't*," said Dan, with foolish bitterness.

"Oh, I don't know about that. She's a human being, I suppose—at least that was the impression I got from her parentage."

"What have you got to say against her parents?" demanded Dan, savagely.

"Oh, nothing. I didn't come down to Boston to denounce the Pasmer family."

"I suppose you didn't like their being in a flat; you'd have liked to find them in a house on Commonwealth Avenue or Beacon Street."

"I'll own I'm a snob," said Eunice, with maddening meekness. "So's father."

"They are connected with the best families in the city, and they are in the best society. They do what they please, and they live where they like. They have been so long in Europe that they don't care for those silly distinctions. But what you say doesn't harm them. It's simply disgraceful to you; that's all," said Dan, furiously.

"I'm glad it's no worse, Dan," said his sister, with a tranquil smile. "And if you'll stop prancing up and down the room, and take a seat, and behave yourself in a Christian manner, I'll talk with you; and if you don't, I won't. Do you suppose I'm going to be bullied into liking them?"

"You can like them or not, as you please," said Dan, sullenly; but he sat down, and waited decently for his sister to speak. "But you can't abuse them—at least in my presence."

"I didn't know men lost their heads as well as their hearts," said Eunice. "Perhaps it's only an exchange, though, and it's Miss Pasmer's head." Dan started, but did not say anything, and Eunice smoothly continued: "No, I don't believe it is. She looked like a sensible girl, and she talked sensibly. I should think she had a very *good* head. She has good manners, and she's extremely pretty, and very graceful. I'm surprised she should be in love with such a simpleton."

"Oh, go on! Abuse *me* as much as you like," said Dan. He was at once soothed by her praise of Alice.

"No, it isn't necessary to go on; the case is a little too obvious. But I think she will do very well. I hope you're not marrying the whole family, though. I suppose that it's always a question of which shall be scooped up. They will want to scoop you up, and we shall want to scoop her up. I dare say Ma'am Pasmer has her little plan; what is it?"

Dan started at this touch on the quick, but he controlled himself, and said, with dignity, "I have my own plans."

"Well, you know what mother's are," returned Eunice, easily. "You seem so cheerful that I suppose yours are quite the same, and you're just keeping them for a surprise." She laughed provokingly, and Dan burst forth again:

"You seem to live to give people pain. You take a fiendish delight in torturing others. But if you think you can influence me in the slightest degree, you're very much mistaken."

"Well, well, *there*! It *sha'n't* be teased any more, so it sha'n't! It *shall* have its own way, it shall, and nobody shall say a *word* against its little girly's mother." Eunice rose from her chair, and patted Dan on the head as she passed to the adjoining room. He caught her hand and flung it violently away; she shrieked with delight in his childish resentment, and left him sulking. She was gone two or three minutes, and when she came back it was in quite a different mood, as often happens with women in a little lapse of time.

"Dan, I think Miss Pasmer is a beautiful girl, and I know we shall all like her, if you don't set us against her by your arrogance. Of course we don't know anything about her yet, and *you* don't, really; but she seems a very lovable little thing, and if she's rather silent and undemonstrative, why, she'll be all the better for you: you've got demonstration enough for twenty. And I think the family are well enough. Mrs. Pasmer is thoroughly harmless; and Mr. Pasmer is a most dignified personage; his eyebrows alone are worth the price of admission." Dan could not help smiling. "All that there is about it is, you mustn't expect to drive people into raptures about them, and expect them to go grovelling round on their knees because you do."

"Oh, I know I'm an infernal idiot," said Dan, yielding to the mingled sarcasm and flattery. "It's because I'm so anxious, and you all seem so confoundedly provisional about it. Eunice, what do you suppose father really thinks?"

Eunice seemed tempted to a relapse into her teasing, but she did not yield. "Oh, *father's* all right—from your point of view. He's been ridiculous from the first; perhaps that's the reason he doesn't feel obliged to expatiate and expand a great deal at present."

"Do you think so?" cried Dan, instantly adopting her as an ally.

"Well, if I *say* so, oughtn't it to be enough?"

"It depends upon what else you say. Look here, now, Eunice!" Dan said, with a laughing mixture of fun and earnest, "what are you going to say to mother? It's no use being disagreeable, is it? Of course I don't contend for ideal perfection anywhere, and I don't expect it. But there isn't anything experimental about this thing, and don't you think we had better all make the best of it?"

"That sounds very impartial."

"It *is* impartial. I'm a purely disinterested spectator."

"Oh, quite."

"And don't you suppose I understand Mr. and Mrs. Pasmer quite as well as you do? All I say is that Alice is simply the noblest girl that ever breathed, and—"

"Now you're talking *sense*, Dan!"

"Well, what are you going to say when you get home, Eunice? Come!"

"That we had better make the best of it."

"And what else?"

"That you're hopelessly infatuated; and that she will twist you round her finger."

"Well?"

"But that you've had your own way so much, it will do you good to have somebody else's awhile."

"I guess you're pretty solid," said Dan, after thinking it over for a moment. "I don't believe you're going to make it hard for me, and I know you can make it just what you please. But I want you to be frank with mother. Of course I wish you felt about the whole affair just as I do, but if you're right on the main question, I don't care for the rest. I'd rather mother would know just how you feel about it," said Dan, with a sigh for the honesty which he felt to be not immediately attainable in his own case.

"Well, I'll see what can be done," Eunice finally assented.

Whatever her feelings were in regard to the matter, she must have satisfied herself that the situation was not to be changed by her disliking it, and she began to talk so sympathetically with Dan that she soon had the whole story of his love out of him. They laughed a good deal together at it, but it convinced her that he had not been hoodwinked into the engagement. It is always the belief of a young man's family, especially his mother and sisters, that unfair means have been used to win him, if the family of his betrothed are unknown to them; and it was a relief, if not exactly a comfort, for Eunice Mavering to find that Alice was as great a simpleton as Dan, and perhaps a sincerer simpleton.

XXXII

A WEEK LATER, in fulfillment of the arrangement made by Mrs. Pasmer and Eunice Mavering, Alice and her mother returned the formal visit of Dan's people.

While Alice stood before the mirror in one of the sumptuously furnished rooms assigned them, arranging a ribbon for the effect upon Dan's mother after dinner, and regarding its relation to her serious beauty, Mrs. Pasmer came in out of her chamber adjoining, and began to inspect the formal splendor of the place.

"What a perfect *man's* house!" she said, peering about. "You can see that everything has been done to order. They have their own taste; they're artistic enough for that—or the father is—and they've given orders to have things done so and so, and the New York upholsterer has come up and taken the measure of the rooms and done it. But it isn't like New York, and it isn't individual. The whole house is just like those girls' tailor-made costumes in character. They were made in New York, but they don't wear them with the New York style; there's no more atmosphere about them than if they were young men dressed up. There isn't a thing lacking in the house here; there's an awful completeness; but even the ornaments seem laid on, like the hot and cold water. I never saw a handsomer, more uninviting room than that drawing-room. I suppose the etchings will come some time after supper. What do you think of it all, Alice?"

"Oh, I don't know. They must be very rich," said the girl, indifferently.

"You can't tell. Country people of a certain kind are apt to put everything on their backs and their walls and floors. Of course such a house here doesn't mean what it would in town." She examined the texture of the carpet more critically, and the curtains; she had no shame about a curiosity that made her daughter shrink.

"Don't, mamma!" pleaded the girl. "What if they should come?"

"They won't come," said Mrs. Pasmer; and her notice

being called to Alice, she made her take off the ribbon. "You're better without it."

"I'm so nervous I don't know what I'm doing," said Alice, removing it, with a whimper.

"Well, I can't have you breaking down!" cried her mother, warningly: she really wished to shake her, as a culmination of her own conflicting emotions. "Alice, stop this instant! Stop it, I say!"

"But if I don't like her?" whimpered Alice.

"You're not going to marry *her*. Now stop! Here, bathe your eyes; they're all red. Though I don't know that it matters. Yes, they'll expect you to have been crying," said Mrs. Pasmer, seeing the situation more and more clearly. "It's perfectly natural." But she took some cologne on a handkerchief, and recomposed Alice's countenance for her. "There, the color becomes you, and I never saw your eyes look so bright."

There was a pathos in their brilliancy which of course betrayed her to the Mavering girls. It softened Eunice, and encouraged Minnie, who had been a little afraid of the Pasmers. They both kissed Alice with sisterly affection. Their father merely saw how handsome she looked, and Dan's heart seemed to melt in his breast with tenderness.

In recognition of the different habits of their guests, they had dinner instead of tea. The Portuguese cook had outdone himself, and course followed course in triumphal succession. Mrs. Pasmer praised it all with a sincerity that took away a little of the zest she felt in making flattering speeches.

Everything about the table was perfect, but in a man's fashion, like the rest of the house. It lacked the atmospheric charm, the otherwise indefinable grace, which a woman's taste gives. It was in fact Elbridge Mavering's taste which had characterized the whole; the daughters simply accepted and approved.

"Yes," said Eunice, "we haven't much else to do; so we eat. And Joe does his best to spoil us."

"Joe?"

"Joe's the cook. All Portuguese cooks are Joe."

"How very amusing!" said Mrs. Pasmer. "You *must* let me speak of your grapes. I never saw anything so—well!—*except* your roses."

"There you touch father in *two* tender spots. He cultivates both."

"Really? Alice, *did* you ever see anything like these roses?"

Alice looked away from Dan a moment, and blushed to find that she had been looking so long at him.

"Ah, *I* have," said Mr. Mavering, gallantly.

"Does he often do it?" asked Mrs. Pasmer, in an obvious aside to Eunice.

Dan answered for him. "He never had such a chance before."

Between coffee, which they drank at table, and tea, which they were to take in Mrs. Mavering's room, they acted upon a suggestion from Eunice that her father should show Mrs. Pasmer his rose-house. At one end of the dining-room was a little apse of glass full of flowering plants growing out of the ground, and with a delicate fountain tinkling in their midst. Dan ran before the rest, and opened two glass doors in the further side of this half-bubble, and at the same time with a touch flashed up a succession of brilliant lights in some space beyond, from which there gushed in a wave of hot-house fragrance, warm, heavy, humid. It was a pretty little effect for guests new to the house, and was part of Elbridge Mavering's pleasure in this feature of his place. Mrs. Pasmer responded with generous sympathy, for if she really liked anything with her whole heart, it was an effect, and she traversed the half-bubble by its pebbled path, showering praises right and left with a fulness and accuracy that missed no detail, while Alice followed silently, her hand in Minnie Mavering's, and cold with suppressed excitement. The rose-house was divided by a wall, pierced with frequent doorways, over which the trees were trained and the roses hung; and on either side were ranks of rare and costly kinds, weighed down with bud and bloom. The air was thick with their breath and the pungent odors of the rich soil from which they grew, and the glass roof was misted with the mingled exhalations.

Mr. Mavering walked beside Alice, modestly explaining the difficulties of rose culture, and his method of dealing with the red spider. He had a stout knife in his hand, and he cropped long, heavy-laden stems of roses from the walls and the beds, casually giving her their different names, and laying them along his arm in a massive sheaf.

Mrs. Pasmer and Eunice had gone forward with Dan, and were waiting for them at the thither end of the rose-house.

"Alice! just imagine: the grapery is beyond this," cried the girl's mother.

"It's a cold grapery," said Mr. Mavering. "I hope you'll see it to-morrow."

"Oh, why not to-night?" shouted Dan.

"Because it's a *cold* grapery," said Eunice; "and after this rose-house, it's an arctic grapery. You're crazy, Dan."

"Well, I want Alice to see it, anyway," he persisted, wilfully. "There's nothing like a cold grapery by starlight. I'll get some wraps." They all knew that he wished to be alone with her a moment, and the three women, consenting with their hearts, protested with their tongues, following him in his flight with their chorus, and greeting his return. He muffled her to the chin in a fur-lined overcoat, which he had laid hands on the first thing, and her mother, still protesting, helped to tie a scarf over her hair so as not to disarrange it. "Here," he pointed, "we can run through it, and it's worth seeing. Better come," he said to the others as he opened the door, and hurried Alice down the path under the keen sparkle of the crystal roof, blotched with the leaves and bunches of the vines. Coming out of the dense, sensuous, vaporous air of the rose-house into this clear, thin atmosphere, delicately penetrated with the fragrance, pure and cold, of the fruit, it was as if they had entered another world. His arm crept round her in the odorous obscurity. "Look up! See the stars through the vines!" But when she lifted her face he bent his upon it for a wild kiss.

"Don't! don't!" she murmured. "I want to think; I don't know what I'm doing."

"Neither do I. I feel as if I were a blessed ghost."

Perhaps it is only in these ecstasies of the senses that the soul ever reaches self-consciousness on earth; and it seems to be only the man-soul which finds itself even in this abandon. The woman-soul has always something else to think of.

"What shall we do," said the girl, "if we— Oh, I dread to meet your mother! Is she like either of your sisters?"

"No," he cried, joyously; "she's like *me*. If you're not afraid of me, and you don't seem to be—"

"You're all I have—you're all I have in the world. Do you think she'll like me? Oh, *do* you love me, Dan?"

"You darling! you divine—" The rest was a mad embrace. "If you're not afraid of me, you won't mind mother. I wanted you here alone for just a last word, to tell you you needn't be afraid; to tell you to— But I needn't tell you how to act. You mustn't treat her as an invalid, you must treat her like any one else; that's what she likes. But you'll know what's best, Alice. Be yourself, and she'll like you well enough. I'm not afraid."

XXXIII

WHEN SHE ENTERED Mrs. Mavering's room Alice first saw the pictures, the bric-à-brac, the flowers, the dazzle of lights, and then the invalid propped among her pillows, and vividly expectant of her. She seemed all eager eyes to the girl, aware next of the strong resemblance to Dan in her features, and of the careful toilet the sick woman had made for her. To youth all forms of suffering are abhorrent, and Alice had to hide a repugnance at sight of this spectre of what had once been a pretty woman. Through the egotism with which so many years of flattering subjection in her little world had armed her, Mrs. Mavering probably did not feel the girl's shrinking, or, if she did, took it for the natural embarrassment which she would feel. She had satisfied herself that she was looking her best, and that her cap and the lace jacket she wore were very becoming, and softened her worst points; the hangings of her bed and the richly embroidered crimson silk coverlet were part of the coquetry of her costume, from which habit had taken all sense of ghastliness; she was proud of them, and she was not aware of the scent of drugs that insisted through the odor of the flowers.

She lifted herself on her elbow as Dan approached with Alice, and the girl felt as if an intense light had been thrown upon her from head to foot in the moment of searching scrutiny that followed. The invalid's set look broke into a smile, and she put out her hand, neither hot nor cold, but of a dry, neutral, spiritual temperature, and pulled Alice down and kissed her.

"Why, child, your hand's like ice!" she exclaimed, without preamble. "We used to say that came from a warm heart."

"I guess it comes from a cold grapery in this case, mother," said Dan, with his laugh. "I've just been running Alice through it. And perhaps a little excitement—"

"Excitement?" echoed his mother. "Cold grapery, I dare say, and very silly of *you*, Dan; but there's no occasion for excitement, as if we were strangers. Sit down in that chair, my dear. And, Dan, you go round to the other side of the bed; I want Alice all to myself. I saw your photograph a week ago, and I've thought about you for ages since, and wondered whether you would approve of your old friend."

"Oh yes," whispered the girl, suppressing a tremor; and Dan's eyes were suffused with grateful tears at his mother's graciousness.

Alice's reticence seemed to please the invalid. "I hope you'll like *all* your old friends here; you've begun with the worst among us, but perhaps you like him the best *because* he's the worst; *I* do."

"You may believe just half of that, Alice," cried Dan.

"Then believe the best half, or the half you like best," said Mrs. Mavering. "There must be something good in him if you like him. Have they welcomed you home, my dear?"

"We've all made a stagger at it," said Dan, while Alice was faltering over the words which were so slow to come.

"Don't try to answer my formal stupidities. You *are* welcome, and that's enough, and more than enough of speeches. Did you have a comfortable journey up?"

"Oh, very."

"Was it cold?"

"Not at all. The cars were very hot."

"Have you had any snow yet at Boston?"

"No, none at all yet."

"Now I feel that we're talking sense. I hope you found everything in your room? I can't look after things as I would like, and so I inquire."

"There's everything," said Alice. "We're very comfortable."

"I'm very glad. I had Dan look; he's my house-keeper; he understands me better than my girls; he's like me, more. That's what makes us so fond of each other; it's a kind of personal vanity. But he has his good points, Dan has. He's very amiable, and I was too, at his age—and till I came here. But I'm not going to tell you of his good points; I dare say you've found them out. I'll tell you about his bad ones. He says you're very serious. Are you?" She pressed the girl's hand, which she had kept in hers, and regarded her keenly.

Alice dropped her eyes at the odd question. "I don't know," she faltered. "Sometimes."

"Well, that's good. Dan's frivolous."

"Oh, *sometimes*—only sometimes!" he interposed.

"He's frivolous, and he's very light-minded; but he's none the worse for that."

"Oh, thank you," said Dan; and Alice, still puzzled, laughed provisionally.

"No; I want you to understand that. He's light-hearted too, and that's a great thing in this world. If you're serious you'll be apt to be heavy-hearted, and then you'll find Dan of use. And I hope he'll know how to turn your seriousness to account too. He needs something to keep him down—to keep him from blowing away. Yes, it's very well for people to be opposites. Only they must understand each other. If they do that, then they get along. Light-heartedness or heavy-heartedness comes to the same thing if they know how to use it for each other. You see, I've got to be a great philosopher lying here; nobody dares contradict me or interrupt me when I'm constructing my theories, and so I get them perfect."

"I wish I could hear them all," said Alice, with sincerity that made Mrs. Mavering laugh as light-heartedly as Dan himself, and that seemed to suggest the next thing to her.

"You can for the asking, almost any time. Are you a very truthful person, my dear? Don't take the trouble to deny it if you are," she added, at Alice's stare. "You see I'm not at all conventional, and you needn't be. Come! tell the truth for once, at any rate. Are you habitually truthful?"

"Yes, I think I am," said Alice, still staring.

"Dan's not," said his mother, quietly.

"Oh, see here, now, mother! Don't give me away!"

"He'll tell the truth in extremity, of course, and he'll tell it if it's pleasant, always; but if you don't expect much more of him you won't be disappointed; and you can make him of great use."

"You see where I got it, anyway, Alice," said Dan, laughing across the bed at her.

"Yes, you got it from me: I own it. A great part of my life was made up of making life pleasant to others by fibbing. I stopped it when I came here."

"Oh, not altogether, mother!" urged her son. "You mustn't be too hard on yourself."

She ignored his interruption. "You'll find Dan a great convenience with that agreeable habit of his. You can get him to make all your verbal excuses for you (he'll do it beautifully), and dictate all the thousand and one little lying notes you'll have to write; he won't mind it in the least, and it will save you a great wear and tear of conscience."

"Go on, mother, go on," said Dan, with delighted eyes that asked of Alice if it were not all perfectly charming.

"And you can come in with your habitual truthfulness where Dan wouldn't know what to do, poor fellow. You'll have the moral courage to come right to the point when he would like to shilly-shally, and you can be frank while he's trying to think how to make y-e-s spell no."

"Any other little compliments, mother?" suggested Dan.

"No," said Mrs. Mavering; "that's all. I thought I'd better have it off my mind; I knew you'd never get it off yours, and Alice had better know the worst. It *is* the worst, my dear, and if I talked of him till doomsday I couldn't say any more harm of him. I needn't tell you how sweet he is; you know that, I'm sure; but you can't know yet how gentle and forbearing he is, how patient, how full of kindness to every living soul, how unselfish, how—"

She lost her voice. "Oh, come now, mother," Dan protested, huskily.

Alice did not say anything; she bent over, without repugnance, and gathered the shadowy shape into her strong young arms, and kissed the wasted face, whose unearthly coolness was like the leaf of a flower against her lips. "He never gave me a moment's trouble," said the mother, "and I'm sure he'll make you happy. How kind of you not to be afraid of me—"

"Afraid!" cried the girl, with passionate solemnity. "I shall never feel safe away from you!"

The door opened upon the sound of voices, and the others came in.

Mrs. Pasmer did not wait for an introduction, but with an affectation of impulse which she felt Mrs. Mavering would penetrate and respect, she went up to the bed and presented herself. Dan's mother smiled hospitably upon her, and they had some playful words about their children. Mrs. Pasmer neatly conveyed the regrets of her husband, who had hoped up to the last moment that the heavy cold he had taken would let him come with her; and the invalid made her guest sit down on the right hand of her bed, which seemed to be the place of honor, while her husband took Dan's place on the left, and admired his wife's skill in fence. At the end of her encounter with Mrs. Pasmer she called out with her strong voice, "Why don't you get your banjo, Minnie, and play something?"

"A banjo? Oh, do!" cried Mrs. Pasmer. "It's so picturesque and interesting! I heard that young ladies had taken it up, and I should so like to hear it!" She had turned to Mrs. Mavering again, and she now beamed winningly upon her.

Alice regarded the girl with a puzzled frown as she brought her banjo in from another room and sat down with it. She relaxed the severity of her stare a little as Minnie played one wild air after another, singing some of them with an evidence of training in her naïve effectiveness. There were some Mexican songs which she had learned in a late visit to their country, and some creole melodies caught up in a winter's sojourn in Louisiana. The elder sister accompanied her on the piano, not with the hard, resolute proficiency which one might have expected of Eunice Mavering, but with a sympathy which was perhaps the expression of her share of the family kindliness.

"Your children seem to have been everywhere," said Mrs. Pasmer, with a sigh of flattering envy. "Oh, you're not going to stop!" she pleaded, turning from Mrs. Mavering to Minnie.

"I think Dan had better do the rheumatic uncle now," said Eunice, from the piano.

"Oh yes! the rheumatic uncle — do," said Mrs. Pasmer. "*We* know the rheumatic uncle," she added, with a glance at Alice. Dan looked at her too, as if doubtful of her approval; and then he told in character a Yankee story which he had worked up from the talk of his friend the foreman. It made them all laugh.

Mrs. Pasmer was the gayest; she let herself go, and throughout the evening she flattered right and left, and said, in her good-night to Mrs. Mavering, that she had never imagined so delightful a time. "Oh, Mrs. Mavering, I don't wonder your children love their home. It's a revelation."

XXXIV

S HE'S A CAT, Dan," said his mother, quietly, and not without liking, when he looked in for his good-night kiss after the rest were gone; "a perfect tabby. But your Alice is sublime."

"Oh, mother—"

"She's a little *too* sublime for *me*. But you're young, and you can stand it."

Dan laughed with delight. "Yes, I think I can, mother. All I ask is the chance."

"Oh, you're very much in love, both of you; there's no doubt about that. What I mean is that she's very high strung, very intense. She has ideals—any one can see that."

Dan took it all for praise. "Yes," he said, eagerly, "that's what I told you. And that will be the best thing about it for me. I have *no* ideals."

"Well, you must find out what hers are, and live up to them."

"Oh, there won't be any trouble about that," said Dan, buoyantly.

"You must help *her* to find them out too." He looked puzzled. "You mustn't expect the child to be too definite at first, nor to be always right, even when she's full of ideals. You must be very patient with her, Dan."

"Oh, I *will*, mother! You know that. How could I ever be impatient with Alice?"

"Very forbearing, and very kind, and indefatigably forgiving. Ask your father how to behave."

Dan promised to do so, with a laugh at the joke. It had never occurred to him that his father was particularly exemplary in these things, or that his mother idolized him for what seemed to Dan simply a matter-of-course endurance of her sick whims and freaks and moods. He broke forth into a vehement protest of his good intentions, to which his mother did not seem very attentive. After a while she asked,

"Is she always so silent, Dan?"

"Well, not with *me*, mother. Of course she was a little embarrassed; she didn't know exactly what to say, I suppose—"

"Oh, I rather liked that. At least she isn't a rattle-pate. And we shall get acquainted; we shall like each other. She will understand me when you bring her home here to live with us, and—"

"Yes," said Dan, rising rather hastily, and stooping over to his mother. "I'm not going to let you talk any more now, or we shall have to suffer for it to-morrow night."

He got gayly away before his mother could amplify a suggestion which spoiled a little his pleasure in the praises—he thought they were unqualified and enthusiastic praises—she had been heaping upon Alice. He wished to go to bed with them all sweet and unalloyed in his thought, to sleep, to dream upon his perfect triumph.

Mrs. Pasmer was a long time in undressing, and in calming down after the demands which the different events of the evening had made upon her resources.

"It has certainly been a very *mixed* evening, Alice," she said, as she took the pins out of her back hair and let it fall; and she continued to talk as she went back and forth between their rooms. "What do you think of banjo-playing for young ladies? Isn't it rather rowdy? Decidedly rowdy, *I* think. And Dan's Yankee story! I expected to see the old gentleman get up and perform some trick."

"I suppose they do it to amuse Mrs. Mavering," said Alice, with cold displeasure.

"Oh, it's quite *right*," tittered Mrs. Pasmer. "It would be as much as their lives are worth if they didn't. You can see that she rules them with a rod of iron. *What* a will! I'm glad you're not going to come under her sway; I really think you couldn't be safe from her in the same hemisphere; it's well you're going abroad at once. They're a very self-concentrated family, don't you think—very self-satisfied? Of course that's the danger of living off by themselves as they do: they get to thinking there's nobody else in the world. You would simply be absorbed by them; it's a hair-breadth escape. How splendidly Dan contrasts with the others! Oh, *he's* delightful; he's a man of the world. Give me the *world*, after all! And he's so considerate of their rustic conceit! *What* a house! It's perfectly baronial—and ridiculous. In any other country it would mean something—society, entertainments, troops of guests; but here it doesn't mean anything but money. Not that money isn't a very good thing; I wish we had more of it. But now you see how very little it can do by itself. You looked very well, Alice, and behaved with great dignity; perhaps too much. You ought to enter a little more into the spirit of things, even if you don't respect them. That oldest girl isn't particularly pleased, I fancy, though it doesn't matter really."

Alice replied to her mother from time to time with absent yeses and noes; she sat by the window looking out on the hillside lawn before the house; the moon had risen, and poured a flood of snowy light over it, in which the cold statues dimly shone, and the firs, in clumps and singly, blackened with an inky solidity. Beyond wandered the hills, their bare pasturage broken here and there by blotches of woodland.

After her mother had gone to bed she turned her light down and resumed her seat by the window, pressing her hot forehead against the pane, and losing all sense of the scene without in the whirl of her thoughts.

After this evening of gay welcome in Dan's family, and those moments of tenderness with him, her heart was troubled. She now realized her engagement as something exterior to herself and her own family, and confronted for the first time its responsibilities, its ties, and its claims. It was not enough to be everything to Dan; she could not be that unless she were something to his family. She did not realize this vividly, but with the remoteness which all verities except those of sensation have for youth.

Her uneasiness was full of exultation, of triumph; she knew she had been admired by Dan's family, and she experienced the sweetness of having pleased them for his sake; his happy eyes shone before her; but she was touched in her self-love by what her mother had coarsely characterized in them. They had regarded her liking them as a matter of course; his mother had ignored her even in pretending to decry Dan to her. But again this was very remote, very momentary. It was no nearer, no more lasting on the surface of her happiness, than the flying whiffs of thin cloud that chased across the moon and lost themselves in the vast blue around it.

XXXV

People came to the first of Mrs. James Bellingham's receptions with the expectation of pleasure which the earlier receptions of the season awaken even in the oldest and wisest. But they tried to dissemble their eagerness in a fashionable tardiness. "We get later and later," said Mrs. Brinkley to John Munt, as she sat watching the slow gathering of the crowd. By half past eleven it had not yet hidden Mrs. Bellingham, where she stood near the middle of the room, from the pleasant corner they had found after accidentally arriving together. Mr. Brinkley had not come; he said he might not be too old for receptions, but he was too good; in either case he preferred to stay at home. "We used to come at nine o'clock, and now we come at— I'm getting into a quotation from Mother Goose, I think."

"I thought it was Browning," said Munt, with his witticism manner. Neither he nor Mrs. Brinkley was particularly glad to be together, but at Mrs. James Bellingham's it was well not to fling any companionship away till you were sure of something else. Besides, Mrs. Brinkley was indolent and good-natured, and Munt was active and good-natured, and they were well fitted to get on for ten or fifteen minutes. While they talked she kept an eye out for other acquaintance, and he stood alert to escape at the first chance. "How is it we are here so early— or rather you are?" she pursued, irrelevantly.

"Oh, I don't know," said Munt, accepting the implication of his superior fashion with pleasure. "I never mind being among the first. It's rather interesting to see people come in—don't you think?"

"That depends a good deal on the people. I don't find a great variety in their smirks and smiles to Mrs. Bellingham; I seem to be doing them all myself. And there's a monotony about their apprehension and helplessness when they're turned adrift that's altogether too much like my own. No, Mr. Munt, I can't agree with you that it's interesting to see people come in. It's altogether too autobiographical. What else have you to suggest?"

"I'm afraid I'm at the end of my string," said Munt. "I

suppose we shall see the Pasmers and young Mavering here
to-night."

Mrs. Brinkley turned and looked sharply at him.

"You've heard of the engagement?" he asked.

"No, decidedly, I haven't. And after his flight from Campobello it's the last thing I expected to hear of. When did it
come out?"

"Only within a few days. They've been keeping it rather
quiet. Mrs. Pasmer told me herself."

Mrs. Brinkley gave herself a moment for reflection. "Well,
if he can stand it, I suppose I can."

"That isn't exactly what people are saying to Mrs. Pasmer,
Mrs. Brinkley," suggested Munt, with his humorous manner.

"I dare say they're trying to make her believe that her
daughter is sacrificed. That's the way. But she knows better."

"There's no doubt but she's informed herself. She put me
through my catechism about the Maverings the day of the
picnic down there."

"Do you know them?"

" 'Bridge Mavering and I were at Harvard together."

"Tell me about them." Mrs. Brinkley listened to Munt's
praises of his old friend with an attention superficially divided
with the people to whom she bowed and smiled. The room
was filling up. "Well," she said at the end, "he's a sweet young
fellow. I hope he likes his Pasmers."

"I guess there's no doubt about his liking one of them—
the principal one."

"Yes, if she *is* the principal one." There was an implication
in everything she said that Dan Mavering had been hoodwinked by Mrs. Pasmer. Mature ladies always like to imply
something of the sort in these cases. They like to ignore the
prime agency of youth and love, and pretend that marriage is
a game that parents play at with us, as if we were in an old
comedy; it is a tradition. "Will he take her home to live?"

"No. I heard that they're all going abroad—for a year or
two at least."

"Ah! I *thought* so," cried Mrs. Brinkley. She looked up with
whimsical pleasure in the uncertainty of an old gentleman
who was staring hard at her through his glasses. "Well," she
said, with a pleasant sharpness, "do you make me out?"

"As nearly as my belief in your wisdom will allow," said the old gentleman, as distinctly as his long white mustache and an apparent absence of teeth behind it would let him. John Munt had eagerly abandoned the seat he was keeping at Mrs. Brinkley's side, and had launched himself into the thickening crowd. The old gentleman, who was lank and tall, folded himself down into it. He continued as tranquilly as if seated quite alone with Mrs. Brinkley, and not minding that his voice, with the senile crow in it, made itself heard by others. "I'm always surprised to find sensible people at these things of Jane's. They're most extraordinary things. Jane's idea of society is to turn a herd of human beings loose in her house, and see what will come of it. She has no more sense of hospitality or responsibility than the Elements, or Divine Providence. You may come here and have a good time—if you can get it; she won't object; or you may die of solitude and inanition; she'd never know it. I don't know but it's rather sublime in her. It's like the indifference of fate; but it's rather rough on those who don't understand it. She likes to see her rooms filled with pretty dresses, but she has no social instincts and no social inspiration whatever. She lights and heats and feeds her guests, and then she leaves them to themselves. She's a kind woman, Jane is, a very good-natured woman, and I really think she'd be grieved if she thought any one went away unhappy, but she does nothing to make them at home in her house—absolutely nothing."

"Perhaps she does all they deserve for them. I don't know that any one acquires merit by coming to an evening party; and it's impossible to be personally hospitable to everybody in such a crowd."

"Yes, I've sometimes taken that view of it. And yet if you ask a stranger to your house, you establish a tacit understanding with him that you won't forget him after you have him there. I like to go about and note the mystification of strangers who've come here with some notion of a little attention. It's delightfully poignant; I suffer with them; it's a cheap luxury of woe; I follow them through all the turns and windings of their experience. Of course the theory is that being turned loose here with the rest, they may speak to anybody; but the fact is they can't. Sometimes I should like to hail some of these unfriended spirits, but I haven't the courage. I'm not individually bashful, but I have a thousand years of Anglo-Saxon civilization behind me. I've just seen two pretty women cast away in a corner, and clinging to a small water-color on the wall with a show of interest that would melt a heart of stone. Why do you come, Mrs. Brinkley? I should really like to know. You're not obliged to."

"No," said Mrs. Brinkley, lowering her voice instinctively, as if to bring his down. "I suppose I come from force of habit. I've been coming a long time, you know. Why do you come?"

"Because I can't sleep. If I could sleep, I should be at home in bed." A weariness came into his thin face and dim eyes that was pathetic, and passed into a whimsical sarcasm. "I'm not one of the great leisure class, you know, that voluntarily turns night into day. Do you know what I go about saying now?"

"Something amusing, I suppose."

"You'd better not be so sure of that. I've discovered a fact, or rather I've formulated an old one. I've always been troubled how to classify people here, there are so many exceptions; and I've ended by broadly generalizing them as women and men."

Mrs. Brinkley was certainly amused at this. "It seems to me that there you've been anticipated by nature—not to mention art."

"Oh, not in my particular view. The women in America represent the aristocracy which exists everywhere else in both sexes. You are born to the patrician leisure; you have the accomplishments and the clothes and manners and ideals; and we men are a natural commonalty, born to business, to newspapers, to cigars, and horses. This natural female aristocracy of ours establishes the forms, usages, places, and times of society. The epicene aristocracies of other countries turn night into day in their social pleasures, and our noblesse sympathetically follows their example. You ladies, who can lie till noon next day, come to Jane's reception at eleven o'clock, and you drag along with you a herd of us brokers, bankers, merchants, lawyers, and doctors, who must be at our offices and counting-rooms before nine in the morning. The hours of us work-people are regulated by the wholesome industries of the great democracy which we're a part of; and the hours of our wives and daughters by the deleterious pleasures of the Old World aristocracy. That's the reason we're not all at home in bed."

"I thought you were not at home in bed because you couldn't sleep."

"I know it. And you've no idea how horrible a bed is that you can't sleep in." The old man's voice broke in a tremor. "Ah, it's a bed of torture! I spend many a wicked hour in mine, envying St. Lawrence his gridiron. But what do you think of my theory?"

"It's a very pretty theory. My only objection to it is that it's too flattering. You know I rather prefer to abuse my sex; and to be set up as a natural aristocracy—I don't know that I can quite agree to that, even to account satisfactorily for my being at your sister-in-law's reception."

"You're too modest, Mrs. Brinkley."

"No, really. There ought to be some men among us—men without morrows. Now why don't you and my husband set an example to your sex? Why don't you relax your severe sense of duty? Why need you insist upon being at your offices every morning at nine? Why don't you fling off these habits of life-long industry, and be gracefully indolent in the interest of the higher civilization?"

Bromfield Corey looked round at her with a smile of relish for her satire. Her husband was a notoriously lazy man, who had chosen to live restrictedly upon an inherited property rather than increase it by the smallest exertion.

"Do you think we could get Andy Pasmer to join us?"

"No, I can't encourage you with that idea. You must get on without Mr. Pasmer; he's going back to Europe with his son-in-law."

"Do you mean that their girl's married?"

"No—engaged. It's just out."

"Well, I must say Mrs. Pasmer has made use of her time." He too liked to imply that it was all an effect of her manœuvring, and that the young people had nothing to do with it; this survival from European fiction dies hard. "Who is the young man?"

Mrs. Brinkley gave him an account of Dan Mavering as she

had seen him at Campobello, and of his family as she just heard of them. "Mr. Munt was telling me about them as you came up."

"Why, was that John Munt?"

"Yes; didn't you know him?"

"No," said Corey, sadly. "I don't know anybody nowadays. I seem to be going to pieces every way. I don't call sixty-nine such a very great age."

"Not at all!" cried Mrs. Brinkley. "I'm fifty-four myself, and Brinkley's sixty."

"But I feel a thousand years old. I don't see people, and when I do I don't know 'em. My head's in a cloud." He let it hang heavily; then he lifted it, and said: "He's a nice, comfortable fellow, Munt is. Why didn't he stop and talk a bit?"

"Well, Munt's modest, you know; and I suppose he thought he might be the third that makes company a crowd. Besides, nobody stops and talks a bit at these things. They're afraid of boring or being bored."

"Yes, they're all in as unnatural a mood as if they were posing for a photograph. I wonder who invented this sort of thing? Do you know," said the old man, "that I think it's rather worse with us than with any other people? We're a simple, sincere folk, domestic in our instincts, not gregarious or frivolous in any way; and when we're wrenched away from our firesides, and packed in our best clothes into Jane's gilded saloons, we feel vindictive; we feel wicked. When the Boston being abandons himself—or herself—to fashion, she suffers a depravation into something quite lurid. She has a bad conscience, and she hardens her heart with talk that's tremendously cynical. It's amusing," said Corey, staring round him purblindly at the groups and files of people surging and eddying past the corner where he sat with Mrs. Brinkley.

"No; it's shocking," said his companion. "At any rate, you mustn't say such things, even if you think them. I can't let you go too far, you know. These young people think it heavenly, here."

She took with him the tone that elderly people use with those older than themselves who have begun to break; there were authority and patronage in it. At the bottom of her heart she thought that Bromfield Corey should not have been allowed to come; but she determined to keep him safe and harmless as far as she could.

From time to time the crowd was a stationary mass in front of them; then it dissolved and flowed away, to gather anew; there were moments when the floor near them was quite vacant; then it was inundated again with silken trains. From another part of the house came the sound of music, and most of the young people who passed went two and two, as if they were partners in the dance, and had come out of the ball-room between dances. There was a good deal of nervous talk, politely subdued, among them; but it was not the note of unearthly rapture which Mrs. Brinkley's conventional claim had implied; it was self-interested, eager, anxious; and was probably not different from the voice of good society anywhere.

XXXVI

"WHY, THERE'S Dan Mavering now!" said Mrs. Brinkley, rather to herself than to her companion. "And alone!"

Dan's face showed above most of the heads and shoulders about him; it was flushed, and looked troubled and excited. He caught sight of Mrs. Brinkley, and his eyes brightened joyfully. He slipped quickly through the crowd, and bowed over her hand, while he stammered out, without giving her a chance for reply till the end: "Oh, Mrs. Brinkley, I'm so glad to see you! I'm going—I want to ask a great favor of you, Mrs. Brinkley. I want to bring—I want to introduce some friends of mine to you—some ladies, Mrs. Brinkley; very nice people I met last summer at Portland. Their father—General Wrayne—has been building some railroads down East, and they're very nice people; but they don't know any one—any ladies—and they've been looking at the pictures ever since they came. They're very good pictures; but it isn't an exhibition!" He broke down with a laugh.

"Why, of course, Mr. Mavering; I shall be delighted," said Mrs. Brinkley, with a hospitality rendered reckless by her sympathy with the young fellow. "By all means!"

"Oh, thanks!—thank you ever so much!" said Dan. "I'll bring them to you—they'll understand!" He slipped into the crowd again.

Corey made an offer of going. Mrs. Brinkley stopped him with her fan. "No—stay, Mr. Corey. Unless you wish to go. I fancy it's the people you were talking about, and you must help me through with them."

"I ask nothing better," said the old man, unresentful of Dan's having not even seemed to see him, in his generous preoccupation. "I should like to see how you'll get on, and perhaps I can be of use."

"Of course you can—the greatest."

"But why hasn't he introduced them to his Pasmers? What? Eh? Oh!" Corey made these utterances in response to a sharper pressure of Mrs. Brinkley's fan on his arm.

Dan was opening a way through the crowd before them for

525

two ladies, whom he now introduced. "Mrs. Frobisher, Mrs. Brinkley; and Miss Wrayne."

Mrs. Brinkley cordially gave her hand to the ladies, and said, "May I introduce Mr. Corey? Mr. Mavering, let me introduce you to Mr. Corey." The old man rose and stood with the little group.

Dan's face shone with flattered pride and joyous triumph. He bubbled out some happy incoherencies about the honor and pleasure, while at the same time he beamed with tender gratitude upon Mrs. Brinkley, who was behaving with a gracious, humorous kindliness to the aliens cast upon her mercies. Mrs. Frobisher, after a half-hour of Boston society, was not that presence of easy gayety which crossed Dan's path on the Portland pavement the morning of his arrival from Campobello; but she was still a handsome, effective woman, of whom you would have hesitated to say whether she was showy or distinguished. Perhaps she was a little of both, with an air of command bred of supremacy in frontier garrisons; her sister was like her in the way that a young girl may be like a young matron. They blossomed alike in the genial atmosphere of Mrs. Brinkley and of Mr. Corey. He began at once to make bantering speeches with them both. The friendliness of an old man and a stout elderly woman might not have been their ideal of success at an evening party, used as they were to the unstinted homage of young captains and lieutenants, but a brief experience of Mrs. Bellingham's hospitality must have taught them humility; and when a stout, elderly gentleman, whose baldness was still trying to be blond, joined the group, the spectacle was not without its points of resemblance to a social ovation. Perhaps it was a Boston social ovation.

"Hallo, Corey!" said this stout gentleman, whom Mrs. Brinkley at once introduced as Mr. Bellingham, and whose salutation Corey returned with a "Hallo, Charles!" of equal intimacy.

Mr. Bellingham caught at the name of Frobisher. "Mrs. Major Dick Frobisher?"

"Mrs. Colonel now, but Dick always," said the lady, with immediate comradery. "Do you know my husband?"

"I should think so!" said Bellingham; and a talk of common

interest and mutual reminiscence sprang up between them. Bellingham graphically depicted his meeting with Colonel Frobisher the last time he was out on the Plains, and Mrs. Frobisher and Miss Wrayne discovered to their great satisfaction that he was the brother of Mrs. Stephen Blake, of Omaha, who had come out to the fort once with her husband, and captured the garrison, as they said. Mrs. Frobisher accounted for her present separation from her husband, and said she had come on for a while to be with her father and sister, who both needed more looking after than the Indians. Her father had left the army, and was building railroads.

Miss Wrayne, when she was not appealed to for confirmation or recollection by her sister, was having a lively talk with Corey and Mrs. Brinkley; she seemed to enter into their humor; and no one paid much attention to Dan Mavering. He hung upon the outskirts of the little group, proffering unrequited sympathy and applause; and at last he murmured something about having to go back to some friends, and took himself off. Mrs. Frobisher and Miss Wrayne let him go with a certain shade—the lightest, and yet evident—of not wholly satisfied pique: women know how to accept a reparation on account, and without giving a receipt in full.

Mrs. Brinkley gave him her hand with an effort of compassionate intelligence and appreciation of the sacrifice he must have made in leaving Alice. "May I congratulate you?" she murmured.

"Oh yes, indeed; thank you, Mrs. Brinkley," he gushed, tremulously; and he pressed her hand hard, and clung to it, as if he would like to take her with him.

Neither of the older men noticed his going. They were both taken in their elderly way with these two handsome young women, and they professed regret—Bellingham that his mother was not there, and Corey, that neither his wife nor daughters had come, whom they might otherwise have introduced. They did not offer to share their acquaintance with any one else, but they made the most of it themselves, as if knowing a good thing when they had it. Their devotion to Mrs. Frobisher and her sister heightened the curiosity of such people as noticed it, but it would be wrong to say that it moved any in that self-limited company with a strong wish to know the ladies. The time comes to every man, no matter how great a power he may be in society, when the general social opinion retires him for senility, and this time had come for Bromfield Corey. He could no longer make or mar any success; and Charles Bellingham was so notoriously amiable, so deeply compromised by his inveterate habit of liking nearly every one, that his notice could not distinguish or advantage a newcomer.

He and Corey took the ladies down to supper. Mrs. Brinkley saw them there together, and a little later she saw old Corey wander off, forgetful of Miss Wrayne. She saw Dan Mavering, but not the Pasmers, and then, when Corey forgot Miss Wrayne, she saw Dan, forlorn and bewildered-looking, approach the girl, and offer her his arm for the return to the drawing-room; she took it with a bright, cold smile, making white rings of ironical depreciation around the pupils of her eyes.

"What is that poor boy doing, I wonder?" said Mrs. Brinkley to herself.

XXXVII

THE NEXT MORNING Dan Mavering knocked at Boardman's door before the reporter was up. This might have
been any time before one o'clock, but it was really at half past
nine. Boardman wanted to know who was there, and when
Mavering had said it was he, Boardman seemed to ponder the
fact awhile before Mavering heard him getting out of bed and
coming barefooted to the door. He unlocked it, and got back
into bed; then he called out, "Come in," and Mavering
pushed the door open impatiently. But he stood blank and
silent, looking helplessly at his friend. A strong glare of
winter light came in through the naked sash—for Boardman
apparently not only did not close his window-blinds, but did
not pull down his curtains, when he went to bed—and shone
upon his gay, shrewd face where he lay, showing his pop-corn
teeth in a smile at Mavering.

"Prefer to stand?" he asked, by-and-by, after Mavering had
remained standing in silence, with no signs of proposing to
sit down or speak. Mavering glanced at the only chair in the
room: Boardman's clothes dripped and dangled over it.
"Throw 'em on the bed," he said, following Mavering's
glance.

"I'll take the bed myself," said Mavering; and he sat down
on the side of it, and was again suggestively silent.

Boardman moved his head on the pillow, as he watched
Mavering's face, with the agreeable sense of personal security
which we all feel in viewing trouble from the outside. "You
seem balled up about something."

Mavering sighed heavily. "Balled up? It's no word for it.
Boardman, I'm done for. Yesterday I was the happiest fellow
in the world, and now— Yes, it's all over with me, and it's
my own fault, as usual. *Look* at that!" He jerked Boardman a
note which he had been holding fast in his hand, and got
up and went to look himself at the wide range of chimney-
pots and slated roofs which Boardman's dormer-window
commanded.

"Want me to read it?" Boardman asked; and Mavering nodded without glancing round. It dispersed through the air of

Boardman's room, as he unfolded it, a thin, elect perfume, like a feminine presence, refined and strict; and Boardman involuntarily passed his hand over his rumpled hair, as if to make himself a little more personable before reading the letter.

"DEAR MR. MAVERING,—I enclose the ring you gave me the other day, and I release you from the promise you gave with it. I am convinced that you wronged yourself in offering either without your whole heart, and I care too much for your happiness to let you persist in your sacrifice.

"In begging that you will not uselessly attempt to see me, but that you will consider this note final, I know you will do me the justice not to attribute an ungenerous motive to me. I shall rejoice to hear of any good that may befall you, and I shall try not to envy any one through whom it comes.

"Yours sincerely,   ALICE PASMER.

"P.S.—I say nothing of circumstances or of persons; I feel that any comment of mine upon them would be idle."

Mavering looked up at the sound Boardman made in refolding the letter. Boardman grinned, with sparkling eyes. "Pretty neat," he said.

"Pretty infernally neat," roared Mavering.

"Do you suppose she means business?"

"Of course she means business. Why shouldn't she?"

"I don't know. Why should she?"

"Why, I'll tell you, Boardman. I suppose I shall have to tell you if I'm going to get any good out of you; but it's a dose." He came away from the window, and swept Boardman's clothes off the chair preparatory to taking it.

Boardman lifted his head nervously from the pillow.

"Oh, I'll put them on the bed, if you're so punctilious!" cried Mavering.

"I don't mind the clothes," said Boardman. "I thought I heard my watch knock on the floor in my vest pocket. Just take it out, will you, and see if you've stopped it?"

"Oh, confound your old Waterbury! All the world's stopped; why shouldn't your watch stop too?" Mavering tugged it out of the pocket, and then shoved it back disdainfully. "You couldn't stop that thing with anything short of a sledge-hammer; it's rattling away like a mowing-machine.

You know those Portland women—those ladies I spent the day with when you were down there at the regatta—the day I came from Campobello—Mrs. Frobisher and her sister?" He agglutinated one query to another till he saw a light of intelligence dawn in Boardman's eye. "Well, they're at the bottom of it, I suppose. I was introduced to them on Class Day, and I ought to have shown them some attention there; but the moment I saw Alice—Miss Pasmer—I forgot all about 'em. But they didn't seem to have noticed it much, and I made it all right with 'em that day at Portland; and they came up in the fall, and I made an appointment with them to drive out to Cambridge and show them the place. They were to take me up at the Art Museum; but that was the day I met Miss Pasmer, and I—I forgot about those women again."

Boardman was one of those who seldom laugh; but his grin expressed all the malicious enjoyment he felt. He said nothing in the impressive silence which Mavering let follow at this point.

"Oh, you think it was funny?" cried Mavering. "I thought it was funny too; but Alice herself opened my eyes to what I'd done, and I always intended to make it all right with them when I got the chance. I supposed she wished me to."

Boardman grinned afresh.

"She told me I must; though she seemed to dislike my having been with them the day after she'd thrown me over. But if"—Mavering interrupted himself to say, as the grin widened on Boardman's face—"if you think it was any case of vulgar jealousy, you're very much mistaken, Boardman. She isn't capable of it, and she was so magnanimous about it that I made up my mind to do all I could to retrieve myself. I felt that it was my duty to *her*. Well, last night at Mrs. Jim Bellingham's reception—"

A look of professional interest replaced the derision in Boardman's eyes. "Any particular occasion for the reception? Given in honor of anybody?"

"I'll contribute to your society notes some other time, Boardman," said Mavering, haughtily. "I'm speaking to a friend, not an interviewer. Well, whom should I see after the first waltz—I'd been dancing with Alice, and we were taking a turn through the drawing-room, and she hanging on my arm, and I knew everybody saw how it was, and I was feeling well—whom should I see but these women. They were in a corner by themselves, looking at a picture, and trying to look as if they were doing it voluntarily. But I could see at a glance that they didn't know anybody; and I knew they had better be in the heart of the Sahara without acquaintances than where they were; and when they bowed forlornly across the room to me, my heart was in my mouth, I felt so sorry for them; and I told Alice who they were; and I supposed she'd want to rush right over to them with me—"

"And did she rush?" asked Boardman, filling up a pause which Mavering made in wiping his face.

"How infernally hot you have it in here!" He went to the window and threw it up, and then did not sit down again, but continued to walk back and forth as he talked. "She didn't seem to know who they were at first, and when I made her understand she hung back, and said, 'Those *showy* things?' and I must say I think she was wrong; they were dressed as quietly as nine-tenths of the people there; only they *are* rather large, handsome women. I said I thought we ought to go and speak to them, they seemed stranded there; but she didn't seem to see it; and when I persisted, she said, 'Well, you go if you think best; but take me to mamma.' And I supposed it was all right; and I told Mrs. Pasmer I'd be back in a minute, and then I went off to those women. And after I'd talked with them awhile I saw Mrs. Brinkley sitting with old Bromfield Corey in another corner, and I got them across and introduced them, after I'd explained to Mrs. Brinkley who they were; and they began to have a good time, and I—didn't."

"Just so," said Boardman.

"I thought I hadn't been gone any while at all from Alice; but the weather had changed by the time I had got back. Alice was pretty serious, and she was engaged two or three dances deep; and I could see her looking over the fellows' shoulders, as she went round and round, pretty pale. I hung about till she was free; but then she couldn't dance with me; she said her head ached, and she made her mother take her home before supper; and I mooned round like my own ghost awhile, and then *I* went home. And as if that wasn't enough, I could see by the looks of those other women—old Corey forgot Miss Wrayne in the supper-room, and I had to take her back—that I hadn't made it right with *them*, even; they were as hard and smooth as glass. I'd ruined myself, and ruined myself for nothing."

Mavering flung Boardman's chair over, and seated himself on its rungs.

"I went to bed, and waited for the next thing to happen. I found my thunder-bolt waiting for me when I woke up. I didn't know what it was going to be, but when I felt a ring through the envelop of that note I knew what it *was*. I mind-read that note before I opened it."

"Give it to the Society for Psychical Research," suggested Boardman. "Been to breakfast?"

"Breakfast!" echoed Mavering. "Well, now, Boardman, what use do you suppose I've got for breakfast under the circumstances?"

"Well, not very much; but your story's made me pretty hungry. Would you mind turning your back, or going out and sitting on the top step of the stairs landing, or something, while I get up and dress?"

"Oh, I can go, if you want to get rid of me," said Mavering, with unresentful sadness. "But I hoped you might have something to suggest, Boardy."

"Well, I've suggested two things, and you don't like either. Why not go round and ask to see the old lady?"

"Mrs. Pasmer?"

"Yes."

"Well, I thought of that. But I didn't like to mention it, for fear you'd sit on it. When would you go?"

"Well, about as quick as I could get there. It's early for a call, but it's a peculiar occasion, and it'll show your interest in the thing. You can't very well let it cool on your hands, unless you mean to accept the situation."

"What do you mean?" demanded Mavering, getting up and standing over Boardman. "Do you think I could accept the situation, as you call it, and live?"

"You did once," said Boardman. "You couldn't, unless you could fix it up with Mrs. Frobisher's sister."

Mavering blushed. "It was a different thing altogether then. I could have broken off then, but I tell you it would kill me now. I've got in too deep. My whole life's set on that girl. You can't understand, Boardman, because you've never been there; but I *couldn't* give her up."

"All right. Better go and see the old lady without loss of time; or the old man, if you prefer."

Mavering sat down on the edge of the bed again. "Look here, Boardman, what do you mean?"

"By what?"

"By being so confoundedly heartless. Did you suppose that I wanted to pay those women any attention last night from an interested motive?"

"Seems to have been Miss Pasmer's impression."

"Well, you're mistaken. She had no such impression. She would have too much self-respect, too much pride, magnanimity. She would know that after such a girl as she is I couldn't think of any other woman; the thing is simply impossible."

"That's the theory."

"Theory? It's the *practice!*"

"Certain exceptions."

"There's no exception in my case. No, sir! I tell you this thing is for all time — for eternity. It makes me or it mars me, once for all. She may listen to me or she may not listen, but as long as she lives there's no other woman alive for me."

"Better go and tell her so. You're wasting your arguments on me."

"Why?"

"Because I'm convinced already. Because people always marry their first and only loves. Because people never marry twice for love. Because I've never seen you hit before, and I know you never could be again. Now go and convince Miss Pasmer. She'll believe you, because she'll know that she can never care for any one but you, and you naturally can't care for anybody but her. It's a perfectly clear case. All you've got to do is to set it before her."

"If I were you, I wouldn't try to work that cynical racket, Boardman," said Mavering. He rose, but he sighed drearily, and regarded Boardman's grin with lack-lustre absence. But he went away without saying anything more, and walked mechanically toward the Cavendish. As he rang at the door of

Mrs. Pasmer's apartments he recalled another early visit he had paid there; he thought how joyful and exuberant he was then, and how crushed and desperate now. He was not without youthful satisfaction in the disparity of his different moods; it seemed to stamp him as a man of large and varied experience.

XXXVIII

M RS. PASMER was genuinely surprised to see Mavering, and he pursued his advantage—if it was an advantage—by coming directly to the point. He took it for granted that she knew all about the matter, and he threw himself upon her mercy without delay.

"Mrs. Pasmer, you must help me about this business with Alice," he broke out at once. "I don't know what to make of it; but I know I can explain it. Of course," he added, smiling ruefully, "the two statements don't hang together; but what I mean is that if I can find out what the trouble is, I can make it all right, because there's nothing wrong about it; don't you see?"

Mrs. Pasmer tried to keep the mystification out of her eye; but she could not even succeed in seeming to do so, which she would have liked almost as well.

"Don't you know what I mean?" asked Dan.

Mrs. Pasmer chanced it. "That Alice was a—little out of sorts last night?" she queried, leadingly.

"Yes," said Mavering, fervently. "And about her—her writing to me."

"Writing to you?" Mrs. Pasmer was going to ask, when Dan gave her the letter.

"I don't know whether I ought to show it, but I must. I must have your help, and I can't, unless you understand the case."

Mrs. Pasmer had begun to read the note. It explained what the girl herself had refused to give any satisfactory reason for—her early retirement from the reception, her mysterious disappearance into her own room on reaching home, and her resolute silence on the way. Mrs. Pasmer had known that there must be some trouble with Dan, and she had suspected that Alice was vexed with him on account of those women; but it was beyond her cheerful imagination that she should go to such lengths in her resentment. She could conceive of her wishing to punish him, to retaliate her suffering on him; but to renounce him for it was another thing; and she did not attribute to her daughter any other motive than she would

536

have felt herself. It was always this way with Mrs. Pasmer: she followed her daughter accurately up to a certain point; beyond that she did not believe the girl knew herself what she meant; and perhaps she was not altogether wrong. Girlhood is often a turmoil of wild impulses, ignorant exaltations, mistaken ideals, which really represent no intelligent purpose, and come from disordered nerves, ill-advised reading, and the erroneous perspective of inexperience. Mrs. Pasmer felt this, and she was tempted to break into a laugh over Alice's heroics; but she preferred to keep a serious countenance, partly because she did not feel the least seriously. She was instantly resolved not to let this letter accomplish anything more than Dan's temporary abasement, and she would have preferred to shorten this to the briefest moment possible. She liked him, and she was convinced that Alice could never do better, if half so well. She would now have preferred to treat him with familiar confidence, to tell him that she had no idea of Alice's writing him that nonsensical letter, and he was not to pay the least attention to it, for of course it meant nothing; but another principle of her complex nature came into play, and she silently folded the note and returned it to Dan, trembling before her.

"Well?" he quavered.

"Well," returned Mrs. Pasmer, judicially, while she enjoyed his tremor, whose needlessness inwardly amused her—"well, of course, Alice was—"

"Annoyed, I know. And it was all my fault—or my misfortune. But I assure you, Mrs. Pasmer, that I thought I was doing something that would please her—in the highest and noblest way. Now don't you know I did?"

Mrs. Pasmer again wished to laugh, but in the face of Dan's tragedy she had to forbear. She contented herself with saying: "Of course. But perhaps it wasn't the best time for pleasing her just in that *way*."

"It was then or never. I can see now—why, I could see all the time—just how it might look; but I supposed Alice wouldn't care for that, and if I hadn't tried to make some reparation then to Mrs. Frobisher and her sister, I never could. Don't you see?"

"Yes, certainly. But—"

"And Alice herself told me to go and look after them," interposed Mavering. He suppressed, a little uncandidly, the fact of her first reluctance.

"But you know it was the first time you had been out together?"

"Yes."

"And naturally she would wish to have you a good deal to herself, or at least not seeming to run after other people."

"Yes, yes; I know that."

"And no one ever likes to be taken at their word in a thing like that."

"I ought to have thought of that, but I didn't. I wish I had gone to you first, Mrs. Pasmer. Somehow it seems to me as if I were very young and inexperienced; I didn't use to feel so. I wish you were always on hand to advise me, Mrs. Pasmer." Dan hung his head, and his face, usually so gay, was blotted with gloom.

"Will you take my advice now?" asked Mrs. Pasmer.

"Indeed I will!" cried the young fellow, lifting his head. "What is it?"

"See Alice about this."

Dan jumped to his feet, and the sunshine broke out over his face again. "Mrs. Pasmer, I promised to take your advice, and I'll *do* it. I *will* see her. But how? Where? Let me have your advice on that point too."

They began to laugh together, and Dan was at once inexpressibly happy. Those two light natures thoroughly comprehended each other.

Mrs. Pasmer had proposed his seeing Alice with due seriousness, but now she had a longing to let herself go; she felt all the pleasure that other people felt in doing Dan Mavering a pleasure, and something more, because he was so perfectly intelligible to her. She let herself go.

"You might stay to breakfast."

"Mrs. Pasmer, I *will*—I will do that *too*. I'm awfully hungry, and I put myself in your hands."

"Let me see," said Mrs. Pasmer, thoughtfully, "how it can be contrived."

"Yes," said Mavering, ready for a panic. "How? She wouldn't stand a surprise?"

"No; I had thought of that."

"No behind-a-screen or next-room business?"

"No," said Mrs. Pasmer, with a light sigh. "Alice is peculiar. I'm afraid she wouldn't like it."

"Isn't there any little ruse she *would* like?"

"I can't think of any. Perhaps I'd better go and tell her you're here and wish to see her."

"Do you think you'd better?" asked Dan, doubtfully. "Perhaps she won't come."

"She will come," said Mrs. Pasmer, confidently. She did not say that she thought Alice would be curious to know why he had come, and that she was too just to condemn him unheard.

But she was right about the main point. Alice came, and Dan could see with his own weary eyes that she had not slept either.

She stopped just inside the portière, and waited for him to speak. But he could not, though a smile from his sense of the absurdity of their seriousness hovered about his lips. His first impulse was to rush upon her and catch her in his arms, and perhaps this might have been well, but the moment for it passed, and then it became impossible.

"Well?" she said at last, lifting her head, and looking at him with impassioned solemnity. "You wished to see me? I hoped you wouldn't. It would have spared me something. But perhaps I had no right to your forbearance."

"Alice, how can you say such things to me?" asked the young fellow, deeply hurt.

She responded to his tone. "I'm sorry if it wounds you. But I only mean what I say."

"You've a right to my forbearance, and not only that, but to my—my life; to everything that I am," cried Dan, in a quiver of tenderness at the sight of her and the sound of her voice. "Alice, why did you write me that letter? why did you send me back my ring?"

"Because," she said, looking him seriously in the face—"because I wished you to be free, to be happy."

"Well, you've gone the wrong way about it. I can never be free from you; I never can be happy without you."

"I did it for your good, then, which ought to be above

your happiness. Don't think I acted hastily. I thought it over all night long. I didn't sleep—"

"Neither did I," interposed Dan.

"And I saw that I had no claim to you; that you never could be truly happy with me—"

"I'll take the chances," he interrupted. "Alice, you don't suppose I cared for those women any more than the ground under your feet, do you? I don't suppose I should ever have given them a second thought if you hadn't seemed to feel so badly about my neglecting them; and I thought you'd be pleased to have me try to make it up to them if I could."

"I know your motive was good—the noblest. Don't think that I did you injustice, or that I was vexed because you went away with them."

"You sent me."

"Yes; and now I give you up to them altogether. It was a mistake, a crime, for me to think we could be anything to each other when our love began with a wrong to some one else."

"With a wrong to some one else?"

"You neglected them on Class Day after you saw me."

"Why, of course I did. How could I help it?"

A flush of pleasure came into the girl's pale face; but she banished it, and continued, gravely, "Then at Portland you were with them all day."

"You'd given me up—you'd thrown me over, Alice," he pleaded.

"I know that; I don't blame you. But you made them believe that you were very much interested in them."

"I don't know what I did. I was perfectly desperate."

"Yes; it was my fault. And then when they came to meet you at the Museum, I had made you forget them; I'd made you wound them and insult them again. No. I've thought it all out, and we never could be happy. Don't think that I do it from any resentful motive."

"Alice! how could I think that? Of *you*!"

"I have tried—prayed—to be purified from that, and I believe that I have been."

"You never had a selfish thought."

"And I have come to see that you were perfectly right in what you did last night. At first I was wounded."

"Oh, did I *wound* you, Alice?" he grieved.

"But afterward I could see that you belonged to them, and not me, and—and I give you up to them. Yes, freely, fully."

Alice stood there, beautiful, pathetic, austere, and Dan had halted in the spot to which he had advanced, when her eye forbade him to approach nearer. He did not mean to joke, and it was in despair that he cried out: "But *which*, Alice? There are *two* of them."

"Two?" she repeated, vaguely.

"Yes; Mrs. Frobisher and Miss Wrayne. You can't give me up to both of them."

"Both?" she repeated again. She could not condescend to specify; it would be ridiculous, and as it was, she felt her dignity hopelessly shaken. The tears came into her eyes.

"Yes. And neither of them wants me—they haven't got any use for me. Mrs. Frobisher is married already, and Miss Wrayne took the trouble last night to let me feel that, so far as she was concerned, I hadn't made it all right, and couldn't. I thought I had rather a cold parting with you, Alice, but it was quite tropical to what you left me to." A faint smile, mingled with a blush of relenting, stole into her face, and he hurried on. "I don't suppose I tried very hard to thaw her out. I wasn't much interested. If you must give me up, you must give me up to some one else, for they don't want me, and I don't want them." Alice's head drooped lower, and he could come nearer now without her seeming to know it. "But why need you give me up? There's really no occasion for it, I assure you."

"I wished," she explained, "to show you that I loved you for something above yourself and myself—far above either—"

She stopped, and dropped the hand which she had raised to fend him off; and he profited by the little pause she made to take her in his arms without seeming to do so. "Well," he said, "I don't believe I was formed to be loved on a very high plane. But I'm not too proud to be loved for my own sake; and I don't think there's anything above you, Alice."

"Oh yes, there is! I don't deserve to be happy, and that's the reason why I'm not allowed to be happy in any noble way. I can't bear to give you up; you know I can't; but you ought to give me up—indeed you ought. I have ideals, but I can't live up to them. You ought to go. You ought to leave me." She accented each little sentence by vividly pressing herself to his heart, and he had the wisdom or the instinct to treat their reconciliation as nothing settled, but merely provisional in its nature.

"Well, we'll see about that. I don't want to go till after breakfast, anyway; your mother says I may stay, and I'm awfully hungry. If I see anything particularly base in you, perhaps I sha'n't come back to lunch."

Dan would have liked to turn it all off into a joke, now that the worst was apparently over; but Alice freed herself from him, and held him off with her hand set against his breast. "Does mamma know about it?" she demanded, sternly.

"Well, she knows there's been some misunderstanding," said Dan, with a laugh that was anxious, in view of the clouds possibly gathering again.

"How much?"

"Well, I can't say exactly." He would not say that he did not know, but he felt that he could truly say that he could not say.

She dropped her hand, and consented to be deceived. Dan caught her again to his breast; but he had an odd, vague sense of doing it carefully, of using a little of the caution with which one seizes the stem of a rose between the thorns.

"I can bear to be ridiculous with *you*," she whispered, with an implication which he understood.

"You haven't been ridiculous, dearest," he said; and his tension gave way in a convulsive laugh, which partially expressed his feeling of restored security, and partly his amusement in realizing how the situation would have pleased Mrs. Pasmer if she could have known it.

Mrs. Pasmer was seated behind her coffee biggin at the breakfast table when he came into the room with Alice, and she lifted an eye from its glass bulb long enough to catch his flying glance of exultation and admonition. Then, while she regarded the chemical struggle in the bulb, with the rapt eye of a magician reading fate in his crystal ball, she questioned herself how much she should know, and how much she should ignore. It was a great moment for Mrs. Pasmer, full of delicious choice. "Do you understand this process, Mr. Mavering?" she said, glancing up at him warily for further instruction.

"I've seen it done," said Dan, "but I never knew how it was managed. I always thought it was going to blow up; but it seemed to me that if you were good and true and very meek, and had a conscience void of offence, it wouldn't."

"Yes, that's what it seems to depend upon," said Mrs. Pasmer, keeping her eye on the bulb. She dodged suddenly forward and put out the spirit-lamp. "Now have your coffee!" she cried, with a great air of relief. "You must need it by this time," she said, with a little low cynical laugh—"both of you!"

"Did you always make coffee with a biggin in France, Mrs. Pasmer?" asked Dan; and he laughed out the last burden that lurked in his heart.

Mrs. Pasmer joined him. "No, Mr. Mavering. In France you don't need a biggin. I set mine up when we went to England."

Alice looked darkly from one of these light spirits to the other, and then they all shrieked together.

They went on talking volubly from that, and they talked as far away from what they were thinking about as possible. They talked of Europe, and Mrs. Pasmer said where they would live and what they would do when they all got back there together. Dan abetted her, and said that they must cross in June. Mrs. Pasmer said that she thought June was a good month. He asked if it were not the month of the marriages too, and she answered that he must ask Alice about that. Alice blushed and laughed her sweet reluctant laugh, and said she did not know; she had never been married.

It was silly, but it was delicious; it made them really one family. Deep in his consciousness a compunction pierced and teased Dan. But he said to himself that it was all a joke about their European plans, or else his people would consent to it if he really wished it.

XXXIX

A PERIOD of entire harmony and tenderness followed the episode which seemed to threaten the lovers with the loss of each other. Mavering forbore to make Alice feel that in attempting a sacrifice which consulted only his good and ignored his happiness, and then failing in it so promptly, she had played rather a silly part. After one or two tentative jokes in that direction he found the ground unsafe, and with the instinct which served him in place of more premeditated piety he withdrew, and was able to treat the affair with something like religious awe. He was obliged, in fact, to steady Alice's own faith in it, and to keep her from falling under dangerous self-condemnation in that and other excesses of un-instructed self-devotion. This brought no fatigue to his robust affection, whatever it might have done to a heart more tried in such exercises. Love acquaints youth with many things in character and temperament which are none the less interesting because it never explains them; and Dan was of such a make that its revelations of Alice were charming to him because they were novel. He had thought her a person of such serene and flawless wisdom that it was rather a relief to find her subject to gusts of imprudence, to unexpected passions and resentments, to foibles and errors, like other people. Her power of cold reticence, which she could employ at will, was something that fascinated him almost as much as that habit of impulsive concession which seemed to come neither from her will nor her reason. He was a person himself who was so eager to give other people pleasure that he quivered with impatience to see them happy through his words or acts; he could not bear to think that any one to whom he was speaking was not perfectly comfortable in regard to him; and it was for this reason perhaps that he admired a girl who could prescribe herself a line of social conduct, and follow it out regardless of individual pangs, who could act from ideals and principles, and not from emotions and sympathies. He knew that she had the emotions and sympathies, for there were times when she lavished them on him; and that she could seem without them was another proof of that depth of nature which he liked to imagine had first attracted him to her. Dan Mavering had never been able to snub any one in his life; it gave him a great respect for Alice that it seemed not to cost her an effort or a regret, and it charmed him to think that her severity was part of the unconscious sham which imposed her upon the world for a person of inflexible design and invariable constancy to it. He was not long in seeing that she shared this illusion, if it was an illusion, and that perhaps the only person besides himself who was in the joke was her mother. Mrs. Pasmer and he grew more and more into each other's confidence in talking Alice over, and he admired the intrepidity of this lady, who was not afraid of her daughter even in the girl's most topping moments of self-abasement. For his own part, these moods of hers never failed to cause him confusion and anxiety. They commonly intimated themselves parenthetically in the midst of some blissful talk they were having, and overcast his clear sky with retrospective ideals of conduct or presentimental plans for contingencies that might never occur. He found himself suddenly under condemnation for not having reproved her at a given time when she forced him to admit she had seemed unkind or cold to others; she made him promise that even at the risk of alienating her affections he would make up for her deficiencies of behavior in such matters whenever he noticed them. She now praised him for what he had done for Mrs. Frobisher and her sister at Mrs. Bellingham's reception; she said it was generous, heroic. But Mavering rested satisfied with his achievement in that instance, and did not attempt anything else of the kind. He did not reason from cause to effect in regard to it: a man's love is such that while it lasts he cannot project its object far enough from him to judge it reasonable or unreasonable; but Dan's instincts had been disciplined and his perceptions sharpened by that experience. Besides, in bidding him take this impartial and even admonitory course toward her, she stipulated that they should maintain to the world a perfect harmony of conduct which should be an outward image of the union of their lives. She said that anything less than a continued self-sacrifice of one to the other was not worthy of the name of love, and that she should not be happy unless he required this of her. She said that they ought each to find out what was the most distasteful thing which they could mutually require, and then do it; she asked him to try to think what she most hated, and let her do that for him; as for her, she only asked to ask nothing of him.

Mavering could not worship enough this nobility of soul in her, and he celebrated it to Boardman with the passionate need of imparting his rapture which a lover feels. Boardman acquiesced in silence, with a glance of reserved sarcasm, or contented himself with laconic satire of his friend's general condition, and avoided any comment that might specifically apply to the points Dan made. Alice allowed him to have this confidant, and did not demand of him a report of all he said to Boardman. A main fact of their love, she said, must be their utter faith in each other. She had her own confidante, and the disparity of years between her and Miss Cotton counted for nothing in the friendship which their exchange of trust and sympathy cemented. Miss Cotton, in the freshness of her sympathy and the ideality of her inexperience, was in fact younger than Alice, at whose feet, in the things of soul and character, she loved to sit. She never said to her what she believed: that a girl of her exemplary principles, a nature conscious of such noble ideals, so superior to other girls, who in her place would be given up to the happiness of the moment, and indifferent to the sense of duty to herself and to others, was sacrificed to a person of Mavering's gay, bright nature and trivial conception of life. She did not deny his sweetness; that was perhaps the one saving thing about him; and she confessed that he simply adored Alice; that counted for everything, and it was everything in his favor that he could appreciate such a girl. She hoped, she prayed, that Alice might never realize how little depth he had; that she might go through life and never suspect it. If she did so, then they might be happy together to the end, or at least Alice might never know she was unhappy.

Miss Cotton never said these things in so many words; it is doubtful if she ever said them in any form of words; with her sensitive anxiety not to do injustice to any one, she took Dan's part against those who viewed the engagement as she allowed it to appear only to her secret heart. She defended him the more eagerly because she felt that it was for Alice's sake, and that everything must be done to keep her from knowing how people looked at the affair, even to changing people's minds. She said to all who spoke to her of it that of course Alice was superior to him, but he was devoted to her, and he would grow into an equality with her. He was naturally very refined, she said, and if he was not a very serious person, he was amiable beyond anything. She alleged many little incidents of their acquaintance at Campobello in proof of her theory that he had an instinctive appreciation of Alice, and she was sure that no one could value her nobleness of character more than he. She had seen them a good deal together since their engagement, and it was beautiful to see his manner with her. They were opposites, but she counted a good deal upon that very difference in their temperaments to draw them to each other.

It was an easy matter to see Dan and Alice together. Their engagement came out in the usual way: it had been announced to a few of their nearest friends, and intelligence of it soon spread from their own set through society generally; it had been published in the Sunday papers while it was still in the tender condition of a rumor, and had been denied by some of their acquaintance and believed by all.

The Pasmer cousinship had been just in the performance of the duties of blood toward Alice since the return of her family from Europe, and now did what was proper in the circumstances. All who were connected with her called upon her and congratulated her; they knew Dan, the younger of them, much better than they knew her; and though he had shrunk from the nebulous bulk of social potentiality which every young man is to that much smaller nucleus to which definite betrothal reduces him, they could be perfectly sincere in calling him the sweetest fellow that ever was, and too lovely to live.

In such a matter Mr. Pasmer was naturally nothing; he could not be less than he was at other times, but he was not more; and it was Mrs. Pasmer who shared fully with her daughter the momentary interest which the engagement gave Alice with all her kindred. They believed, of course, that they recognized in it an effect of her skill in managing; they agreed to suppose that she had got Mavering for Alice, and to ignore the beauty and passion of youth as factors in the case. The closest of the kindred, with the romantic delicacy of Americans in such things, approached the question of Dan's position and prospects, and heard with satisfaction the good accounts which Mrs. Pasmer was able to give of his father's prosperity. There had always been more or less apprehension among them of a time when a family subscription would be necessary for Bob Pasmer, and in the relief which the new situation gave them some of them tried to remember having known Dan's father in college, but it finally came to their guessing that they must have heard John Munt speak of him.

Mrs. Pasmer had a supreme control in the affair. She believed with the rest—so deeply is this delusion seated—that she had made the match; but knowing herself to have used no dishonest magic in the process, she was able to enjoy it with a clean conscience. She grew fonder of Dan; they understood each other; she was his refuge from Alice's ideals, and helped him laugh off his perplexity with them. They were none the less sincere because they were not in the least frank with each other. She let Dan beat about the bush to his heart's content, and waited for him at the point which she knew he was coming to, with an unconsciousness which he knew was factitious; neither of them got tired of this, or failed freshly to admire the other's strategy.

XL

IT CANNOT be pretended that Alice was quite pleased with the way her friends took her engagement, or rather the way in which they spoke of Dan. It seemed to her that she alone, or she chiefly, ought to feel that sweetness and loveliness of which every one told her, as if she could not have known it. If he was sweet and lovely to every one, how was he different to her, except in degree? Ought he not to be different in kind? She put the case to Miss Cotton, whom it puzzled, while she assured Alice that he *was* different in kind to her, though he might not seem so; the very fact that he was different in degree proved that he was different in kind. This logic sufficed for the moment of its expression, but it did not prevent Alice from putting the case to Dan himself. At one of those little times when she sat beside him alone and rearranged his necktie, or played with his watch chain, or passed a critical hand over his cowlick, she asked him if he did not think they ought to have an ideal in their engagement. What ideal? he asked. He thought it was all solid ideal through and through. "Oh," she said, "be more and more to each other." He said he did not see how that could be; if there was anything more of him, she was welcome to it, but he rather thought she had it all. She explained that she meant being less to others; and he asked her to explain that.

"Well, when we're anywhere together, don't you think we ought to show how different we are to each other from what we are to any one else?"

Dan laughed. "I'm afraid we do, Alice. I always supposed one ought to hide that little preference as much as possible. You don't want me to be dangling after you every moment?"

"No-o-o. But not—dangle after others."

Dan sighed a little—a little impatiently. "Do I dangle after others?"

"Of course not. But show that we're thoroughly united in all our tastes and feelings, and—like and dislike the same persons."

"I don't think that will be difficult," said Dan.

She was silent a moment, and then she said, "You don't like to have me bring up such things?"

"Oh yes, I do. I wish to be and do just what you wish."

"But I can see, I can understand, that you would sooner pass the time without talking of them. You like to be perfectly happy, and not to have any cares when—when you're with me this way?"

"Well, yes, I suppose I do," said Dan, laughing again. "I suppose I rather do like to keep pleasure and duty apart. But there's nothing you can wish, Alice, that isn't a pleasure to me."

"I'm very different," said the girl. "I can't be at peace unless I know that I have a right to be so. But now, after this, I'm going to do your way. If it's your way, it'll be the right way—for me." She looked sublimely resolved, with a grand lift of the eyes, and Dan caught her to him in a rapture, breaking into laughter.

"Oh, don't! Mine's a bad way—the worst kind of a way," he cried.

"It makes everybody like you, and mine makes nobody like me."

"It makes *me* like you, and that's quite enough. I don't want other people to like you!"

"Yes, that's what I mean!" cried Alice; and now she flung herself on his neck, and the tears came. "Do you suppose it can be very pleasant to have everybody talking of you as if everybody loved you as much—as much as *I* do?" She clutched him tighter and sobbed.

"Oh, Alice! Alice! Alice! Nobody could ever be what you are to me!" He soothed and comforted her with endearing words and touches; but before he could have believed her half consoled she pulled away from him, and asked, with shining eyes, "Do you think Mr. Boardman is a good influence in your life?"

"Boardman!" cried Mavering, in astonishment. "Why, I thought you liked Boardman?"

"I do; and I respect him very much. But that isn't the question. Don't you think we ought to ask ourselves how others influence us?"

"Well, I don't see much of Boardy nowadays; but I like to

drop down and touch earth in Boardy once in a while—I'm in the air so much. Board has more common-sense, more solid chunk-wisdom, than anybody I know. He's kept me from making a fool of myself more times—"

"Wasn't he with you that day with—with those women in Portland?"

Dan winced a little, and then laughed. "No, he wasn't. That was the trouble. Boardman was off on the press boat. I thought I told you. But if you object to Boardman—"

"I don't. You mustn't think I object to people when I ask you about them. All that I wished was that you should think yourself what sort of influence he was. *I* think he's a very good influence."

"He's a splendid fellow, Boardman is, Alice!" cried Dan. "You ought to have seen how he fought his way through college on such a little money, and never skulked or felt mean. He wasn't appreciated for it; the men don't notice these things much; but he didn't *want* to have it noticed; always acted as if it was neither here nor there; and now I guess he sends out home whatever he has left after keeping soul and body together every week."

He spoke, perhaps, with too great an effect of relief. Alice listened, as it seemed, to his tone rather than his words, and said, absently:

"Yes, that's grand. But I don't want you to act as if you were afraid of me in such things."

"Afraid?" Dan echoed.

"I don't mean actually afraid, but as if you thought I couldn't be reasonable; as if you supposed I didn't expect you to make mistakes or to be imperfect."

"Yes, I know you're very reasonable, and you're more patient with me than I deserve; I know all that, and it's only my wish to come up to your standard, I suppose, that gives me that apprehensive appearance."

"That was what vexed me with you there at Campobello, when you—asked me—"

"Yes, I know."

"You ought to have understood me better. You ought to know now that I don't wish you to do anything on my account, but because it's something we owe to others."

"Oh, excuse me! I'd much rather do it for you," cried Dan; but Alice looked so grave, so hurt, that he hastened on: "How in the world does it concern others whether we are devoted or not, whether we're harmonious and two-souls-with-but-a-single-thought, and all that?" He could not help being light about it.

"*How?*" Alice repeated. "Won't it give them an idea of what—what—of how much—how truly—if we care for each other—how people *ought* to care? We don't do it for ourselves. That would be selfish and disgusting. We do it because it's something that we owe to the idea of being engaged—of having devoted our lives to each other, and would show—would teach—"

"Oh yes! I know what you mean," said Dan, and he gave way in a sputtering laugh. "But they wouldn't understand. They'd only think we were spoons on each other; and if they noticed that I cooled off toward people I'd liked, and warmed up toward those you liked, they'd say you made me."

"Should you care?" asked Alice, sublimely, withdrawing a little from his arm.

"Oh no! only on your account," he answered, checking his laugh.

"You needn't on my account," she returned. "If we sacrifice some little preferences to each other, isn't that right? I shall be glad to sacrifice all of mine to you. Isn't our—marriage to be full of such sacrifices? I expect to give up everything to you." She looked at him with a sad severity.

He began to laugh again. "Oh no, Alice! Don't do that! I couldn't stand it. I want some little chance at the renunciations myself."

She withdrew still further from his side, and said, with a cold anger, "It's that detestable Mrs. Brinkley."

"Mrs. Brinkley!" shouted Dan.

"Yes; with her pessimism. I have heard her talk. She influences you. Nothing is sacred to her. It was she who took up with those army women that night."

"Well, Alice, I must say you can give things as ugly names as the next one. I haven't seen Mrs. Brinkley the whole winter, except in your company. But she has more sense than all the other women I know."

"Oh, thank you!"

"You know I don't mean you," he pushed on. "And she isn't a pessimist. She's very kind-hearted, and that night she was very polite and good to those army women, as you call them, when you had refused to say a word or do anything for them."

"I knew it had been rankling in your mind all along," said the girl. "I expected it to come out sooner or later. And you talk about renunciation! You never forget nor forgive the slightest thing. But I don't *ask* your forgiveness."

"Alice!"

"No. You are as hard as iron. You have that pleasant outside manner that makes people think you're very gentle and yielding, but all the time you're like adamant. I would rather die than ask your forgiveness for anything, and you'd rather let me than give it."

"Well, then, I ask *your* forgiveness, Alice, and I'm sure you won't let me die without it."

They regarded each other a moment. Then the tenderness gushed up in their hearts, a passionate tide, and swept them into each other's arms.

"Oh, Dan," she cried, "how sweet you are! how good! how lovely! Oh, how wonderful it is! I wanted to hate you, but I couldn't. I couldn't do anything but love you. Yes, now I understand what love is, and how it can do everything, and last forever."

XLI

MAVERING CAME to lunch the next day, and had a word with Mrs. Pasmer before Alice came in. Mr. Pasmer usually lunched at the club.

"We don't see much of Mrs. Saintsbury nowadays," he suggested.

"No; it's a great way to Cambridge," said Mrs. Pasmer, stifling, in a little sigh of apparent regret for the separation, the curiosity she felt as to Dan's motive in mentioning Mrs. Saintsbury. She was very patient with him when he went on.

"Yes, it *is* a great way. And a strange thing about it is that when you're living here it's a good deal farther from Boston to Cambridge than it is from Cambridge to Boston."

"Yes," said Mrs. Pasmer; "every one notices that."

Dan sat absently silent for a time before he said, "Yes, I guess I must go out and see Mrs. Saintsbury."

"Yes, you ought. She's very fond of you. You and Alice ought both to go."

"Does Mrs. Saintsbury like me?" asked Dan. "Well, she's awfully nice. Don't you think she's awfully fond of formulating people?"

"Oh, everybody in Cambridge does that. They don't gossip; they merely accumulate materials for the formulation of character."

"And they 'get there just the same!'" cried Dan. "Mrs. Saintsbury used to think she had got *me* down pretty fine," he suggested.

"Yes?" said Mrs. Pasmer, with an indifference which they both knew she did not feel.

"Yes. She used to accuse me of preferring to tack, even in a fair wind."

He looked inquiringly at Mrs. Pasmer; and she said, "How ridiculous!"

"Yes, it was. Well, I suppose I *am* rather circuitous about some things."

"Oh, not at all!"

"And I suppose I'm rather a trial to Alice in that way."

554

He looked at Mrs. Pasmer again, and she said: "I don't believe you are, in the least. You can't tell what is trying to a girl."

"No," said Dan, pensively, "*I* can't." Mrs. Pasmer tried to render the interest in her face less vivid. "*I* can't tell where she's going to bring up. Talk about *tacking*!"

"Do you mean the abstract girl, or Alice?"

"Oh, the abstract girl," said Dan, and they laughed together. "You think Alice is very straightforward, don't you?"

"Very," said Mrs. Pasmer, looking down with a smile—"for a girl."

"Yes, that's what I mean. And don't you think the most circuitous kind of fellow would be pretty direct compared with the straightforwardest kind of girl?"

There was a rueful defeat and bewilderment in Dan's face that made Mrs. Pasmer laugh. "What has she been doing now?" she asked.

"Mrs. Pasmer," said Dan, "you and I are the only frank and open people I know. Well, she began to talk last night about influence—the influence of other people on us; and she killed off nearly all the people I like before I knew what she was up to, and she finished with Mrs. Brinkley. I'm glad she didn't happen to think of *you*, Mrs. Pasmer, or I shouldn't be associating with you at the present moment." This idea seemed to give Mrs. Pasmer inexpressible pleasure. Dan went on: "Do you quite see the connection between our being entirely devoted to each other and my dropping Mrs. Brinkley?"

"I don't know," said Mrs. Pasmer. "Alice doesn't like satirical people."

"Well, of course not. But Mrs. Brinkley is such an admirer of hers."

"I dare say she tells you so."

"Oh, but she *is*!"

"I don't deny it," said Mrs. Pasmer. "But if Alice feels something inimical—*antipatico*—in her atmosphere, it's no use talking."

"Oh no, it's no use talking, and I don't know that I want to *talk*." After a pause, Mavering asked, "Mrs. Pasmer, don't you think that where two people are going to be entirely devoted to each other, and self-sacrificing to each other, they ought to divide, and one do all the devotion, and the other all the self-sacrifice?"

Mrs. Pasmer was amused by the droll look in Dan's eyes. "I think they ought to be willing to share evenly," she said.

"Yes; that's what I say—share and share alike. I'm not selfish about those little things." He blew off a long sighing breath. "Mrs. Pasmer, don't you think we ought to have an ideal of conduct?"

Mrs. Pasmer abandoned herself to laughter. "Oh, Dan! Dan! You will be the death of me."

"We will die together, then, Mrs. Pasmer. Alice will kill *me*." He regarded her with a sad sympathy in his eye as she laughed and laughed with delicious intelligence of the case. The intelligence was perfect, from their point of view; but whether it fathomed the girl's whole intention or aspiration is another matter. Perhaps this was not very clear to herself. At any rate, Mavering did not go any more to see Mrs. Brinkley, whose house he had liked to drop into. Alice went several times, to show, she said, that she had no feeling in the matter; and Mrs. Brinkley, when she met Dan, forbore to embarrass him with questions or reproaches; she only praised Alice to him.

There were not many other influences that Alice cut him off from; she even exposed him to some influences that might have been thought deleterious. She made him go and call alone upon certain young ladies whom she specified, and she praised several others to him, though she did not praise them for the same things that he did. One of them was a girl to whom Alice had taken a great fancy, such as often buds into a romantic passion between women; she was very gentle and mild, and she had none of that strength of will which she admired in Alice. One night there was a sleighing party to a hotel in the suburbs, where they had dancing and then supper. After the supper they danced "Little Sally Waters" for a *finale*, instead of the Virginia Reel, and Alice would not go on the floor with Dan; she said she disliked that dance; but she told him to dance with Miss Langham. It became a gale of fun, and in the height of it Dan slipped and fell with his partner. They laughed it off, with the rest, but after awhile the girl began to cry; she had received a painful bruise. All the way home, while the others laughed and sang and chattered, Dan was troubled about this poor girl; his anxiety became a joke with the whole sleighful of people.

When he parted with Alice at her door, he said, "I'm afraid I hurt Miss Langham; I feel awfully about it."

"Yes; there's no doubt of that. Good-night!"

She left him to go off to his lodging, hot and tingling with indignation at her injustice. But kindlier thoughts came to him before he slept, and he fell asleep with a smile of tenderness for her on his lips. He could see how he was wrong to go out with any one else when Alice said she disliked the dance; he ought not to have taken advantage of her generosity in appointing him a partner; it was trying for her to see him make that ludicrous tumble, of course; and perhaps he had overdone the attentive sympathy on the way home. It flattered him that she could not help showing her jealousy; that is flattering, at first; and Dan was able to go and confess all but this to Alice. She received his submission magnanimously, and said that she was glad it had happened, because his saying this showed that now they understood each other perfectly. Then she fixed her eyes on his, and said, "I've just been round to see Lilly, and she's as well as ever; it was only a nervous shock."

Whether Mavering was really indifferent to Miss Langham's condition, or whether the education of his perceptions had gone so far that he consciously ignored her, he answered, "That was splendid of you, Alice."

"No," she said; "it's you that are splendid; and you always are. Oh, I wonder if I can ever be worthy of you!"

Their mutual forgiveness was very sweet to them, and they went on praising each other. Alice suddenly broke away from this weakening exchange of worship, and said, with that air of coming to business which he had learned to recognize and dread a little, "Dan, don't you think I ought to write to your mother?"

"Write to my mother? Why, you *have* written to her. You wrote as soon as you got back, and she answered you."

"Yes; but write regularly? Show that I think of her all the time? When I really think I'm going to take you from her, I seem so cruel and heartless!"

"Oh, *I* don't look at it in that light, Alice."

"Don't joke! And when I think that we're going away to leave her, for several years, perhaps, as soon as we're married, I can't make it seem right. I know how she depends upon your being near her, and seeing her every now and then; and to go off to Europe for years, perhaps— Of course you can be of use to your father there; but do you think it's right toward your mother? I want you to think."

Dan thought, but his thinking was mainly to the effect that he did not know what she was driving at. Had she got any inkling of that plan of his mother's for them to come and stay a year or two at the Falls after their marriage? He always expected to be able to reconcile that plan with the Pasmer plan of going at once; to his optimism the two were not really incompatible; but he did not wish them prematurely confronted in Alice's mind. Was this her way of letting him know that she knew what his mother wished, and that she was willing to make the sacrifice? Or was it just some vague longing to please him by a show of affection toward his family, an unmediated impulse of reparation? He had an impulse himself to be frank with Alice, to take her at her word, and to allow that he did not like the notion of going abroad. This was Dan's notion of being frank; he could still reserve the fact that he had given his mother a tacit promise to bring Alice home to live, but he postponed even this. He said: "Oh, I guess that'll be all right, Alice. At any rate, there's no need to think about it yet awhile. That can be arranged."

"Yes," said Alice; "but don't you think I'd better get into the habit of writing regularly to your mother now, so that there needn't be any break when we go abroad?" He could see now that she had no idea of giving that plan up, and he was glad that he had not said anything. "I think," she continued, "that I shall write to her once a week, and give her a full account of our life from day to day; it'll be more like a diary; and then, when we get over there, I can keep it up without any effort, and she won't feel so much that you've gone."

She seemed to refer the plan to him, and he said it was capital. In fact, he did like the notion of a diary; that sort of historical view would involve less danger of precipitating a discussion of the two schemes of life for the future. "It's awfully kind of you, Alice, to propose such a thing, and you mustn't make it a burden. Any sort of little sketchy record will do; mother can read between the lines, you know."

"It won't be a burden," said the girl, tenderly. "I shall seem to be doing it for your mother, but I know I shall be doing it for you. I do everything for you. Do you think it's right?"

"Oh, it must be," said Dan, laughing. "It's so pleasant."

"Oh," said the girl, gloomily; "that's what makes me doubt it."

XLII

Eunice Mavering acknowledged Alice's first letter. She said that her mother read it aloud to them all, and had been delighted with the good account she gave of Dan, and fascinated with all the story of their daily doings and sayings. She wished Eunice to tell Alice how fully she appreciated her thoughtfulness of a sick old woman, and that she was going to write herself and thank her. But Eunice added that Alice must not be surprised if her mother was not very prompt in this, and she sent messages from all the family, affectionate for Alice, and polite for her father and mother.

Alice showed Dan the letter, and he seemed to find nothing noticeable in it. "She says your mother will write later," Alice suggested.

"Yes. You ought to feel very much complimented by that. Mother's autographs are pretty uncommon," he said, smiling.

"Why, doesn't she write? Can't she? Does it tire her?" asked Alice.

"Oh yes, she can write, but she hates to. She gets Eunice or Minnie to write usually."

"Dan," cried Alice, intensely, "why didn't you tell me?"

"Why, I thought you knew it," he explained, easily. "She likes to read, and likes to talk, but it bores her to write. I don't suppose I get more than two or three pencil scratches from her in the course of a year. She makes the girls write. But you needn't mind her not writing. You may be sure she's glad of your letters."

"It makes me seem very presumptuous to be writing to her when there's no chance of her answering," Alice grieved. "It's as if I had passed over your sisters' heads. I ought to have written to them."

"Oh, well, you can do that now," said Dan, soothingly.

"No. No, I can't do it now. It would be ridiculous." She was silent, and presently she asked, "Is there anything else about your mother that I ought to know?" She looked at him with a sort of impending discipline in her eyes which he had learned to dread; it meant such a long course of things, such a very great variety of atonement and expiation for him, that he could not bring himself to confront it steadily.

His heart gave a feeble leap; he would have gladly told her all that was in it, and he meant to do so at the right time, but this did not seem the moment. "I can't say that there is," he answered, coldly.

In that need of consecrating her happiness which Alice felt she went a great deal to church in those days. Sometimes she felt the need almost of defence against her happiness, and a vague apprehension mixed with it. Could it be right to let it claim her whole being, as it seemed to do? That was the question which she once asked Dan, and it made him laugh, and catch her to him in a rapture that served for the time, and then left her to more morbid doubts. Evidently he could not follow her in them; he could not even imagine them; and while he was with her they seemed to have no verity or value. But she talked them over very hypothetically and impersonally with Miss Cotton, in whose sympathy they resumed all their import, and gained something more. In the idealization which the girl underwent in this atmosphere all her thoughts and purposes had a significance which she would not of herself, perhaps, have attached to them. They discussed them and analyzed them with a satisfaction in the result which could not be represented without an effect of caricature. They measured Alice's romance together, and evolved from it a sublimation of responsibility, of duty, of devotion, which Alice found it impossible to submit to Dan when he came with his simple-hearted, single-minded purpose of getting Mrs. Pasmer out of the room, and sitting down with his arm around Alice's waist. When he had accomplished this it seemed sufficient in itself, and she had to think, to struggle to recall things beyond it, above it. He could not be made to see at such times how their lives could be more in unison than they were. When she proposed doing something for him which he knew was disagreeable to her, he would not let her; and when she hinted at anything she wished him to do for her because she knew it was disagreeable to him, he consented so promptly, so joyously, that she perceived he could not have given the least thought to it.

She felt every day that they were alien in their tastes and

aims; their pleasures were not the same, and though it was sweet, though it was charming, to have him give up so willingly all his preferences, she felt, without knowing that the time must come when this could not be so, that it was all wrong.

"But these very differences, these antagonisms, if you wish to call them so," suggested Miss Cotton, in talking Alice's misgivings over with her, "aren't they just what will draw you together more and more? Isn't it what attracted you to each other? The very fact that you are such perfect counterparts—"

"Yes," the girl assented, "that's what we're taught to believe." She meant by the novels, to which we all trust our instruction in such matters, and her doubt doubly rankled after she had put it to silence.

She kept on writing to Dan's mother, though more and more perfunctorily; and now Eunice and now Minnie Mavering acknowledged her letters. She knew that they must think she was silly, but having entered by Dan's connivance upon her folly, she was too proud to abandon it.

At last, after she had ceased to expect it, came a letter from his mother, not a brief note, but a letter which the invalid had evidently tasked herself to make long and full, in recognition of Alice's kindness in writing to her so much. The girl opened it, and after a verifying glance at the signature, began to read it with a thrill of tender triumph, and the fond prevision of the greater pleasure of reading it again with Dan.

But after reading it once through, she did not wait for him before reading it again and again. She did this with bewilderment, intershot with flashes of conviction, and then doubts of this conviction. When she could misunderstand no longer, she rose quietly and folded the letter, and put it carefully back into its envelop and into her writing-desk, where she sat down and wrote, in her clearest and firmest hand, this note to Mavering:

"I wish to see you immediately.

"ALICE PASMER."

XLIII

DAN HAD LEARNED, with a lover's keenness, to read Alice's moods in the most colorless wording of her notes. She was rather apt to write him notes, taking back or reaffirming the effect of something that had just passed between them. Her notes were tempered to varying degrees of heat and cold, so fine that no one else would have felt the difference, but sensible to him in their subtlest intention.

Perhaps a mere witness of the fact would have been alarmed by a note which began without an address, except that on the envelop, and ended its peremptory brevity with the writer's name signed in full. Dan read calamity in it, and he had all the more trouble to pull himself together to meet it because he had parted with unusual tenderness from Alice the night before, after an evening in which it seemed to him that their ideals had been completely reconciled.

The note came, as her notes were apt to come, while Dan was at breakfast, which he was rather luxurious about for so young a man, and he felt formlessly glad afterward that he had drunk his first cup of coffee before he opened it, for it chilled the second cup, and seemed to take all character out of the omelet.

He obeyed it, wondering what the doom menaced in it might be, but knowing that it was doom, and leaving his breakfast half finished, with a dull sense of the tragedy of doing so.

He would have liked to ask for Mrs. Pasmer first, and interpose a moment of her cheerful unreality between himself and his interview with Alice, but he decided that he had better not do this, and they met at once, with the width of the room between them. Her look was one that made it impassable to the simple impulse he usually had to take her in his arms and kiss her. But as she stood holding out a letter to him, with the apparent intention that he should come and take it, he traversed the intervening space and took it.

"Why, it's from mother!" he said, joyously, with a glance at the handwriting.

"Will you please explain it?" said Alice, and Dan began to read it.

It began with a good many excuses for not having written before, and went on with a pretty expression of interest in Alice's letters and gratitude for them; Mrs. Mavering assured the girl that she could not imagine what a pleasure they had been to her. She promised herself that they should be great friends, and she said that she looked forward eagerly to the time, now drawing near, when Dan should bring her home to them. She said she knew Alice would find it dull at the Falls except for him, but they would all do their best, and she would find the place very different from what she had seen it in the winter. Alice could make believe that she was there just for the summer, and Mrs. Mavering hoped that before the summer was gone she would be so sorry for a sick old woman that she would not even wish to go with it. This part of the letter, which gave Dan away so hopelessly, as he felt, was phrased so touchingly that he looked up from it with moist eyes to the hard cold judgment in the eyes of Alice.

"Will you please explain it?" she repeated.

He tried to temporize. "Explain what?"

Alice was prompt to say, "Had you promised your mother to take me home to live?"

Dan did not answer.

"You promised *my* mother to go abroad. What else have you promised?" He continued silent, and she added, "You are a faithless man." They were the words of Romola, in the romance, to Tito; she had often admired them; and they seemed to her equally the measure of Dan's offence.

"Alice—"

"Here are your letters and remembrances, Mr. Mavering." Dan mechanically received the packet she had been holding behind her; with a perverse freak of intelligence he observed that though much larger now, it was tied up with the same ribbon which had fastened it when Alice returned his letters and gifts before. "Good-by. I wish you every happiness consistent with your nature."

She bowed coldly, and was about to leave him, as she had planned; but she had not arranged that he should be standing in front of the door, and he was there, with no apparent intention of moving.

"Will you allow me to pass?" she was forced to ask, however, haughtily.

"No!" he retorted, with a violence that surprised him. "I will not let you pass till you have listened to me—till you tell me why you treat me so. I won't stand it—I've had enough of this kind of thing."

It surprised Alice too a little, and after a moment's hesitation she said, "I will listen to you," so much more gently than she had spoken before that Dan relaxed his imperative tone, and began to laugh. "But," she added, and her face clouded again, "it will be of no use. My mind is made up *this* time. Why should we talk?"

"Why, because mine isn't," said Dan. "What is the matter, Alice? Do you think I would force you, or even ask you, to go home with me to live unless you were entirely willing? It could only be a temporary arrangement anyway."

"That isn't the question," she retorted. "The question is whether you've promised your mother one thing and me another."

"Well, I don't know about *promising*," said Dan, laughing a little more uneasily, but still laughing. "As nearly as I can remember, I wasn't consulted about the matter. *Your* mother proposed one thing, and *my* mother proposed another."

"And *you* agreed to *both*. That is quite enough—quite characteristic!"

Dan flushed, and stopped laughing. "I don't know what you mean by characteristic. The thing didn't have to be decided at once, and I didn't suppose it would be difficult for either side to give way, if it was judged best. I was sure my mother wouldn't insist."

"It seems very easy for your family to make sacrifices that are not likely to be required of them."

"You mustn't criticise my mother!" cried Dan.

"I have *not* criticised her. You insinuate that we would be too selfish to give up, if it were for the best."

"I do nothing of the kind, and unless you are determined to quarrel with me you wouldn't say so."

"I don't wish a quarrel; none is necessary," said Alice, coldly.

"You accuse me of being treacherous—"

"I didn't say treacherous!"

"Faithless, then. It's a mere quibble about words. I want you to take that back."

"I can't take it back; it's the truth. Aren't you faithless, if you let us go on thinking that you're going to Europe, and let your mother think that we're coming home to live after we're married?"

"No! I'm simply leaving the question open!"

"Yes," said the girl, sadly, "you *like* to leave questions open. That's your way."

"Well, I suppose I do till it's necessary to decide them. It saves the needless effusion of talk," said Dan, with a laugh; and then, as people do in a quarrel, he went back to his angry mood, and said: "Besides, I supposed you would be glad of the chance to make some sacrifice for me. You're always asking for it."

"Thank you, Mr. Mavering," said Alice, "for reminding me of it; nothing is sacred to you, it seems. I can't say that *you* have ever sought any opportunities of self-sacrifice."

"I wasn't allowed time to do so; they were always presented."

"Thank you again, Mr. Mavering. All this is quite a revelation. I'm glad to know how you really felt about things that you seemed so eager for."

"Alice, you know that I would do anything for you!" cried Dan, ruing his precipitate words.

"Yes; that's what you've repeatedly told me. I used to believe it."

"And I always believed what *you* said. You said at the picnic that day that you thought I would like to live at Ponkwasset Falls if my business was there—"

"That is not the point!"

"And now you quarrel with me because my mother wishes me to do so."

Alice merely said: "I don't know why I stand here allowing you to intimidate me in my father's house. I demand that you shall stand aside and let me pass."

"I'll not oblige you to leave the room," said Dan. "*I* will go. But if I go, you will understand that I don't come back."

"I hoped that," said the girl.

"Very well. Good-morning, Miss Pasmer."

She inclined her head slightly in acknowledgment of his bow, and he whirled out of the room and down the dim narrow passageway into the arms of Mrs. Pasmer, who had resisted as long as she could her curiosity to know what the angry voices of himself and Alice meant.

"Oh, Mr. Mavering, is it you?" she buzzed; and she flung aside one pretence for another in adding, "Couldn't Alice make you stay to breakfast?"

Dan felt a rush of tenderness in his heart at the sound of the kind, humbugging little voice. "No, thank you, Mrs. Pasmer, I couldn't stay, thank you. I—I thank you very much. I—good-by, Mrs. Pasmer." He wrung her hand, and found his way out of the apartment door, leaving her to clear up the mystery of his flight and his broken words as she could.

"Alice," she said, as she entered the room, where the girl had remained, "what have you been doing now?"

"Oh, nothing," she said, with a remnant of her scorn for Dan qualifying her tone and manner to her mother. "I've dismissed Mr. Mavering."

"Then you want him to come to lunch?" asked her mother. "I should advise him to refuse."

"I don't think he'd accept," said Alice. Then, as Mrs. Pasmer stood in the door, preventing her egress, as Dan had done before, she asked, meekly: "Will you let me pass, mamma? My head aches."

Mrs. Pasmer, whose easy triumphs in so many difficult circumstances kept her nearly always in good temper, let herself go, at these words, in vexation very uncommon with her. "Indeed I shall not!" she retorted. "And you will please sit down here and tell me what you mean by dismissing Mr. Mavering. I'm tired of your whims and caprices."

"I can't talk," began the girl, stubbornly.

"Yes, I think you can," said her mother. "At any rate, *I* can. Now what is it all?"

"Perhaps this letter will explain," said Alice, continuing to dignify her enforced submission with a tone of unabated hauteur; and she gave her mother Mrs. Mavering's letter, which Dan had mechanically restored to her.

Mrs. Pasmer read it, not only without indignation, but apparently without displeasure. But she understood perfectly what the trouble was, when she looked up and asked, cheerfully, "Well?"

"Well!" repeated Alice, with a frown of astonishment. "Don't you see that he's promised us one thing and her another, and that he's false to both?"

"I don't know," said Mrs. Pasmer, recovering her good-humor in view of a situation that she felt herself able to cope with. "Of course he has to temporize, to manage a little. She's an invalid, and of course she's very exacting. He has to humor her. How do you know he has promised her? He hasn't promised *us*."

"Hasn't *promised* us?" Alice gasped.

"No. He's simply fallen in with what we've said. It's because he's so sweet and yielding, and can't bear to refuse. I can understand it perfectly."

"Then if he hasn't promised us, he's deceived us all the more shamefully, for he's made us *think* he had."

"He hasn't *me*," said Mrs. Pasmer, smiling at the stormy virtue in her daughter's face. "And what if you *should* go home awhile with him—for the summer, say? It couldn't last longer, much; and it wouldn't hurt us to wait. I suppose he hoped for something of that kind."

"Oh, it isn't that," groaned the girl, in a kind of bewilderment. "I could have gone there with him joyfully, and lived all my days, if he'd only been frank with me."

"Oh no, you couldn't," said her mother, with cozy security. "When it comes to it, you don't like giving up any more than other people. It's very hard for you to give up; he sees that— he knows it, and he doesn't really like to ask any sort of sacrifice from you. He's afraid of you."

"Don't I know that?" demanded Alice, desolately. "I've known it from the first, and I've felt it all the time. It's all a mistake, and has been. We never could understand each other. We're too different."

"That needn't prevent your understanding him. It needn't

prevent you from seeing how really kind and good he is—how faithful and constant he is."

"Oh, you say that—you praise him—because you like him."

"Of course I do. And can't you?"

"No. The least grain of deceit—of temporizing, you call it—spoils everything. It's over," said the girl, rising, with a sigh, from the chair she had dropped into. "We're best apart; we could only have been wretched and wicked together."

"What did you say to him, Alice?" asked her mother, unshaken by her rhetoric.

"I told him he was a faithless person."

"Then you were a cruel girl," cried Mrs. Pasmer, with sudden indignation; "and if you were not my daughter I could be glad he had escaped you. I don't know where you got all those silly, romantic notions of yours about these things. You certainly didn't get them from me," she continued, with undeniable truth, "and I don't believe you get them from your Church. It's just as Miss Anderson said: your Church makes allowance for human nature, but you make none."

"I shouldn't go to Julie Anderson for instruction in such matters," said the girl, with cold resentment.

"I wish you would go to her for a little common-sense—or somebody," said Mrs. Pasmer. "Do you know what talk this will make?"

"I don't care for the talk. It would be worse than talk to marry a man whom I couldn't trust—who wanted to please me so much that he had to deceive me, and was too much afraid of me to tell me the truth."

"You headstrong girl!" said her mother, impartially admiring at the same time the girl's haughty beauty.

There was an argument in reserve in Mrs. Pasmer's mind which perhaps none but an American mother would have hesitated to urge; but it is so wholly our tradition to treat the important business of marriage as a romantic episode that even she could not bring herself to insist that her daughter should not throw away a chance so advantageous from every worldly point of view. She could only ask, "If you break this engagement, what do you expect to do?"

"The engagement is broken. I shall go into a sisterhood."

"You will do nothing of the kind, with my consent," said Mrs. Pasmer. "I will have no such nonsense. Don't flatter yourself that I will. Even if I approved of such a thing, I should think it wicked to let you do it. You're always fancying yourself doing something very devoted, but I've never seen you ready to give up your own will, or your own comfort even, in the slightest degree. And Dan Mavering, if he were twice as temporizing and—circuitous"—the word came to her from her talk with him—"would be twice too good for you. I'm going to breakfast."

XLIV

THE DIFFICULTY in life is to bring experience to the level of expectation, to match our real emotions in view of any great occasion with the ideal emotions which we have taught ourselves that we ought to feel. This is all the truer when the occasion is tragical: we surprise ourselves in a helplessness to which the great event, death, ruin, lost love, reveals itself slowly, and at first wears the aspect of an unbroken continuance of what has been, or at most of another incident in the habitual sequence.

Dan Mavering came out into the bright winter morning knowing that his engagement was broken, but feeling it so little that he could not believe it. He failed to realize it, to seize it for a fact, and he could not let it remain that dumb and formless wretchedness, without proportion or dimensions, which it now seemed to be, weighing his life down. To verify it, to begin to outlive it, he must instantly impart it, he must tell it, he must see it with others' eyes. This was the necessity of his youth and of his sympathy, which included himself as well as the rest of the race in its activity. He had the usual environment of a young man who has money. He belonged to clubs, and he had a large acquaintance among men of his own age, who lived a life of greater leisure, or were more absorbed in business, but whom he met constantly in society. For one reason or another, or for no other reason than that he was Dan Mavering and liked every one, he liked them all. He thought himself great friends with them; he dined and lunched with them; and they knew the Pasmers, and all about his engagement. But he did not go to any of them now with the need he felt to impart his calamity, to get the support of some other's credence and opinion of it. He went to a friend whom, in the way of his world, he met very seldom, but whom he always found, as he said, just where he had left him.

Boardman never made any sign of suspecting that he was put on and off, according to Dan's necessity or desire for comfort or congratulation; but it was part of their joke that Dan's coming to him always meant something decisive in his experiences. The reporter was at his late breakfast, which his landlady furnished him in his room, though, as Mrs. Nash said, she never gave meals, but a cup of coffee and an egg or two, yes.

"Well?" he said, without looking up.

"Well, I'm done for!" cried Dan.

"Again?" asked Boardman.

"Again! The other time was nothing, Boardman—I knew it wasn't anything; but this—this is final."

"Go on," said Boardman, looking about for his "individual" salt-cellar, which he found under the edge of his plate; and Mavering laid the whole case before him. As he made no comment on it for a while, Dan was obliged to ask him what he thought of it. "Well," he said, with the smile that showed the evenness of his pretty teeth, "there's a kind of wild justice in it." He admitted this, with the object of meeting Dan's views in an opinion.

"So *you* think I'm a faithless man *too*, do you?" demanded Mavering, stormily.

"Not from your point of view," said Boardman, who kept on quietly eating and drinking.

Mavering was too amiable not to feel Boardman's innocence of offence in his unperturbed behavior. "There was no faithlessness about it, and you know it," he went on, half laughing, half crying, in his excitement, and making Boardman the avenue of an appeal really addressed to Alice. "I was ready to do what either side decided."

"Or both," suggested Boardman.

"Yes, or both," said Dan, boldly accepting the suggestion. "It wouldn't have cost *me* a pang to give up if I'd been in the place of either."

"I guess that's what she could never understand," Boardman mused aloud.

"And I could never understand how any one could fail to see that that was what I intended—expected: that it would all come out right of itself—naturally." Dan was still addressing Alice in this belated reasoning. "But to be accused of bad faith—of trying to deceive any one—"

"Pretty rough," said Boardman.

"Rough? It's more than I can stand!"

"Well, you don't seem to be asked to stand it," said Boardman, and Mavering laughed forlornly with him at his joke, and then walked away and looked out of Boardman's dormer-window on the roofs below, with their dirty, smoke-stained February snow. He pulled out his handkerchief and wiped his face with it. When he turned round, Boardman looked keenly at him, and asked, with an air of caution, "And so it's all up?"

"Yes, it's all up," said Dan, hoarsely.

"No danger of a relapse?"

"What do you mean?"

"No danger of having my sympathy handed over later to Miss Pasmer for examination?"

"I guess you can speak up freely, Boardman," said Dan, "if that's what you mean. Miss Pasmer and I are quits."

"Well, then, I'm glad of it. She wasn't the one for you. She isn't fit for you."

"What's the reason she isn't?" cried Dan. "She's the most beautiful and noble girl in the world, and the most conscientious, and the best—if she *is* unjust to me."

"No doubt of that. I'm not attacking her, and I'm not defending you."

"What are you doing, then?"

"Simply saying that I don't believe you two would ever understand each other. You haven't got the same point of view, and you couldn't make it go. Both out of a scrape."

"I don't know what you mean by a scrape," said Dan, resenting the word more than the idea. Boardman tacitly refused to modify or withdraw it, and Dan said, after a sulky silence, in which he began to dramatize a meeting with his family: "I'm going home; I can't stand it here. What's the reason you can't come with me, Boardman?"

"Do you mean to your rooms?"

"No; to the Falls."

"Thanks. Guess not."

"*Why* not?"

"Don't care about being a fifth wheel."

"Oh, pshaw, now, Boardman! Look here, you *must* go. I want you to go. I—I want your support. That's it. I'm all broken up, and I couldn't stand that three hours' pull alone. They'll be glad to see you—all of them. Don't you suppose they'll be glad to see you? They're always glad; and they'll understand."

"I don't believe you want me to go yourself. You just think you do."

"No. I really do want you, Boardman. I want to talk it all over with you. I do want you. I'm not fooling."

"Don't think I could get away." Yet he seemed to be pleased with the notion of the Falls; it made him smile.

"Well, see," said Mavering, disconsolately. "I'm going round to my rooms now, and I'll be there till two o'clock; train's at 2.30." He went toward the door, where he faced about. "And you don't think it would be of any use?"

"Any use—what?" asked Boardman.

"Trying to—to—to make it up."

"How should I know?"

"No, no; of course you couldn't," said Dan, miserably downcast. All the resentment which Alice's injustice had roused in him had died out; he was suffering as helplessly and hopelessly as a child. "Well!" he sighed, as he swung out of the door.

Boardman found him seated at his writing-desk in his smoking jacket when he came to him, rather early, and on the desk were laid out the properties of the little play which had come to a tragic close. There were some small bits of jewelry, among the rest a ring of hers which Alice had been letting him wear; a lock of her hair, which he had kept, for the greater convenience of kissing, in the original parcel, tied with crimson ribbon; a succession of flowers which she had worn, more and more dry and brown with age; one of her gloves, which he had found and kept from the day they first met in Cambridge; a bunch of withered blueberries tied with sweet-grass, whose odor filled the room, from the picnic at Campobello; scraps of paper with her writing on them, and cards; several photographs of her, and piles of notes and letters.

"Look here," said Dan, knowing it was Boardman without turning round, "what am I to do about these things?"

Boardman respectfully examined them over his shoulder. "Don't know what the usual ceremony is," he said. He ventured to add, referring to the heaps of letters, "Seems to have been rather epistolary, doesn't she?"

"Oh, don't talk of her as if she were dead!" cried Dan. "I've been feeling as if she were." All at once he dropped his head among these witnesses of his loss, and sobbed.

Boardman appeared shocked, and yet somewhat amused; he made a soft, low sibilation between his teeth.

Dan lifted his head. "Boardman, if you ever give me away!"

"Oh, I don't suppose it's very hilarious," said Boardman, with vague kindness. "Packed yet?" he asked, getting away from the subject, as something he did not feel himself fitted to deal with consecutively.

"I'm only going to take a bag," said Mavering, going to get some clothes down from a closet where his words had a sepulchral reverberation.

"Can't I help?" asked Boardman, keeping away from the sad memorials of Dan's love strewn about on the desk, and yet not able to keep his eyes off them across the room.

"Well, I don't know," said Dan. He came out with his armful of coats and trousers, and threw them on the bed. "Are you going?"

"If I could believe you wanted me to."

"Good!" cried Mavering, and the fact seemed to brighten him immediately. "If you want to, stuff these things in, while I'm doing up these other things." He nodded his head sidewise toward the desk.

"All right," said Boardman.

His burst of grief must have relieved Dan greatly. He set about gathering up the relics on the desk, and getting a suitable piece of paper to wrap them in. He rejected several pieces as inappropriate. "I don't know what kind of paper to do these things up in," he said at last.

"Any special kind of paper required?" Boardman asked, pausing in the act of folding a pair of pantaloons so as not to break the fall over the boot.

"I didn't know there was, but there seems to be," said Dan.

"Silver paper seems to be rather more for cake and that sort of thing," suggested Boardman. "Kind of mourning too, isn't it—silver?"

"I don't know," said Dan. "But I haven't got any silver paper."

"Newspaper wouldn't do?"

"Well, *hardly*, Boardman," said Dan, with sarcasm.

"Well," said Boardman, "I should have supposed that nothing could be simpler than to send back a lot of love-letters; but the question of paper seems insuperable. Manila paper wouldn't do either. And then comes string. What kind of string are you going to tie it up with?"

"Well, we won't start that question till we get to it," answered Dan, looking about. "If I could find some kind of a box—"

"Haven't you got a collar box? Be the very thing!" Boardman had gone back to the coats and trousers, abandoning Dan to the subtler difficulties in which he was involved.

"They've all got labels," said Mavering, getting down one marked "The Tennyson," and another lettered "The Clarion," and looking at them with cold rejection.

"Don't see how you're going to send these things back at all, then. Have to keep them, I guess." Boardman finished his task, and came back to Dan.

"I guess I've got it now," said Mavering, lifting the lid of his desk, and taking out a large stiff envelop, in which a set of photographic views had come.

"Seems to have been made for it," Boardman exulted, watching the envelop, as it filled up, expand into a kind of shapely packet. Dan put the things silently in, and sealed the parcel with his ring. Then he turned it over to address it, but the writing of Alice's name for this purpose seemed too much for him, in spite of Boardman's humorous support throughout.

"Oh, *I* can't do it," he said, falling back in his chair.

"Let me," said his friend, cheerfully ignoring his despair. He philosophized the whole transaction, as he addressed the package, rang for a messenger, and sent it away, telling him to call a cab for ten minutes past two.

"Mighty good thing in life that we move by steps. Now on the stage, or in a novel, you'd have got those things together, and addressed 'em, and despatched 'em, in just the right kind of paper, with just the right kind of string round it, at a dash; and then you'd have had time to go up and lean your head against something and soliloquize, or else think unutterable things. But here you see how a merciful Providence blocks

your way all along. You've had to fight through all sorts of
sordid little details to the grand tragic result of getting off
Miss Pasmer's letters, and when you reach it you don't mind
it a bit."

"Don't I?" demanded Dan, in as hollow a voice as he could.
"You'd joke at a funeral, Boardman."

"I've seen some pretty cheerful funerals," said Boardman.
"And it's this principle of steps, of degrees, of having to do
this little thing and that little thing, that keeps funerals from
killing the survivors. I suppose this is worse than a funeral—
look at it in the right light. You mourn as one without hope,
don't you? Live through it too, I suppose."

He made Dan help get the rest of his things into his bag,
and with one little artifice and another prevented him from
stagnating in despair. He dissented from the idea of waiting
over another day to see if Alice would not relent when she
got her letters back, and send for Dan to come and see her.

"Relent a great deal more when she finds you've gone out
of town, if she sends for you," he argued; and he got Dan
into the cab and off to the station, carefully making him an
active partner in the whole undertaking, even to checking his
own bag.

Before he bought his own ticket he appealed once more to
Dan.

"Look here! I feel like a fool going off with you on this
expedition. Be honest for once, now, Mavering, and tell me
you've thought better of it, and don't want me to go!"

"Yes—yes, I do. Oh yes, you've got to go. I—I do want
you. I—you make me see things in just the right light, don't
you know. That idea of yours about little steps—it's braced
me all up. Yes—"

"You're such an infernal humbug," said Boardman, "I can't
tell whether you want me or not. But I'm in for it now, and
I'll go." Then he bought his ticket.

XLV

BOARDMAN PUT HIMSELF in charge of Mavering, and took him into the smoking-car. It was impossible to indulge a poetic gloom there without becoming unpleasantly conspicuous in the smoking and euchre and profanity. Some of the men were silent and dull, but no one was apparently very unhappy, and perhaps if Dan had dealt in absolute sincerity with himself, even he would not have found himself wholly so. He did not feel as he had felt when Alice rejected him. Then he was wounded to the quick through his vanity, and now, in spite of all, in spite of the involuntary tender swaying of his heart toward her through the mere force of habit, in spite of some remote compunctions for his want of candor with her, he was supported by a sense of her injustice, her hardness. Related with this was an obscure sense of escape, of liberation, which, however he might silence and disown it, was still there. He could not help being aware that he had long relinquished tastes, customs, purposes, ideals, to gain a peace that seemed more and more fleeting and uncertain, and that he had submitted to others which, now that the moment of giving pleasure by his submission was passed, he recognized as disagreeable. He felt a sort of guilt in his enlargement; he knew, by all that he had ever heard or read of people in his position, that he ought to be altogether miserable; and yet this consciousness of relief persisted. He told himself that a very tragical thing had befallen him; that his broken engagement was the ruin of his life and the end of his youth, and that he must live on an old and joyless man, wise with the knowledge that comes to decrepitude and despair; he imagined a certain look for himself, a gait, a name, that would express this; but all the same he was aware of having got out of something. Was it a bondage, a scrape, as Boardman called it? He thought he must be a very light, shallow, and frivolous nature not to be utterly broken up by his disaster.

"I don't know what I'm going home for," he said, hoarsely, to Boardman.

"Kind of a rest, I suppose," suggested his friend.

"Yes, I guess that's it," said Dan. "I'm tired."

It seemed to him that this was rather fine; it was a fatigue of the soul that he was to rest from. He remembered the apostrophic close of a novel in which the heroine dies after much emotional suffering. "Quiet, quiet heart!" he repeated to himself. Yes, he too had died to hope, to love, to happiness.

As they drew near their journey's end he said, "I don't know how I'm going to break it to them."

"Oh, probably break itself," said Boardman. "These things usually do."

"Yes, of course," Dan assented.

"Know from your looks that something's up. Or you might let me go ahead a little and prepare them."

Dan laughed. "It was awfully good of you to come, Boardman. I don't know what I should have done without you."

"Nothing I like more than these little trips. Brightens you up to see the misery of others; makes you feel that you're on peculiarly good terms with Providence. Haven't enjoyed myself so much since that day in Portland." Boardman's eyes twinkled.

"Yes," said Dan, with a deep sigh, "it's a pity it hadn't ended there."

"Oh, I don't know. You won't have to go through with it again. Something that had to come, wasn't it? Never been satisfied if you hadn't tried it. Kind of aching void before, and now you've got enough."

"Yes, I've got enough," said Dan, "if *that's* all."

When they got out of the train at Ponkwasset Falls, and the conductor and the brakeman, who knew Dan as his father's son, and treated him with the distinction due a representative of an interest valued by the road, had bidden him a respectfully intimate good-night, and he began to climb the hill to his father's house, he recurred to the difficulty before him in breaking the news to his family. "I wish I could have it over in a flash. I wish I'd thought to telegraph it to them."

"Wouldn't have done," said Boardman. "It would have given 'em time to formulate questions and conjectures, and now the astonishment will take their breath away till you can get your second wind, and then—you'll be all right."

"You think so?" asked Dan, submissively.

"*Know* so. You see, if you could have had it over in a flash, it would have knocked you flat. But now you've taken all the little steps, and you've got a lot more to take, and you're all braced up. See? You're like rock, now—adamant." Dan laughed in forlorn perception of Boardman's affectionate irony. "Little steps are the thing. You'll have to go in now and meet your family, and pass the time of day with each one, and talk about the weather, and account for my being along, and ask how they all are; and by the time you've had dinner, and got settled with your legs out in front of the fire, you'll be just in the mood for it. Enjoy telling them all about it."

"Don't, Boardman," pleaded Dan. "Boardy, I believe if I could get in and up to my room without anybody's seeing me, I'd let you tell them. There don't seem to be anybody about, and I think we could manage it."

"It wouldn't work," said Boardman. "Got to do it yourself."

"Well, then, wait a minute," said Dan, desperately; and Boardman knew that he was to stay outside while Dan reconnoitred the interior. Dan opened one door after another till he stood within the hot, brilliantly lighted hall. Eunice Mavering was coming down the stairs, hooded and wrapped for a walk on the long verandas before supper.

"Dan!" she cried.

"It's all up, Eunice," he said at once, as if she had asked him about it. "My engagement's off."

"*Oh*, I'm so glad!" She descended upon him with outstretched arms, but stopped herself before she reached him. "It's a hoax. What do you mean? Do you really mean it, Dan?"

"I guess I mean it. But don't— Hold on! Where's Minnie?"

Eunice turned and ran back upstairs. "Minnie! Min!" she called on her way. "Dan's engagement's off."

"I don't believe it!" answered Minnie's voice, joyously, from within some room. It was followed by her presence, with successive inquiries. "How do you know? Did you get a letter? When did it happen? Oh, *isn't* it too good?"

Minnie was also dressed for the veranda promenade, which they always took when the snow was too deep. She caught sight of her brother as she came down. "Why, Dan's here! Dan, I've been thinking about you all day." She kissed him, which Eunice was now reminded to do too.

"Yes, it's true, Minnie," said Dan, gravely. "I came up to tell you. It don't seem to distress you much."

"Dan!" said his sister, reproachfully. "You know I didn't mean to say anything. I only felt so glad to have you back again."

"I understand, Minnie—I don't blame you. It's all right. How's mother? Father up from the works yet? I'm going to my room."

"Indeed you're not!" cried Eunice, with elder-sisterly authority. "You shall tell us about it first."

"Oh no! Let him go, Eunice!" pleaded Minnie. "Poor Dan! And I don't think we ought to go to walk when—"

Dan's eyes dimmed, and his voice weakened a little at her sympathy. "Yes, go. I'm tired—that's all. There isn't anything to tell you, hardly. Miss Pasmer—"

"Why, he's pale!" cried Minnie. *"Eunice!"*

"Oh, it's just the heat in here." Dan really felt a little sick and faint with it, but he was not sorry to seem affected by the day's strain upon his nerves.

The girls began to take off their wraps. "Don't. I'll go out with you. Boardman's out there."

"Boardman! What nonsense!" exclaimed Eunice.

"He'll like to hear your opinion of it," Dan began; but his sister pulled the doors open, and ran out to see if he really meant that too.

Whether Boardman had heard her, or had discreetly withdrawn out of ear-shot at the first sound of voices, she could not tell, but she found him some distance away from the snow-box on the piazza. "Dan's just managed to tell us you were here," she said, giving him her hand. "I'm glad to see you. Do come in."

"Came along as a sort of Job's comforter," Boardman explained, as he followed her in; and he had the silly look that the man who feels himself superfluous must wear.

"Then you know about it?" said Eunice, while Minnie Mavering and he were shaking hands.

"Yes, Boardman knows; *he* can tell you about it," said Dan, from the hall chair he had dropped into. He rose and made his way to the stairs, with the effect of leaving the whole thing to them.

His sisters ran after him, and got him upstairs and into his room, with Boardman's semi-satirical connivance, and Eunice put up the window, while Minnie went to get some cologne to wet his forehead. Their efforts were so successful that he revived sufficiently to drive them out of his room, and make them go and show Boardman to his.

"You know the way, Mr. Boardman," said Eunice, going before him, while Minnie followed timorously, but curious for what he should say. She lingered on the threshold, while her sister went in and pulled the electric apparatus which lighted the gas-burners. "I suppose Dan didn't break it?" she said, turning sharply upon him.

"No; and I don't think he was to blame," said Boardman, inferring her reserved anxiety.

"Oh, I'm quite sure of that," said Eunice, rejecting what she had asked for. "You'll find everything, Mr. Boardman. It was kind of you to come with Dan. Supper's at seven."

"How *severe* you were with him!" murmured Minnie, following her away.

"Severe with *Dan?*"

"No—with Mr. Boardman."

"What nonsense! I had to be. I couldn't let him defend Dan to me. Couple of silly boys!"

After a moment Minnie said, "*I* don't think he's silly."

"Who?"

"Mr. Boardman."

"Well, Dan is, then, to bring him at such a time. But I suppose he felt that he couldn't get here without him. What a boy! Think of such a child being engaged! I hope we sha'n't hear any more of such nonsense for *one* while again—at least till Dan's got his growth."

They went down into the library, where, in their excitement, they sat down with most of their out-door things on.

Minnie had the soft contrary-mindedness of gentle natures. "I should like to know *how* you would have had Dan bear it," she said, rebelliously.

"How? Like a man. Or like a woman. How do you suppose

Miss Pasmer's bearing it? Do you suppose she's got some friend to help her?"

"If she's broken it, she doesn't need any one," urged Minnie.

"Well," said Eunice, with her high scorn of Dan unabated, "I never could have liked that girl, but I certainly begin to respect her. I think I could have got on with her—now that it's no use. I declare," she broke off, "we're sitting here sweltering to death! What *are* we keeping our things on for?" She began to tear hers violently off and to fling them on chairs, scolding, and laughing at the same time with Minnie, at their absent-mindedness.

A heavy step sounded on the veranda without.

"There's father!" she cried, vividly, jumping to her feet and running to the door, while Minnie, in a nervous bewilderment, ran off upstairs to her room. Eunice flung the door open. "Well, father, we've got Dan back again." And at a look of quiet question in his eye she hurried on: "His engagement's broken, and he's come up here to tell us, and brought Mr. Boardman along to help."

"Where is he?" asked the father, with his ruminant quiet, pulling off first one sleeve of his overcoat, and pausing for Eunice's answer before he pulled off the other.

XLVI

H<small>E'S UP IN</small> his room, resting from the effort." She laughed nervously, and her father made no comment. He took off his arctics, and then went creaking upstairs to Dan's room. But at the door he paused, with his hand on the knob, and turned away to his own room without entering.

Dan must have heard him; in a few minutes he came to him.

"Well, Dan," said his father, shaking hands.

"I suppose Eunice has told you? Well, I want to tell you why it happened."

There was something in his father that always steadied Dan and kept him to the point. He now put the whole case fairly and squarely, and his candor and openness seemed to him to react and characterize his conduct throughout. He did not realize that this was not so till his father said at the close, with mild justice, "You were to blame for letting the thing run on so at loose ends."

"Yes, of course," said Dan, seeing that he was. "But there was no intention of deceiving any one—of bad faith—"

"Of course not."

"I thought it could be easily arranged whenever it came to the point."

"If you'd been older, you wouldn't have thought that. You had women to deal with on both sides. But if it's all over, I'm not sorry. I always admired Miss Pasmer, but I've been more and more afraid you were not suited to each other. Your mother doesn't know you're here?"

"No, sir, I suppose not. Do you think it will distress her?"

"How did your sisters take it?"

Dan gave a rueful laugh. "It seemed to be rather a popular move with them."

"I will see your mother first," said the father.

He left them when they went into the library after supper, and a little later Dan and Eunice left Boardman in charge of Minnie there.

He looked after their unannounced withdrawal in comic

584

consciousness. "It's no use pretending that I'm not a pretty large plurality here," he said to Minnie.

"Oh, I'm *so* glad you came!" she cried, with a kindness which was as real as if it had been more sincere.

"Do you think mother will feel it much?" asked Dan, anxiously, as he went upstairs with Eunice.

"Well, she'll hate to lose a correspondent—such a regular one," said Eunice, and the affair being so far beyond any other comment, she laughed the rest of the way to their mother's room.

The whole family had in some degree that foible which affects people who lead isolated lives; they come to think that they are the only people who have their virtues; they exaggerate these, and they conceive a kindness even for the qualities which are not their virtues. Mrs. Mavering's life was secluded again from the family seclusion, and their peculiarities were intensified in her. Besides, she had some very marked peculiarities of her own, and these were also intensified by the solitude to which she was necessarily left so much. She meditated a great deal upon the character of her children, and she liked to analyze and censure it both in her own mind and openly in their presence. She was very trenchant and definite in these estimates of them; she liked to ticket them, and then ticket them anew. She explored their ancestral history on both sides for the origin of their traits, and there were times when she reduced them in formula to mere congeries of inherited characteristics. If Eunice was self-willed and despotic, she was just like her grandmother Mavering; if Minnie was all sentiment and gentle stubbornness, it was because two aunts of hers, one on either side, were exactly so; if Dan loved pleasure and beauty, and was sinuous and uncertain in so many ways, and yet was so kind and faithful and good, as well as shilly-shallying and undecided, it was because her mother, and her mother's father, had these qualities in the same combination.

When she took her children to pieces before their faces, she was sharp and admonitory enough with them. She warned them of what their characters would bring them to if they did not look out; but perhaps because she beheld them so hopelessly the present effect of the accumulated tendencies of the

family past, she was tender and forgiving to their actions. The
mother came in there, and superseded the student of heredity:
she found excuse for them in the perversity of circumstance,
in the peculiar hardship of the case, in the malignant misbe-
havior of others.

As Dan entered, with the precedence his father and sister
yielded him as the principal actor in the scene which must
follow, she lifted herself vigorously in bed, and propped herself on the elbow of one arm while she stretched the other
toward him.

"I'm glad of it, Dan!" she called, at the moment he opened
the door, and as he came toward her she continued, with the
amazing velocity of utterance peculiar to nervous sufferers of
her sex: "I know all about it, and I don't blame you a bit!
And I don't blame *her*! Poor helpless young things! But it's a
perfect mercy it's all over; it's the greatest deliverance I ever
heard of! You'd have been eaten up alive. I saw it and I knew
it from the very first moment, and I've lived in fear and trembling for you. You could have got on well enough if you'd
been left to yourselves, but that you couldn't have been nor
hope to be as long as you breathed, from the meddling and
the machinations and the malice of that unscrupulous and un-
conscionable old *Cat*!"

By the time Mrs. Mavering had hissed out the last word she
had her arm round her boy's neck and was clutching him,
safe and sound after his peril, to her breast; and between her
kissing and crying she repeated her accusals and denunciations
with violent volubility.

Dan could not have replied to them in that effusion of gratitude and tenderness he felt for his mother's partisanship; and
when she went on in almost the very terms of his self-defence,
and told him that he had done as he had because it was easy
for him to yield, and he could not imagine a Cat who would
put her daughter up to entrapping him into a promise that
she knew must break his mother's heart, he found her so
right on the main point that he could not help some question
of Mrs. Pasmer in his soul. Could she really have been at the
bottom of it all? She was very sly, and she might be very false,
and it was certainly she who had first proposed their going

abroad together. It looked as if it might be as his mother said, and at any rate it was no time to dispute her, and he did not say a word in behalf of Mrs. Pasmer, whom she continued to rend in a thousand pieces and scatter to the winds till she had to stop breathless.

"Yes! It's quite as I expected! She did everything she could to trap you into it. She fairly flung that poor girl at you. She laid her plans so that you couldn't say no—she understood your character from the start!—and then, when it came out by accident, and she saw that she had older heads to deal with, and you were not going to be *quite* at her mercy, she dropped the mask in an instant, and made Alice break with you. Oh, I could see through her from the beginning! And the next time, Dan, I advise you, as you never suspect anybody yourself, to consult with somebody who doesn't take people for what they seem, and not to let yourself be flattered out of your senses, even if you see your father is."

Mrs. Mavering dropped back on her pillows, and her husband smiled patiently at their daughter.

Dan saw his patient smile and understood it; and the injustice which his father bore made him finally unwilling to let another remain under it. Hard as it was to oppose his mother in anything when she was praising him so sweetly and comforting him in the moment of his need, he pulled himself together to protest: "No, no, mother! I don't think Mrs. Pasmer was to blame; I don't believe she had anything to do with it. She's always stood my friend—"

"Oh, I've no doubt she's made you *think* so, Dan," said his mother, with unabated fondness for him; "and you think so because you're so simple and good, and never suspect evil of any one. It's this hideous optimism that's killing everything—"

A certain note in the invalid's falling voice seemed to warn her hearers of an impending change that could do no one good. Eunice rose hastily and interrupted: "Mother, Mr. Boardman's here. He came up with Dan. May Minnie come in with him?"

Mrs. Mavering shot a glance of inquiry at Dan, and then let a swift inspection range over all the details of the room, and finally concentrate itself on the silk and lace of her bed, over which she passed a smoothing hand. "Mr. Boardman?" she cried, with instantly recovered amiability. "Of course she may!"

XLVII

I N BOSTON the rumor of Dan's broken engagement was followed promptly by a denial of it; both the rumor and the denial were apparently authoritative; but it gives the effect of a little greater sagacity to distrust rumors of all kinds, and most people went to bed, after the teas and dinners and receptions and clubs at which the fact was first debated, in the self-persuasion that it was not so. The next day they found the rumor still persistent; the denial was still in the air too, but it seemed weaker; at the end of the third day it had become a question as to which broke the engagement, and why; by the end of a week it was known that Alice had broken the engagement, but the reason could not be ascertained.

This was not for want of asking, more or less direct. Pasmer, of course, went and came at his club with perfect immunity. Men are quite as curious as women, but they set business bounds to their curiosity, and do not dream of passing these. With women who have no business of their own, and cannot quell themselves with the reflection that this thing or that is not their affair, there is no question so intimate that they will not put it to some other woman; perhaps it is not so intimate, or perhaps it will not seem so; at any rate, they chance it. Mrs. Pasmer was given every opportunity to explain the facts to the ladies whom she met, and if she was much afflicted by Alice's behavior, she had a measure of consolation in using her skill to baffle the research of her acquaintance. After each encounter of the kind she had the pleasure of reflecting that absolutely nothing more than she meant had become known. The case never became fully known through her; it was the girl herself who told it to Miss Cotton in one of those moments of confidence which are necessary to burdened minds; and it is doubtful if more than two or three people ever clearly understood it; most preferred one or other of several mistaken versions which society finally settled down to.

The paroxysm of self-doubt, almost self-accusal, in which Alice came to Miss Cotton moved the latter to the deepest sympathy, and left her with misgivings which became an intolerable anguish to her conscience. The child was so afflicted at what she had done, not because she wished to be reconciled with her lover, but because she was afraid she had been unjust, been cruelly impatient and peremptory with him; she seemed to Miss Cotton so absolutely alone and friendless with her great trouble, she was so helpless, so hopeless, she was so anxious to do right, and so fearful she had done wrong, that Miss Cotton would not have been Miss Cotton if she had not taken her in her arms and assured her that in everything she had done she had been sublimely and nobly right, a lesson to all her sex in such matters forever. She told her that she had always admired her, but that now she idolized her; that she felt like going down on her knees and simply worshipping her.

"Oh, *don't* say that, Miss Cotton!" pleaded Alice, pulling away from her embrace, but still clinging to her with her tremulous, cold little hands. "I can't bear it! I'm wicked and hard—you don't *know* how bad I am; and I'm afraid of being weak, of doing more harm yet. Oh, I wronged him cruelly in ever letting him get engaged to me! But now what you've said will support me. If *you* think I've done right— It must seem strange to you that I should come to you with my trouble instead of my mother; but I've *been* to her, and—and we think alike on so few subjects, don't you know—"

"Yes, yes; I know, dear!" said Miss Cotton, in the tender folly of her heart, with the satisfaction which every woman feels in being more sufficient to another in trouble than her natural comforters.

"And I wanted to know how *you* saw it; and now, if you feel as you say, I can never doubt myself again."

She tempested out of Miss Cotton's house, all tearful under the veil she had pulled down, and as she shut the door of her coupé, Miss Cotton's heart jumped into her throat with an impulse to run after her, to recall her, to recant, to modify everything.

From that moment Miss Cotton's trouble began, and it became a torment that mounted and gave her no peace till she imparted it. She said to herself that she should suffer to the utmost in this matter, and if she spoke to any one, it must not be to some one who had agreed with her about Alice, but to some hard, skeptical nature, some one who would look at it from a totally different point of view, and would punish her for her error, if she had committed an error, in supporting and consoling Alice. All the time she was thinking of Mrs. Brinkley; Mrs. Brinkley had come into her mind at once; but it was only after repeated struggles that she could get the strength to go to her.

Mrs. Brinkley, sacredly pledged to secrecy, listened with a sufficiently dismaying air to the story which Miss Cotton told her in the extremity of her fear and doubt.

"Well," she said at the end, "have you written to Mr. Mavering?"

"Written to Mr. Mavering?" gasped Miss Cotton.

"Yes—to tell him she wants him back."

"Wants him back?" Miss Cotton echoed again.

"That's what she came to you for."

"*Oh*, Mrs. Brinkley!" moaned Miss Cotton, and she stared at her in mute reproach.

Mrs. Brinkley laughed. "I don't say she knew that she came for that; but there's no doubt that she did; and she went away bitterly disappointed with your consolation and support. She didn't want anything of the kind—you may comfort yourself with that reflection, Miss Cotton."

"Mrs. Brinkley," said Miss Cotton, with a severity which ought to have been extremely effective from so mild a person, "do you mean to accuse that poor child of dissimulation—of deceit—in such—a—a—"

"No!" shouted Mrs. Brinkley; "she didn't know what she was doing any more than you did; and she went home perfectly heart-broken; and I hope she'll stay so, for the good of all parties concerned."

Miss Cotton was so bewildered by Mrs. Brinkley's interpretation of Alice's latent motives that she let the truculent hostility of her aspiration pass unheeded. She looked helplessly about, and seemed faint, so that Mrs. Brinkley, without appearing to notice her state, interposed the question of a little sherry. When it had been brought, and Miss Cotton had sipped the glass that trembled in one hand while her emotion shattered a biscuit with the other, Mrs. Brinkley went on: "I'm glad the engagement is broken, and I hope it will never be mended. If what you tell me of her reason for breaking it is true—"

"Oh, I feel so *guilty* for telling you! I'd no right to! Please never speak of it!" pleaded Miss Cotton.

"—Then I feel more than ever that it was all a mistake, and that to help it on again would be a—crime."

Miss Cotton gave a small jump at the word, as if she had already committed the crime: she had longed to do it.

"Yes; I mean to say that they are better parted than plighted. If matches are made in heaven, I believe some of them are *un*made there too. They're not adapted to each other; there's too great a disparity."

"You mean," began Miss Cotton, from her prepossession of Alice's superiority, "that she's—"

"Altogether his inferior, intellectually and morally."

"Oh, I can't admit *that*!" cried Miss Cotton, glad to have Mrs. Brinkley go too far, and plucking up courage from her excess.

"Intellectually and morally," repeated Mrs. Brinkley, with the mounting conviction which ladies seem to get from mere persistence. "I saw that girl at Campobello; I watched her."

"I never felt that you did her justice!" cried Miss Cotton, with the valor of a hen-sparrow. "There was an antipathy."

"There certainly wasn't a sympathy, I'm happy to say," retorted Mrs. Brinkley. "I know her, and I know her family, root and branch. The Pasmers are the dullest and most selfish people in the world."

"Oh, I don't think *that's* her character," said Miss Cotton, ruffling her feathers defensively.

"Neither do I. She has *no* fixed character. *No* girl has. *Nobody* has. We all have twenty different characters—more characters than gowns—and we put them on and take them off just as often for different occasions. I know *you* think each person is permanently this or that; but my experience is that half the time they're the other thing."

"Then why," said Miss Cotton, winking hard, as some weak people do when they think they are making a point, "do you say that Alice is dull and selfish?"

"I don't—not always, or not simply so. That's the character of the Pasmer blood, but it's crossed with twenty different currents in her, and from somebody that the Pasmer dulness and selfishness must have driven mad she's got a crazy streak of piety; and that's got mixed up in her again with a nonsensical ideal of duty; and everything she does she not only thinks is right, but she thinks it's religious, and she thinks it's unselfish."

"If you'd seen her, if you'd heard her, this morning," said Miss Cotton, "you wouldn't say *that*, Mrs. Brinkley."

Mrs. Brinkley refused this with an impatient gesture. "It isn't what she is now, or seems to be, or thinks she is. It's what she's going to finally harden into—what's going to be her prevailing character. Now Dan Mavering has just the faults that will make such a girl think her own defects are virtues, because they're so different. I tell you Alice Pasmer has neither the head nor the heart to appreciate the goodness, the loveliness, of a fellow like Dan Mavering."

"I think she feels his sweetness fully," urged Miss Cotton. "But she couldn't endure his uncertainty. With her the truth is first of all things."

"Then she's a little goose. If she had the sense to know it, she would know that he might delay and temporize and beat about the bush, but he would be true when it was necessary. I haven't the least doubt in the world but that poor fellow was going on in perfect security, because he felt that it would be so easy for *him* to give up, and supposed it would be just as easy for her. I don't suppose he had a misgiving, and it must have come upon him like a thunder-clap."

"Don't you think," timidly suggested Miss Cotton, "that truth is the first essential in marriage?"

"Of course it is. And if this girl was worthy of Dan Mavering, if she were capable of loving him or anybody else unselfishly, she would have felt his truth even if she couldn't have seen it. I believe this minute that that manœuvring, humbugging mother of hers is a better woman, a kinder woman, than she is."

"Alice says her mother took his part," said Miss Cotton, with a sigh. "She took your view of it."

"She's a sensible woman. But I hope she won't be able to get him into her toils again," continued Mrs. Brinkley, recurring to the conventional estimate of Mrs. Pasmer.

"I can't help feeling—believing—that they'll come to-gether somehow still," murmured Miss Cotton. It seemed to her that she had all along wished this; and she tried to re-member if what she had said to comfort Alice might be con-strued as adverse to a reconciliation.

"I hope they won't, then," said Mrs. Brinkley, "for they couldn't help being unhappy together, with their tempera-ments. There's one thing, Miss Cotton, that's more essential in marriage than Miss Pasmer's instantaneous honesty, and that's patience."

"Patience with wrong?" demanded Miss Cotton.

"Yes, even with wrong; but I meant patience with each other. Marriage is a perpetual pardon, concession, surrender; it's an everlasting giving up; that's the divine thing about it; and that's just what Miss Pasmer could never conceive of, because she is self-righteous and conceited and unyielding. She would make him miserable."

Miss Cotton rose in a bewilderment which did not permit her to go at once. There was something in her mind which she wished to urge, but she could not make it out, though she lingered in vague generalities. When she got a block away from the house it suddenly came to her. Love! If they loved each other, would not all be well with them? She would have liked to run back and put that question to Mrs. Brinkley; but just then she met Brinkley lumbering heavily homeward; she heard his hard breathing from the exertion of bowing to her as he passed.

His wife met him in the hall, and went up to kiss him. He smelt abominably of tobacco smoke.

"Hullo!" said her husband. "What are you after?"

"Nothing," said his wife, enjoying his joke. "Come in here; I want to tell you how I have just sat upon Miss Cotton."

XLVIII

The relations between Dan and his father had always been kindly and trustful; they now became, in a degree that touched and flattered the young fellow, confidential. With the rest of the family there soon ceased to be any reference to his engagement; his sisters were glad, each in her way, to have him back again, and whatever they may have said between themselves, they said nothing to him about Alice. His mother appeared to have finished with the matter the first night; she had her theory, and she did it justice; and when Mrs. Mavering had once done a thing justice, she did not bring it up again unless somebody disputed it. But nobody had defended Mrs. Pasmer after Dan's feeble protest in her behalf; Mrs. Mavering's theory was accepted with obedience if not conviction; the whole affair dropped, except between Dan and his father.

Dan was certainly not so gay as he used to be; he was glad to find that he was not so gay. There had been a sort of mercy in the suddenness of the shock; it benumbed him, and the real stress and pain came during the long weeks that followed, when nothing occurred to vary the situation in any manner; he did not hear a word about Alice from Boston, nor any rumor of her people.

At first he had intended to go back with Boardman and face it out; but there seemed no use in this, and when it came to the point he found it impossible. Boardman went back alone, and he put Dan's things together in his rooms at Boston and sent them to him, so that Dan remained at home.

He set about helping his father at the business with unaffected docility. He tried not to pose, and he did his best to bear his loss and humiliation with manly fortitude. But his whole life had not set so strongly in one direction that it could be sharply turned aside now and not in moments of forgetfulness press against the barriers almost to bursting. Now and then, when he came to himself from the wonted tendency, and remembered that Alice and he, who had been all in all to each other, were now nothing, the pain was so sharp, so astonishing, that he could not keep down a groan, which he then tried to turn off with a cough, or a snatch of song, or a whistle, looking wildly round to see if any one had noticed.

Once this happened when his father and he were walking silently home from the works, and his father said, without touching him or showing his sympathy except in his tone of humorously frank recognition, "Does it still hurt a little occasionally, Dan?"

"Yes, sir, it hurts," said the son; and he turned his face aside, and whistled through his teeth.

"Well, it's a trial, I suppose," said his father, with his gentle, soft half-lisp. "But there are greater trials."

"How, greater?" asked Dan, with sad incredulity. "I've lost all that made life worth living; and it's all my own fault, too."

"Yes," said his father; "I think she was a good girl."

"Good!" cried Dan; the word seemed to choke him.

"Still, I doubt if it's all your fault." Dan looked round at him. He added, "And I think it's perhaps for the best as it is."

Dan halted, and then said, "Oh, I suppose so," with dreary resignation, as they walked on.

"Let us go round by the paddock," said his father, "and see if Pat's put the horses up yet. You can hardly remember your mother, before she became an invalid, I suppose," he added, as Dan mechanically turned aside with him from the path that led to the house into that leading to the barn.

"No; I was such a little fellow," said Dan.

"Women give up a great deal when they marry," said the elder. "It's not strange that they exaggerate the sacrifice, and expect more in return than it's in the nature of men to give them. I should have been sorry to have you marry a woman of an exacting disposition."

"I'm afraid she was exacting," said Dan. "But she never asked more than was right."

"And it's difficult to do all that's right," suggested the elder.

"I'm sure you always have, father," said the son.

The father did not respond. "I wish you could remember your mother when she was well," he said. Presently he added, "I think it isn't best for a woman to be too much in love with her husband."

Dan took this to himself, and he laughed harshly. "She's been able to dissemble her love at last."

His father went on, "Women keep the romantic feeling longer than men; it dies out of us very soon—perhaps too soon."

"You think I couldn't have come to time?" asked Dan. "Well, as it's turned out, I won't have to."

"No man can be all a woman wishes him to be," said his father. "It's better for the disappointment to come before it's too late."

"I was to blame," said Dan, stoutly. "She was all right."

"You were to blame in the particular instance," his father answered. "But in general the fault was in her—or her temperament. As long as the romance lasted she might have deluded herself, and believed you were all she imagined you; but romance can't last, even with women. I don't like your faults, and I don't want you to excuse them to yourself. I don't like your chancing things, and leaving them to come out all right of themselves; but I've always tried to make you children see all your qualities in their true proportion and relation."

"Yes; I know that, sir," said Dan.

"Perhaps," continued his father, as they swung easily along, shoulder to shoulder, "I may have gone too far in that direction because I was afraid that you might take your mother too seriously in the other—that you might not understand that she judged you from her nerves and not her convictions. It's part of her malady, of her suffering, that her inherited Puritanism clouds her judgment, and makes her see all faults as of one size and equally damning. I wish you to know that she was not always so, but was once able to distinguish differences in error, and to realize that evil is of ill-will."

"Yes; I know that," said Dan. "She is now—when she feels well."

"Harm comes from many things, but evil is of the heart. I wouldn't have you condemn yourself too severely for harm that you didn't intend—that's remorse—that's insanity; and I wouldn't have you fall under the condemnation of another's invalid judgment."

"Thank you, father," said Dan.

They had come up to the paddock behind the barn, and they laid their arms on the fence while they looked over at the horses which were still there. The beasts, in their rough winter coats, some bedaubed with frozen clots of the mud in which they had been rolling earlier in the afternoon, stood motionless in the thin, keen breeze that crept over the hillside from the March sunset, and blew their manes and tails out toward Dan and his father. Dan's pony sent him a gleam of recognition from under his frowzy bangs, but did not stir.

"Bunch looks like a caterpillar," he said, recalling the time when his father had given him the pony; he was a boy then, and the pony was as much to him, it went through his mind, as Alice had ever been. Was it all a jest, an irony? he asked himself.

"He's getting pretty old," said his father. "Let's see: you were only twelve."

"Ten," said Dan. "We've had him thirteen years."

Some of the horses pricked up their ears at the sound of their voices. One of them bit another's neck; the victim threw up his heels and squealed.

Pat called from the stable, "Heigh, you divils!"

"I think he'd better take them in," said Dan's father; and he continued, as if it were all the same subject, "I hope you'll have seen something more of the world before you fall in love the next time."

"Thank you; there won't be any next time. But do you consider the world such a school of morals, then? I supposed it was a very bad place."

"We seem to have been all born into it," said the father. He lifted his arms from the fence, and Dan mechanically followed him into the stable. A warm, homely smell of hay and of horses filled the place; a lantern glimmered, a faint blot, in the loft where Pat was pitching some hay forward to the edge of the boards; the naphtha gas weakly flared from the jets beside the harness-room, whence a smell of leather issued and mingled with the other smell. The simple, earthy wholesomeness of the place appealed to Dan and comforted him. The hay began to tumble from the loft with a pleasant rustling sound.

His father called up to Pat, "I think you'd better take the horses in now."

"Yes, sir: I've got the box-stalls ready for 'em."

Dan remembered how he and Eunice used to get into the box-stall with his pony, and play at circus with it; he stood up on the pony, and his sister was the ring-master. The picture of his careless childhood reflected a deeper pathos upon his troubled present, and he sighed again.

His father said, as they moved on through the barn: "Some of the best people I've ever known were what were called worldly people. They are apt to be sincere, and they have none of the spiritual pride, the conceit of self-righteousness, which often comes to people who are shut up by conscience or circumstance to the study of their own motives and actions."

"I don't think she was one of that kind," said Dan.

"Oh, I don't know that she was. But the chances of happiness, of goodness, would be greater with a less self-centred person—for you."

"Ah, yes! For *me!*" said Dan, bitterly. "Because I hadn't it in me to be frank with her. With a man like me, a woman had better be a little scampish too! Father, I could get over the loss; she might have died, and I could have got over that; but I can't get over being to blame."

"I don't think I'd indulge in any remorse," said his father. "There's nothing so useless, so depraving, as that. If you see your wrong, it's for your warning, not for your destruction."

Dan was not really feeling very remorseful; he had never felt that he was much to blame; but he had an intellectual perception of the case, and he thought that he ought to feel remorseful; it was this persuasion that he took for an emotion. He continued to look very disconsolate.

"Come," said his father, touching his arm, "I don't want you to brood upon these things. It can do no manner of good. I want you to go to New York next week and look after that Lafflin process. If it's what he thinks—if he can really cast his brass patterns without air-holes—it will revolutionize our business. I want to get hold of him."

The Portuguese cook was standing in the basement door which they passed at the back of the house. He saluted father and son with a glittering smile.

"Hello, Joe!" said Dan.

"Ah, Joe!" said the father; he touched his hat to the cook, who snatched his cap off.

"What a brick you are, father!" thought Dan. His heart leaped at the notion of getting away from Ponkwasset; he perceived how it had been irking him to stay. "If you think I could manage it with Lafflin—"

"Oh, I think you could. He's another slippery chap."

Dan laughed for pleasure and pain at his father's joke.

XLIX

IN NEW YORK Dan found that Lafflin had gone to Washington, to look up something in connection with his patent. In his eagerness to get away from home, Dan had supposed that his father meant to make a holiday for him, and he learned with a little surprise that he was quite in earnest about getting hold of the invention. He wrote home of Lafflin's absence, and he got a telegram in reply ordering him to follow on to Washington.

The sun was shining warm on the asphalt when he stepped out of the Pennsylvania Depot with his bag in his hand, and put it into the hansom that drove up for him. The sky overhead was of an intense blue that made him remember the Boston sky as pale and gray; when the hansom tilted out into the Avenue he had a joyous glimpse of the White House, of the Capitol swimming like a balloon in the cloudless air. A keen March breeze swept the dust before him, and through its veil the classic Treasury Building showed like one edifice standing perfect amid ruin represented by the jag-tooth irregularities of the business architecture along the wide street.

He had never been in Washington before, and he had a confused sense of having got back to Rome, which he remembered from his boyish visit. Throughout his stay he seemed to be coming up against the façade of the Temple of Neptune; but it was the Patent Office, or the Treasury Building, or the White House, and under the gay Southern sky this reversion to the sensations of a happier time began at once, and made itself a lasting relief. He felt a lift in his spirits from the first. They gave him a room at Wormley's, where the chairs comported themselves as self-respectfully upon two or three legs as they would have done at Boston upon four; the cooking was excellent, and a mercenary welcome glittered from all the kind black faces about him. After the quiet of Ponkwasset and the rush of New York, the lazy ease of the hotel pleased him; the clack of boots over its pavements, the clouds of tobacco smoke, the Southern and Western accents, the spectacle of people unexpectedly encountering and recognizing each other in the office and the dining-room, all helped to restore him to a hopefuler mood. Without asking his heart too curiously why, he found it lighter; he felt that he was still young.

In the weather he had struck a cold wave, and the wind was bitter in the streets, but they were full of sun; he found the grass green in sheltered places, and in one of the circles he plucked a blossomed spray from an adventurous forsythia. This happened when he was walking from Wormley's to the Arlington by a roundabout way of his own involuntary invention, and he had the flowers in his button-hole when Lafflin was pointed out to him in the reading-room there, and he introduced himself. Lafflin had put his hat far back on his head, and was intensely chewing a toothpick, with an air of rapture from everything about him. He seemed a very simple soul to Dan's inexperience of men, and the young fellow had no difficulty in committing him to a fair conditional arrangement. He was going to stay some days in Washington, and he promised other interviews, so that Dan thought it best to stay too. He used a sheet of the Arlington letter-paper in writing his father of what he had done; and then, as Lafflin had left him, he posted his letter at the clerk's desk, and wandered out through a corridor different from that which he had come in by. It led by the door of the ladies' parlor, and at the sound of women's voices Dan halted. For no other reason than that such voices always irresistibly allured him, he went in, putting on an air of having come to look for some one. There were two or three groups of ladies receiving friends in different parts of the room. At the window a girl's figure silhouetted itself against the keen light, and as he advanced into the room, peering about, it turned with a certain vividness that seemed familiar. This young lady, whoever she was, had the advantage of Dan in seeing him with the light on his face, and he was still in the dark about her, when she advanced swiftly upon him, holding out her hand.

"You don't seem to know your old friends, Mr. Mavering," and the manly tones left him no doubt.

He felt a rush of gladness, and he clasped her hand and clung to it as if he were not going to let it go again, bubbling out incoherencies of pleasure at meeting her. "Why, Miss Anderson! You here? What a piece of luck! Of course I

couldn't see you against the window—make you out. But
something looked familiar—and the way you turned! And
when you started toward me! I'm awfully glad! When—
where are you—that is—"

Miss Anderson kept laughing with him, and bubbled back
that she was very glad too, and she was staying with her aunt
in that hotel, and they had been there a month, and didn't he
think Washington was charming? But it was too bad he had
just got there with that blizzard. The weather had been perfectly divine till the day before yesterday.

He took the spray of forsythia out of his button-hole. "I
can believe it. I found this in one of the squares, and I think it
belongs to you." He offered it with a bow and a laugh, and
she took it in the same humor.

"What is the language of forsythia?" she asked.

"It has none—only expressive silence, you know."

A middle-aged lady came in, and Miss Anderson said, "My
aunt, Mr. Mavering."

"Mr. Mavering will hardly remember me," said the lady,
giving him her hand. He protested that he should indeed, but
she had really made but a vague impression upon him at
Campobello. He knew that she was there with Miss Anderson; he had been polite to her, as he was to all women; but he
had not noticed her much, and in his heart he had a slight for
her, as compared with the Boston people he was more naturally thrown with; he certainly had not remembered that she
was a little hard of hearing.

Miss Van Hook was in a steel-gray effect of dress, and she
had carried this up into her hair, of which she wore two short
vertical curls on each temple.

She did not sit down, and Dan perceived that the ladies
were going out. In her tailor-made suit of close-fitting serge,
and her Paris bonnet carried like a crest on her pretty little
head, Miss Anderson was charming. She had a short veil that
came across the base of her lively nose, and left her mouth
and chin to make the most of themselves, unprejudiced by its
irregularity.

Dan felt it a hardship to part with them, but he prepared to
take himself off. Miss Anderson asked him how long he was
to be in Washington, and said he must come to see them; they

meant to stay two weeks yet, and then they were going to Old Point Comfort; they had their rooms engaged.

He walked down to their carriage with the ladies and put them into it, and Miss Anderson still kept him talking there.

Her aunt said: "Why shouldn't you come with us, Mr. Mavering? We're going to Mrs. Secretary Miller's reception."

Dan gave himself a glance. "I don't know—if you want me?"

"We want you," said Miss Anderson.

"Very well, then, I'll go."

He got in, and they began rolling over that smooth Washington asphalt which makes talk in a carriage as easy as in a drawing-room. Dan kept saying to himself, "Now she's going to bring up Campobello"; but Miss Anderson never recurred to their former meeting, and except for the sense of old acquaintance which was manifest in her treatment of him, he might have thought that they had never met before. She talked of Washington and its informal delights, and of those plans which her aunt had made, like every one who spends a month in Washington, to spend all the remaining winters of her life there.

It seemed to Dan that Miss Anderson was avoiding Campobello on his account; he knew from what Alice had told him that there had been much surmise about their affair after he had left the island, and he suspected that Miss Anderson thought the subject was painful to him. He wished to reassure her. He asked at the first break in the talk about Washington, "How are the Trevors?"

"Oh, quite well," she said, promptly availing herself of the opening. "Have you seen any of our Campobello friends lately in Boston?"

"No; I've been at home for the last month—in the country." He scanned her face to see if she knew anything of his engagement. But she seemed honestly ignorant of everything since Campobello; she was not just the kind of New York girl who would visit in Boston, or have friends living there; probably she had never heard of his engagement. Somehow this seemed to simplify matters for Dan. She did not ask specifically after the Pasmers; but that might have been because of the sort of break in her friendship with Alice after that night at the Trevors'; she did not ask specifically after Mrs. Brinkley or any of the others.

At Mrs. Secretary Miller's door there was a rapid arrival and departure of carriages, of coupés, of hansoms, and of herdics, all managed by a man in plain livery, who opened and shut the doors, and sent the drivers off without the intervention of a policeman: it is the genius of Washington, which distinguishes it from every other capital, from every other city, to make no show of formality, of any manner of constraint anywhere. People were swarming in and out, coming and going on foot as well as by carriage. The blandest of colored uncles received their cards in the hall and put them into a vast tray heaped up with pasteboard, smiling affectionately upon them as if they had done him a favor.

"Don't you *like* them?" asked Dan of Miss Anderson: he meant the Southern negroes.

"I *adoye* them," she responded, with equal fervor. "You must study some new types here for next summer," she added.

Dan laughed, and winced too. "Yes!" Then he said, solemnly, "I am not going to Campobello next summer."

They fell into a stream of people tending toward an archway between the drawing-rooms, where Mrs. Secretary Miller stood with two lady friends who were helping her receive. They smiled wearily but kindly upon the crowd, for whom the Secretary's wife had a look of impartial hospitality. She could not have known more than one in fifty; and she met them all with this look at first, breaking into incredulous recognition when she found a friend. "Don't go away yet," she said, cordially, to Miss Van Hook and her niece, and she held their hands for a moment with a gentle look of relief and appeal which included Dan. "Let me introduce you to Mrs. Tolliver and to Miss Dixon."

These ladies said that it was not necessary in regard to Miss Anderson and Miss Van Hook; and as the crowd pushed them on, Dan felt that they had been received with distinction.

The crowd expressed the national variety of rich and poor, plain and fashionable, urbane and rustic; they elbowed and shouldered each other upon a perfect equality in a place where all were as free to come as to the White House; and they jostled quaint groups of almond-eyed legations in the yellows and purples of the East, who looked dreamily on as if puzzled past all surmise by the scene. Certain young gentlemen with the unmistakable air of being European or South American *attachés* found their way about on their little feet, which the stalwart boots of the republican masses must have imperilled, and smiled with a faint diplomatic superiority, not visibly admitted, but all the same indisputable. Several of these seemed to know Miss Anderson, and took her presentation of Mavering with exaggerated effusion.

"I want to introduce you to my cousin over yonder," she said, getting rid of a minute Brazilian under-secretary, and putting her hand on Dan's arm to direct him: "Mrs. Justice Averill."

Miss Van Hook, keeping her look of severe vigilance, really followed her energetic niece, who took the lead, as a young lady must whenever she and her chaperon meet on equal terms.

Mrs. Justice Averill, who was from the far West somewhere, received Dan with the ease of the far East, and was talking London and Paris to him before the end of the third minute. It gave Dan a sense of liberation, of expansion; he filled his lungs with the cosmopolitan air in a sort of intoxication; without formulating it, he felt, with the astonishment which must always attend the Bostonian's perception of the fact, that there is a great social life in America outside of Boston. At Campobello he had thought Miss Anderson a very jolly girl, bright, and up to all sorts of things, but in the presence of the portable Boston there he could not help regarding her with a sort of tolerance, which he now blushed for: he thought he had been a great ass. She seemed to know all sorts of nice people, and she strove with generous hospitality to make him have a good time. She said it was Cabinet day, and that all the Secretaries' wives were receiving, and she told him he had better make the rounds with them. He assented very willingly, and at six o'clock he was already so much in the spirit of this free and simple society, so much opener and therefore so much wiser than any other, that he professed a profound disappointment with the two or three Cabinet

ladies whose failure to receive brought his pleasure to a premature close.

"But I suppose you're going to Mrs. Whittington's to-
night?" Miss Anderson said to him, as they drove up to
Wormley's, where she set him down. Miss Van Hook had
long ceased to say anything: Dan thought her a perfect
duenna. "You know you can go late there," she added.

"No, I can't go at all," said Dan. "I don't know them."

"They're New England people," urged Miss Anderson, as
if to make him try to think that he was asked to Mrs. Whittington's.

"I don't know more than half the population of New England," said Dan, with apparent levity, but real forlornness.

"If you'd like to go—if you're sure you've no other engagement—"

"Oh, I'm certain of that!"

"—We would come for you."

"Do!"

"At half past ten, then."

Miss Anderson explained to her aunt, who cordially confirmed her invitation, and they both shook hands with him
upon it, and he backed out of the carriage with a grin of
happiness on his face; it remained there while he wrote out
the order for his dinner, which they require at Wormley's in
holograph. The waiter reflected his smile with ethnical warm-
heartedness. For a moment Dan tried to think what it was he
had forgotten; he thought it was some other dish; then he
remembered that it was his broken heart. He tried to subdue
himself; but there was something in the air of the place, the
climate, perhaps, or a pleasant sense of its facile social life,
that kept him buoyant in spite of himself. He went out after
dinner, and saw part of a poor play, and returned in time to
dress for his appointment with Miss Anderson. Her aunt was
with her, of course; she seemed to Dan more indefatigable
than she was by day. He could not think her superfluous, and
she was very good-natured. She made little remarks full of
conventional wisdom, and appealed to his judgment on several points as they drove along. When they came to a street
lamp where she could see him, he nodded and said yes, or no,
respectfully. Betweentimes he talked with Miss Anderson,

who lectured him upon Washington society, and prepared him for the difference he was to find between Mrs. Whittington's evening of invited guests and the cabinet ladies' afternoon of volunteer guests.

"Volunteer guests is good," he laughed. "Do you mean that anybody can go?"

"Anybody that is able to be about. This is Cabinet day. There's a Supreme Court day, and a Senators' day, and a Representatives' day. Do you mean to say you weren't going to call upon your Senator?"

"I didn't know I had any."

"Neither did I till I came here. But you've got two; everybody's got two. And the President's wife receives three times a week, and the President has two or three days. They say the public days at the White House are great fun. I've been to some of the invited, or semi-invited, or official evenings."

He could not see that difference from the great public receptions which Miss Anderson had promised him, at Mrs. Whittington's, though he pretended afterward that he had done so. The people were more uniformly well dressed, there were not so many of them, and the hostess was sure of knowing her acquaintances at first glance; but there was the same ease, the same unconstraint, the same absence of provincial anxiety, which makes Washington a lighter and friendlier London. There were rather more sallow *attachés*; in their low-cut white waistcoats, with small brass buttons, they moved more consciously about, and looked weightier personages than several foreign ministers who were present.

Dan was soon lost from the side of Miss Anderson, who more and more seemed to him important socially. She seemed, in her present leadership, to know more of life than he; to be maturer. But she did not abuse her superiority; she kept an effect of her last summer's friendliness for him throughout. Several times, finding herself near him, she introduced him to people.

Guests kept arriving till midnight. Among the latest, when Dan had lost himself far from Boston in talk with a young lady from Richmond, who spoke with a slur of her vowels that fascinated him, came Mr. and Mrs. Brinkley. He felt himself grow pale and inattentive to his pretty Virginian. That accent of Mrs. Brinkley's recalled him to his history. He hoped that she would not see him; but in another moment he was greeting her with a warmth which Bostonians seldom show in meeting at Boston.

"When did you come to Washington?" she asked, trying to keep her consciousness out of her eyes, which she let dwell kindly upon him.

"Day before yesterday—no, yesterday. It seems a month, I've seen and done so much," he said, with his laugh. "Miss Anderson's been showing me the whole of Washington society. Have you been here long?"

"Since morning," said Mrs. Brinkley. And she added, "Miss Anderson?"

"Yes—Campobello, don't you know?"

"Oh, yes. Is she here to-night?"

"I came with her and her aunt."

"Oh, yes."

"How is all Boston?" asked Dan, boldly.

"I don't know; I'm just going down to Old Point Comfort to ask. Every other house on the Back Bay has been abandoned for the Hygeia." Mrs. Brinkley stopped, and then she asked, "Are you just up from there?"

"No; but I don't know but I shall go."

"Hello, Mavering!" said her husband, coming up and taking his hand into his fat grasp. "On your way to Fortress Monroe? Better come with us. Why, Munt!"

He turned to greet this other Bostonian, who had hardly expressed his joy at meeting with his fellow-townsmen when the hostess rustled softly up, and said, with the irony more or less friendly which everybody uses in speaking of Boston, or recognizing the intellectual pre-eminence of its people, "I'm not going to let you keep this feast of reason all to yourselves. I want you to leaven the whole lump," and she began to disperse them, and to introduce them about right and left.

Dan tried to find his Virginian again, but she was gone. He found Miss Anderson; she was with her aunt. "Shall we be tearing you away?" she asked.

"Oh no. I'm quite ready to go."

His nerves were in a tremble. Those Boston faces and voices had brought it all back again; it seemed as if he had met Alice. He was silent and incoherent as they drove home, but Miss Anderson apparently did not want to talk much, and apparently did not notice his reticence.

He fell asleep with the pang in his heart which had been there so often.

When Dan came down to breakfast he found the Brinkleys at a pleasant place by one of the windows, and after they had exchanged a pleased surprise with him that they should all happen to be in the same hotel, they asked him to sit at their table.

There was a bright sun shining, and the ache was gone out of Dan's heart. He began to chatter gayly with Mrs. Brinkley about Washington.

"Oh, better come on to Fortress Monroe," said her husband. "Better come on with us."

"No, I can't just yet," said Dan. "I've got some business here that will keep me for a while. Perhaps I may run down there a little later."

"Miss Anderson seems to have a good deal of business in Washington too," observed Brinkley, with some hazy notion of saying a pleasant rallying thing to the young man. He wondered at the glare his wife gave him. With those panned oysters before him he had forgotten all about Dan's love affair with Miss Pasmer.

Mrs. Brinkley hastened to make the mention of Miss Anderson as impersonal as possible.

"It was so nice to meet her again. She *is* such an honest, wholesome creature, and so bright, and full of sense. She always made me think of the broad daylight. I always liked that girl."

"Yes; *isn't* she jolly?" said Dan, joyously. "She seems to know everybody here. It's a great piece of luck for me. They're going to take a house in Washington next winter."

"Yes; I know that stage," said Mrs. Brinkley. "Her aunt's an amusingly New-Yorky respectability. I don't think you'd find just such Miss Mitford curls as hers in all Boston."

"Yes, they *are* like the portraits, aren't they?" said Dan, delighted. "She's very nice, don't you think?"

"Very. But Miss Anderson is more than that. I was disposed to be critical of her at Campobello for a while, but she wore extremely well. All at once you found yourself admiring her uncommon common-sense."

"Yes! That's just it!" cried Dan. "She *is* so sensible!"

"I think she's very pretty," said Mrs. Brinkley.

"Well, her nose," suggested Dan. "It seems a little—capricious."

"It's a trifle bizarre, I suppose. But what beautiful eyes! And her figure! I declare that girl's carriage is something superb."

"Yes, she has a magnificent walk."

"Walks with her carriage," mused Brinkley, aloud.

His wife did not regard him. "I don't know what Miss Anderson's principles are, but her practices are perfect. I never knew her do an unkind or shabby thing. She seems very good and very wise. And that deep voice of hers has such a charm. It's so restful. You feel as if you could repose upon it for a thousand years. Well! You *will* get down before we leave?"

"Yes, I will," said Dan. "I'm here after a man who's after a patent, and as soon as I can finish up my business with him I believe I *will* run down to Fortress Monroe."

"This eleven-o'clock train will get you there at six," said Brinkley. "Better telegraph for your rooms."

"Or, let us know," said Mrs. Brinkley, "and we'll secure them for you."

"Oh, *thank* you," said Dan.

He went away feeling that Mrs. Brinkley was the pleasantest woman he ever met. He knew that she had talked Miss Anderson so fully in order to take away the implication of her husband's joke, and he admired her tact. He thought of this as he loitered along the street from Wormley's to the Arlington, where he was going to find Miss Anderson, by an appointment of the night before, and take a walk with her; and thinking of tact made him think of Mrs. Pasmer. Mrs. Pasmer was full of tact; and how kind she had always been to him! She had really been like a mother to him; he was sure she had understood him; he believed she had defended him; with a futility of which he felt the pathos, he made her defend him now to Alice. Alice was very hard and cold, as when he saw her last; her mother's words fell upon her as upon a stone;

even Mrs. Pasmer's tears, which Dan made her shed, had no effect upon the haughty girl. Not that he cared now.

The blizzard of the previous days had whirled away; the sunshine lay still, with a warm glisten and sparkle, on the asphalt which seemed to bask in it, and which it softened to the foot. He loitered by the gate of the little park or plantation where the statue of General Jackson is riding a cock-horse to Banbury Cross, and looked over at the French-Italian classicism of the White House architecture with a pensive joy at finding pleasure in it, and then he went on to the Arlington.

Miss Anderson was waiting for him in the parlor, and they went a long walk up the avenues and across half the alphabet in the streets, and through the pretty squares and circles, where the statues were sometimes beautiful and always picturesque, and the sparrows made a vernal chirping in the naked trees and on the green grass. In two or three they sat down on the iron benches and rested.

They talked and talked—about the people they knew, and of whom they found that they thought surprisingly alike, and about themselves, whom they found surprisingly alike in a great many things, and then surprisingly unlike. Dan brought forward some points of identity which he and Alice had found in themselves; it was just the same with Miss Anderson. She found herself rather warm with the seal-skin sacque she had put on; she let him carry it on his arm while they walked, and then lay it over her shoulders when they sat down. He felt a pang of self-reproach, as if he had been inconstant to Alice. This was an old habit of feeling, formed during the months of their engagement, when, at her inspiration, he was always bringing himself to book about something. He replied to her bitterly, in the colloquy which began to hold itself in his mind, and told her that she had no claim upon him now; that if his thoughts wandered from her it was her fault, not his; that she herself had set them free. But in fact he was like all young men, with a thousand potentialities of loving. There was no aspect of beauty that did not tenderly move him; he could not help a soft thrill at the sight of any pretty shape, the sound of any piquant voice; and Alice had merely been the synthesis of all that was most charming to his fancy. This is a truth which it is the convention of the poets and the novelists to deny; but it is also true that she might have remained the sum of all that was loveliest if she would, or if she could.

It was chiefly because she would not or could not that his glance recognized the charm of Miss Anderson's back hair, both in its straying gossamer and in the loose mass in which it was caught up under her hat, when he laid her sacque on her shoulders. They met that afternoon at a Senator's, and in the house of a distinguished citizen, to whose wife Dan had been presented at Mrs. Whittington's, and who had somehow got his address, and sent him a card for her evening. They encountered here with a jocose old friendliness, and a profession of being tired of always meeting Miss Anderson and Mr. Mavering. He brought her salad and ice, and they made an appointment for another walk in the morning, if it was fine.

He carried her some flowers. A succession of fine days followed, and they walked every morning. Sometimes Dan was late, and explained that it was his patent-right man had kept him. She was interested in the patent-right man, whom Dan began to find not quite so simple as at first, but she was not exacting with him about his want of punctuality; she was very easy-going; she was not always ready herself. When he began to beat about the bush, to talk insincerities, and to lose himself in intentionless plausibilities, she waited with serene patience for him to have done, and met him on their habitual ground of frankness and reality as if he had not left it. He got to telling her all his steps with his patent-right man, who seemed to be growing more and more slippery, and who presently developed a demand for funds. Then she gave him some very shrewd, practical advice, and told him to go right into the hotel office and telegraph to his father while she was putting on her bonnet.

"Yes," he said, "that's what I thought of doing." But he admired her for advising him; he said to himself that Miss Anderson was the kind of girl his father would admire. She was good, and she was of the world too; that was what his father meant. He imagined himself arriving home and saying, "Well, father, you know that despatch I sent you about Lafflin's wanting money?" and telling him about Miss Anderson.

Then he fancied her acquainted with his sisters and visiting them, and his father more and more fond of her, and perhaps in declining health, and eager to see his son settled in life; and he pictured himself telling her that he had done with love forever, but if she could accept respect, fidelity, gratitude, he was ready to devote his life to her; she refused him, but they always remained good friends and comrades; she married another, perhaps Boardman—while Dan was writing out his telegram, and he broke into whispered maledictions on his folly, which attracted the notice of the operator.

One morning when he sent up his name to Miss Anderson, whom he did not find in the hotel parlor, the servant came back with word that Miss Van Hook would like to have him come up to their rooms. But it was Miss Anderson who met him at the door.

"It seemed rather formal to send you word that Miss Van Hook was indisposed, and Miss Anderson would be unable to walk this morning, and I thought perhaps you'd rather come up and get my regrets in person. And I wanted you to see our view."

She led the way to the window for it, but they did not look at it, though they sat down there apparently for the purpose. Dan put his hat beside his chair, and observed some inattentive civilities in inquiring after Miss Van Hook's health, and in hearing that it was merely a bad headache, one of a sort in which her niece hated to leave her to serve herself with the wet compresses which Miss Van Hook always wore on her forehead for it.

"One thing: it's decided us to be off for Fortress Monroe at last. We shall go by the boat to-morrow, if my aunt's better."

"To-morrow?" said Dan. "What's to become of me when you're gone?"

"Oh, we shall not take the whole population with us," suggested Miss Anderson.

"I wish you would take me. I told Mrs. Brinkley I would come while she was there, but I'm afraid I can't get off. Lafflin is developing into all sorts of strange propositions."

"I think you'd better look out for that man," said Miss Anderson.

"Oh, I do nothing without consulting my father. But I shall miss you."

"Thank you," said the girl, gravely.

"I don't mean in a business capacity only."

They both laughed, and Dan looked about the room, which he found was a private hotel parlor, softened to a more domestic effect by the signs of its prolonged occupation by two refined women. On a table stood a leather photograph envelop with three cabinet pictures in it. Along the top lay a spray of withered forsythia. Dan's wandering eyes rested on it. Miss Anderson went and softly closed the door opening into the next room.

"I was afraid our talking might disturb my aunt," she said, and on her way back to him she picked up the photograph case and brought it to the light. "These are my father and mother. We live at Yonkers; but I'm with my aunt a good deal of the time in town—even when I'm at home." She laughed at her own contradictory statement, and put the case back without explaining the third figure—a figure in uniform. Dan conjectured a military brother, or from her indifference perhaps a militia brother, and then forgot about him. But the partial Yonkers residence accounted for traits of unconventionality in Miss Anderson which he had not been able to reconcile with the notion of an exclusively New York breeding. He felt the relief, the sympathy, the certainty of intelligence which every person whose life has been partly spent in the country feels at finding that a suspected cockney has also had the outlook into nature and simplicity.

On the Yonkers basis they became more intimate, more personal, and Dan told her about Ponkwasset Falls, and his mother and sisters; he told her about his father, and she said she should like to see his father; she thought he must be like her father.

All at once, and for no reason that he could think of afterward, except, perhaps, the desire to see the case with her eyes, he began to tell her of his affair with Alice, and how and why it was broken off; he told the whole truth in regard to that, and did not spare himself.

She listened without once speaking, but without apparent surprise at the confidence, though she may have felt surprised.

At times she looked as if her thoughts were away from what he was saying.

He ended with: "I'm sure I don't know why I've told you all this. But I wanted you to know about me. The worst."

Miss Anderson said, looking down, "I always thought she was a very conscientious giyl." Then, after a pause, in which she seemed to be overcoming an embarrassment in being obliged to speak of another in such a conviction: "I think she was very moybid. She was like ever so many New England giyls that I've met. They seem to want some excuse for suffering, and they must suffer, even if it's through somebody else. I don't know; they're romantic, New England giyls are; they have too many ideals."

Dan felt a balm in this; he too had noticed a superfluity of ideals in Alice; he had borne the burden of realizing some of them; they all seemed to relate in objectionable degree to his perfectionation. So he said, gloomily: "She was very good. And I was to blame."

"Oh yes!" said Miss Anderson, catching her breath in a queer way; "she seyved you right."

She rose abruptly, as if she had heard her aunt speak, and Dan perceived that he had been making a long call.

He went away dazed and dissatisfied; he knew now that he ought not to have told Miss Anderson about his affair, unless he meant more by his confidence than he really did—unless he meant to follow it up.

He took leave of her, and asked her to make his adieux to her aunt; but the next day he came down to the boat to see them off. It seemed to him that their interview had ended too hastily; he felt sore and restless over it; he hoped that something more conclusive might happen. But at the boat Miss Anderson and her aunt were inseparable. Miss Van Hook said she hoped they should soon see him at the Hygeia, and he replied that he was not sure that he should be able to come, after all.

Miss Anderson called something after him as he turned from them to go ashore. He ran back eagerly to know what it was. "Better look out for that Mr. Lafflin of yours," she repeated.

"Oh! oh yes," he said, indefinitely disappointed. "I shall

keep a sharp eye on *him*." He was disappointed, but he could not have said what he had hoped or expected her to say. He was humbled before himself for having told Miss Anderson about his affair with Alice, and had wished she would say something that he might scramble back to his self-esteem upon. He had told her all that partly from mere weakness, from his longing for the sympathy which he was always so ready to give, and partly from the willingness to pose before her as a broken heart, to dazzle her by the irony and persiflage with which he could treat such a tragical matter; but he could not feel that he had succeeded. The sum of her comment had been that Alice had served him right. He did not know whether she really believed that, or merely said it to punish him for some reason; but he could never let it be the last word. He tingled as he turned to wave his handkerchief to her on the boat, with the suspicion that she was laughing at him; and he could not console himself with any hero of a novel who had got himself into just such a box. There were always circumstances, incidents, mitigations, that kept the hero still a hero, and ennobled the box into an unjust prison cell.

L

O N THE LONG sunny piazza of the Hygeia Mrs. Brinkley and Miss Van Hook sat and talked in a community of interest which they had not discovered during the summer before at Campobello, and with an equality of hearing which the sound of the waves washing almost at their feet established between them. In this pleasant noise Miss Van Hook heard as well as any one, and Mrs. Brinkley gradually realized that it was the trouble of having to lift her voice that had kept her from cultivating a very agreeable acquaintance before. The ladies sat in a secluded corner, wearing light wraps that they had often found comfortable at Campobello in August, and from time to time attested to each other their astonishment that they needed no more at Old Point in early April.

They did this not only as a just tribute to the amiable climate, but as a relief from the topic which had been absorbing them, and to which they constantly returned.

"No," said Mrs. Brinkley, with a sort of finality, "I think it is the best thing that could possibly have happened to him. He is bearing it in a very manly way, but I fancy he has felt it deeply, poor fellow. He's never been in Boston since, and I don't believe he'd come here if he'd any idea how many Boston people there were in the hotel—we swarm! It would be very painful to him."

"Yes," said Miss Van Hook, "young people seem to feel those things."

"Of course he's going to get over it. That's what young people do too. At his age he can't help being caught with every pretty face and every pretty figure, even in the midst of his woe, and it's only a question of time till he seizes some pretty hand and gets drawn out of it altogether."

"I think that would be the case with my niece too," said Miss Van Hook, "if she wasn't kept in it by a sense of loyalty. I don't believe she really cares much for Lieutenant Willing any more; but he sees no society where he's stationed, of course, and his constancy is a—a rebuke and a—a—an incentive to her. They were engaged a long time ago—just after he left West Point—and we've always been in hopes that he would be removed to some post where he could meet other ladies and become interested in some one else. But he never has, and so the affair remains. It's most undesirable they should marry, and in the mean time she won't break it off, and it's spoiling her chances in life."

"It is too bad," sighed Mrs. Brinkley; "but of course you can do nothing. I see that."

"No, we can do nothing. We have tried everything. I used to think it was because she was so dull there at Yonkers with her family, and brooded upon the one idea all the time, that she could not get over it; and at first it did seem when she came to me that she would get over it. She is very fond of gayety—of young men's society; and she's had plenty of little flirtations that didn't mean anything, and never amounted to anything. Every now and then a letter would come from the wilds where he was stationed, and spoil it all. She seemed to feel a sort of chivalrous obligation because he was so far off and helpless and lonely."

"Yes, I understand," said Mrs. Brinkley. "What a pity she couldn't be made to feel that that didn't deepen the obligation at all!"

"I've tried to make her," said Miss Van Hook, "and I've been everywhere with her. One winter we were up the Nile, and another in Nice, and last winter we were in Rome. She met young men everywhere, and had offers upon offers; but it was of no use. She remained just the same, and till she met Mr. Mavering in Washington I don't believe—"

Miss Van Hook stopped, and Mrs. Brinkley said, "And yet she always seemed to me particularly practical and level-headed—as the men say."

"So she is. But she is really very romantic about some things; and when it comes to a matter of that kind, girls are about all alike, don't you think?"

"Oh yes," said Mrs. Brinkley, hopelessly; and both ladies looked out over the water, where the waves came rolling in one after another to waste themselves on the shore as futilely as if they had been lives.

In the evening Miss Anderson got two letters from the clerk, at the hour when the ladies all flocked to his desk with the eagerness for letters which is so engaging in them. One she pulled open and glanced at with a sort of impassioned indifference; the other she read in one intense moment, and then ran it into her pocket, and with her hand still on it hurried vividly flushing to her room, and read and read it again with constantly mounting emotion.

"WORMLEY'S HOTEL, *Washington, April 7, 188 –.*

"DEAR MISS ANDERSON, — I have been acting on your parting advice to look out for that Mr. Lafflin of mine, and I have discovered that he is an unmitigated scamp. Consequently there is nothing more to keep me in Washington, and I should now like your advice about coming to Fortress Monroe. Do you find it malarial? On the boat your aunt asked me to come, but you said nothing about it, and I was left to suppose that you did not think it would agree with me. Do you still think so? or what do you think? I know you think it was uncalled-for and in extremely bad taste for me to tell you what I did the other day; and I have thought so too. There is only one thing that could justify it — that is, I think it might justify it — if you thought so. But I do not feel sure that you would like to know it, or, if you knew it, would like it. I've been rather slow coming to the conclusion myself, and perhaps it's only the beginning of the end, and not the conclusion — if there is such a difference. But the question now is whether I may come and tell you what I think it is — justify myself, or make things worse than they are now. I don't know that they can be worse, but I think I should like to try. I think your presence would inspire me.

"Washington is a wilderness since Miss —— Van Hook left. It is not a howling wilderness simply because it has not enough left in it to howl; but it has all the other merits of a wilderness.

"Yours sincerely,
                    "D. F. MAVERING."

After a second perusal of this note, Miss Anderson recurred to the other letter which she had neglected for it, and read it with eyes from which the tears slowly fell upon it. Then she sat a long time at her table with both letters before her, and did not move, except to take her handkerchief out of her pocket and dry her eyes, from which the tears began at once to drip again. At last she started forward, and caught pen and paper toward her, biting her lip and frowning as if to keep herself firm; and she said to the central figure in the photograph case which stood at the back of the table, "I will, I *will*! *You* are a *man*, anyway."

She sat down, and by a series of impulses she wrote a letter, with which she gave herself no pause till she put it in the clerk's hands, to whom she ran down-stairs with it, kicking her skirt into wild whirls as she ran, and catching her foot in it and stumbling.

"Will it go—go to-night?" she demanded, tragically.

"Just in time," said the clerk, without looking up, and apparently not thinking that her tone betrayed any unusual amount of emotion in a lady posting a letter; he was used to intensity on such occasions.

The letter ran:

"Dear Mr. Mavering,—We shall now be here so short a time that I do not think it advisable for you to come.

"Your letter was rather enigmatical, and I do not know whether I understood it exactly. I suppose you told me what you did for good reasons of your own, and I did not think much about it. I believe the question of taste did not come up in my mind.

"My aunt joins me in kindest regards.

"Yours very sincerely,
"Julia V. H. Anderson."

"P.S.—I think that I ought to return your letter. I know that you would not object to my keeping it, but it does not seem right. I wish to ask your congratulations. I have been engaged for several years to Lieutenant Willing, of the army. He has been transferred from his post in Montana to Fort Hamilton at New York, and we are to be married in June.

"J. V. H. A."

The next morning Mrs. Brinkley came up from breakfast in a sort of duplex excitement, which she tried to impart to her husband; he stood with his back toward the door, bending forward to the glass for a more accurate view of his face, from which he had scraped half the lather in shaving.

She had two cards in her hand. "Miss Van Hook and Miss Anderson have gone. They went this morning. I found their P. P. C.'s by my plate."

Mr. Brinkley made an inarticulate noise for comment, and assumed the contemptuous sneer which some men find convenient for shaving the lower lip.

"And guess who's come, of all people in the world?"

"I don't know," said Brinkley, seizing his chance to speak.

"The Pasmers!—Alice and her mother! Isn't it awful?"

Mr. Brinkley had entered upon a very difficult spot at the corner of his left jaw. He finished it before he said, "I don't see anything awful about it, so long as Pasmer hasn't come too."

"But Dan Mavering! He's in Washington, and he may come down here any day. Just think how shocking that would be!"

"Isn't that rather a theory?" asked Mr. Brinkley, finding such opportunities for conversation as he could. "I dare say Mrs. Pasmer would be very glad to see him."

"I've no *doubt* she would," said Mrs. Brinkley. "But it's the worst thing that could happen—for him. And I feel like writing him not to come—telegraphing him."

"You know how the man made a fortune in Chicago," said her husband, drying his razor tenderly on a towel before beginning to strop it. "I advise you to let the whole thing alone. It doesn't concern us in any way whatever."

"Then," said Mrs. Brinkley, "there ought to be a committee to take it in hand and warn him."

"I dare say you could make one up among the ladies. But don't be the first to move in the matter."

"I really believe," said his wife, with her mind taken off the point by the attractiveness of a surmise which had just occurred to her, "that Mrs. Pasmer would be capable of following him down if she knew he was in Washington."

"Yes, if she knew. But she probably doesn't."

"Yes," said Mrs. Brinkley, disappointedly. "I think the sudden departure of the Van Hooks must have had something to do with Dan Mavering."

"Seems a very influential young man," said her husband. "He attracts and repels people right and left. Did you speak to the Pasmers?"

"No; you'd better, when you go down. They've just come into the dining-room. The girl looks like death."

"Well, I'll talk to her about Mavering. That'll cheer her up."

Mrs. Brinkley looked at him for an instant as if she really thought him capable of it. Then she joined him in his laugh.

L I

Mrs. Brinkley had theorized Alice Pasmer as simply and primitively selfish, like the rest of the Pasmers in whom the family traits prevailed.

When Mavering stopped coming to her house after his engagement, she justly suspected that it was because Alice had forbidden him, and she had rejoiced at the broken engagement as an escape for Dan; she had frankly said so, and she had received him back into full favor at the first moment in Washington. She liked Miss Anderson, and she had hoped, with the interest which women feel in every such affair, that her flirtation with him might become serious. But now this had apparently not happened. Julia Anderson was gone with mystifying precipitation, and Alice Pasmer had come with an unexpectedness which had the aspect of fatality.

Mrs. Brinkley felt bound, of course, since there was no open enmity between them, to meet the Pasmers on the neutral ground of the Hygeia with conventional amiability. She was really touched by the absent wanness of the girl's look, and by the later-coming recognition which shaped her mouth into a pathetic smile. Alice did not look like death quite, as Mrs. Brinkley had told her husband, with the necessity her sex has for putting its superlatives before its positives; but she was pale and thin, and she moved with a languid step when they all met at night, after Mrs. Brinkley had kept out of the Pasmers' way during the day.

"She has been ill all the latter part of the winter," said Mrs. Pasmer to Mrs. Brinkley that night in the corner of the spreading hotel parlors, where they found themselves. Mrs. Pasmer did not look well herself; she spoke with her eyes fixed anxiously on the door Alice had just passed out of. "She is going to bed, but I know I shall find her awake whenever I go."

"Perhaps," suggested Mrs. Brinkley, "this soft, heavy sea-air will put her to sleep." She tried to speak dryly and indifferently, but she could not; she was, in fact, very much interested by the situation, and she was touched, in spite of her distaste for them both, by the evident unhappiness of mother and daughter. She knew what it came from, and she said to herself that they deserved it; but this did not altogether fortify her against their pathos. "I can hardly keep awake myself," she added, gruffly.

"I hope it may help her," said Mrs. Pasmer; "the doctor strongly urged our coming."

"Mr. Pasmer isn't with you?" said Mrs. Brinkley, feeling that it was decent to say something about him.

"No; he was detained." Mrs. Pasmer did not explain the cause of his detention, and the two ladies slowly waved their fans a moment in silence. "Are there many Boston people in the house?" Mrs. Pasmer asked.

"It's full of them," cried Mrs. Brinkley.

"I had scarcely noticed," sighed Mrs. Pasmer; and Mrs. Brinkley knew that this was not true. "Alice takes up all my thoughts," she added; and this might be true enough. She leaned a little forward, and asked, in a low, entreating voice, over her fan, "Mrs. Brinkley, have you seen Mr. Mavering lately?"

Mrs. Brinkley considered this a little too bold, a little too brazen. Had they actually come South in pursuit of him? It was shameless, and she let Mrs. Pasmer know something of her feeling in the shortness with which she answered, "I saw him in Washington the other day—for a moment." She shortened the time she had spent in Dan's company so as to cut Mrs. Pasmer off from as much comfort as possible, and she stared at her in open astonishment.

Mrs. Pasmer dropped her eyes and fingered the edge of her fan with a submissiveness that seemed to Mrs. Brinkley the perfection of duplicity; she wanted to shake her. "I knew," sighed Mrs. Pasmer, "that you had always been such a friend of his."

It is the last straw which breaks the camel's back; Mrs. Brinkley felt her moral vertebræ give way; she almost heard them crack; but if there was really a detonation, she drowned the noise with a harsh laugh. "Oh, he had *other* friends in Washington. I met him everywhere with Miss Anderson." This statement conflicted with the theory of her single instant with Dan, but she felt that in such a cause, in the cause of giving pain to a woman like Mrs. Pasmer, the deflection from exact truth was justifiable. She hurried on: "I rather expected he might run down here, but now that they're gone, I don't suppose he'll come. You remember Miss Anderson's aunt, Miss Van Hook?"

"Oh yes," said Mrs. Pasmer.

"She was here with her."

"Miss Van Hook was such a New York type—of a certain kind," said Mrs. Pasmer. She rose, with a smile at once so conventional, so heroic, and so pitiful that Mrs. Brinkley felt the remorse of a generous victor.

She went to her room, hardening her heart, and she burst in with a flood of voluble exasperation that threatened all the neighboring rooms with overflow.

"Well," she cried, "they have shown their hands completely. They have simply come here to hound Dan Mavering down, and get him into their toils again. Why, the woman actually said as much! But I fancy I have given her a fit of insomnia that will enable her to share her daughter's vigils. Really, such impudence I never heard of!"

"Do you want everybody in the corridor to hear of it?" asked Brinkley, from behind a newspaper.

"I know *one* thing," continued Mrs. Brinkley, dropping her voice a couple of octaves. "They will never get him here, if *I* can help it. He won't come, anyway, now Miss Anderson is gone; but I'll make assurance doubly sure by writing him *not* to come; I'll tell him they've gone, and that we are going too."

"You had better remember the man in Chicago," said her husband.

"Well, this *is* my business—or I'll *make* it my business!" cried Mrs. Brinkley. She went on talking rapidly, rising with great excitement in her voice at times, and then remembering to speak lower; and her husband apparently read on through most of her talk, though now and then he made some comment that seemed of almost inspired aptness.

"The way they both made up to me was disgusting. But I know the girl is just a tool in her mother's hands. Her mother seemed actually passive in comparison. For skilful wheedling I could fall down and worship that woman; I really admire her. As long as the girl was with us she kept herself in the background and put the girl at me. It was simply a masterpiece."

"How do you know she put her at you?" asked Brinkley.

"How? By the way she seemed *not* to do it! And because from what I know of that stupid Pasmer pride it would be perfectly impossible for any one who *was* a Pasmer to take her deprecatory manner toward me of herself. You ought to have seen it! It was simply perfect."

"Perhaps," said Brinkley, with a remote dreaminess, "she was truly sorry."

"Truly stuff! No, indeed; she hates me as much as ever—more!"

"Well, then, maybe she's doing it because she hates you—doing it for her soul's good—sort of penance, sort of atonement to Mavering."

Mrs. Brinkley turned round from her dressing-table to see what her husband meant, but the newspaper hid him. We all know that our own natures are mixed and contradictory, but we each attribute to others a logical consistency which we never find in any one out of the novels. Alice Pasmer was cold and reticent, and Mrs. Brinkley, who had lived half a century in a world full of paradoxes, could not imagine her subject to gusts of passionate frankness; she knew the girl to be proud and distant, and she could not conceive of an abject humility and longing for sympathy in her heart. If Alice felt, when she saw Mrs. Brinkley, that she had a providential opportunity to punish herself for her injustice to Dan, the fact could not be established upon Mrs. Brinkley's theory of her. If the ascetic impulse is the most purely selfish impulse in human nature, Mrs. Brinkley might not have been mistaken in suspecting her of an ignoble motive, though it might have had for the girl the last sublimity of self-sacrifice. The woman who disliked her and pitied her knew that she had no arts, and rather than adopt so simple a theory of her behavior as her husband had advanced, she held all the more strenuously to her own theory that Alice was practising her mother's arts.

This was inevitable, partly from the sense of Mrs. Pasmer's artfulness which everybody had, and partly from the allegiance which we pay—and women especially like to pay—to the tradition of the playwrights and the novelists that social results of all kinds are the work of deep, and more or less darkling design on the part of other women—such other women as Mrs. Pasmer.

Mrs. Brinkley continued to talk, but the god spoke no more from behind the newspaper; and afterward Mrs. Brinkley lay a long time awake, hardening her heart. But she was haunted to the verge of her dreams by that girl's sick look, by her languid walk, and by the effect which she had seen her own words take upon Mrs. Pasmer—an effect so admirably disowned, so perfectly obvious. Before she could get to sleep she was obliged to make a compromise with her heart, in pursuance of which, when she found Mrs. Pasmer at breakfast alone in the morning, she went up to her, and said, holding her hand a moment, "I hope your daughter slept well last night?"

"No," said Mrs. Pasmer, slipping her hand away. "I can't say that she did."

There was probably no resentment expressed in the way she withdrew her hand, but the other thought there was.

"I wish I could do something for her," she cried.

"Oh, thank you," said Mrs. Pasmer. "It's very good of you." And Mrs. Brinkley fancied she smiled rather bitterly.

LII

M<small>RS.</small> B<small>RINKLEY</small> went out upon the seaward veranda of the hotel with this bitterness of Mrs. Pasmer's smile in her thoughts; and it disposed her to feel more keenly the quality of Miss Pasmer's smile. She found the girl standing there at a remote point of that long stretch of planking, and looking out over the water; she held with both hands across her breast the soft chuddah shawl which the wind caught and fluttered away from her waist. She was alone, and as Mrs. Brinkley's compunctions goaded her nearer, she fancied that she saw Alice master a primary dislike in her face, and put on a look of pathetic propitiation. She did not come forward to meet Mrs. Brinkley, who liked better her waiting to be approached; but she smiled gratefully when Mrs. Brinkley put out her hand, and she took it with a very cold one.

"You must find it chilly here," said the elder woman.

"I had better be out in the air all I could, the doctor said," answered Alice.

"Well, then, come with me round the corner; there's a sort of recess there, and you won't be blown to pieces," said Mrs. Brinkley, with authority. They sat down together in the recess, and she added: "I used to sit here with Miss Van Hook; she could hear better in the noise the waves made. I hope it isn't too much for you?"

"Oh no," said Alice. "Mamma said you told her they were here." Mrs. Brinkley reassured herself from this; Miss Van Hook's name had rather slipped out; but of course Mrs. Pasmer had not repeated what she had said about Dan in this connection. "I wish I could have seen Julia," Alice went on. "It would have been quite like Campobello again."

"Oh, quite," said Mrs. Brinkley, with a short breath, and not knowing whither this tended. Alice did not leave her in doubt.

"I should like to have seen her, and begged her pardon for the way I treated her the last part of the time there. I feel as if I could make my whole *life* a reparation," she added, passionately.

629

Mrs. Brinkley believed that this was the mere frenzy of sentimentality, the exaltation of a selfish asceticism; but at the break in the girl's voice and the aversion of her face she could not help a thrill of motherly tenderness for her. She wanted to tell her that she was an unconscious humbug, bent now as always on her own advantage, and really indifferent to others; she also wanted to comfort her, and tell her that she exaggerated, and was not to blame. She did neither, but when Alice turned her face back, she seemed encouraged by Mrs. Brinkley's look to go on: "I didn't appreciate her then; she was very generous and high-minded—too high-minded for me to understand, even. But we don't seem to know how good others are till we wrong them."

"Yes, that is very true," said Mrs. Brinkley. She knew that Alice was obviously referring to the breach between herself and Miss Anderson following the night of the Trevor theatricals, and the dislike for her that she had shown with a frankness some of the ladies had thought brutal. Mrs. Brinkley also believed that her words had a tacit meaning, and she would have liked to have the hardness to say she had seen an unnamed victim of Alice doing his best to console the other she had specified. But she merely said, dryly, "Yes; perhaps that's the reason why we're allowed to injure people."

"It must be," said Alice, simply. "Did Miss Anderson ever speak of me?"

"No, I can't remember that she ever did." Mrs. Brinkley did not feel bound to say that she and Miss Van Hook had discussed her at large, and agreed perfectly about her.

"I should like to see her; I should like to write to her."

Mrs. Brinkley felt that she ought not to suffer this intimate tendency in the talk.

"You must find a great many other acquaintances in the hotel, Miss Pasmer."

"Some of the Frankland girls are here, and the two Bellinghams. I have hardly spoken to them yet. Do you think that where you have even been in the right, if you have been harsh, if you have been hasty, if you haven't made allowances, you ought to offer some atonement?"

"Really, I can't say," said Mrs. Brinkley, with a smile of distaste. "I'm afraid your question isn't quite in my line of thinking; it's more in Miss Cotton's way. You'd better ask her some time."

"No," said Alice, sadly; "she would flatter me."

"Ah? I always supposed she was very conscientious."

"She's conscientious, but she likes me too well."

"Oh!" commented Mrs. Brinkley to herself, "then you know I don't like you, and you'll use me in one way, if you can't in another. Very well!" But she found the girl's trust touching somehow, though the sentimentality of her appeal seemed as tawdry as ever.

"I knew you would be just," added Alice, wistfully.

"Oh, I don't know about atonements!" said Mrs. Brinkley, with an effect of carelessness. "It seems to me that we usually make them for our own sake."

"I have thought of that," said Alice, with a look of expectation.

"And we usually astonish other people when we offer them."

"Yes?"

"Either they don't like it, or else they don't feel so much injured as we had supposed."

"Oh, but there's no question—"

"If Miss Anderson—"

"Miss Anderson? Oh—oh yes!"

"If Miss Anderson—*for example*," pursued Mrs. Brinkley, "felt aggrieved with you— But really I've no right to enter into your affairs, Miss Pasmer."

"Oh, yes, yes! do! I asked you to," the girl implored.

"I doubt if it will help matters for her to know that you regret anything; and if she shouldn't happen to have thought that you were unjust to her, it would make her uncomfortable for nothing."

"Do you think so?" asked the girl, with a disappointment that betrayed itself in her voice and eyes.

"I never feel myself competent to advise," said Mrs. Brinkley. "I can criticise—anybody can—and I do, pretty freely; but advice is a more serious matter. Each of us must act from herself—from what she thinks is right."

"Yes, I see. Thank you so much, Mrs. Brinkley."

"After all, we have a right to do ourselves good, even when

we pretend that it's good to others, if we don't do them any harm."

"Yes, I see." Alice looked away, and then seemed about to speak again; but one of Mrs. Brinkley's acquaintance came up, and the girl rose with a frightened air and went away.

"Alice's talk with you this morning did her *so* much good!" said Mrs. Pasmer, later. "She has always felt so badly about Miss Anderson!"

Mrs. Brinkley saw that Mrs. Pasmer wished to confine the meaning of their talk to Miss Anderson, and she assented, with a penetration of which she saw that Mrs. Pasmer was gratefully aware.

She grew more tolerant of both the Pasmers as the danger of greater intimacy from them, which seemed to threaten at first, seemed to pass away. She had not responded to their advances, but there was no reason why she should not be civil to them; there had never been any open quarrel with them. She often found herself in talk with them, and was amused to note that she was the only Bostonian whom they did not keep aloof from.

It could not be said that she came to like either of them better. She still suspected Mrs. Pasmer of design, though she developed none beyond manœuvring Alice out of the way of people whom she wished to avoid; and she still found the girl, as she had always thought her, an egotist whose best impulses toward others had a final aim in herself. She thought her very crude in her ideas—cruder than she had seemed at Campobello, where she had perhaps been softened by her affinition with the gentler and kindlier nature of Dan Mavering. Mrs. Brinkley was never tired of saying that he had made the most fortunate escape in the world, and though Brinkley owned he was tired of hearing it, she continued to say it with a great variety of speculation. She recognized that in most girls of Alice's age many traits are in solution, waiting their precipitation into character by the chemical contact which time and chances must bring, and that it was not fair to judge her by the present ferment of hereditary tendencies; but she rejoiced all the same that it was not Dan Mavering's character which was to give fixity to hers. The more she saw of the girl the more she was con-

vinced that two such people could only make each other unhappy; from day to day, almost from hour to hour, she
resolved to write to Mavering and tell him not to come.

She was sure that the Pasmers wished to have the affair on
again, and part of her fascination with a girl whom she neither liked nor approved was her belief that Alice's health had
broken under the strain of her regrets and her despair. She
did not get better from the change of air; she grew more
listless and languid, and more dependent upon Mrs. Brinkley's chary sympathy. The older woman asked herself again
and again what made the girl cling to her? Was she going to
ask her finally to intercede with Dan? or was it really a de-
spairing atonement to him, the most disagreeable sacrifice she
could offer, as Mr. Brinkley had stupidly suggested? She believed that Alice's selfishness and morbid sentiment were
equal to either.

Brinkley generally took the girl's part against his wife, and
in a heavy, jocose way tried to cheer her up. He did little
things for her; fetched and carried chairs and cushions and
rugs, and gave his attentions the air of pleasantries. One of his
offices was to get the ladies' letters for them in the evening,
and one night he came in beaming with a letter for each of
them where they sat together in the parlor. He distributed
them into their laps.

"Hello! I've made a mistake," he said, putting down his
hand to take back the letter he had dropped in Miss Pasmer's
lap. "I've given you my wife's letter."

The girl glanced at it, gave a moaning kind of cry, and fell
back in her chair, hiding her face in her hands.

Mrs. Brinkley possessed herself of the other letter, and
though past the age when ladies wish to kill their husbands
for their stupidity, she gave Brinkley a look of massacre which
mystified even more than it murdered his innocence. He had
to learn later from his wife's more explicit fury what the
women had all known instantly.

He showed his usefulness in gathering Alice up and getting
her to her mother's room.

"*Oh*, Mrs. Brinkley," implored Mrs. Pasmer, following her
to the door, "*Is* Mr. Mavering coming here?"

"I don't know—I can't say—I haven't read the letter yet."

"Oh, *do* let me know when you've read it, won't you? I don't know what we shall do."

Mrs. Brinkley read the letter in her own room. "You go down," she said to her husband, with unabated ferocity, "and telegraph Dan Mavering at Wormley's *not to come*. Say we're going away at once."

Then she sent Mrs. Pasmer a slip of paper on which she had written, "Not coming."

It has been the experience of every one to have some alien concern come into his life and torment him with more anxiety than any affair of his own. This is, perhaps, a hint from the Infinite Sympathy which feels for us all, that none of us can hope to free himself from the troubles of others, that we are each bound to each by ties which, for the most part, we cannot perceive, but which, at the moment their stress comes, we cannot break.

Mrs. Brinkley lay awake and raged impotently against her complicity with the unhappiness of that distasteful girl and her more than distasteful mother. In her revolt against it she renounced the interest she had felt in that silly boy, and his ridiculous love business, so really unimportant to her whatever turn it took. She asked herself what it mattered to her whether those children marred their lives one way or another way. There was a lurid moment before she slept when she wished Brinkley to go down and recall her telegram; but he refused to be a fool at so much inconvenience to himself.

Mrs. Brinkley came to breakfast feeling so much more haggard than she found either of the Pasmers looking that she was able to throw off her lingering remorse for having told Mavering not to come. She had the advantage also of doubt as to her precise motive in having done so; she had either done so because she had judged it best for him not to see Miss Pasmer again, or else she had done so to relieve the girl from the pain of an encounter which her mother evidently dreaded for her. If one motive seemed at moments outrageously meddling and presumptuous, the other was so nobly good and kind that it more than counterbalanced it in Mrs. Brinkley's mind, who knew very well, in spite of her doubt, that she had acted from a mixture of both. With this conviction, it was both a comfort and a pang to find by the register of the hotel, which she furtively consulted, that Dan had not arrived by the morning boat, as she groundlessly feared and hoped he might have done.

In any case, however, and at the end of all the ends, she had that girl on her hands more than ever; and believing as she did that Dan and Alice had only to meet in order to be reconciled, she felt that the girl whom she had balked of her prey was her innocent victim. What right had she to interfere? Was he not her natural prey? If he liked being a prey, who was lawfully to forbid him? He was not perfect; he would know how to take care of himself, probably; in marriage things equalized themselves. She looked at the girl's thin cheeks and lack-lustre eyes, and pitied and hated her with that strange mixture of feeling which our victims inspire in us.

She walked out on the veranda with the Pasmers after breakfast, and chatted awhile about indifferent things; and Alice made an effort to ignore the event of the night before with a pathos which wrung Mrs. Brinkley's heart, and with a gay resolution which ought to have been a great pleasure to such a veteran dissembler as her mother. She said she had never found the air so delicious; she really believed it would begin to do her good now; but it was a little fresh just there, and with her eyes she invited her mother to come with her round the corner into that sheltered recess, and invited Mrs. Brinkley not to come.

It was that effect of resentment which is lighter even than a touch, the waft of the arrow's feather; but it could wound a guilty heart, and Mrs. Brinkley sat down where she was, realizing with a pang that the time when she might have been everything to this unhappy girl had just passed forever, and henceforth she could be nothing. She remained musing sadly upon the contradictions she had felt in the girl's character, the confusion of good and evil, the potentialities of misery and harm, the potentialities of bliss and good; and she felt less and less satisfied with herself. She had really presumed to interfere with Fate; perhaps she had interfered with Providence. She would have given anything to recall her act; and then with a flash she realized that it was quite possible to recall it. She could telegraph Mavering to come;

and she rose, humbly and gratefully, as if from an answered prayer, to go and do so.

She was not at all a young woman, and many things had come and gone in her life that ought to have fortified her against surprise; but she wanted to scream like a little frightened girl as Dan Mavering stepped out of the parlor door toward her. The habit of not screaming, however, prevailed, and she made a tolerably successful effort to treat him with decent composure.

She gave him a rigid hand. "Where in the *world* did you come from? Did you get my telegram?"

"No. Did you get my letter?"

"Yes."

"Well, I took a notion to come right on after I wrote, and I started on the same train with it. But they said it was no use trying to get into the Hygeia, and I stopped last night at the little hotel in Hampton. I've just walked over, and Mr. Brinkley told me you were out here somewhere. That's the whole story, I believe." He gave his nervous laugh, but it seemed to Mrs. Brinkley that it had not much joy in it.

"Hush!" she said, involuntarily, receding to her chair, and sinking back into it again. He looked surprised. "You know the Van Hooks are gone?"

He laughed harshly. "I should think they were dead from your manner, Mrs. Brinkley. But I didn't come to see the Van Hooks. What made you think I did?"

He gave her a look which she found so dishonest, so really insincere, that she resolved to abandon him to Providence as soon as she could. "Oh, I didn't know but there had been some little understanding at Washington."

"Perhaps on their part. They were people who seemed to take a good many things for granted, but they could hardly expect to control other people's movements."

He looked sharply at Mrs. Brinkley, as if to question how much she knew; but she had now measured him, and she said, "Oh! then the visit's to me?"

"Entirely," cried Dan. The old sweetness came into his laughing eyes again, and went to Mrs. Brinkley's heart. She wished him to be happy, somehow; she would have done anything for him; she wished she knew what to do. Ought she to tell him the Pasmers were there? Ought she to make up some excuse and get him away before he met them? She felt herself getting more and more bewildered and helpless. Those women might come round that corner any moment, and then she knew that the first sight of Alice's face would do or undo everything with Dan. Did she wish them reconciled? Did she wish them forever parted? She no longer knew what she wished; she only knew that she had no right to wish anything. She continued to talk on with Dan, who grew more and more at ease, and did most of the talking, while Mrs. Brinkley's whole being narrowed itself to the question, Would the Pasmers come back that way, or would they go round the farther corner, and get into the hotel by another door?

The suspense seemed interminable; they must have already gone that other way. Suddenly she heard the pushing back of chairs in that recess. She could not bear it. She jumped to her feet.

"Just wait a moment, Mr. Mavering! I'll join you again. Mr. Brinkley is expecting— I must—"

One morning of the following June Mrs. Brinkley sat well forward in the beautiful church where Dan and Alice were to be married. The lovely day became a still lovelier day within, enriched by the dyes of the stained windows through which it streamed; the still place was dim yet bright with it; the figures painted on the walls had a soft distinctness; a body of light seemed to irradiate from the depths of the dome like lamplight.

There was a subdued murmur of voices among the people in the pews; they were in a sacred edifice without being exactly at church, and they might talk; now and then a muffled, nervous laugh escaped. A delicate scent of flowers from the masses in the chancel mixed with the light and the prevailing silence. There was a soft, continuous rustle of drapery as the ladies advanced up the thickly carpeted aisles on the arms of the young ushers and compressed themselves into place in the pews.

Two or three people whom she did not know were put into the pew with Mrs. Brinkley, but she kept her seat next the aisle; presently an usher brought up a lady who sat down beside her, and then for a moment or two seemed to sink and rise, as if on the springs of an intense excitement.

It was Miss Cotton, who, while this process of quiescing lasted, appeared not to know Mrs. Brinkley. When she became aware of her, all was lost again. "Mrs. *Brinkley!*" she cried, as well as one can cry in whisper. "Is it *possible?*"

"I have my doubts," Mrs. Brinkley whispered back. "But we'll suppose the case."

"Oh, it's *all* too good to be true! How I envy you being the means of bringing them together, Mrs. Brinkley!"

"Means?"

"Yes; they owe it all to you; you needn't try to deny it; he's told every one!"

"I was sure *she* hadn't," said Mrs. Brinkley, remembering how Alice had marked an increasing ignorance of any part she might have had in the affair from the first moment of her reconciliation with Dan; she had the effect of feeling that she had sacrificed enough to Mrs. Brinkley; and Mrs. Brinkley had been restored to all the original strength of her conviction that she was a solemn little unconscious egotist, and Dan was as unselfish and good as he was unequal to her exactions.

"Oh *no!*" said Miss Cotton. "She couldn't!" implying that Alice would be too delicate to speak of it.

"Do you see any of his family here?" asked Mrs. Brinkley.

"Yes; over there—up front." Miss Cotton motioned with her eyes toward a pew in which Mrs. Brinkley distinguished an elderly gentleman's down-misted bald head and the back of a young lady's bonnet. "His father and sister; the other's a bridemaid; mother bed-ridden and couldn't come."

"They might have brought her in an arm-chair," suggested Mrs. Brinkley, ironically, "on such an occasion. But perhaps they don't take much interest in such a patched-up affair."

"Oh, yes they do!" exclaimed Miss Cotton. "They idolize Alice."

"And Mrs. Pasmer and Mister, too?"

"I don't suppose that so much matters."

"They know how to acquiesce, I've no doubt."

"Oh yes! You've heard? The young people are going abroad

first with her family for a year, and then they come back to live with his—where the Works are."

"Poor fellow!" said Mrs. Brinkley.

"Why, Mrs. Brinkley, do you still feel that way?" asked Miss Cotton, with a certain distress. "It seems to me that if ever two young people had the promise of happiness, *they* have. Just see what their love has done for them already!"

"And you still think that in these cases love can do everything?"

Miss Cotton was about to reply, when she observed that the people about her had stopped talking. The bridegroom, with his best man, in whom his few acquaintances there recognized Boardman with some surprise, came over the chancel from one side.

Miss Cotton bent close to Mrs. Brinkley and whispered rapidly: "Alice found out Mr. Mavering wished it, and insisted on his having him. It was a great concession, but she's perfectly magnanimous. Poor fellow! how he *does* look!"

Alice, on her father's arm, with her bridemaids, of whom the first was Minnie Mavering, mounted the chancel steps, where Mr. Pasmer remained standing till he advanced to give away the bride. He behaved with great dignity, but seemed deeply affected; the ladies in the front pews said they could see his face twitch; but he never looked handsomer.

The two clergymen came from the back of the chancel in their white surplices. The ceremony proceeded to the end.

The young couple drove at once to the station, where they were to take the train for New York, and wait there a day or two for Mrs. and Mr. Pasmer before they all sailed.

As they drove along, Alice held Dan's wrist in the cold clutch of her trembling little ungloved hand, on which her wedding-ring shone. "Oh, dearest! let us be good!" she said. "I will try my best. I will try not to be exacting and unreasonable, and I know I can. I won't even make any conditions, if you will always be frank and open with me, and tell me everything!"

He leaned over and kissed her behind the drawn curtains. "I will, Alice! I will indeed! I won't keep anything from you after this."

He resolved to tell her all about Julia Anderson at the right moment, when Alice was in the mood, and as soon as he thoroughly understood what he had really meant himself.

If he had been different she would not have asked him to be frank and open; if she had been different, he might have been frank and open. This was the beginning of their married life.

ANNIE KILBURN

I.

AFTER THE DEATH of Judge Kilburn his daughter came back to America. They had been eleven winters in Rome, always meaning to return, but staying on from year to year, as people do who have nothing definite to call them home. Toward the last Miss Kilburn tacitly gave up the expectation of getting her father away, though they both continued to say that they were going to take passage as soon as the weather was settled in the spring. At the date they had talked of for sailing he was lying in the Protestant cemetery, and she was trying to gather herself together, and adjust her life to his loss. This would have been easier with a younger person, for she had been her father's pet so long, and then had taken care of his helplessness with a devotion which was finally so motherly, that it was like losing at once a parent and a child when he died, and she remained with the habit of giving herself when there was no longer any one to receive the sacrifice. He had married late, and in her thirty-first year he was seventy-eight; but the disparity of their ages, increasing toward the end through his infirmities, had not loosened for her the ties of custom and affection that bound them; she had seen him grow more and more fitfully cognisant of what they had been to each other since her mother's death, while she grew the more tender and fond with him. People who came to condole with her seemed not to understand this, or else they thought it would help her to bear up if they treated her bereavement as a relief from hopeless anxiety. They were all surprised when she told them she still meant to go home.

"Why, my dear," said one old lady, who had been away from America twenty years, "*this* is home! You've lived in this apartment longer now than the oldest inhabitant has lived in most American towns. What are you talking about? Do you mean that you are going back to Washington?"

"Oh no. We were merely staying on in Washington from force of habit, after father gave up practice. I think we shall go back to the old homestead, where we used to spend our summers, ever since I can remember."

643

"And where is that?" the old lady asked, with the sharpness which people believe must somehow be good for a broken spirit.

"It's in the interior of Massachusetts—you wouldn't know it: a place called Hatboro'."

"No, I certainly shouldn't," said the old lady, with superiority. "Why Hatboro', of all the ridiculous reasons?"

"It was one of the first places where they began to make straw hats; it was a nickname at first, and then they adopted it. The old name was Dorchester Farms. Father fought the change, but it was of no use; the people wouldn't have it Farms after the place began to grow; and by that time they had got used to Hatboro'. Besides, I don't see how it's any worse than Hatfield, in England."

"It's very American."

"Oh, it's American. We have Boxboro' too, you know, in Massachusetts."

"And you are going from Rome to Hatboro', Mass.," said the old lady, trying to present the idea in the strongest light by abbreviating the name of the State.

"Yes," said Miss Kilburn. "It will be a change, but not so much of a change as you would think. It was father's wish to go back."

"Ah, my *dear!*" cried the old lady. "You're letting that weigh with you, I see. Don't do it! If it wasn't wise, don't you suppose that the last thing he could wish you to do would be to sacrifice yourself to a sick whim of his?"

The kindness expressed in the words touched Annie Kilburn. She had a certain beauty of feature; she was nearsighted; but her eyes were brown and soft, her lips red and full; her dark hair grew low, and played in little wisps and rings on her temples, where her complexion was clearest; the bold contour of her face, with its decided chin and the rather large salient nose, was like her father's; it was this, probably, that gave an impression of strength, with a wistful qualification. She was at that time rather thin, and it could have been seen that she would be handsomer when her frame had rounded out in fulfilment of its generous design. She opened her lips to speak, but shut them again in an effort at self-control before she said—

"But I really wish to do it. At this moment I would rather be in Hatboro' than in Rome."

"Oh, very well," said the old lady, gathering herself up as one does from throwing away one's sympathy upon an unworthy object; "if you really *wish* it——"

"I know that it must seem preposterous and—and almost ungrateful that I should think of going back, when I might just as well stay. Why, I've a great many more friends here than I have there; I suppose I shall be almost a stranger when I get there, and there's no comparison in congeniality; and yet I feel that I must go back. I can't tell you why. But I have a longing; I feel that I must try to be of some use in the world—try to do some good—and in Hatboro' I think I shall know how." She put on her glasses, and looked at the old lady as if she might attempt an explanation, but, as if a clearer vision of the veteran worldling discouraged her, she did not make the effort.

"*Oh!*" said the old lady. "If you want to be of use, and do good——" She stopped, as if then there were no more to be said by a sensible person. "And shall you be going soon?" she asked. The idea seemed to suggest her own departure, and she rose after speaking.

"Just as soon as possible," answered Miss Kilburn. Words take on a colour of something more than their explicit meaning from the mood in which they are spoken: Miss Kilburn had a sense of hurrying her visitor away, and the old lady had a sense of being turned out-of-doors, that the preparations for the homeward voyage might begin instantly.

II.

MANY TIMES after the preparations began, and many times after they were ended, Miss Kilburn faltered in doubt of her decision; and if there had been any will stronger than her own to oppose it, she might have reversed it, and stayed in Rome. All the way home there was a strain of misgiving in her satisfaction at doing what she believed to be for the best, and the first sight of her native land gave her a shock of emotion which was not unmixed joy. She felt forlorn among people who were coming home with all sorts of high expectations, while she only had high intentions.

These dated back a good many years; in fact, they dated back to the time when the first flush of her unthinking girlhood was over, and she began to question herself as to the life she was living. It was a very pleasant life, ostensibly. Her father had been elected from the bench to Congress, and had kept his title and his repute as a lawyer through several terms in the House before he settled down to the practice of his profession in the courts at Washington, where he made a good deal of money. They passed from boarding to housekeeping, in the easy Washington way, after their impermanent Congressional years, and divided their time between a comfortable little place in Nevada Circle and the old homestead in Hatboro'. He was fond of Washington, and robustly content with the world as he found it there and elsewhere. If his daughter's compunctions came to her through him, it must have been from some remoter ancestry; he was not apparently characterised by their transmission, and probably she derived them from her mother, who died when she was a little girl, and of whom she had no recollection. Till he began to break, after they went abroad, he had his own way in everything; but as men grow old or infirm they fall into subjection to their womenkind; their rude wills yield in the suppler insistence of the feminine purpose; they take the colour of the feminine moods and emotions; the cycle of life completes itself where it began, in helpless dependence upon the sex; and Rufus Kilburn did not escape the common lot. He was often complaining and unlovely, as aged and ailing men must be;

perhaps he was usually so; but he had moments when he recognised the beauty of his daughter's aspiration with a spiritual sympathy, which showed that he must always have had
an intellectual perception of it. He expressed with rhetorical
largeness and looseness the longing which was not very definite in her own heart, and mingled with it a strain of homesickness poignantly simple and direct for the places, the
scenes, the persons, the things, of his early days. As he failed
more and more, his homesickness was for natural aspects
which had wholly ceased to exist through modern changes
and improvements, and for people long since dead, whom he
could find only in an illusion of that environment in some
other world. In the pathos of this situation it was easy for his
daughter to keep him ignorant of the passionate rebellion
against her own ideals in which she sometimes surprised herself. When he died, all counter-currents were lost in the tidal
revulsion of feeling which swept her to the fulfilment of what
she hoped was deepest and strongest in her nature, with
shame for what she hoped was shallowest, till that moment of
repulsion in which she saw the thickly roofed and many-
towered hills of Boston grow up out of the western waves.

She had always regarded her soul as the battlefield of two
opposite principles, the good and the bad, the high and the
low. God made her, she thought, and He alone; He made
everything that she was; but she would not have said that He
made the evil in her. Yet her belief did not admit the existence
of Creative Evil; and so she said to herself that she herself was
that evil, and she must struggle against herself; she must
question whatever she strongly wished because she strongly
wished it. It was not logical; she did not push her postulates
to their obvious conclusions; and there was apt to be the
same kind of break between her conclusions and her actions
as between her reasons and her conclusions. She acted impul-
sively, and from a force which she could not analyse. She indulged reveries so vivid that they seemed to weaken and
exhaust her for the grapple with realities; the recollection of
them abashed her in the presence of facts.

With all this, it must not be supposed that she was mor-
bidly introspective. Her life had been apparently a life of
cheerful acquiescence in worldly conditions; it had been, in

some measure, a life of fashion, or at least of society. It had not been without the interests of other girls' lives, by any means; she had sometimes had fancies, flirtations, but she did not think she had been really in love, and she had refused some offers of marriage for that reason.

III.

THE INDUSTRY of making straw hats began at Hatboro',
as many other industries have begun in New England,
with no great local advantages, but simply because its founder
happened to live there, and to believe that it would pay.
There was a railroad, and labour of the sort he wanted was
cheap and abundant in the village and the outlying farms. In
time the work came to be done more and more by machinery,
and to be gathered into large shops. The buildings increased
in size and number; the single line of the railroad was multi-
plied into four, and in the region of the tracks several large,
ugly, windowy wooden bulks grew up for shoe shops; a
stocking factory followed; yet this business activity did not
warp the old village from its picturesqueness or quiet. The
railroad tracks crossed its main street; but the shops were all
on one side of them, with the work-people's cottages and
boarding-houses, and on the other were the simple, square,
roomy old mansions, with their white paint and their green
blinds, varied by the modern colour and carpentry of French-
roofed villas. The old houses stood quite close to the street,
with a strip of narrow door-yard before them; the new ones
affected a certain depth of lawn, over which their owners personally pushed a clucking hand-mower in the summer evenings after tea. The fences had been taken away from the new
houses, in the taste of some of the Boston suburbs; they generally remained before the old ones, whose inmates resented
the ragged effect that their absence gave the street. The irregularity had hitherto been of an orderly and harmonious kind,
such as naturally follows the growth of a country road into a
village thoroughfare. The dwellings were placed nearer or further from the sidewalk as their builders fancied, and the elms
that met in a low arch above the street had an illusive symme-
try in the perspective; they were really set at uneven intervals,
and in a line that wavered capriciously in and out. The street
itself lounged and curved along, widening and contracting
like a river, and then suddenly lost itself over the brow of an
upland which formed a natural boundary of the village. Beyond this was South Hatboro', a group of cottages built by

city people who had lately come in—idlers and invalids, the
former for the cool summer, and the latter for the dry winter.
At chance intervals in the old village new side streets
branched from the thoroughfare to the right and the left, and
here and there a Queen Anne cottage showed its chimneys
and gables on them. The roadway under the elms that kept it
dark and cool with their hovering shade, and swept the
wagon-tops with their pendulous boughs at places, was un-
paved; but the sidewalks were asphalted to the last dwelling
in every direction, and they were promptly broken out in
winter by the public snow-plough.

Miss Kilburn saw them in the spring, when their usefulness
was least apparent, and she did not know whether to praise
the spirit of progress which showed itself in them as well as in
other things at Hatboro'. She had come prepared to have misgivings, but she had promised herself to be just; she thought
she could bear the old ugliness, if not the new. Some of the
new things, however, were not so ugly; the young stationmaster was handsome in his railroad uniform, and pleasanter
to the eye than the veteran baggage-master, incongruous in
his stiff silk cap and his shirt sleeves and spectacles. The station itself, one of Richardson's, massive and low, with red-
tiled, spreading veranda roofs, impressed her with its fitness,
and strengthened her for her encounter with the business architecture of Hatboro', which was of the florid, ambitious
New York type, prevalent with every American town in the
early stages of its prosperity. The buildings were of pink
brick, faced with granite, and supported in the first story by
columns of painted iron; flat-roofed blocks looked down over
the low-wooden structures of earlier Hatboro', and a large
hotel had pushed back the old-time tavern, and planted itself
flush upon the sidewalk. But the stores seemed very good,
as she glanced at them from her carriage, and their show-
windows were tastefully arranged; the apothecary's had an
interior of glittering neatness unsurpassed by an Italian apothecary's; and the provision-man's, besides its symmetrical array
of pendent sides and quarters indoors, had banks of fruit and
vegetables without, and a large aquarium with a spraying
fountain in its window.

Bolton, the farmer who had always taken care of the

Kilburn place, came to meet her at the station and drive her home. Miss Kilburn had bidden him drive slowly, so that she could see all the changes, and she noticed the new town-hall, with which she could find no fault; the Baptist and Methodist churches were the same as of old; the Unitarian church seemed to have shrunk as if the architecture had sympathised with its dwindling body of worshippers; just beyond it was the village green, with the soldiers' monument, and the tall white-painted flag-pole, and the four small brass cannon threatening the points of the compass at its base.

"Stop a moment, Mr. Bolton," said Miss Kilburn; and she put her head quite out of the carriage, and stared at the figure on the monument.

It was strange that the first misgiving she could really make sure of concerning Hatboro' should relate to this figure, which she herself was mainly responsible for placing there. When the money was subscribed and voted for the statue, the committee wrote out to her at Rome as one who would naturally feel an interest in getting something fit and economical for them. She accepted the trust with zeal and pleasure; but she overruled their simple notion of an American volunteer at rest, with his hands folded on the muzzle of his gun, as intolerably hackneyed and commonplace. Her conscience, she said, would not let her add another recruit to the regiment of stone soldiers standing about in that posture on the tops of pedestals all over the country; and so, instead of going to an Italian statuary with her fellow-townsmen's letter, and getting him to make the figure they wanted, she doubled the money and gave the commission to a young girl from Kansas, who had come out to develop at Rome the genius recognised at Topeka. They decided together that it would be best to have something ideal, and the sculptor promptly imagined and rapidly executed a design for a winged Victory, poising on the summit of a white marble shaft, and clasping its hands under its chin, in expression of the grief that mingled with the popular exultation. Miss Kilburn had her doubts while the work went on, but she silenced them with the theory that when the figure was in position it would be all right.

Now that she saw it in position she wished to ask Mr.

Bolton what was thought of it, but she could not nerve herself to the question. He remained silent, and she felt that he was sorry for her. "Oh, may I be very humble; may I be helped to be very humble!" she prayed under her breath. It seemed as if she could not take her eyes from the figure; it was such a modern, such an American shape, so youthfully inadequate, so simple, so sophisticated, so like a young lady in society indecorously exposed for a *tableau vivant*. She wondered if the people in Hatboro' felt all this about it; if they realised how its involuntary frivolity insulted the solemn memory of the slain.

"Drive on, please," she said gently.

Bolton pulled the reins, and as the horses started he pointed with his whip to a church at the other side of the green. "That's the new Orthodox church," he explained.

"Oh, is it?" asked Miss Kilburn. "It's very handsome, I'm sure." She was not sensible of admiring the large Romanesque pile very much, though it was certainly not bad, but she remembered that Bolton was a member of the Orthodox church, and she was grateful to him for not saying anything about the soldiers' monument.

"We sold the old buildin' to the Catholics, and they moved it down ont' the side street."

Miss Kilburn caught the glimmer of a cross where he beckoned, through the flutter of the foliage.

"They had to razee the steeple some to git their cross on," he added; and then he showed her the high-school building as they passed, and the Episcopal chapel, of blameless church-warden's Gothic, half hidden by its Japanese ivy, under a branching elm, on another side street.

"Yes," she said, "that was built before we went abroad."

"I disremember," he said absently. He let the horses walk on the soft, darkly shaded road, where the wheels made a pleasant grinding sound, and set himself sidewise on his front seat, so as to talk to Miss Kilburn more at his ease.

"I d' know," he began, after clearing his throat, with a conscious air, "as you know we'd got a new minister to our church."

"No, I hadn't heard of it," said Miss Kilburn, with her mind full of the monument still. "But I might have heard and forgotten it," she added. "I was very much taken up toward the last before I left Rome."

"Well, come to think," said Bolton; "I don't know 's you'd had time to heard. He hain't been here a great while."

"Is he—satisfactory?" asked Miss Kilburn, feeling how far from satisfactory the Victory was, and formulating an explanatory apology to the committee in her mind.

"Oh yes, he's satisfactory enough, as far forth as that goes. He's talented, and he's right up with the times. Yes, he's progressive. I guess they got pretty tired of Mr. Rogers, even before he died; and they kept the supply a-goin' till—all was blue, before they could settle on anybody. In fact they couldn't seem to agree on anybody till Mr. Peck come."

Miss Kilburn had got as far, in her tacit interview with the committee, as to have offered to replace at her own expense the Victory with a Volunteer, and she seemed to be listening to Bolton with rapt attention.

"Well, it's like this," continued the farmer. "He's progressive in his idees, 'n' at the same time he's spiritual-minded; and so I guess he suits pretty well all round. Of course you can't suit everybody. There's always got to be a dog in the manger, it don't matter where you go. But if anybody was to ask me, I should say Mr. Peck suited. Yes, I don't know but what I should."

Miss Kilburn instantaneously closed her transaction with the committee, removed the Victory, and had the Volunteer unveiled with appropriate ceremonies, opened with prayer by the Rev. Mr. Peck.

"Peck?" she said. "Did you tell me his name was Peck?"

"Yes, ma'am; Rev. Julius W. Peck. He's from down Penobscotport way, in Maine. I guess he's all right."

Miss Kilburn did not reply. Her mind had been taken off the monument for the moment by her dislike for the name of the new minister, and the Victory had seized the opportunity to get back.

Bolton sighed deeply, and continued in a strain whose diffusiveness at last became perceptible to Miss Kilburn through her own humiliation. "There's some in every community that's bound to complain, I don't care what you do to accommodate 'em; and what I done, I done as much to stop their

clack as anything, and give him the right sort of a start off, an'
I guess I did. But Mis' Bolton she didn't know but what
you'd look at it in the light of a libbutty, and I didn't know
but what you *would* think I no business to done it."

He seemed to be addressing a question to her, but she only
replied with a dazed frown, and Bolton was obliged to go on.

"I didn't let him room in your part of the house; that is to
say, not sleep there; but I thought, as you was comin' home,
and I better be airin' it up some, anyway, I might as well let
him set in the old Judge's room. If you think it was more
than I had a right to do, I'm willin' to pay for it. Git up!"
Bolton turned fully round toward his horses, to hide the
workings of emotion in his face, and shook the reins like a
desperate man.

"What *are* you talking about, Mr. Bolton?" cried Miss
Kilburn. "*Whom* are you talking about?"

Bolton answered, with a kind of violence, "Mr. Peck; I took
him to board, first off."

"You took him to *board*?"

"Yes. I know it wa'n't just accordin' to the letter o' the law,
and the old Judge was always pootty p'tic'lah. But I've took
care of the place goin' on twenty years now, and I hain't never
had a chick nor a child in it before. The child," he continued,
partly turning his face round again, and beginning to look
Miss Kilburn in the eye, "wa'n't one to touch anything, anyway, and we kep' her in our part all the while; Mis' Bolton
she couldn't seem to let her out of her sight, she got so fond
of her, and she used to follow me round among the hosses
like a kitten. I declare, I *miss* her."

Bolton's face, the colour of one of the lean ploughed fields
of Hatboro', and deeply furrowed, lighted up with real
feeling, which he tried to make go as far in the work of reconciling Miss Kilburn as if it had been factitious.

"But I don't understand," she said. "What child are you
talking about?"

"Mr. Peck's."

"Was he married?" she asked, with displeasure, she did not
know why.

"Well, yes, he *had* been," answered Bolton. "But she'd be'n
in the asylum ever since the child was born."

"Oh," said Miss Kilburn, with relief; and she fell back upon the seat from which she had started forward.

Bolton might easily have taken her tone for that of disgust. He faced round upon her once more. "It was kind of queer, his havin' the child with him, an' takin' most the care of her himself; and so, as I *say*, Mis' Bolton and me we took him in, as much to stop folks' mouths as anything, till they got kinder used to it. But we didn't take him into your part, as I *say*; and as *I* say, I'm willin' to pay you whatever you say for the use of the old Judge's study. I presume that part of it *was* a libbutty."

"It was all perfectly right, Mr. Bolton," said Miss Kilburn.

"His wife died anyway, more than a year ago," said Bolton, as if the fact completed his atonement to Miss Kilburn. "*Git* ep! I told him from the start that it had got to be a temporary thing, an' 't I only took him till he could git settled somehow. I guess he means to go to house-keepin', if he can git the right kind of a house-keeper; he wants an old one. If it was a young one, I guess he wouldn't have any great trouble, if he went about it the right way." Bolton's sarcasm was merely a race sarcasm. He was a very mild man, and his thick-growing eyelashes softened and shadowed his grey eyes, and gave his lean face pathos.

"You could have let him stay till he had found a suitable place," said Miss Kilburn.

"Oh, I wa'n't goin' to do *that*," said Bolton. "But I'm 'bliged to you just the same."

They came up in sight of the old square house, standing back a good distance from the road, with a broad sweep of grass sloping down before it into a little valley, and rising again to the wall fencing the grounds from the street. The wall was overhung there by a company of magnificent elms, which turned and formed one side of the avenue leading to the house. Their tops met and mixed somewhat incongruously with those of the stiff dark maples which more densely shaded the other side of the lane.

Bolton drove into their gloom, and then out into the wide sunny space at the side of the house where Miss Kilburn had alighted so often with her father. Bolton's dog, grown now so very old as to be weak-minded, barked crazily at his master, and then, recognising him, broke into an imbecile whimper,

and went back and coiled his rheumatism up in the sun on a
warm stone before the door. Mrs. Bolton had to step over
him as she came out, formally supporting her right elbow
with her left hand as she offered the other in greeting to Miss
Kilburn, with a look of question at her husband.

Miss Kilburn intercepted the look, and began to laugh.

All was unchanged, and all so strange; it seemed as if her
father must both get down with her from the carriage and
come to meet her from the house. Her glance involuntarily
took in the familiar masses and details; the patches of short
tough grass mixed with decaying chips and small weeds un-
derfoot, and the spacious June sky overhead; the fine network
and blisters of the cracking and warping white paint on the
clapboarding, and the hills beyond the bulks of the village
houses and trees; the wood-shed stretching with its low board
arches to the barn, and the milk-pans tilted to sun against the
underpinning of the L, and Mrs. Bolton's pot plants in the
kitchen window.

"Did you think I could be hard about such a thing as that?
It was perfectly right. O Mrs. Bolton!" She stopped laughing
and began to cry; she put away Mrs. Bolton's carefully offered
hand, she threw herself upon the bony structure of her
bosom, and buried her face sobbing in the leathery folds of
her neck.

Mrs. Bolton suffered her embrace above the old dog, who
fled with a cry of rheumatic apprehension from the sweep of
Miss Kilburn's skirts, and then came back and snuffed at them
in a vain effort to recall her.

"Well, go in and lay down by the stove," said Mrs. Bolton,
with a divided interest, while she beat Miss Kilburn's back
with her bony palm in sign of sympathy. But the dog went
off up the lane, and stood there by the pasture bars, barking
abstractedly at intervals.

IV.

MISS KILBURN found that the house had been well aired for her coming, but an old earthy and mouldy smell, which it took days and nights of open doors and windows to drive out, stole back again with the first turn of rainy weather. She had fires built on the hearths and in the stoves, and after opening her trunks and scattering her dresses on beds and chairs, she spent most of the first week outside of the house, wandering about the fields and orchards to adjust herself anew to the estranged features of the place. The house she found lower-ceiled and smaller than she remembered it. The Boltons had kept it up very well, and in spite of the earthy and mouldy smell, it was conscientiously clean. There was not a speck of dust anywhere; the old yellowish-white paint was spotless; the windows shone. But there was a sort of frigidity in the perfect order and repair which repelled her, and she left her things tossed about, as if to break the ice of this propriety. In several places, within and without, she found marks of the faithful hand of Bolton in economical patches of the wood-work; but she was not sure that they had not been there eleven years before; and there were darnings in the carpets and curtains, which affected her with the same mixture of novelty and familiarity. Certain stale smells about the place (minor smells as compared with the prevalent odour) con-fused her; she could not decide whether she remembered them of old, or was reminded of the odours she used to catch in passing the pantry on the steamer.

Her father had never been sure that he would not return any next year or month, and the house had always been ready to receive them. In his study everything was as he left it. His daughter looked for signs of Mr. Peck's occupation, but there were none; Mrs. Bolton explained that she had put him in a table from her own sitting-room to write at. The Judge's desk was untouched, and his heavy wooden arm-chair stood pulled up to it as if he were in it. The ranks of law-books, in their yellow sheep-skin, with their red titles above and their black titles below, were in the order he had taught Mrs. Bolton to replace them in after dusting; the stuffed owl on a shelf above the mantel looked down with a clear solemnity in its gum-copal eyes, and Mrs. Bolton took it from its perch to show Miss Kilburn that there was not a moth on it, nor the sign of a moth.

Miss Kilburn experienced here that refusal of the old associations to take the form of welcome which she had already felt in the earth and sky and air outside; in everything there was a sense of impassable separation. Her dead father was no nearer in his wonted place than the trees of the orchard, or the outline of the well-known hills, or the pink of the familiar sunsets. In her rummaging about the house she pulled open a chest of drawers which used to stand in the room where she slept when a child. It was full of her own childish clothing, a little girl's linen and muslin; and she thought with a throe of despair that she could as well hope to get back into these outgrown garments, which the helpless piety of Mrs. Bolton had kept from the rag-bag, as to think of re-entering the relations of the life so long left off.

It surprised her to find how cold the Boltons were; she had remembered them as always very kind and willing; but she was so used now to the ways of the Italians and their showy affection, it was hard for her to realise that people could be both kind and cold. The Boltons seemed ashamed of their feelings, and hid them; it was the same in some degree with all the villagers when she began to meet them, and the fact slowly worked back into her consciousness, wounding its way in. People did not come to see her at once. They waited, as they told her, till she got settled, before they called, and then they did not appear very glad to have her back.

But this was not altogether the effect of their temperament. The Kilburns had made a long summer always in Hatboro', and they had always talked of it as home; but they had never passed a whole year there since Judge Kilburn first went to Congress, and they were not regarded as full neighbours or permanent citizens. Miss Kilburn, however, kept up her childhood friendships, and she and some of the ladies called one another by their Christian names, but they believed that she met people in Washington whom she liked better; the winters she spent there certainly weakened the ties between them, and when it came to those eleven years in Rome, the letters they exchanged grew rarer and rarer, till they stopped altogether. Some of the girls went away; some died; others became dead and absent to her in their marriages and household cares.

After waiting for one another, three of them came together to see her one day. They all kissed her, after a questioning glance at her face and dress, as if they wanted to see whether she had grown proud or too fashionable. But they were themselves apparently much better dressed, and certainly more richly dressed. In a place like Hatboro', where there is no dinner-giving, and evening parties are few, the best dress is a street costume, which may be worn for calls and shopping, and for church and all public entertainments. The well-to-do ladies make an effect of outdoor fashion, in which the poorest shop hand has her part; and in their turn they share her indoor simplicity. These old friends of Annie's wore bonnets and frocks of the latest style and costly material.

They let her make the advances, receiving them with blank passivity, or repelling them with irony, according to the several needs of their self-respect, and talking to one another across her. One of them asked her when her hair had begun to turn, and they each told her how thin she was, but promised her that Hatboro' air would bring her up. At the same time they feigned humility in regard to everything about Hatboro' but the air; they laughed when she said she intended now to make it her home the whole year round, and said they guessed she would be tired of it long before fall; there were plenty of summer folks that passed the winter as long as the June weather lasted. As they grew more secure of themselves, or less afraid of one another in her presence, their voices rose; they laughed loudly at nothing, and they yelled in a nervous chorus at times, each trying to make herself heard above the others.

She asked them about the social life in the village, and they told her that a good many new people had really settled there, but they did not know whether she would like them; they were not the old Hatboro' style. Annie showed them some of the things she had brought home, especially Roman views, and they said now she ought to give an evening in the church parlour with them.

"You'll have to come to our church, Annie," said Mrs.

Putney. "The Unitarian doesn't have preaching once in a month, and Mr. Peck is *very* liberal."

"He's 'most *too* liberal for some," said Emmeline Gerrish. Of the three she had grown the stoutest, and from being a slight, light-minded girl, she had become a heavy matron, habitually censorious in her speech. She did not mean any more by it, however, than she did by her girlish frivolity, and if she was not supported in her severity, she was apt to break down and disown it with a giggle, as she now did.

"Well, I don't know about his being *too* liberal," said Mrs. Wilmington, a large red-haired blonde, with a lazy laugh. "He makes you feel that you're a pretty miserable sinner." She made a grimace of humorous disgust.

"Mr. Gerrish says that's just the trouble," Mrs. Gerrish broke in. "Mr. Peck don't put stress enough on the promises. That's what Mr. Gerrish says. You must have been surprised, Annie," she added, "to find that he'd been staying in your house."

"I was glad Mrs. Bolton invited him," answered Annie sincerely, but not instantly.

The ladies waited, with an exchange of glances, for her reply, as if they had talked the matter over beforehand, and had agreed to find out just how Annie Kilburn felt about it.

"Oh, I guess he paid his board," said Mrs. Wilmington, jocosely rejecting the implication that he had been the guest of the Boltons.

"I don't see what he expects to do with that little girl of his, without any mother, that way," said Mrs. Gerrish. "He ought to get married."

"Perhaps he will, when he's waited a proper time," suggested Mrs. Putney demurely.

"Well, his wife's been the same as dead ever since the child was born. I don't know what you call a proper time, Ellen," argued Mrs. Gerrish.

"I presume a minister feels differently about such things," Mrs. Wilmington remarked indolently.

"I don't see why a minister should feel any different from anybody else," said Mrs. Gerrish. "It's his duty to do it on his child's account. I don't see why he don't have the remains brought to Hatboro', anyway."

They debated this point at some length, and they seemed to forget Annie. She listened with more interest than her concern in the last resting-place of the minister's dead wife really inspired. These old friends of hers seemed to have lost the sensitiveness of their girlhood without having gained tenderness in its place. They treated the affair with a nakedness that shocked her. In the country and in small towns people come face to face with life, especially women. It means marrying, child-bearing, household cares and burdens, neighbourhood gossip, sickness, death, burial, and whether the corpse appeared natural. But ever so much kindness goes with their disillusion; they are blunted, but not embittered.

They ended by recalling Annie to mind, and Mrs. Putney said: "I suppose you haven't been to the cemetery yet? They've got it all fixed up since you went away—drives laid out, and paths cut through, and everything. A good many have put up family tombs, and they've taken away the old iron fences round the lots, and put granite curbing. They mow the grass all the time. It's a perfect garden." Mrs. Putney was a small woman, already beginning to wrinkle. She had married a man whom Annie remembered as a mischievous little boy, with a sharp tongue and a nervous temperament; her father had always liked him when he came about the house, but Annie had lost sight of him in the years that make small boys and girls large ones, and he was at college when she went abroad. She had an impression of something unhappy in her friend's marriage.

"I think it's *too* much fixed up myself," said Mrs. Gerrish. She turned suddenly to Annie: "You going to have your father fetched home?"

The other ladies started a little at the question and looked at Annie; it was not that they were shocked, but they wanted to see whether she would not be so.

"No," she said briefly. She added, helplessly, "It wasn't his wish."

"I should have thought he would have liked to be buried alongside of your mother," said Mrs. Gerrish. "But the Judge always *was* a little peculiar. I presume you can have the name and the date put on the monument just the same."

Annie flushed at this intimate comment and suggestion

from a woman whom as a girl she had never admitted to
familiarity with her, but had tolerated her because she was
such a harmless simpleton, and hung upon other girls whom
she liked better. The word monument cowed her, however.
She was afraid they might begin to talk about the soldiers'
monument. She answered hastily, and began to ask them
about their families.

Mrs. Wilmington, who had no children, and Mrs. Putney,
who had one, spoke of Mrs. Gerrish's large family. She had
four children, and she refused the praises of her friends for
them, though she celebrated them herself. "You ought to
have seen the two little girls that Ellen lost, Annie," she said.
"Ellen Putney, I don't see how you ever got over that. Those
two lovely, healthy children gone, and poor little Winthrop
left! I always did say it was too hard."

She had married a clerk in the principal dry-goods store,
who had prospered rapidly, and was now one of the first business men of the place, and had an ambition to be a leading
citizen. She believed in his fitness to deal with the questions
of religion and education which he took part in, and was always quoting Mr. Gerrish. She called him Mr. Gerrish so
much that other people began to call him so too. But Mrs.
Putney's husband held out against it, and had the habit of
returning the little man's ceremonious salutations with an
easy, "Hello, Billy," "Good morning, Billy." It was his theory
that this was good for Gerrish, who might otherwise have
forgotten when everybody called him Billy. He was one of the
old Putneys; and he was a lawyer by profession.

Mrs. Wilmington's husband had come to Hatboro' since
Annie's long absence began; he had capital, and he had
started a stocking-mill in Hatboro'. He was much older than
his wife, whom he had married after a protracted widower-
hood. She had one of the best houses and the most richly
furnished in Hatboro'. She and Mrs. Putney saw Mrs. Gerrish
at rare intervals, and in observance of some notable fact of
their girlish friendship like the present.

In pursuance of the subject of children, Mrs. Gerrish said
that she sometimes had a notion to offer to take Mr. Peck's
little girl herself till he could get fixed somehow, but Mr. Gerrish would not let her. Mr. Gerrish said Mr. Peck had better

get married himself if he wanted a step-mother for his little girl. Mr. Gerrish was peculiar about keeping a family to itself.

"Well, you'll think *we've* come to board with you *too*," said Mrs. Putney, in reference to Mr. Peck.

The ladies all rose, and having got upon their feet, began to shout and laugh again—like girls, they implied.

They stayed and talked a long time after rising, with the same note of unsparing personality in their talk. Where there are few public interests and few events, as in such places, there can be no small-talk, nothing of the careless touch-and-go of larger societies. Every one knows all the others, and knows the worst of them. People are not unkind; they are mutually and freely helpful; but they have only themselves to occupy their minds. Annie's friends had also to distinguish themselves to her from the rest of the villagers, and it was easiest to do this by an attitude of criticism mingled with large allowance. They ended a dissection of the community by saying that they believed there was no place like Hatboro', after all.

In the contagion of their perfunctory gaiety Annie began to scream and laugh too, as she followed them to the door, and stood talking to them while they got into Mrs. Wilmington's extension-top carry-all. She answered with deafening promises, when they put their bonnets out of the carry-all and called back to her to be sure to come soon to see them soon.

V.

MRS. BOLTON made no advances with Annie toward the discussion of her friends; but when Annie asked about their families, she answered with the incisive directness of a country-bred woman. She delivered her judgments as she went about her work, the morning after the ladies' visit, while Annie sat before the breakfast-table, which she had given her leave to clear. As she passed in and out from the dining-room to the kitchen she kept talking; she raised her voice in the further room, and lowered it when she drew near again. She wore a dismal calico wrapper, which made no compromise with the gauntness of her figure; her reddish-brown hair, which grew in a fringe below her crown, was plaited into small tags or tails, pulled up and tied across the top of her head, the bare surfaces of which were curiously mottled with the dye which she sometimes put on her hair. Behind, this was gathered up into a small knob pierced with a single hair-pin; the arrangement left Mrs. Bolton's visage to the un-restricted expression of character. She did not let it express toward Annie any expectation of the confidential relations that are supposed to exist between people who have been a long time master and servant. She had never recognised her relations with the Kilburns in these terms. She was a mature Yankee single woman, of confirmed self-respect, when she first came as house-keeper to Judge Kilburn, twenty years ago, and she had not changed her nature in changing her condition by her marriage with Oliver Bolton; she was childless, unless his comparative youth conferred a sort of adoptive maternity upon her.

Annie went into her father's study, where she had lit the fire in the Franklin-stove on her way to breakfast. It had come on to rain during the night, after the fine yesterday which Mrs. Gerrish had denounced to its face as a weather-breeder. At first it rained silently, stealthily; but toward morning Annie heard the wind rising, and when she looked out of her window after daylight she found a fierce north-easterly storm drenching and chilling the landscape. Now across the flat-tened and tangled grass of the lawn the elms were writhing in the gale, and swinging their long lean boughs to and fro; from another window she saw the cuffed and hustled maples ruffling their stiff masses of foliage, and shuddering in the storm. She turned away, with a sigh of the luxurious melancholy which a north-easter inspires in people safely sheltered from it, and sat down before her fire. She recalled the three women who had visited her the day before, in the better-remembered figures of their childhood and young girlhood; and their present character did not seem a broken promise. Nothing was really disappointed in it but the animal joy, the hopeful riot of their young blood, which must fade and die with the happiest fate. She perceived that what they had come to was not unjust to what they had been; and as our own fate always appears to us unaccomplished, a thing for the distant future to fulfil, she began to ask herself what was to be the natural sequence of such a temperament, such mental and moral traits, as hers. Had her life been so noble in anything but vague aspirations that she could ever reasonably expect the destiny of grand usefulness which she had always unreasonably expected? The question came home to her with such pain, in the light of what her old playmates had become, that she suddenly ceased to enjoy the misery of the storm out-of-doors, or the purring content of the fire on the hearth of the stove at her feet; the book she had taken down to read fell unopened into her lap, and she gave herself up to a half-hour of such piercing self-question as only a high-minded woman can endure when the flattering promises of youth have grown vague and few.

There is no condition of life that is wholly acceptable, but none that is not tolerable when once it establishes itself; and while Annie Kilburn had never consented to be an old maid, she had become one without great suffering. At thirty-one she could not call herself anything else; she often called herself an old maid, with the mental reservation that she was not one. She was merely unmarried; she might marry any time. Now, when she assured herself of this, as she had done many times before, she suddenly wondered if she should ever marry; she wondered if she had seemed to her friends yesterday like a person who would never marry. Did one carry such a thing in one's looks? Perhaps they idealised her; they had not seen her since she was twenty, and perhaps they still thought of her as a young girl. It now seemed to her as if she had left her youth in Rome, as in Rome it had seemed to her that she should find it again in Hatboro'. A pang of aimless, unlocalised homesickness passed through her; she realised that she was alone in the world. She rose to escape the pang, and went to the window of the parlour which looked toward the street, where she saw the figure of a young man draped in a long indiarubber gossamer coat fluttering in the wind that pushed him along as he tacked on a southerly course; he bowed and twisted his head to escape the lash of the rain. She watched him till he turned into the lane leading to the house, and then, at a discreeter distance, she watched him through the window at the other corner, making his way up to the front door in the teeth of the gale. He seemed to have a bundle under his arm, and as he stepped into the shelter of the portico, and freed his arm to ring, she discovered that it was a bundle of books. Whether Mrs. Bolton did not hear the bell, or whether she heard it and decided that it would be absurd to leave her work for it, when Miss Kilburn, who was so much nearer, could answer it, she did not come, even at a second ring, and Annie was forced to go to the door herself, or leave the poor man dripping in the cold wind outside.

She had made up her mind, at sight of the books, that he was a canvasser for some subscription book, such as used to come in her father's time, but when she opened to him he took off his hat with a great deal of manner, and said "Miss Kilburn?" with so much insinuation of gentle disinterestedness, that it flashed upon her that it might be Mr. Peck.

"Yes," she said, with confusion, while the flash of conjecture faded away.

"Mr. Brandreth," said her visitor, whom she now saw to be much younger than Mr. Peck could be. He looked not much more than twenty-two or twenty-three; his damp hair waved and curled upon his temples and forehead, and his blue eyes lightened from a beardless and freshly shaven face. "I called this morning because I felt sure of finding you at home."

He smiled at his reference to the weather, and Annie smiled too as she again answered, "Yes?" She did not want his books,

but she liked something that was cheerful and enthusiastic in
him; she added, "Won't you step into the study?"

"Thanks, yes," said the young man, flinging off his gossamer, and hanging it up to drip into the pan of the hat rack.
He gathered up his books from the chair where he had laid
them, and held them at his waist with both hands, while he
bowed her precedence beside the study door.

"I don't know," he began, "but I ought to apologise for
coming on a day like this, when you were not expecting to be
interrupted."

"Oh no; I'm not at all busy. But you must have had courage to brave a storm like this."

"No. The truth is, Miss Kilburn, I was very anxious to see
you about a matter I have at heart––that I desire your help
with."

"He wants me," Annie thought, "to give him the use of my
name as a subscriber to his book"—there seemed really to be
a half-dozen books in his bundle—"and he's come to me
first."

"I had expected to come with Mrs. Munger—she's a great
friend of mine; you haven't met her yet, but you'll like her;
she's the leading spirit in South Hatboro'—and we were
coming together this morning; but she was unexpectedly
called away yesterday, and so I ventured to call alone."

"I'm very glad to see you, Mr. Brandreth," Annie said.
"Then Mrs. Munger has subscribed already, and I'm only second fiddle, after all," she thought.

"The truth is," said Mr. Brandreth, "I'm the factotum, or
teetotum, of the South Hatboro' ladies' book club, and I've
been deputed to come and see if you wouldn't like to join it."

"Oh!" said Annie, and with a thrill of dismay she asked
herself how much she had let her manner betray that she had
supposed he was a book agent. "I shall be very glad indeed,
Mr. Brandreth."

"Mrs. Munger was sure you would," said Mr. Brandreth
joyously. "I've brought some of the books with me—the
last," he said; and Annie had time to get into a new social
attitude toward him during their discussion of the books. She
chose one, and Mr. Brandreth took her subscription, and
wrote her name in the club book.

"One of the reasons," he said, "why I would have preferred to come with Mrs. Munger is that she is so heart and soul with me in my little scheme. She could have put it before you in so much better light than I can. But she was called away so suddenly."

"I hope for no serious cause," said Annie.

"Oh no! It's just to Cambridge. Her son is one of the Freshman Nine, and he's been hit by a ball."

"Oh!" said Annie.

"Yes; it's a great pity for Mrs. Munger. But I come to you for advice as well as co-operation, Miss Kilburn. You must have met a great many English people in Rome, and heard some of them talk about it. We're thinking, some of the young people here, about getting up some outdoor theatricals, like Lady Archibald Campbell's, don't you know. You know about them?" he added, at the blankness in her face.

"I read accounts of them in the English papers. They must have been very—original. But do you think that in a community like Hatboro'—— Are there enough who could—enter into the spirit?"

"Oh yes, indeed!" cried Mr. Brandreth ardently. "You've no idea what a place Hatboro' has got to be. You've not been about much yet, Miss Kilburn?"

"No," said Annie; "I haven't really been off our own place since I came. I've seen nobody but two or three old friends, and we naturally talked more about old times than anything else. But I hear that there are great changes."

"Yes," said Mr. Brandreth. "The social growth has been even greater than the business growth. You've no idea! People have come in for the winter as well as the summer. South Hatboro', where we live—you must see South Hatboro', Miss Kilburn!—is quite a famous health resort. A great many Boston doctors send their patients to us now, instead of Colorado or the Adirondacks. In fact, that's what brought *us* to Hatboro'. My mother couldn't have lived, if she had tried to stay in Melrose. One lung all gone, and the other seriously affected. And people have found out what a charming place it is for the summer. It's cool; and it's so near, you know; the gentlemen can run out every night—only an hour and a quarter from town, and expresses both ways. All very agreeable people, too; and cultivated. Mr. Fellows, the painter, makes a long summer; he bought an old farm-house, and built a studio; Miss Jennings, the flower-painter, has a little box there, too; Mr. Chapley, the publisher, of New York, has built; the Misses Clevinger, and Mrs. Valence, are all near us. There's one family from Chicago—quite nice—New England by birth, you know; and Mrs. Munger, of course; so that there's a very pleasant variety."

"I certainly had no idea of it," said Annie.

"I knew you couldn't have," said Mr. Brandreth, "or you wouldn't have felt any doubt about our having the material for the theatricals. You see, I want to interest all the nice people in it, and make it a whole-town affair. I think it's a great pity for some of the old village families and the summer folks, as they call us, not to mingle more than they do, and Mrs. Munger thinks so too; and we've been talking you over, Miss Kilburn, and we've decided that you could do more than anybody else to help on a scheme that's meant to bring them together."

"Because I'm neither summer folks nor old village families?" asked Annie.

"Because you're both," retorted Mr. Brandreth.

"I don't see that," said Annie; "but we'll suppose the case, for the sake of argument. What do you expect me to do in theatricals, in-doors or out? I never took part in anything of the kind; I can't see an inch beyond the end of my nose without glasses; I never could learn the simplest thing by heart; I'm clumsy and awkward; I get confused."

"Oh, my dear Miss Kilburn, spare yourself! We don't expect you to take part in the play. I don't admit that you're what you say at all; but we only want you to lend us your countenance."

"Oh, is that all? And what do you expect to do with my countenance?" Annie said, with a laugh of misgiving.

"Everything. We know how much influence your name has—one of the old Hatboro' names—in the community, and all that; and we do want to interest the whole community in our scheme. We want to establish a Social Union for the work-people, don't you know, and we think it would be much nicer if it seemed to originate with the old village people."

Annie could not resist an impression in favour of the scheme. It gave definition to the vague intentions with which she had returned to Hatboro'; it might afford her a chance to make reparation for the figure on the soldiers' monument.

"I'm not sure," she began. "If I knew just what a Social Union is——"

"Well, at first," Mr. Brandreth interposed, "it will only be a reading-room, supplied with the magazines and papers, and well lighted and heated, where the work-people—those who have no families especially—could spend their evenings. Afterward we should hope to have a kitchen, and supply tea and coffee—and oysters, perhaps—at a nominal cost; and ice-cream in the summer."

"But what have your outdoor theatricals to do—— But of course. You intend to give the proceeds——"

"Exactly. And we want the proceeds to be as large as possible. We propose to give our time and money to getting the thing up in the best shape, and then we want all the villagers to give their half-dollars and make it a success every way."

"I see," said Annie.

"We want it to be successful, and we want it to be distinguished; we want to make it unique. Mrs. Munger is going to give her grounds and the decorations, and there will be a supper afterward, and a little dance."

"Such things are a great deal of trouble," said Annie, with a smile, from the vantage-ground of her larger experience. "What do you propose to do—what play?"

"Well, we've about decided upon some scenes from *Romeo and Juliet*. They would be very easy to set, outdoors, don't you know, and everybody knows them, and they wouldn't be hard to do. The ballroom in the house of the Capulets could be made to open on a kind of garden terrace—Mrs. Munger has a lovely terrace in her grounds for lawn-tennis—and then we could have a minuet on the grass. You know Miss Mather introduces a minuet in that scene, and makes a great deal of it. Or, I forgot. She's come up since you went away."

"Yes; I hadn't heard of her. Isn't a minuet at Verona in the time of the Scaligeri rather——"

"Well, yes, it is, rather. But you've no idea how pretty it is. And then, you know, we could have the whole of the balcony scene, and other bits that we choose to work in—perhaps parts of other acts that would suit the scene."

"Yes, it would be charming; I can see how very charming it could be made."

"Then we may count upon you?" he asked.

"Yes, yes," she said; "but I don't really know what I'm to do."

Mr. Brandreth had risen; but he sat down again, as if glad to afford her any light he could throw upon the subject.

"How am I to 'influence people,' as you say?" she continued. "I'm quite a stranger in Hatboro'; I hardly know anybody."

"But a great many people know *you*, Miss Kilburn. Your name is associated with the history of the place, and you could do everything for us. You *won't* refuse!" cried Mr. Brandreth winningly. "For instance, you know Mrs. Wilmington."

"Oh yes; she's an old girl-friend of mine."

"Then you know how enormously clever she is. She can do anything. We want her to take an active part—the part of the Nurse. She's delightfully funny. But you know her peculiar temperament—how she hates initiative of all kinds; and we want somebody to bring Mr. Wilmington round. If we could get them committed to the scheme, and a man like Mr. Putney—he'd make a capital Mercutio—it would go like wildfire. We want to interest the churches, too. The object is so worthy, and the theatricals will be so entirely unobjectionable in every respect. We have the Unitarians and Universalists, of course. The Baptists and Methodists will be hard to manage; but the Orthodox are of so many different shades; and I understand the new minister, Mr. Peck, is very liberal. He was here in your house, I believe."

"Yes; but I never saw him," said Annie. "He boarded with the farmer. I'm a Unitarian myself."

"Of course. It would be a great point gained if we could interest him. Every care will be taken to have the affair unobjectionable. You see, the design is to let everybody come to the theatricals, and only those remain to the supper and dance whom we invite. That will keep out the socially objectionable element—the shoe-shop hands and the straw-shop girls."

"Oh," said Annie. "But isn't the—the Social Union for just that class?"

"Yes, it's *expressly* for them, and we intend to organise a system of entertainments—lectures, concerts, readings—for the winter, and keep them interested the whole year round in it. The object is to show them that the best people in the community have their interests at heart, and wish to get on common ground with them."

"Yes," said Annie, "the object is certainly very good."

Mr. Brandreth rose again, and put out his hand. "Then you will help us?"

"Oh, I don't know about that yet."

"At least you won't hinder us?"

"Certainly not."

"Then I consider you in a very hopeful condition, Miss Kilburn, and I feel that I can safely leave you to Mrs. Munger. She is coming to see you as soon as she gets back."

Annie found herself sadder when he was gone, and she threw herself upon the old feather-cushioned lounge to enjoy a reverie in keeping with the dreary storm outside. Was it for this that she had left Rome? She had felt, as every American of conscience feels abroad, the drawings of a duty, obscure and indefinable, toward her country, the duty to come home and do something for it, be something in it. This is the impulse of no common patriotism; it is perhaps a sense of the opportunity which America supremely affords for the race to help itself, and for each member of it to help all the rest.

But from the moment Annie arrived in Hatboro' the difficulty of being helpful to anything or any one had increased upon her with every new fact that she had learned about it and the people in it. To her they seemed terribly self-sufficing. They seemed occupied and prosperous, from her front parlour window; she did not see anybody going by who appeared to be in need of her; and she shrank from a more thorough exploration of the place. She found she had fancied necessity coming to her and taking away her good works, as it were, in a basket; but till Mr. Brandreth appeared with his scheme, nothing had applied for her help. She had always hated theatricals; they bored her; and yet the Social Union was a good object, and if this scheme would bring her acquainted in Hatboro' it might be the stepping-stone to something better, something really or more ideally useful. She wondered what South Hatboro' was like; she would get Mrs. Bolton's opinion, which, if severe, would be just. She would ask Mrs. Bolton about Mrs. Munger, too. She would tell Mrs. Bolton to tell Mr. Peck to call to dine. Would it be thought patronising to Mr. Peck?

The fire from the Franklin-stove diffused a drowsy comfort through the room, the rain lashed the window-panes, and the wind shrilled in the gable. Annie fell off to sleep. When she woke up she heard Mrs. Bolton laying the table for her one o'clock dinner, and she knew it was half-past twelve, because Mrs. Bolton always laid the table just half an hour beforehand. She went out to speak to Mrs. Bolton.

There was no want of distinctness in Mrs. Bolton's opinion, but Annie felt that there was a want of perspective and proportion in it, arising from the narrowness of Mrs. Bolton's experience and her ignorance of the world; she was farm-bred, and she had always lived upon the outskirts of Hatboro', even when it was a much smaller place than now. But Mrs. Bolton had her criterions, and she believed in them firmly; in a time when agnosticism extends among cultivated people to every region of conjecture, the social convictions of Mrs. Bolton were untainted by misgiving. In the first place, she despised laziness, and as South Hatboro' was the summer home of open and avowed disoccupation, of an idleness so entire that it had to seek refuge from itself in all manner of pastimes, she held its population in a contempt to which her meagre phrase did imperfect justice. From time to time she had to stop altogether, and vent it in "Wells!" of varying accents and inflections, but all expressive of aversion, and in snorts and sniffs still more intense in purport.

Then she held that people who had nothing else to do ought at least to be exemplary in their lives, and she was merciless to the goings-on in South Hatboro', which had penetrated on the breath of scandal to the elder village. When Annie came to find out what these were, she did not think them dreadful; they were small flirtations and harmless intimacies between the members of the summer community, which in the imagination of the village blackened into guilty intrigue. On the tongues of some, South Hatboro' was another Gomorrah; Mrs. Bolton believed the worst, especially of the women.

"I hear," said Mrs. Bolton, "that them women come up here for *rest*. I don't know what they want to rest *from*; but if it's from doin' nothin' all winter long, I guess they go back to the city poot' near's tired's they come."

Perhaps Annie felt that it was useless to try to enlighten her in regard to the fatigues from which the summer sojourner in the country escapes so eagerly; the cares of giving and going to lunches and dinners; the labour of afternoon teas; the late hours and the heavy suppers of evening receptions; the drain of charity-doing and play-going; the slavery of amateur art study, and parlour readings, and *musicales*; the writing of invitations and acceptances and refusals; the trying on of dresses; the calls made and received. She let her talk on, and tried to figure, as well as she could from her talk, the form and magnitude of the task laid upon her by Mr. Brandreth, of reconciling Old Hatboro' to South Hatboro', and uniting them in a common enterprise.

"Mrs. Bolton," she said, abruptly leaving the subject at last, "I've been thinking whether I oughtn't to do something about Mr. Peck. I don't want him to feel that he was unwelcome to me in my house; I should like him to feel that I approved of his having been here."

As this was not a question, Mrs. Bolton, after the fashion of country people, held her peace, and Annie went on—

"Does he never come to see you?"

"Well, he was here last night," said Mrs. Bolton.

"Last *night*!" cried Annie. "Why in the world didn't you let me know?"

"I didn't know as you wanted to know," began Mrs. Bolton, with a sullen defiance mixed with pleasure in Annie's reproach. "He was out there in my settin'-room with his little girl."

"But don't you see that if you didn't let me know he was here it would look to him as if I didn't wish to meet him—as if I had told you that you were not to introduce him?"

Probably Mrs. Bolton believed too that a man's mind was agile enough for these conjectures; but she said she did not suppose he would take it in that way; she added that he stayed longer than she expected, because the little girl seemed to like it so much; she always cried when she had to go away.

"Do you mean that she's attached to the place?" demanded Annie.

"Well, yes, she is," Mrs. Bolton admitted. "And the cat."

Annie had a great desire to tell Mrs. Bolton that she had behaved very stupidly. But she knew Mrs. Bolton would not stand that, and she had to content herself with saying, severely, "The next time he comes, let me know without fail, please. What is the child like?" she asked.

"Well, I guess it must favour the mother, if anything. It don't seem to take after him any."

"Why don't you have it here often, then," asked Annie, "if it's so much attached to the place?"

"Well I didn't know as you wanted to have it round," replied Mrs. Bolton bluntly.

Annie made a "Tchk!" of impatience with her obtuseness, and asked, "Where is Mr. Peck staying?"

"Well, he's staying at Mis' Warner's till he can get settled."

"Is it far from here?"

"It's down in the north part of the village—Over the Track."

"Is Mr. Bolton at home?"

"Yes, he is," said Mrs. Bolton, with the effect of not intending to deny it.

"Then I want him to hitch up—now—at once—right away—and go and get the child and bring her here to dinner with me." Annie got so far with her severity, feeling that it was needed to mask a proceeding so romantic, perhaps so silly. She added timidly, "Can he do it?"

"I d' know but what he can," said Mrs. Bolton, dryly, and whatever her feeling really was in regard to the matter, her manner gave no hint of it. Annie did not know whether Bolton was going on her errand or not, from Mrs. Bolton, but in ten or twelve minutes she saw him emerge from the avenue into the street, in the carry-all, tightly curtained against the storm. Half an hour later he returned, and his wife set down in the library a shabbily dressed little girl, with her cheeks bright and her hair curling from the weather, and staring at Annie, and rather disposed to cry. She said hastily, "Bring in the cat, Mrs. Bolton; we're going to have the cat to dinner with us."

This inspiration seemed to decide the little girl against crying. The cat was equipped with a doily, and actually provided with dinner at a small table apart; the child did not look at it as Annie had expected she would, but remained with her eyes fastened on Annie herself. She did not stir from the spot where Mrs. Bolton had put her down, but she let Annie take her up and arrange her in a chair, with large books graduated to the desired height under her, and made no sign of satisfaction or disapproval. Once she looked round, when Mrs. Bolton finally went out after bringing in the last dish for dinner, and then fastened her eyes on Annie again, twisting her head shyly round to follow her in every gesture and expression as Annie fitted on a napkin under her chin, cut up her meat, poured her milk, and buttered her bread. She answered nothing to the chatter which Annie tried to make lively and entertaining, and made no sound but that of a broken and suppressed breathing. Annie had forgotten to ask her name of Mrs. Bolton, and she asked it in vain of the child herself, with a great variety of circumlocution; she was so unused to children that she was ashamed to invent any pet name for her; she called her, in what she felt to be a stiff and school-mistressly fashion, "Little Girl," and talked on at her, growing more and more nervous herself without perceiving that the child's condition was approaching a climax. She had taken off her glasses, from the notion that they embarrassed her guest, and she did not see the pretty lips beginning to curl, nor the searching eyes clouding with tears; the storm of sobs that suddenly burst upon her astounded her.

"Mrs. Bolton! Mrs. Bolton!" she screamed, in hysterical helplessness. Mrs. Bolton rushed in, and with an instant perception of the situation, caught the child to her bony breast, and fled with it to her own room, where Annie heard its wails die gradually away amid murmurs of comfort and reassurance from Mrs. Bolton.

She felt like a great criminal and a great fool; at the same time she was vexed with the stupid child which she had meant so well by, and indignant with Mrs. Bolton, whose flight with it had somehow implied a reproach of her behaviour. When she could govern herself, she went out to Mrs. Bolton's room, where she found the little one quiet enough, and Mrs. Bolton tying on the long apron in which she cleared up the dinner and washed the dishes.

"I guess she'll get along now," she said, without the critical tone which Annie was prepared to resent. "She was scared some, and she felt kind of strange, I presume."

"Yes, and I behaved like a simpleton, dressing up the cat, I suppose," answered Annie. "But I thought it would amuse her."

"You can't tell how children will take a thing. I don't believe they like anything that's out of the common—well, not a great deal."

There was a leniency in Mrs. Bolton's manner which encouraged Annie to go on and accuse herself more and more, and then an unresponsive blankness that silenced her. She went back to her own rooms; and to get away from her shame, she began to write a letter.

It was to a friend in Rome, and from the sense we all have that a letter which is to go such a great distance ought to be a long letter, and from finding that she had really a good deal to say, she let it grow so that she began apologising for its length half a dozen pages before the end. It took her nearly the whole afternoon, and she regained a little of her self-respect by ridiculing the people she had met.

VI.

TOWARD five o'clock Annie was interrupted by a knock at her door, which ought to have prepared her for something unusual, for it was Mrs. Bolton's habit to come and go without knocking. But she called "Come in!" without rising from her letter, and Mrs. Bolton entered with a stranger. The little girl clung to his forefinger, pressing her head against his leg, and glancing shyly up at Annie. She sprang up, and, "This is Mr. Peck, Miss Kilburn," said Mrs. Bolton.

"How do you do?" said Mr. Peck, taking the hand she gave him.

He was gaunt, without being tall, and his clothes hung loosely about him, as if he had fallen away in them since they were made. His face was almost the face of the caricature American: deep, slightly curved vertical lines enclosed his mouth in their parenthesis; a thin, dust-coloured beard fell from his cheeks and chin; his upper lip was shaven. But instead of the slight frown of challenge and self-assertion which marks this face in the type, his large blue eyes, set near together, gazed sadly from under a smooth forehead, extending itself well up toward the crown, where his dry hair dropped over it.

"I am very glad to see you, Mr. Peck," said Annie; "I've wanted to tell you how pleased I am that you found shelter in my old home when you first came to Hatboro'."

Mr. Peck's trousers were short and badly kneed, and his long coat hung formlessly from his shoulders; she involuntarily took a patronising tone toward him which was not habitual with her.

"Thank you," he said, with the dry, serious voice which seemed the fit vocal expression of his presence; "I have been afraid that it seemed like an intrusion to you."

"Oh, not the least," retorted Annie. "You were very welcome. I hope you're comfortably placed where you are now?"

"Quite so," said the minister.

"I'd heard so much of your little girl from Mrs. Bolton, and her attachment to the house, that I ventured to send for her to-day. But I believe I gave her rather a bad quarter of an

678

hour, and that she liked the place better under Mrs. Bolton's *régime*."

She expected some deprecatory expression of gratitude from him, which would relieve her of the lingering shame she felt for having managed so badly, but he made none.

"It was my fault. I'm not used to children, and I hadn't taken the precaution to ask her name——"

"Her name is Idella," said the minister.

Annie thought it very ugly, but, with the intention of saying something kind, she said, "What a quaint name!"

"It was her mother's choice," returned the minister. "Her own name was Ella, and my mother's name was Ida; she combined the two."

"Oh!" said Annie. She abhorred those made-up names in which the New England country people sometimes indulge their fancy, and Idella struck her as a particularly repulsive invention; but she felt that she must not visit the fault upon the little creature. "Don't you think you could give me another trial some time, Idella?" She stooped down and took the child's unoccupied hand, which she let her keep, only twisting her face away to hide it in her father's pantaloon leg. "Come now, won't you give me a forgiving little kiss?" Idella looked round, and Annie made bold to gather her up.

Idella broke into a laugh, and took Annie's cheeks between her hands.

"Well, I declare!" said Mrs. Bolton. "You never can tell what that child will do next."

"I never can tell what I will do next myself," said Annie. She liked the feeling of the little, warm, soft body in her arms, against her breast, and it was flattering to have triumphed where she had seemed to fail so desperately. They had all been standing, and she now said, "Won't you sit down, Mr. Peck?" She added, by an impulse which she instantly thought ill-advised, "There is something I would like to speak to you about."

"Thank you," said Mr. Peck, seating himself beyond the stove. "We must be getting home before a great while. It is nearly tea-time."

"I won't detain you unduly," said Annie.

Mrs. Bolton left them at her hint of something special to

say to the minister. Annie could not have had the face to speak of Mr. Brandreth's theatricals in that grim presence; and as it was, she resolved to put forward their serious object. She began abruptly: "Mr. Peck, I've been asked to interest myself for a Social Union which the ladies of South Hatboro' are trying to establish for the operatives. I suppose you haven't heard anything of the scheme?"

"No, I hadn't," said Mr. Peck.

He was one of those people who sit very high, and he now seemed taller and more impressive than when he stood.

"It is certainly a very good object," Annie resumed; and she went on to explain it at second-hand from Mr. Brandreth as well as she could. The little girl was standing in her lap, and got between her and Mr. Peck, so that she had to look first around one side of her and then another to see how he was taking it.

He nodded his head, and said gravely, "Yes," and "Yes," and "Yes," at each significant point of her statement. At the end he asked: "And are the means forthcoming? Have they raised the money for renting and furnishing the rooms?"

"Well, no, they haven't yet, or not quite, as I understand."

"Have they tried to interest the working people themselves in it? If they are to value its benefits, it ought to cost them something—self-denial, privation even."

"Yes, I know," Annie began.

"I'm not satisfied," the minister pursued, "that it is wise to provide people with even harmless amusements that take them much away from their homes. These things are invented by well-to-do people who have no occupation, and think that others want pastimes as much as themselves. But what working people want is rest, and what they need are decent homes where they can take it. Besides, unless they help to support this union out of their own means, the better sort among them will feel wounded by its existence, as a sort of superfluous charity."

"Yes, I see," said Annie. She saw this side of the affair with surprise. The minister seemed to have thought more about such matters than she had, and she insensibly receded from her first hasty generalisation of him, and paused to reapproach him on another level. The little girl began to play with her glasses, and accidentally knocked them from her nose. The minister's face and figure became a blur, and in the purblindness to which she was reduced she had a moment of clouded volition in which she was tempted to renounce, and even oppose, the scheme for a Social Union, in spite of her promise to Mr. Brandreth. But she remembered that she was a consistent and faithful person, and she said: "The ladies have a plan for raising the money, and they've applied to me to second it—to use my influence somehow among the villagers to get them interested; and the working people can help too if they choose. But I'm quite a stranger amongst those I'm expected to influence, and I don't at all know how they will take it." The minister listened, neither prompting nor interrupting. "The ladies' plan is to have an entertainment at one of the cottages, and charge an admission, and devote the proceeds to the union." She paused. Mr. Peck still remained silent, but she knew he was attentive. She pushed on. "They intend to have a—a representation, in the open air, of one of Shakespeare's plays, or scenes from one——"

"Do you wish me," interrupted the minister, "to promote the establishment of this union? Is that why you speak to me of it?"

"Why, I don't know *why* I speak to you of it," she replied with a laugh of embarrassment, to which he was cold, apparently. "I certainly couldn't ask you to take part in an affair that you didn't approve."

"I don't know that I disapprove of it. Properly managed, it might be a good thing."

"Yes, of course. But I understand why you might not sympathise with that part of it, and that is why I told you of it," said Annie.

"What part?"

"The—the—theatricals."

"Why not?" asked the minister.

"I know—Mrs. Bolton told me you were very liberal," Annie faltered on; "but I didn't expect you as a—— But of course——"

"I read Shakespeare a great deal," said Mr. Peck. "I have never been in the theatre; but I should like to see one of his plays represented where it could cause no one to offend."

"Yes," said Annie, "and this would be by amateurs, and there could be no *possible* 'offence in it.' I wished to know how the general idea would strike you. Of course the ladies would be only too glad of your advice and co-operation. Their plan is to sell tickets to every one for the theatricals, and to a certain number of invited persons for a supper, and a little dance afterward on the lawn."

"I don't know if I understand exactly," said the minister.

Annie repeated her statement more definitely, and explained, from Mr. Brandreth, as before, that the invitations were to be given so as to eliminate the shop-hand element from the supper and dance.

Mr. Peck listened quietly. "That would prevent my taking part in the affair," he said, as quietly as he had listened.

"Of course—dancing," Annie began.

"It is not that. Many people who hold strictly to the old opinions now allow their children to learn dancing. But I could not join at all with those who were willing to lay the foundations of a Social Union in a social disunion—in the exclusion of its beneficiaries from the society of their benefactors."

He was not sarcastic, but the grotesqueness of the situation as he had sketched it was apparent. She remembered now that she had felt something incongruous in it when Mr. Brandreth exposed it, but not deeply.

The minister continued gently: "The ladies who are trying to get up this Social Union proceed upon the assumption that working people can neither see nor feel a slight; but it is a great mistake to do so."

Annie had the obtuseness about those she fancied below her which is one of the consequences of being brought up in a superior station. She believed that there was something to say on the other side, and she attempted to say it.

"I don't know that you could call it a slight exactly. People can ask those they prefer to a social entertainment."

"Yes—if it is for their own pleasure."

"But even in a public affair like this the work-people would feel uncomfortable and out of place, wouldn't they, if they stayed to the supper and the dance? They might be exposed to greater suffering among those whose manners and breeding were different, and it might be very embarrassing all round. Isn't there that side to be regarded?"

"You beg the question," said the minister, as unsparingly as if she were a man. "The point is whether a Social Union beginning in social exclusion could ever do any good. What part do these ladies expect to take in maintaining it? Do they intend to spend their evenings there, to associate on equal terms with the shoe-shop and straw-shop hands?"

"I don't suppose they do, but I don't know," said Annie dryly; and she replied by helplessly quoting Mr. Brandreth: "They intend to organise a system of lectures, concerts, and readings. They wish to get on common ground with them."

"They can never get on common ground with them in that way," said the minister. "No doubt they think they want to do them good; but good is from the heart, and there is no heart in what they propose. The working people would know that at once."

"Then you mean to say," Annie asked, half alarmed and half amused, "that there can be no friendly intercourse with the poor and the well-to-do unless it is based upon social equality?"

"I will answer your question by asking another. Suppose you were one of the poor, and the well-to-do offered to be friendly with you on such terms as you have mentioned, how should you feel toward them?"

"If you make it a personal question——"

"It makes itself a personal question," said the minister dispassionately.

"Well, then, I trust I should have the good sense to see that social equality between people who were better dressed, better taught, and better bred than myself was impossible, and that for me to force myself into their company was not only bad taste, but it was foolish. I have often heard my father say that the great superiority of the American practice of democracy over the French ideal was that it didn't involve any assumption of social equality. He said that equality before the law and in politics was sacred, but that the principle could never govern society, and that Americans all instinctively recognised it. And I believe that to try to mix the different classes would be un-American."

Mr. Peck smiled, and this was the first break in his seriousness. "We don't know what is or will be American yet. But we will suppose you are quite right. The question is, how would you feel toward the people whose company you wouldn't force yourself into?"

"Why, of course," Annie was surprised into saying, "I suppose I shouldn't feel very kindly toward them."

"Even if you knew that they felt kindly toward you?"

"I'm afraid that would only make the matter worse," she said, with an uneasy laugh.

The minister was silent on his side of the stove.

"But do I understand you to say," she demanded, "that there can be no love at all, no kindness, between the rich and the poor? God tells us all to love one another."

"Surely," said the minister. "Would you suffer such a slight as your friends propose, to be offered to any one you loved?"

She did not answer, and he continued, thoughtfully: "I suppose that if a poor person could do a rich person a kindness which cost him some sacrifice, he might love him. In that case there could be love between the rich and the poor."

"And there could be no love if a rich man did the same?"

"Oh yes," the minister said—"upon the same ground. Only, the rich man would have to make a sacrifice first that he would really feel."

"Then you mean to say that people can't do any good at all with their money?" Annie asked.

"Money is a palliative, but it can't cure. It can sometimes create a bond of gratitude perhaps, but it can't create sympathy between rich and poor."

"But *why* can't it?"

"Because sympathy—common feeling—the sense of fraternity—can spring only from like experiences, like hopes, like fears. And money cannot buy these."

He rose, and looked a moment about him, as if trying to recall something. Then, with a stiff obeisance, he said, "Good evening," and went out, while she remained daunted and bewildered, with the child in her arms, as unconscious of having kept it as he of having left it with her.

Mrs. Bolton must have reminded him of his oversight, for after being gone so long as it would have taken him to walk to her parlour and back, he returned, and said simply, "I forgot Idella."

He put out his hands to take her, but she turned perversely from him, and hid her face in Annie's neck, pushing his hands away with a backward reach of her little arm.

"Come, Idella!" he said. Idella only snuggled the closer.

Mrs. Bolton came in with the little girl's wraps; they were very common and poor, and the thought of getting her something prettier went through Annie's mind.

At sight of Mrs. Bolton the child turned from Annie to her older friend.

"I'm afraid you have a woman-child for your daughter, Mr. Peck," said Annie, remotely hurt at the little one's fickleness.

Neither Mr. Peck nor Mrs. Bolton smiled, and with some vague intention of showing him that she could meet the poor on common ground by sharing their labours, she knelt down and helped Mrs. Bolton tie on and button on Idella's things.

VII.

NEXT MORNING the day broke clear after the long storm, and Annie woke in revolt against the sort of subjection in which she had parted from Mr. Peck. She felt the need of showing Mrs. Bolton that, although she had been civil to him, she had no sympathy with his ideas; but she could not think of any way to formulate her opposition, and all she could say in offence was, "Does Mr. Peck usually forget his child when he starts home?"

"I don't know as he doos," answered Mrs. Bolton simply. "He's rather of an absent-minded man, and I suppose he's like other men when he gets talking."

"The child's clothes were disgracefully shabby!" said Annie, vexed that her attack could come to no more than this.

"I presume," said Mrs. Bolton, "that if he kept more of his money for himself, he could dress her better."

"Oh, that's the way with these philanthropists," said Annie, thinking of Hollingsworth, in *The Blithedale Romance*, the only philanthropist whom she had really ever known. "They are always ready to sacrifice the happiness and comfort of any one to the general good."

Mrs. Bolton stood a moment, and then went out without replying; but she looked as offended as Annie could have wished. About ten o'clock the bell rang, and she came gloomily into the study, and announced that Mrs. Munger was in the parlour.

Annie had already heard an authoritative rustling of skirts, and she was instinctively prepared for the large, vigorous woman who turned upon her from the picture she had been looking at on the wall, and came toward her with the confident air of one sure they must be friends. Mrs. Munger was dressed in a dark, firm woollen stuff, which communicated its colour, if not its material, to the matter-of-fact bonnet which she wore on her plainly dressed hair. In one of her hands, which were cased in driving gloves of somewhat insistent evidence, she carried a robust black silk sun-umbrella, and the effect of her dress otherwise might be summarised in the statement that where other women would have worn lace, she seemed to wear leather. She had not only leather gloves, and a broad leather belt at her waist, but a leather collar; her watch was secured by a leather cord, passing round her neck, and the stubby tassel of her umbrella stick was leather: she might be said to be in harness. She had a large, handsome face, no longer fresh, but with an effect of exemplary cleanness, and a pair of large grey eyes that suggested the notion of being newly washed, and that now looked at Annie with the assumption of fully understanding her.

"Ah, Miss Kilburn!" she said, without any of the wonted preliminaries of introduction and greeting. "I should have come long ago to see you, but I've been dispersed over the four quarters of the globe ever since you came, my dear. I got home last night on the nine o'clock train, in the last agonies of that howling tempest. Did you ever know anything like it? I see your trees have escaped. I wonder they weren't torn to shreds."

Annie took her on her own ground of ignoring their past non-acquaintance. "Yes, it was awful. And your son—how did you leave him? Mr. Brandreth——"

"Oh yes, poor little man! I found him waiting for me at home last night, and he told me he had been here. He was blowing about in the storm all day. Such a spirit! There was nothing serious the matter; the bridge of the nose was all right; merely the cartilage pushed aside by the ball."

She had passed so lightly from Mr. Brandreth's heroic spirit to her son's nose that Annie, woman as she was, and born to these bold bounds over sequence, was not sure where they had arrived, till Mrs. Munger added: "Jim's used to these things. I'm thankful it wasn't a finger, or an eye. What is *that?*" She jumped from her chair, and swooped upon the Spanish-Roman water-colour Annie had stood against some books on the table, pending its final disposition.

"It's only a Guerra," said Annie. "My things are all scattered about still; I have scarcely tried to get into shape yet."

Mrs. Munger would not let her interpose any idea of there being a past between them. She merely said: "You knew the Herricks at Rome, of course. I'm in hopes I shall get them here when they come back. I want you to help me colonise Hatboro' with the right sort of people: it's so easy to get the wrong sort! But, so far, I think we've succeeded beyond our wildest dreams. It's easy enough to get nice people together at the seaside; but inland! No; it's only a very few nice people who will come into the country for the summer; and we propose to make Hatboro' a winter colony too; that gives us agreeable invalids, you know; it gave us the Brandreths. He told you of our projected theatricals, I suppose?"

"Yes," said Annie non-committally, "he did."

"I know just how you feel about it, my dear," said Mrs. Munger. " 'Been there myself,' as Jim says. But it grows upon you. I'm glad you didn't refuse outright;" and Mrs. Munger looked at her with eyes of large expectance.

"No, I didn't," said Annie, obliged by this expectance to say something. "But to tell you the truth, Mrs. Munger, I don't see how I'm to be of any use to you or to Mr. Brandreth."

"Oh, take a cab and go about, like Boots and Brewer, you know, for the Veneerings." She said this as if she knew about the humour rather than felt it. "We are placing all our hopes of bringing round the Old Hatborians in you."

"I'm afraid you're mistaken about my influence," said Annie. "Mr. Brandreth spoke of it, and I had an opportunity of trying it last night, and seeing just what it amounted to."

"Yes?" Mrs. Munger prompted, with an increase of expectance in her large clear eyes, and of impartiality in her whole face.

"Mr. Peck was here," said Annie reluctantly, "and I tried it on him."

"Yes?" repeated Mrs. Munger, as immutably as if she were sitting for her photograph and keeping the expression.

Annie broke from her reluctance with a sort of violence which carried her further than she would have gone otherwise. She ridiculed Mr. Peck's appearance and manner, and laughed at his ideas to Mrs. Munger. She had not a good conscience in it, but the perverse impulse persisted in her. There seemed no other way in which she could assert herself against him.

Mrs. Munger listened judicially, but she seemed to take in only what Mr. Peck had thought of the dance and supper; at the end she said, rather vacantly, "What nonsense!"

"Yes; but I'm afraid he thinks it's wisdom, and for all practical purposes it amounts to that. You see what my 'influence' has done at the outset, Mrs. Munger. He'll never give way on such a point."

"Oh, very well, then," said Mrs. Munger, with the utmost lightness and indifference, "we'll drop the idea of the invited supper and dance."

"Do you think that would be well?" asked Annie.

"Yes; why not? It's only an idea. I don't think you've made at all a bad beginning. It was very well to try the idea on some one who would be frank about it, and wouldn't go away and talk against it," said Mrs. Munger, rising. "I want you to come with me, my dear."

"To see Mr. Peck? Excuse me. I don't think I could," said Annie.

"No; to see some of his parishioners," said Mrs. Munger. "His deacons, to begin with, or his deacons' wives."

This seemed so much less than calling on Mr. Peck that Annie looked out at Mrs. Munger's basket-phaeton at her gate, and knew that she would go with very little more urgency.

"After all, you know, you're not one of his congregation; he may yield to them," said Mrs. Munger. "We must *have* him—if only because he's hard to get. It'll give us an idea of what we've got to contend with."

It had a very practical sound; it was really like meeting the difficulties on their own ground, and it overcame the question of taste which was rising in Annie's mind. She demurred a little more upon the theory of her uselessness; but Mrs. Munger insisted, and carried her off down the village street.

The air sparkled full of sun, and a breeze from the southwest frolicked with the twinkling leaves of the overarching elms, and made their shadows dance on the crisp roadway, packed hard by the rain, and faced with clean sand, which crackled pleasantly under Mrs. Munger's phaeton wheels. She talked incessantly. "I think we'll go first to Mrs. Gerrish's, and then to Mrs. Wilmington's. You know them?"

"Oh yes; they were old girl friends."

"Then you know why I go to Mrs. Gerrish's first. She'll care a great deal, and Mrs. Wilmington won't care at all.

She's a delicious creature, Mrs. Wilmington—don't you think? That large, indolent nature; Mr. Brandreth says she makes him think of 'the land in which it seemed always afternoon.' "

Annie remembered Lyra Goodman as a long, lazy, red-haired girl who laughed easily; and she could not readily realise her in the character of a Titianesque beauty with a gift for humorous dramatics, which she had filled out into during the years of her absence from Hatboro'; but she said "Oh yes," in the necessity of polite acquiescence, and Mrs. Munger went on talking—

"She's the only one of the Old Hatboro' people, so far as I know them, who has any breadth of view. Whoa!" She pulled up suddenly beside a stout, short lady in a fashionable walking dress, who was pushing an elegant perambulator with one hand, and shielding her complexion with a crimson sun-umbrella in the other.

"Mrs. Gerrish!" Mrs. Munger called; and Mrs. Gerrish, who had already looked around at the approaching phaeton, and then looked away, so as not to have seemed to look, stopped abruptly, and after some exploration of the vicinity, discovered where the voice came from.

"Oh, Mrs. Munger!" she called back, bridling with pleasure at being greeted in that way by the chief lady of South Hatboro', and struggling to keep up a dignified indifference at the same time. "Why, Annie!" she added.

"Good morning, Emmeline," said Annie; she annexed some irrelevancies about the weather, which Mrs. Munger swept away with business-like robustness.

"We were driving down to your house to find you. I want to see the principal ladies of your church, and talk with them about our Social Union. You've heard about it?"

"Well, nothing very particular," said Mrs. Gerrish: she had probably heard nothing at all. After a moment she asked, "Have you seen Mrs. Wilmington yet?"

"No, I haven't," cried Mrs. Munger. "The fact is, I wanted to talk it over with you and Mr. Gerrish first."

"Oh!" said Mrs. Gerrish, brightening. "Well, I was just going right there. I guess he's in."

"Well, we shall meet there, then. Sorry I can't offer you a

seat. But there's nothing but the rumble, and that wouldn't hold you *all*."

Mrs. Munger called this back after starting her pony. Mrs. Gerrish did not understand, and screamed, *"What?"*

Mrs. Munger repeated her joke at the top of her voice.

"Oh, I can walk!" Mrs. Gerrish yelled at the top of hers. Both the ladies laughed at their repartee.

"She's as jealous of Mrs. Wilmington as a cat," Mrs. Munger confided to Annie as they drove away; "and she's just as pleased as Punch that I've spoken to her first. Mrs. Wilmington won't mind. She's so delightfully indifferent, it really renders her almost superior; you might forget that she was a village person. But this has been an immense stroke. I don't know," she mused, "whether I'd better let her get there first and prepare her husband, or do it myself. No; I'll let *her*. I'll stop here at Gates's."

She stopped at the pavement in front of a provision store, and a pale, stout man, in the long over-shirt of his business, came out to receive her orders. He stood, passing his hand through the top of a barrel of beans, and listened to Mrs. Munger with a humorous, patient smile.

"Mr. Gates, I want you to send me up a leg of lamb for dinner—a large one."

"Last year's, then," suggested Gates.

"No; *this* year's," insisted Mrs. Munger; and Gates gave way with the air of pacifying a wilful child, which would get, after all, only what he chose to allow it.

"All right, ma'am; a large leg of this year's lamb—grown to order. Any peas, spinnage, cucumbers, sparrowgrass?"

"Southern, I suppose?" said Mrs. Munger.

"Well, not if you want to call 'em native," said Gates.

"Yes, I'll take two bunches of asparagus, and some peas."

"Any strawberries?—natives?" suggested Gates.

"Nonsense!"

"Same thing; natives of Norfolk."

"You had better be honest with *me*, Mr. Gates," said Mrs. Munger. "Yes, I'll take a couple of boxes."

"All right! Want 'em nice, and the biggest ones at the bottom of the box?"

"Yes, I do."

"That's what I thought. Some customers wants the big ones on top; but I tell 'em it's all foolishness; just vanity." Gates laughed a dry, hacking little laugh at his drollery, and kept his eyes on Annie. She smiled at last, with permissive recognition, and Gates came forward. "Used to know your father pretty well; but I can't keep up with the young folks any more." He was really not many years older than Annie; he rubbed his right hand on the inside of his long shirt, and gave it her to shake. "Well, you haven't been about much for the last nine or ten years, that's a fact."

"Eleven," said Annie, trying to be gay with the hand-shaking, and wondering if this were meeting the lower classes on common ground, and what Mr. Peck would think of it.

"That so?" queried Gates. "Well, I declare! No wonder you've grown!" He hacked out another laugh, and stood on the curb-stone looking at Annie a moment. Then he asked, "Anything else, Mrs. Munger?"

"No; that's all. Tell me, Mr. Gates, how *do* Mr. Peck and Mr. Gerrish get on?" asked Mrs. Munger in a lower tone.

"Well," said Gates, "he's workin' round—the deacon's workin' round gradually, I guess. I guess if Mr. Peck was to put in a little more brimstone, the deacon'd be all right. He's a great hand for brimstone, you know, the deacon is."

Mrs. Munger laughed again, and then she said, with a pros-elyting sigh, "It's a pity you couldn't all find your way into the Church."

"Well, may be it *would* be a good thing," said Gates, as Mrs. Munger gathered up her reins and chirped to her pony.

"He isn't a member of Mr. Peck's church," she explained to Annie; "but he's one of the society, and his wife's very devout Orthodox. He's a great character, we think, and he'll treat you very well, if you keep on the right side of him. They say he cheats awfully in the weight, though."

VIII.

Mrs. Munger drove across the street, and drew up before a large, handsomely ugly brick dry-goods store, whose showy windows had caught Annie's eye the day she arrived in Hatboro'.

"I see Mrs. Gerrish has got here first," Mrs. Munger said, indicating the perambulator at the door, and she dismounted and fastened her pony with a weight, which she took from the front of the phaeton. On either door jamb of the store was a curved plate of polished metal, with the name Gerrish cut into it in black letters; the sills of the wide windows were of metal, and bore the same legend. At the threshold a very prim, ceremonious little man, spare and straight, met Mrs. Munger with a ceremonious bow, and a solemn "How do you do, ma'am? how do you do? I hope I see you well," and he put a small dry hand into the ample clasp of Mrs. Munger's gauntlet.

"Very well indeed, Mr. Gerrish. Isn't it a lovely morning? You know Miss Kilburn, Mr. Gerrish."

He took Annie's hand into his right and covered it with his left, lifting his eyes to look her in the face with an old-merchant-like cordiality.

"Why, yes, indeed! Delighted to see her. Her father was one of my best friends. I may say that I owe everything that I am to Squire Kilburn; he advised me to stick to commerce when I once thought of studying law. Glad to welcome you back to Hatboro', Miss Kilburn. You see changes on the surface, no doubt, but you'll find the genuine old feeling here. Walk right back, ladies," he continued, releasing Annie's hand to waft them before him toward the rear of the store. "You'll find Mrs. Gerrish in my room there—my Growlery, as I call it." He seemed to think he had invented the name. "And Mrs. Gerrish tells me that you've really come back," he said, leaning decorously toward Annie as they walked, "with the intention of taking up your residence permanently among us. You will find very few places like Hatboro'."

As he spoke, walking with his hands clasped behind him, he glanced to right and left at the shop-girls on foot behind the counter, who dropped their eyes under their different bangs as they caught his glance, and bridled nervously. He denied them the use of chewing-gum; he permitted no conversation, as he called it, among them; and he addressed no jokes or idle speeches to them himself. A system of grooves overhead brought to his counting-room the cash from the clerks in wooden balls, and he returned the change, and kept the accounts, with a pitiless eye for errors. The women were afraid of him, and hated him with bitterness, which exploded at crises in excesses of hysterical impudence.

His store was an example of variety, punctuality, and quality. Upon the theory, for which he deserved the credit, of giving to a country place the advantages of one of the great city establishments, he was gradually gathering, in their fashion, the small commerce into his hands. He had already opened his bazaar through into the adjoining store, which he had bought out, and he kept every sort of thing desired or needed in a country town, with a tempting stock of articles before unknown to the shopkeepers of Hatboro'. Everything was of the very quality represented; the prices were low, but inflexible, and cash payments, except in the case of some rich customers of unimpeachable credit, were invariably exacted; at the same time every reasonable facility for the exchange or return of goods was afforded. Nothing could exceed the justice and fidelity of his dealing with the public. He had even some effects of generosity in his dealing with his dependants; he furnished them free seats in the churches of their different persuasions, and he closed every night at six o'clock, except Saturday, when the shop hands were paid off, and made their purchases for the coming week.

He stepped lightly before Annie and Mrs. Munger, and pushed open the ground-glass door of his office for them. It was like a bank parlour, except for Mrs. Gerrish sitting in her husband's leather-cushioned swivel chair, with her last-born in her lap; she greeted the others noisily, without trying to rise.

"You see we are quite at home here," said Mr. Gerrish.

"Yes, and very snug you are, too," said Mrs. Munger, taking one half of the leather lounge, and leaving the other half to Annie. "I don't wonder Mrs. Gerrish likes to visit you here."

Mr. Gerrish laughed, and said to his wife, who moved provisionally in her chair, seeing he had none, "Sit, my dear; I prefer my usual perch." He took a high stool beside a desk, and gathered a ruler in his hand.

"Well, I may as well begin at the beginning," said Mrs. Munger, "and I'll try to be short, for I know these are business hours."

"Take all the time you want, Mrs. Munger," said Mr. Gerrish affably. "It's my idea that a good business man's business can go on without him, when necessary."

"Of course!" Mrs. Munger sighed. "If everybody had your *system*, Mr. Gerrish!" She went on and succinctly expanded the scheme of the Social Union. "I suppose I can't deny that the idea occurred to *me*," she concluded, "but we can't hope to develop it without the co-operation of the ladies of Old Hatboro', and I've come, first of all, to Mrs. Gerrish."

Mr. Gerrish bowed his acknowledgments of the honour done his wife, with a gravity which she misinterpreted.

"I think," she began, with her censorious manner and accent, "that these people have too much done for them *now*. They're perfectly spoiled. Don't you, Annie?"

Mr. Gerrish did not give Annie time to answer. "I differ with you, my dear," he cut in. "It is my opinion—— Or I don't know but you wish to confine this matter entirely to the ladies?" he suggested to Mrs. Munger.

"Oh, I'm only too proud and glad that you feel interested in the matter!" cried Mrs. Munger. "Without the gentlemen's practical views, we ladies are such feeble folk—mere conies in the rocks."

"I am as much opposed as Mrs. Gerrish—or any one—to acceding to unjust demands on the part of my clerks or other employees," Mr. Gerrish began.

"Yes, that's what I mean," said his wife, and broke down with a giggle.

He went on, without regarding her: "I have always made it a rule, as far as business went, to keep my own affairs entirely in my own hands. I fix the hours, and I fix the wages, and I fix all the other conditions, and I say plainly, 'If you don't like them, do/me,' or 'don't stay,' and I never have any difficulty."

"I'm su/,d Mrs. Munger, "that if all the employers in the coun/ould take such a stand, there would soon be an end of l/r troubles. I think we're too concessive."

"And too, Mrs. Munger!" cried Mrs. Gerrish, glad of the occ/1 to be censorious and of the finer lady's opinion at the / time. "That's what I meant. Don't you, Annie?"

"I'm/aid I don't understand exactly," Annie replied.

Mr./rrish kept his eye on Mrs. Munger's face, now arrange/r indefinite photography, as he went on. "That is exact/hat I say to them. That is what I said to Mr. Marvin one /r ago, when he had that trouble in his shoe shop. I said,/ou're too concessive.' I said, 'Mr. Marvin, if you give thos/ellows an inch, they'll take an ell. Mr. Marvin,' said I, 'you/ got to begin by being your own master, if you want to b master of anybody else. You've got to put your foot dow/, as Mr. Lincoln said; and as I say, you've got to keep it dow/.'"

/rs. Gerrish looked at the other ladies for admiration, and /rs. Munger said, rapidly, without disarranging her face—

"Oh yes. And how much misery could be saved in such cases by a little firmness at the outset!"

"Mr. Marvin differed with me," said Mr. Gerrish sorrowfully. "He agreed with me on the main point, but he said that too many of his hands had been in his regiment, and he couldn't lock them out. He submitted to arbitration. And what is arbitration?" asked Mr. Gerrish, levelling his ruler at Mrs. Munger. "It is postponing the evil day."

"Exactly," said Mrs. Munger, without winking.

"Mr. Marvin," Mr. Gerrish proceeded, "may be running very smoothly now, and sailing before the wind all—all—nicely; but I tell you his house is built upon the sand." He put his ruler by on the desk very softly, and resumed with impressive quiet: "I never had any trouble but once. I had a porter in this store who wanted his pay raised. I simply said that I made it a rule to propose all advances of salary myself, and I should submit to no dictation from any one. He told me to go to—a place that I will not repeat, and I told him to walk out of my store. He was under the influence of liquor at the time, I suppose. I understand that he is drinking very hard. He does nothing to support his family whatever, and from all that I can gather, he bids fair to fill a drunkard's grave inside of six months."

Mrs. Munger seized her opportunity. "Yes; and it is just such cases as this that the Social Union is designed to meet. If this man had some such place to spend his evenings—and bring his family if he chose—where he could get a cup of good coffee for the same price as a glass of rum—— Don't you see?"

She looked round at the different faces, and Mr. Gerrish slightly frowned, as if the vision of the Social Union interposing between his late porter and a drunkard's grave, with a cup of good coffee, were not to his taste altogether; but he said: "Precisely so! And I was about to make the remark that while I am very strict—and obliged to be—with those under me in business, *no* one is more disposed to promote such objects as this of yours."

"I was *sure* you would approve of it," said Mrs. Munger. "That is why I came to you—to you and Mrs. Gerrish— first," said Mrs. Munger. "I was sure you would see it in the right light." She looked round at Annie for corroboration, and Annie was in the social necessity of making a confirmatory murmur.

Mr. Gerrish ignored them both in the more interesting work of celebrating himself. "I may say that there is not an institution in this town which I have not contributed my humble efforts to—to—establish, from the drinking fountain in front of this store, to the soldiers' monument on the village green."

Annie turned red; Mrs. Munger said shamelessly, "That beautiful monument!" and looked at Annie with eyes full of gratitude to Mr. Gerrish.

"The schools, the sidewalks, the water-works, the free library, the introduction of electricity, the projected system of drainage, and *all* the various religious enterprises at various times, I am proud—I am humbly proud—that I have been allowed to be the means of doing—sustaining——"

He lost himself in the labyrinths of his sentence, and Mrs. Munger came to his rescue: "I fancy Hatboro' wouldn't be

Hatboro' without *you*, Mr. Gerrish! And you *don't* think that Mr. Peck's objection will be seriously felt by other leading citizens?"

"*What* is Mr. Peck's objection?" demanded Mr. Gerrish, perceptibly bristling up at the name of his pastor.

"Why, he talked it over with Miss Kilburn last night, and he objected to an entertainment which wouldn't be open to all—to the shop hands and everybody." Mrs. Munger explained the point fully. She repeated some things that Annie had said in ridicule of Mr. Peck's position regarding it. "If you *do* think that part would be bad or impolitic," Mrs. Munger concluded, "we could drop the invited supper and the dance, and simply have the theatricals."

She bent upon Mr. Gerrish a face of candid deference that filled him with self-importance almost to bursting.

"No!" he said, shaking his head, and "No!" closing his lips abruptly, and opening them again to emit a final "No!" with an explosive force which alone seemed to save him. "Not at all, Mrs. Munger; not on any account! I am surprised at Mr. Peck, or rather I am *not* surprised. He is not a practical man—not a man of the world; and I should have much preferred to hear that he objected to the dancing and the play; I could have understood that; I could have gone with him in that to a certain extent, though I can see no harm in such things when properly conducted. I have a great respect for Mr. Peck; I was largely instrumental in getting him here; but he is altogether wrong in this matter. We are not obliged to go out into the highways and the hedges until the bidden guests have—er— declined."

"Exactly," said Mrs. Munger. "I never thought of that."

Mrs. Gerrish shifted her baby to another knee, and followed her husband with her eyes, as he dismounted from his stool and began to pace the room.

"I came into this town a poor boy, without a penny in my pocket, and I have made my own way, every inch of it, unaided and alone. I am a thorough believer in giving every one an equal chance to rise and to—get along; I would not throw an obstacle in anybody's way; but I do not believe—I do *not* believe—in pampering those who have not risen, or have made no effort to rise."

"It's their wastefulness, in nine cases out of ten, that keeps them down," said Mrs. Gerrish.

"I don't care *what* it is, I don't *ask* what it is, that keeps them down. I don't expect to invite my clerks or Mrs. Gerrish's servants into my parlour. I will meet them at the polls, or the communion table, or on any proper occasion; but a man's home is *sacred*. I will not allow my wife or my children to associate with those whose—whose—whose idleness, or vice, or whatever, has kept them down in a country where—where everybody stands on an equality; and what I will not do myself, I will not ask others to do. I make it a rule to do unto others as I would have them do unto me. It is all nonsense to attempt to introduce those one-ideaed notions into—put them in practice."

"Yes," said Mrs. Munger, with deep conviction, "that is my own feeling, Mr. Gerrish, and I'm glad to have it corroborated by your experience. Then you *wouldn't* drop the little invited dance and supper?"

"I will tell you how I feel about it, Mrs. Munger," said Mr. Gerrish, pausing in his walk, and putting on a fine, patronising, gentleman-of-the-old-school smile. "You may put me down for any number of tickets—five, ten, fifteen—and you may command me in anything I can do to further the objects of your enterprise, if you will *keep* the invited supper and dance. But I should not be prepared to do anything if they are dropped."

"What a comfort it is to meet a person who knows his own mind!" exclaimed Mrs. Munger.

"Got company, Billy?" asked a voice at the door; and it added, "Glad to see *you* here, Mrs. Gerrish."

"Ah, Mr. Putney! Come in. Hope I see you well, sir!" cried Mr. Gerrish. "Come in!" he repeated, with jovial frankness. "Nobody but friends here."

"I don't know about that," said Mr. Putney, with whimsical perversity, holding the door ajar. "I see that arch-conspirator from South Hatboro'," he said, looking at Mrs. Munger.

He showed himself, as he stood holding the door ajar, a lank little figure, dressed with reckless slovenliness in a suit of old-fashioned black; a loose neckcloth fell stringing down his shirt front, which his unbuttoned waistcoat exposed, with its stains from the tobacco upon which his thin little jaws worked mechanically, as he stared into the room with flamy blue eyes; his silk hat was pushed back from a high, clear forehead; he had yesterday's stubble on his beardless cheeks; a heavy moustache and imperial gave dash to a cast of countenance that might otherwise have seemed slight and effeminate.

"Yes; but I'm in charge of Miss Kilburn, and you needn't be afraid of me. Come in. We wish to consult you," cried Mrs. Munger. Mrs. Gerrish cackled some applausive incoherencies.

Putney advanced into the room, and dropped his burlesque air as he approached Annie.

"Miss Kilburn, I must apologise for not having called with Mrs. Putney to pay my respects. I have been away; when I got back I found she had stolen a march on me. But I'm going to make Ellen bring me at once. I don't think I've been in your house since the old Judge's time. Well, he was an able man, and a good man; I was awfully fond of the old Judge, in a boy's way."

"Thank you," said Annie, touched by something gentle and honest in his words.

"He was a Christian gentleman," said Mr. Gerrish, with authority.

Putney said, without noticing Mr. Gerrish, "Well, I'm glad you've come back to the old place, Miss Kilburn—I almost said Annie."

"I shouldn't have minded, Ralph," she retorted.

"Shouldn't you? Well, that's right." Putney continued, ignoring the laugh of the others at Annie's sally: "You'll find Hatboro' pretty exciting, after Rome, for a while, I suppose. But you'll get used to it. It's got more of the modern improvements, I'm told, and it's more public-spirited—more snap to it. I'm told that there's more enterprise in Hatboro', more real *crowd* in South Hatboro' alone, than there is in the Quirinal and the Vatican put together."

"You had better come and live at South Hatboro', Mr. Putney; that would be just the atmosphere for you," said Mrs. Munger, with aimless hospitality. She said this to every one.

"Is it about coming to South Hatboro' you want to consult me?" asked Putney.

"Well, it is, and it isn't," she began.

"Better be honest, Mrs. Munger," said Putney. "You can't do anything for a client who won't be honest with his attorney. That's what I have to continually impress upon the reprobates who come to me. I say, 'It don't matter what you've done; if you expect me to get you off, you've got to make a clean breast of it.' They generally do; they see the sense of it."

They all laughed, and Mr. Gerrish said, "Mr. Putney is one of Hatboro's privileged characters, Miss Kilburn."

"Thank you, Billy," returned the lawyer, with mock-tenderness. "Now, Mrs. Munger, out with it!"

"You'll have to tell him sooner or later, Mrs. Munger!" said Mrs. Gerrish, with overweening pleasure in her acquaintance with both of these superior people. "He'll get it out of you anyway." Her husband looked at her, and she fell silent.

Mrs. Munger swept her with a tolerant smile as she looked up at Putney. "Why, it's really Miss Kilburn's affair," she began; and she laid the case before the lawyer with a fulness that made Annie wince.

Putney took a piece of tobacco from his pocket, and tore off a morsel with his teeth. "Excuse me, Annie! It's a beastly habit. But it's saved me from something worse. *You* don't know what I've been; but anybody in Hatboro' can tell you. I made my shame so public that it's no use trying to blink the past. You don't have to be a hypocrite in a place where everybody's seen you in the gutter; that's the only advantage I've got over my fellow-citizens, and of course I abuse it; that's nature, you know. When I began to pull up I found that tobacco helped me; I smoked and chewed both; now I only chew. Well," he said, dropping the pathetic simplicity with which he had spoken, and turning with a fierce jocularity from the shocked and pitying look in Annie's face to Mrs. Munger, "what do you propose to do? Brother Peck's head seems to be pretty level, in the abstract."

"Yes," said Mrs. Munger, willing to put the case impartially; "and I should be perfectly willing to drop the invited dance and supper, if it was thought best, though I must say I don't at all agree with Mr. Peck in principle. I don't see what would become of society."

"You ought to be in politics, Mrs. Munger," said Putney.

"Your readiness to sacrifice principle to expediency shows what a reform will be wrought when you ladies get the suffrage. What does Brother Gerrish think?"

"No, no," said Mrs. Munger. "We want an impartial opinion."

"I always think as Brother Gerrish thinks," said Putney. "I guess you better give up the fandango; hey, Billy?"

"No, sir; no, Mr. Putney," answered the merchant nervously. "I can't agree with you. And I will tell you why, sir."

He gave his reasons, with some abatement of pomp and detail, and with the tremulous eagerness of a solemn man who expects a sarcastic rejoinder. "It would be a bad precedent. This town is full now of a class of persons who are using every opportunity to—to abuse their privileges. And this would be simply adding fuel to the flame."

"Do you really think so, Billy?" asked the lawyer, with cool derision. "Well, we all abuse our privileges at every opportunity, of course; I was just saying that I abused mine; and I suppose those fellows would abuse theirs if you happened to hurt their wives' and daughters' feelings. And how are you going to manage? Aren't you afraid that they will hang around, after the show, indefinitely, unless you ask all those who have not received invitations to the dance and supper to clear the grounds, as they do in the circus when the minstrels are going to give a performance not included in the price of admission? Mind, I don't care anything about your Social Union."

"Oh, but *surely!*" cried Mrs. Munger, "you *must* allow that it's a good object."

"Well, perhaps it is, if it will keep the men away from the rum-holes. Yes, I guess it is. You won't sell liquor?"

"We expect to furnish coffee at cost price," said Mrs. Munger, smiling at Putney's joke.

"And good navy-plug too, I hope. But you see it would be rather awkward, don't you? You see, Annie?"

"Yes, I see," said Annie. "I hadn't thought of that part before."

"And you didn't agree with Brother Peck on general principles? There we see the effect of residence abroad," said Putney. "The uncorrupted—or I will say the uninterrupted—

Hatborian has none of those aristocratic predilections of yours, Annie. He grows up in a community where there is neither poverty nor richness, and where political economy can show by the figures that the profligate shop hands get nine-tenths of the profits, and starve on 'em, while the good little company rolls in luxury on the other tenth. But you've got used to something different over there, and of course Brother Peck's ideas startled you. Well, I suppose I should have been just so myself."

"Mr. Putney has never felt just right about the working-men since he lost the boycotters' case," said Mr. Gerrish, with a snicker.

"Oh, come now, Billy, why did you give me away?" said Putney, with mock suffering. "Well, I suppose I might as well own up, Mrs. Munger; it's no use trying to keep it from *you*; you know it already. Yes, Annie, I defended some poor devils here for combining to injure a non-union man—for doing once just what the big manufacturing Trusts do every day of the year with impunity; and I lost the case. I expected to. I told 'em they were wrong, but I did my best for 'em. 'Why, you fools,' said I—that's the way I talk to 'em, Annie; I call 'em pet names; they like it; they're used to 'em; they get 'em every day in the newspapers—'you fools,' said I, 'what do you want to boycott for, when you can *vote*? What do you want to break the laws for, when you can *make* 'em? You idiots, you,' said I, 'what do you putter round for, persecuting non-union men, that have as good a right to earn their bread as you, when you might make the whole United States of America a Labour Union?' Of course I didn't say that in court."

"Oh, how delicious you are, Mr. Putney!" said Mrs. Munger.

"Glad you like me, Mrs. Munger," Putney replied.

"Yes, you're delightful," said the lady, recovering from the effects of the drollery which they had all pretended to enjoy, Mr. Gerrish, and Mrs. Gerrish by his leave, even more than the others. "But you're not candid. All this doesn't help us to a conclusion. Would you give up the invited dance and supper, or wouldn't you? That's the question."

"And no shirking, hey?" asked Putney.

"No shirking."

Putney glanced through a little transparent space in the ground-glass windows framing the room, which Mr. Gerrish used for keeping an eye on his salesladies to see that they did not sit down.

"Hello!" he exclaimed. "There's Dr. Morrell. Let's put the case to him." He opened the door and called down the store, "Come in here, Doc!"

"What?" called back an amused voice; and after a moment steps approached, and Dr. Morrell hesitated at the open door. He was a tall man, with a slight stoop; well dressed; full bearded; with kind, boyish blue eyes that twinkled in fascinating friendliness upon the group. "Nobody sick here, I hope?"

"Walk right in, sir! come in, Dr. Morrell," said Mr. Gerrish. "Mrs. Munger and Mrs. Gerrish you know. Present you to Miss Kilburn, who has come to make her home among us after a prolonged residence abroad. Dr. Morrell, Miss Kilburn."

"No, there's nobody sick here, in one sense," said Putney, when the doctor had greeted the ladies. "But we want your advice all the same. Mrs. Munger is in a pretty bad way morally, Doc."

"Don't you mind Mr. Putney, doctor!" screamed Mrs. Gerrish.

Putney said, with respectful recognition of the poor woman's attempt to be arch, "I'll try to keep within the bounds of truth in stating the case, Mrs. Gerrish."

He went on to state it, with so much gravity and scrupulosity, and with so many appeals to Mrs. Munger to correct him if he were wrong, that the doctor was shaking with laughter when Putney came to an end with unbroken seriousness. At each repetition of the facts, Annie's relation to them grew more intolerable; and she suspected Putney of an intention to punish her. "Well, what do you say?" he demanded of the doctor.

"Ha, ha, ha! ah, ha, ha!" laughed the doctor, shutting his eyes and throwing back his head.

"Seems to consider it a *laughing* matter," said Putney to Mrs. Munger.

"Yes; and that is all your fault," said Mrs. Munger, trying, with the ineffectiveness of a large woman, to pout.

"No, no, I'm not laughing," began the doctor.

"Smiling, perhaps," suggested Putney.

The doctor went off again. Then, "I beg—I *beg* your pardon, Mrs. Munger," he resumed. "But it isn't a professional question, you know; and I—I really couldn't judge—have any opinion on such a matter."

"No shirking," said Putney. "That's what Mrs. Munger said to me."

"Of course not," gurgled the doctor. "You ladies will know what to do. I'm sure *I* shouldn't," he added.

"Well, I must be going," said Putney. "Sorry to leave you in this fix, Doc." He flashed out of the door, and suddenly came back to offer Annie his hand. "I beg your pardon, Annie. I'm going to make Ellen bring me round. Good morning." He bowed cursorily to the rest.

"Wait—I'll go with you, Putney," said the doctor.

Mrs. Munger rose, and Annie with her. "We must go too," she said. "We've taken up Mr. Gerrish's time most unconscionably," and now Mr. Gerrish did not urge her to remain.

"Well, good-bye," said Mrs. Gerrish, with a genteel prolongation of the last syllable.

Mr. Gerrish followed his guests down the store, and even out upon the sidewalk, where he presided with unheeded hospitality over the superfluous politeness of Putney and Dr. Morrell in putting Mrs. Munger and Annie into the phaeton. Mrs. Munger attempted to drive away without having taken up her hitching weight.

"I suppose that there isn't a post in this town that my wife hasn't tried to pull up in that way," said Putney gravely.

The doctor doubled himself down with another fit of laughing.

Annie wanted to laugh too, but she did not like his laughing. She questioned if it were not undignified. She felt that it might be disrespectful. Then she asked herself why he should respect her.

IX.

"THAT WAS a great success," said Mrs. Munger, as they drove away. Annie said nothing, and she added, "Don't you think so?"

"Well, I confess," said Annie, "I don't see how, exactly. Do you mean with regard to Mr. Gerrish?"

"Oh no; I don't care anything about him," said Mrs. Munger, touching her pony with the tip of her whip-lash. "He's an odious little creature, and I knew that he would go for the dance and supper because Mr. Peck was opposed to them. He's one of the anti-Peck party in his church, and that is the reason I spoke to him. But I meant the other gentlemen. You saw how they took it."

"I saw that they both made fun of it," said Annie.

"Yes; that's just the point. It's so fortunate they were frank about it. It throws a new light on it; and if that's the way nice people are going to look at it, why, we must give up the idea. I'm quite prepared to do so. But I want to see Mrs. Wilmington first."

"Mrs. Munger," said Annie uneasily, "I would rather not see Mrs. Wilmington with you on this subject; I should be of no use."

"My dear, you would be of the *greatest* use," persisted Munger, and she laid her arm across Annie's lap, as if to prevent her jumping out of the phaeton. "As Mrs. Wilmington's old friend, you will have the greatest influence with her."

"But I don't know that I wish to influence her in favour of the supper and dance; I don't know that I believe in them," said Annie, cowed and troubled by the affair.

"That doesn't make the slightest difference," said Mrs. Munger impartially. "All you will have to do is to keep still. I will put the case to her."

She checked the pony before the bar which the flagman at the railroad crossing had let down, while a long freight train clattered deafeningly by, and then drove bumping and jouncing across the tracks. "I suppose you remember what 'Over the Track' means in Hatboro'?"

"Oh yes," said Annie, with a smile. "Social perdition at the least. You don't mean that Mrs. Wilmington lives 'Over the Track'?"

"Yes. It isn't so bad as it used to be, socially. Mr. Wilmington has built a very fine house on this side, and there are several pretty Queen Anne cottages going up."

They drove along under the elms which here stood somewhat at random about the wide, grassless street, between the high, windowy bulks of the shoe shops and hat shops. The dust gradually freed itself from the cinders about the tracks, and it hardened into a handsome, newly made road beyond the houses of the shop hands. They passed some open lots, and then, on a pleasant rise of ground, they came to a stately residence, lifted still higher on its underpinning of granite blocks. It was built in a Boston suburban taste of twenty years ago, with a lofty mansard-roof, and it was painted the stone-grey colour which was once esteemed for being so quiet. The lawn before it sloped down to the road, where it ended smoothly at the brink of a neat stone wall. A black asphalt path curved from the steps by which you mounted from the street to the steps by which you mounted to the heavy portico before the massive black walnut doors.

The ladies were shown into the music-room, from which the notes of a piano were sounding when they rang, and Mrs. Wilmington rose from the instrument to meet them. A young man who had been standing beside her turned away. Mrs. Wilmington was dressed in a light morning dress with a Watteau fall, whose delicate russets and faded reds and yellows heightened the richness of her complexion and hair.

"Why, Annie," she said, "how glad I am to see you! And you too, Mrs. Munger. How *vurry* nice!" Her words took value from the thick mellow tones of her voice, and passed for much more than they were worth intrinsically. She moved lazily about and got them into chairs, and was not resentful when Mrs. Munger broke out with "How hot you have it!" "Have we? We had the furnace lighted yesterday, and we've been in all the morning, and so we hadn't noticed. Jack, won't you shut the register?" she drawled over her shoulder. "This is my nephew, Mr. Jack Wilmington, Miss Kilburn. Mr. Wilmington and Mrs. Munger are old friends."

The young fellow bowed silently, and Annie instantly took

a dislike to him, his heavy jaw, long eyes, and low forehead almost hidden under a thick bang. He sat down cornerwise on a chair, and listened, with a scornful thrust of his thick lips, to their talk.

Mrs. Munger was not abashed by him. She opened her budget with all her robust authority, and once more put Annie to shame. When she came to the question of the invited supper and dance, and having previously committed Mrs. Wilmington in favour of the general scheme, asked her what she thought of that part, Mr. Jack Wilmington answered for her—

"I should think you had a right to do what you please about it. It's none of the hands' business if you don't choose to ask them."

"Yes, that's what any one would think—in the abstract," said Mrs. Munger.

"Now, little boy," said Mrs. Wilmington, with indolent amusement, putting out a silencing hand in the direction of the young man, "don't you be so fast. You let your aunty speak for herself. I don't know about not letting the hands stay to the dance and supper, Mrs. Munger. You know I might feel 'put upon.' I used to be one of the hands myself. Yes, Annie, there was a time after you went away, and after father died, when I actually fell so low as to work for an honest living."

"I think I heard, Lyra," said Annie; "but I had forgotten." The fact, in connection with what had been said, made her still more uncomfortable.

"Well, I didn't work very hard, and I didn't have to work long. But I was a hand, and there's no use trying to deny it. As Mr. Putney says, he and I have our record, and we don't have to make any pretences. And the question is, whether I ought to go back on my fellow-hands."

"Oh, but Mrs. *Wilmington!*" said Mrs. Munger, with intense deprecation, "that's such a very different thing. You were not brought up to it; it was just temporary; and besides——"

"And besides, there was Mr. Wilmington, I know. He was very opportune. I might have been a hand at this moment if Mr. Wilmington had not come along and invited me to be a head—the head of his house. But I don't know, Annie, whether I oughtn't to remember my low beginnings."

"I suppose we all like to be consistent," answered Annie aimlessly, uneasily.

"Yes," Mrs. Munger broke in; "but they were *not* your beginnings, Mrs. Wilmington; they were your incidents—your accidents."

"It's very pretty of you to say so, Mrs. Munger," drawled Mrs. Wilmington. "But I guess I must oppose the little invited dance and supper, on principle. We all like to be consistent, as Annie says—even if we're inconsistent in the attempt," she added, with a laugh.

"Very well, then," exclaimed Mrs. Munger, "we'll *drop* them. As I said to Miss Kilburn on our way here, 'if Mrs. Wilmington is opposed to them, we'll drop them.' "

"Oh, am I such an influential person?" said Mrs. Wilmington, with a shrug. "It's rather awful—isn't it, Annie?"

"Not at all!" Mrs. Munger answered for Annie. "We've just been talking the matter over with Mr. Putney and Dr. Morrell, and they're both opposed. You're merely the straw that breaks the camel's back, Mrs. Wilmington."

"Oh, *thank* you! That's a great relief."

"Well—and now the question is, will you take the part of the Nurse or not in the dramatics?" asked Mrs. Munger, returning to business.

"Well, I must think about that, and I must ask Mr. Wilmington. Jack," she called over her shoulder to the young man at the window, "do you think your uncle would approve of me as Juliet's Nurse?"

"You'd better ask him," growled the young fellow.

"Well," said Mrs. Wilmington, with another laugh, "I'll think it over, Mrs. Munger."

"Thank you," said Mrs. Munger. "And now we must really be going," she added, pulling out her watch by its leathern guard.

"Not till you've had lunch," said Mrs. Wilmington, rising with the ladies. "You must stay. Annie, I shall not excuse you."

"Well," said Mrs. Munger, complying without regard to Annie, "all this diplomacy is certainly very exhausting."

"Lunch will be on the table in one moment," returned Mrs. Wilmington, as the ladies sat down again provisionally. "Will you join us, Jack?"

"No; I'm going to the office," said the nephew, bowing himself out of the room.

"Jack's learning to be superintendent," said Mrs. Wilmington, lifting her teasing voice to make him hear her in the hall, "and he's been spending the whole morning here."

In the richly appointed dining-room—a glitter of china and glass and a mass of carven oak—the table was laid for two.

"Put another plate, Norah," said Mrs. Wilmington carelessly.

There was bouillon in teacups, chicken cutlets in white sauce, and luscious strawberries.

"*What* a cook!" cried Mrs. Munger, over the cutlets.

"Yes, she's a treasure; I don't deny it," said Mrs. Wilmington.

X.

By the end of May most of the summer folk had come to their cottages in South Hatboro'. One after another the ladies called upon Annie. They all talked to her of the Social Union, and it seemed to be agreed that it was fully in train, though what was really in train was the entertainment to be given at Mrs. Munger's for the benefit of the Union; the Union always dropped out of the talk as soon as the theatricals were mentioned.

When Annie went to return these visits she scarcely recognised even the shape of the country, once so familiar to her, of which the summer settlement had possessed itself. She found herself in a strange world—a world of colonial and Queen Anne architecture, where conscious lines and insistent colours contributed to an effect of posing which she had never seen off the stage. But it was not a very large world, and after the young trees and hedges should have grown up and helped to hide it, she felt sure that it would be a better world. In detail it was not so bad now, but the whole was a violent effect of porches, gables, chimneys, galleries, loggias, balconies, and jalousies, which nature had not yet had time to palliate.

Mrs. Munger was at home, and wanted her to spend the day, to drive out with her, to stay to lunch. When Annie would not do any of these things, she invited herself to go with her to call at the Brandreths'. But first she ordered her to go out with her to see the place where they intended to have the theatricals: a pretty bit of natural boscage—white birches, pines, and oaks—faced by a stretch of smooth turf, where a young man in a flannel blazer was painting a tennis-court in the grass. Mrs. Munger introduced him as her Jim, and the young fellow paused from his work long enough to bow to her: his nose now seemed in perfect repair.

Mr. Brandreth met them at the door of his mother's cottage. It was a very small cottage on the outside, with a good deal of stained glass *en évidence* in leaded sashes; where the sashes were not leaded and the glass not stained, the panes were cut up into very large ones, with little ones round them. Everything was very old-fashioned inside. The door opened directly into a wainscoted square hall, which had a large fireplace with gleaming brass andirons, and a carved mantel carried to the ceiling. It was both baronial and colonial in its decoration; there was part of a suit of imitation armour under a pair of moose antlers on one wall, and at one side of the fireplace there was a spinning-wheel, with a tuft of flax ready to be spun. There were Japanese swords on the lowest mantel-shelf, together with fans and vases; a long old flint-lock musket stretched across the panel above. Mr. Brandreth began to show things to Annie, and to tell how little they cost, as soon as the ladies entered. His mother's voice called from above, "Now, Percy, you stop till *I* get there!" and in a moment or two she appeared from behind a *portière* in one corner. Before she shook hands with the ladies, or allowed any kind of greeting, she pulled the *portière* aside, and made Annie admire the snug concealment of the staircase. Then she made her go upstairs and see the chambers, and the second-hand colonial bedsteads, and the andirons everywhere, and the old chests of drawers and their brasses; and she told her some story about each, and how Percy picked it up and had it repaired. When they came down, the son took Annie in hand again and walked her over the ground-floor, ending with the kitchen, which was in the taste of an old New England kitchen, with hard-seated high-backed chairs, and a kitchen table with curiously turned legs, which he had picked up in the hen-house of a neighbouring farmer for a song. There was an authentic crane in the dining-room fireplace, which he had found in a heap of scrap-iron at a blacksmith's shop, and had got for next to nothing. The sideboard he had got at an old second-hand shop in the North End; and he believed it was an heirloom from the house of one of the old ministers of the North End Church. Everything, nearly, in the Brandreth cottage was an heirloom, though Annie could not remember afterward any object that had been an heirloom in the Brandreth family.

When she went back with Mr. Brandreth to the hall, which seemed to be also the drawing-room, she found that Mrs. Brandreth had lighted the fire on the hearth, though it was rather a warm day without, for the sake of the effect. She was sitting in the chimney-seat, and shielding her face from the blaze with an old-fashioned feather hand-screen.

"Now don't you think we have a lovely little home?" she demanded.

Mrs. Munger began to break out in its praise, but she shook the screen silencingly at her.

"No, no! I want Miss Kilburn's unbiassed opinion. Don't you speak, Mrs. Munger! Now haven't we?"

Mrs. Brandreth made Annie assent to the superiority of her cottage in detail. She recapitulated the different facts of the architecture and furnishing, from each of which she seemed to acquire personal merit, and she insisted that Percy should show some of them again. "We think it's a little picture," she concluded, and once more Annie felt obliged to murmur her acquiescence.

At last Mrs. Munger said that she must go to lunch, and was going to take Annie with her; Annie said she must lunch at home; and then Mrs. Brandreth pressed them both to stay to lunch with her. "You shall have a cup of tea out of a piece of real Satsuma," she said; but they resisted. "I don't believe," she added, apparently relieved by their persistence, and losing a little anxiety of manner, "that Percy's had any chance to consult you on a very important point about your theatricals, Miss Kilburn."

"Oh, that will do some other time, mother," said Mr. Brandreth.

"No, no! Now! And you can have Mrs. Munger's opinion too. You know Miss Sue Northwick is going to be Juliet?"

"No!" shouted Mrs. Munger. "I thought she had refused positively. When did she change her mind?"

"She's just sent Percy a note. We were talking it over when you came, and Percy was going over to tell you."

"Then it is *sure* to be a success," said Mrs. Munger, with a solemnity of triumph.

"Yes, but Percy feels that it complicates one point more than ever——"

"It's a question that always comes up in amateur dramatics," said Mr. Brandreth, with reluctance, "and it always will; and of course it's particularly embarrassing in *Romeo and*

Juliet. If they don't show any affection—it's very awkward and stiff; and if——"

"I never approved of those liberties on the stage," said Mrs. Brandreth. "I tell Percy that it's my principal objection to it. I can't make it seem nice. But he says that it's essential to the effect. Now *I* say that they might just incline their heads toward each other without *actually*, you know. But Percy is afraid that it won't do, especially in the parting scene on the balcony—so passionate, you know—it won't do simply to—— They must *act* like lovers. And it's such a great point to get Miss Sue Northwick to take the part, that he mustn't risk losing her by anything that might seem——"

"Yes," said Mrs. Munger, with deep concern.

Mr. Brandreth looked very unhappy. "It's an embarrassing point. We can't change the play, and so the difficulty must be met and disposed of at once."

He did not look at either of the ladies, but Mrs. Munger referred the matter to Annie with a glance of impartiality. His mother also turned her eyes upon Annie. "Percy thought that you must have seen so much of amateur dramatics in Europe that you could tell him just how to do."

"Perhaps you could consult Miss Northwick herself," said Annie dryly, after a moment of indignation, and another of amusement.

"I thought of that," said Mrs. Brandreth; "but as Percy's to be Romeo—— You see he wishes the play to be a success artistically; but if it's to succeed socially, he must have Miss Northwick, and she might resign at the first suggestion of——"

"Bessie Chapley would certainly have been better. She's so outspoken you could have put the case right to her," said Mrs. Munger.

"Yes," said Mr. Brandreth gloomily.

"But we shall find out a way. Why, you can settle it at rehearsal!"

"Perhaps at rehearsal," said Mr. Brandreth, with a pensive absence of mind.

Mrs. Munger crushed his hand and his mother's in her leathern grasp, and took Annie away with her. "It isn't lunch-time yet," she explained, when they were out of earshot, "but

I saw she was simply killing you, and so I made the excuse. She has no mercy. There's time enough for you to make your calls before lunch, and then you can come home with me."

Annie suggested that this would not do after refusing Mrs. Brandreth.

"Why, it would never have done to *accept*!" Mrs. Munger cried. "They didn't dream of it!" At the next place she said: "This is the Clevingers'. *They're* some of our all-the-year-round people too." She opened the door without ringing, and let herself noisily in. "This is the way we run in, without ceremony, everywhere. It's quite one family. That's the charm of the place. We expect to take each other as we find them."

Her freedom did not find the ladies off their guard anywhere. At all the houses there was a skurrying of feet and a flashing of skirts out of the room or up the stairs, and there was an interval for a thorough study of the features of the room before the hostess came in, with the effect of coming in just as she was. She had naturally always made some change in her dress, and Annie felt that she had not really liked being run in upon. Everywhere they talked to her about the theatricals; and they talked across her to Mrs. Munger, about one another, pretty freely.

"Well, that's all there is of us at present," said Mrs. Munger, coming down the main road with her from the last place, "and you see just what we are. It's a neighbourhood where everybody's just adapted to everybody else. It's not a mere mush of concession, as Emerson says; people are perfectly outspoken; but there's the greatest good feeling, and no vulgar display, or lavish expenditure, or—anything."

Annie walked slowly homeward. She was tired, and she was now aware of having been extremely bored by the South Hatboro' people. She was very censorious of them, as we are of other people when we have reason to be discontented with ourselves. They were making a pretence of simplicity and unconventionality; but they had brought each her full complement of servants with her, and each was apparently giving herself in the summer to the unrealities that occupied her during the winter. Everywhere Annie had found the affectation of intellectual interests, and the assumption that these were the highest interests of life: there could be no doubt that culture was the ideal of South Hatboro', and several of the ladies complained that in the summer they got behind with their reading, or their art, or their music. They said it was even more trouble to keep house in the country than it was in town; sometimes your servants would not come with you; or, if they did, they were always discontented, and you did not know what moment they would leave you.

Annie asked herself how her own life was in any wise different from that of these people. It had received a little more light into it, but as yet it had not conformed itself to any ideal of duty. She too was idle and vapid, like the society of which her whole past had made her a part, and she owned to herself, groaning in spirit, that it was no easier to escape from her tradition at Hatboro' than it was at Rome.

When she reached her own house again, Mrs. Bolton called to her from the kitchen threshold as she was passing the corner on her way to the front door: "Mis' Putney's b'en here. I guess you'll find a note from her on the parlour table."

Annie fired in resentment of the uncouthness. It was Mrs. Bolton's business to come into the parlour and give her the note, with a respectful statement of the facts. But she did not tell her so; it would have been useless.

Mrs. Putney's note was an invitation to a family tea for the next evening.

XI.

PUTNEY met Annie at the door, and led her into the parlour beside the hall. He had a little crippled boy on his right arm, and he gave her his left hand. In the parlour he set his burden down in a chair, and the child drew up under his thin arms a pair of crutches that stood beside it. His white face had the eager purity and the waxen translucence which we see in sufferers from hip-disease.

"This is our Winthrop," said his father, beginning to talk at once. "We receive the company and do the honours while mother's looking after the tea. We only keep one undersized girl," he explained more directly to Annie, "and Ellen has to be chief cook and bottlewasher herself. She'll be in directly. Just lay off your bonnet anywhere."

She was taking in the humility of the house and its belongings while she received the impression of an unimagined simplicity in its life from his easy explanations. The furniture was in green terry, the carpet a harsh, brilliant tapestry; on the marble-topped centre table was a big clasp Bible and a basket with a stereoscope and views; the marbleised iron shelf above the stove-pipe hole supported two glass vases and a French clock under a glass bell; through the open door, across the oil-cloth of the hallway, she saw the white-painted pine balusters of the steep, cramped stairs. It was clear that neither Putney nor his wife had been touched by the æsthetic craze; the parlour was in the tastelessness of fifteen years before; but after the decoration of South Hatboro', she found a delicious repose in it. Her eyes dwelt with relief on the wall-paper of French grey, sprigged with small gilt flowers, and broken by a few cold engravings and framed photographs.

Putney himself was as little decorated as the parlour. He had put on a clean shirt, but the bulging bosom had broken away from its single button, and showed two serrated edges of ragged linen; his collar lost itself from time to time under the rise of his plastron scarf band, which kept escaping from the stud that ought to have held it down behind. His hair was brushed smoothly across a forehead which looked as innocent and gentle as the little boy's.

"We don't often give these festivities," he went on, "but you don't come home once in twelve years every day, Annie. I can't tell you how glad I am to see you in our house; and Ellen's just as excited as the rest of us; she was sorry to miss you when she called."

"You're very kind, Ralph. I can't tell *you* what a pleasure it was to come, and I'm not going to let the trouble I'm giving spoil my pleasure."

"Well, that's right," said Putney. "*We* sha'n't either." He took out a cigar and put it into his mouth. "It's only a dry smoke. Ellen makes me let up on my chewing when we have company, and I must have something in my mouth, so I get a cigar. It's a sort of compromise. I'm a terribly nervous man, Annie; you can't imagine. If it wasn't for the grace of God, I think I should fly to pieces sometimes. But I guess that's what holds me together—that and Winthy here. I dropped him on the stairs out there, when I was drunk, one night. I saw you looking at them; I suppose you've been told; it's all right. I presume the Almighty knows what He's about; but sometimes He appears to save at the spigot and waste at the bung-hole, like the rest of us. He let me cripple my boy to reform me."

"Don't, Ralph!" said Annie, with a voice of low entreaty. She turned and spoke to the child, and asked him if he would not come to see her.

"What?" he asked, breaking with a sort of absent-minded start from his intentness upon his father's words.

She repeated her invitation.

"Thanks!" he said, in the prompt, clear little pipe which startles by its distinctness and decision on the lips of crippled children. "I guess father'll bring me some day. Don't you want I should go out and tell mother she's here?" he asked his father.

"Well, if you want to, Winthrop," said his father.

The boy swung himself lightly out of the room on his crutches, and his father turned to her. "Well, how does Hatboro' strike you, anyway, Annie? You needn't mind being honest with me, you know."

He did not give her a chance to say, and she was willing to let him talk on, and tell her what he thought of Hatboro' himself. "Well, it's like every other place in the world, at every moment of history—it's in a transition state. The theory is, you know, that most places are at a standstill the greatest part of the time; they haven't begun to move, or they've stopped moving; but I guess that's a mistake; they're moving all the while. I suppose Rome itself was in a transition state when you left?"

"Oh, very decidedly. It had ceased to be old and was becoming new."

"Well, that's just the way with Hatboro'. There *is* no old Hatboro' any more; and there never was, as your father and mine could tell us if they were here. They lived in a painfully transitional period, poor old fellows! But, for all that, there is a difference. They lived in what was really a New England village, and we live now in a sprawling American town; and by American of course I mean a town where at least one-third of the people are raw foreigners or rawly extracted natives. The old New England ideal characterises them all, up to a certain point, socially; it puts a decent outside on most of 'em; it makes 'em keep Sunday, and drink on the sly. We got in the Irish long ago, and now they're part of the conservative element. We got in the French Canadians, and some of them are our best mechanics and citizens. We're getting in the Italians, and as soon as they want something better than bread and vinegar to eat, they'll begin going to Congress and boycotting and striking and forming pools and trusts just like any other class of law-abiding Americans. There used to be some talk of the Chinese, but I guess they've pretty much blown over. We've got Ah Lee and Sam Lung here, just as they have everywhere, but their laundries don't seem to increase. The Irish are spreading out into the country and scooping in the farms that are not picturesque enough for the summer folks. You can buy a farm anywhere round Hatboro' for less than the buildings on it cost. I'd rather the Irish would have the land than the summer folks. They make an honest living off it, and the other fellows that come out to roost here from June till October simply keep somebody else from making a living off it, and corrupt all the poor people in sight by their idleness and luxury. That's what I tell 'em at South Hatboro'. They don't like it, but I guess they believe it; anyhow they have to hear it. They'll tell you in self-defence that J. Milton Northwick is a practical farmer, and sells his butter for a dollar a pound. He's done more than anybody else to improve the breeds of cattle and horses; and he spends fifteen thousand a year on his place. It can't return him five; and that's the reason he's a curse and a fraud."

"Who *is* Mr. Northwick, Ralph?" Annie interposed. "Everybody at South Hatboro' asked me if I'd met the Northwicks."

"He's a very great and good man," said Putney. "He's worth a million, and he runs a big manufacturing company at Ponkwasset Falls, and he owns a fancy farm just beyond South Hatboro'. He lives in Boston, but he comes out here early enough to dodge his tax there, and let poorer people pay it. He's got miles of cut stone wall round his place, and conservatories and gardens and villas and drives inside of it, and he keeps up the town roads outside at his own expense. Yes, we feel it such an honour and advantage to have J. Milton in Hatboro' that our assessors practically allow him to fix the amount of tax here himself. People who can pay only a little at the highest valuation are assessed to the last dollar of their property and income; but the assessors know that this wouldn't do with Mr. Northwick. They make a guess at his income, and he always pays their bills without asking for abatement; they think themselves wise and public-spirited men for doing it, and most of their fellow-citizens think so too. You see it's not only difficult for a rich man to get into the kingdom of heaven, Annie, but he makes it hard for other people.

"Well, as I was saying, socially the old New England element is at the top of the heap here. That's so everywhere. The people that are on the ground first, it don't matter much who they are, have to manage pretty badly not to leave their descendants in social ascendency over all newer comers for ever. Why, I can see it in my own case. I can see that I was a sort of fetich to the bedevilled fancy of the people here when I was seen drunk in the streets every day, just because I was one of the old Hatboro' Putneys; and when I began to hold up, there wasn't a man in the community that wasn't proud and flattered to help me. Curious, isn't it? It made me sick of myself and ashamed of them, and I just made up my mind, as soon as I got straight again, I'd give all my help to the men that hadn't a tradition. That's what I've done, Annie. There isn't any low, friendless rapscallion in this town that hasn't got me for his friend—and Ellen. We've been in all the strikes with the men, and all their fool boycottings and kicking over the traces generally. Anybody else would have been turned out of respectable society for one-half that I've done, but it tolerates me because I'm one of the old Hatboro' Putneys. You're one of the old Hatboro' Kilburns, and if you want to have a mind of your own and a heart of your own, all you've got to do is to have it. They'll like it; they'll think it's original. That's the reason South Hatboro' got after you with that Social Union scheme. They were right in thinking you would have a great deal of influence. I was sorry you had to throw it against Brother Peck."

Annie felt herself jump at this climax, as if she had been touched on an exposed nerve. She grew red, and tried to be angry, but she was only ashamed and tempted to lie out of the part she had taken. "Mrs. Munger," she said, "gave that a very unfair turn. I didn't mean to ridicule Mr. Peck. I think he was perfectly sincere. The scheme of the invited dance and supper has been entirely given up. And I don't care for the project of the Social Union at all."

"Well, I'm glad to hear it," said Putney, indifferently, and he resumed his analysis of Hatboro'—

"We've got all the modern improvements here, Annie. I suppose you'd find the modern improvements, most of 'em, in Sheol: electric light, Bell telephone, asphalt sidewalks, and city water—though I don't know about the water; and I presume they haven't got a public library or an opera-house— perhaps they *have* got an opera-house in Sheol: you see I use the Revised Version, it don't sound so much like swearing. But, as I was saying——"

Mrs. Putney came in, and he stopped with the laugh of a man who knows that his wife will find it necessary to account for him and apologise for him.

The ladies kissed each other. Mrs. Putney was dressed in

the black silk of a woman who has one silk; she was red from the kitchen, but all was neat and orderly in the hasty toilet which she must have made since leaving the cook-stove. A faint, mixed perfume of violet sachet and fricasseed chicken attended her.

"Well, as you were saying, Ralph?" she suggested.

"Oh, I was just tracing a little parallel between Hatboro' and Sheol," replied her husband.

Mrs. Putney made a *tchk* of humorous patience, and laughed toward Annie for sympathy. "Well, then, I guess you needn't go on. Tea's ready. Shall we wait for the doctor?"

"No; doctors are too uncertain. We'll wait for him while we're eating. That's what fetches him the soonest. I'm hungry. Ain't you, Win?"

"Not so very," said the boy, with his queer promptness. He stood resting himself on his crutches at the door, and he now wheeled about, and led the way out to the living-room, swinging himself actively forward. It seemed that his haste was to get to the dumb-waiter in the little china closet opening off the dining-room, which was like the papered inside of a square box. He called to the girl below, and helped pull it up, as Annie could tell by the creaking of the rope, and the light jar of the finally arriving crockery. A half-grown girl then appeared, and put the dishes on at the places indicated with nods and looks by Mrs. Putney, who had taken her place at the table. There was a platter of stewed fowl, and a plate of high-piled waffles, sweltering in successive courses of butter and sugar. In cut-glass dishes, one at each end of the table, there were canned cherries and pine-apple. There was a square of old-fashioned soda biscuit, not broken apart, which sent up a pleasant smell; in the centre of the table was a shallow vase of strawberries.

It was all very good and appetising; but to Annie it was pathetically old-fashioned, and helped her to realise how wholly out of the world was the life which her friends led.

"Winthrop," said Putney, and the father and mother bowed their heads.

The boy dropped his over his folded hands, and piped up clearly: "Our Father, which art in heaven, help us to remember those who have nothing to eat. Amen!"

"That's a grace that Win got up himself," his father explained, beginning to heap a plate with chicken and mashed potato, which he then handed to Annie, passing her the biscuit and the butter. "We think it suits the Almighty about as well as anything."

"I suppose you know Ralph of old, Annie?" said Mrs. Putney. "The only way he keeps within bounds at all is by letting himself perfectly loose."

Putney laughed out his acquiescence, and they began to talk together about old times. Mrs. Putney and Annie recalled the childish plays and adventures they had together, and one dreadful quarrel. Putney told of the first time he saw Annie, when his father took him one day for a call on the old judge, and how the old judge put him through his paces in American history, and would not admit the theory that the battle of Bunker's Hill could have been fought on Breed's Hill. Putney said that it was years before it occurred to him that the judge must have been joking: he had always thought he was simply ignorant.

"I used to set a good deal by the battle of Bunker's Hill," he continued. "I thought the whole Revolution and subsequent history revolved round it, and that it gave us all liberty, equality, and fraternity at a clip. But the Lord always finds some odd jobs to look after next day, and I guess He didn't clear 'em all up at Bunker's Hill."

Putney's irony and piety were very much of a piece apparently, and Annie was not quite sure which this conclusion was. She glanced at his wife, who seemed satisfied with it in either case. She was waiting patiently for him to wake up to the fact that he had not yet given her anything to eat; after helping Annie and the boy, he helped himself, and pending his wife's pre-occupation with the tea, he forgot her.

"Why didn't you throw something at me?" he roared, in grief and self-reproach. "There wouldn't have been a loose piece of crockery on this side of the table if I hadn't got my tea in time."

"Oh, I was listening to Annie's share in the conversation," said Mrs. Putney; and her husband was about to say something in retort of her thrust when a tap on the front door was heard.

"Come in, come in, Doc!" he shouted. "Mrs. Putney's just been helped, and the tea is going to begin."

Dr. Morrell's chuckle made answer for him, and after time enough to put down his hat, he came in, rubbing his hands and smiling, and making short nods round the table. "How d' ye do, Mrs. Putney? How d' ye do, Miss Kilburn? Winthrop?" He passed his hand over the boy's smooth hair and slipped into the chair beside him.

"You see, the reason why we always wait for the doctor in this formal way," said Putney, "is that he isn't in here more than seven nights of the week, and he rather stands on his dignity. Hand round the doctor's plate, my son," he added to the boy, and he took it from Annie, to whom the boy gave it, and began to heap it from the various dishes. "Think you can lift that much back to the doctor, Win?"

"I guess so," said the boy coolly.

"What is flooring Win at present," said his father, "and getting him down and rolling him over, is that problem of the robin that eats half a pint of grasshoppers and then doesn't weigh a bit more than he did before."

"When he gets a little older," said the doctor, shaking over his plateful, "he'll be interested to trace the processes of his father's thought from a guest and half a peck of stewed chicken, to a robin and half a pint of——"

"Don't, doctor!" pleaded Mrs. Putney. "He won't have the least trouble if he'll keep to the surface."

Putney laughed impartially, and said: "Well, we'll take the doctor out and weigh him when he gets done. We expected Brother Peck here this evening," he explained to Dr. Morrell. "You're our sober second thought—— Well," he broke off, looking across the table at his wife with mock anxiety. "Anything wrong about that, Ellen?"

"Not as far as I'm concerned, Mrs. Putney," interposed the doctor. "I'm glad to be here on any terms. Go on, Putney."

"Oh, there isn't anything more. You know how Miss Kilburn here has been round throwing ridicule on Brother Peck, because he wants the shop-hands treated with common decency, and my idea was to get the two together and see how she would feel."

Dr. Morrell laughed at this with what Annie thought was

unnecessary malice; but he stopped suddenly, after a glance at her, and Putney went on—

"Brother Peck pleaded another engagement. Said he had to go off into the country to see a sick woman that wasn't expected to live. You don't remember the Merrifields, do you, Annie? Well, it doesn't matter. One of 'em married West, and her husband left her, and she came home here and got a divorce; I got it for her. She's the one. As a consumptive, she had superior attractions for Brother Peck. It isn't a case that admits of jealousy exactly, but it wouldn't matter to Brother Peck anyway. If he saw a chance to do a good action, he'd wade through blood."

"Now look here, Ralph," said Mrs. Putney, "there's such a thing as letting yourself *too* loose."

"Well, *gore*, then," said Putney, buttering himself a biscuit.

The boy, who had kept quiet till now, seemed reached by this last touch, and broke into a high, crowing laugh, in which they all joined except his father.

"Gore suits Winthy, anyway," he said, beginning to eat his biscuit. "I met one of the deacons from Brother Peck's last parish, in Boston, yesterday. He asked me if we considered Brother Peck anyways peculiar in Hatboro', and when I said we thought he was a little too luxurious, the deacon came out with a lot of things. The way Brother Peck behaved toward the needy in that last parish of his made it simply uninhabitable to the standard Christian. They had to get rid of him somehow—send him away or kill him. Of course the deacon said they didn't want to *kill* him."

"Where was his last parish?" asked the doctor.

"Down on the Maine coast somewhere. Penobscotport, I believe."

"And was he indigenous there?"

"No, I believe not; he's from Massachusetts. Farm-boy and then mill-hand, I understand. Self-helped to an education; divinity student with summer intervals of waiting at table in the mountain hotels probably. Drifted down Maine way on his first call and stuck; but I guess he won't stick here very long. Annie's friend Mr. Gerrish is going to look after Brother Peck before a great while." He laughed to see her blush, and went on. "You see, Brother Gerrish has got a high ideal of what a

Christian minister ought to be; he hasn't said much about it, but I can see that Brother Peck doesn't come up to it. Well, Brother Gerrish has got a good many ideals. He likes to get anybody he can by the throat, and squeeze the difference of opinion out of 'em."

"There, now, Ralph," his wife interposed, "you let Mr. Gerrish alone. *You* don't like people to differ with you, either. Is your cup out, doctor?"

"Thank you," said the doctor, handing it up to her. "And you mean Mr. Gerrish doesn't like Mr. Peck's doctrine?" he asked of Putney.

"Oh, I don't know that he objects to his doctrine; he can't very well; it's 'between the leds of the Bible,' as the Hardshell Baptist said. But he objects to Brother Peck's walk and conversation. He thinks he walks too much with the poor, and converses too much with the lowly. He says he thinks that the pew-owners in Mr. Peck's church and the people who pay his salary have some rights to his company that he's bound to respect."

The doctor relished the irony, but he asked, "Isn't there something to say on that side?"

"Oh yes, a good deal. There's always something to say on both sides, even when one's a wrong side. That's what makes it all so tiresome—makes you wish you were dead." He looked up, and caught his boy's eye fixed with melancholy intensity upon him. "I hope you'll never look at both sides when you grow up, Win. It's mighty uncomfortable. You take the right side, and stick to that. Brother Gerrish," he resumed, to the doctor, "goes round taking the credit of Brother Peck's call here; but the fact is he opposed it. He didn't like his being so indifferent about the salary. Brother Gerrish held that the labourer was worthy of his hire, and if he didn't inquire what his wages were going to be, it was a pretty good sign that he wasn't going to earn them."

"Well, there was some logic in that," said the doctor, smiling as before.

"Plenty. And now it worries Brother Gerrish to see Brother Peck going round in the same old suit of clothes he came here in, and dressing his child like a shabby little Irish girl. He says that he who provideth not for those of his own household is worse than a heathen. That's perfectly true. And he would like to know what Brother Peck does with his money, anyway. He would like to insinuate that he loses it at poker, I guess; at any rate, he can't find out whom he gives it to, and he certainly doesn't spend it on himself."

"From your account of Mr. Peck," said the doctor, "I should think Brother Gerrish might safely object to him as a certain kind of sentimentalist."

"Well, yes, he might, looking at him from the outside. But when you come to talk with Brother Peck, you find yourself sort of frozen out with a most unexpected, hard-headed cold-bloodedness. Brother Peck is plain common-sense itself. He seems to be a man without an illusion, without an emotion."

"Oh, not so bad as that!" laughed the doctor.

"Ask Miss Kilburn. She's talked with him, and she hates him."

"No, I don't, Ralph," Annie began.

"Oh, well, then, perhaps he only made you hate yourself," said Putney. There was something charming in his mockery, like the teasing of a brother with a sister; and Annie did not find the atonement to which he brought her altogether painful. It seemed to her really that she was getting off pretty easily, and she laughed with hearty consent at last.

Winthrop asked solemnly, "How did he do that?"

"Oh, I can't tell exactly, Winthrop," she said, touched by the boy's simple interest in this abstruse point. "He made me feel that I had been rather mean and cruel when I thought I had only been practical. I can't explain; but it wasn't a comfortable feeling, my dear."

"I guess that's the trouble with Brother Peck," said Putney. "He doesn't make you feel comfortable. He doesn't flatter you up worth a cent. There was Annie expecting him to take the most fervent interest in her theatricals, and her Social Union, and coo round, and tell her what a noble woman she was, and beg her to consider her health, and not overwork herself in doing good; but instead of that he simply showed her that she was a moral Cave-Dweller, and that she was living in a Stone Age of social brutalities; and of course she hated him."

"Yes, that was the way, Winthrop," said Annie; and they all laughed with her.

"Now you take them into the parlour, Ralph," said his wife, rising, "and tell them how he made *you* hate him."

"I shouldn't like anything better," replied Putney. He lifted the large ugly kerosene lamp that had been set on the table when it grew dark during tea, and carried it into the parlour with him. His wife remained to speak with her little helper, but she sent Annie with the gentlemen.

"Why, there isn't a great deal of it—more spirit than letter, so to speak," said Putney, when he put down the lamp in the parlour. "You know how I like to go on about other people's sins, and the world's wickedness generally; but one day Brother Peck, in that cool, impersonal way of his, suggested that it was not a wholly meritorious thing to hate evil. He went so far as to say that perhaps we could not love them that despitefully used us if we hated their evil so furiously. He said it was a good deal more desirable to understand evil than to hate it, for then we could begin to cure it. Yes, Brother Peck let in a good deal of light on me. He rather insinuated that I must be possessed by the very evils I hated, and that was the reason I was so violent about them. I had always supposed that I hated other people's cruelty because I was merciful, and their meanness because I was magnanimous, and their intolerance because I was generous, and their conceit because I was modest, and their selfishness because I was disinterested; but after listening to Brother Peck a while I came to the conclusion that I hated these things in others because I was cruel myself, and mean, and bigoted, and conceited, and piggish; and that's why I've hated Brother Peck ever since—just like you, Annie. But he didn't reform me, I'm thankful to say, any more than he did you. I've gone on just the same, and I suppose I hate more infernal scoundrels and loathe more infernal idiots to-day than ever; but I perceive that I'm no part of the power that makes for righteousness as long as I work that racket; and now I sin with light and knowledge, anyway. No, Annie," he went on, "I can understand why Brother Peck is not the success with women, and feminine temperaments like me, that his virtues entitle him to be. What we feminine temperaments want is a prophet, and Brother Peck doesn't prophesy worth a cent. He doesn't pretend to be authorised in any sort of way; he has a sneaking style of being no better than you are, and of being rather stumped by some of the truths he finds out. No, women like a good prophet about as well as they do a good doctor. Now if you, if you could unite the two functions, Doc——"

"Sort of medicine-man?" suggested Morrell.

"Exactly! The aborigines understood the thing. Why, I suppose that a real live medicine-man could go through a community like this and not leave a sinful soul nor a sore body in it among the ladies—perfect faith cure."

"But what did you say to Mr. Peck, Ralph?" asked Annie. "Didn't you attempt any defence?"

"No," said Putney. "He had the advantage of me. You can't talk back at a man in the pulpit."

"Oh, it was a sermon?"

"I suppose the other people thought so. But I knew it was a private conversation that he was publicly holding with me."

Putney and the doctor began to talk of the nature and origin of evil, and Annie and the boy listened. Putney took high ground, and attributed it to Adam. "You know, Annie," he explained, "I don't *believe* this; but I like to get a scientific man that won't quite deny Scripture or the good old Bible premises, and see him suffer. Hello! you up yet, Winthrop? I guess I'll go through the form of carrying you to bed, my son."

When Mrs. Putney rejoined them, Annie said she must go, and Mrs. Putney went upstairs with her, apparently to help her put on her things, but really to have that talk before parting which guest and hostess value above the whole evening's pleasure. She showed Annie the pictures of the little girls that had died, and talked a great deal about their sickness and their loveliness in death. Then they spoke of others, and Mrs. Putney asked Annie if she had seen Lyra Wilmington lately. Annie told of her call with Mrs. Munger, and Mrs. Putney said: "I *like* Lyra, and I always did. I presume she isn't very happily married; he's too old; there couldn't have been any love on her part. But she would be a better woman than she is if she had children. Ralph says," added Mrs. Putney, smiling, "that he knows she would be a good mother, she's such a good aunt."

Annie put her two hands impressively on the hands of her friend folded at her waist. "Ellen, what *does* it mean?"

"Nothing more than what you saw, Annie. She must have—or she *will* have—some one to amuse her; to be at her beck and call; and it's best to have it all in the family, Ralph says."

"But isn't it—doesn't he think it's—odd?"

"It makes talk."

They moved a little toward the door, holding each other's hands. "Ellen, I've had a *lovely* time!"

"And so have I, Annie. I thought you'd like to meet Dr. Morrell."

"Oh yes, indeed!"

"And I can't tell you what a night this has been for Ralph. He likes you so much, and it isn't often that he has a chance to talk to *two* such people as you and Dr. Morrell."

"How brilliant he is!" Annie sighed.

"Yes, he's a very able man. It's very fortunate for Hatboro' to have such a doctor. He and Ralph are great cronies. I never feel uneasy now when Ralph's out late—I know he's been up at the doctor's office, talking. I——"

Annie broke in with a laugh. "I've no doubt Dr. Morrell is all you say, Ellen, but I meant Ralph when I spoke of brilliancy. He has a great future, I'm sure."

Mrs. Putney was silent for a moment. "I'm satisfied with the present, so long as Ralph——" The tears suddenly gushed out of her eyes, and ran down over the fine wrinkles of her plump little cheeks.

"Not quite so much loud talking, please," piped a thin, high voice from a room across the stairs landing.

"Why, dear little soul!" cried Annie. "I forgot he'd gone to bed."

"Would you like to see him?" asked his mother.

She led the way into the room where the boy lay in a low bed near a larger one. His crutches lay beside it. "Win sleeps in our room yet. He can take care of himself quite well. But when he wakes in the night he likes to reach out and touch his father's hand."

The child looked mortified.

"I wish I could reach out and touch *my* father's hand when I wake in the night," said Annie.

The cloud left the boy's face. "I can't remember whether I said my prayers, mother, I've been thinking so."

"Well, say them over again, to me."

The men's voices sounded in the hall below, and the ladies found them there. Dr. Morrell had his hat in his hand.

"Look here, Annie," said Putney, "*I* expected to walk home with you, but Doc Morrell says he's going to cut me out. It looks like a put-up job. I don't know whether you're in it or not, but there's no doubt about Morrell."

Mrs. Putney gave a sort of gasp, and then they all shouted with laughter, and Annie and the doctor went out into the night. In the imperfect light which the electrics of the main street flung afar into the little avenue where Putney lived, and the moon sent through the sidewalk trees, they struck against each other as they walked, and the doctor said, "Hadn't you better take my arm, Miss Kilburn, till we get used to the dark?"

"Yes, I think I had, decidedly," she answered; and she hurried to add: "Dr. Morrell, there is something I want to ask you. You're their physician, aren't you?"

"The Putneys? Yes."

"Well, then, you can tell me——"

"Oh no, I can't, if you ask me as their physician," he interrupted.

"Well, then, as their friend. Mrs. Putney said something to me that makes me very unhappy. I thought Mr. Putney was out of all danger of his—trouble. Hasn't he perfectly reformed? Does he ever——"

She stopped, and Dr. Morrell did not answer at once. Then he said seriously: "It's a continual fight with a man of Putney's temperament, and sometimes he gets beaten. Yes, I guess you'd better know it."

"Poor Ellen!"

"They don't allow themselves to be discouraged. As soon as he's on his feet they begin the fight again. But of course it prevents his success in his profession, and he'll always be a second-rate country lawyer."

"Poor Ralph! And so brilliant as he is! He could be anything."

"We must be glad if he can be something, as it is."

"Yes, and how happy they seem together, all three of them! That child worships his father; and how tender Ralph is of him! How good he is to his wife; and how proud she is of him! And that awful shadow over them all the time! I don't see how they live!"

The doctor was silent for a moment, and finally said: "They have the peace that seems to come to people from the presence of a common peril, and they have the comfort of people who never blink the facts."

"I think Ralph is terrible. I wish he'd let other people blink the facts a little."

"Of course," said the doctor, "it's become a habit with him now, or a mania. He seems to speak of his trouble as if mentioning it were a sort of conjuration to prevent it. I wouldn't venture to check him in his way of talking. He may find strength in it."

"It's all terrible!"

"But it isn't by any means hopeless."

"I'm so glad to hear you say so. You see a great deal of them, I believe?"

"Yes," said the doctor, getting back from their seriousness, with apparent relief. "Pretty nearly every day. Putney and I consider the ways of God to man a good deal together. You can imagine that in a place like Hatboro' one would make the most of such a friend. In fact, anywhere."

"Yes, of course," Annie assented. "Dr. Morrell," she added, in that effect of continuing the subject with which one breaks away from it, "do you know much about South Hatboro'?"

"I have some patients there."

"I was there this morning——"

"I heard of you. They all take a great interest in your theatricals."

"In *my* theatricals? Really this is too much! Who has made them my theatricals, I should like to know? Everybody at South Hatboro' talked as if I had got them up."

"And haven't you?"

"No. I've had nothing to do with them. Mr. Brandreth

spoke to me about them a week ago, and I was foolish enough to go round with Mrs. Munger to collect public opinion about her invited dance and supper; and now it appears that I have invented the whole affair."

"I certainly got that impression," said the doctor, with a laugh lurking under his gravity.

"Well, it's simply atrocious," said Annie. "I've nothing at all to do with either. I don't even know that I approve of their object."

"Their object?"

"Yes. The Social Union."

"Oh! Oh yes. I had forgot about the object," and now the doctor laughed outright.

"It seems to have dropped into the background with everybody," said Annie, laughing too.

"You like the unconventionality of South Hatboro'?" suggested the doctor, after a little silence.

"Oh, very much," said Annie. "I was used to the same thing abroad. It might be an American colony anywhere on the Continent."

"I suppose," said the doctor musingly, "that the same conditions of sojourn and disoccupation *would* produce the same social effects anywhere. Then you must feel quite at home in South Hatboro'!"

"Quite! It's what I came back to avoid. I was sick of the life over there, and I wanted to be of some use here, instead of wasting all my days."

She stopped, resolved not to go on if he took this lightly, but the doctor answered her with sufficient gravity: "Well?"

"It seemed to me that if I could be of any use in the world anywhere, I could in the place where I was born, and where my whole childhood was spent. I've been at home a month now, the most useless person in Hatboro'. I did catch at the first thing that offered — at Mr. Brandreth and his ridiculous Social Union and theatricals, and brought all this trouble on myself. I talked to Mr. Peck about them. You know what his views are?"

"Only from Putney's talk," said the doctor.

"He didn't merely disapprove of the dance and supper, but he had some very peculiar notions about the relations of the different classes in general," said Annie; and this was the point she had meant circuitously to lead up to when she began to speak of South Hatboro', though she theoretically despised all sorts of feminine indirectness.

"Yes?" said the doctor. "What notions?"

"Well, he thinks that if you have money, you *can't* do good with it."

"That's rather odd," said Dr. Morrell.

"I don't state it quite fairly. He meant that you can't make any kindness with it between yourself and the—the poor."

"That's odd too."

"Yes," said Annie anxiously. "You can impose an obligation, he says, but you can't create sympathy. Of course Ralph exaggerates what I said about him in connection with the invited dance and supper, though I don't justify what I did say; and if I'd known then, as I do now, what his history had been, I should have been more careful in my talk with him. I should be very sorry to have hurt his feelings, and I suppose people who've come up in that way are sensitive?"

She suggested this, and it was not the reassurance she was seeking to have Dr. Morrell say, "Naturally."

She continued, with an effort: "I'm afraid I didn't respect his sincerity, and I ought to have done that, though I don't at all agree with him on the other points. It seems to me that what he said was shocking, and perfectly—impossible."

"Why, what was it?" asked the doctor.

"He said there could be no real kindness between the rich and poor, because all their experiences of life were different. It amounted to saying that there ought not to *be* any wealth. Don't you think so?"

"Really, I've never thought about it," returned Dr. Morrell. After a moment he asked, "Isn't it rather an abstraction?"

"Don't say that!" said Annie nervously. "It's the *most* concrete thing in the world!"

The doctor laughed with enjoyment of her convulsive emphasis; but she went on: "I don't think life's worth living if you're to be shut up all your days to the intelligence merely of your own class."

"Who said you were?"

"Mr. Peck."

"And what was your inference from the fact? That there oughtn't to be any classes?"

"Of course it won't do to say that. There *must* be social differences. Don't you think so?"

"I don't know," said Dr. Morrell. "I never thought of it in that light before. It's a very curious question." He asked, brightening gaily after a moment of sober pause, "Is that the whole trouble?"

"Isn't it enough?"

"No; I don't think it is. Why didn't you tell him that you didn't want any gratitude?"

"Not *want* any?" she demanded.

"Oh!" said Dr. Morrell, "I didn't know but you thought it was enough to *give*."

Annie believed that he was making fun of her, and she tried to make her resentful silence dignified; but she only answered sadly: "No; it isn't enough for me. Besides, he made me see that you can't give sympathy where you can't receive it."

"Well, that *is* bad," said the doctor, and he laughed again. "Excuse me," he added. "I see the point. But why don't you forget it?"

"Forget it!"

"Yes. If you can't help it, why need you worry about it?"

She gave a kind of gasp of astonishment. "Do you really think that would be right?" She edged a little away from Dr. Morrell, as if with distrust.

"Well, no; I can't say that I do," he returned thoughtfully, without seeming to have noticed her withdrawal. "I don't suppose I was looking at the moral side. It's rather out of my way to do that. If a physician let himself get into the habit of doing that, he might regard nine-tenths of the diseases he has to treat as just penalties, and decline to interfere."

She fancied that he was amused again, rather than deeply concerned, and she determined to make him own his personal complicity in the matter if she could. "Then you *do* feel sympathy with your patients? You find it necessary to do so?"

The doctor thought a moment. "I take an interest in their diseases."

"But you want them to get well?"

"Oh, certainly. I'm bound to do all I can for them as a physician."

"Nothing more?"

"Yes; I'm sorry for them—for their families, if it seems to be going badly with them."

"And—and as—as—— Don't you care at all for your work as a part of what every one ought to do for others—as humanity, philan——" She stopped the offensive word.

"Well, I can't say that I've looked at it in that light exactly," he answered. "I suspect I'm not very good at generalising my own relations to others, though I like well enough to speculate in the abstract. But don't you think Mr. Peck has overlooked one important fact in his theory? What about the people who have grown rich from being poor, as most Americans have? They have the same experiences, and why can't they sympathise with those who have remained poor?"

"I never thought of that. Why didn't I ask him that?" She lamented so sincerely that the doctor laughed again. "I think that Mr. Peck——"

"Oh no! oh no!" said the doctor, in an entreating, coaxing tone, expressive of a satiety with the subject that he might very well have felt; and he ended with another laugh, in which, after a moment of indignant self-question, she joined him.

"Isn't that delicious?" he exclaimed; and she involuntarily slowed her pace with his.

The spicy scent of sweet-currant blossoms hung in the dewy air that wrapped one of the darkened village houses. From a syringa bush before another, as they moved on, a denser perfume stole out with the wild song of a cat-bird hidden in it; the music and the odour seemed braided together. The shadows of the trees cast by the electrics on the walks were so thick and black that they looked palpable; it seemed as if she could stoop down and lift them from the ground. A broad bath of moonlight washed one of the house fronts, and the white-painted clapboards looked wet with it.

They talked of these things, of themselves, and of their own traits and peculiarities; and at her door they ended far from Mr. Peck and all the perplexities he had suggested.

She had told Dr. Morrell of some things she had brought home with her, and had said she hoped he would find time to come and see them. It would have been stiff not to do it, and she believed she had done it in a very off-hand, business-like way. But she continued to question whether she had.

XII.

MISS NORTHWICK called upon Annie during the week, with excuses for her delay and for coming alone. She seemed to have intentions of being polite; but she constantly betrayed her want of interest in Annie, and disappointed an expectation of refinement which her physical delicacy awakened. She asked her how she ever came to take up the Social Union, and answered for her that of course it had the attraction of the theatricals, and went on to talk of her sister's part in them. The relation of the Northwick family to the coming entertainment, and an impression of frail mottled wrists and high thin cheeks, and an absence of modelling under affluent drapery, was the main effect of Miss Northwick's visit.

When Annie returned it, she met the younger sister, whom she found a great beauty. She seemed very cold, and of a *hauteur* which she subdued with difficulty; but she was more consecutively polite than her sister, and Annie watched with fascination her turns of the head, her movements of leopard swiftness and elasticity, the changing lights of her complexion, the curves of her fine lips, the fluttering of her thin nostrils.

A very new basket phaeton stood glittering at Annie's door when she got home, and Mrs. Wilmington put her head out of the open parlour window.

"How d' ye do, Annie?" she drawled, in her tender voice. "Won't you come in? You see I'm in possession. I've just got my new phaeton, and I drove up at once to crush you with it. Isn't it a beauty?"

"You're too late, Lyra," said Annie. "I've just come from the Northwicks, and another crushing beauty has got in ahead of your phaeton."

"Oh, *poor* Annie!" Lyra began to laugh with agreeable intelligence. "*Do* come in and tell me about it!"

"Why is that girl going to take part in the theatricals? She doesn't care to please any one, does she?"

"I didn't know that people took part in theatricals for that, Annie. I thought they wanted to please themselves and

738

mortify others. *I* do. But then I may be different. Perhaps Miss Northwick wants to please Mr. Brandreth."

"Do you mean it, Lyra?" demanded Annie, arrested on her threshold by the charm of this improbability.

"Well, I don't know; they're opposites. But, upon second thoughts, you needn't come in, Annie. I want you to take a drive with me, and try my new phaeton," said Lyra, coming out.

Annie now looked at it with that irresolution of hers, and Lyra commanded: "Get right in. We'll go down to the Works. You've never met my husband yet; have you, Annie?"

"No, I haven't, Lyra. I've always just missed him somehow. He seems to have been perpetually just gone to town, or not got back."

"Well, he's really at home now. And I don't mean at the house, which isn't home to him, but the Works. You've never seen the Works either, have you?"

"No, I haven't."

"Well, then, we'll just go round there, and kill two birds with one stone. I ought to show off my new phaeton to Mr. Wilmington first of all; he gave it to me. It would be kind of conjugal, or filial, or something. You know Mr. Wilmington and I are not exactly contemporaries, Annie?"

"I heard he was somewhat your senior," said Annie reluctantly.

Lyra laughed. "Well, I always say we were born in the same century, *any*way."

They came round into the region of the shops, and Lyra checked her pony in front of her husband's factory. It was not imposingly large, but, as Mrs. Wilmington caused Annie to observe, it was as big as the hat shops and as ugly as the shoe shops.

The structure trembled with the operation of its industry, and as they mounted the wooden steps to the open outside door, an inner door swung ajar for a moment, and let out a roar mingled of the hum and whirl and clash of machinery and fragments of voice, borne to them on a whiff of warm, greasy air. "Of course it doesn't smell very nice," said Lyra.

She pushed open the door of the office, and finding its first apartment empty, led the way with Annie to the inner room, where her husband sat writing at a table.

"George, I want to introduce you to Miss Kilburn."

"Oh yes, yes, yes," said her husband, scrambling to his feet, and coming round to greet Annie. He was a small man, very bald, with a serious and wrinkled forehead, and rather austere brows; but his mouth had a furtive curl at one corner, which, with the habit he had of touching it there with the tip of his tongue, made Annie think of a cat that had been at the cream. "I've been hoping to call with Mrs. Wilmington to pay my respects; but I've been away a great deal this season, and—and—— We're all very happy to have you home again, Miss Kilburn. I've often heard my wife speak of your old days together at Hatboro'."

They fenced with some polite feints of interest in each other, the old man standing beside his writing-table, and staying himself with a shaking hand upon it.

Lyra interrupted them. "Well, I think now that Annie is here, we'd better not let her get away without showing her the Works."

"Oh—oh—decidedly! I'll go with you, with great pleasure. Ah!" He bustled about, putting the things together on his table, and then reaching for the Panama hat on a hook behind it. There was something pathetic in his eagerness to do what Lyra bade him, and Annie fancied in him the uneasy consciousness which an elderly husband might feel in the presence of those who met him for the first time with his young wife. At the outer office door they encountered Jack Wilmington.

"I'll show them through," he said to his uncle; and the old man assented with, "Well, perhaps you'd better, Jack," and went back to his room.

The Wilmington Stocking-Mills spun their own threads, and the first room was like what Annie had seen before in cotton factories, with a faint smell of oil from the machinery, and a fine snow of fluff in the air, and catching to the white-washed walls and the foul window sashes. The tireless machines marched back and forth across the floor, and the men who watched them with suicidal intensity ran after them bare-footed when they made off with a broken thread, spliced it, and then escaped from them to their stations again. In other rooms, where there was a stunning whir of spindles, girls and women were at work; they looked after Lyra and her nephew from under cotton-frowsed bangs; they all seemed to know her, and returned her easy, kindly greetings with an effect of liking. From time to time, at Lyra's bidding, the young fellow explained to Annie some curious feature of the processes; in the room where the stockings were knitted she tried to understand the machinery that wrought and seemed to live before her eyes. But her mind wandered to the men and women who were operating it, and who seemed no more a voluntary part of it than all the rest, except when Jack Wilmington curtly ordered them to do this or that in illustration of some point he was explaining. She wearied herself, as people do in such places, in expressing her wonder at the ingenuity of the machinery; it was a relief to get away from it all into the room, cool and quiet, where half a dozen neat girls were counting and stamping the stockings with different numbers. "Here's where *I* used to work," said Lyra, "and here's where I first met Mr. Wilmington. The place is *full* of romantic associations. The stockings are all one *size*, Annie; but people like to wear different numbers, and so we try to gratify them. Which number do *you* wear? Or don't you wear the Wilmington machine-knit? *I* don't. Well, they're not *dreams* exactly, Annie, when all's said and done for them."

When they left the mill she asked Annie to come home to tea with her, saying, as if from a perception of her dislike for the young fellow, that Jack was going to Boston.

They had a long evening together, after Mr. Wilmington took himself off after tea to his study, as he called it, and remained shut in there. Annie was uneasily aware of him from time to time, but Lyra had apparently no more disturbance from his absence than from his presence, which she had managed with a frank acceptance of everything it suggested. She talked freely of her marriage, not as if it were like others, but for what it was. She showed Annie over the house, and she ended with a display of the rich dresses which he was always buying her, and which she never wore, because she never went anywhere.

Annie said she thought she would at least like to go to the

seaside somewhere during the summer, but "No," Lyra said; "it would be too much trouble, and you know, Annie, I always did hate *trouble*. I don't want the care of a cottage, and I don't want to be poked into a hotel, so I stay in Hatboro'." She said that she had always been a village girl, and did not miss the interests of a larger life, as she caught glimpses of them in South Hatboro', or want the bother of them. She said she studied music a little, and confessed that she read a good deal, novels mostly, though the library was handsomely equipped with well-bound general literature.

At moments it all seemed no harm; at others, the luxury in which this life was so contentedly sunk oppressed Annie like a thick, close air. Yet she knew that Lyra was kind to many of the poor people about her, and did a great deal of good, as the phrase is, with the superfluity which it involved no self-denial to give from. But Mr. Peck had given her a point of view, and though she believed she did not agree with him, she could not escape from it.

Lyra told her much about people in Hatboro', and characterised them all so humorously, and she seemed so good-natured, in her ridicule which spared nobody.

She shrieked with laughter about Mr. Brandreth when Annie told her of his mother's doubt whether his love-making with Miss Northwick ought to be tacit or explicit in the kissing and embracing between Romeo and Juliet.

"Don't you think, Annie, we'd better refer him to Mr. Peck? I *should* like to hear Mr. Brandreth and Mr. Peck discussing it. I must tell Jack about it. I might get him to ask Sue Northwick, and get her ideas."

"Has Mr. Wilmington known the Northwicks long?" Annie asked.

"He used to go to their Boston house when he was at Harvard."

"Oh, then," said Annie, "perhaps *he* accounts for her playing Juliet; though, as Tybalt, I don't see exactly how he——"

"Oh, it's at the rehearsals, you know, that the fun is, and then it don't matter what part you have."

Annie lay awake a long time that night. She was sure that she ought not to like Lyra if she did not approve of her, and that she ought not to have gone home to tea with her and spent the evening with her unless she fully respected her. But she had to own to herself that she did like her, and enjoyed hearing her soft drawl. She tried to think how Jack Wilmington's having gone to Boston for the evening made it somehow less censurable for her to spend it with Lyra, even if she did not approve of her. As she drowsed, this became perfectly clear.

XIII.

IN THE PROCESS of that expansion from a New England village to an American town of which Putney spoke, Hatboro' had suffered one kind of deterioration which Annie could not help noticing. She remembered a distinctly intellectual life, which might still exist in its elements, but which certainly no longer had as definite expression. There used to be houses in which people, maiden aunts and hale grandmothers, took a keen interest in literature, and read the new books and discussed them, some time after they had ceased to be new in the publishing centres, but whilst they were still not old. But now the grandmothers had died out, and the maiden aunts had faded in, and she could not find just such houses anywhere in Hatboro'. The decay of the Unitarians as a sect perhaps had something to do with the literary lapse of the place: their highly intellectualised belief had favoured taste in a direction where the more ritualistic and emotional religions did not promote it: and it is certain that they were no longer the leading people.

It would have been hard to say just who these leading people were. The old political and juristic pre-eminence which the lawyers had once enjoyed was a tradition; the learned professions yielded in distinction to the growing wealth and plutocratic influence of the prosperous manufacturers; the situation might be summed up in the fact that Colonel Marvin of the shoe interest and Mr. Wilmington now filled the place once held by Judge Kilburn and Squire Putney. The social life in private houses had undoubtedly shrunk; but it had expanded in the direction of church sociables, and it had become much more ecclesiastical in every way, without becoming more religious. As formerly, some people were acceptable, and some were not; but it was, as everywhere else, more a question of money; there was an aristocracy and a commonalty, but there was a confusion and a more ready convertibility in the materials of each.

The social authority of such a person as Mrs. Gerrish was not the only change that bewildered Annie, and the effort to extend her relations with the village people was one from which she shrank till her consciousness had more perfectly adjusted itself to the new conditions. Meanwhile Dr. Morrell came to call the night after their tea at the Putneys', and he fell into the habit of coming several nights in the week, and staying late. Sometimes he was sent for at her house by sick people, and he must have left word at his office where he was to be found.

He had spent part of his student life in Europe, and he looked back to his travel there with a fondness that the Old World inspires less and less in Americans. This, with his derivation from one of the unliterary Boston suburbs, and his unambitious residence in a place like Hatboro', gave her a sense of provinciality in him. On his part, he apparently found it droll that a woman of her acquaintance with a larger life should be willing to live in Hatboro' at all, and he seemed incredulous about her staying after summer was over. She felt that she mystified him, and sometimes she felt the pursuit of a curiosity which was a little too like a psychical diagnosis. He had a way of sitting beside her table and playing with her paper-cutter, while he submitted with a quizzical smile to her endeavours to turn him to account. She did not mind his laughing at her eagerness (a woman is willing enough to join a man in making fun of her femininity if she believes that he respects her), and she tried to make him talk about Hatboro', and tell her how she could be of use among the working people. She would have liked very much to know whether he gave his medical service gratis among them, and whether he found it a pleasure and a privilege to do so. There was one moment when she would have liked to ask him to let her be at the charges of his more indigent patients, but with the words behind her lips she perceived that it would not do. At the best, it would be taking his opportunity from him and making it hers. She began to see that one ought to have a conscience about doing good.

She let the chance of proposing this impossibility go by; and after a little silence Dr. Morrell seemed to revert, in her interest, to the economical situation in Hatboro'.

"You know that most of the hands in the hat-shops are from the farms around; and some of them own property here in the village. I know the owner of three small houses who's always worked in the shops. You couldn't very well offer help to a landed proprietor like that?"

"No," said Annie, abashed in view of him.

"I suppose you ought to go to a factory town like Fall River, if you really wanted to deal with overwork and squalor."

"I'm beginning to think there's no such thing anywhere," she said desperately.

The doctor's eyes twinkled sympathetically. "I don't know whether Benson earned his three houses altogether in the hat-shops. He 'likes a good horse,' as he says; and he likes to trade it for a better; I know that from experience. But he's a great friend of mine. Well, then, there are more women than men in the shops, and they earn more. I suppose that's rather disappointing too."

"It is, rather."

"But, on the other hand, the work only lasts eight months of the year, and that cuts wages down to an average of a dollar a day."

"Ah!" cried Annie. "There's some hope in *that*! What do they do when the work stops?"

"Oh, they go back to their country-seats."

"All?"

"Perhaps not all."

"I *thought* so!"

"Well, you'd better look round among those that stay."

Even among these she looked in vain for destitution; she could find that in satisfactory degree only in straggling veterans of the great army of tramps which once overran country places in the summer.

She would have preferred not to see or know the objects of her charity, and because she preferred this she forced herself to face their distasteful misery. Mrs. Bolton had orders to send no one from the door who asked for food or work, but to call Annie and let her judge the case. She knew that it was folly, and she was afraid it was worse, but she could not send the homeless creatures away as hungry or poor as they came. They filled her gentlewoman's soul with loathing; but if she kept beyond the range of the powerful corporeal odour that enveloped them, she could experience the luxury of pity for them. The filthy rags that caricatured them, their sick or sodden faces, always frowsed with a week's beard, represented typical poverty to her, and accused her comfortable state with a poignant contrast; and she consoled herself as far as she could with the superstition that in meeting them she was fulfilling a duty sacred in proportion to the disgust she felt in the encounter.

The work at the hat-shops fell off after the spring orders, and did not revive till the beginning of August. If there was less money among the hands and their families who remained than there was in time of full work, the weather made less demand upon their resources. The children lived mostly out-of-doors, and seemed to have always what they wanted of the season's fruit and vegetables. They got these too late from the decaying lots at the provision stores, and too early from the nearest orchards; and Dr. Morrell admitted that there was a good deal of sickness, especially among the little ones, from this diet. Annie wondered whether she ought not to offer herself as a nurse among them; she asked him whether she could not be of use in that way, and had to confess that she knew nothing about the prevailing disease.

"Then, I don't think you'd better undertake it," he said. "There are too many nurses there already, such as they are. It's the dull time in most of the shops, you know, and the women have plenty of leisure. There are about five volunteer nurses for every patient, not counting the grandmothers on both sides. I think they would resent any outside aid."

"Ah, I'm always on the outside! But can't I send—I mean carry—them anything nourishing, any little dishes——"

"Arrowroot is about all the convalescents can manage." She made a note of it. "But jelly and chicken broth are always relished by their friends."

"Dr. Morrell, I must ask you not to turn me into ridicule, if you please. I cannot permit it."

"I beg your pardon—I do indeed, Miss Kilburn. I didn't mean to ridicule you. I began seriously, but I was led astray by remembering what becomes of most of the good things sent to sick people."

"I know," she said, breaking into a laugh. "I have eaten lots of them for my father. And is arrowroot the only thing?"

The doctor reflected gravely. "Why, no. There's a poor little life now and then that might be saved by the sea-air. Yes, if you care to send some of my patients, with a mother and a grandmother apiece, to the seaside——"

"Don't say another word, doctor," cried Annie. "You make me *so* happy! I will—I will send their whole families. And you won't, you *won't* let a case escape, will you, doctor?" It was a break in the iron wall of uselessness which had closed her in; she behaved like a young girl with an invitation to a ball.

When the first patient came back well from the seaside her rejoicing overflowed in exultation before the friends to whom she confessed her agency in the affair. Putney pretended that he could not see what pleasure she could reasonably take in restoring the child to the sort of life it had been born to; but that was a matter she would not consider, theoretically or practically.

She began to go outside of Dr. Morrell's authority; she looked up two cases herself, and, upon advising with their grandmothers, sent them to the seaside, and she was at the station when the train came in with the young mother and the still younger aunt of one of the sick children. She did not see the baby, and the mother passed her with a stare of impassioned reproach, and fell sobbing on the neck of her husband, waiting for her on the platform. Annie felt the blood drop back upon her heart. She caught at the girlish aunt, who was looking about her with a sense of the interest which attached to herself as a party to the spectacle.

"Oh, Rebecca, where is the child?"

"Well, there, Miss Kilburn, I'm *ril* sorry to tell you, but I guess the sea-air didn't do it a great deal of good, if any. I tell Maria she'll see it in the right light after a while, but of course she can't, first off. Well, there! *Somebody's* got to look after it. You'll excuse *me*, Miss Kilburn."

Annie saw her run off to the baggage-car, from which the baggage-man was handing out a narrow box. The ground reeled under her feet; she got the public depot carriage and drove home.

She sent for Dr. Morrell, and poured out the confession of her error upon him before he could speak. "I am a murderess," she ended hysterically. "Don't deny it!"

"I think you can be got off on the ground of insanity, Miss Kilburn, if you go on in this way," he answered.

Her desperation broke in tears. "Oh, what shall I do— what shall I do? I've killed the child!"

"Oh no, you haven't," he retorted. "I know the case. The only hope for it was the sea-air; I was going to ask you to send it——"

She took down her handkerchief and gave him a piercing look. "Dr. Morrell, if you are lying to me——"

"I'm not lying, Miss Kilburn," he answered. "You've done a very unwarrantable thing in both of the cases that you sent to the seaside on your own responsibility. One of them I certainly shouldn't have advised sending, but it's turned out well. You've no more credit for it, though, than for this that died; and you won't think I'm lying, perhaps, when I say you're equally to blame in both instances."

"I—I beg your pardon," she faltered, with dawning comfort in his severity. "I didn't mean—I didn't intend to say——"

"I know it," said Dr. Morrell, allowing himself to smile. "Just remember that you blundered into doing the only thing left to be done for Mrs. Savor's child; and—don't try it again. That's all."

He smiled once more, and at some permissive light in her face, he began even to laugh.

"You—you're horrible!"

"Oh no, I'm not," he gasped. "All the tears in the world wouldn't help; and my laughing hurts nobody. I'm sorry for you, and I'm sorry for the mother; but I've told you the truth—I have indeed; and you *must* believe me."

The child's father came to see her the next night. "Rebecca she seemed to think that you felt kind of bad, may be, because Maria wouldn't speak to you when she first got off the cars yesterday, and I don't say she done exactly right, myself. The way I look at it, and the way I tell Maria *she'd* ought to, is like this: You done what you done for the best, and we wa'n't *obliged* to take your advice anyway. But of course Maria she'd kind of set her heart on savin' it, and she can't seem to get over it right away." He talked on much longer to the same effect, tilted back in his chair, and looking down, while he covered and uncovered one of his knees with his straw hat. He had the usual rustic difficulty in getting away, but Annie was glad to keep him, in her gratitude for his kindness. Besides, she could not let him go without satisfying a suspicion she had.

"And Dr. Morrell—have you seen him for Mrs. Savor— have you——" She stopped, for shame of her hypocrisy.

"No, 'm. We hain't seen him *sence*. I guess she'll get along."

It needed this stroke to complete her humiliation before the single-hearted fellow.

"I—I suppose," she stammered out, "that you—your wife, wouldn't like me to come to the—I can understand that; but oh! if there is anything I can do for you—flowers—or my carriage—or helping anyway——"

Mr. Savor stood up. "I'm much obliged to *you*, Miss Kilburn; but we thought we hadn't better wait, well not a great while, and—the funeral was this afternoon. Well, I wish you good evening."

She met the mother, a few days after, in the street; with an impulse to cross over to the other side she advanced straight upon her.

"Mrs. Savor! What can I say to you?"

"Oh, I don't presume but what you meant for the best, Miss Kilburn. But I guess I shall know what to do next time. I kind of felt the whole while that it was a resk. But it's all right now."

Annie realised, in her resentment of the poor thing's uncouth sorrow, that she had spoken to her with the hope of getting, not giving, comfort.

"Yes, yes," she confessed. "I was to blame." The bereaved mother did not gainsay her, and she felt that, whatever was the justice of the case, she had met her present deserts.

She had to bear the discredit into which the seaside fell with the mothers of all the other sick children. She tried to bring Dr. Morrell once to the consideration of her culpability in the case of those who might have lived if the case of Mrs. Savor's baby had not frightened their mothers from sending them to the seaside; but he refused to grapple with the problem. She was obliged to believe him when he said he should not have advised sending any of the recent cases there; that the disease was changing its character, and such a course could have done no good.

"Look here, Miss Kilburn," he said, after scanning her face sharply, "I'm going to leave you a little tonic. I think you're rather run down."

"Well," she said passively.

XIV.

IT WAS in her revulsion from the direct beneficence which had proved so dangerous that Annie was able to give herself to the more general interests of the Social Union. She had not the courage to test her influence for it among the workpeople whom it was to entertain and elevate, and whose cooperation Mr. Peck had thought important; but she went about among the other classes, and found a degree of favour and deference which surprised her, and an ignorance of what lay so heavy on her heart which was still more comforting. She was nowhere treated as the guilty wretch she called herself; some who knew of the facts had got them wrong; and she discovered what must always astonish the inquirer below the pretentious surface of our democracy—an indifference and an incredulity concerning the feelings of people of lower station which could not be surpassed in another civilisation. Her concern for Mrs. Savor was treated as a great trial for Miss Kilburn; but the mother's bereavement was regarded as something those people were used to, and got over more easily than one could imagine.

Annie's mission took her to the ministers of the various denominations, and she was able to overcome any scruples they might have about the theatricals by urging the excellence of their object. As a Unitarian, she was not prepared for the liberality with which the matter was considered; the Episcopalians of course were with her; but the Universalist minister himself was not more friendly than the young Methodist preacher, who volunteered to call with her on the pastor of the Baptist church, and help present the affair in the right light; she had expected a degree of narrow-mindedness, of bigotry, which her sect learned to attribute to others in the militant period before they had imbibed so much of its own tolerance.

But the recollection of what had passed with Mr. Peck remained a reproach in her mind, and nothing that she accomplished for the Social Union with the other ministers was important. In her vivid reveries she often met him, and combated his peculiar ideas, while she admitted a wrong in her

own position, and made every expression of regret, and
parted from him on the best terms, esteemed and complimented in high degree; in reality she saw him seldom, and
still more rarely spoke to him, and then with a distance and
consciousness altogether different from the effects dramatised
in her fancy. Sometimes during the period of her interest in
the sick children of the hands, she saw him in their houses, or
coming and going outside; but she had no chance to speak
with him, or else said to herself that she had none, because
she was ashamed before him. She thought he avoided her;
but this was probably only a phase of the impersonality which
seemed characteristic of him in everything. At these times she
felt a strange pathos in the lonely man whom she knew to be
at odds with many of his own people, and she longed to interpret herself more sympathetically to him, but actually confronted with him she was sensible of something cold and even
hard in the nimbus her compassion cast about him. Yet even
this added to the mystery that piqued her, and that loosed her
fancy to play, as soon as they parted, in conjecture about his
past life, his marriage, and the mad wife who had left him
with the child he seemed so ill-fitted to care for. Then, the
next time they met she was abashed with the recollection of
having unwarrantably romanced the plain, simple, homely little man, and she added an embarrassment of her own to that
shyness of his which kept them apart.

Except for what she had heard Putney say, and what she
learned casually from the people themselves, she could not
have believed he ever did anything for them. He came and
went so elusively, as far as Annie was concerned, that she
knew of his presence in the houses of sickness and death usually by his little girl, whom she found playing about in the
street before the door with the children of the hands. She
seemed to hold her own among the others in their plays and
their squabbles; if she tried to make up to her, Idella smiled,
but she would not be approached, and Annie's heart went out
to the little mischief in as helpless goodwill as toward the
minister himself.

She used to hear his voice through the summer-open windows when he called upon the Boltons, and wondered if
some accident would not bring them together, but she had to

send for Mrs. Bolton at last, and bid her tell Mr. Peck that she would like to see him before he went away, one night. He came, and then she began a parrying parley of preliminary nothings before she could say that she supposed he knew the ladies were going on with their scheme for the establishment of the Social Union; he admitted vaguely that he had heard something to that effect, and she added that the invited dance and supper had been given up.

He remained apparently indifferent to the fact, and she hurried on: "And I ought to say, Mr. Peck, that nearly every one—every one whose opinion you would value—agreed with you that it would have been extremely ill-advised, and—and shocking. And I'm quite ashamed that I should not have seen it from the beginning; and I hope—I hope you will forgive me if I said things in my—my excitement that must have—I mean not only what I said to you, but what I said to others; and I assure you that I regret them, and——"

She went on and repeated herself at length, and he listened patiently, but as if the matter had not really concerned either of them personally. She had to conclude that what she had said of him had not reached him, and she ended by confessing that she had clung to the Social Union project because it seemed the only thing in which her attempts to do good were not mischievous.

Mr. Peck's thin face kindled with a friendlier interest than it had shown while the question at all related to himself, and a light of something that she took for humorous compassion came into his large, pale blue eyes. At least it was intelligence; and perhaps the woman nature craves this as much as it is supposed to crave sympathy; perhaps the two are finally one.

"I want to tell you something, Mr. Peck—an experience of mine," she said abruptly, and without trying to connect it obviously with what had gone before, she told him the story of her ill-fated beneficence to the Savors. He listened intently, and at the end he said: "I understand. But that is sorrow you have caused, not evil; and what we intend in goodwill must not rest a burden on the conscience, no matter how it turns out. Otherwise the moral world is no better than a crazy dream, without plan or sequence. You might as well rejoice in an evil deed because good happened to come of it."

"Oh, I *thank* you!" she gasped. "You don't know what a load you have lifted from me!"

Her words feebly expressed the sense of deliverance which overflowed her heart. Her strength failed her like that of a person suddenly relieved from some great physical stress or peril; but she felt that he had given her the truth, and she held fast by it while she went on.

"If you knew, or if any one knew, how difficult it is, what a responsibility, to do the least thing for others! And once it seemed so simple! And it seems all the more difficult, the more means you have for doing good. The poor people seem to help one another without doing any harm, but if *I* try it——"

"Yes," said the minister, "it is difficult to help others when we cease to need help ourselves. A man begins poor, or his father or grandfather before him—it doesn't matter how far back he begins—and then he is in accord and full understanding with all the other poor in the world; but as he prospers he withdraws from them and loses their point of view. Then when he offers help, it is not as a brother of those who need it, but a patron, an agent of the false state of things in which want is possible; and his help is not an impulse of the love that ought to bind us all together, but a compromise proposed by iniquitous social conditions, a peace-offering to his own guilty consciousness of his share in the wrong."

"Yes," said Annie, too grateful for the comfort he had given her to question words whose full purport had not perhaps reached her. "And I assure you, Mr. Peck, I feel very differently about these things since I first talked with you. And I wish to tell you, in justice to myself, that I had no idea then that—that—you were speaking from your own experience when you—you said how working people looked at things. I didn't know that you had been—that is, that——"

"Yes," said the minister, coming to her relief, "I once worked in a cotton-mill. Then," he continued, dismissing the personal concern, "it seems to me that I saw things in their right light, as I have never been able to see them since——"

"And how brutal," she broke in, "how cruel and vulgar, what I said must have seemed to you!"

"I fancied," he continued evasively, "that I had authority to set myself apart from my fellow-workmen, to be a teacher and guide to the true life. But it was a great error. The true life was the life of work, and no one ever had authority to turn from it. Christ Himself came as a labouring man."

"That is true," said Annie; and his words transfigured the man who spoke them, so that her heart turned reverently toward him. "But if you had been meant to work in a mill all your life," she pursued, "would you have been given the powers you have, and that you have just used to save me from despair?"

The minister rose, and said, with a sigh: "No one was meant to work in a mill all his life. Good night."

She would have liked to keep him longer, but she could not think how, at once. As he turned to go out through the Boltons' part of the house, "Won't you go out through my door?" she asked, with a helpless effort at hospitality.

"Oh, if you wish," he answered submissively.

When she had closed the door upon him she went to speak with Mrs. Bolton. She was in the kitchen mixing flour to make bread, and Annie traced her by following the lamp-light through the open door. It discovered Bolton sitting in the outer doorway, his back against one jamb and his stocking-feet resting against the base of the other.

"Mrs. Bolton," Annie began at once, making herself free of one of the hard kitchen chairs, "how is Mr. Peck getting on in Hatboro'?"

"I d' know as I know just what you mean, Miss Kilburn," said Mrs. Bolton, on the defensive.

"I mean, is there a party against him in his church? Is he unpopular?"

Mrs. Bolton took some flour and sprinkled it on her bread-board; then she lifted the mass of dough out of the trough before her, and let it sink softly upon the board.

"I d' know as you can say he's unpoplah. He ain't poplah with some. Yes, there's a party—the Gerrish party."

"Is it a strong one?"

"It's pretty strong."

"Do you think it will prevail?"

"Well, most o' folks don't know *what* they want; and if

there's some folks that know what they *don't* want, they can generally keep from havin' it."

Bolton made a soft husky prefatory noise of protest in his throat, which seemed to stimulate his wife to a more definite assertion, and she cut in before he could speak—

"*I* should say that unless them that stood Mr. Peck's friends first off, and got him here, done something to keep him, his enemies wa'n't goin' to take up his cause."

Annie divined a personal reproach for Bolton in the apparent abstraction.

"Oh, now, you'll see it 'll all come out right in the end, Pauliny," he mildly opposed. "There ain't any such great feelin' about Mr. Peck; nothin' but what 'll work itself off perfec'ly natural, give it time. It 's goin' to come out all right."

"Yes, at the day o' jedgment," Mrs. Bolton assented, plunging her fists into the dough, and beginning to work a contempt for her husband's optimism into it.

"Yes, an' a good deal before," he returned. "There's always somethin' to objec' to every minister; we ain't any of us perfect, and Mr. Peck's got his failin's; he hain't built up the church quite so much as some on 'em expected but what he would; and there's some that don't like his prayers; and some of 'em thinks he ain't doctrinal enough. But I guess, take it all round, he suits pretty well. It 'll come out all right, Pauliny. You'll see."

A pause ensued, of which Annie felt the awfulness. It seemed to her that Mrs. Bolton's impatience with this intolerable hopefulness must burst violently. She hastened to interpose. "I think the trouble is that people don't fully understand Mr. Peck at first. But they do finally."

"Yes; take time," said Bolton.

"Take eternity, I guess, for some," retorted his wife. "If you think William B. Gerrish is goin' to work round with time——" She stopped for want of some sufficiently rejectional phrase, and did not go on.

"The way I look at it," said Bolton, with incorrigible courage, "is like this: When it comes to anything like askin' Mr. Peck to resign, it 'll develop his strength. You can't tell how strong he is without you try to git red of him. I 'most wish it would come, once, fair and square."

"I'm sure you're right, Mr. Bolton," said Annie. "I don't believe that your church would let such a man go when it really came to it. Don't they all feel that he has great ability?"

"Oh, I guess they appreciate him as far forth as ability goes. Some on 'em complains that he's a little *too* intellectial, if anything. But I tell 'em it's a good fault; it's a thing that can be got over in time."

Mrs. Bolton had ceased to take part in the discussion. She finished kneading her dough, and having fitted it into two baking-pans and dusted it with flour, she laid a clean towel over both. But when Annie rose she took the lamp from the mantel-shelf, where it stood, and held it up for her to find her way back to her own door.

Annie went to bed with a spirit lightened as well as chastened, and kept saying over the words of Mr. Peck, so as to keep fast hold of the consolation they had given her. They humbled her with a sense of his wisdom and insight; the thought of them kept her awake. She remembered the tonic that Dr. Morrell had left with her, and after questioning whether she really needed it now, she made sure by getting up and taking it.

XV.

THE SPRING had filled and flushed into summer. Bolton had gone over the grass on the slope before the house, and it was growing thick again, dark green above the yellow of its stubble, and the young generation of robins was foraging in it for the callow grasshoppers. Some boughs of the maples were beginning to lose the elastic upward lift of their prime, and to hang looser and limper with the burden of their foliage. The elms drooped lower toward the grass, and swept the straggling tops left standing in their shade.

The early part of September had been fixed for the theatricals. Annie refused to have anything to do with them, and the preparations remained altogether with Brandreth. "The minuet," he said to her one afternoon, when he had come to report to her as a co-ordinate authority, "is going to be something exquisite, I assure you. A good many of the ladies studied it in the Continental times, you know, when we had all those Martha Washington parties—or, I forgot you were out of the country—and it will be done perfectly. We're going to have the ball-room scene on the tennis-court just in front of the evergreens, don't you know, and then the balcony scene in the same place. We have to cut some of the business between Romeo and Juliet, because it's too long, you know, and some of it's too—too passionate; we couldn't do it properly, and we've decided to leave it out. But we sketch along through the play, and we have Friar Laurence coming with Juliet out of his cell onto the tennis-court and meeting Romeo; so that tells the story of the marriage. You can't imagine what a Mercutio Mr. Putney makes; he throws himself into it heart and soul, especially where he fights with Tybalt and gets killed. I give him lines there out of other scenes too; the tennis-court sets that part admirably; they come out of a street at the side. I think the scenery will surprise you, Miss Kilburn. Well, and then we have the Nurse and Juliet, and the poison scene—we put it into the garden, on the tennis-court, and we condense the different acts so as to give an idea of all that's happened, with Romeo banished, and all that. Then he comes back from Mantua, and we have the tomb scene set at one side of the tennis-court just opposite the street scene; and he fights with Paris; and then we have Juliet come to the door of the tomb—it's a liberty, of course; but we couldn't arrange the light inside—and she stabs herself and falls on Romeo's body, and that ends the play. You see, it gives a notion of the whole action, and tells the story pretty well. I think you'll be pleased."

"I've no doubt I shall," said Annie. "Did you make the adaptation yourself, Mr. Brandreth?"

"Well, yes, I did," Mr. Brandreth modestly admitted. "It's been a good deal of work, but it's been a pleasure too. *You* know how that is, Miss Kilburn, in your charities."

"*Don't* speak of my charities, Mr. Brandreth. I'm not a charitable person."

"You won't get people to believe *that*," said Mr. Brandreth. "Everybody knows how much good you do. But, as I was saying, my idea was to give a notion of the whole play in a series of passages or tableaux. Some of my friends think I've succeeded so well in telling the story, don't you know, without a change of scene, that they're urging me to publish my arrangement for the use of out-of-door theatricals."

"I should think it would be a very good idea," said Annie. "I suppose Mr. Chapley would do it?"

"Well, I don't know—I don't know," Mr. Brandreth answered, with a note of trouble in his voice. "I'm afraid not," he added sadly. "Miss Kilburn, I've been put in a very unfair position by Miss Northwick's changing her mind about Juliet, after the part had been offered to Miss Chapley. I've been made the means of a seeming slight to Miss Chapley, when, if it hadn't been for the cause, I'd rather have thrown up the whole affair. She gave up the part instantly when she heard that Miss Northwick wished to change her mind, but all the same I know——"

He stopped, and Annie said encouragingly: "Yes, I see. But perhaps she doesn't really care."

"That's what she said," returned Mr. Brandreth ruefully. "But I don't know. I have never spoken of it with her since I went to tell her about it, after I got Miss Northwick's note."

"Well, Mr. Brandreth, I think you've really been victimised;

and I don't believe the Social Union will ever be worth what it's costing."

"I was sure you would appreciate—would understand;" and Mr. Brandreth pressed her hand gratefully in leave-taking.

She heard him talking with some one at the gate, whose sharp, "All right, my son!" identified Putney.

She ran to the door to welcome him.

"Oh, you're *both* here!" she rejoiced, at sight of Mrs. Putney too.

"I can send Ellen home," suggested Putney.

"Oh *no*, indeed!" said Annie, with single-mindedness at which she laughed with Mrs. Putney. "Only it seemed too good to have you both," she explained, kissing Mrs. Putney. "I'm *so* glad to see you!"

"Well, what's the reason?" Putney dropped into a chair and began to rock nervously. "Don't be ashamed: we're *all* selfish. Has Brandreth been putting up any more jobs on you?"

"No, no! Only giving me a hint of his troubles and sorrows with those wretched Social Union theatricals. Poor young fellow! I'm sorry for him. He is really very sweet and unselfish. I like him."

"Yes, Brandreth is one of the most lady-like fellows I ever saw," said Putney. "That Juliet business has pretty near been the death of him. *I* told him to offer Miss Chapley some other part—Rosaline, the part of the young lady who was dropped; but he couldn't seem to see it. Well, and how come on the good works, Annie?"

"The good works! Ralph, tell me: *do* people think me a charitable person? Do they suppose I've done or can do any good whatever?" She looked from Putney to his wife, and back again with comic entreaty.

"Why, aren't you a charitable person? Don't you do any good?" he asked.

"No!" she shouted. "Not the least in the world!"

"It is pretty rough," said Putney, taking out a cigar for a dry smoke; "and nobody will believe me when I report what you say, Annie. Mrs. Munger is telling round that she don't see how you can live through the summer at the rate you're going. She's got it down pretty cold about your taking

Brother Peck's idea of the invited dance and supper, and joining hands with him to save the vanity of the self-respecting
poor. She says that your suppression of that one unpopular
feature has done more than anything else to promote the success of the Social Union. You ought to be glad Brother Peck is
coming to the show."

"To the theatricals?"

Putney nodded his head. "That's what he says. I believe
Brother Peck is coming to see how the upper classes amuse
themselves when they really try to benefit the lower classes."

Annie would not laugh at his joke. "Ralph," she asked, "is
it true that Mr. Peck is so unpopular in his church? Is he really
going to be turned out—dismissed?"

"Oh, I don't know about that. But they'll bounce him if
they can."

"And can nothing be done? Can't his friends unite?"

"Oh, they're united enough now; what they're afraid of is
that they're not numerous enough. Why don't you buy in,
Annie, and help control the stock? That old Unitarian concern
of yours isn't ever going to get into running order again, and
if you owned a pew in Ellen's church you could have a vote in
church meeting, after a while, and you could lend Brother
Peck your moral support now."

"I never liked that sort of thing, Ralph. I shouldn't believe
with your people."

"Ellen's people, please. *I* don't believe with them either.
But I always vote right. Now you think it over."

"No, I shall not think it over. I don't approve of it. If I
should take a pew in your church it would be simply to hear
Mr. Peck preach, and contribute toward his——"

"Salary? Yes, that's the way to look at it in the beginning. I
knew you'd work round. Why, Annie, in a year's time you'll
be trying to *buy* votes for Brother Peck."

"I should *never* vote," she retorted. "And I shall keep myself
out of all temptation by not going to your church."

"Ellen's church," Putney corrected.

She went the next Sunday to hear Mr. Peck preach, and
Putney, who seemed to see her the moment she entered the
church, rose, as the sexton was showing her up the aisle, and
opened the door of his pew for her with ironical welcome.

"You can always have a seat with us, Annie," he mocked, on their way out of the church together.

"Thank you, Ralph," she answered boldly. "I'm going to speak to the sexton for a pew."

XVI.

A WIRE had been carried from the village to the scene of the play at South Hatboro', and electric globes fizzed and hissed overhead, flooding the open tennis-court with the radiance of sharper moonlight, and stamping the thick velvety shadows of the shrubbery and tree-tops deep into the raw green of the grass along its borders.

The spectators were seated on the verandas and terraced turf at the rear of the house, and they crowded the sides of the court up to a certain point, where a cord stretched across it kept them from encroaching upon the space intended for the action. Another rope enclosed an area all round them, where chairs and benches were placed for those who had tickets. After the rejection of the exclusive feature of the original plan, Mrs. Munger had liberalised more and more: she caused it to be known that all who could get into her grounds would be welcome on the outside of that rope, even though they did not pay anything; but a large number of tickets had been sold to the hands, as well as to the other villagers, and the area within the rope was closely packed. Some of the boys climbed the neighbouring trees, where from time to time the town authorities threatened them, but did not really dislodge them.

Annie, with other friends of Mrs. Munger, gained a reserved seat on the veranda through the drawing-room windows; but once there, she found herself in the midst of a sufficiently mixed company.

"How do, Miss Kilburn? That you? Well, I declare!" said a voice that she seemed to know, in a key of nervous excitement. Mrs. Savor's husband leaned across his wife's lap and shook hands with Annie. "William thought I better come," Mrs. Savor seemed called upon to explain. "I got to do *something*. Ain't it just too cute for anything the way they got them screens worked into the shrubbery down they-ar? It's like the cycloraymy to Boston; you can't tell where the ground ends and the paintin' commences. Oh, I do want 'em to *begin*!"

Mr. Savor laughed at his wife's impatience, and she said

playfully: "What you laughin' at? I guess you're full as excited as what I be, when all's said and done."

There were other acquaintances of Annie's from Over the Track, in the group about her, and upon the example of the Savors they all greeted her. The wives and sweethearts tittered with self-derisive expectation; the men were gravely jocose, like all Americans in unwonted circumstances, but they were respectful to the coming performance, perhaps as a tribute to Annie. She wondered how some of them came to have those seats, which were reserved at an extra price; she did not allow for that self-respect which causes the American workman to supply himself with the best his money can buy while his money lasts.

She turned to see who was on her other hand. A row of three small children stretched from her to Mrs. Gerrish, whom she did not recognise at first. "Oh, Emmeline!" she said; and then, for want of something else, she added, "Where is Mr. Gerrish? Isn't he coming?"

"He was detained at the store," said Mrs. Gerrish, with cold importance; "but he will be here. May I ask, Annie," she pursued solemnly, "how you got here?"

"How did I get here? Why, through the windows. Didn't you?"

"May I ask who had charge of the arrangements?"

"I don't know, I'm sure," said Annie. "I suppose Mrs. Munger."

A burst of music came from the dense shadow into which the group of evergreens at the bottom of the tennis-court deepened away from the glister of the electrics. There was a deeper hush; then a slight jarring and scraping of a chair beyond Mrs. Gerrish, who leaned across her children and said, "He's come, Annie—right through the parlour window!" Her voice was lifted to carry above the music, and all the people near were able to share the fact that righted Mrs. Gerrish in her own esteem.

From the covert of the low pines in the middle of the scene Miss Northwick and Mr. Brandreth appeared hand in hand, and then the place filled with figures from other apertures of the little grove and through the artificial wings at the sides, and walked the minuet. Mr. Fellows, the painter, had helped with the costumes, supplying some from his own artistic properties, and mediævalising others; the Boston costumers had been drawn upon by the men; and they all moved through the stately figures with a security which discipline had given them. The broad solid colours which they wore took the light and shadow with picturesque effectiveness; the masks contributed a sense of mystery novel in Hatboro', and kept the friends of the dancers in exciting doubt of their identity; the strangeness of the audience to all spectacles of the sort held its judgment in suspense. The minuet was encored, and had to be given again, and it was some time before the applause of the repetition allowed the characters to be heard when the partners of the minuet began to move about arm in arm, and the drama properly began. When the applause died away it was still not easy to hear; a boy in one of the trees called, "Louder!" and made some of the people laugh, but for the rest they were very orderly throughout.

Toward the end of the fourth act Annie was startled by a child dashing itself against her knees, and breaking into a gurgle of shy laughter as children do.

"Why, you little witch!" she said to the uplifted face of Idella Peck. "Where is your father?"

"Oh, somewhere," said the child, with entire ease of mind.

"And your hat?" said Annie, putting her hand on the curly bare head—"where's your hat?"

"On the ground."

"On the ground—where?"

"Oh, I don't know," said Idella lightly, as if the pursuit bored her.

Annie pulled her up on her lap. "Well, now, you stay here with me, if you please, till your papa or your hat comes after you."

"My—hat—can't—come—after—me!" said the child, turning back her head, so as to laugh her sense of the joke in Annie's face.

"No matter; your papa can, and I'm going to keep you."

Idella let her head fall back against Annie's breast, and began to finger the rings on the hand which Annie laid across her lap to keep her.

"For goodness gracious!" said Mrs. Savor, "who you got there, Miss Kilburn?"

"Mr. Peck's little girl."

"Where'd she spring from?"

Mrs. Gerrish leaned forward and spoke across the six legs of her children, who were all three standing up in their chairs: "You don't mean to say that's Idella Peck? Where's her father?"

"Somewhere, she says," said Annie, willing to answer Mrs. Gerrish with the child's nonchalance.

"Well, that's great!" said Mrs. Gerrish. "I should think he better be looking after her—or some one."

The music ceased, and the last act of the play began. Before it ended, Idella had fallen asleep, and Annie sat still with her after the crowd around her began to break up. Mrs. Savor kept her seat beside Annie. She said, "Don't you want I should spell you a little while, Miss Kilburn?" She leaned over the face of the sleeping child. "Why, she ain't much more than a baby! William, you go and see if you can't find Mr. Peck. I'm goin' to stay here with Miss Kilburn." Her husband humoured her whim, and made his way through the knots and clumps of people toward the rope enclosing the tennis-court. "Won't you let me hold her, Miss Kilburn?" she pleaded again.

"No, no; she isn't heavy; I like to hold her," replied Annie. Then something occurred to her, and she started in amazement at herself.

"Or yes, Mrs. Savor, you *may* take her a while;" and she put the child into the arms of the bereaved creature, who had fallen desolately back in her chair. She hugged Idella up to her breast, and hungrily mumbled her with kisses, and moaned out over her, "Oh dear! Oh my! Oh my!"

XVII.

THE PEOPLE beyond the rope had nearly all gone away, and Mr. Savor was coming back across the court with Mr. Peck. The players appeared from the grove at the other end of the court in their vivid costumes, chatting and laughing with their friends, who went down from the piazzas and terraces to congratulate them. Mrs. Munger hurried about among them, saying something to each group. She caught sight of Mr. Peck and Mr. Savor, and she ran after them, arriving with them where Annie sat.

"I hope you were not anxious about Idella," Annie said, laughing.

"No; I didn't miss her at once," said the minister simply; "and then I thought she had merely gone off with some of the other children who were playing about."

"You shall talk all that over later," said Mrs. Munger. "Now, Miss Kilburn, I want you and Mr. Peck and Mr. and Mrs. Savor to stay for a cup of coffee that I'm going to give our friends out there. Don't you think they deserve it? Wasn't it a wonderful success? They must be frightfully exhausted. Just go right out to them. I'll be with you in one moment. Oh yes, the child! Well, bring her into the house, Mrs. Savor; I'll find a place for her, and then you can go out with me."

"I guess you won't get Maria away from her very easy," said Mr. Savor, laughing. His wife stood with the child's cheek pressed tight against hers.

"Oh, I'll manage that," said Mrs. Munger. "I'm counting on Mrs. Savor." She added in a hurried undertone to Annie: "I've asked a number of the workpeople to stay—representative workpeople, the foremen in the different shops and their families—and you'll find your friends of all classes together. It's a great day for the Social Union!" she said aloud. "I'm sure *you* must feel that, Mr. Peck. Miss Kilburn and I have to thank you for saving us from a great mistake at the outset, and now your staying," she continued, "will give it just the appearance we want. I'm going to keep your little girl as a hostage, and you shall not go till I let you. Come, Mrs.

Savor!" She bustled away with Mrs. Savor, and Mr. Peck reluctantly accompanied Annie down over the lawn.

He was silent, but Mr. Savor was hilarious. "Well, Mr. Putney," he said, when he joined the group of which Putney was the centre, "you done that in apple-pie order. I never see anything much better than the way you carried on with Mrs. Wilmington."

"Thank you, Mr. Savor," said Putney; "I'm glad you liked it. You couldn't say I was trying to flatter her up much, anyway."

"No, no!" Mr. Savor assented, with delight in the joke.

"Well, Annie," said Putney. He shook hands with her, and Mrs. Putney, who was there with Dr. Morrell, asked her where she had sat.

"We kept looking all round for you."

"Yes," said Putney, with his hand on his boy's shoulder, "we wanted to know how you liked the Mercutio."

"Ralph, it was incomparable!"

"Well, that will do for a beginning. It's a little cold, but it's in the right spirit. You mean that the Mercutio wasn't comparable to the Nurse."

"Oh, Lyra was wonderful!" said Annie. "Don't you think so, Ellen?"

"She was Lyra," said Mrs. Putney definitely.

"No; she wasn't Lyra at all!" retorted Annie. "That was the marvel of it. She was Juliet's nurse."

"Perhaps she was a little of both," suggested Putney. "What did you think of the performance, Mr. Peck? I don't want a personal tribute, but if you offer it, I shall not be ungrateful."

"I have been very much interested," said the minister. "It was all very new to me. I realised for the first time in my life the great power that the theatre must be. I felt how much the drama could do—how much good."

"Well, that's what we're after," said Putney. "We had no personal motive; good, right straight along, was our motto. Nobody wanted to outshine anybody else. I kept my Mercutio down all through, so's not to get ahead of Romeo or Tybalt in the public esteem. Did our friends outside the rope catch on to my idea?" Mr. Peck smiled at the banter, but he seemed not to know just what to say, and Putney went on:

"That's why I made it so bad. I didn't want anybody to go home feeling sorry that Mercutio was killed. I don't suppose Winthrop could have slept."

"You won't sleep yourself to-night, I'm afraid," said his wife.

"Oh, Mrs. Munger has promised me a particularly weak cup of coffee. She has got us all in, it seems, for a sort of supper, in spite of everything. I understand it includes representatives of all the stations and conditions present except the outcasts beyond the rope. I don't see what you're doing here, Mr. Peck."

"Was Mr. Peck really outside the rope?" Annie asked Dr. Morrell, as they dropped apart from the others a little.

"I believe he gave his chair to one of the women from the outside," said the doctor.

Annie moved with him toward Lyra, who was joking with some of the hands.

With all her good-nature, she had the effect of patronising them, as she stood talking about the play with them in her drawl, which she had got back to again. They were admiring her, in her dress of the querulous old nurse, and told her how they never would have known her. But there was an insincerity in the effusion of some of the more nervous women, and in the reticence of the others, who were holding back out of self-respect.

She met Annie and Morrell with eager relief. "Well, Annie?"

"Perfect!"

"Well, now, that's very nice; you can't go beyond perfect, you know. I *did* do it pretty well, didn't I? Poor Mr. Brandreth! Have you seen him? You must say something comforting to him. He's really been sacrificed in this business. You know he wanted Miss Chapley. She would have made a lovely Juliet. Of course she blames him for it. She thinks he wanted to make up to Miss Northwick, when Miss Northwick was just flinging herself at Jack. Look at her!"

Jack Wilmington and Miss Sue Northwick were standing together near her father and a party of her friends, and she was smiling and talking at him. Eyes, lips, gestures, attitude expressed in the proud girl a fawning eagerness to please the man, who received her homage rather as if it bored him. His indifferent manner may have been one secret of his power over her, and perhaps she was not capable of all the suffering she was capable of inflicting.

Lyra turned to walk toward the house, deflecting a little in the direction of her nephew and Miss Northwick. "Jack!" she drawled over the shoulder next them as she passed, "I wish you'd bring your aunty's wrap to her on the piazza."

"Why, stay here!" Putney called after her. "They're going to fetch the refreshments out here."

"Yes, but I'm tired, Ralph, and I can't sit on the grass, at my age."

She moved on, with her sweeping, lounging pace, and Jack Wilmington, after a moment's hesitation, bowed to Miss Northwick and went after her.

The girl remained apart from her friends, as if expecting his return.

Silhouetted against the bright windows, Lyra waited till Jack Wilmington reappeared with a shawl and laid it on her shoulders. Then she sank into a chair. The young man stood beside her talking down upon her. Something restive and insistent expressed itself in their respective attitudes. He sat down at her side.

Miss Northwick joined her friends carelessly.

"Ah, Miss Kilburn," said Mr. Brandreth's voice at Annie's ear, "I'm glad to find you. I've just run home with mother—she feels the night air—and I was afraid you would slip through our fingers before I got back. This little business of the refreshments was an afterthought of Mrs. Munger's, and we meant it for a surprise—we knew you'd approve of it in the form it took." He looked round at the straggling work-people, who represented the harmonisation of classes, keeping to themselves as if they had been there alone.

"Yes," Annie was obliged to say; "it's very pleasant." She added: "You must all be rather hungry, Mr. Brandreth. If the Social Union ever gets on its feet, it will have *you* to thank more than any one."

"Oh, don't speak of me, Miss Kilburn! Do you know, we've netted about two hundred dollars. Isn't that pretty good, doctor?"

"Very," said the doctor. "Hadn't we better follow Mrs. Wilmington's example, and get up under the piazza roof? I'm afraid you'll be the worse for the night air, Miss Kilburn. Putney," he called to his friend, "we're going up to the house."

"All right. I guess that's a good idea."

The doctor called to the different knots and groups, telling them to come up to the house. Some of the workpeople slipped away through the grounds and did not come. The Northwicks and their friends moved toward the house.

Mrs. Munger came down the lawn to meet her guests. "Ah, that's right. It's much better in-doors. I was just coming for you." She addressed herself more particularly to the Northwicks. "Coffee will be ready in a few moments. We've met with a little delay."

"I'm afraid we must say good night at once," said Mr. Northwick. "We had arranged to have our friends and some other guests with us at home. And we're quite late now."

Mrs. Munger protested. "Take our Juliet from us! Oh, Miss Northwick, how can I thank you enough? The whole play turned upon you!"

"It's just as well," she said to Annie, as the Northwicks and their friends walked across the lawn to the gate, where they had carriages waiting. "They'd have been difficult to manage, and everybody else will feel a little more at home without them. Poor Mr. Brandreth, I'm sure *you* will! I did pity you so, with such a Juliet on your hands!"

In-doors the representatives of the lower classes were less at ease than they were without. Some of the ministers mingled with them, and tried to form a bond between them and the other villagers. Mr. Peck took no part in this work; he stood holding his elbows with his hands, and talking with a perfunctory air to an old lady of his congregation.

The young ladies of South Hatboro', as Mrs. Munger's assistants, went about impartially to high and low with trays of refreshments. Annie saw Putney, where he stood with his wife and boy, refuse coffee, and she watched him anxiously when the claret-cup came. He waved his hand over it, and said, "No; I'll take some of the lemonade." As he lifted a glass of it toward his lips he stopped and made as if to put it down again, and his hand shook so that he spilled some of it. Then he dashed it off, and reached for another glass. "I want some more," he said, with a laugh; "I'm thirsty." He drank a second glass, and when he saw a tray coming toward Annie, where Dr. Morrell had joined her, he came over and exchanged his empty glass for a full one.

"Not much to brag of as lemonade," he said, "but first-rate rum punch."

"Look here, Putney," whispered the doctor, laying his hand on his arm, "don't you take any more of that. Give me that glass!"

"Oh, all right!" laughed Putney, dashing it off. "You're welcome to the tumbler, if you want it, Doc."

XVIII.

MRS. MUNGER'S guests kept on talking and laughing. With the coffee and the punch there began to be a little more freedom. Some prohibitionists among the working people went away when they found that the lemonade was punch; but Mrs. Munger did not know it, and she saw the ideal of a Social Union figuratively accomplished in her own house. She stirred about among her guests till she produced a fleeting, empty good-fellowship among them. One of the shoe-shop hands, with an inextinguishable scent of leather and the character of a droll, seconded her efforts with noisy jokes. He proposed games, and would not be snubbed by the refusal of his boss to countenance him, he had the applause of so many others. Mrs. Munger approved of the idea.

"Don't you think it would be great fun, Mrs. Gerrish?" she asked.

"Well, now, if Squire Putney would lead off," said the joker, looking round.

Putney could not be found, nor Dr. Morrell.

"They're off somewhere for a smoke," said Mrs. Munger. "Well, that's right. I want everybody to feel that my house is their own to-night, and to come and go just as they like. Do you suppose Mr. Peck is offended?" she asked, under her breath, as she passed Annie. "He *couldn't* feel that this is the same thing; but I can't see him anywhere. He wouldn't go without taking leave, you don't suppose?"

Annie joined Mrs. Putney. They talked at first with those who came to ask where Putney and the doctor were; but finally they withdrew into a little alcove from the parlour, where Mrs. Munger approved of their being when she discovered them; they must be very tired, and ought to rest on the lounge there. Her theory of the exhaustion of those who had taken part in the play embraced their families.

The time wore on toward midnight, and her guests got themselves away with more or less difficulty as they attempted the formality of leave-taking or not. Some of the hands who thought this necessary found it a serious affair; but most of them slipped off without saying good night to Mrs. Munger or expressing that rapture with the whole evening from beginning to end which the ladies of South Hatboro' professed. The ladies of South Hatboro' and Old Hatboro' had met in a general intimacy not approached before, and they parted with a flow of mutual esteem. The Gerrish children had dropped asleep in nooks and corners, from which Mr. Gerrish hunted them up and put them together for departure, while his wife remained with Mrs. Munger, unable to stop talking, and no longer amenable to the looks with which he governed her in public.

Lyra came downstairs, hooded and wrapped for departure, with Jack Wilmington by her side. "Why, *Ellen!*" she said, looking into the little alcove from the hall. "Are you here yet? And Annie! Where in the world is Ralph?" At the pleading look with which Mrs. Putney replied, she exclaimed: "Oh, it's what I was afraid of! I don't see what the woman could have been about! But of course she didn't think of poor Ralph. Ellen, let me take you and Winthrop home! Dr. Morrell will be sure to bring Ralph."

"Well," said Mrs. Putney passively, but without rising.

"Annie can come too. There's plenty of room. Jack can walk."

Jack Wilmington joined Lyra in urging Annie to take his place. He said to her, apart, "Young Munger has been telling me that Putney got at the sideboard and carried off the rum. I'll stay and help look after him."

A crazy laugh came into the parlour from the piazza outside, and the group in the alcove started forward. Putney stood at a window, resting one arm on the bar of the long lower sash, which was raised to its full height, and looking ironically in upon Mrs. Munger and her remaining guests. He was still in his Mercutio dress, but he had lost his plumed cap, and was bareheaded. A pace or two behind him stood Mr. Peck, regarding the effect of this apparition upon the company with the same dreamy, indrawn presence he had in the pulpit.

"Well, Mrs. Munger, I'm glad I got back in time to tell you how much I've enjoyed it. Brother Peck wanted me to go home, but I told him, Not till I've thanked Mrs. Munger,

Brother Peck; not till I've drunk her health in her own old particular Jamaica." He put to his lips the black bottle which he had been holding in his right hand behind him; then he took it away, looked at it, and flung it rolling along the piazza floor. "Didn't get hold of the inexhaustible bottle that time; never do. But it's a good article; a better article than you used to sell on the sly, Bill Gerrish. You'll excuse my helping myself, Mrs. Munger; I knew you'd want me to. Well, it's been a great occasion, Mrs. Munger." He winked at the hostess. "You've had your little invited supper, after all. You're a manager, Mrs. Munger. You've made even the wrath of Brother Peck to praise you."

The ladies involuntarily shrank backward as Putney suddenly entered through the window and gained the corner of the piano at a dash. He stayed himself against it, slightly swaying, and turned his flaming eyes from one to another, as if questioning whom he should attack next.

Except for the wild look in them, which was not so much wilder than they wore in all times of excitement, and an occasional halt at a difficult word, he gave no sign of being drunk. The liquor had as yet merely intensified him.

Mrs. Munger had the inspiration to treat him as one caresses a dangerous lunatic. "I'm sure you're very kind, Mr. Putney, to come back. Do sit down!"

"Why?" demanded Putney. "Everybody else standing."

"That's true," said Mrs. Munger. "I'm sure I don't know why——"

"Oh yes, you do, Mrs. Munger. It's because they want to have a good view of a man who's made a fool of himself——"

"Oh, now, Mr. *Putney!*" said Mrs. Munger, with hospitable deprecation. "I'm sure no one wants to do anything of the kind." She looked round at the company for corroboration, but no one cared to attract Putney's attention by any sound or sign.

"But I'll tell you what," said Putney, with a savage burst, "that a woman who puts hell-fire before a poor devil who can't keep out of it when he sees it, is better worth looking at."

"Mr. Putney, I assure you," said Mrs. Munger, "that it was

the *mildest* punch! And I really didn't think—I didn't remember——"

She turned toward Mrs. Putney with her explanation, but Putney seemed to have forgotten her, and he turned upon Mr. Gerrish, "How's that drunkard's grave getting along that you've dug for your porter?" Gerrish remained prudently silent. "I know you, Billy. You're all right. You've got the pull on your conscience; we all have, one way or another. Here's Annie Kilburn, come back from Rome, where she couldn't seem to fix it up with hers to suit her, and she's trying to get round it in Hatboro' with good works. Why, there isn't any occasion for good works in Hatboro'. I could have told you that before you came," he said, addressing Annie directly. "What we want is faith, and lots of it. The church is going to pieces because we haven't got any faith."

His hand slipped from the piano, and he dropped heavily back upon a chair that stood near. The concussion seemed to complete in his brain the transition from his normal dispositions to their opposite, which had already begun. "Bill Gerrish has done more for Hatboro' than any other man in the place. He's the only man that holds the church together, because he knows the value of *faith*." He said this without a trace of irony, glaring at Annie with fierce defiance. "You come back here, and try to set up for a saint in a town where William B. Gerrish has done—has done more to establish the dry-goods business on a metro-me-tro-politan basis than any other man out of New York or Boston."

He stopped and looked round, mystified, as if this were not the point which he had been aiming at.

Lyra broke into a spluttering laugh, and suddenly checked herself. Putney smiled slightly. "Pretty good, eh? Say, where was I?" he asked slyly. Lyra hid her face behind Annie's shoulder. "What's that dress you got on? What's all this about, anyway? Oh yes, I know. *Romeo and Juliet*—Social Union. Well," he resumed, with a frown, "there's too much *Romeo and Juliet*, too much Social Union, in this town already." He stopped, and seemed preparing to launch some deadly phrase at Mrs. Wilmington, but he only said, "You're all right, Lyra."

"Mrs. Munger," said Mr. Gerrish, "we must be going. Good night, ma'am. Mrs. Gerrish, it's time the children were at home."

"Of course it is," said Putney, watching the Gerrishes getting their children together. He waved his hand after them, and called out, "William Gerrish, you're a man; I honour you."

He laid hold of the piano and pulled himself to his feet, and seemed to become aware, for the first time, of his wife, where she stood with their boy beside her.

"What you doing here with that child at this time of night?" he shouted at her, all that was left of the man in his eyes changing into the glare of a pitiless brute. "Why don't you go home? You want to show people what I did to him? You want to publish my shame, do you? Is that it? Look here!"

He began to work himself along toward her by help of the piano. A step was heard on the piazza without, and Dr. Morrell entered through the open window.

"Come now, Putney," he said gently. The other men closed round them.

Putney stopped. "What's this? Interfering in family matters? You better go home and look after your own wives, if you got any. Get out the way, 'n' you mind your own business, Doc. Morrell. You meddle too much." His speech was thickening and breaking. "You think science going do everything—evolution! Talk me about evolution! What's evolution done for Hatboro'? 'Volved Gerrish's store. One day of Christianity—real Christianity—— Where's that boy? If I get hold of him——"

He lunged forward, and Jack Wilmington and young Munger stepped before him.

Mrs. Putney had not moved, nor lost the look of sad, passive vigilance which she had worn since her husband reappeared.

She pushed the men aside.

"Ralph, behave yourself! *Here's* Winthrop, and we want you to take us home. Come now!" She passed her arm through his, and the boy took his other hand. The action, so full of fearless custom and wonted affection from them both, seemed with her words to operate another total change in his mood.

"All right; I'm going, Ellen. Got to say good night Mrs. Munger, that's all." He managed to get to her, with his wife on his arm and his boy at his side. "Want to thank you for a pleasant evening, Mrs. Munger—want to thank you——"

"And *I* want to thank you *too*, Mrs. Munger," said Mrs. Putney, with an intensity of bitterness no repetition of the words could give. "It's been a pleasant evening for *me!*"

Putney wished to stop and explain, but his wife pulled him away.

Dr. Morrell and Annie followed to get them safely into the carriage; he went with them, and when she came back Mrs. Munger was saying: "I will leave it to Mr. Wilmington, or any one, if I'm to blame. It had quite gone out of my head about Mr. Putney. There was plenty of coffee, besides, and if everything that could harm particular persons had to be kept out of the way, society couldn't go on. We ought to consider the greatest good of the greatest number." She looked round from one to another for support. No one said anything, and Mrs. Munger, trembling on the verge of a collapse, made a direct appeal: "Don't you think so, Mr. Peck?"

The minister broke his silence with reluctance. "It's sometimes best to have the effect of error unmistakable. Then we are sure it's error."

Mrs. Munger gave a sob of relief into her handkerchief. "Yes, that's just what I say."

Lyra bent her face on her arm, and Jack Wilmington put his head out of the window where he stood.

Mr. Peck remained staring at Mrs. Munger, as if doubtful what to do. Then he said: "You seem not to have understood me, ma'am. I should be to blame if I left you in doubt. You have been guilty of forgetting your brother's weakness, and if the consequence has promptly followed in his shame, it is for you to realise it. I wish you a good evening."

He went out with a dignity that thrilled Annie. Lyra leaned toward her and said, choking with laughter, "He's left Idella asleep upstairs. We haven't *any* of us got *perfect* memories, have we?"

"Run after him!" Annie said to Jack Wilmington, in undertone, "and get him into my carriage. I'll get the little girl. Lyra, *don't* speak of it."

"Never!" said Mrs. Wilmington, with delight. "I'm solid for Mr. Peck every time."

XIX.

Aᴺᴺɪᴇ ᴍᴀᴅᴇ ᴜᴘ a bed for Idella on a wide, old-fashioned lounge in her room, and put her away in it, swathed in a night-gown which she found among the survivals of her own childish clothing in that old chest of drawers. When she woke in the morning she looked across at the little creature, with a tender sense of possession and protection suffusing her troubled recollections of the night before. Idella stirred, stretched herself with a long sigh, and then sat up and stared round the strange place as if she were still in a dream.

"Would you like to come in here with me?" Annie suggested from her bed.

The child pushed back her hair with her little hands, and after waiting to realise the situation to the limit of her small experience, she said, with a smile that showed her pretty teeth, "Yes."

"Then come."

Idella tumbled out of bed, pulling up the night-gown, which was too long for her, and softly thumped across the carpet. Annie leaned over and lifted her up, and pressed the little face to her own, and felt the play of the quick, light breath over her cheek.

"Would you like to stay with me—live with me—Idella?" she asked.

The child turned her face away, and hid a roguish smile in the pillow. "I don't know."

"Would you like to be my little girl?"

"No."

"No? Why not?"

"Because—because"—she seemed to search her mind—"because your night-gowns are too long."

"Oh, is that all? That's no reason. Think of something else."

Idella rubbed her face hard on the pillow. "You dress up cats."

She lifted her face, and looked with eyes of laughing malice into Annie's, and Annie pushed her face against Idella's neck and cried, "You're a rogue!"

The little one screamed with laughter and gurgled: "Oh, you tickle! You tickle!"

They had a childish romp, prolonged through the details of Idella's washing and dressing, and Annie tried to lose, in her frolic with the child, the anxieties that had beset her waking; she succeeded in confusing them with one another in one dull, indefinite pain.

She wondered when Mr. Peck would come for Idella, but they were still at their belated breakfast when Mrs. Bolton came in to say that Bolton had met the minister on his way up, and had asked him if Idella might not stay the week out with them.

"I don' know but he done more'n he'd ought. But she can be with us the rest part, when you've got done with her."

"I haven't begun to get done with her," said Annie. "I'm glad Mr. Bolton asked."

After breakfast Bolton himself appeared, to ask if Idella might go up to the orchard with him. Idella ran out of the room and came back with her hat on, and tugging to get into her shabby little sack. Annie helped her with it, and Idella tucked her hand into Bolton's loose, hard fist, and gave it a pull toward the door.

"Well, I don't see but what she's goin'," he said.

"Yes; you'd better ask her the next time if *I* can go," said Annie.

"Well, why don't you?" asked Bolton, humouring the joke. "I guess you'd enjoy it about as well as any. We're just goin' for a basket of wind-falls for pies. I guess we ain't a-goin' to be gone a great while."

Annie watched them up the lane from the library window with a queer grudge at heart; Bolton stiffly lumbering forward at an angle of forty-five degrees, the child whirling and dancing at his side, and now before and now after him.

At the sound of wheels on the gravel before the front door, Annie turned away with such an imperative need of its being Dr. Morrell's buggy that it was almost an intolerable disappointment to find it Mrs. Munger's phaeton.

Mrs. Munger burst in upon her in an excitement which somehow had an effect of premeditation.

"Miss Kilburn, I wish to know what you think of Mr. and

Mrs. Putney's behaviour to me, and Mr. Peck's, in my own house, last night. They are friends of yours, and I wish to know if you approve of it. I come to you *as* their friend, and I am sure you will feel as I do that my hospitality has been abused. It was an outrage for Mr. Putney to get intoxicated in my house; and for Mr. Peck to attack me as he did before everybody, because Mr. Putney had taken advantage of his privileges, was abominable. I am not a member of his church; and even if I were, he would have had no right to speak so to me."

Annie felt the blood fly to her head, and she waited a moment to regain her coolness. "I wonder you came to ask me, Mrs. Munger, if you were so sure that I agreed with you. I'm certainly Mr. and Mrs. Putney's friend, and so far as admiring Mr. Peck's sincerity and goodness is concerned, I'm *his* friend. But I'm obliged to say that you're mistaken about the rest."

She folded her hands at her waist, and stood up very straight, looking firmly at Mrs. Munger, who made a show of taking a new grip of her senses as she sank unbidden into a chair.

"Why, what do you mean, Miss Kilburn?"

"It seems to me that I needn't say."

"Why, but you must! You *must*, you know. I can't be *left* so! I must know where I *stand*! I must be sure of my *ground*! I can't go on without understanding just how much you mean by my being mistaken."

She looked Annie in the face with eyes superficially expressive of indignant surprise, and Annie perceived that she wished to restore herself in her own esteem by browbeating some one else into the affirmation of her innocence.

"Well, if you must know, Mrs. Munger, I mean that you ought to have remembered Mr. Putney's infirmity, and that it was cruel to put temptation in his way. Everybody knows that he can't resist it, and that he is making such a hard fight to keep out of it. And then, if you press me for an opinion, I must say that you were not justifiable in asking Mr. Peck to take part in a social entertainment when we had explicitly dropped that part of the affair."

Mrs. Munger had not pressed Annie for an opinion on this point at all; but in their interest in it they both ignored the fact. Mrs. Munger tacitly admitted her position in retorting, "He needn't have stayed."

"You made him stay—you remember how—and he couldn't have got away without being rude."

"And you think he wasn't rude to scold me before my guests?"

"He told you the truth. He didn't wish to say anything, but you forced him to speak, just as you have forced me."

"Forced *you*? Miss Kilburn!"

"Yes. I don't at all agree with Mr. Peck in many things, but he is a good man, and last night he spoke the truth. I shouldn't be speaking it if I didn't tell you I thought so."

"Very well, then," said Mrs. Munger, rising. "After this you can't expect me to have anything to do with the Social Union; you couldn't *wish* me to, if that's your opinion of my character."

"I haven't expressed any opinion of your character, Mrs. Munger, if you'll remember, please; and as for the Social Union, I shall have nothing further to do with it myself."

Annie drew herself up a little higher, and silently waited for her visitor to go.

But Mrs. Munger remained.

"I don't believe Mrs. Putney herself would say what you have said," she remarked, after an embarrassing moment. "If it were really so I should be willing to make any reparation— to acknowledge it. Will you go with me to Mrs. Putney's? I have my phaeton here, and——"

"I shouldn't dream of going to Mrs. Putney's with you."

Mrs. Munger urged, with the effect of invincible argument: "I've been down in the village, and I've talked to a good many about it—some of them hadn't heard of it before—and I must say, Miss Kilburn, that people generally take a very different view of it from what you do. They think that my hospitality has been shamefully abused. Mr. Gates said he should think I would have Mr. Putney arrested. But I don't care for all that. What I wish is to prove to you that I am right; and if I can go with you to call on Mrs. Putney, I shall not care what any one else says. Will you come?"

"Certainly not," cried Annie.

They both stood a moment, and in this moment Dr.

Morrell drove up, and dropped his hitching-weight beyond Mrs. Munger's phaeton.

As he entered she said: "We will let Dr. Morrell decide. I've been asking Miss Kilburn to go with me to Mrs. Putney's. I think it would be a graceful and proper thing for me to do, to express my sympathy and interest, and to hear what Mrs. Putney really has to say. Don't *you* think I ought to go to see her, doctor?"

The doctor laughed. "I can't prescribe in matters of social duty. But what do you want to see Mrs. Putney for?"

"What for? Why, doctor, on account of Mr. Putney—what took place last night."

"Yes? What was that?"

"What was *that*? Why, his strange behaviour—his—his intoxication."

"Was he intoxicated? Did you think so?"

"Why, you were there, doctor. Didn't you think so?"

Annie looked at him with as much astonishment as Mrs. Munger.

The doctor laughed again. "You can't always tell when Putney's joking; he's a great joker. Perhaps he was hoaxing."

"Oh doctor, do you think he *could* have been?" said Mrs. Munger, with clasped hands. "It would make me the happiest woman in the world! I'd forgive him all he's made me suffer. But *you're* joking *now*, doctor?"

"You can't tell when people are joking. If I'm not, does it follow that I'm really intoxicated?"

"Oh, but that's nonsense, Dr. Morrell. That's mere—what do you call it?—chop logic. But I don't mind it. I grasp at a straw." Mrs. Munger grasped at a straw of the mind, to show how. "But what *do* you mean?"

"Well, Mrs. Putney wasn't intoxicated last night, but she's not well this morning. I'm afraid she couldn't see you."

"Just as you *say*, doctor," cried Mrs. Munger, with mounting cheerfulness. "I *wish* I knew just how much you meant, and how little." She moved closer to the doctor, and bent a look of candid fondness upon him. "But I know you're trying to mystify me."

She pursued him with questions which he easily parried, smiling and laughing. At the end she left him to Annie, with adieux that were almost radiant. "Anyhow, I shall take the benefit of the doubt, and if Mr. Putney was hoaxing, I shall not give myself away. *Do* find out what he means, Miss Kilburn, won't you?" She took hold of Annie's unoffered hand, and pressed it in a double leathern grasp, and ran out of the room with a lightness of spirit which her physical bulk imperfectly expressed.

XX.

"WELL?" said Annie, to the change which came over Morrell's face when Mrs. Munger was gone.

"Oh, it's a miserable business! He must go on now to the end of his debauch. He's got past doing any mischief, I'm thankful to say. But I had hoped to tide him over a while longer, and now that fool has spoiled everything. Well!"

Annie's heart warmed to his vexation, and she postponed another emotion. "Yes, she *is* a fool. I wish you had qualified the term, doctor."

They looked at each other solemnly, and then laughed. "It won't do for a physician to swear," said Morrell. "I wish you'd give me a cup of coffee. I've been up all night."

"With Ralph?"

"With Putney."

"You shall have it instantly; that is, as instantly as Mrs. Bolton can kindle up a fire and make it." She went out to the kitchen, and gave the order with an imperiousness which she softened in Dr. Morrell's interest by explaining rather fully to Mrs. Bolton.

When she came back she wanted to talk seriously, tragically, about Putney. But the doctor would not. He said that it paid to sit up with Putney, drunk or sober, and hear him go on. He repeated some things Putney said about Mr. Peck, about Gerrish, about Mrs. Munger.

"But why did you try to put her off in that way—to make her believe he wasn't intoxicated?" asked Annie, venting her postponed emotion, which was of disapproval.

"I don't know. It came into my head. But she knows better."

"It was rather cruel; not that she deserves any mercy. She caught so at the idea."

"Oh yes, I saw that. She'll humbug herself with it, and you'll see that before night there'll be two theories of Putney's escapade. I think the last will be the popular one. It will jump with the general opinion of Putney's ability to carry anything out. And Mrs. Munger will do all she can to support it."

Mrs. Bolton brought in the coffee-pot, and Annie hesitated a moment, with her hand on it, before pouring out a cup.

"I don't like it," she said.

"I know you don't. But you can say that it wasn't Putney who hoaxed Mrs. Munger, but Dr. Morrell."

"Oh, you didn't either of you hoax her."

"Well, then, there's no harm done."

"I'm not so sure."

"And you won't give me any coffee?"

"Oh yes, I'll give you some *coffee*," said Annie, with a sigh of baffled scrupulosity that made them both laugh.

He broke out again after he had begun to drink his coffee.

"Well?" she demanded, from her own lapse into silence.

"Oh, nothing! Only Putney. He wants Brother Peck, as he calls him, to unite all the religious elements of Hatboro' in a church of his own, and send out missionaries to the heathen of South Hatboro' to preach a practical Christianity. He makes South Hatboro' stand for all that's worldly and depraved."

"Poor Ralph! Is that the way he talks?"

"Oh, not all the time. He talks a great many other ways."

"I wonder you can laugh."

"He's been very severe on Brother Peck for neglecting the discipline of his child. He says he ought to remember his duty to others, and save the community from having the child grow up into a capricious, wilful woman. Putney was very hard upon your sex, Miss Kilburn. He attributed nearly all the trouble in the world to women's wilfulness and caprice."

He looked across the table at her with his merry eyes, whose sweetness she felt even in her sudden preoccupation with the notion which she now launched upon him, leaning forward and pushing some books and magazines aside, as if she wished to have nothing between her need and his response.

"Dr. Morrell, what should you think of my asking Mr. Peck to give me his little girl?"

"To give you his——"

"Yes. Let me take Idella—keep her—adopt her! I've nothing to do, as you know very well, and she'd be an occupation; and it would be far better for her. What Ralph says is true.

She's growing up without any sort of training; and I think if she keeps on she will be mischievous to herself and every one else."

"Really?" asked the doctor. "Is it so bad as that?"

"Of course not. And of course I don't want Mr. Peck to renounce all claim to his child; but to let me have her for the present, or indefinitely, and get her some decent clothes, and trim her hair properly, and give her some sort of instruction——"

"May I come in?" drawled Mrs. Wilmington's mellow voice, and Annie turned and saw Lyra peering round the edge of the half-opened library door. "I've been discreetly hemming and scraping and hammering on the wood-work so as not to overhear, and I'd have gone away if I hadn't been afraid of being overheard."

"Oh, come in, Lyra," said Annie; and she hoped that she had kept the spirit of resignation with which she spoke out of her voice.

Dr. Morrell jumped up with an apparent desire to escape that wounded and exasperated her. She put out her hand quite haughtily to him and asked, "Oh, must you go?"

"Yes. How do you do, Mrs. Wilmington? You'd better get Miss Kilburn to give you a cup of her coffee."

"Oh, I will," said Lyra. She forbore any reference, even by a look, to the intimate little situation she had disturbed.

Morrell added to Annie: "I like your plan. It's the best thing you could do."

She found she had been keeping his hand, and in the revulsion from wrath to joy she violently wrung it.

"I'm *so* glad!" She could not help following him to the door, in the hope that he would say something more, but he did not, and she could only repeat her rapturous gratitude in several forms of incoherency.

She ran back to Mrs. Wilmington. "Lyra, what do you think of my taking Mr. Peck's little girl?"

Mrs. Wilmington never allowed herself to seem surprised at anything; she was, in fact, surprised at very few things. She had got into the easiest chair in the room, and she answered from it, with a luxurious interest in the affair, "Well, you know what people will say, Annie."

"No, I don't. *What* will they say?"

"That you're after Mr. Peck pretty openly."

Annie turned scarlet. "And when they find I'm *not*?" she demanded with severity, that had no effect upon Lyra.

"Then they'll say you couldn't get him."

"They may say what they please. What do you think of the plan?"

"I think it would be the greatest blessing for the poor little thing," said Lyra, with a nearer approach to seriousness than she usually made. "And the greatest care for you," she added, after a moment.

"I shall not care for the care. I shall be glad of it—thankful for it," cried Annie fervidly.

"If you can get it," Lyra suggested.

"I believe I can get it. I believe I can make Mr. Peck see that it's a duty. I shall ask him to regard it as a charity to me—as a mercy."

"Well, that's a good way to work upon Mr. Peck's feelings," said Lyra demurely. "Was that the plan that Dr. Morrell approved of so highly?"

"Yes."

"I didn't know but it was some course of treatment. You pressed his hand so affectionately. I said to myself, Well, Annie's either an enthusiastic patient, or else——"

"What?" demanded Annie, at the little stop Lyra made.

"Well, you know what people do *say*, Annie."

"What?"

"Why, that you're very much out of health, or——" Lyra made another of her tantalising stops.

"Or what?"

"Or Dr. Morrell is very much in love."

"Lyra, I can't allow you to say such things to me."

"No; that's what I've kept saying to myself all the time. But you would have it *out* of me. *I* didn't want to say it."

It was impossible to resist Lyra's pretended deprecation. Annie laughed. "I suppose I can't help people's talking, and I ought to be too old to care."

"You ought, but you're not," said Lyra flatteringly. "Well, Annie, what do you think of our little evening at Mrs. Munger's in the dim retrospect? Poor Ralph! What did the

doctor say about him?" She listened with so keen a relish for
the report of Putney's sayings that Annie felt as if she had
been turning the affair into comedy for Lyra's amusement.
"Oh dear, I wish I could hear him! I thought I should have
died last night when he came back, and began to scare everybody blue with his highly personal remarks. I wish he'd had
time to get round to the Northwicks."

"Lyra," said Annie, nerving herself to the office; "don't you
think it was wicked to treat that poor girl as you did?"

"Well, I suppose that's the way some people might look at
it," said Lyra dispassionately.

"Then how—*how* could you do it?"

"Oh, it's easy enough to behave wickedly, Annie, when
you feel like it," said Lyra, much amused by Annie's fervour,
apparently. "Besides, I don't know that it was so *very* wicked.
What makes you think it was?"

"Oh, it wasn't that merely. Lyra, may I—*may* I speak to
you plainly, frankly—like a sister?" Annie's heart filled with
tenderness for Lyra, with the wish to help her, to save a person who charmed her so much.

"Well, like a *step*-sister, you may," said Lyra demurely.

"It wasn't for her sake alone that I hated to see it. It was for
your sake—for *his* sake."

"Well, that's very kind of you, Annie," said Lyra, without
the least resentment. "And I know what you mean. But it
really doesn't hurt either Jack or me. I'm not very goody-
goody, Annie; I don't pretend to be; but I'm not very baddy-
baddy either. I assure you"—Lyra laughed mischievously—
"I'm one of the very few persons in Hatboro' who are better
than they should be."

"I know it, Lyra—I know it. But you have no right to keep
him from taking a fancy to some young girl—and marrying
her; to keep him to yourself; to make people talk."

"There's something in that," Lyra assented, with impartiality. "But I don't think it would be well for Jack to marry
yet; and if I see him taking a fancy to any real nice girl,
I sha'n't interfere with him. But I shall be very *particular*,
Annie."

She looked at Annie with such a droll mock earnest, and
shook her head with such a burlesque of grandmotherly solic-

itude, that Annie laughed in spite of herself. "Oh, Lyra, Lyra!"

"And as for me," Lyra went on, "I assure you I don't care for the little bit of harm it does me."

"But you ought—you ought!" cried Annie. "You ought to respect yourself enough to care. You ought to respect other women enough."

"Oh, I guess I'd let the balance of the sex slide, Annie," said Lyra.

"No, you mustn't; you can't. We are all bound together; we owe everything to each other."

"Isn't that rather Peckish?" Lyra suggested.

"I don't know. But it's true, Lyra. And I shouldn't be ashamed of getting it from Mr. Peck."

"Oh, I didn't say you would be."

"And I hope you won't be hurt with me. I know that it's a most unwarrantable thing to speak to you about such a matter; but you know why I do it."

"Yes, I suppose it's because you like me; and I appreciate that, I assure you, Annie."

Lyra was soberer than she had yet been, and Annie felt that she was really gaining ground. "And your husband; you ought to respect *him*——"

Lyra laughed out with great relish. "Oh, now, Annie, you *are* joking! Why in the *world* should I respect Mr. Wilmington? An old man like him marrying a young girl like me!" She jumped up and laughed at the look in Annie's face. "Will you go round with me to the Putneys? I thought Ellen might like to see us."

"No, no. I can't go," said Annie, finding it impossible to recover at once from the quite unanswerable blow her sense of decorum—she thought it her moral sense—had received.

"Well, you'll be glad to have *me* go, anyway," said Lyra. She saw Annie shrinking from her, and she took hold of her, and pulled her up and kissed her. "You dear old thing! I wouldn't hurt your feelings for the world. And whichever it is, Annie, the parson or the doctor, I wish him joy."

That afternoon, as Annie was walking to the village, the doctor drove up to the sidewalk, and stopped near her. "Miss Kilburn, I've got a letter from home. They write me about my mother in a way that makes me rather anxious, and I shall run down to Chelsea this evening."

"Oh, I'm sorry for your bad news. I hope it's nothing serious."

"She's old; that's the only cause for anxiety. But of course I must go."

"Oh yes, indeed. I do hope you'll find all right with her."

"Thank you very much. I'm sorry that I must leave Putney at such a time. But I leave him with Mr. Peck, who's promised to be with him. I thought you'd like to know."

"Yes, I do; it's very kind of you—very kind indeed."

"Thank you," said the doctor. It was not the phrase exactly, but it served the purpose of the cordial interest in which they parted as well as another.

XXI.

D URING THE DAYS that Mr. Peck had consented to leave
Idella with her Annie took the whole charge of the
child, and grew into an intimacy with her that was very
sweet. It was not necessary to this that Idella should be always tractable and docile, which she was not, but only that
she should be affectionate and dependent; Annie found that
she even liked her to be a little baddish; it gave her something to forgive; and she experienced a perverse pleasure in
discovering that the child of a man so self-forgetful as Mr.
Peck was rather more covetous than most children. It also
amused her that when some of Idella's shabby playmates
from Over the Track casually found their way to the woods
past Annie's house, and tried to tempt Idella to go with
them, the child disowned them, and ran into the house from
them; so soon was she alienated from her former life by her
present social advantages. She apparently distinguished between Annie and the Boltons, or if not quite this, she
showed a distinct preference for her company, and for her
part of the house. She hung about Annie with a flattering
curiosity and interest in all she did. She lost every trace of
shyness with her, but developed an intense admiration for
her in every way—for her dresses, her rings, her laces, for
the elegancies that marked her a gentlewoman. She pronounced them prettier than Mrs. Warner's things, and the
house prettier and larger.

"Should you like to live with me?" Annie asked.

The child seemed to reflect. Then she said, with the indirec-
tion of her age and sex, pushing against Annie's knee, "I don't
know what your name is."

"Have you never heard my name? It's Annie. How do you
like it?"

"It's—it's too short," said the child, from her readiness
always to answer something that charmed Annie.

"Well, then you can make it longer. You can call me Aunt
Annie. I think that will be better for a little girl; don't you?"

"Mothers can whip, but aunts can't," said Idella, bringing

a practical knowledge, acquired from her observation of life Over the Track, to a consideration of the proposed relation.

"I know *one* aunt who won't," said Annie, touched by the reply.

Saturday evening Idella's father came for her; and with a preamble which seemed to have been unnecessary when he understood it, Annie asked him to let her keep the child, at least till he had settled himself in a house of his own, or, she hinted, in some way more comfortable for Idella than he was now living. In her anxiety to make him believe that she was not taking too great a burden on her hands, she became slowly aware that no fear of this had apparently troubled him, and that he was looking at the whole matter from a point outside of questions of polite ceremonial, even of personal feeling.

She was vexed a little with his insensibility to the favour she meant the child, and she could not help trying to make him realise it. "I don't promise always to be the best guide, philosopher, and friend that Idella could have"—she took this light tone because she found herself afraid of him—"but I think I shall be a little improvement on some of her friends Over the Track. At least, if she wants my cat, she shall have it without fighting for it."

Mr. Peck looked up with question, and she went on to tell him of a struggle which she had seen one day between Idella and a small Irish boy for a kitten; it really belonged to the boy, but Idella carried it off.

The minister listened attentively. At the end: "Yes," he said, "that lust of possession is something all but impossible, even with constant care, to root out of children. I have tried to teach Idella that nothing is rightfully hers except while she can use it; but it is hard to make her understand, and when she is with other children she forgets."

Annie could not believe at first that he was serious, and then she was disposed to laugh. "Really, Mr. Peck," she began, "I can't think it's so important that a little thing like Idella should be kept from coveting a kitten as that she should be kept from using naughty words and from scratching and biting."

"I know," Mr. Peck consented. "That is the usual way of looking at such things."

"It seems to me," said Annie, "that it's the common-sense way."

"Perhaps. But upon the whole, I don't agree with you. It is bad for the child to use naughty words and to scratch and bite; that's part of the warfare in which we all live; but it's worse for her to covet, and to wish to keep others from having."

"I don't wonder you find it hard to make her understand that."

"Yes, it's hard with all of us. But if it is ever to be easier we must begin with the children."

He was silent, and Annie did not say anything. She was afraid that she had not helped her cause. "At least," she finally ventured, "you can't object to giving Idella a little rest from the fray. Perhaps if she finds that she can get things without fighting for them, she'll not covet them so much."

"Yes," he said, with a dim smile that left him sad again, "there is some truth in that. But I'm not sure that I have the right to give her advantages of any kind, to lift her above the lot, the chance, of the least fortunate——"

"Surely, we are bound to provide for those of our own household," said Annie.

"Who are those of our own household?" asked the minister. "All mankind are those of our own household. These are my mother and my brother and my sister."

"Yes, I know," said Annie, somewhat eagerly quitting this difficult ground. "But you can leave her with me at least till you get settled," she faltered, "if you don't wish it to be for longer."

"Perhaps it may not be for long," he answered, "if you mean my settlement in Hatboro'. I doubt," he continued, lifting his eyes to the question in hers, "whether I shall remain here."

"Oh, I hope you will," cried Annie. She thought she must make a pretence of misunderstanding him. "I supposed you were very much satisfied with your work here."

"I am not satisfied with myself in my work," replied the

minister; "and I know that I am far from acceptable to many others in it."

"You are acceptable to those who are best able to appreciate you, Mr. Peck," she protested, "and to people of every kind. I'm sure it's only a question of time when you will be thoroughly acceptable to all. I want you to understand, Mr. Peck," she added, "that I was shocked and ashamed the other night at your being tricked into countenancing a part of the entertainment you were promised should be dropped. I had nothing to do with it."

"It was very unimportant, after all," the minister said, "as far as I was concerned. In fact, I was interested to see the experiment of bringing the different grades of society together."

"It seems to me it was an utter failure," suggested Annie.

"Quite. But it was what I expected."

There appeared an uncandour in this which Annie could not let pass even if it imperilled her present object to bring up the matter of past contention. "But when we first talked of the Social Union you opposed it because it wouldn't bring the different classes together."

"Did you understand that? Then I failed to make myself clear. I wished merely to argue that the well-meaning ladies who suggested it were not intending a social union at all. In fact, such a union in our present condition of things, with its division of classes, is impossible—as Mrs. Munger's experiment showed—with the best will on both sides. But, as I said, the experiment was interesting, though unimportant, except as it resulted in heart-burning and offence."

They were on the same ground, but they had reached it from starting-points so opposite that Annie felt it very unsafe. In her fear of getting into some controversy with Mr. Peck that might interfere with her designs regarding Idella, she had a little insincerity in saying: "Mrs. Munger's bad faith in that was certainly unimportant compared with her part in poor Mr. Putney's misfortune. That was the worst thing; that's what I *can't* forgive."

Mr. Peck said nothing to this, and Annie, somewhat daunted by his silence, proceeded. "I've had the satisfaction of telling her what I thought on both points. But Ralph—Mr.

Putney—I hear, has escaped this time with less than his usual——"

She did not know what lady-like word to use for spree, and so she stopped.

Mr. Peck merely said, "He has shown great self-control;" and she perceived that he was not going to say more. He listened patiently to the reasons she gave for not having offered Mrs. Putney anything more than passive sympathy at a time when help could only have cumbered and kindness wounded her, but he made no sign of thinking them either necessary or sufficient. In the meantime he had not formally consented to Idella's remaining with her, and Annie prepared to lead back to that affair as artfully as she could.

"I really want you to believe, Mr. Peck, that I think very differently on *some* points from what I did when we first talked about the Social Union, and I have you to thank for seeing things in a new light. And you needn't," she added lightly, "be afraid of my contaminating Idella's mind with any wicked ideas. I'll do my best to keep her from coveting kittens or property of any kind; though I've always heard my father say that civilisation was founded upon the instinct of ownership, and that it was the only thing that had advanced the world. And if you dread the danger of giving her advantages, as you say, or bettering her worldly lot," she continued, with a smile for his quixotic scruples, "why, I'll do my best to reduce her blessings to a minimum; though I don't see why the poor little thing shouldn't get some good from the inequalities that there always must be in the world."

"I am not sure there always must be inequalities in the world," answered the minister.

"There always have been," cried Annie.

"There always had been slavery, up to a certain time," he replied.

"Oh, but surely you don't compare the two!" Annie pleaded with what she really regarded as a kind of lunacy in the good man. "In the freest society, I've heard my father say, there is naturally an upward and downward tendency; a perfect level is impossible. Some must rise, and some must sink."

"But what do you mean by rising? If you mean in material things, in wealth and the power over others that it gives——"

"I don't mean that altogether. But there are other ways—in cultivation, refinement, higher tastes and aims than the great mass of people can have. You have risen yourself, Mr. Peck."

"I have risen, as you call it," he said, with a meek sufferance of the application of the point to himself. "Those who rise above the necessity of work for daily bread are in great danger of losing their right relation to other men, as I said when we talked of this before."

A point had remained in Annie's mind from her first talk with Dr. Morrell. "Yes; and you said once that there could be no sympathy between the rich and the poor—no real love— because they had not had the same experience of life. But how is it about the poor who become rich? They have had the same experience."

"Too often they make haste to forget that they were poor; they become hard masters to those they have left behind them. They are eager to identify themselves with those who have been rich longer than they. Some working-men who now see this clearly have the courage to refuse to rise. Miss Kilburn, why should I let you take my child out of the conditions of self-denial and self-help to which she was born?"

"I don't know," said Annie rather blankly. Then she added impetuously: "Because I love her and want her. I don't—I *won't*—pretend that it's for her sake. It's for *my* sake, though I can take better care of her than you can. But I'm all alone in the world; I've neither kith nor kin; nothing but my miserable money. I've set my heart on the child; I must have her. At least let me keep her a while. I will be honest with you, Mr. Peck. If I find I'm doing her harm and not good, I'll give her up. I should wish you to feel that she is yours as much as ever, and if you *will* feel so, and come often to see her—I—I shall—be very glad, and——" she stopped, and Mr. Peck rose.

"Where is the child?" he asked, with a troubled air; and she silently led the way to the kitchen, and left him at the door to Idella and the Boltons. When she ventured back later he was gone, but the child remained.

Half exultant and half ashamed, she promised herself that

she really would be true as far as possible to the odd notions of the minister in her treatment of his child. When she undressed Idella for bed she noticed again the shabbiness of her poor little clothes. She went through the bureau that held her own childish things once more, but found them all too large for Idella, and too hopelessly antiquated. She said to herself that on this point at least she must be a law to herself.

She went down to see Mrs. Bolton. "Isn't there some place in the village where they have children's ready-made clothes for sale?" she asked.

"Mr. Gerrish's," said Mrs. Bolton briefly.

Annie shook her head, drawing in her breath. "I shouldn't want to go there. Is there nowhere else?"

"There's a Jew place. They say he cheats."

"I dare say he doesn't cheat more than most Christians," said Annie, jumping from her chair. "I'll try the Jew place. I want you to come with me, Mrs. Bolton."

They went together, and found a dress that they both decided would fit Idella, and a hat that matched it.

"I don't know as he'd like to have anything quite so nice," said Mrs. Bolton coldly.

"I don't know as he has anything to say about it," said Annie, mimicking Mrs. Bolton's accent and syntax.

They both meant Mr. Peck. Mrs. Bolton turned away to hide her pleasure in Annie's audacity and extravagance.

"Want I should carry 'em?" she asked, when they were out of the store.

"No, I can carry them," said Annie.

She put them where Idella must see them as soon as she woke.

It was late before she slept, and Idella's voice broke upon her dreams. The child was sitting up in her bed, gloating upon the dress and hat hung and perched upon the chair-back in the middle of the room. "Oh, whose is it? Whose is it? Whose is it?" she screamed; and as Annie lifted herself on her elbow, and looked over at her: "Is it mine? Is it mine?"

Annie had thought of playing some joke; of pretending not to understand; of delaying the child's pleasure; playing with it; teasing. But in the face of this rapturous longing, she could only answer, "Yes."

"Mine? My very own? To have? To keep always?"

"Yes."

Idella sprang from her bed, and flew upon the things with a primitive, greedy transport in their possession. She could scarcely be held long enough to be washed before the dress could be put on.

"Be careful—be careful not to get it soiled now," said Annie.

"No; I won't spoil it." She went quietly down-stairs, and when Annie followed, she found her posing before the long pier-glass in the parlour, and twisting and turning for this effect and that. All the morning she moved about prim and anxious; the wild-wood flower was like a hot-house blossom wired for a bouquet. At the church door she asked Idella, "Would you rather sit with Mrs. Bolton?"

"No, no," gasped the child intensely; "with *you!*" and she pushed her hand into Annie's, and held fast to it.

Annie's question had been suggested by a belated reluctance to appear before so much of Hatboro' in charge of the minister's child. But now she could not retreat, and with Idella's hand in hers she advanced blushing up the aisle to her pew.

XXII.

THE FARMERS' carry-alls filled the long shed beside the church, and their leathern faces looked up, with their wives' and children's, at Mr. Peck where he sat high behind the pulpit; a patient expectance suggested itself in the men's bald or grizzled crowns, and in the fantastic hats and bonnets of their women folks. The village ladies were all in the perfection of their street costumes, and they compared well with three or four of the ladies from South Hatboro', but the men with them spoiled all by the inadequacy of their fashion. Mrs. Gates, the second of her name, was very stylish, but the provision-man had honestly the effect of having got for the day only into the black coat which he had bought ready-made for his first wife's funeral. Mr. Wilmington, who appeared much shorter than his wife as he sat beside her, was as much inferior to her in dress; he wore, with the carelessness of a rich man who could afford simplicity, a loose alpaca coat and a cambric neckcloth, over which he twisted his shrivelled neck to catch sight of Annie, as she rustled up the aisle. Mrs. Gerrish—so much as could be seen of her—was a mound of bugled velvet, topped by a small bonnet, which seemed to have gone much to a fat black pompon; she sat far within her pew, and their children stretched in a row from her side to that of Mr. Gerrish, next the door. He did not look round at Annie, but kept an attitude of fixed self-concentration, in harmony with the severe old-school respectability of his dress; his wife leaned well forward to see, and let all her censure appear in her eyes.

Colonel Marvin, of the largest shoe-shop, showed the side of his large florid face, with the kindly smile that seemed to hang loosely upon it; and there was a good number of the hat-shop and shoe-shop hands of different ages and sexes scattered about. The gallery, commonly empty or almost so, showed groups and single figures dropped about here and there on its seats.

The Putneys were in their pew, the little lame boy between the father and mother, as their custom was. They each looked up at her as she passed, and smiled in the slight measure of recognition which people permit themselves in church. Putney was sitting with his head hanging forward in pathetic dejection; his face, when he first lifted it to look at Annie in passing, was haggard, but otherwise there was no consciousness in it of what had passed since they had sat there the Sunday before. When his glance took in Idella too, in her sudden finery, a light of friendly mocking came into it, and seemed to comment the relation Annie had assumed to the child.

Annie's pew was just in front of Lyra's, and Lyra pursed her mouth in burlesque surprise as Annie got into it with Idella and turned round to lift the child to the seat. While Mr. Peck was giving out the hymn, Lyra leaned forward and whispered—

"Don't imagine that this turnout is *all* on your account, Annie. He's going to preach against the Social Union and the social glass."

The banter echoed a mechanical expectation in Annie's heart, which was probably present in many others there. It was some time before she could cast it out, even after he had taken his text, "I am the Resurrection and the Life," and she followed him with a mechanical disappointment at his failure to meet it.

He began by saying that he wished to dissociate his text in his hearers' minds from the scent of the upturned earth, and the fall of clods upon the coffin lid, and he asked them to join him in attempting to find in it another meaning beside that which it usually carried. He believed that those words of Christ ought to speak to us of this world as well as the next, and enjoin upon us the example which we might all find in Him, as well as promise us immortality with Him. As the minister went on, Annie followed him with the interest which her belief that she heard between the words inspired, and occasionally in a discontent with what seemed a mystical, almost a fantastical, quality of his thought.

"There is an evolution," he continued, "in the moral as well as in the material world, and good unfolds in greater good; that which was once best ceases to be in that which is better. In the political world we have striven forward to liberty as to the final good, but with this achieved we find that liberty is only a means and not an end, and that we shall abuse it as a means if we do not use it, even sacrifice it, to promote equality; or in other words, equality is the perfect work, the evolution of liberty. Patriotism has been the virtue which has secured an image of brotherhood, rude and imperfect, to large numbers of men within certain limits, but nationality must perish before the universal ideal of fraternity is realised. Charity is the holiest of the agencies which have hitherto wrought to redeem the race from savagery and despair; but there is something holier yet than charity, something higher, something purer and further from selfishness, something into which charity shall willingly grow and cease, and that is *justice*. Not the justice of our Christless codes, with their penalties, but the instinct of righteous shame which, however dumbly, however obscurely, stirs in every honest man's heart when his superfluity is confronted with another's destitution, and which is destined to increase in power till it becomes the social as well as the individual conscience. Then, in the truly Christian state, there shall be no more asking and no more giving, no more gratitude and no more merit, no more charity, but only and evermore justice; all shall share alike, and want and luxury and killing toil and heartless indolence shall all cease together.

"It is in the spirit of this justice that I believe Christ shall come to judge the world; not to condemn and punish so much as to reconcile and to right. We live in an age of seeming preparation for indefinite war. The lines are drawn harder and faster between the rich and the poor, and on either side the forces are embattled. The working-men are combined in vast organisations to withstand the strength of the capitalists, and these are taking the lesson and uniting in trusts. The smaller industries are gone, and the smaller commerce is being devoured by the larger. Where many little shops existed one huge factory assembles manufacture; one large store, in which many different branches of trade are united, swallows up the small dealers. Yet in the labour organisations, which have their bad side, their weak side, through which the forces of hell enter, I see evidence of the fact that the poor have at last had pity on the poor, and will no more betray and underbid and desert one another, but will stand and fall together as brothers; and the monopolies, though they are founded upon ruin, though they know no pity and no relenting, have a final significance which we must not lose sight of. They prophesy the end of competition; *they eliminate* one element of strife, of rivalry, of warfare. But woe to them through whose evil this good comes, to any man who prospers on to ease and fortune, forgetful or ignorant of the ruin on which his success is built. For that death the resurrection and the life seem not to be. Whatever his creed or his religious profession, his state is more pitiable than that of the sceptic, whose words perhaps deny Christ, but whose works affirm Him. There has been much anxiety in the Church for the future of the world abandoned to the godlessness of science, but I cannot share it. If God is, nothing exists but from Him. He directs the very reason that questions Him, and Christ rises anew in the doubt of him that the sins of Christendom inspire. So far from dreading such misgiving as comes from contemplating the disparity between the Church's profession and her performance, I welcome it as another resurrection and a new life."

The minister paused and seemed about to resume, when a scuffling and knocking noise drew all eyes toward the pew of the Gerrish family. Mr. Gerrish had risen and flung open the door so sharply that it struck against the frame-work of the pew, and he stood pulling his children, whom Mrs. Gerrish urged from behind, one after another, into the aisle beside him. One of them had been asleep, and he now gave way to the alarm which seizes a small boy suddenly awakened. His mother tried to still him, stooping over him and twitching him by the hand, with repeated " 'Sh! 'sh's!" as mothers do, till her husband got her before him, and marched his family down the aisle and out of the door. The noise of their feet over the floor of the vestibule died away upon the stone steps outside. The minister allowed the pause he had made to prolong itself painfully. He wavered, after clearing his throat, as if to go on with his sermon, and then he said sadly, "Let us pray!"

XXIII.

PUTNEY STOPPED with his wife and boy and waited for Annie at the corner of the street where their ways parted. She had eluded Lyra Wilmington in coming down the aisle, and she had hurried to escape the sensation which broke into eager talk among the people before they got out of church, and which began with question whether one of the Gerrish children was sick, and ended in the more satisfactory conviction that Mr. Gerrish was offended at something in the sermon.

"Well, Annie," said Putney, with a satirical smile.

"Oh, Ralph—Ellen—what does it mean?"

"It means that Brother Gerrish thought Mr. Peck was hitting at him in that talk about the large commerce, and it means business," said Putney. "Brother Gerrish has made a beginning, and I guess it's the beginning of the end, unless we're all ready to take hold against him. What are you going to do?"

"Do? Anything! Everything! It was abominable! It was atrocious!" she shuddered out with disgust. "How could he imagine that Mr. Peck would do such a thing?"

"Well, he's imagined it. But he doesn't mean to stay out of church; he means to put Brother Peck out."

"We mustn't let him. That would be outrageous."

"That's the way Ellen and I feel about it," said Putney; "but we don't know how much of a party there is with us."

"But everybody—everybody must feel the same way about Mr. Gerrish's behaviour? I don't see how you can be so quiet about it—you and Ellen!"

Annie looked from one to another indignantly, and Putney laughed.

"We're not *feeling* quietly about it," said Mrs. Putney.

Putney took out a piece of tobacco, and bit off a large corner, and began to chew vehemently upon it. "Hello, Idella!" he said to the little girl, holding by Annie's hand and looking up intently at him, with childish interest in what he was eating. "What a pretty dress you've got on!"

"It's mine," said the child. "To keep."

"Is that so? Well, it's a beauty."

"I'm going to wear it all the time."

"Is that so? Well, now, you and Winthrop step on ahead a little; I want to see how you look in it. Splendid!" he said, as she took the boy's hand and looked back over her shoulder for Putney's applause. "Lyra tells us you've adopted her for the time being, Annie. I guess you'll have your hands full. But, as I was going to say, about feeling differently, my experience is that there's always a good-sized party for the perverse, simply because it seems to answer a need in human nature. There's a fascination in it; a man feels as if there must be something in it besides the perversity, and because it's so obviously wrong it must be right. Don't you believe but what a good half of the people in church to-day are pretty sure that Gerrish had a good reason for behaving indecently. The very fact that he did so carries conviction to some minds, and those are the minds we have got to deal with. When he gets up in the next Society meeting there's a mighty great danger that he'll have a strong party to back him."

"I can't believe it," Annie broke out, but she was greatly troubled. "What do you think, Ellen; that there's any danger of his carrying the day against Mr. Peck?"

"There's a great deal of dissatisfaction with Mr. Peck already, you know, and I guess Ralph's right about the rest of it."

"Well, I'm glad I've taken a pew. I'm with you for Mr. Peck, Ralph, heart and soul."

"As Brother Brandreth says about the Social Union. Well, that's right. I shall count upon you. And speaking of the Social Union, I haven't seen you, Annie, since that night at Mrs. Munger's. I suppose you don't expect me to say anything in self-defence?"

"No, Ralph, and you needn't; *I've* defended you sufficiently—justified you."

"That won't do," said Putney. "Ellen and I have thought that all out, and we find that I—or something that stood for me—was to blame, whoever else was to blame, too; we won't mention the hospitable Mrs. Munger. When Dr. Morrell had to go away Brother Peck took hold with me, and he suggested good resolutions. I told him I'd tried 'em, and they never did me the least good; but his sort really seemed to work. I don't know whether they would work again; Ellen thinks they would. *I* think we sha'n't ever need anything again; but that's what I always think when I come out of it—like a man with chills and fever."

"It was Dr. Morrell who asked Mr. Peck to come," said Mrs. Putney; "and it turned out for the best. Ralph got well quicker than he ever did before. Of course, Annie," she explained, "it must seem strange to you hearing us talk of it as if it were a disease; but that's just like what it is—a raging disease; and I can't feel differently about anything that happens in it, though I do blame people for it." Annie followed with tender interest the loving pride that exonerated and idealised Putney in the words of the woman who had suffered so much with him, and must suffer. "I couldn't help speaking as I did to Mrs. Munger."

"She deserved it every word," said Annie. "I wonder you didn't say more."

"Oh, hold on!" Putney interposed. "We'll allow that the local influences were malarial, but I guess we can't excuse the invalid altogether. That's Brother Peck's view; and I must say I found it decidedly tonic; it helped to brace me up."

"I think he was too severe with you altogether," said his wife.

Putney laughed. "It was all I could do to keep Ellen from getting up and going out of church too, when Brother Gerrish set the example. She's a Gerrishite at heart."

"Well, remember, Ralph," said Annie, "that I'm with you in whatever you do to defeat that man. It's a good cause—a righteous cause—the cause of justice; and we must do everything for it," she said fervently.

"Yes, any enormity is justifiable against injustice," he suggested, "or the unjust; it's the same thing."

"You know I don't mean that. I can trust you."

"I shall keep within the law, at any rate," said Putney.

"Well, Mrs. Bolton!" Annie called out, when she entered her house, and she pushed on into the kitchen; she had not the patience to wait for her to bring in the dinner before speaking about the exciting event at church. But Mrs. Bolton would not be led up to the subject by a tacit invitation, and after a suspense in which her zeal for Mr. Peck began to take a colour of resentment toward Mrs. Bolton, Annie demanded, "What do you think of Mr. Gerrish's scandalous behaviour?"

Mrs. Bolton gave herself time to put a stick of wood into the stove, and to punch it with the stove-lid handle before answering. "I don't know as it's anything more than I expected."

Annie went on: "It was shameful! Do you suppose he really thought Mr. Peck was referring to him in his sermon?"

"I presume he felt the cap fit. But if it hadn't b'en one thing, 'twould b'en another. Mr. Peck was bound to roil the brook for Mr. Gerrish's drinkin', wherever he stood, up stream or down."

"Yes. He *is* a wolf! A wolf in sheep's clothing," said Annie excitedly.

"I d'know as you can call him a *wolf*, exactly," returned Mrs. Bolton dryly. "He's got his good points, I presume."

Annie was astounded. "Why, Mrs. Bolton, you're surely not going to justify him?"

Mrs. Bolton erected herself from cutting a loaf of her best bread into slices, and stood with the knife in her hand, like a figure of Justice. "Well, I *guess* you no need to ask me a question like that, Miss Kilburn. I hain't obliged to make up to Mr. Peck, though, for what I done in the beginnin' by condemnin' everybuddy else without mercy now." Mrs. Bolton's eyes did not flash fire, but they sent out an icy gleam that went as sharply to Annie's heart.

Bolton came in from feeding the horse and cow in the barn, with a mealy tin pan in his hand, from which came a mild, subdued radiance like that of his countenance. He was not sensible of arriving upon a dramatic moment, and he said, without noticing the attitude of either lady: "I see you walkin' home with Mr. Putney, Miss Kilburn. What'd *he* say?"

"You mean about Mr. Gerrish? He thinks as we all do; that it was a challenge to Mr. Peck's friends, and that we must take it up."

A light of melancholy satisfaction shone from Bolton's deeply shaded eyes. "Well, he ain't one to lose time, not a great deal. I presume he's goin' to work?"

"At once," said Annie. "He says Mr. Gerrish will be sure to

bring his grievance up at the next Society meeting, and we must be ready to meet him, and out-talk him and out-vote him." She reported these phrases from Putney's lips.

"Well, I guess if it was out-talkin', Mr. Putney wouldn't have much trouble about it. And as far forth as votin' goes, I don't believe but what we can carry the day."

"We couldn't," said Mrs. Bolton from the pantry, where she had gone to put the bread away in its stone jar, "if it was left to the church." She accented the last word with the click of the jar lid, and came out.

"Well, it ain't a church question. It's a Society question."

Mrs. Bolton replied, on her passage to the dining-room with the plate of sliced bread: "I can't make it seem right to have the minister a Society question. Seems to me that the church members 'd ought have the say."

"Well, you can't make the discipline over to suit everybody," said Bolton. "I presume it was ordered for a wise purpose."

"Why, land alive, Oliver Bolton," his wife shouted back from the remoteness to which his words had followed her, "the statute provisions and rules of the Society wa'n't ordered by Providence."

"Well, not directly, as you may say," said Bolton, beginning high, and lowering his voice as she rejoined them, "but I presume the hearts of them that made them was moved."

Mrs. Bolton could not combat a position of such unimpregnable piety in words, but she permitted herself a contemptuous sniff, and went on getting the things into the dining-room.

"And I guess it's all goin' to work together for good. I ain't afraid any but what it's goin' to come out all right. But we got to be up and doin', as they say about 'lection times. The Lord helps them that helps themselves," said Bolton, and then, as if he felt the weakness of this position as compared with that of entire trust in Providence, he winked his mild eyes, and added, "if they're on the right side, and put their faith in His promises."

"Well, your dinner's ready now," Mrs. Bolton said to Annie.

Idella had clung fast to Annie's hand; as Annie started toward the dining-room she got before her, and whispered vehemently.

"What?" asked Annie, bending down; she laughed, in lifting her head, "I promised Idella you'd let us have some preserves to-day, Mrs. Bolton."

Mrs. Bolton smiled with grim pleasure. "I see all the while her mind was set on something. She ain't one to let you forget *your* promises. Well, I guess if Mr. Peck had a little more of *her* disposition there wouldn't be much doubt about the way it would all come out."

"Well, you don't often see pairents take after their children," said Bolton, venturing a small joke.

"No, nor husbands after their wives, either," said Mrs. Bolton sharply. "The more's the pity."

XXIV.

D R. MORRELL came to see Annie late the next Wednesday evening.

"I didn't know you'd come back," she said. She returned to the rocking-chair, from which she came forward to greet him, and he dropped into an easy seat near the table piled with books and sewing.

"I didn't know it myself half an hour ago."

"Really? And is this your first visit? I must be a very interesting case."

"You are—always. How have you been?"

"I? I hardly know whether I've been at all," she answered, in mechanical parody of his own reply. "So many other things have been of so much more importance."

She let her eyes rest full upon his, with a sense of returning comfort and safety in his presence, and after a deep breath of satisfaction, she asked, "How did you leave your mother?"

"Very much better—entirely out of danger."

"It's so odd to think of any one's having a family. To me it seems the normal condition not to have any relatives."

"Well, we can't very well dispense with mothers," said the doctor. "We have to begin with them, at any rate."

"Oh, I don't object to them. I only wonder at them."

They fell into a cosy and mutually interesting talk about their separate past, and he gave her glimpses of the life, simple and studious, he had led before he went abroad. She confessed to two mistakes in which she had mechanically persisted concerning him; one that he came from Charlestown instead of Chelsea, and the other that his first name was Joseph instead of James. She did not own that she had always thought it odd he should be willing to remain in a place like Hatboro', and that it must argue a strangely unambitious temperament in a man of his ability. She diverted the impulse to a general satire of village life, and ended by saying that she was getting to be a perfect villager herself.

He laughed, and then, "How has Hatboro' been getting along?" he asked.

"Simply seething with excitement," she answered. "But I

should hardly know where to begin if I tried to tell you," she added. "It seems such an age since I saw you."

"Thank you," said the doctor.

"I didn't mean to be *quite* so flattering; but you have certainly marked an epoch. Really, I *don't* know where to begin. I wish you'd seen somebody else first—Ralph and Ellen, or Mrs. Wilmington."

"I might go and see them now."

"No; stay, now you're here, though I know I shall not do justice to the situation." But she was able to possess him of it with impartiality, even with a little humour, all the more because she was at heart intensely partisan and serious. "No one knows what Mr. Gerrish intends to do next. He has kept quietly about his business; and he told some of the ladies who tried to interview him that he was not prepared to talk about the course he had taken. He doesn't seem to be ashamed of his behaviour; and Ralph thinks that he's either satisfied with it, and intends to let it stand as a protest, or else he's going to strike another blow on the next business meeting. But he's even kept Mrs. Gerrish quiet, and all we can do is to unite Mr. Peck's friends provisionally. Ralph's devoted himself to that, and he says he has talked forty-eight hours to the day ever since."

"Is he——"

"Yes; perfectly! I could hardly believe it when I saw him at church on Sunday. It was like seeing one risen from the dead. What he must have gone through, and Ellen! She told me how Mr. Peck had helped him in the struggle. She attributes everything to him. But of course you think he had nothing to do with it."

"What makes you think that?" he asked.

"Oh, I don't know. Wouldn't that naturally be the attitude of Science?"

"Toward religion? Perhaps. But I'm not Science—with a large S. May be that's the reason why I left the case with Mr. Peck," said the doctor, smiling. "Putney didn't leave off my medicine, did he?"

"He never got well so soon before. They both say that. I didn't think you could be so narrow-minded, Dr. Morrell. But of course your scientific bigotry couldn't admit the effect of the moral influence. It would be too much like a miracle; you would have to allow for a mystery."

"I have to allow for a good many," said the doctor. "The world is full of mysteries for me, if you mean things that science hasn't explored yet. But I hope that they'll all yield to the light, and that somewhere there'll be light enough to clear up even the spiritual mysteries."

"Do you really?" she demanded eagerly. "Then you believe in a life hereafter? You believe in a moral government of the——"

He retreated, laughing, from her ardent pursuit. "Oh, I'm not going to commit myself. But I'll go so far as to say that I like to hear Mr. Peck preach, and that I want him to stay. I don't say he had nothing to do with Putney's straightening up. Putney had a great deal to do with it himself. What does he think Mr. Peck's chances are?"

"If Mr. Gerrish tries to get him dismissed? He doesn't know; he's quite in the dark. He says the party of the perverse—the people who think Mr. Gerrish must have had some good reason for his behaviour, simply because they can't see any—is unexpectedly large; and it doesn't help matters with the more respectable people that the most respectable, like Mr. Wilmington and Colonel Marvin, are Mr. Peck's friends. They think there must be something wrong if such good men are opposed to Mr. Gerrish."

"And I suspect," said Dr. Morrell soberly, "that Putney's championship isn't altogether an advantage. The people all concede his brilliancy, and they are prouder of him on account of his infirmity; but I guess they like to feel their superiority to him in practical matters. They admire him, but they don't want to follow him."

"Oh, I suppose so," said Annie disconsolately. "And I imagine that Mr. Wilmington's course is attributed to Lyra, and that doesn't help Mr. Peck much with the husbands of the ladies who don't approve of her."

The doctor tacitly declined to touch this delicate point. He asked, after a pause, "You'll be at the meeting?"

"I couldn't keep away. But I've no vote, that's the worst. I can only suffer in the cause." The doctor smiled. "You must go, too," she added eagerly.

"Oh, I shall go; I couldn't keep away either. Besides, I can vote. How are you getting on with your little *protégée?*"

"Idella? Well, it isn't such a simple matter as I supposed, quite. Did you ever hear anything about her mother?"

"Nothing more than what every one has. Why?" asked the doctor, with scientific curiosity. "Do you find traits that the father doesn't account for?"

"Yes. She is very vain and greedy and quick-tempered."

"Are those traits uncommon in children?"

"In such a degree I should think they were. But she's very affectionate, too, and you can do anything with her through her love of praise. She puzzles me a good deal. I wish I knew something about her mother. But Mr. Peck himself is a puzzle. With all my respect for him and regard and admiration, I can't help seeing that he's a very imperfect character."

Doctor Morrell laughed. "There's a great deal of human nature in man."

"There isn't enough in Mr. Peck," Annie retorted. "From the very first he has said things that have stirred me up and put me in a fever; but he always seems to be cold and passive himself."

"Perhaps he *is* cold," said the doctor.

"But has he any *right* to be so?" retorted Annie, with certainly no coldness of her own.

"Well, I don't know. I never thought of the right or wrong of a man's being what he was born. Perhaps we might justly blame his ancestors."

Annie broke into a laugh at herself: "Of course. But don't you think that a man who is able to put things as he does— who can make you see, for example, the stupidity and cruelty of things that always seemed right and proper before—don't you think that he's guilty of a kind of hypocrisy if he doesn't *feel* as well as see?"

"No, I can't say that I do," said the doctor, with pleasure in the feminine excess of her demand. "And there are so many ways of feeling. We're apt to think that our own way is the only way, of course; but I suppose that most philanthropists—men who have done the most to better conditions— have been people of cold temperaments; and yet you can't say they are unfeeling."

"No, certainly. Do you think Mr. Peck is a real philanthropist?"

"How you do get back to the personal always!" said Dr. Morrell. "What makes you ask?"

"Because I can't understand his indifference to his child. It seems to me that real philanthropy would begin at home. But twice he has distinctly forgotten her existence, and he always seems bored with it. Or not that quite; but she seems no more to him than any other child."

"There's something very curious about all that," said the doctor. "In most things the greater includes the less, but in philanthropy it seems to exclude it. If a man's heart is open to the whole world, to all men, it's shut sometimes against the individual, even the nearest and dearest. You see I'm willing to admit all you can say against a rival practitioner."

"Oh, I understand," said Annie. "But I'm not going to gratify your spite." At the same time she tacitly consented to the slight for Mr. Peck which their joking about him involved. In such cases we excuse our disloyalty as merely temporary, and intend to turn serious again and make full amends for it. "He made very short work," she continued, "of that notion of yours that there could be any good feeling between the poor and the rich who had once been poor themselves."

"Did I have any such notion as that?"

She recalled the time and place of its expression to him, and he said, "Oh yes! Well?"

"He says that rich people like that are apt to be the hardest masters, and are eager to forget they ever were poor, and are only anxious to identify themselves with the rich."

Dr. Morrell seemed to enjoy this immensely. "That does rather settle it," he said recreantly.

She tried to be severe with him, but he only kept on laughing and joking; she was aware that he was luring her away from her seriousness.

Mrs. Bolton brought in the lamp, and set it on the library table, showing her gaunt outline a moment against it before she left it to throw its softened light into the parlour where they sat. The autumn moonshine, almost as mellow, fell in through the open windows, which let in the shrilling of the crickets and grasshoppers, and wafts of the warm night wind.

"Does life," Annie was asking, at the end of half an hour, "seem more simple or more complicated as you live on? That sounds awfully abstruse, doesn't it? And I don't know why I'm always asking you abstruse things, but I am."

"Oh, I don't mind it," said the doctor. "Perhaps I haven't lived on long enough to answer this particular question; I'm only thirty-six, you know."

"*Only?* I'm thirty-one, and I feel a hundred!" she broke in.

"You don't look it. But I believe I rather like abstruse questions. You know Putney and I have discussed a great many. But just what do you mean by this particular abstraction?"

He took from the table a large ivory paper-knife which he was in the habit of playing with in his visits, and laid first one side and then the other side of its smooth cool blade in the palm of his left hand, as he leaned forward, with his elbows on his knees, and bent his smiling eyes keenly upon her.

She stopped rocking herself, and said imperatively, "Will you please put that back, Dr. Morrell?"

"This paper-knife?"

"Yes. And not look at me just in that way? When you get that knife and that look, I feel a little too much as if you were diagnosing me."

"Diagnosticating," suggested the doctor.

"Is it? I always supposed it was diagnosing. But it doesn't matter. It wasn't the name I was objecting to."

He put the knife back and changed his posture, with a smile that left nothing of professional scrutiny in his look. "Very well, then; you shall diagnose yourself."

"Diagnosticate, please."

"Oh, I thought you preferred the other."

"No, it sounds undignified, now that I know there's a larger word. Where was I?"

"The personal bearing of the question whether life isn't more and more complicated?"

"How did you know it had a personal bearing?"

"I suspected as much."

"Yes, it has. I mean that within the last four or five months—since I've been in Hatboro'—I seem to have lost my old point of view; or, rather, I don't find it satisfactory any more. I'm ashamed to think of the simple plans, or dreams, that I came home with. I hardly remember what they were; but I must have expected to be a sort of Lady Bountiful here; and now I think a Lady Bountiful one of the most mischievous persons that could infest any community."

"You don't mean that charity is played out?" asked the doctor.

"In the old-fashioned way, yes."

"But they say poverty is on the increase. What is to be done?"

"Justice," said Annie. "Those who do most of the work in the world ought to share in its comforts as a right, and not be put off with what we idlers have a mind to give them from our superfluity as a grace."

"Yes, that's all very true. But what till justice *is* done?"

"Oh, we must continue to do charity," cried Annie, with self-contempt that amused him. "But don't you see how much more complicated it is? That's what I meant by life not being simple any more. It was easy enough to do charity when it used to seem the right and proper remedy for suffering; but now, when I can't make it appear a finality, but only something provisional, temporary—— Don't you see?"

"Yes, I see. But I don't see how you're going to help it. At the same time, I'll allow that it makes life more difficult."

For a moment they were both serious and silent. Then she said: "Sometimes I think the fault is all in myself, and that if I were not so sophisticated and—and—selfish, I should find the old way of doing good just as effective and natural as ever. Then again, I think the conditions are all wrong, and that we ought to be fairer to people, and then we needn't be so good to them. I should prefer that. I hate being good to people I don't like, and I can't like people who don't interest me. I think I must be very hard-hearted."

The doctor laughed at this.

"Oh, I know," said Annie, "I know the fraudulent reputation I've got for good works."

"Your charity to tramps is the opprobrium of Hatboro'," the doctor consented.

"Oh, I don't mind that. It's easy when people ask you for food or money, but the horrible thing is when they ask you for work. Think of me, who never did anything to earn a cent in my life, being humbly asked by a fellow-creature to let him work for something to eat and drink! It's hideous! It's abominable! At first I used to be flattered by it, and try to conjure up something for them to do, and to believe that I was helping the deserving poor. Now I give all of them money, and tell them that they needn't even pretend to work for it. *I* don't work for my money, and I don't see why they should."

"They'd find that an unanswerable argument if you put it to them," said the doctor. He reached out his hand for the paper-cutter, and then withdrew it in a way that made her laugh.

"But the worst of it is," she resumed, "that I don't love any of the people that I help, or hurt, whichever it is. I did feel remorseful toward Mrs. Savor for a while, but I didn't love her, and I knew that I only pitied myself through her. Don't you see?"

"No, I don't," said the doctor.

"You don't, because you're too polite. The only kind of creature that I can have any sympathy with is some little wretch like Idella, who is perfectly selfish and naughty every way, but seems to want me to like her, and a reprobate like Lyra, or some broken creature like poor Ralph. I think there's something in the air, the atmosphere, that won't allow you to live in the old way if you've got a grain of conscience or humanity. I don't mean that *I* have. But it seems to me as if the world couldn't go on as it has been doing. Even here in America, where I used to think we had the millennium because slavery was abolished, people have more liberty, but they seem just as far off as ever from justice. That is what paralyses me and mocks me and laughs in my face when I remember how I used to dream of doing good after I came home. I had better stayed at Rome."

The doctor said vaguely, "I'm glad you didn't," and he let his eyes dwell on her with a return of the professional interest which she was too lost in her self-reproach to be able to resent.

"I blame myself for trying to excuse my own failure on the plea that things generally have gone wrong. At times it seems to me that I'm responsible for having lost my faith in what I used to think was the right thing to do; and then again it seems as if the world were all so bad that no real good could be done in the old way, and that my faith is gone because there's nothing for it to rest on any longer. I feel that something must be done; but I don't know what."

"It would be hard to say," said the doctor.

She perceived that her exaltation amused him, but she was too much in earnest to care. "Then we are guilty—all guilty—till we find out and begin to do it. If the world has come to such a pass that you can't do anything but harm in it——"

"Oh, is it so bad as that?" he protested.

"It's *quite* as bad," she insisted. "Just see what mischief I've done since I came back to Hatboro'. I took hold of that miserable Social Union because I was outside of all the life about me, and it seemed my only chance of getting into it; and I've done more harm by it in one summer than I could undo in a lifetime. Just think of poor Mr. Brandreth's love affair with Miss Chapley broken off, and Lyra's lamentable triumph over Miss Northwick, and Mrs. Munger's duplicity, and Ralph's escapade—all because I wanted to do good!"

A note of exaggeration had begun to prevail in her self-upbraiding, which was real enough, and the time came for him to suggest, "I think you're a little morbid, Miss Kilburn."

"Morbid? Of course I am! But that doesn't alter the fact that everything is wrong, does it?"

"Everything?"

"Why, you don't pretend yourself, do you, that everything is right?"

"A true American ought to do so, oughtn't he?" teased the doctor. "One mustn't be a bad citizen."

"But if you *were* a bad citizen?" she persisted.

"Oh, then I might agree with you on some points. But I shouldn't say such things to my patients, Miss Kilburn."

"It would be a great comfort to them if you did," she sighed.

The doctor broke out in a laugh of delight at her perfervid concentration. "Oh, no, no! They're mostly nervous women, and it would be the death of them—if they understood me. In fact, what's the use of brooding upon such ideas? We can't hurry any change, but we can make ourselves uncomfortable."

"Why should I be comfortable?" she asked, with a solemnity that made him laugh again.

"Why shouldn't you be?"

"Yes, that's what I often ask myself. But I can't be," she said sadly.

They had risen, and he looked at her with his professional interest now openly dominant, as he stood holding her hand. "I'm going to send you a little more of that tonic, Miss Kilburn."

She pulled her hand away. "No, I shall not take any more medicine. You think everything is physical. Why don't you ask at once to see my tongue?"

He went out laughing, and she stood looking wistfully at the door he had passed through.

XXV.

THE BELL on the orthodox church called the members of Mr. Peck's society together for the business meeting with the same plangent, lacerant note that summoned them to worship on Sundays. Among those who crowded the house were many who had not been there before, and seldom in any place of the kind. There were admirers of Putney: workmen of rebellious repute and of advanced opinions on social and religious questions; nonsuited plaintiffs and defendants of shady record, for whom he had at one time or another done what he could. A good number of the summer folk from South Hatboro' were present, with the expectation of something dramatic, which every one felt, and every one hid with the discipline that subdues the outside of life in a New England town to a decorous passivity.

At the appointed time Mr. Peck rose to open the meeting with prayer; then, as if nothing unusual were likely to come before it, he declared it ready to proceed to business. Some people who had been gathering in the vestibule during his prayer came in; and the electric globes, which had been recently hung above the pulpit and on the front of the gallery in substitution of the old gas chandelier, shed their moony glare upon a house in which few places were vacant. Mr. Gerrish, sitting erect and solemn beside his wife in their pew, shared with the minister and Putney the tacit interest of the audience.

He permitted the transaction of several minor affairs, and Mr. Peck, as Moderator, conducted the business with his habitual exactness and effect of far-off impersonality. The people waited with exemplary patience, and Putney, who lounged in one corner of his pew, gave no more sign of excitement, with his chin sunk in his rumpled shirt-front, than his sad-faced wife at the other end of the seat.

Mr. Gerrish rose, with the air of rising in his own good time, and said, with dry pomp, "Mr. Moderator, I have prepared a resolution, which I will ask you to read to this meeting."

He held up a paper as he spoke, and then passed it to the minister, who opened and read it—

"*Whereas,* It is indispensable to the prosperity and well-being of any and every organisation, and especially of a Christian church, that the teachings of its minister be in accord with the convictions of a majority of its members upon vital questions of eternal interest, with the end and aim of securing the greatest efficiency of that body in the community, as an example and a shining light before men to guide their steps in the strait and narrow path; therefore

"*Resolved,* That a committee of this society be appointed to inquire if such is the case in the instance of the Rev. Julius W. Peck, and be instructed to report upon the same."

A satisfied expectation expressed itself in the silence that followed the reading of the paper, whatever pain and shame were mixed with the satisfaction. If the contempt of kindly usage shown in offering such a resolution without warning or private notice to the minister shocked many by its brutality, still it was satisfactory to find that Mr. Gerrish had intended to seize the first chance of airing his grievance, as everybody had said he would do.

Mr. Peck looked up from the paper and across the intervening pews at Mr. Gerrish. "Do I understand that you move the adoption of this resolution?"

"Why, certainly, sir," said Mr. Gerrish, with an accent of supercilious surprise.

"You did not say so," said the minister gently. "Does any one second Brother Gerrish's motion?"

A murmur of amusement followed Mr. Peck's reminder to Mr. Gerrish, and an ironical voice called out—

"Mr. Moderator!"

"Mr. Putney."

"I think it important that the sense of the meeting should be taken on the question the resolution raises. I therefore second the motion for its adoption."

Putney sat down, and the murmur now broadened into something like a general laugh, hushed as with a sudden sense of the impropriety.

Mr. Gerrish had gradually sunk into his seat, but now he rose again, and when the minister formally announced the motion before the meeting, he called, sharply, "Mr. Moderator!"

"Brother Gerrish," responded the minister, in recognition.

"I wish to offer a few remarks in support of the resolution which I have had the honour—the duty, I *would* say—of laying before this meeting." He jerked his head forward at the last word, and slid the fingers of his right hand into the breast of his coat like an orator, and stood very straight. "I have no desire, sir, to make this the occasion of a personal question between myself and my pastor. But, sir, the question has been forced upon me against my will and my—my consent; and I was obliged on the last ensuing Sabbath, when I sat in this place, to enter my public protest against it.

"Sir, I came into this community a poor boy, without a penny in my pocket, and unaided and alone and by my own exertions I have built up one of the business interests of the place. I will not stoop to boast of the part I have taken in the prosperity of this place; but I will say that no public object has been wanting—that my support has not been wanting—from the first proposition to concrete the sidewalks of this village to the introduction of city waterworks and an improved system of drainage, and—er—electric lighting. So much for my standing in a public capacity! As for my business capacity, I would gladly let that speak for itself, if that capacity had not been turned in the sanctuary itself against the personal reputation which every man holds dearer than life itself, and which has had a deadly blow aimed at it through that—that very capacity. Sir, I have established in this town a business which I may humbly say that in no other place of the same numerical size throughout the commonwealth will you find another establishment so nearly corresponding to the wants and the—er—facilities of a great city. In no other establishment in a place of the same importance will you find the interests and the demands and the necessities of the whole community so carefully considered. In no other——"

Putney got upon his feet and called out, "Mr. Moderator, will Brother Gerrish allow me to ask him a single question?"

Mr. Peck put the request, and Mr. Gerrish involuntarily made a pause, in which Putney pursued—

"My question is simply this: doesn't Brother Gerrish think it would help us to get at the business in hand sooner if he would print the rest of his advertisement in the Hatboro' *Register*?"

A laugh broke out all over the house as Putney dropped back into his seat. Mr. Gerrish stood apparently undaunted.

"I will attend to you presently, sir," he said, with a school-masterly authority which made an impression in his favour with some. "And I thank the gentleman," he continued, turning again to address the minister, "for recalling me from a side issue. As he acknowledges in the suggestion which he intended to wound my feelings, but I can assure him that my self-respect is beyond the reach of slurs and innuendoes; I care little for them; I care not what quarter they originate from, or have their—their origin; and still less when they spring from a source notoriously incompetent and unworthy to command the respect of this community, which has abused all its privileges and trampled the forbearance of its fellow-citizens under foot, until it has become a—a byword in this place, sir."

Putney sprang up again with, "Mr. Moderator——"

"No, sir! no, sir!" pursued Gerrish; "I will not submit to your interruptions. I have the floor, and I intend to keep it. I intend to challenge a full and fearless scrutiny of my motives in this matter, and I intend to probe those motives in others. Why do we find, sir, on the one side of this question as its most active exponent a man outside of the church in orga-nising a force within this society to antagonise the most cherished convictions of that church? We do not asperse his motives; but we ask if these motives coincide with the rela-tions which a Christian minister should sustain to his flock as expressed in the resolution which I have had the privilege to offer, more in sorrow than in anger."

Putney made some starts to rise, but quelled himself, and finally sank back with an air of ironical patience. Gerrish's per-sonalities had turned public sentiment in his favour. Colonel Marvin came over to Putney's pew and shook hands with him before sitting down by his side. He began to talk with him in whisper while Gerrish went on——

"But on the other hand, sir, what do we see? I will not allude to myself in this connection, but I am well aware, sir, that I represent a large and growing majority of this church in the stand I have taken. We are tired, sir—and I say it to you openly, sir, what has been bruited about in secret long enough—of having what I may call a one-sided gospel preached in this church and from this pulpit. We enter our protest against the neglect of very essential elements of Christianity—not to say *the* essential—the representation of Christ as—a—a spirit as well as a life. Understand me, sir, we do not object, neither I nor any of those who agree with me, to the preaching of Christ as a life. That is all very well in its place, and it is the wish of every true Christian to conform and adapt his own life as far as—as circumstances will permit of. But when I come to this sanctuary, and *they* come, Sabbath after Sabbath, and hear nothing said of my Redeemer as a—means of salvation, and nothing of Him crucified; and when I find the precious promises of the gospel ignored and neglected continually and—and all the time, and each discourse from yonder pulpit filled up with generalities—glittering generalities, as has been well said by another—in relation to and connection with mere conduct, I am disappointed, sir, and dissatisfied, and I feel to protest against that line of—of preaching. During the last six months, Sabbath after Sabbath, I have listened in vain for the ministrations of the plain gospel and the tenets under which we have been blessed as a church and as—a—people. Instead of this I have heard, as I have said—and I repeat it without fear of contradiction—nothing but one-idea appeals and mere moralisings upon duty to others, which a child and the veriest tyro could not fail therein; and I have culminated—or rather it has been culminated to me—in a covert attack upon my private affairs and my way of conducting my private business in a manner which I could not overlook. For that reason, and for the reasons which I have recapitulated—and I challenge the closest scrutiny—I felt it my duty to enter my public protest and to leave this sanctuary, where I have worshipped ever since it was erected, with my family. And I now urge the adoption of the foregoing resolution because I believe that your usefulness has come to an end to the vast majority of the constituent members of this church; and—and that is all."

Mr. Gerrish stopped so abruptly that Putney, who was engaged in talk with Colonel Marvin, looked up with a startled air, too late to secure the floor. Mr. Peck recognized Mr. Gates, who stood with his wrists caught in either hand across his middle, and looked round with a quizzical glance before he began to speak. Putney lifted his hand in playful threatening toward Colonel Marvin, who got away from him with a face of noiseless laughter, and went and joined Mr. Wilmington where he sat with his wife, who entered into the talk between the men.

"Mr. Moderator," said Gates, "I don't know as I expected to take part in this debate; but you can't always tell what's going to happen to you, even if you're only a member of the church by marriage, as you might say. I presume, though, that I have a right to speak in a meeting like this, because I *am* a member of the society in my own right, and I've got its interests at heart as much as any one. I don't know but what I got the interests of Hatboro' at heart too, but I can't be certain; sometimes you can't; sometimes you think you've got the common good in view, and you come to look a little closer and you find it's the uncommon good; that is to say, it's not so much the public weal you're after as what it is the private weal. But that's neither here nor there. I haven't got anything to say against identifying yourself with things in general; I don't know but what it's a good way; all is, it's apt to make you think you're personally attacked when nobody is meant in particular. *I* think that's what's partly the matter with Brother Gerrish here. I heard that sermon, and I didn't suppose there was anything in it to hurt any one especially; and I was consid'ably surprised to see that Mr. Gerrish seemed to take it to himself, somehow, and worry over it; but I didn't really know just what the trouble was till he explained here to-night. All I was thinking was when it come to that about large commerce devouring the small— sort of lean and fat kine—I wished Jordan and Marsh could hear that, or Stewart's in New York, or Wanamaker's in Philadelphia. *I* never *thought* of Brother Gerrish once; and I don't presume one out of a hundred did either. I——" The electric light immediately over Gates's head began to hiss and sputter, and to suffer the sort of syncope which overtakes electric lights at such times, and to leave the house in darkness. Gates waited, standing, till it revived, and then added: "I guess I hain't got anything more to say, Mr. Moderator. If I had it's gone from me now. I'm more used to speaking by kerosene, and I always lose my breath when an electric light begins that way."

Putney was on his legs in good time now, and secured recognition before Mr. Wilmington, who made an effort to catch the moderator's eye. Gates had put the meeting in good-humoured expectation of what they might now have from Putney. They liked Gates's points very well, but they hoped from Putney something more cruel and unsparing, and the greater part of those present must have shared his impatience with Mr. Wilmington's request that he would give way to him for a moment. Yet they all probably felt the same curiosity about what was going forward, for it was plain that Mr. Wilmington and Colonel Marvin were conniving at the same point. Marvin had now gone to Mr. Gerrish, and had slipped into the pew beside him with the same sort of hand-shake he had given Putney.

"Will my friend Mr. Putney give way to me for a moment?" asked Mr. Wilmington.

"I don't see why I should do that," said Putney.

"I assure him that I will not abuse his courtesy, and that I will yield the floor to him at any moment."

Putney hesitated a moment, and then, with the contented laugh of one who securely bides his time, said, "Go ahead."

"It is simply this," said Mr. Wilmington, with a certain formal neatness of speech: "The point has been touched by the last speaker, which I think suggested itself to all who heard the remarks of Brother Gerrish in support of his resolution, and the point is simply this—whether he has not misapplied the words of the discourse by which he felt himself aggrieved, and whether he has not given them a particular bearing foreign to the intention of their author. If, as I believe, this is the case, the whole matter can be easily settled by a private conference between the parties, and we can be saved the public appearance of disagreement in our society. And I would now ask Brother Gerrish, in behalf of many who take this view with me, whether he will not consent to reconsider the matter, and whether, in order to arrive at the end proposed, he will not, for the present at least, withdraw the resolution he has offered?"

Mr. Wilmington sat down amidst a general sensation,

which was heightened by Putney's failure to anticipate any action on Gerrish's part. Gerrish rapidly finished something he was saying to Colonel Marvin, and then half rose, and said, "Mr. Moderator, I withdraw my resolution—for the time being, and—for the present, sir," and sat down again.

"Mr. Moderator," Putney called sharply, from his place, "this is altogether unparliamentary. That resolution is properly before the meeting. Its adoption has been moved and seconded, and it cannot be withdrawn without leave granted by a vote of the meeting. I wish to discuss the resolution in all its bearings, and I think there are a great many present who share with me a desire to know how far it represents the sense of this society. I don't mean as to the supposed personal reflections which it was intended to punish; that is a very small matter, and as compared with the other questions involved, of no consequence whatever." Putney tossed his head with insolent pleasure in his contempt of Gerrish. His nostrils swelled, and he closed his little jaws with a firmness that made his heavy black moustache hang down below the corners of his chin. He went on with a wicked twinkle in his eye, and a look all round to see that people were waiting to take his next point. "I judge my old friend Brother Gerrish by myself. My old friend Gerrish cares no more really about personal allusions than I do. What he really had at heart in offering his resolution was not any supposed attack upon himself or his shop from the pulpit of this church. He cared no more for that than I should care for a reference to my notorious habits. These are things that we feel may be safely left to the judgment, the charitable judgment, of the community, which will be equally merciful to the man who devours widows' houses and to the man who 'puts an enemy in his mouth to steal away his brains.' "

"Mr. Moderator," said Colonel Marvin, getting upon his feet.

"No, sir!" shouted Putney fiercely; "I can't allow you to speak. Wait till I get done!" He stopped, and then said gently "Excuse me, Colonel; I really must go on. I'm speaking now in behalf of Brother Gerrish, and he doesn't like to have the speaking on his side interrupted."

"Oh, all right," said Colonel Marvin amiably; "go on."

"What my old friend William Gerrish really designed in offering that resolution was to bring into question the kind of Christianity which has been preached in this place by our pastor—the one-sided gospel, as he aptly called it—and what he and I want to get at is the opinion of the society on that question. Has the gospel preached to us here been one-sided or hasn't it? Brother Gerrish says it has, and Brother Gerrish, as I understand, doesn't change his mind on that point, if he does on any, in asking to withdraw his resolution. He doesn't expect Mr. Peck to convince him in a private conference that he has been preaching an all-round gospel. I don't contend that he has; but I suppose I'm not a very competent judge. I don't propose to give you the opinion of one very fallible and erring man, and I don't set myself up in judgment of others; but I think it's important for all parties concerned to know what the majority of this society think on a question involving its future. That importance must excuse—if anything can excuse—the apparent want of taste, of humanity, of decency, in proposing the inquiry at a meeting over which the person chiefly concerned would naturally preside, unless he were warned to absent himself. Nobody cares for the contemptible point, the wholly insignificant question, whether allusion to Mr. Gerrish's variety store was intended or not. What we are all anxious to know is whether he represents any considerable portion of this society in his general attack upon its pastor. I want a vote on that, and I move the previous question."

No one stopped to inquire whether this was parliamentary or not. Putney sat down, and Colonel Marvin rose to say that if a vote was to be taken, it was only right and just that Mr. Peck should somehow be heard in his own behalf, and half a dozen voices from all parts of the church supported him. Mr. Peck, after a moment, said, "I think I have nothing to say;" and he added, "Shall I put the question?"

"Question!" "Question!" came from different quarters.

"It is moved and seconded that the resolution before the meeting be adopted," said the minister formally. "All those in favour will say ay." He waited for a distinct space, but there was no response; Mr. Gerrish himself did not vote. The minister proceeded, "Those opposed will say no."

The word burst forth everywhere, and it was followed by

laughter and inarticulate expressions of triumph and mocking. "Order! order!" called the minister gravely, and he announced, "The noes have it."

The electric light began to suffer another syncope. When it recovered, with the usual fizzing and sputtering, Mr. Peck was on his feet, asking to be relieved from his duties as moderator, so that he might make a statement to the meeting. Colonel Marvin was voted into the chair, but refused formally to take possession of it. He stood up and said, "There is no place where we would rather hear you than in that pulpit, Mr. Peck."

"I thank you," said the minister, making himself heard through the approving murmur; "but I stand in this place only to ask to be allowed to leave it. The friendly feeling which has been expressed toward me in the vote upon the resolution you have just rejected is all that reconciles me to its defeat. Its adoption might have spared me a duty which I find painful. But perhaps it is best that I should discharge it. As to the sermon which called forth that resolution it is only just to say that I intended no personalities in it, and I humbly entreat any one who felt himself aggrieved to believe me." Every one looked at Gerrish to see how he took this; he must have felt it the part of self-respect not to change countenance. "My desire in that discourse was, as always, to present the truth as I had seen it, and try to make it a help to all. But I am by no means sure that the author of the resolution was wrong in arraigning me before you for neglecting a very vital part of Christianity in my ministrations here. I think with him, that those who have made an open profession of Christ have a claim to the consolation of His promises, and to the support which good men have found in the mysteries of faith; and I ask his patience and that of others who feel that I have not laid sufficient stress upon these. My shortcoming is something that I would not have you overlook in any survey of my ministry among you; and I am not here now to defend that ministry in any point of view. As I look back over it, by the light of the one ineffable ideal, it seems only a record of failure and defeat." He stopped, and a sympathetic dissent ran through the meeting. "There have been times when I was ready to think that the fault was not in me, but in my office, in the church, in religion. We all have these moments of clouded vision, in which we ourselves loom up in illusory grandeur above the work we have failed to do. But it is in no such error that I stand before you now. Day after day it has been borne in upon me that I had mistaken my work here, and that I ought, if there was any truth in me, to turn from it for reasons which I will give at length should I be spared to preach in this place next Sabbath. I should have willingly acquiesced if our parting had come in the form of my dismissal at your hands. Yet I cannot wholly regret that it has not taken that form, and that in offering my resignation, as I shall formally do to those empowered by the rules of our society to receive it, I can make it a means of restoring concord among you. It would be affectation in me to pretend that I did not know of the dissension which has had my ministry for its object if not its cause; and I earnestly hope that with my withdrawal that dissension may cease, and that this church may become a symbol before the world of the peace of Christ. I conjure such of my friends as have been active in my behalf to unite with their brethren in a cause which can alone merit their devotion. Above all things I beseech you to be at peace one with another. Forbear, forgive, submit, remembering that strife for the better part can only make it the worse, and that for Christians there can be no rivalry but in concession and self-sacrifice."

Colonel Marvin forgot his office and all parliamentary proprieties in the tide of emotion that swept over the meeting when the minister sat down. "I am glad," he said, "that no sort of action need be taken now upon Mr. Peck's proposed resignation, which I for one cannot believe this society will ever agree to accept."

Others echoed his sentiment; they spoke out, sitting and standing, and addressed themselves to no one, till Putney moved an adjournment, which Colonel Marvin sufficiently recollected himself to put to a vote, and declare carried.

Annie walked home with the Putneys and Dr. Morrell. She was aware of something unwholesome in the excitement which ran so wholly in Mr. Peck's favour, but abandoned herself to it with feverish helplessness.

"Ah-h-h!" cried Putney, when they were free of the crowd

which pressed upon him with questions and conjectures and comments. "What a slump!—what a slump! That blessed, short-legged little seraph has spoilt the best sport that ever was. Why, he's sent that fool of a Gerrish home with the conviction that he was right in the part of his attack that was the most vilely hypocritical, and he's given that heartless scoundrel the pleasure of feeling like an honest man. I should like to rap Mr. Peck's head up against the back of his pulpit, and I should like to knock the skulls of Colonel Marvin and Mr. Wilmington together and see which was the thickest. Why, I had Gerrish fairly by the throat at last, and I was just reaching for the balm of Gilead with my other hand to give him a dose that would have done him for one while! Ah, it's too bad, too bad! Well! well! But—haw! haw! haw!—didn't Gerrish tangle himself up beautifully in his rhetoric? I guess we shall fix Brother Gerrish yet, and I don't think we shall let Brother Peck off without a tussle. I'm going to try print on Brother Gerrish. I'm going to ask him in the Hatboro' *Register*—he doesn't advertise, and the editor's as independent as a lion where a man don't advertise——"

"Indeed he's not going to do anything of the kind, Annie," said Mrs. Putney. "I shall not let him. I shall make him drop the whole affair now, and let it die out, and let us be at peace again, as Mr. Peck says."

"There seemed to be a good deal of sense in that part of it," said Dr. Morrell. "I don't know but he was right to propose himself as a peace-offering; perhaps there's no other way out."

"Well," said Mrs. Putney, "whether he goes or stays, I think we owe him that much. Don't you, Annie?"

"Oh yes!" sighed Annie, from the exaltation to which the events of the evening had borne her. "And we mustn't let him go. It would be a loss that every one would feel; that——"

"I'm tired of this fighting," Mrs. Putney broke in, "and I think it's ruining Ralph every way. He hasn't slept the last two nights, and he's been all in a quiver for the last fortnight. For my part I don't care what happens now, I'm not going to have Ralph mixed up in it any more. I think we ought all to forgive and forget. I'm willing to overlook everything, and I believe others are the same."

"You'd better ask Mrs. Gerrish the next time she calls," Putney interposed.

Mrs. Putney stopped, and took her hand from her husband's arm. "Well, after what Mr. Gerrish said to-night about you, I *don't* think Emmeline had better call *very* soon!"

"Ha, ha, ha! Ha, ha, ha!" shrieked Putney, and his laugh flapped back at them in derisive echo from the house-front they were passing. "I guess Brother Peck had better stay and help fight it out. It won't be *all* brotherly love after he goes— or sisterly either."

XXVI.

ANNIE KNEW from the light in the kitchen window that Mrs. Bolton, who had not gone to the meeting, was there, and she inferred from the silence of the house that Bolton had not yet come home. She went up to her room, and after a glance at Idella asleep in her crib, she began to lay off her things. Then she sat down provisionally by the open window, and looked out into the still autumnal night. The air was soft and humid, with a scent of smoke in it from remote forest fires. The village lights showed themselves dimmed by the haze that thickened the moonless dark.

She heard steps on the gravel of the lane, and then two men talking, one of whom she knew to be Bolton. In a little while the back entry door was opened and shut, and after a brief murmur of voices in the library Mrs. Bolton knocked on the door-jamb of the room where Annie sat.

"What is it, Mrs. Bolton?"

"You in bed yet?"

"No; I'm here by the window. What is it?"

"Well, I don't know but what you'll think it's pretty late for callers, but Mr. Peck is down in the library. I guess he wants to speak with you about Idella. I told him he better see *you*."

"I will come right down."

She followed Mrs. Bolton to the foot of the stairs, where she kept on to the kitchen, while Annie turned into the library. Mr. Peck stood beside her father's desk, resting one hand on it and holding his hat in the other.

"Won't you be seated, Mr. Peck?"

"I thank you. It's only for a moment. I am going away to-morrow, and I wish to speak with you about Idella."

"Yes, certainly. But surely you are not going to leave Hatboro', Mr. Peck! I hoped—we all did—that after what you had seen of the strong feeling in your favour to-night you would reconsider your determination and stay with us!" She went on impetuously. "You must know—you must understand now—how much good you can do here—more than any one else—more than you could do anywhere else. I don't believe that you realise how much depends upon your staying here. You can't stop the dissensions by going away; it will only make them worse. You saw how Colonel Marvin and Mr. Wilmington were with you; and Mr. Gates—all classes. I oughtn't to speak—to attempt to teach you your duty; I'm not of your church; and I can only tell you how it seems to me: that you never can find another place where your principles—your views——"

He waited for her to go on; but she really had nothing more to say, and he began: "I am not hoping for another charge elsewhere, at least not for the present; but I am satisfied that my usefulness here is at an end, and I do not think that my going away will make matters worse. Whether I go or stay, the dissensions will continue. At any rate, I believe that there are those who need help more, and whom I can help more, in another field——"

"Yes," she broke in, with a woman's relevancy to the immediate point, "there is nothing to do here."

He went on as if she had not spoken: "I am going to Fall River to-morrow, where I have heard that there is work for me——"

"In the mills!" she exclaimed, recurring in thought to what he had once said of his work in them. "Surely you don't mean that!" The sight, the smell, the tumult of the work she had seen that day in the mill with Lyra came upon her with all their offence. "To throw away all that you have learnt, all that you have become to others!"

"I am less and less confident that I have become anything useful to others in turning aside from the life of toil and presuming to attempt the guidance of those who remained in it. But I don't mean work in the mills," he continued, "or not at first, or not unless it seems necessary to my work with those who work in them. I have a plan—or if it hardly deserves that name, a design—of being useful to them in such ways as my own experience of their life in the past shall show me in the light of what I shall see among them now. I needn't trouble you with it."

"Oh yes!" she interposed.

"I do not expect to preach at once, but only to teach in one of the public schools, where I have heard of a vacancy, and—and—perhaps otherwise. With those whose lives are made up of hard work there must be room for willing and peaceful service. And if it should be necessary that I should work in the mills in order to render this, then I will do so; but at present I have another way in view—a social way that shall bring me into immediate relations with the people." She still tried to argue with him, to prove him wrong in going away, but they both ended where they began. He would not or could not explain himself further. At last he said: "But I did not come to urge this matter. I have no wish to impose my will, my theory, upon any one, even my own child."

"Oh yes—Idella!" Annie broke in anxiously. "You will leave her with me, Mr. Peck, won't you? You don't know how much I'm attached to her. I see her faults, and I shall not spoil her. Leave her with me at least till you see your way clear to having her with you, and then I will send her to you."

A trouble showed itself in his face, ordinarily so impassive, and he seemed at a loss how to answer her; but he said: "I— appreciate your kindness to her, but I shall not ask you to be at the inconvenience longer than till to-morrow. I have arranged with another to take her until I am settled, and then bring her to me."

Annie sat intensely searching his face, with her lips parted to speak. "*Another!*" she said, and the wounded feeling, the resentment of his insensibility to her good-will, that mingled in her heart, must have made itself felt in her voice, for he went on reluctantly—

"It is a family in which she will be brought up to work and to be helpful to herself. They will join me with her. You know the mother—she has lost her own child—Mrs. Savor."

At the name, Annie's spirit fell; the tears started from her eyes. "Yes, she must have her. It is just—it is the only expiation. Don't you remember that it was I who sent Mrs. Savor's baby to the sea-shore, where it died?"

"No; I had forgotten," said the minister, aghast. "I am sorry——"

"It doesn't matter," said Annie lifelessly; "it had to be." After a pause, she asked quietly, "If Mrs. Savor is going to work in the mills, how can she make a home for the child?"

"She is not going into the mills," he answered. "She will keep house for us all, and we hope to have others who are without homes of their own join us in paying the expenses and doing the work, so that all may share its comfort without gain to any one upon their necessity of food and shelter."

She did not heed his explanation, but suddenly entreated: "Let me go with you. I will not be a trouble to you, and I will help as well as I can. I can't give the child up! Why—why" —the thought, crazy as it would have once seemed, was now such a happy solution of the trouble that she smiled hopefully—"why shouldn't I go with Mr. and Mrs. Savor, and help to make a home for Idella there? You will need money to begin your work; I will give you mine. I will give it up—I will give it all up. I will give it to any good object that you approve; or you may have it, to do what you think best with; and I will go with Idella and I will work in the mills there— or anything."

He shook his head, and for the first time in their acquaintance he seemed to feel compassion for her. "It isn't possible. I couldn't take your money; I shouldn't know what to do with it."

"You know what to do with your own," she broke in. "You do good with that!"

"I'm afraid I do harm with it too," he returned. "It's only a little, but little as it has been, I can no longer meet the responsibility it brings."

"But if you took my money," she urged, "you could devote your life to preaching the truth, to writing and publishing books, and all that; and so could others: don't you see?"

He shook his head. "Perhaps others; but I have done with preaching for the present. Later I may have something to say. Now I feel sure of nothing, not even of what I've been saying here."

"Will you send for Idella? When she goes with the Savors I will come too!"

He looked at her sorrowfully. "I think you are a good woman, and you mean what you say. But I am sorry you say it, if any words of mine have caused you to say it, for I know you cannot do it. Even for me it is hard to go back to those associations, and for you they would be impossible."

"You will see," she returned, with exaltation. "I will take

Idella to the Savors' to-morrow—or no; I'll have them come here!"

He stood looking at her in perplexity. At last he asked, "Could I see the child?"

"Certainly!" said Annie, with the lofty passion that possessed her, and she led him up into the chamber where Idella lay sleeping in Annie's own crib.

He stood beside it, gazing long at the little one, from whose eyes he shaded the lamp. Then he said, "I thank you," and turned away.

She followed him down-stairs, and at the door she said: "You think I will not come; but I will come. Don't you believe that?"

He turned sadly from her. "You might come, but you couldn't stay. You don't know what it is; you can't imagine it, and you couldn't bear it."

"I will come, and I will stay," she answered; and when he was gone she fell into one of those intense reveries of hers—a rapture in which she prefigured what should happen in that new life before her. At its end Mr. Peck stood beside her grave, reading the lesson of her work to the multitude of grateful and loving poor who thronged to pay the last tribute to her memory. Putney was there with his wife, and Lyra regretful of her lightness, and Mrs. Munger repentant of her mendacities. They talked together in awe-stricken murmurs of the noble career just ended. She heard their voices, and then she began to ask herself what they would really say of her proposing to go to Fall River with the Savors and be a mill-hand.

XXVII.

ANNIE did not sleep. After lying a long time awake she took some of the tonic that Dr. Morrell had left her, upon the chance that it might quiet her; but it did no good. She dressed herself, and sat by the window till morning.

The breaking day showed her purposes grotesque and monstrous. The revulsion that must come, came with a tide that swept before it all prepossessions, all affections. It seemed as if the child, still asleep in her crib, had heard what she said, and would help to hold her to her word.

She choked down a crust of bread with the coffee she drank at breakfast, and instead of romping with Idella at her bath, she dressed the little one silently, and sent her out to Mrs. Bolton. Then she sat down again in the sort of daze in which she had spent the night, and as the day passed, her revolt from what she had pledged herself to do mounted and mounted. It was like the sort of woman she was, not to think of any withdrawal from her pledges; they were all the more sacred with her because they had been purely voluntary, insistent; the fact that they had been refused made them the more obligatory.

She thought some one would come to break in upon the heavy monotony of the time; she expected Ralph or Ellen, or at least Lyra; but she only saw Mrs. Bolton, and heard her about her work. Sometimes the child stole back from the kitchen or the barn, and peeped in upon her with a roguish expectance which her gloomy stare defeated, and then it ran off again.

She lay down in the afternoon and tried to sleep; but her brain was inexorably alert, and she lay making inventory of all the pleasant things she was to leave for that ugly fate she had insisted on. A swarm of fancies gave every detail of the parting dramatic intensity. Amidst the poignancy of her regrets, her shame for her recreancy was sharper still.

By night she could bear it no longer. It was Dr. Morrell's custom to come nearly every night; but she was afraid, because he had walked home with her from the meeting the night before, he might not come now, and she sent for him. It was in quality of medicine-man, as well as physician, that she wished to see him; she meant to tell him all that had passed with Mr. Peck; and this was perfectly easy in the interview she forecast; but at the sound of his buggy wheels in the lane a thought came that seemed to forbid her even to speak of Mr. Peck to him. For the first time it occurred to her that the minister might have inferred a meaning from her eagerness and persistence infinitely more preposterous than even the preposterous letter of her words. A number of little proofs of the conjecture flashed upon her: his anxiety to get away from her, his refusal to let her believe in her own constancy of purpose, his moments of bewilderment and dismay. It needed nothing but this to add the touch of intolerable absurdity to the horror of the whole affair, and to snatch the last hope of help from her.

She let Mrs. Bolton go to the door, and she did not rise to meet the doctor; she saw from his smile that he knew he had a moral rather than a physical trouble to deal with, but she did not relax the severity of her glare in sympathy, as she was tempted from some infinite remoteness to do.

When he said, "You're not well," she whispered solemnly back, "Not at all."

He did not pursue his inquiry into her condition, but said, with an irrelevant cheerfulness that piqued her, "I was coming here this evening at any rate, and I got your message on the way up from my office."

"You are very kind," she said, a little more audibly.

"I wanted to tell you," he went on, "of what a time Putney and I have had to-day working up public sentiment for Mr. Peck, so as to keep him here."

Annie did not change her position, but the expression of her glance changed.

"We've been round in the enemy's camp, everywhere; and I've committed Gerrish himself to an armed neutrality. That wasn't difficult. The difficulty was in another quarter—with Mr. Peck himself. He's more opposed than any one else to his stay in Hatboro'. You know he intended going away this morning?"

"Did he?" Annie asked dishonestly. The question obliged her to say something.

"Yes. He came to Putney before breakfast to thank him and take leave of him, and to tell him of the plan he had for——Imagine what!"

"I don't know," said Annie, hoarsely, after an effort, as if the untruth would not come easily. "I am worse than Mrs. Munger," she thought.

"For going to Fall River to teach school among the mill-hands' children! And to open a night-school for the hands themselves."

The doctor waited for her sensation, and in its absence he looked so disappointed that she was forced to say, "To teach school?"

Then he went on briskly again. "Yes. Putney laboured with him on his knees, so to speak, and got him to postpone his going till to-morrow morning; and then he came to me for help. We enlisted Mrs. Wilmington in the cause, and we've spent the day working up the Peck sentiment to a fever-heat. It's been a very queer campaign; three Gentiles toiling for a saint against the elect, and bringing them all over at last. We've got a paper, signed by a large majority of the members of the church—the church, not the society—asking Mr. Peck to remain; and Putney's gone to him with the paper, and he's coming round here to report Mr. Peck's decision. We all agreed that it wouldn't do to say anything about his plan for the future, and I fancy some of his people signed our petition under the impression that they were keeping a valuable man out of another pulpit."

Annie accompanied the doctor's words, which she took in to the last syllable, with a symphony of conjecture as to how the change in Mr. Peck's plans, if they prevailed with him, would affect her, and the doctor had not ceased to speak before she perceived that it would be deliverance perfect and complete, however inglorious. But the tacit drama so vividly preoccupied her with its minor questions of how to descend to this escape with dignity that still she did not speak, and he took up the word again.

"I confess I've had my misgivings about Mr. Peck, and about his final usefulness in a community like this. In spite of all that Putney can say of his hard-headedness, I'm afraid that he's a good deal of a dreamer. But I gave way to Putney, and I hope you'll appreciate what I've done for your favourite."

"You are very good," she said, in mechanical acknowledgment: her mind was set so strenuously to break from her dishonest reticence that she did not know really what she was saying. "Why—why do you call him a dreamer?" She cast about in that direction at random.

"Why? Well, for one thing, the reason he gave Putney for giving up his luxuries here: that as long as there was hardship and overwork for underpay in the world, he must share them. It seems to me that I might as well say that as long as there were dyspepsia and rheumatism in the world, I must share them. Then he has a queer notion that he can go back and find instruction in the working-men—that they alone have the light and the truth, and know the meaning of life. I don't say anything against them. My observation and my experience is that if others were as good as they are in the ratio of their advantages, Mr. Peck needn't go to them for his ideal. But their conditions warp and dull them; they see things askew, and they don't see them clearly. I might as well expose myself to the small-pox in hopes of treating my fellow-sufferers more intelligently."

She could not perceive where his analogies rang false; they only overwhelmed her with a deeper sense of her own folly.

"But I don't know," he went on, "that a dreamer is such a desperate character, if you can only keep him from trying to realise his dreams; and if Mr. Peck consents to stay in Hatboro', perhaps we can manage it." He drew his chair a little toward the lounge where she reclined, and asked, with the kindliness that was both personal and professional, "What seems to be the matter?"

She started up. "There is nothing—nothing that medicine can help. Why do you call him my favourite?" she demanded violently. "But you have wasted your time. If he had made up his mind to what you say, he would never give it up—never in the world!" she added hysterically. "If you've interfered between any one and his duty in this world, where it seems as if hardly any one had any duty, you've done a very unwarrantable thing." She was aware from his stare that her words were incoherent, if not from the words themselves, but she hurried on: "I am going with him. He was here last night, and I told him I would. I will go with the Savors, and we will keep the child together; and if they will take me, I shall go to work in the mills; and I shall not care what people think, if it's right——"

She stopped and weakly dropped back on the lounge, and hid her face in the pillow.

"I really don't understand." The doctor began, with a physician's carefulness, to unwind the coil she had flung down to him. "Are the Savors going, and the child?"

"He will give her the child for the one they lost—you know how! And they will take it with them."

"But you—what have you——"

"I must have the child too! I can't give it up, and I shall go with them. There's no other way. You don't know. I've given him my word, and there is no hope!"

"He asked you," said the doctor, to make sure he had heard aright—"he asked you—advised you—to go to work in a cotton-mill?"

"No;" she lifted her face to confront him. "He told me *not* to go; but I said I would."

They sat staring at each other in a silence which neither of them broke, and which promised to last indefinitely. They were still in their daze when Putney's voice came through the open hall door.

"Hello! hello! hello! Hello, Central! *Can't* I make you hear, any one?" His steps advanced into the hall, and he put his head in at the library doorway. "Thought you'd be here," he said, nodding at the doctor. "Well, doctor, Brother Peck's beaten us again. He's going."

"Going?" the doctor echoed.

"Yes. It's no use. I put the whole case before him, and I argued it with a force of logic that would have fetched the twelfth man with eleven stubborn fellows against him on a jury; but it didn't fetch Brother Peck. He was very appreciative and grateful, but he believes he's got a call to give up the ministry, for the present at least. Well, there's some consolation in supposing he may know best, after all. It seemed to us that he had a great opportunity in Hatboro', but if he turns his back on it, perhaps it's a sign he wasn't equal to it. The doctor told you what we've been up to, Annie?"

"Yes," she answered faintly, from the depths of the labyrinth in which she was plunged again.

"I'm sorry for your news about him," said the doctor. "I hoped he was going to stay. It's always a pity when such a man lets his sympathies use him instead of using them. But we must always judge that kind of crank leniently, if he doesn't involve other people in his craze."

She knew that he was shielding and trying to spare her, and she felt inexpressibly degraded by the terms of his forbearance. She could not accept, and she had not the strength to refuse it; and Putney said: "I've not seen anything to make me doubt his sanity; but I must say the present racket shakes my faith in his common-sense, and I rather held by that, you know. But I suppose no man, except the kind of a man that a woman would be if she were a man—excuse me, Annie—is ever absolutely right. I suppose the truth is a constitutional thing, and you can't separate it from the personal consciousness, and so you get it coloured and heated by personality when you get it fresh. That is, we can see what the absolute truth was, but never what it is."

Putney amused himself in speculating on these lines with more or less reference to Mr. Peck, and did not notice that the doctor and Annie gave him only a silent assent. "As to misleading any one else, Mr. Peck's following in his new religion seems to be confined to the Savors, as I understand. They are going with him to help him set up a sort of co-operative boarding-house. Well, I don't know where we shall get a hotter gospeller than Brother Peck. Poor old fellow! I hope he'll get along better in Fall River. It *is* something to be out of reach of Gerrish."

The doctor asked, "When is he going?"

"Why, he's gone by this time, I suppose," said Putney. "I tried to get him to think about it overnight, but he wouldn't. He's anxious to go and get back, so as to preach his last sermon here Sunday, and he's taken the 9.10, if he hasn't changed his mind." Putney looked at his watch.

"Let's hope he hasn't," said Dr. Morrell.

"Which?" asked Putney.

"Changed his mind. I'm sorry he's coming back."

Annie knew that he was talking at her, though he spoke to Putney; but she was powerless to protest.

XXVIII.

THEY WENT AWAY together, leaving her to her despair, which had passed into a sort of torpor by the following night, when Dr. Morrell came again, out of what she knew must be mere humanity; he could not respect her any longer. He told her, as if for her comfort, that Putney had gone to the depot to meet Mr. Peck, who was expected back in the eight-o'clock train, and was to labour with him all night long if necessary to get him to change, or at least postpone, his purpose. The feeling in his favour was growing. Putney hoped to put it so strongly to him as a proof of duty that he could not resist it.

Annie listened comfortlessly. Whatever happened, nothing could take away the shame of her weakness now. She even wished, feebly, vaguely, that she might be forced to keep her word.

A sound of running on the gravel-walk outside and a sharp pull at the door-bell seemed to jerk them both to their feet.

Some one stepped into the hall panting, and the face of William Savor showed itself at the door of the room where they stood. "Doc—Doctor Morrell, come—come quick! There's been an accident—at—the depot. Mr.—Peck——" He panted out the story, and Annie saw rather than heard how the minister tried to cross the track from his train, where it had halted short of the station, and the flying express from the other quarter caught him from his feet, and dropped the bleeding fragment that still held his life beside the rail a hundred yards away, and then kept on in brute ignorance into the night.

"Where is he? Where have you got him?" the doctor demanded of Savor.

"At my house."

The doctor ran out of the house, and she heard his buggy whirl away, followed by the fainter sound of Savor's feet as he followed running, after he had stopped to repeat his story to the Boltons. Annie turned to the farmer. "Mr. Bolton, get the carry-all. I must go."

"And me too," said his wife.

"Why, no, Pauliny; I guess you better stay. I guess it'll come out all right in the end," Bolton began. "I guess William has exaggerated some, may be. Anyrate, who's goin' to look after the little girl if you come?"

"*I* am," Mrs. Bolton snapped back. "She's goin' with me."

"Of course she is. Be quick, Mr. Bolton!" Annie called from the stairs, which she had already mounted half-way.

She caught up the child, limp with sleep, from its crib, and began to dress it. Idella cried, and fought away the hands that tormented her, and made herself now very stiff and now very lax; but Annie and Mrs. Bolton together prevailed against her, and she was dressed, and had fallen asleep again in her clothes while the women were putting on their hats and sacks, and Bolton was driving up to the door with the carry-all.

"Why, I can see," he said, when he got out to help them in, "just how William's got his idee about it. His wife's an excitable kind of a woman, and she's sent him off lickety-split after the doctor without looking to see what the matter was. There hain't never been anybody hurt at our depot, and it don't stand to reason——"

"Oliver Bolton, *will* you hush that noise?" shrieked his wife. "If the world was burnin' up you'd say it was nothing but a chimbley on fire som'er's."

"Well, well, Pauliny, have it your own way, have it your own way," said Bolton. "I ain't sayin' but what there's *some-thin'* in William's story; but you'll see 't he's exaggerated. Git up!"

"Well, do hurry, and *do* be still!" said his wife.

"Yes, yes. It's all right, Pauliny; all right. Soon's I'm out the lane, you'll see 't I'll drive *fast* enough."

Mrs. Bolton kept a grim silence, against which her husband's babble of optimism played like heat-lightning on a night sky.

Idella woke with the rush of cold air, and in the dark and strangeness began to cry, and wailed heart-breakingly between her fits of louder sobbing, and then fell asleep again before they reached the house where her father lay dying.

They had put him in the best bed in Mrs. Savor's little guest-room, and when Annie entered, the minister was apologising to her for spoiling it.

"Now don't you say one word, Mr. Peck," she answered him. "It's all right. I ruthah see you layin' there just 's you be than plenty of folks that——" She stopped for want of an apt comparison, and at sight of Annie she said, as if he were a child whose mind was wandering: "Well, I declare, if here ain't Miss Kilburn come to see you, Mr. Peck! And Mis' Bolton! Well, the land!"

Mrs. Savor came and shook hands with them, and in her character of hostess urged them forward from the door, where they had halted. "Want to see Mr. Peck? Well, he's real comf'table now; ain't he, Dr. Morrell? We got him all fixed up nicely, and he ain't in a bit o' pain. It's his spine that's hurt, so 't he don't feel nothin'; but he's just as clear in his mind as what you or I be. *Ain't* he, doctor?"

"He's not suffering," said Dr. Morrell, to whom Annie's eye wandered from Mrs. Savor, and there was something in his manner that made her think the minister was not badly hurt. She went forward with Mr. and Mrs. Bolton, and after they had both taken the limp hand that lay outside the covering, she touched it too. It returned no pressure, but his large, wan eyes looked at her with such gentle dignity and intelligence that she began to frame in her mind an excuse for what seemed almost an intrusion.

"We were afraid you were hurt badly, and we thought—we thought you might like to see Idella—and so—we came. She is in the next room."

"Thank you," said the minister. "I presume that I am dying; the doctor tells me that I have but a few hours to live."

Mrs. Savor protested, "Oh, I guess you ain't a-goin' to die *this* time, Mr. Peck." Annie looked from Dr. Morrell to Putney, who stood with him on the other side of the bed, and experienced a shock from their gravity without yet being able to accept the fact it implied. "There's plenty of folks," continued Mrs. Savor, "hurt worse'n what you be that's alive to-day and as well as ever they was."

Bolton seized his chance. "It's just what I said to Pauliny, comin' along. 'You'll see,' said I, 'Mr. Peck'll be out as spry as any of us before a great while.' That's the way I felt about it from the start."

"All you got to do is to keep up courage," said Mrs. Savor.

"That's so; that's half the battle," said Bolton.

There were numbers of people in the room and at the door of the next. Annie saw Colonel Marvin and Jack Wilmington. She heard afterward that he was going to take the same train to Boston with Mr. Peck, and had helped to bring him to the Savors' house. The stationmaster was there, and some other railroad employés.

The doctor leaned across the bed and lifted slightly the arm that lay there, taking the wrist between his thumb and finger. "I think we had better let Mr. Peck rest a while," he said to the company generally. "We're doing him no good."

The people began to go; some of them said, "Well, good night!" as if they would meet again in the morning. They all made the pretence that it was a slight matter, and treated the wounded man as if he were a child. He did not humour the pretence, but said "Good-bye" in return for their "Good night" with a quiet patience.

Mrs. Savor hastened after her retreating guests. "I ain't a-goin' to let you go without a sup of coffee," she said. "I want you should all stay and git some, and I don't believe but what a little of it would do Mr. Peck good."

The surface of her lugubrious nature was broken up, and whatever was kindly and cheerful in its depths floated to the top; she was almost gay in the demand which the calamity made upon her. Annie knew that she must have seen and helped to soothe the horror of mutilation which she could not even let her fancy figure, and she followed her foolish bustle and chatter with respectful awe.

"Rebecca'll have it right off the stove in half a minute now," Mrs. Savor concluded; and from a further room came the cheerful click of cups, and then a wandering whiff of the coffee; life in its vulgar kindliness touched and made friends with death, claiming it a part of nature too.

The night at Mrs. Munger's came back to Annie from the immeasurable remoteness into which all the past had lapsed. She looked up at Dr. Morrell across the bed.

"Would you like to speak with Mr. Peck?" he asked officially. "Better do it now," he said, with one of his short nods.

Putney came and set her a chair. She would have liked to fall on her knees beside the bed; but she took the chair, and drew the minister's hand into hers, stretching her arm above his head on the pillow. He lay like some poor little wounded boy, like Putney's Winthrop; the mother that is in every woman's heart gushed out of hers in pity upon him, mixed with filial reverence. She had thought that she should confess her baseness to him, and ask his forgiveness, and offer to fulfil with the people he had chosen for the guardians of his child that interrupted purpose of his. But in the presence of death, so august, so simple, all the concerns of life seemed trivial, and she found herself without words. She sobbed over the poor hand she held. He turned his eyes upon her and tried to speak, but his lips only let out a moaning, shuddering sound, inarticulate of all that she hoped or feared he might prophesy to shape her future.

Life alone has any message for life, but from the beginning of time it has put its ear to the cold lips that must for ever remain dumb.

XXIX.

THE EVENING after the funeral Annie took Idella, with the child's clothes and toys in a bundle, and Bolton drove them down Over the Track to the Savors'. She had thought it all out, and she perceived that whatever the minister's final intention might have been, she was bound by the purpose he had expressed to her, and must give up the child. For fear she might be acting from the false conscientiousness of which she was beginning to have some notion in herself, she put the case to Mrs. Bolton. She knew what she must do in any event, but it was a comfort to be stayed so firmly in her duty by Mrs. Bolton, who did not spare some doubts of Mrs. Savor's fitness for the charge, and reflected a subdued censure even upon the judgment of Mr. Peck himself, as she bustled about and helped Annie get Idella and her belongings ready. The child watched the preparations with suspicion. At the end, when she was dressed, and Annie tried to lift her into the carriage, she broke out in sudden rebellion; she cried, she shrieked, she fought; the two good women who were obeying the dead minister's behest were obliged to descend to the foolish lies of the nursery; they told her she was going on a visit to the Savors, who would take her on the cars with them, and then bring her back to Aunt Annie's house. Before they could reconcile her to this fabled prospect they had to give it verisimilitude by taking off her everyday clothes and putting on her best dress.

She did not like Mrs. Savor's house when she came to it, nor Mrs. Savor, who stopped, all blowzed and work-deranged from trying to put it in order after the death in it, and gave Idella a motherly welcome. Annie fancied a certain surprise in her manner, and her own ideal of duty was put to proof by Mrs. Savor's owning that she had not expected Annie to bring Idella to her right away.

"If I had not done it at once, I never could have done it," Annie explained.

"Well, I presume it's a cross," said Mrs. Savor, "and I don't feel right to take her. If it wa'n't for what her father——"

" 'Sh!" Annie said, with a significant glance.

"It's an ugly house!" screamed the child. "I want to go back to my Aunt Annie's house. I want to go on the cars."

"Yes, yes," answered Mrs. Savor, blindly groping to share in whatever cheat had been practised on the child, "just as soon as the cars starts. Here, William, you take her out and show her the pretty coop you be'n makin' the pigeons, to keep the cats out."

They got rid of her with Savor's connivance for the moment, and Annie hastened to escape.

"We had to tell her she was going a journey, or we never could have got her into the carriage," she explained, feeling like a thief.

"Yes, yes. It's all right," said Mrs. Savor. "I see you'd be'n putting up some kind of job on her the minute she mentioned the cars. Don't you fret any, Miss Kilburn. Rebecca and me'll get along with her, you needn't be afraid."

Annie could not look at the empty crib where it stood in its alcove when she went to bed; and she cried upon her own pillow with heart-sickness for the child, and with a humiliating doubt of her own part in hurrying to give it up without thought of Mrs. Savor's convenience. What had seemed so noble, so exemplary, began to wear another colour; and she drowsed, worn out at last by the swarming fears, shames, and despairs, which resolved themselves into a fantastic medley of dream images. There was a cat trying to get at the pigeons in the coop which Mr. Savor had carried Idella to see. It clawed and miauled at the lattice-work of lath, and its caterwauling became like the cry of a child, so like that it woke Annie from her sleep, and still kept on. She lay shuddering a moment; it seemed as if the dead minister's ghost flitted from the room, while the crying defined and located itself more and more, till she knew it a child's wail at the door of her house. Then she heard, "Aunt Annie! Aunt Annie!" and soft, faint thumps as of a little fist upon the door panels.

She had no experience of more than one motion from her bed to the door, which the same impulse flung open and let her crush to her breast the little tumult of sobs and moans from the threshold.

"Oh, wicked, selfish, heartless wretch!" she stormed out

over the child. "But now I will never, never, never give you up! Oh, my poor little baby! my darling! God has sent you back to me, and I will keep you, I don't care what happens! What a cruel wretch I have been—oh, what a cruel wretch, my pretty!—to tear you from your home! But now you shall never leave it; no one shall take you away." She gripped it in a succession of fierce hugs, and mumbled it—face and neck, and little cold wet hands and feet—with her kisses; and all the time she did not know the child was in its night-dress like herself, or that her own feet were bare, and her drapery as scanty as Idella's.

A sense of the fact evanescently gleamed upon her with the appearance of Mrs. Bolton, lamp in hand, and the instantaneous appearance and disappearance of her husband at the back door through which she emerged. The two women spent the first moments of the lamp-light in making certain that Idella was sound and whole in every part, and then in making uncertain for ever how she came to be there. Whether she had wandered out in her sleep, and found her way home with dream-led feet, or whether she had watched till the house was quiet, and then stolen away, was what she could not tell them, and must always remain a mystery.

"I don't believe but what Mr. Bolton had better go and wake up the Savors. You got to keep her for the night, I presume, but they'd ought to know where she is, and you can take her over there agin, come daylight."

"*Mrs.* Bolton!" shouted Annie, in a voice so deep and hoarse that it shook the heart of a woman who had never known fear of man. "If you say such a thing to me—if you ever say such a thing again—I—I—I will *hit* you! Send Mr. Bolton for Idella's things—right away!"

"Land!" said Mrs. Savor, when Bolton, after a long conciliatory preamble, explained that he did not believe Miss Kilburn felt a great deal like giving the child up again. "*I* don't want it without it's satisfied to stay. I see last night it was just breakin' its heart for her, and I told William when we first missed her this mornin', and he was in such a pucker about her, I bet anything he was a mind to that the child had gone back to Miss Kilburn's. That's just the words I used;

didn't I, Rebecca? I couldn't stand it to have no child *grievin'* around."

Beyond this sentimental reluctance, Mrs. Savor later confessed to Annie herself that she was really accepting the charge of Idella in the same spirit of self-sacrifice as that in which Annie was surrendering it, and that she felt, when Mr. Peck first suggested it, that the child was better off with Miss Kilburn; only she hated to say so. Her husband seemed to think it would make up to her for the one they lost, but nothing could really do that.

XXX.

I N A REVERIE of rare vividness following her recovery of the minister's child, Annie Kilburn dramatised an escape from all the failures and humiliations of her life in Hatboro'. She took Idella with her and went back to Rome, accomplishing the whole affair so smoothly and rapidly that she wondered at herself for not having thought of such a simple solution of her difficulties before. She even began to put some little things together for her flight, while she explained to old friends in the American colony that Idella was the orphan child of a country minister, which she had adopted. That old lady who had found her motives in returning to Hatboro' insufficient questioned her sharply *why* she had adopted the minister's child, and did not find her answers satisfactory. They were such as also failed to pacify inquiry in Hatboro', where Annie remained, in spite of her reverie; but people accepted the fact, and accounted for it in their own way, and approved it, even though they could not quite approve her.

The dramatic impressiveness of the minister's death won him undisputed favour, yet it failed to establish unity in his society. Supply after supply filled his pulpit, but the people found them all unsatisfactory when they remembered his preaching, and could not make up their minds to any one of them. They were more divided than ever, except upon the point of regretting Mr. Peck. But they distinguished, in honouring his memory. They revered his goodness and his wisdom, but they regarded his conduct of life as unpractical. They said there never was a more inspired teacher, but it was impossible to follow him, and he could not himself have kept the course he had marked out. They said, now that he was beyond recall, no one else could have built up the church in Hatboro' as he could, if he could only have let impracticable theories alone. Mr. Gerrish called many people to witness that this was what he had always said. He contended that it was the *spirit* of the gospel which you were to follow. He said that if Mr. Peck had gone to teaching among the mill-hands, he would have been sick of it inside of six weeks; but he was a good Christian man, and no one wished less than Mr. Gerrish to reproach him for what was, after all, more an error of the head than the heart. His critics had it their own way in this, for he had not lived to offer that full exposition of his theory and justification of his purpose which he had been expected to give on the Sunday after he was killed; and his death was in no wise exegetic. It said no more to his people than it had said to Annie; it was a mere casualty; and his past life, broken and unfulfilled, with only its intimations and intentions of performance, alone remained.

When people learned, as they could hardly help doing from Mrs. Savor's volubility, what his plan with regard to Idella had been, they instanced that in proof of the injuriousness of his idealism as applied to real life; and they held that she had been remanded in that strange way to Miss Kilburn's charge for some purpose which she must not attempt to cross. As the minister had been thwarted in another intent by death, it was a sign that he was wrong in this too, and that she could do better by the child than he had proposed.

This was the sum of popular opinion; and it was further the opinion of Mrs. Gerrish, who gave more attention to the case than many others, that Annie had first taken the child because she hoped to get Mr. Peck, when she found she could not get Dr. Morrell; and that she would have been very glad to be rid of it if she had known how, but that she would have to keep it now for shame's sake.

For shame's sake certainly, Annie would have done several other things, and chief of these would have been never to see Dr. Morrell again. She believed that he not only knew the folly she had confessed to him, but that he had divined the cowardice and meanness in which she had repented it, and she felt intolerably disgraced before the thought of him. She had imagined mainly because of him that escape to Rome which never has yet been effected, though it might have been attempted if Idella had not wakened ill from the sleep she sobbed herself into when she found herself safe in Annie's crib again.

She had taken a heavy cold, and she moped lifelessly about during the day, and drowsed early again in the troubled cough-broken slumber.

"That child ought to have the doctor," said Mrs. Bolton,

with the grim impartiality in which she masked her inter-
ference.

"Well," said Annie helplessly.

At the end of the lung fever which followed, "It was a narrow chance," said the doctor one morning; "but now I
needn't come any more unless you send for me."

Annie stood at the door, where he spoke with his hand on
the dash-board of his buggy before getting into it.

She answered with one of those impulses that come from
something deeper than intention. "I will send for you, then—
to tell you how generous you are," and in the look with
which she spoke she uttered the full meaning that her words
withheld.

He flushed for pleasure of conscious desert, but he had to
laugh and turn it off lightly. "I don't think I could come for
that. But I'll look in to see Idella unprofessionally."

He drove away, and she remained at her door looking up at
the summer blue sky that held a few soft white clouds, such as
might have overhung the same place at the same hour thou-
sands of years before, and such as would lazily drift over it in
a thousand years to come. The morning had an immeasurable
vastness, through which some crows flying across the pasture
above the house sent their voices on the spacious stillness. A
perception of the unity of all things under the sun flashed and
faded upon her, as such glimpses do. Of her high intentions,
nothing had resulted. An inexorable centrifugality had
thrown her off at every point where she tried to cling. Nothing of what was established and regulated had desired her
intervention; a few accidents and irregularities had alone accepted it. But now she felt that nothing withal had been lost;
a magnitude, a serenity, a tolerance, intimated itself in the
universal frame of things, where her failure, her recreancy, her
folly, seemed for the moment to come into true perspective,
and to show venial and unimportant, to be limited to itself,
and to be even good in its effect of humbling her to patience
with all imperfection and shortcoming, even her own. She
was aware of the cessation of a struggle that has never since
renewed itself with the old intensity; her wishes, her propen-
sities, ceased in that degree to represent evil in conflict with
the portion of good in her; they seemed so mixed and inter-

woven with the good that they could no longer be antago-
nised; for the moment they seemed in their way even wiser
and better, and ever after to be the nature out of which good
as well as evil might come.

As she remained standing there, Mr. Brandreth came round
the corner of the house, looking very bright and happy.

"Miss Kilburn," he said abruptly, "I want you to congratulate me. I'm engaged to Miss Chapley."

"Are you indeed, Mr. Brandreth? I do congratulate you
with all my heart. She is a lovely girl."

"Yes, it's all right now," said Mr. Brandreth. "I've come to
tell you the first one, because you seemed to take an interest
in it when I told you of the trouble about the Juliet. We
hadn't come to any understanding before that, but that
seemed to bring us both to the point, and—and we're engaged. Mother and I are going to New York for the winter;
we think she can risk it; and at anyrate she won't be separated
from me; and we shall be back in our little home next May.
You know that I'm to be with Mr. Chapley in his business?"

"Why, no! This is *great* news, Mr. Brandreth! I don't know
what to say."

"You're very kind," said the young man, and for the third
or fourth time he wrung her hand. "It isn't a partnership, of
course; but he thinks I can be of use to him."

"I know you can!" Annie adventured.

"We are very busy getting ready—nearly everybody else is
gone—and mother sent her kindest regards—you know she
don't make calls—and I just ran up to tell you. Well, *good*-
bye!"

"*Good*-bye! Give my love to your mother, and to your—to
Miss Chapley."

"I will." He hurried off, and then came running back. "Oh,
I forgot! About the Social Union fund. You know we've got
about two hundred dollars from the theatricals, but the matter seems to have stopped there, and some of us think there'd
better be some other disposition of the money. Have you any
suggestion to make?"

"No, none."

"Then I'll tell you. It's proposed to devote the money to
beautifying the grounds around the soldiers' monument.

They ought to be fenced and planted with flowers—turned into a little public garden. Everybody appreciates the interest you took in the Union, and we hoped you'd be pleased with that disposition of the money."

"It is very kind," said Annie, with a meek submission that must have made him believe she was deeply touched.

"As I'm not to be here this winter," he continued, "we thought we had better leave the whole matter in your hands, and the money has been deposited in the bank subject to your order. It was Mrs. Munger's idea. I don't think she's ever felt just right about that evening of the dramatics, don't you know. *Good*-bye!"

He ran off to escape her thanks for this proof of confidence in her taste and judgment, and he was gone beyond her protest before she emerged from her daze into a full sense of the absurdity of the situation.

"Well, it's a very simple matter to let the money lie in the bank," said Dr. Morrell, who came that evening to make his first unprofessional visit, and received with pure amusement the account of the affair, which she gave him with a strong infusion of vexation.

"The way I was involved in this odious Social Union business from the first, and now have it left on my hands in the end, is maddening. Why, I can't get rid of it!" she replied.

"Then, perhaps," he comfortably suggested, "it's a sign you're not intended to get rid of it."

"What *do* you mean?"

"Why don't you go on," he irresponsibly adventured further, "and establish a Social Union?"

"Do you *mean* it?"

"What was that notion of his"—they usually spoke of the minister pronominally—"about getting the Savors going in a co-operative boarding-house at Fall River? Putney said something about it."

Annie explained, as she had heard it from him, and from the Savors since his death, the minister's scheme for a club, in which the members should contribute the labour and the provisions, and should live cheaply and wholesomely under the management of the Savors at first, and afterward should continue them in charge, or not, as they chose. "He seemed to have thought it out very carefully. But I supposed, of course, it was unpractical."

"Was that why you were going in for it?" asked the doctor; and then he spared her confusion in adding: "I don't see why it was unpractical. It seems to me a very good notion for a Social Union. Why not try it here? There isn't the same pressing necessity that there is in a big factory town; but you have the money, and you have the Savors to make a beginning."

His tone was still half bantering; but it had become more and more serious, so that she could say in earnest: "But the money is one of the drawbacks. It was Mr. Peck's idea that the working people ought to do it all themselves."

"Well, I should say that two-thirds of that money in the bank had come from them. They turned out in great force to Mr. Brandreth's theatricals. And wouldn't it be rather high-handed to use their money for anything but the Union?"

"You don't suppose," said Annie hotly, "that I would spend a cent of it on the grounds of that idiotic monument? I would pay for having it blown up with dynamite! No, I can't have anything more to do with the wretched affair. My touch is fatal." The doctor laughed, and she added: "Besides, I believe most heartily with Mr. Peck that no person of means and leisure can meet working people except in the odious character of a patron, and if I didn't respect them, I respect myself too much for that. If I were ready to go in with them and start the Social Union on his basis, by helping do house-work — *scullion*-work — for it, and eating and living with them, I might try; but I know from experience I'm not. I haven't the need, and to pretend that I have, to forego my comforts and luxuries in a make-believe that I haven't them, would be too ghastly a farce, and I won't."

"Well, then, don't," said the doctor, bent more perhaps on carrying his point in argument than on promoting the actual establishment of the Social Union. "But my idea is this: Take two-thirds or one-half of that money, and go to Savor, and say: 'Here! This is what Mr. Brandreth's theatricals swindled the shop-hands out of. It's honestly theirs, at least to control; and if you want to try that experiment of Mr. Peck's here in Hatboro', it's yours. We people of leisure, or comparative leisure, have really nothing in common with you people who work with your hands for a living; and as we really can't be friends with you, we won't patronise you. We won't advise you, and we won't help you; but here's the money. If you fail, you fail; and if you succeed, you won't succeed by our aid and comfort.' "

The plan that Annie and Doctor Morrell talked over half in joke took a more and more serious character in her sense of duty to the minister's memory and the wish to be of use, which was not extinct in her, however she mocked and defied it. It was part of the irony of her fate that the people who were best able to counsel with her in regard to it were Lyra, whom she could not approve, and Jack Wilmington, whom she had always disliked. He was able to contribute some facts about the working of the Thayer Club at the Harvard Memorial Hall in Cambridge, and Lyra because she had been herself a hand, and would not forget it, was of use in bringing the scheme into favour with the hands. They felt easy with her, as they did with Putney, and for much the same reason: it is one of the pleasing facts of our conditions that people who are socially inferior like best those above them who are morally anomalous. It was really through Lyra that Annie got at the working people, and when it came to a formal conference, there was no one who could command their confidence like Putney, whom they saw mad-drunk two or three times a year, but always pulling up and fighting back to sanity against the enemy whose power some of them had felt too.

No theory is so perfect as not to be subject to exceptions in the experiment, and in spite of her conviction of the truth of Mr. Peck's social philosophy, Annie is aware, through her simple and frank relations with the hands in a business matter, of mutual kindness which it does not account for. But perhaps the philosophy and the experiment were not contradictory; perhaps it was intended to cover only the cases in which they had no common interest. At anyrate, when the Peck Social Union, as its members voted to call it, at the suggestion of one of their own number, got in working order, she was as cordially welcomed to the charge of its funds and accounts as if she had been a hat-shop hand or a shoe-binder. She is really of use, for its working is by no means ideal, and with her wider knowledge she has suggested improvements

and expedients for making both ends meet which were sometimes so reluctant to meet. She has kept a conscience against
subsidising the Union from her own means; and she even accepts for her services a small salary, which its members think
they ought to pay her. She owns this ridiculous, like all the
make-believe work of rich people; a travesty which has no
reality except the little sum it added to the greater sum of her
superabundance. She is aware that she is a pensioner upon the
real members of the Social Union for a chance to be useful,
and that the work they let her do is the right of some one
who needs it. She has thought of doing the work and giving
the pay to another; but she sees that this would be pauperis-
ing and degrading another. So she dwells in a vicious circle,
and waits, and mostly forgets, and is mostly happy.

The Social Union itself, though not a brilliant success in all
points, is still not a failure; and the promise of its future is in
the fact that it continues to have a present. The people of
Hatboro' are rather proud of it, and strangers visit it as one of
the possible solutions of one of the social problems. It is predicted that it cannot go on; that it must either do better or do
worse; but it goes on the same.

Putney studies its existence in the light of his own infirmity, to which he still yields from time to time, as he has
always done. He professes to find there a law which would
account for a great many facts of human experience otherwise
inexplicable. He does not attempt to define this occult preser-
vative principle, but he offers himself and the Social Union as
proofs of its existence; and he argues that if they can only last
long enough they will finally be established in a virtue and
prosperity as great as those of Mr. Gerrish and his store.

Annie sometimes feels that nothing else can explain the
maintenance of Lyra Wilmington's peculiar domestic relations
at the point which perpetually invites comment and never jus-
tifies scandal. The situation seems to her as lamentable as ever.
She grieves over Lyra, and likes her, and laughs with her; she
no longer detests Jack Wilmington so much since he showed
himself so willing and helpful about the Social Union; she
thinks there must be a great deal of good in him, and sometimes she is sorry for him, and longs to speak again to Lyra
about the wrong she is doing him. One of the dangers of

having a very definite point of view is the temptation of abus-
ing it to read the whole riddle of the painful earth. Annie has
permitted herself to think of Lyra's position as one which
would be impossible in a state of things where there was neither poverty nor riches, and there was neither luxury on one
hand to allure, nor the fear of want to constrain on the other.

When her recoil from the fulfilment of her volunteer pledge
to Mr. Peck brought her face to face with her own weakness,
there were two ways back to self-respect, either of which she
might take. She might revert to her first opinion of him, and
fortify herself in that contempt and rejection of his ideas, or
she might abandon herself to them, with a vague intention of
reparation to him, and accept them to the last insinuation of
their logic. This was what she did, and while her life remained
the same outwardly, it was inwardly all changed. She never
could tell by what steps she reached her agreement with the
minister's philosophy; perhaps, as a woman, it was not possible she should; but she had a faith concerning it to which
she bore unswerving allegiance, and it was Putney's delight to
witness its revolutionary effect on an old Hatboro' Kilburn,
the daughter of a shrewd lawyer and canny politician like her
father, and the heir of an aristocratic tradition, a gentlewoman born and bred. He declared himself a reactionary in
comparison with her, and had the habit of taking the conservative side against her. She was in the joke of this; but it was
a real trouble to her for a time that Dr. Morrell, after admit-
ting the force of her reasons, should be content to rest in a
comfortable inconclusion as to his conduct, till one day she
reflected that this was what she was herself doing, and that
she differed from him only in the openness with which she
proclaimed her opinions. Being a woman, her opinions were
treated by the magnates of Hatboro' as a good joke, the
harmless fantasies of an old maid, which she would get rid of
if she could get anybody to marry her; being a lady, and very
well off, they were received with deference, and she was left
to their uninterrupted enjoyment. Putney amused himself by
saying that she was the fiercest apostle of labour that never
did a stroke of work; but no one cared half so much for all
that as for the question whether her affair with Dr. Morrell
was a friendship or a courtship. They saw an activity of atten-

tion on his part which would justify the most devout belief in the latter, and yet they were confronted with the fact that it so long remained eventless. The two theories, one that she was amusing herself with him, and the other that he was just playing with her, divided public opinion, but they did not molest either of the parties to the mystery; and the village, after a season of acute conjecture, quiesced into that sarcastic sufferance of the anomaly into which it may have been noticed that small communities are apt to subside from such occasions. Except for some such irreconcilable as Mrs. Gerrish, it was a good joke that if you could not find Dr. Morrell in his office after tea, you could always find him at Miss Kilburn's. Perhaps it might have helped solve the mystery if it had been known that she could not accept the situation, whatever it really was, without satisfying herself upon two points, which resolved themselves into one in the process of the inquiry.

She asked, apparently as preliminary to answering a question of his, "Have you heard that gossip about my—being in—caring for the poor man?"

"Yes."

"And did you—what did you think?"

"That it wasn't true. I knew if there were anything in it, you couldn't have talked him over with me."

She was silent. Then she said, in a low voice: "No, there couldn't have been. But not for that reason alone, though it's very delicate and generous of you to think of it, very large-minded; but because it *couldn't* have been. I could have worshipped him, but I couldn't have loved him—any more," she added, with an implication that entirely satisfied him, "than I could have worshipped *you*."

THE END.

Chronology

1837   Born March 1, second son, second child among eight siblings, in Martinsville (now Martins Ferry), Ohio, to Mary Dean Howells, of Irish and Pennsylvania Dutch descent, and William Cooper Howells, a Welsh-born printer and publisher whose utopian yearnings and lively mind led him from deism and the Democrats to Swedenborgianism and the Whigs and who provided literate and challenging influences unusual in a post-frontier household.

1840–47   Father buys Whig paper, *Hamilton Intelligencer*, and moves to Hamilton, Ohio. Howells' early assistance as typesetter allows little formal schooling.

1848–50   Father loses *Intelligencer* because of his Free Soil convictions. Takes on *Dayton Transcript* and fails again, despite bitter struggle in which Howells works long, hard hours typesetting and delivering papers. Father, with businessmen brothers, establishes family utopian commune at Eureka Mills, Ohio, but abandons it after a year when brothers withdraw financial support.

1851–52   Free Soil Party hires father as legislative reporter in Columbus, the state capital, for *Ohio State Journal*, in which Howells, now a printer's apprentice, has a poem published on March 23, 1852. Father accepts editorship of abolitionist *Ashtabula Sentinel*, in radical Western Reserve. Family moves to Ashtabula in summer of 1852 and that winter to Jefferson, the county seat, where they begin to prosper.

1853–57   Howells combines full-time work as *Sentinel*'s printer with rigorous self-education, learning Spanish, French, Latin, and later German, which leads to one of his prime "literary passions," Heinrich Heine. He suffers periodic nervous collapses (not fully overcome until his marriage), which bring about humiliating failure as city editor of *Cincinnati Gazette*. Writes and publishes prolifically—journalism, verse, essays—and works on novels.

1858   Becomes city editor and columnist of the *Ohio State Journal*, part of Governor Salmon P. Chase's political organization. Howells' cleverness, wit, and shy charm win him professional and social success in the provincial capital.

1859–60 Poems, stories, and reviews in *Atlantic Monthly*, *National Era*, *Saturday Press*, and *The Dial*, his first book (*Poems of Two Friends*, 1859, with John James Piatt), and sympathetic writing about John Brown's raid on Harpers Ferry bring national attention. With proceeds ($199) of Lincoln campaign biography (in *Lives and Speeches of Abraham Lincoln and Hannibal Hamlin*, 1860), he makes pilgrimage East to meet literary figures of New England—James T. Fields and James Russell Lowell of the *Atlantic*, Holmes, Hawthorne, Emerson, Thoreau—and of New York—Whitman and the *Saturday Press* "Bohemians." Goes to Brattleboro, Vermont, to meet family of Elinor Mead, whom he has known since she visited her cousin, Rutherford B. Hayes, in Ohio the winter before; they become engaged.

1861–64 Lincoln Administration awards Howells U.S. Consulate in Venice, where he lives for duration of Civil War. Marries Elinor Mead in Paris, December 24, 1862, and daughter Winifred is born December 17, 1863. Studies Italian, Dante, Venetian art; discovers plays of Carlo Goldoni which reflect his own interest in life of lower classes. Elinor, from a cultivated family that includes artists and architects (as well as the utopian John Humphrey Noyes), contributes to his artistic education. Writes humorous anti-romantic travel letters for *Boston Advertiser* and prepares them for book form, but failure to sell poetry or fiction leads to despair about literary career. In July 1864 Lowell writes him to praise his *Advertiser* letters and to accept a long article, "Recent Italian Comedy," for *North American Review*. With new confidence, tours Italy gathering material for another travel book.

1865 Returns to United States on four-month leave; resigns consulate to begin literary career. In November joins E. L. Godkin's *Nation* in New York.

1866–70 Moves to Cambridge to become assistant editor of *Atlantic*; assigned to supervise production, review books, and recruit new talent. Enters the "old Cambridge" of Longfellow and C. E. Norton, the "proper Boston" of Holmes and Lowell, and the international literary set of Fields. Begins lifelong friendships with William and Henry James, also from a Swedenborgian family, and with Mark Twain. In 1868 mother dies and son, John Mead, is born. *Venetian Life* published in 1866; *Italian Journeys*, 1867; *Suburban Sketches*, 1870.

1871–80 Succeeds Fields as editor of *Atlantic* and has house built for family in Cambridge, where daughter Mildred is born September 1872; in 1878 has another house, Redtop, built in nearby Belmont, Massachusetts. Under his direction *Atlantic* serializes fiction of Henry James and Mark Twain and reflects current Cambridge concern with Darwinism and, after Crash of 1873, socioeconomic theory. Howells' reviews show growing interest in native and European realism, especially Turgenev's work. *Their Wedding Journey*, 1871; *A Chance Acquaintance, Poems*, 1873; *A Foregone Conclusion*, 1874; "Private Theatricals," serially, 1875 (published in book form as *Mrs. Farrell*, 1921); *Sketch of the Life and Character of Rutherford B. Hayes, The Parlor Car*, 1876; *Out of the Question: A Comedy*, 1877; *The Lady of the Aroostook*, 1879; *The Undiscovered Country*, 1880.

1881–84 Resigns *Atlantic* editorship to write full time. After taking family abroad for the sake of Winifred's health, moves to Boston where he associates with journalists, clergymen, and others actively concerned with social reform. "The Sleeping Car," inaugurating a series of popular Christmas farces, appears in 1882 in *Harper's*, and Howells begins writing for the *Century*, where an essay praising Henry James provokes international "Realism War." Publishes *Dr. Breen's Practice*, 1881; *A Modern Instance*, 1882; and writes *Indian Summer* and *The Rise of Silas Lapham*.

1885 In the spring a sudden, overwhelming sense of guilt—a Swedenborgian "vastation"—turns Howells to Tolstoy and deeper, more radical social inquiries. Winifred suffers a relapse; her Boston debut is canceled and Howells leaves Boston house and moves family to suburban hotel. In October he signs with Harper & Brothers the most lucrative contract offered an American author up to that time; he is to furnish a book a year and a monthly *Harper's* column, "The Editor's Study," and he gives Harper &

Brothers first refusal of all work. *The Rise of Silas Lapham*, *Tuscan Cities* published.

1886–90   Closest sibling, Victoria, dies of malaria. Howells declines Chair at Harvard held earlier by Longfellow and Lowell, and family wanders in search of a cure for Winifred, whose illness, misdiagnosed as "neurasthenic," is fatal in March 1889. Parents guilt-stricken and deeply grieved. "The Editor's Study" champions realism, Tolstoy, Dostoevsky, Hamlin Garland, and Emily Dickinson; it also reflects Howells' attraction (shared by his wife) to socialism, his commitment to democracy, and his opposition to social injustice. In 1887 he becomes the only prominent American writer to risk a public plea for Chicago anarchists unjustly convicted of murder in the Haymarket Riots. Hostile press reactions to his plea for executive clemency briefly threaten his career. *Indian Summer, Poems, The Minister's Charge*, 1886; *April Hopes*, 1887; *Annie Kilburn*, 1888; *A Hazard of New Fortunes, The Shadow of a Dream, A Boy's Town*, 1890.

1891–93   Lets Harper contract expire and does free-lance writing again, including experimental poetry. Moves to New York to edit *Cosmopolitan*, for which he writes the utopian *Altrurian Sketches*. Begins a series of major radical essays— socialist, feminist, anti-racist, anti-imperialist—but his plan to make *Cosmopolitan* a center for literary radicals ends when he resigns in conflict with its millionaire owner. *An Imperative Duty, Criticism and Fiction*, 1891; *The Quality of Mercy*, 1892; *The World of Chance, The Coast of Bohemia*, 1893.

1894–98   Travels occasionally—visits son John, who is studying architecture in France, in 1894, Carlsbad, Germany, in 1897, lecture tours in 1897 and 1899. Emerging as a declared "Ibsenian," he befriends new generation of realists, including Stephen Crane and H. B. Fuller, and sponsors Crane's *Maggie*, Paul Lawrence Dunbar's *Lyrics of Lowly Life*, and Abram Cahan's *Yekl*. Father dies August 1894. *A Traveler from Altruria*, 1894; *My Literary Passions, Stops of Various Quills*, 1895; *Impressions and Experiences*, 1896; *The Landlord at Lion's Head*, 1897; *The Story of a Play*, 1898.

1899–1903 Harper & Brothers fails and is placed in receivership, but J. P. Morgan rescues it and puts Colonel George Harvey in charge; Howells agrees to conduct monthly column, "Editor's Easy Chair." Here and in Harvey's *North American Review*, over the next decade, Howells continues his literary and social criticism from a realist, socialist, anti-imperialist perspective. He reviews Thorstein Veblen and Frank Norris favorably, and introduces Charles W. Chesnutt in the *Atlantic*. *Their Silver Wedding Journey*, 1899; *Literary Friends and Acquaintance*, 1900; *A Pair of Patient Lovers, Heroines of Fiction*, "Professor Barrett Wendell's Notions of American Literature," 1901; *The Kentons, Literature and Life*, "Émile Zola," "Frank Norris," 1902.

1904–09   Howells receives Litt. D. from Oxford, 1904, and is elected first president of American Academy of Arts and Letters, 1908. He writes tributes to John Hay and Mark Twain, Tolstoy and Ibsen, begins friendship with G. B. Shaw, and travels—to Italy in 1908, England and the Continent in 1909. *The Son of Royal Langbrith*, 1904; *London Films, 1905; Certain Delightful English Towns*, 1906; *Through the Eye of the Needle*, 1907; *Fennel and Rue, Roman Holidays*, 1908; *Seven English Cities*, 1909.

1910–14   Mark Twain dies in April, Elinor Mead Howells in May 1910. Howells travels to England and then to Bermuda and Spain. His old audience is dying out and he has difficulty placing fiction in magazines. After publication of six volumes, the projected "Library Edition" of his works is aborted by commercial publishers' quarrels. Tries unsuccessfully to obtain Nobel Prize for Henry James in 1911. *My Mark Twain, Imaginary Interviews*, 1910; writes *The Vacation of the Kelwyns* (published posthumously 1920); *New Leaf Mills, Familiar Spanish Travels*, 1913.

1915–19   The American Academy of Arts and Letters inaugurates Howells Medal for fiction in 1915; presents the first to Howells. Declares support for World War I, and contributes poem to *The Book of the Homeless*, anthology edited by Edith Wharton published in 1916 to aid refugees. Praises the "new poetry" of Robert Frost, Vachel Lindsay, Edgar Lee Masters, and E. A. Robinson. *The Daughter of the Storage, The Leatherwood God, Years of My Youth*, 1916.

1920   Dies of pneumonia May 11, in New York.

Note on the Texts

The texts of two of the three novels printed in this volume are those of the Indiana University Press's *A Selected Edition of W. D. Howells*, prepared in accordance with the standards of the Modern Language Association's Center for Editions of American Authors and approved by that organization. *The Minister's Charge; Or, The Apprenticeship of Lemuel Barker* (volume 14, 1978), edited by David J. Nordloh and David Kleinman, and *April Hopes* (volume 15, 1974), edited by Don L. Cook, James P. Elliott, and David J. Nordloh, were published with full textual apparatus by the Indiana University Press. The text of *Annie Kilburn*, not yet included in *A Selected Edition*, is that of the first American book edition published by Harper & Brothers, New York, in 1888, but dated 1889. The three novels are presented in this volume in the order of their initial publication.

The history of composition and publication of the three novels is similar. By this point in his career, Howells had devised the system of selling the serialization rights to his novels on the basis of an idea, a few sentences of description, or a brief summary of the theme or situation he intended to develop. The magazine would begin publishing the serial while Howells was writing it, and he would simultaneously compose future installments and correct proof for installments already set in type. As each monthly installment was set in type and sent to him for correction and revision, Howells returned a set of corrected proofs to the magazine and then sent another copy to David Douglas, his publisher in Edinburgh. (No manuscripts or proofs of any of the three novels included here are known to be extant.)

In the absence of international copyright laws, Howells and Douglas had worked out a scheme to protect the copyright in Great Britain. From the proof sheets supplied by Howells, Douglas had his printers, T. & A. Constable, set each installment in type in Edinburgh and print a few copies, which Douglas registered at Stationers' Hall in London and deposited with appropriate British libraries prior to the sale of that magazine installment in England. When all the installments were set in type, Douglas had stereotype plates made, from which about a thousand copies of the novel were printed and issued by his firm as the English edition. The plates were then sent to America where they were used to print the American edition. Depending on how much time he had, Howells sometimes made additional revisions in a later set of serial proofs after he had sent corrected proofs to Douglas. These revisions would appear in the magazine serial, but not in the book edition. In some cases he had time to make revisions in the standing type after the deposit copies had been pulled, or even in the stereotype plates after they arrived in America.

The Indiana editors of *The Minister's Charge* selected the serial version of the novel that appeared in *The Century Illustrated Monthly Magazine* from February through December 1886 for their copy-text. They had determined that, although the British and American book editions were printed later than the magazine version, Howells entered his final corrections and decisions on magazine proofs after he had already sent earlier proof sheets to Edinburgh for Douglas to use in setting type and making stereotype plates for the book edition. For example, in Chapter X Howells changed the redundant "in the city of Boston" to "Boston" (89.12); the few other substantive variants between serial and book version are of the same kind. The book also contains English spellings and punctuation automatically inserted by the printer. In consequence, the chronologically earliest publication of the novel, the magazine serial, constitutes the closest approach to both the author's manuscript and the author's final intention. Therefore the text of *The Minister's Charge* in *A Selected Edition of W. D. Howells* is the serial, with fifteen necessary editorial emendations—fourteen for spelling or punctuation and one for grammar. That text is printed here.

A similar pattern of publication was noted in the Indiana *April Hopes*, serialized in *Harper's Monthly* from February through November 1887. The nature of the differences between the book edition and the serial convinced the Indiana editors that here as well Howells continued to make corrections after he sent Douglas the proofs from which the type for the book edition was set. The only exception to this pattern existed in the first seven chapters (installment one of the

serial), in which four word substitutions and the deletion of
one substantial passage in the deposit copy appear to be authorial. The editors emended these five variants into the serial
text, along with nine corrections of errors in spelling or fact
in the remaining pages of the book. This text of *April Hopes*
from *A Selected Edition* is printed here.

Annie Kilburn poses a more complex problem than do the
other two novels in this volume. The serial text, appearing in
Harper's Monthly from June through November 1888, probably
preserves Howells' punctuation and spelling with less corruption than either the deposit copy or the book edition. However, collation reveals that both the deposit copy and the
book edition contain variants that not only appear authorial
in their extensiveness and tone, but conform better than the
serial readings to the ultimate emphasis and outcome of the
narrative. The two longest variant passages (one in Chapter V
and the other in Chapter XX) reflect Howells' early uncertainty about the plot line he was to develop and his later
strengthening of theme and character. In Chapter V, at the
end of the first serial installment, Mrs. Bolton describes to
Annie the behavior of the young Mr. Brandreth and the
middle-aged Mrs. Munger that leads her to believe that they
are engaged in what Annie describes as "a flirtation." The passage appears in neither the deposit copy nor the book. (See
the notes to this volume, 674.22.) The relationship between
the two characters is not developed in the remainder of the
book, and indeed Mrs. Munger and Mr. Brandreth fade from
Howells' plot after Chapter XIX. So it seems unlikely that
Howells added this isolated description of the affair in late
proofs of the serial.

There are more variants in the first of the six deposit parts
(Chapters I – V) than in all the other parts combined, and
their effect is to reduce Howells' intrusion into his narrative
and to remove solecisms and verbal extravagances. In at least
fifteen cases, the change either occurs first in the book or further revises a passage already revised in the deposit part. An
example of a change first occurring in the book appears after
"others" at 659.32, where the book omits a long sentence
present in both the serial and the deposit copy: "Two of them
were really women of very good minds; the other was a sim-

pleton; but in these moments of demonstration they were all alike, and collectively they were inferior in mind and manners to the worst of their number." An example of continued revision occurs at 663.20, where the paragraph in the serial began with the sentence: "They went out on a tide of the most tolerant hilarity and exuberant local pride. Each felt that she had not made a good impression, but blamed the others for it, while she laughed and screamed to keep her spirits up. In the contagion . . ." The first sentence was cut from the deposit copy, and the book omitted both sentences. Another kind of revision was made at 649.23, where the serial version had the owners pushing their hand-mowers "every summer evening" rather than "in the summer evenings." The frequency of alterations decreases radically after the first three installments. However, Chapter XX contains a final major substantive difference, where an important interchange between Annie and Lyra, not in the serial ("And I hope . . . girl like me!", 792.16–26), appears first in the deposit copy and is retained in the book edition.

Thus the process of revision appears to have been cumulative from serial proofs, to copyright deposit parts, to the book edition. There are nearly fifty verbal variants among the three texts, about one-third of those introduced after the deposit parts were printed and before the stereotype plates were made. In no case, except for the correction of obvious errors, does the book text return to a serial reading. Therefore, the Harper & Brothers edition, published late in 1888 (but dated on the title page 1889), best represents Howells' intentions for the novel, even though some of his spelling and punctuation preferences may be lost; that text is printed here.

This volume presents the texts of the editions chosen for inclusion here but does not attempt to reproduce features of their typographic design, such as the display capitalization of chapter openings. The texts are printed without change except for the correction of typographical errors. (The few errors found in *The Minister's Charge* and *April Hopes* will also be corrected in the next printings of those volumes in *A Selected Edition of W. D. Howells*.) Spelling, punctuation, and capitalization are often expressive features, and they are not altered, even when inconsistent or irregular. The following is a list of typographical errors corrected, cited by page and line number: 23.15, proposing—"; 44.29, No. 2334; 95.19, make Sarah; 149.37, was favor; 177.25, around; 257.8, *è buono*; 300.18, Sybil; 621.27, P.S.; 669.30, 'Oh; 683.22, 'I; 686.16, better.'; 695.32, 'I; 696.1, 'don't; 698.4, Gerrish.; 700.22, Gerrish.; 704.37, ha.; 705.13, going,; 713.6, Mrs; 725.19, 'Gore; 739.24, 'I; 761.11, Putney; 768.11, I; 783.38, affair.'; 789.10, May; 793.7, 'Oh; 797.3, 'You; 806.38, To; 816.32, but she; 819.12, 'But; 830.31, him; 845.39, 'Let's.

Notes

In the notes below, the reference numbers denote page and line of the present volume (the line count includes chapter headings). No note is made for material included in a standard desk-reference book. For more detailed notes, references to other studies, and further biographical background than is contained in the Chronology, see: *Selected Letters of W. D. Howells (1902–1920)*, six volumes (Boston: Twayne Publishers, 1979–83), edited by Christoph K. Lohmann et al.; *Life in Letters of William Dean Howells*, two volumes (Garden City, N.Y.: Doubleday, Doran & Co., 1928), edited by Mildred Howells; and Edwin H. Cady, *The Road to Realism: The Early Years 1837–1885 of William Dean Howells* (Syracuse: Syracuse University Press, 1956) and *The Realist at War: The Mature Years 1885–1920 of William Dean Howells* (Syracuse: Syracuse University Press, 1958).

THE MINISTER'S CHARGE

3.34   make . . . reason] Milton, *Paradise Lost*, Book II, lines 113–14.

16.26   Nilsson] The Swedish soprano and violinist Christine Nilsson (1843–1921) performed in Boston several times in the 1870s.

29.17–19   Washington . . . sick] The statue of George Washington is by Thomas Ball (1819–1911), and the bronze statue of Edward Everett is by William Wetmore Story (1819–95). The Ether Monument by John Quincy Adams Ward (1830–1910) depicts the Good Samaritan as a turbaned figure holding a stricken youth.

30.39   Bloomer dress] Introduced by Elizabeth Smith Miller, daughter of the philanthropist Gerrit Smith (1797–1874), an advocate of women's dress reform. The dress was adopted c. 1851 by the feminist and reformer Amelia Jenks Bloomer (1818–94).

52.39–40   the Island] Deer Island, between Boston Bay and Boston Harbor, was the site of the workhouse for convicts.

66.33–67.13   Wayfarer's . . . Street Home] The city Lodge for Wayfarers was on Hawkins Street, and the Chardon Street Home was a charitable shelter for pregnant and homeless women.

97.19   Tito Melema] The handsome, dashing, and unscrupulous young Greek in *Romola* (first published in serial form July 1862– August 1863).

109.8   Quaker's meetin'] At meetings of the Religious Society of Friends, members sit in silence unless someone is moved to speak.

110.11–24   *Set . . . consumed.*]   Song of Solomon 8:6–7.

132.20   Museum]   The stock company at the Boston Museum theater on Tremont Street was considered one of the nation's finest and was often joined by outstanding guest artists. The theater was established in 1841 and closed in 1893.

132.24   Jefferson's . . . *Acres*]   Joseph Jefferson (1829–1905), one of the most popular American actors of his day, rewrote the part of Bob Acres for his 1880 production of Richard Sheridan's *The Rivals* (1775). He toured in the role of Acres for several years.

182.8–12   Williams . . . Prang.]   The art dealers, Williams and Everett, maintained a showroom on Washington Street. L. Prang and Company lithographed greeting cards.

189.15   Development Theory]   An evolutionary theory.

189.31   Fast Day]   Until 1895, the governor of Massachusetts annually proclaimed a day of fasting and prayer, usually the fourth Monday in April.

197.20–22   Now o'er . . . sleep—ah]   Cf. *Macbeth*, II, i, 49–51.

201.34   'Nymph . . . remembered!']   *Hamlet*, III, i, 88–89.

202.15–16   'The falling . . . love!']   From Richard Edwards's (1523?–66) "Amantium Irae," in *The Paradise of Dainty Devises* (1576).

216.7   Billy Ducks]   Billet-doux; literally "sweet (i.e., love) note."

226.6   Seaside Library]   A series of cheap reprints of popular novels first published in 1877 by George P. Munro.

248.14   "What . . . Tom?"]   In *The Rise of Silas Lapham*, Tom Corey, the son of Bromfield Corey, married Lapham's daughter, Penelope. Tom had joined the Kanawha Paint Company of West Virginia and New York after the failure of Lapham's firm.

248.28   bant]   Diet. The terms "bantingism" and "to bant" were coined after William Banting (1797–1878) published his diet regime in *Letter on Corpulence, Addressed to the Public* (England, 1863; America, 1864). The pamphlet was reprinted through 1902.

251.1   a Buttons]   A page or serving boy whose jacket traditionally was adorned with rows of buttons.

257.8   "*Novanta . . . dentro.*"]   "Ninety of a hundred, one beautiful on the outside is good within."

274.5–8   that prisoner . . . between them.]   The protagonist in Edgar Allan Poe's "The Pit and the Pendulum" (1843).

293.22   there . . . case]   See *The Rise of Silas Lapham*, Chapter XVIII.

307.31   Penitentes . . . Mexico] The secret lay order which arose in the southwestern United States practiced flagellation and re-enacted the crucifixion during Holy Week. The order was condemned by the archbishop of Santa Fe in 1889.

308.24–25   "Remember . . . with them,"] Hebrews 13:3.

308.38   telegrapher's strike] On July 19, 1883, the Brotherhood of Telegraphers of the United States and Canada, which included 15,000 members from every rank, went on strike. Their demands, some of which were especially designed to help women employees, included eight-hour day shifts and seven-hour night shifts, equal pay for men and women, and a 15 percent wage increase, with extra Sunday pay. A number of union members remained at work and the companies quickly began hiring new employees, causing the strike to be broken on August 15. Many of the strike activists lost their jobs.

APRIL HOPES

323.15–16   your sisters . . . aunts] A variation of this phrase runs through "I Am the Monarch of the Sea," Act I, in Gilbert and Sullivan's *H.M.S. Pinafore* (1878); e.g., "And so do his sisters, and his cousins and his aunts! / His sisters and his cousins / Whom he reckons up by dozens, / And his aunts!"

338.24–25   Salvini's . . . Booth's] On tour in America in 1886, the Italian actor Tommaso Salvini (1829–1916) portrayed Othello to Edwin Booth's (1833–93) Iago for a week in Boston.

362.24   Mr. . . . *Mail*] Charles Reade's play, originally *The Courier of Lyons* (1854), was one of the most popular in the repertoire of the English actor and theater manager Henry Irving (1838–1905). The melodrama featured sudden disappearances and reappearances.

365.8   the *Events*] This fictitional newspaper also appears in *A Modern Instance* and *The Rise of Silas Lapham*.

379.13–14   "You . . . eyes."] Cf. Sir Joseph Porter in Act II: "My amazement—my surprise— / You may learn from the expression of my eyes!"

383.26–31   *Fumée . . . Gentilshommes*] The English translations of the Russian titles are *Smoke* (1867) and *The Nest of Gentlefolks* (or *The Nest of the Landed Gentry*) (1858); the latter first appeared in English as *Liza*.

383.34–35   I don't . . . built "] For Emerson on translations see "Books," in *Society and Solitude* (1870): "I should as soon think of swimming across Charles River when I wish to go to Boston, as of reading all my books in originals when I have them rendered for me in my mother-tongue."

402.22–23   It was . . . heaven]   Cf. Matthew 19:24: "And again I tell you it is easier for a camel to go through the eye of a needle than for a rich man to enter the kingdom of God."

404.32–33   'Legend of Pornic']   "Gold Hair: A Story of Pornic" in *Dramatis Personæ* (1864).

432.3   'a mush of concession']   From "Friendship" in *Essays: First Series* (1847).

433.19   *Punch's* advice]   Cf. *Punch's Almanac* (1845): "Advice to persons about to marry—Don't."

452.13   Colonel Newcome]   In William Thackeray's *The Newcomes* (1853–55), Col. Newcome is a naïve, honorable, but pathetic old gentleman.

533.12   Society . . . Research]   Founded in London in 1882 by Frederic Myers, Richard Hodgson, and others. William James organized its first American branch in Boston in 1884.

542.34   coffee biggin]   Biggin is defined by the *Oxford English Dictionary* as: "A kind of coffee-pot containing a strainer for the infusion of the coffee, without allowing the grains to mix with the infusion." The device was patented by a Mr. Biggin, c. 1800.

564.27–28   "You . . . man."]   Cf. George Eliot's *Romola* (1862–63), Chapter 32: "You are a treacherous man!"

ANNIE KILBURN

661.14–19   cemetery . . . garden."]   The first garden cemetery in the United States was Mount Auburn Cemetery in the Boston suburbs of Cambridge and Watertown. Established in 1831 by the physician and botanist Jacob Bigelow (1786–1879) and designed by the landscape architect Alexander Wadsworth, it changed the pattern from the earlier burial grounds to the memorial parks that came to predominate in America.

668.15   Lady Archibald Campbell]   The Scottish dramatist and actress, née Jane Sevilla Callander.

670.36   Miss Mather]   Margaret Mather (1859?–98) first appeared in *Romeo and Juliet* in 1885.

670.39–40   minuet . . . Scaligeri]   Romeo Montague and Juliet Capulet traditionally lived in Verona during the rule of the Scaliger or della Scala family (1260–1387). The minuet came into fashion in the late 17th century.

674.22   enterprise.]   The passage that appeared in the serial version following this sentence is given here:
   "What sort of person is Mr. Brandreth, Mrs. Bolton?" she asked, finally.

"Well, I suppose I'd ought to apologize to you for not comin' quicker to open the door for him," began Mrs. Bolton.

"You didn't come at all," said Annie, with an amused willingness to let her get at Mr. Brandreth in her own way.

"Well, no; you're right. I don't presume I did, or 't I *should*. I guess I'd let him staid and soaked it out, if I'd had *my* way."

"Why, what is there wrong about him?"

"Wrong? There ain't *any*thing about him. He don't amount to a row of pins. He *is* the greatest— Well, 'f I was his mother I guess I wouldn't stand it long to have him following round with that Mrs. Munger the way he doos."

"Why, Mrs. Bolton, you don't mean to say that Mr. Brandreth and Mrs. Munger are carrying on a flirtation?"

"I don't know what you call it. He's taggin' her round all the while, or her him."

"But, Mrs. Bolton! She's got a son in college! Where *is* her husband?"

"She *says* he's out West somewhere; Sent Paul or Sent Louis. He hain't never troubled Hatboro' any. I guess he ain't never goin' to, either. But she's got plenty of money, and I don't suppose but what it's her money he's after. I guess if she *could* get a divorce she wouldn't let the church hinder her— well, not a great deal."

Annie had heard so much worse talk about very good people in the American colony at Rome that these dark hints of Mrs. Bolton's did not alarm her.

688.17–18   Boots . . . Veneerings]   Characters in Charles Dickens' *Our Mutual Friend* (first published in serial form May 1864–November 1865).

696.17–18   put . . . Lincoln said;]   In an address to the New Jersey General Assembly at Trenton, February 21, 1861, President-elect Lincoln, referring to Southern secession, said: "But it may be necessary to put the foot down firmly."

700.35   Quirinal]   The Quirinal Papal Palace, built in Rome in the 16th century, served as the home of the kings of Italy from 1870–1946.

720.8   "Who . . . Ralph?"]   J. Milton Northwick became a central character in *The Quality of Mercy* (1892). Ralph Putney also figures prominently in the book.

726.13–14   Hard-shell Baptist]   A body of strict American Baptists, also known as the Old-School, Primitive, or Anti-Mission Baptists.

826.15–16   glittering . . . another]   Rufus Choate (1799–1859) called the ideas in the Declaration of Independence "glittering and sounding generalities" in a letter to the Maine Whig State Central Committee, August 9, 1856.

827.30–33   Jordan . . . Philadelphia]   Luxurious department stores.

864.2   riddle . . . earth.]   Alfred, Lord Tennyson (1809–92), "The Palace of Art," line 213.

Cataloging Information

Howells, William Dean, 1837–1920.
  Novels 1886–1888.
  Edited by Don L. Cook.

  (The Library of America ; 44)
  Contents: Minister's charge—April hopes—Annie Kilburn.
  I. Title: Minister's charge. II. Title: April hopes.
  III. Title: Annie Kilburn. IV. Series.
PS2022   1989   813'.4   88–82728
ISBN 0–940450–51–8 (alk. paper)

For a list of titles in the Library of America, write:
The Library of America
14 East 60th Street
New York, New York 10022

*This book is set in 10 point Linotron Galliard,
a face designed for photocomposition by Matthew Carter
and based on the sixteenth-century face Granjon. The paper
is acid-free Ecusta Nyalite and meets the requirements for permanence of the American National Standards Institute. The binding
material is Brillianta, a 100% woven rayon cloth made by
Van Heek-Scholco Textielfabrieken, Holland. The composition is by Haddon Craftsmen, Inc., and The
Clarinda Company. Printing and binding
by R. R. Donnelley & Sons Company.
Designed by Bruce Campbell.*